WILLA CATHER

MY ÁNTONIA

THE TROLL GARDEN

SELECTED SHORT STORIES

WILLA CATHER

MY ÁNTONIA
THE TROLL GARDEN
SELECTED SHORT STORIES

GRAMERCY BOOKS
NEW YORK • AVENEL

This 1994 edition is published by Gramercy Books,
distributed by Outlet Book Company, Inc.,
a Random House Company,
40 Engelhard Avenue, Avenel,
New Jersey 07001.

Random House
New York • Toronto • London • Sydney • Auckland

Printed and bound in the United States of America

Library of Congress Cataloging-in-Publication Data
Cather, Willa, 1873–1947.
[Selections. 1993]
My Ántonia; The troll garden; selected short stories / Willa Cather.
p. cm.
ISBN 0-517-10031-2
I. Title.
PS3505.A87A6 1993
813′.52—dc20 93-36988
CIP

8 7 6 5 4 3 2 1

Editor's Note. Certain characterizations and language of the author should be viewed as arising from the context of the time in which these stories were written. Any offense to modern sensibilities is unintended and does not reflect the attitudes of the editor or publisher of this current edition.

Contents

Introduction

MORE THAN seventy-five years after its publication, *My Ántonia* retains its place as one of the finest novels of the twentieth century. To read this masterpiece side by side with the author's early short stories in this new collection is to open a window into the life and development of a true American artist.

The sixteen years that encompass the stories—between 1896 and 1912—were a spectacular period of growth for Willa Cather. Her attitude toward the early stories, however, is well known: she put them behind her and hoped they would be forgotten. And yet to fully appreciate her achievement, the early work is invaluable. When it came to the lives of her own characters, she held this view herself, often repeating a favorite phrase from the French historian Michelet: "The end is nothing; the road is all." She declared in the preface to the 1921 edition of *The Song of the Lark,* "Success is never so interesting as struggle—not even to the successful."

These early stories clearly demonstrate that early struggle. For in some ways Willa Cather was born an artist, and in other ways she grew into the artist that she was born to be. Apparent in the stories collected here are traces of later designs, and glimpses into a galaxy of future Cather heroines.

To that end, it is enlightening to look at the stories in the sequence they were written—that is, beginning with Part Three of this collection—to see how they fit into the writer's life and to observe the growth of one of America's dominant literary voices.

Willa Cather was born in Virginia's Back Creek Valley on December 7, 1873, a date long obscured by the author herself. (As a young writer she subtracted three years from her age, and the date 1876 is carved on her tombstone.) It was but one of many small deceptions that appealed to her. Even as a child she enjoyed embroidering facts to suit her imagination. She had rich material to work from. On both sides, her family traced its American roots back to Revolutionary days. In the Civil War, family members were divided—some staunchly Unionist, others defenders of the Confederacy. The rift within her own family reverberated through her childhood. Poor health forced her grandparents and one of her uncles to move west, to Nebraska, and when Willa was nine years old her father decided to join them. She would return to memories of Virginia at the very end of her life, but the wrenching move west, from the comfortable and settled Virginia to the raw prairie, transformed the matrix of her life and in various ways forever dominated her art.

In *My Ántonia* the orphaned Jim Burden, the most memorable in a long line of Cather narrators, takes his first look at the prairie and says, "I wanted to walk straight on through the red grass and over the edge of the world, which could not be very far away." When the Cathers first arrived in Nebraska they went directly to her grandfather's house out on the Continental Divide—the house that was vividly re-created in *My Ántonia* and where young Jim spends his first night. Forever after, the Divide came to symbolize in Cather's mind the division that ran straight through her heart.

After about a year on the bleak prairie, the Cathers moved into the bustling small town of Red Cloud, a railhead where the Burlington and Missouri railroads divided. All through the night train whistles blew through "that cold vibrant scream, the world-wide call," stirring the hearts of the restless young people in the lonely, isolated territory.

Willa's father opened a mortgage and loan office and the Cather family—which included seven boys and girls, Grandmother Boak, and Margie, a neighbor from Virginia who moved west with the family—became part of the little community. As a child Willa participated fully in the life of the town and also observed everything going on around her. She was part and parcel of her environment, and yet was completely different. She would retain this duality all of her life. When she was twelve, she cropped her tangle of long auburn hair short as a boy's, adopted shirts and jackets for her daily attire, and wore her father's Civil War cap everywhere she went. In her spare time she liked to dissect frogs and read books. She carefully built her library, inscribing inside each book the name she chose for herself, "Wm. Cather, Jr." She also liked to call herself "William Cather, M.D." and dreamed of becoming a doctor. Young Willa was fascinated by everyone she met, especially the immigrants whose sod houses dotted the lonely Divide. The Danes, Swedes, Czechs, French, Germans, and Bohemians who had moved west to build the railroads and populate the barren land brought with them tales of the old country, music, literature, and languages. Even as a child Willa had a wonderful ear, and for the rest of her life she was able to recapture the color and rhythms of speech from all kinds of people in all kinds of circumstances.

In Red Cloud her best friends were the Miner children, whose parents owned the big general store. Their mother became Mrs. Harley in *My Ántonia.* Annie, the "hired girl" who worked for the Miner family, was a special friend to all the children through all their growing-up years; she became Ántonia herself.

There's no doubt that Willa caused comment and gossip around town, but her family did not try to change her. Her mother seemed to recognize that although she was different, she also had exceptional gifts. No other little girl in town was remotely like young Willa Cather. Willa concluded her high school commencement ceremonies with a ringing address that the local paper called a "masterpiece of oratory." In September of 1889 she set out on her own for Lincoln, where she took a year of college prep, and then matriculated at the University of Nebraska. One of her teachers was so impressed with an essay Willa wrote on Thomas Carlyle that he submitted it without her knowledge to the *Nebraska State Journal.* In that very early work she set down her philosophy of art: "Art of every sort is an exacting master, more so even than Jehovah. He says only 'Thou shalt have no other gods before me.' Art, Science, and Letters cry 'Thou shalt have no other gods at all.' " This was her creed, and she stuck to it for the rest of her life.

Seeing herself in print for the first time had a hypnotic effect on Willa. She set her course to become a great writer and never looked back. But she did not always step smoothly along the path toward artistry. She was admired on campus for her talent but considered an oddity because of her style—she still wore her hair cropped short and stuck to tailored skirts and shirtwaists.

"Peter," her first published story, appeared in a small Boston literary journal, *The Mahogany Tree.* The main character prefigures the character of old Mr. Shimerda in *My Ántonia.* She began to publish more stories in the campus magazine *The Hesperian,* beginning a lifelong pattern of rewriting the same characters until they become full-bodied portraits. The beguiling Lena Lingard of *My Ántonia* appeared in various one-dimensional guises in no fewer than four short stories. By the time she becomes Lena she possesses the attributes of all of her predecessors and more; the character is transformed into a "real" woman who persists in the reader's memory long after the precise context of the story is forgotten.

While still in college Cather began writing play reviews and columns on the arts for the *Nebraska State Journal.* Her stories were also being published in the *Overland Monthly* and the *Nebraska Literary Magazine.* The work poured forth from her pen, some of it brilliant, some overblown. But whatever else she was, she was never boring, either in her opinion or in her expression. After graduation, she applied for a teaching post at the university but failed to receive an appointment. While Cather was respected for her scholarship and her talent, she was too outspoken in her ideas to be universally admired by the university hierarchy.

A college graduate, she returned to Red Cloud and fell into a restless depression. She knew something special was inside her but did not know how to let it out. It was almost a year before she secured a job—the post of editor on the *Home Monthly,* a new family magazine starting up in Pittsburgh. Settled there in a boardinghouse, she went to work, using a half-dozen pen names to pour out a steady stream of stories, articles, reviews, and criticisms. She made friends in the musical, newspaper, and theatrical worlds, and sent back to the *Lincoln Courier* personality profiles of the singers and other artists she met.

She wrote fast and hard to fill the pages of the magazine. One of these hastily contrived potboilers, bylined with one of her pseudonyms, Elizabeth L. Seymour, is included in this collection. "The Burglar's House," published in the December 1896 issue of the *Home Monthly,* is a melodrama featuring a caring mother, forgiving father, and contrite son; the story relies on unlikely coincidences for its denouement. Other young writers working under pressure to meet deadlines—from Dickens and Balzac to Colette—have done far worse. "The Burglar's House" may not be *Catherian* art, but it shows that under extreme pressure Cather took pride in her craftsmanship.

When the *Home Monthly* passed to new ownership in 1897, Willa Cather went immediately to work for the Pittsburgh *Leader.* She was an inexhaustible worker imbued with endless vitality. Between assignments she found time to attend concerts, plays, and musical soirees, which she reviewed freelance for the Lincoln newspapers. She also continued writing short stories.

In 1900 three more stories appeared. "A Singer's Romance" is an early exploration of the prima-donna temperament (reworked from an even earlier story, "Nanette"). Here Cather expresses her conviction that artistic fulfillment is achieved at the expense of human relationships. Fifteen years later she fully expounded this theme in the massive novel

The Song of the Lark. Compared to the magnificent figure of Thea Kronborg in that later work, Selma Schumann seems shallow, but in her matter-of-fact acceptance of her life and fate she is a clear predecessor to Kronborg.

"The Sentimentality of William Tavener" is unique in that it is the only Cather story that combines Virginia and Nebraska settings. She would not return to the Virginia setting again until her last complete novel, when she recaptured her early childhood in *Sapphira and the Slave Girl.* Apart from the Virginia connection, the language and structure of "William Tavener" has an engaging simplicity that suggests Cather's later narrative style.

The third 1900 story, "Eric Hermannson's Soul," is one of the most important of the early tales, virtually a microcosm of her later fiction. The dominant theme of all later Cather work is contrast—contrast between artist and society, ideas and realities, desire and necessity, and above all, that of the soul divided against itself. Here, the accidental encounter between Margaret, the "ultra-refined" and vulnerable woman from the East, and Eric, "the wildest lad on all the Divide," sets in motion East versus West, emotion versus intellectualism. For the first time in her writing, Cather makes explicit the duality in her own nature.

In the spring of 1900, Willa Cather began a new phase of her life and work. It was at this time that she met the wealthy socialite Isabelle McClung, the woman who became her most enduring and most important friend. Isabelle encouraged her to devote herself to serious writing. To assume more control over what she wrote and when, Cather resigned from the *Leader* and took a job teaching English and Latin in the Pittsburgh and Allegheny high schools. She also moved from her boardinghouse into the home of Isabelle's parents. From this stable, comfortable base, she continued to write prodigiously—poetry, fiction, and features for the *Nebraska State Journal* and articles for the Pittsburgh *Gazette.*

In 1902, Cather took her first trip to Europe with Isabelle. For the rest of her life, she traveled constantly, moving with the seasons, looking for new experiences and new places in which to write: the Southwest, England, France, New England, Quebec, and Grand Manaan Island became familiar terrain and settings for new stories.

She always punctuated her frenetic travels and work with trips to Red Cloud to visit her family. In "The Treasure of Far Island" she uses a successful New York playwright to describe her own feelings about returning home. In this story she also includes one particular place that symbolized for her the essence of childhood: the sandbar island in the Republican River, where she and her brothers and their friends camped, read, and spun tall tales. The almost mystical island turns up in story after story, and inspires one of *My Ántonia*'s most beautiful and evocative chapters.

With the publication in 1902 of "The Treasure of Far Island" and "The Professor's Commencement," Willa Cather began to be recognized as a writer of unusual promise. In 1903, her first book, a collection of poetry, *April Twilights,* was received favorably by critics. *The Troll Garden* appeared two years later.

Four of the seven stories in *The Troll Garden* had been previously published; three of them would rank among the finest American short stories written in the twentieth century. "The Sculptor's Funeral" and "A Wagner Matinee" expounded for the first time one of the great Cather themes—the struggle of the individual of unique gifts against an unfavorable environment. In "Paul's Case" Cather seems to conclude that life will betray the sensitive person, artist or not. The heart-wrenching ending of "Paul's Case" displays some of the finest writing in American prose.

The Pittsburgh setting for "Paul's Case" conveys Cather's mixed feelings about the city that she referred to as the birthplace of her writing. Although it was the center of much cultural activity, in "Paul's Case" the city is a crude, mean-spirited character, the cause of Paul's desperation. This story, based on two episodes from her teaching life, was the only Pittsburgh story Cather wrote while she still lived there.

It was Cather's opinion that the three stories especially written for the collection do not hold up. Nevertheless, her voice is beginning to emerge. Although the writing in "The Garden Lodge" is overwrought with heated phrases, the central passage is vividly romantic.

In " 'A Death in the Desert' " the trainman Charley Gaylord prefigures a similar character in *The Song of the Lark.* Charley has nurtured his famous, gifted sister as the brakeman Ray Kennedy would nurture Thea Kronborg.

" 'A Death in the Desert' " is also interesting for its idea that art requires a greater sacrifice from a woman than from a man, a theme that characterizes several later stories. Here, while the singer dies alone, the carefree composer romps around the world, enjoying his celebrity. (Cather later rewrote this story several times but, in the end, decided not to include it in the thirteen-volume Library Edition of her collected works published by Houghton Mifflin between 1937 and 1941.)

By the time *The Troll Garden* was published, Cather was attracting attention around the country. In 1906, S. S. McClure, the publisher of *The Troll Garden*, persuaded her to move to New York and join the staff of his famous muckraking magazine *McClure's*, a publication that thrived in the eye of a journalistic hurricane. The switch from a quiet life of teaching and writing to the mayhem of big-city journalism was one more drastic change for a woman who lived by contrasts. That she handled one as well as the other is testimony to how strong both aspects were in her personality. The straightforward, immensely talented young writer was so successful at *McClure's* that within two years she became its managing editor.

There is no doubt that Willa Cather found working at *McClure's* exhilarating. The job required all of her enormous energy and every minute of her waking hours. The four stories that appeared in 1907 in some ways represent a step backward. "Eleanor's House," "The Willing Muse," "The Profile," and "The Namesake" may in fact have been written earlier, during the Pittsburgh years.

These stories do not seem to have any Cather themes, but they do reveal a progress in craftsmanship. Cather was, first and last, an experimental writer. She had many writing heroes—foremost among them Henry James, Gustave Flaubert, and Guy de Maupassant. Ultimately, all of these early influences disappeared from her style, but the practicing, the turning around and shaping of sentences, paragraphs, and pages, eventually made it possible for her own voice to emerge. At this time in her writing life, she was particularly Jamesian, and her true voice is nearly silent—but not quite.

"The Namesake" is especially interesting in terms of Cather lore. Cather had a young uncle, William Sibert Boak, who had been killed in the Civil War. She considered herself his "namesake" and appropriated his middle name for her own. Although largely written in formal "Jamesian" language, one deeply emotional passage in "The Namesake" is pure Cather—no other writer could have written it. The main character, a painter living in France, has returned to America to settle his father's will and look after an elderly aunt. Sitting in his father's garden, he encounters the memory of a young uncle lost in the Civil War.

> "All the while, the bunting I had run up in the morning flapped fold against fold, heaving and tossing softly in the dark—against a sky so black with rain clouds that I could see above me only the blur of something in the soft, troubled motion.
>
> "The experience of that night, coming so overwhelmingly to a man so dead, almost rent me in pieces. It was the same feeling that artists

> know when we, rarely, achieve truth in our work; the feeling of union with some great force, of purpose and security, of being glad that we have lived. . . . It was as if the earth under my feet had grasped and rooted me, and were pouring its essence into me. I sat there until the dawn of morning, and all night long my life seemed to be pouring out of me and running into the ground."

"The Profile," by contrast, has no true emotional center, although there is a peculiar Cather aspect to this story whose plot turns on a woman's disfiguring scar that covers half her face. According to a member of the *McClure's* staff, who was not a Cather fan, the situation was based on a friend whose face was similarly disfigured. When asked to withdraw the story from the magazine, Cather refused. While she was fully aware that some of her character portrayals caused pain to the real people on whom they were based, stories came first. Virtually every major writer of fiction has made the same choice.

The only Cather theme present in "The Profile" is her abhorrence of physical defects. The painter speaks of the human body as sanctified by Nature's purpose, "but lop away so much as a finger, and you have wounded the creature beyond reparation." The "recurrence" of mutilations, particularly the mutilated hand, runs through Cather's work and is believed to have its origins in a childhood incident when an older child threatened to cut off her hand with a knife. The irony of this obsession was that as Cather grew old, tendons in her writing hand became so inflamed that she often had to wear her arm in a sling; writing—the essence of her life—was painful in the extreme.

The year 1908 was another turning point for Willa Cather. While visiting Boston to research a biography of Mary Baker Eddy for *McClure's* she met Sarah Orne Jewett, the much admired American writer who ultimately showed her how to develop her work to its fullest. Jewett believed that all that was good in her own writing stemmed from the simple and contemplative life she led in her home on the Maine coast. She recommended that Cather separate herself from the chaos of a big-city magazine—the deadlines, dealing with an erratic staff, the demands of socializing in the evening, and being an "important" person. None of these activities, said Jewett, was conducive to great writing.

In a much quoted letter Jewett turned Cather's mind in a new direction: "To work in silence and with all one's heart, that is the writer's lot: he is the only artist who must be solitary, and yet needs the widest outlook on the world."

Also at this time Cather gave up her boardinghouse life and took her first real apartment on Washington Place with Edith Lewis, who became her lifelong companion.

During 1908 she published only one short story, "On the Gull's Road," which appeared in *McClure's* in December. The story is a conventional shipboard romance, the "gull's road" is the sea, and the events are recalled by a male narrator twenty years later. The story brought warm praise from Sarah Jewett, who wrote in a letter, "It made me feel very near to the writer's young and loving heart. . . . It makes me the more sure that you are far on your road toward a fine and long story of a very high class."

The effect of a beautiful woman on the people around her, especially on an impressionable young man, was a purely Cather theme to which she would often return. Yet the romance of the young consul and Mrs. Ebbling is tepid compared to the physical excitement that flows in Cather's later work. In this story, however, she did absorb both the male and female roles, which makes possible the rounded voice later heard in *O Pioneers!* and other works. Willa Cather would never again be so mild in describing sexual passion: in fact, her ability to convey sexual passion between a man and woman without graphically describing the act itself is one of her most distinctive characteristics.

In 1910 Cather began work on her first novel, *Alexander's Bridge.* No stories or poems appeared during that year. But 1911 brought "The Joy of Nelly Deane," a charming, sad tale that years later was enlarged to become *Lucy Gayheart.* In this story, the young girls and children are so vividly written the reader feels he can reach out a hand a touch them.

In the autumn of 1912 *Alexander's Bridge,* a novel about a "bridge builder with a double nature," was published by Houghton Mifflin to generally good reviews—although Cather later passed off the novel as something of an aberration in the larger context of her work.

Cather had taken a leave of absence from *McClure's* to finish *Alexander's Bridge.* Searching for "a quiet center" in which to write, she rented a house with Isabelle in Cherry Valley, west of Albany, New York. In this place, she began a new story. In sharp contrast to the drawing-room setting of *Alexander's Bridge,* she found herself writing about "a kind of country and a kind of people." "The Bohemian Girl" was both a departure from the life she was leading and a return to her very early work. In this story she describes the people she had known as a child, just as she remembered them, imbuing her characters with her own feelings. Here it is Clara Vavrika, her Bohemian girl, who must decide whether to run away with Nils or to stay behind in the country in which she feels safe.

While others commented about the themes of contrast and division in her work, Cather said that her stories were always about "escape." Although she herself had escaped from Red Cloud, she still felt the strong pull to stay home. With Cather, it really doesn't matter which choice her characters make, the result is always unsatisfactory. One chooses to go, another chooses to stay; they are forever divided and pulled in two.

To Cather's surprise, "The Bohemian Girl" was even more popular with the public than *Alexander's Bridge.* At last, here was the real thing. With "The Bohemian Girl" Cather broke through not only to her own natural voice but to a new American *sound.* She would use it for the rest of her life, and with each new work that style would be more and more distilled, until it developed into the great novels of the future.

Already at work on two little Western stories, she was ready to give up her job at *McClure's* and devote herself to her writing. These two pastorals were later combined into her first great novel, *O Pioneers!*—the novel that marked the turning point in her artistic life.

In the fall of 1912, Cather and Edith Lewis moved into 5 Bank Street, her home for the next fifteen years. Nearing forty, Cather was the author a superb collection of short stories and two very different novels. Her third novel, *The Song of the Lark,* fully embodied everything she knew about art. The story of Thea Kronborg was loosely based on the life of Olive Fremstad, the legendary mezzo-soprano. Among all her stories of the artist striving for purity in an uncaring world, *The Song of the Lark* comes closest to revealing that bitter struggle.

During the summer of 1917 Cather visited the little village of Jaffrey, New Hampshire, where she stayed in the Shattuck Inn. After that first visit she went back often, always occupying a small attic room with sloping ceilings that reminded her of her room at home. She worked outdoors, in a tent set up especially for her. Her habit was to write three or four hours in the morning and spend the remainder of the day walking, reading, thinking. It was in Jaffrey, during that first visit, that Willa Cather wrote much of *My Àntonia.*

The book had taken shape in the winter of the previous year. A friend, the writer Elsie Sergeant, recalled Willa coming to tea one afternoon, "flushed and alert from one of her swift wintry walks." Cather picked up a vase filled with scented stock and placed it in the center of a small table. " 'I want my new heroine to be like this,' " Elsie recalled Willa saying, "like a rare object in the middle of a table which one may examine from all sides.' "

Àntonia, she said, embodied all of her feelings about the early years and the immigrants she had known on the prairie. "There is a time in a writer's development," she wrote long after, "when his 'lifeline' and the line of his personal endeavor meet." She supposed she was destined to write *My Àntonia* if she ever wrote anything at all.

In *My Àntonia* Willa Cather achieved the flawless, natural prose that would create a new style of American writing and make Àntonia famous around the world. The story is rooted in the Nebraska landscape and set against the seasons: "On the farm the weather was the great fact, and men's affairs went on underneath it, as the streams creep under the ice." As the seasons evolve and turn, so the story expands and develops, reaches climaxes as the weather peaks, becomes hard and pinched through the gray days of winter, and falls back languidly through the hot days of summer.

She also comes to terms with the narrow-minded bigotry of small-town life that she had exposed in "Paul's Case" and "The Sculptor's Funeral." In a single paragraph, she distills the feelings of a lifetime, as she looks at the pinched town life through the eyes of young Jim Burden:

> There were no other lights burning downtown after nine o'clock. On starlight nights I used to pace up and down those long, cold streets, scowling at the little sleeping houses on either side, with their storm windows and covered back porches. They were flimsy shelters, most of them poorly built of light wood, with spindle porch-posts horribly mutilated by the turning-lathe. Yet for all their frailness, how much jealousy and envy and unhappiness some of them managed to contain! The life that went on in them seemed to me made up of evasions and negations: shifts to save cooking, to save washing and cleaning, devices to propitiate the tongue of gossip. This guarded mode of existence was like living under a tyranny. People's speech, their voices, their very glances, became furtive and repressed. Every individual taste, every natural appetite, was bridled by caution. The people asleep in those houses, I thought, tried to live like the mice in their own kitchens; to make no noise, to leave no trace, to slip over the surface of things in the dark.

The critics did not immediately take to *My Àntonia*. The review in the *New York Times Review of Books* merely summarized the plot; other books, now long forgotten, drew far warmer notices that week. There were exceptions. The New York *Sun* looked into the future: "If a writer is so blessed as to be able, only one or two times, to recapture the past and rekindle the ancient fires, he will leave a name remembered and loved from generation to generation. Of living American writers there is particularly one who has this great gift."

In time, the chorus of acclaim for *My Àntonia* brought huge and lasting fame to its author. In 1934, the International Mark Twain Society voted *My Àntonia* the most memorable and representative American novel of the century.

Between 1912 and 1920 Willa Cather produced an extraordinary body of work. After *My Àntonia,* she continued to mine a rich, seemingly inexhaustible creative lode, writing several masterpieces. In these great years, she gathered many literary honors, including in 1923 the Pulitzer Prize for *One of Ours,* and became one of the most famous women in America. In *My Àntonia* Jim Burden reads his Virgil and lingers over this passage: "For I shall be the first, if I live, to bring the Muse into my country." She had brought the Muse into her country, and she also brought her country to the world. When Sinclair Lewis was awarded the Nobel Prize for Literature in 1930 he said publicly that it should have gone to Willa Cather.

As she grew older, Willa Cather lost much of her vigor and tried to save her energy for her writing. She who always enjoyed fame shunned public life. Her deepest instinct was to reject the modern world.

Throughout her life, Willa Cather wrote lovingly of childhood. She was always able to recall her own childhood vividly—not just the events of it, but the sensation of being a child. In her life, Cather's affection for children was played out in many ways. All through the late 1930s, the child prodigies Yehudi, Hephzibah, and Yalta Menuhin were great favorites of Cather. Every winter, they read Shakespeare with her twice a week in her Park Avenue apartment. Yehudi stored his sled in her closet and on snowy days, Shakespeare aside, they rambled through Central Park together, Yehudi on his sled, the seventy-year-old Cather walking briskly alongside. All through the late 1930s and early 1940s, the Menuhin children were a kind of treasure for the aging writer.

Willa Cather died from a massive cerebral hemorrhage in her Park Avenue apartment on April 24, 1947. She is buried in Jaffrey, New Hampshire, near the Shattuck Inn where, in the deep summer months, she wrote *My Àntonia.* Her epitaph reads: "That is happiness; to be dissolved into something complete and great."

The happiness described belonged to little Jim Burden sitting in the middle of a garden on a summer afternoon, leaning his back against a warm yellow pumpkin, listening to the wind and watching the tall grasses wave, gophers scurry up and down the garden furrows, and grasshoppers jump among the dried vines.

> Nothing happened. I did not expect anything to happen. I was something that lay under the sun and felt it, like the pumpkins, and I did not want to be anything more. I was entirely happy. Perhaps we feel like that when we die and become a part of something entire, whether it is sun and air, or goodness and knowledge. At any rate, that is happiness; to be dissolved into something complete and great. When it comes to one, it comes as naturally as sleep.

JOSLEEN WILSON

New York
1994

MY ÁNTONIA

CONTENTS

To

CARRIE AND IRENE MINER

In Memory of Affections Old and True

INTRODUCTION

LAST SUMMER, in a season of intense heat, Jim Burden and I happened to be crossing Iowa on the same train. He and I are old friends, we grew up together in the same Nebraska town, and we had a great deal to say to each other. While the train flashed through never-ending miles of ripe wheat, by country towns and bright-flowered pastures and oak groves wilting in the sun, we sat in the observation car, where the woodwork was hot to the touch and red dust lay deep over everything. The dust and heat, the burning wind, reminded us of many things. We were talking about what it is like to spend one's childhood in little towns like these, buried in wheat and corn, under stimulating extremes of climate: burning summers when the world lies green and billowy beneath a brilliant sky, when one is fairly stifled in vegetation, in the color and smell of strong weeds and heavy harvests; blustery winters with little snow, when the whole country is stripped bare and gray as sheet-iron. We agreed that no one who had not grown up in a little prairie town could know anything about it. It was a kind of freemasonry, we said.

Although Jim Burden and I both live in New York, I do not see much of him there. He is legal counsel for one of the great Western railways and is often away from his office for weeks together. That is one reason why we seldom meet. Another is that I do not like his wife. She is handsome, energetic, executive, but to me she seems unimpressionable and temperamentally incapable of enthusiasm. Her husband's quiet tastes irritate her, I think, and she finds it worthwhile to play the patroness to a group of young poets and painters of advanced ideas and mediocre ability. She has her own fortune and lives her own life. For some reason, she wishes to remain Mrs. James Burden.

As for Jim, disappointments have not changed him. The romantic disposition which often made him seem very funny as a boy has been one of the strongest elements in his success. He loves with a personal passion the great country through which his railway runs and branches. His faith in it and his knowledge of it have played an important part in its development.

During that burning day when we were crossing Iowa, our talk kept returning to a central figure, a Bohemian girl whom we had both known long ago. More than any other person we remembered, this girl seemed to mean to us the country, the conditions, the whole adventure of our childhood. I had lost sight of her altogether, but Jim had found her again after long years, and had renewed a friendship that meant a great deal to him. His mind was full of her that day. He made me see her again, feel her presence, revived all my old affection for her.

"From time to time I've been writing down what I remember about Ántonia," he told me. "On my long trips across the country, I amuse myself like that, in my stateroom."

When I told him that I would like to read his account of her, he said I should certainly see it—if it were ever finished.

Months afterward, Jim called at my apartment one stormy winter afternoon, carrying a legal portfolio. He brought it into the sitting-room with him, and said, as he stood warming his hands, "Here is the thing about Ántonia. Do you still want to read it? I finished it last night. I didn't take time to arrange it; I simply wrote down pretty much all that her name recalls to me. I suppose it hasn't any form. It hasn't any title, either." He went into the next room, sat down at my desk, and wrote across the face of the portfolio the word *Ántonia.* He frowned at this a moment, then prefixed another word, making it *My Ántonia.* That seemed to satisfy him.

BOOK ONE

The Shimerdas

I

I FIRST HEARD of Ántonia* on what seemed to me an interminable journey across the great midland plain of North America. I was ten years old then; I had lost both my father and mother within a year, and my Virginia relatives were sending me out to my grandparents, who lived in Nebraska. I traveled in the care of a mountain boy, Jake Marpole, one of the "hands" on my father's old farm under the Blue Ridge, who was now going west to work for my grandfather. Jake's experience of the world was not much wider than mine. He had never been in a railway train until the morning when we set out together to try our fortunes in a new world.

We went all the way in day-coaches, becoming more sticky and grimy with each stage of the journey. Jake bought everything the newsboys offered him: candy, oranges, brass collar buttons, a watch-charm, and for me a *Life of Jesse James,* which I remember as one of the most satisfactory books I have ever read. Beyond Chicago we were under the protection of a friendly passenger conductor, who knew all about the country to which we were going and gave us a great deal of advice in exchange for our confidence. He seemed to us an experienced and worldly man who had been almost everywhere; in his conversation he threw out lightly the names of distant states and cities. He wore the rings and pins and badges of different fraternal orders to which he belonged. Even his cuff-buttons were engraved with hieroglyphics, and he was more inscribed than an Egyptian obelisk.

Once when he sat down to chat, he told us that in the immigrant car ahead there was a family from "across the water" whose destination was the same as ours.

"They can't any of them speak English, except one little girl, and all she can say is, 'We go Black Hawk, Nebraska.' She's not much older than you, twelve or thirteen, maybe, and she's as bright as a new dollar. Don't you want to go ahead and see her, Jimmy? She's got the pretty brown eyes, too!"

*The Bohemian name *Ántonia* is strongly accented on the first syllable, like the English name *Anthony,* and the *i* is, of course, given the sound of long *e.* The name is pronounced An′-ton-ee-ah.

This last remark made me bashful, and I shook my head and settled down to *Jesse James.* Jake nodded at me approvingly and said you were likely to get diseases from foreigners.

I do not remember crossing the Missouri River, or anything about the long day's journey through Nebraska. Probably by that time I had crossed so many rivers that I was dull to them. The only thing very noticeable about Nebraska was that it was still, all day long, Nebraska.

I had been sleeping, curled up in a red plush seat, for a long while when we reached Black Hawk. Jake roused me and took me by the hand. We stumbled down from the train to a wooden siding, where men were running about with lanterns. I couldn't see any town, or even distant lights; we were surrounded by utter darkness. The engine was panting heavily after its long run. In the red glow from the fire-box, a group of people stood huddled together on the platform, encumbered by bundles and boxes. I knew this must be the immigrant family the conductor had told us about. The woman wore a fringed shawl tied over her head, and she carried a little tin trunk in her arms, hugging it as if it were a baby. There was an old man, tall and stooped. Two half-grown boys and a girl stood holding oilcloth bundles, and a little girl clung to her mother's skirts. Presently a man with a lantern approached them and began to talk, shouting and exclaiming. I pricked up my ears, for it was positively the first time I had ever heard a foreign tongue.

Another lantern came along. A bantering voice called out: "Hello, are you Mr. Burden's folks? If you are, it's me you're looking for. I'm Otto Fuchs. I'm Mr. Burden's hired man, and I'm to drive you out. Hello, Jimmy, ain't you scared to come so far west?"

I looked up with interest at the new face in the lantern-light. He might have stepped out of the pages of *Jesse James.* He wore a sombrero hat, with a wide leather band and a bright buckle, and the ends of his moustache were twisted up stiffly, like little horns. He looked lively and ferocious, I thought, and as if he had a history. A long scar ran across one cheek and drew the corner of his mouth up in a sinister curl. The top of his left ear was gone, and his skin was brown as an Indian's. Surely this was the face of a desperado. As he walked about the platform in his high-heeled boots, looking for our trunks, I saw that he was a rather slight man, quick and wiry, and light on his feet. He told us we had a long night drive ahead of us and had better be on the hike. He led us to a hitching-bar where two farm-wagons were tied, and I saw the foreign family crowding into one of them. The other was for us. Jake got on the front seat with Otto Fuchs, and I rode on the straw in the bottom of the wagon-box, covered up with a buffalo hide. The immigrants rumbled off into the empty darkness, and we followed them.

I tried to go to sleep, but the jolting made me bite my tongue, and I soon began to ache all over. When the straw settled down, I had a hard bed. Cautiously I slipped from under the buffalo hide, got up on my knees, and peered over the side of the wagon. There seemed to be nothing to see: no fences, no creeks or trees, no hills or fields. If there was a road, I could not make it out in the faint starlight. There was nothing but land: not a country at all, but the material out of which countries are made. No, there was nothing but land—slightly undulating, I knew, because often our wheels ground against the brake as we went down into a hollow and lurched up again on the other side. I had the feeling that the world was left behind, that we had got over the edge of it, and were outside man's jurisdiction. I had never before looked up at the sky when there was not a familiar mountain ridge against it. But this was the complete dome of heaven, all there was of it. I did not believe that my dead father and mother were watching me from up there; they would still be looking for me at the sheepfold down by the creek or along the white road that led to the mountain pastures. I had left even their spirits behind me. The wagon jolted on, carrying me I knew not whither. I don't think I was homesick. If we never arrived anywhere, it did not matter. Between that earth and that sky I felt erased, blotted out. I did not say my prayers that night: here, I felt, what would be would be.

II

I DO NOT REMEMBER our arrival at my grandfather's farm sometime before daybreak, after a drive of nearly twenty miles with heavy workhorses. When I awoke, it was afternoon. I was lying in a little room, scarcely larger than the bed that held me, and the window shade at my head was flapping softly in a warm wind. A tall woman, with wrinkled brown skin and black hair, stood looking down at me; I knew that she must be my grandmother. She had been crying, I could see, but when I opened my eyes she smiled, peered at me anxiously, and sat down on the foot of my bed.

"Had a good sleep, Jimmy?" she asked briskly. Then in a very different tone she said, as if to herself, "My, how you do look like your father!" I remembered that my father had been her little boy; she must often have come to wake him like this when he overslept. "Here are your clean clothes," she went on, stroking my coverlid with her brown hand as she talked. "But first you come down to the kitchen with me, and have a nice warm bath behind the stove. Bring your things; there's nobody about."

"Down to the kitchen" struck me as curious; it was always "out in the kitchen" at home. I picked up my shoes and stockings and followed her through the living room and down a flight of stairs into a basement. This basement was divided into a dining room at the right of the stairs and a kitchen at the left. Both rooms were plastered and whitewashed—the plaster laid directly upon the earth walls, as it used to be in dugouts. The floor was of hard cement. Up under the wooden ceiling there were little half-windows with white curtains, and pots of geraniums and wandering Jew in the deep sills. As I entered the kitchen, I sniffed a pleasant smell of gingerbread baking. The stove was very large, with bright nickel trimmings, and behind it there was a long wooden bench against the wall, and a tin washtub, into which grandmother poured hot and cold water. When she brought the soap and towels, I told her that I was used to taking my bath without help.

"Can you do your ears, Jimmy? Are you sure? Well, now, I call you a right smart little boy."

It was pleasant there in the kitchen. The sun shone into my bathwater through the west half-window, and a big Maltese cat came up and rubbed himself against the tub, watching me curiously. While I scrubbed, my grandmother busied herself in the dining room until I called anxiously, "Grandmother, I'm afraid the cakes are burning!" Then she came laughing, waving her apron before her as if she were shooing chickens.

She was a spare, tall woman, a little stooped, and she was apt to carry her head thrust forward in an attitude of attention, as if she were looking at something, or listening to something, far away. As I grew older, I came to believe that it was only because she was so often thinking of things that were far away. She was quick-footed and energetic in all her movements. Her voice was high and rather shrill, and she often spoke with an anxious inflection, for she was exceedingly desirous that everything should go with due order and decorum. Her laugh, too, was high, and perhaps a little strident, but there was a lively intelligence in it. She was then fifty-five years old, a strong woman, of unusual endurance.

After I was dressed, I explored the long cellar next the kitchen. It was dug out under the wing of the house, was plastered and cemented, with a stairway and an outside door by which the men came and went. Under one of the windows there was a place for them to wash when they came in from work.

While my grandmother was busy about supper, I settled myself on the wooden bench behind the stove and got acquainted with the cat—he caught not only rats and mice, but gophers, I was told. The patch of yellow sunlight on the floor traveled back toward the stairway, and grandmother and I talked about my journey, and about the arrival of the new Bohemian family; she said they were to be our nearest neighbors. We did not talk about the farm in Virginia, which had been her home for so many years. But after the men came in from the fields, and we were all seated at the supper table, then she asked Jake about the old place and about our friends and neighbors there.

My grandfather said little. When he first came in he kissed me and spoke kindly to me, but he was not demonstrative. I felt at once his deliberateness and personal dignity, and was a little in awe of him. The thing one immediately noticed about him was his beautiful, crinkly, snow-white beard. I once heard a missionary say it was like the beard of an Arabian sheik. His bald crown only made it more impressive.

Grandfather's eyes were not at all like those of an old man; they were bright blue, and had a fresh, frosty sparkle. His teeth were white and regular—so sound that he had never been to a dentist in his life. He had a delicate skin, easily roughened by sun and wind. When he was a young man his hair and beard were red; his eyebrows were still coppery.

As we sat at the table, Otto Fuchs and I kept stealing covert glances at each other. Grandmother had told me while she was getting supper that he was an Austrian who came to this country a young boy and had led an adventurous life in the far West among mining camps and cow outfits. His iron constitution was somewhat broken by mountain pneumonia, and he had drifted back to live in a milder country for a while. He had relatives in Bismarck, a German settlement to the north of us, but for a year now he had been working for Grandfather.

The minute supper was over, Otto took me into the kitchen to whisper to me about a pony down in the barn that had been bought for me at a sale; he had been riding him to find out whether he had any bad tricks, but he was a "perfect gentleman," and his name was Dude. Fuchs told me everything I wanted to know: how he had lost his ear in a Wyoming blizzard when he was a stage-driver, and how to throw a lasso. He promised to rope a steer for me before sundown next day. He got out his "chaps" and silver spurs to show them to Jake and me, and his best cowboy boots, with tops stitched in bold design—roses, and true-lover's knots, and undraped female figures. These, he solemnly explained, were angels.

Before we went to bed, Jake and Otto were called up to the living room for prayers. Grandfather put on silver-rimmed spectacles and read several Psalms. His voice was so sympathetic and he read so interestingly that I wished he had chosen one of my favorite chapters in the Book of Kings. I was awed by his intonation of the word "Selah." "He shall choose our inheritance for us, the excellency of Jacob whom He loved. Selah." I had no idea what the word meant; perhaps he had not. But, as he uttered it, it became oracular, the most sacred of words.

Early the next morning I ran out-of-doors to look about me. I had been told that ours was the only wooden house west of Black Hawk—until you came to the Norwegian settlement, where there were several. Our neighbors lived in sod houses and dugouts—comfortable, but not very roomy. Our white frame house, with a storey and half-storey above the basement, stood at the east end of what I might call the farmyard, with the windmill close by the kitchen door. From the windmill the ground sloped westward, down to the barns and granaries and pig-yards. This slope was trampled hard and bare, and washed out in winding gullies by the rain. Beyond the corncribs, at the bottom of the shallow draw, was a muddy little pond, with rusty willow bushes growing about it. The road from the post office came directly by our door, crossed the farmyard, and curved round this little pond, beyond which it began to climb the gentle swell of unbroken prairie to the west. There, along the western skyline it skirted a great cornfield, much larger than any field I had ever seen. This cornfield, and the sorghum patch behind the barn, were the only broken land in sight. Everywhere, as far as the eye could reach, there was nothing but rough, shaggy, red grass, most of it as tall as I.

North of the house, inside the ploughed fire-breaks, grew a thickset strip of box-elder trees, low and bushy, their leaves already turning yellow. This hedge was nearly a quarter of a mile long, but I had to look very hard to see it at all. The little trees were insignificant against the grass. It seemed as if the grass were about to run over them, and over the plum-patch behind the sod chicken-house.

As I looked about me I felt that the grass was the country, as the water is the sea. The red of the grass made all the great prairie the color of wine stains, or of certain seaweeds when they are first washed up. And there was so much motion in it; the whole country seemed, somehow, to be running.

I had almost forgotten that I had a grandmother, when she came out, her sunbonnet on her head, a grain sack in her hand, and asked me if I did not want to go to the garden with her to dig potatoes for dinner.

The garden, curiously enough, was a quarter of a mile from the house, and the way to it led up a shallow draw past the cattle corral. Grandmother called my attention to a stout hickory cane, tipped with copper, which hung by a leather thong from her belt. This, she said, was her rattlesnake cane. I must never go to the garden without a heavy stick or a corn-knife; she had killed a good many rattlers on her way back and forth. A little girl who lived on the Black Hawk road was bitten on the ankle and had been sick all summer.

I can remember exactly how the country looked to me as I walked beside my grandmother along the faint wagon tracks on that early September morning. Perhaps the glide of long railway travel was still with me, for more than anything else I felt motion in the landscape: in the fresh, easy-blowing morning wind, and in the earth itself, as if the shaggy grass were a sort of loose hide, and underneath it herds of wild buffalo were galloping, galloping . . .

Alone, I should never have found the garden—except, perhaps, for the big yellow pumpkins that lay about unprotected by their withering vines—and I felt very little interest in it when I got there. I wanted to walk straight on through the red grass and over the edge of the world, which could not be very far away. The light air about me told me that the world ended here: only the ground and sun and sky were left, and if one went a little farther there would be only sun and sky, and one would float off into them, like the tawny hawks which sailed over our heads making slow shadows on the grass. While Grandmother took the pitchfork we found standing in one of the rows and dug potatoes, while I picked them up out of the soft brown earth and put them into the bag, I kept looking up at the hawks that were doing what I might so easily do.

When Grandmother was ready to go, I said I would like to stay up there in the garden awhile.

She peered down at me from under her sunbonnet. "Aren't you afraid of snakes?"

"A little," I admitted, "but I'd like to stay, anyhow."

"Well, if you see one, don't have anything to do with him. The big yellow and brown ones won't hurt you; they're bull-snakes and help to keep the gophers down. Don't be scared if you see anything look out of that hole in the bank over there. That's a badger hole. He's about as big as a big 'possum, and his face is striped, black and white. He takes a chicken once in a while, but I won't let the men harm him. In a new country a body feels friendly to the animals. I like to have him come out and watch me when I'm at work."

Grandmother swung the bag of potatoes over her shoulder and went down the path, leaning forward a little. The road followed the windings of the draw; when she came to the first bend, she waved at me and disappeared. I was left alone with this new feeling of lightness and content.

I sat down in the middle of the garden, where snakes could scarcely approach unseen, and leaned my back against a warm yellow pumpkin. There were some ground-cherry bushes growing along the furrows, full of fruit. I turned back the papery triangular sheaths that protected the berries and ate a few. All about me giant grasshoppers, twice as big as any I had ever seen, were doing acrobatic feats among the dried vines. The gophers scurried up and down the ploughed ground. There in the sheltered draw-bottom the wind did not blow very hard, but I could hear it singing its humming tune up on the level, and I could see the tall grasses wave. The earth was warm under me, and warm as I crumbled it through my fingers. Queer little red bugs came out and moved in slow squadrons around me. Their backs were polished vermilion, with black spots. I kept as still as I could. Nothing happened. I did not expect anything to happen. I was something that lay under the sun and felt it, like the pumpkins, and I did not want to be anything more. I was entirely happy. Perhaps we feel like that when we die and become a part of something entire, whether it is sun and air, or goodness and knowledge. At any rate, that is happiness; to be dissolved into something complete and great. When it comes to one, it comes as naturally as sleep.

III

On Sunday morning Otto Fuchs was to drive us over to make the acquaintance of our new Bohemian neighbors. We were taking them some provisions, as they had come to live on a wild place where there was no garden or chicken-house, and very little broken land. Fuchs brought up a sack of potatoes and a piece of cured pork from the cellar, and Grandmother packed some loaves of Saturday's bread, a jar of butter, and several pumpkin pies in the straw of the wagon-box. We clambered up to the front seat and jolted off past the little pond and along the road that climbed to the big cornfield.

I could hardly wait to see what lay beyond that cornfield; but there was only red grass like ours, and nothing else, though from the high wagon seat one could look off a long way. The road ran about like a wild thing, avoiding the deep draws, crossing them where they were wide and shallow. And all along it, wherever it looped or ran, the sunflowers grew; some of them were as big as little trees, with great rough leaves and many branches which bore dozens of blossoms. They made a gold ribbon across the prairie. Occasionally one of the horses would tear off with his teeth a plant full of blossoms, and walk along munching it, the flowers nodding in time to his bites as he ate down toward them.

The Bohemian family, Grandmother told me as we drove along, had bought the homestead of a fellow countryman, Peter Krajiek, and had paid him more than it was worth. Their agreement with him was made before they left the old country, through a cousin of his, who was also a relative of Mrs. Shimerda. The Shimerdas were the first Bohemian family to come to this part of the county. Krajiek was their only interpreter, and could tell them anything he chose. They could not speak enough English to ask for advice, or even to make their most pressing wants known. One son, Fuchs said, was well-grown, and strong enough to work the land; but the father was old and frail and knew nothing about farming. He was a weaver by trade, had been a skilled workman on tapestries and upholstery materials. He had brought his fiddle with him, which wouldn't be of much use here, though he used to pick up money by it at home.

"If they're nice people, I hate to think of them spending the winter in that cave of Krajiek's," said Grandmother. "It's no better than a badger hole; no proper dugout at all. And I hear he's made them pay twenty dollars for his old cookstove that ain't worth ten."

"Yes'm," said Otto. "And he's sold 'em his oxen and his two bony old horses for the price of good work-teams. I'd have interfered about the horses—the old man can understand some German—if I'd 'a' thought it would do any good. But Bohemians has a natural distrust of Austrians."

Grandmother looked interested. "Now, why is that, Otto?"

Fuchs wrinkled his brow and nose. "Well, ma'm, it's politics. It would take me a long while to explain."

The land was growing rougher; I was told that we were approaching Squaw Creek, which cut up the west half of the Shimerdas' place and made the land of little value for farming. Soon we could see the broken, grassy clay cliffs which indicated the windings of the stream, and the glittering tops of the cottonwoods and ash trees that grew down in the ravine. Some of the cottonwoods had already turned, and the yellow leaves and shining white bark made them look like the gold and silver trees in fairy tales.

As we approached the Shimerdas' dwelling, I could still see nothing but rough red hillocks, and draws with shelving banks and long roots hanging out where the earth had crumbled away. Presently, against one of those banks, I saw a sort of shed, thatched with the same wine-colored grass that grew everywhere. Near it tilted a shattered windmill frame that had no wheel. We drove up to this skeleton to tie our horses, and then I saw a door and window sunk deep in the draw-bank. The door stood open, and a woman and a girl of fourteen ran out and looked up at us hopefully. A little girl trailed along behind them. The woman had on her head the same embroidered shawl with silk fringes that she wore when she had alighted from the train at Black Hawk. She was not old, but she was certainly not young. Her face was alert and lively, with a sharp chin and shrewd little eyes. She shook Grandmother's hand energetically.

"Very glad, very glad!" she ejaculated. Immediately she pointed to the bank out of which she had emerged and said, "House no good, house no good!"

Grandmother nodded consolingly. "You'll get fixed up comfortable after while, Mrs. Shimerda; make good house."

My grandmother always spoke in a very loud tone to foreigners, as if they were deaf. She made Mrs. Shimerda understand the friendly intention of our visit, and the Bohemian woman handled the loaves of bread and even smelled them, and examined the pies with lively curiosity, exclaiming, "Much good, much thank!"—and again she wrung Grandmother's hand.

The oldest son, Ambrož—they called it Ambrosch—came out of the cave and stood beside his mother. He was nineteen years old, short and broad-backed, with a close-cropped, flat head and a wide, flat face. His hazel eyes were little and shrewd, like his mother's, but more sly and suspicious; they fairly snapped at the food. The family had been living on corncakes and sorghum molasses for three days.

The little girl was pretty, but Án-tonia—they accented the name thus, strongly, when they spoke to her—was still prettier. I remembered what the conductor had said about her eyes. They were big and warm and full of light, like the sun shining on brown pools in the wood. Her skin was brown, too, and in her cheeks she had a glow of rich, dark color. Her brown hair was curly and wild-looking. The little sister, whom they called Yulka (Julka), was fair, and seemed mild and obedient. While I stood awkwardly confronting the two girls, Krajiek came up from the barn to see what was going on. With him was another Shimerda son. Even from a distance one could see that there was something strange about this boy. As he approached us, he began to make uncouth noises, and held up his hands to show us his fingers, which were webbed to the first knuckle, like a duck's foot. When he saw me draw back, he began to crow delightedly, "Hoo, hoo-hoo, hoo-hoo!" like a rooster. His mother scowled and said sternly, "Marek!" then spoke rapidly to Krajiek in Bohemian.

"She wants me to tell you he won't hurt nobody, Mrs. Burden. He was born like that. The others are smart. Ambrosch, he make good farmer." He struck Ambrosch on the back, and the boy smiled knowingly.

At that moment the father came out of the hole in the bank. He wore no hat, and his thick, iron-gray hair was brushed straight back from his forehead. It was so long that it bushed out behind his ears and made him look like the old portraits I remembered in Virginia. He was tall and slender, and his thin shoulders stooped. He looked at us understandingly, then took Grandmother's hand and bent over it. I noticed how white and well-shaped his own hands were. They looked calm, somehow, and skilled. His eyes were melancholy and were set back deep under his brow. His face was ruggedly formed, but it looked like ashes—like something from which all the warmth and light had died out. Everything about this old man was in keeping with his dignified manner. He was neatly dressed. Under his coat he wore a knitted grey vest, and, instead of a collar, a silk scarf of a dark bronze-green, carefully crossed and held together by a red coral pin. While Krajiek was translating for Mr. Shimerda, Ántonia came up to me and held out her hand coaxingly. In a moment we were running up the steep drawside together, Yulka trotting after us.

When we reached the level and could see the gold treetops, I pointed toward them, and Ántonia laughed and squeezed my hand as if to tell me how glad she was I had come. We raced off toward Squaw Creek and did not stop until the ground itself stopped—fell away before us so abruptly that the next step would have been out into the treetops. We stood panting on the edge of the ravine, looking down at the trees and bushes that grew below us. The wind was so strong that I had to hold my hat on, and the girls' skirts were blown out before them. Ántonia seemed to like it; she held her little sister by the hand and chattered away in that language which seemed to me spoken so much more rapidly than mine. She looked at me, her eyes fairly blazing with things she could not say.

"Name? What name?" she asked, touching me on the shoulder. I told her my name, and she repeated it after me and made Yulka say it. She pointed into the gold cottonwood tree behind whose top we stood and said again, "What name?"

We sat down and made a nest in the long red grass. Yulka curled up like a baby rabbit and played with a grasshopper. Ántonia pointed up to the sky and questioned me with her glance. I gave her the word, but she was not satisfied and pointed to my eyes. I told her, and she repeated the word, making it sound like "ice." She pointed up to the sky, then to my eyes, then back to the sky, with movements so quick and impulsive that she distracted me, and I had no idea what she wanted. She got up on her knees and wrung her hands. She pointed to her own eyes and shook her head, then to mine and to the sky, nodding violently.

"Oh," I exclaimed, "blue; blue sky."

She clapped her hands and murmured, "Blue sky, blue eyes," as if it amused her. While we snuggled down there out of the wind, she learned a score of words. She was quick, and very eager. We were so deep in the grass that we could see nothing but the blue sky over us and the gold tree in front of us. It was wonderfully pleasant. After Ántonia had said the new words over and over, she wanted to give me a little chased silver ring she wore on her middle finger. When she coaxed and insisted, I repulsed her quite sternly. I didn't want her ring, and I felt there was something reckless and extravagant about her wishing to give it away to a boy she had never seen before. No wonder Krajiek got the better of these people, if this was how they behaved.

While we were disputing about the ring, I heard a mournful voice calling, "Án-tonia, Án-tonia!" She sprang up like a hare. *"Tatinek! Tatinek!"* she shouted, and we ran to meet the old man who was coming toward us. Ántonia reached him first, took his hand and kissed it. When I came up, he touched my shoulder and looked searchingly down into my face for several seconds. I became somewhat embarrassed, for I was used to being taken for granted by my elders.

We went with Mr. Shimerda back to the dugout, where Grandmother was waiting for me. Before I got into the wagon, he took a book out of his pocket, opened it, and showed me a page with two alphabets, one English and the other Bohemian. He placed this book in my grandmother's hands, looked at her entreatingly, and said, with an earnestness which I shall never forget, "Te-e-ach, te-e-ach my Án-tonia!"

IV

On the afternoon of that same Sunday I took my first long ride on my pony, under Otto's direction. After that Dude and I went twice a week to the post office, six miles east of us, and I saved the men a good deal of time by riding on errands to our neighbors. When we had to borrow anything, or to send about word that there would be preaching at the sod schoolhouse, I was always the messenger. Formerly Fuchs attended to such things after working hours.

All the years that have passed have not dimmed my memory of that first glorious autumn. The new country lay open before me: there were no fences in those days, and I could choose my own way over the grass uplands, trusting the pony to get me home again. Sometimes I followed the sunflower-bordered roads. Fuchs told me that the sunflowers were introduced into that country by the Mormons; that at the time of the persecution, when they left Missouri and struck out into the wilderness to find a place where they could worship God in their own way, the members of the first exploring party, crossing the plains to Utah, scattered sunflower seed as they went. The next summer, when the long trains of wagons came through with all the women and children, they had the sunflower trail to follow. I believe that botanists do not confirm Fuchs's story, but insist that the sunflower was native to those plains. Nevertheless, that legend has stuck in my mind, and sunflower-bordered roads always seem to me the roads to freedom.

I used to love to drift along the pale-yellow cornfields, looking for the damp spots one sometimes found at their edges, where the smartweed soon turned a rich copper color and the narrow brown leaves hung curled like cocoons about the swollen joints of the stem. Sometimes I went south to visit our German neighbors and to admire their catalpa grove, or to see the big elm tree that grew up out of a deep crack in the earth and had a hawk's nest in its branches. Trees were so rare in that country, and they had to make such a hard fight to grow, that we used to feel anxious about them, and visit them as if they were persons. It must have been the scarcity of detail in that tawny landscape that made detail so precious.

Sometimes I rode north to the big prairie-dog town to watch the brown earth-owls fly home in the late afternoon and go down to their nests underground with the dogs. Ántonia Shimerda liked to go with me, and we used to wonder a great deal about these birds of subterranean habit. We had to be on our guard there, for rattlesnakes were always lurking about. They came to pick up an easy living among the dogs and owls, which were quite defenseless against them—took possession of their comfortable houses and ate the eggs and puppies. We felt sorry for the owls. It was always mournful to see them come flying home at sunset and disappear under the earth. But, after all, we felt, winged things who would live like that must be rather degraded creatures. The dog-town was a long way from any pond or creek. Otto Fuchs said he had seen populous dog-towns in the desert where there was no surface water for fifty miles; he insisted that some of the holes must go down to water—nearly two hundred feet, hereabouts. Ántonia said she didn't believe it; that the dogs probably lapped up the dew in the early morning, like the rabbits.

Ántonia had opinions about everything, and she was soon able to make them known. Almost every day she came running across the prairie to have her reading lesson with me. Mrs. Shimerda grumbled, but realized it was important that one member of the family should learn English. When the lesson was over, we used to go up to the watermelon patch behind the garden. I split the melons with an old corn-knife, and we lifted out the hearts and ate them with the juice trickling through our fingers. The white Christmas melons we did not touch, but we watched them with curiosity. They were to be picked late, when the hard frosts had set in, and put away for winter use. After weeks on the ocean, the Shimerdas were famished for fruit. The two girls would wander for miles along the edge of the cornfields, hunting for ground-cherries.

Ántonia loved to help Grandmother in the kitchen and to learn about cooking and housekeeping. She would stand beside her, watching her every movement. We were willing to believe that Mrs. Shimerda was a good housewife in her own country, but she managed poorly under new conditions: the conditions were bad enough, certainly!

I remember how horrified we were at the sour, ashy-gray bread she gave her family to eat. She mixed her dough, we discovered, in an old tin peck-measure that Krajiek had used about the barn. When she took the paste out to bake it, she left smears of dough sticking to the sides of the measure, put the measure on the shelf behind the stove, and let this residue ferment. The next time she made bread, she scraped this sour stuff down into the fresh dough to serve as yeast.

During those first months the Shimerdas never went to town. Krajiek encouraged them in the belief that in Black Hawk they would somehow be mysteriously separated from their money. They hated Krajiek, but they clung to him because he was the only human being with whom they could talk or from whom they could get information. He slept with the old man and the two boys in the dugout barn, along with the oxen. They kept him in their hole and fed him for the same reason that the prairie-dogs and the brown owls house the rattlesnakes—because they did not know how to get rid of him.

V

We knew that things were hard for our Bohemian neighbors, but the two girls were lighthearted and never complained. They were always ready to forget their troubles at home, and to run away with me over the prairie, scaring rabbits or starting up flocks of quail.

I remember Ántonia's excitement when she came into our kitchen one afternoon and announced: "My papa find friends up north with Russian mans. Last night he take me for see, and I can understand very much talk. Nice mans, Mrs. Burden. One is fat and all the time laugh. Everybody laugh. The first time I see my papa laugh in this kawn-tree. Oh, very nice!"

I asked her if she meant the two Russians who lived up by the big dog-town. I had often been tempted to go to see them when I was riding in that direction, but one of them was a wild-looking fellow and I was a little afraid of him. Russia seemed to me more remote than any other country—farther away than China, almost as far as the North Pole. Of all the strange, uprooted people among the first settlers, those two men were the strangest and the most aloof. Their last names were unpronounceable, so they were called Pavel and Peter. They went about making signs to people, and until the Shimerdas came they had no friends. Krajiek could understand them a little, but he had cheated them in a trade, so they avoided him. Pavel, the tall one, was said to be an anarchist; since he had no means of imparting his opinions, probably his wild gesticulations and his generally excited and rebellious manner gave rise to this supposition. He must once have been a very strong man, but now his great frame, with big, knotty joints, had a wasted look, and the skin was drawn tight over his high cheekbones. His breathing was hoarse, and he always had a cough.

Peter, his companion, was a very different sort of fellow; short, bow-legged, and as fat as butter. He always seemed pleased when he met people on the road, smiled and took off his cap to everyone, men as well as women. At a distance, on his wagon, he looked like an old man; his hair and beard were of such a pale flaxen color that they seemed white in the sun. They were as thick and curly as carded wool. His rosy face, with its snub nose, set in this fleece, was like a melon among its leaves. He was usually called Curly Peter or Rooshian Peter.

The two Russians made good farmhands, and in summer they worked out together. I had heard our neighbors laughing when they told how Peter always had to go home at night to milk his cow. Other bachelor homesteaders used canned milk, to save trouble. Sometimes Peter came to church at the sod schoolhouse. It was there I first saw him, sitting on a low bench by the door, his plush cap in his hands, his bare feet tucked apologetically under the seat.

After Mr. Shimerda discovered the Russians, he went to see them almost every evening, and sometimes took Ántonia with him. She said they came from a part of Russia where the language was not very different from Bohemian, and if I wanted to go to their place, she could talk to them for me. One afternoon, before the heavy frosts began, we rode up there together on my pony.

The Russians had a neat log house built on a grassy slope, with a windlass well beside the door. As we rode up the draw, we skirted a big melon patch, and a garden where squashes and yellow cucumbers lay about on the sod. We found Peter out behind his kitchen, bending over a washtub. He was working so hard that he did not hear us coming. His whole body moved up and down as he rubbed, and he was a funny sight from the rear, with his shaggy head and bandy legs. When he straightened himself up to greet us, drops of perspiration were rolling from his thick nose down onto his curly beard. Peter dried his hands and seemed glad to leave his washing. He took us down to see his chickens and his cow that was grazing on the hillside. He told Ántonia that in his country only rich people had cows, but here any man could have one who would take care of her. The milk was good for Pavel, who was often sick, and he could make butter by beating sour cream with a wooden spoon. Peter was very fond of his cow. He patted her flanks and talked to her in Russian while he pulled up her lariat pin and set it in a new place.

After he had shown us his garden, Peter trundled a load of watermelons up the hill in his wheelbarrow. Pavel was not at home. He was off somewhere helping to dig a well. The house I thought very comfortable for two men who were "batching." Besides the kitchen, there was a living room, with a wide double bed built against the wall, properly made up with blue gingham sheets and pillows. There was a little storeroom, too, with a window, where they kept guns and saddles and tools, and old coats and boots. That day the floor was covered with garden things, drying for winter; corn and beans and fat yellow cucumbers. There were no screens or window-blinds in the house, and all the doors and windows stood wide open, letting in flies and sunshine alike.

Peter put the melons in a row on the oilcloth-covered table and stood over them, brandishing a butcher knife. Before the blade got fairly into them, they split of their own ripeness, with a delicious sound. He gave us knives, but no plates, and the top of the table was soon swimming with juice and seeds. I had never seen anyone eat so many melons as Peter ate. He assured us that they were good for one—better than medicine: in his country people lived on them at this time of year. He was very hospitable and jolly. Once, while he was looking at Ántonia, he sighed and told us that if he had stayed at home in Russia perhaps by this time he would have had a pretty daughter of his own to cook and keep house for him. He said he had left his country because of a "great trouble."

When we got up to go, Peter looked about in perplexity for something that would entertain us. He ran into the storeroom and brought out a gaudily painted harmonica, sat down on a bench, and spreading his fat legs apart began to play like a whole band. The tunes were either very lively or very doleful, and he sang words to some of them.

Before we left, Peter put ripe cucumbers into a sack for Mrs. Shimerda and gave us a lard-pail full of milk to cook them in. I had never heard of cooking cucumbers, but Ántonia assured me they were very good. We had to walk the pony all the way home to keep from spilling the milk.

VI

One afternoon we were having our reading lesson on the warm, grassy bank where the badger lived. It was a day of amber sunlight, but there was a shiver of coming winter in the air. I had seen ice on the little horse-pond that morning, and as we went through the garden we found the tall asparagus, with its red berries, lying on the ground, a mass of slimy green.

Tony was barefooted, and she shivered in her cotton dress and was comfortable only when we were tucked down on the baked earth, in the full blaze of the sun. She could talk to me about almost anything by this time. That afternoon she was telling me how highly esteemed our friend the badger was in her part of the world, and how men kept a special kind of dog, with very short legs, to hunt him. Those dogs, she said, went down into the hole after the badger and killed him there in a terrific struggle underground; you could hear the barks and yelps outside. Then the dog dragged himself back, covered with bites and scratches, to be rewarded and petted by his master. She knew a dog who had a star on his collar for every badger he had killed.

The rabbits were unusually spry that afternoon. They kept starting up all about us, and dashing off down the draw as if they were playing a game of some kind. But the little buzzing things that lived in the grass were all dead—all but one. While we were lying there against the warm bank, a little insect of the palest, frailest green hopped painfully out of the buffalo grass and tried to leap into a bunch of bluestem. He missed it, fell back, and sat with his head sunk between his long legs, his antennae quivering, as if he were waiting for something to come and finish him. Tony made a warm nest for him in her hands; talked to him gaily and indulgently in Bohemian. Presently he began to sing for us—a thin, rusty little chirp. She held him close to her ear and laughed, but a moment afterward I saw there were tears in her eyes. She told me that in her village at home there was an old beggar woman who went about selling herbs and roots she had dug up in the forest. If you took her in and gave her a warm place by the fire, she sang old songs to the children in a cracked voice, like this. Old Hata, she was called, and the children loved to see her coming and saved their cakes and sweets for her.

When the bank on the other side of the draw began to throw a narrow shelf of shadow, we knew we ought to be starting homeward; the chill came on quickly when the sun got low, and Ántonia's dress was thin. What were we to do with the frail little creature we had lured back to life by false pretenses? I offered my pockets, but Tony shook her head and carefully put the green insect in her hair, tying her big handkerchief down loosely over her curls. I said I would go with her until we could see Squaw Creek, and then turn and run home. We drifted along lazily, very happy, through the magical light of the late afternoon.

All those fall afternoons were the same, but I never got used to them. As far as we could see, the miles of copper-red grass were drenched in sunlight that was stronger and fiercer than at any other time of the day. The blond cornfields were red gold, the haystacks turned rosy and threw long shadows. The whole prairie was like the bush that burned with fire and was not consumed. That hour always had the exultation of victory, of triumphant ending, like a hero's death—heroes who died young and gloriously. It was a sudden transfiguration, a lifting-up of day.

How many an afternoon Ántonia and I have trailed along the prairie under that magnificence! And always two long black shadows flitted before us or followed after, dark spots on the ruddy grass.

We had been silent a long time, and the edge of the sun sank nearer and nearer the prairie floor, when we saw a figure moving on the edge of the upland, a gun over his shoulder. He was walking slowly, dragging his feet along as if he had no purpose. We broke into a run to overtake him.

"My papa sick all the time," Tony panted as we flew. "He not look good, Jim."

As we neared Mr. Shimerda she shouted, and he lifted his head and peered about. Tony ran up to him, caught his hand and pressed it against her cheek. She was the only one of his family who could rouse the old man from the torpor in which he seemed to live. He took the bag from his belt and showed us three rabbits he had shot, looked at Ántonia with a wintry flicker of a smile and began to tell her something. She turned to me.

"My *tatinek* make me little hat with the skins, little hat for win-ter!" she exclaimed joyfully. "Meat for eat, skin for hat"—she told off these benefits on her fingers.

Her father put his hand on her hair, but she caught his wrist and lifted it carefully away, talking to him rapidly. I heard the name of old Hata. He untied the handkerchief, separated her hair with his fingers, and stood looking down at the green insect. When it began to chirp faintly, he listened as if it were a beautiful sound.

I picked up the gun he had dropped: a queer piece from the old country, short and heavy, with a stag's head on the cock. When he saw me examining it, he turned to me with his faraway look that always made me feel as if I were down at the bottom of a well. He spoke kindly and gravely, and Ántonia translated:

"My *tatinek* say when you are big boy, he give you his gun. Very fine, from Bohemie. It was belong to a great man, very rich, like what you not got here; many fields, many forests, many big house. My papa play for his wedding, and he give my papa fine gun, and my papa give you."

I was glad that this project was one of futurity. There never were such people as the Shimerdas for wanting to give away everything they had. Even the mother was always offering me things, though I knew she expected substantial presents in return. We stood there in friendly silence, while the feeble minstrel sheltered in Ántonia's hair went on with its scratchy chirp. The old man's smile, as he listened, was so full of sadness, of pity for things, that I never afterward forgot it. As the sun sank there came a sudden coolness and the strong smell of earth and drying grass. Ántonia and her father went off hand in hand, and I buttoned up my jacket and raced my shadow home.

VII

MUCH AS I LIKED Ántonia, I hated a superior tone that she sometimes took with me. She was four years older than I, to be sure, and had seen more of the world; but I was a boy and she was a girl, and I resented her protecting manner. Before the autumn was over, she began to treat me more like an equal and to defer to me in other things than reading lessons. This change came about from an adventure we had together.

One day when I rode over to the Shimerdas' I found Ántonia starting off on foot for Russian Peter's house, to borrow a spade Ambrosch needed. I offered to take her on the pony, and she got up behind me. There had been another black frost the night before, and the air was clear and heady as wine. Within a week all the blooming roads had been despoiled, hundreds of miles of yellow sunflowers had been transformed into brown, rattling, burry stalks.

We found Russian Peter digging his potatoes. We were glad to go in and get warm by his kitchen stove and to see his squashes and Christmas melons, heaped in the storeroom for winter. As we rode away with the spade, Ántonia suggested that we stop at the prairie-dog-town and dig into one of the holes. We could find out whether they ran straight down, or were horizontal, like mole-holes; whether they had underground connections; whether the owls had nests down there, lined with feathers. We might get some puppies, or owl eggs, or snakeskins.

The dog-town was spread out over perhaps ten acres. The grass had been nibbled short and even, so this stretch was not shaggy and red like the surrounding country, but gray and velvety. The holes were several yards apart, and were disposed with a good deal of regularity, almost as if the town had been laid out in streets and avenues. One always felt that an orderly and very sociable kind of life was going on there. I picketed Dude down in a draw, and we went wandering about, looking for a hole that would be easy to dig. The dogs were out, as usual, dozens of them, sitting up on their hind legs over the doors of their houses. As we approached, they barked, shook their tails at us, and scurried underground. Before the mouths of the holes were little patches of sand and gravel, scratched up, we supposed, from a long way below the surface.

Here and there, in the town, we came on larger gravel patches, several yards away from any hole. If the dogs had scratched the sand up in excavating, how had they carried it so far? It was on one of these gravel beds that I met my adventure.

We were examining a big hole with two entrances. The burrow sloped into the ground at a gentle angle, so that we could see where the two corridors united, and the floor was dusty from use, like a little highway over which much travel went. I was walking backward, in a crouching position, when I heard Ántonia scream. She was standing opposite me, pointing behind me and shouting something in Bohemian. I whirled round, and there, on one of those dry gravel beds, was the biggest snake I had ever seen. He was sunning himself, after the cold night, and he must have been asleep when Ántonia screamed. When I turned, he was lying in long loose waves, like a letter *W*. He twitched and began to coil slowly. He was not merely a big snake, I thought—he was a circus monstrosity. His abominable muscularity, his loathsome, fluid motion, somehow made me sick. He was as thick as my leg, and looked as if millstones couldn't crush the disgusting vitality out of him. He lifted his hideous little head, and rattled. I didn't run because I didn't think of it—if my back had been against a stone wall I couldn't have felt more cornered. I saw his coils tighten—now he would spring, spring his length, I remembered. I ran up and drove at his head with my spade, struck him fairly across the neck, and in a minute he was all about my feet in wavy loops. I struck now from hate. Ántonia, barefooted as she was, ran up behind me. Even after I had pounded his ugly head flat, his body kept on coiling and winding, doubling and falling back on itself. I walked away and turned my back. I felt seasick.

Ántonia came after me, crying, "O Jimmy, he not bite you? You sure? Why you not run when I say?"

"What did you jabber Bohunk for? You might have told me there was a snake behind me!" I said petulantly.

"I know I am just awful, Jim, I was so scared." She took my handkerchief from my pocket and tried to wipe my face with it, but I snatched it away from her. I suppose I looked as sick as I felt.

"I never know you was so brave, Jim," she went on comfortingly. "You is just like big mans; you wait for him lift his head and then you go for him. Ain't you feel scared a bit? Now we take that snake home and show everybody. Nobody ain't seen in this kawn-tree so big snake like you kill."

She went on in this strain until I began to think that I had longed for this opportunity, and had hailed it with joy. Cautiously we went back to the snake; he was still groping with his tail, turning up his ugly belly in the light. A faint, fetid smell came from him, and a thread of green liquid oozed from his crushed head.

"Look, Tony, that's his poison," I said.

I took a long piece of string from my pocket, and she lifted his head with the spade while I tied a noose around it. We pulled him out straight and measured him by my riding-quirt; he was about five and a half feet long. He had twelve rattles, but they were broken off before they began to taper, so I insisted that he must once have had twenty-four. I explained to Ántonia how this meant that he was twenty-four years old, that he must have been there when white men first came, left on from buffalo and Indian times. As I turned him over, I began to feel proud of him, to have a kind of respect for his age and size. He seemed like the ancient, eldest Evil. Certainly his kind have left horrible unconscious memories in all warm-blooded life. When we dragged him down into the draw, Dude sprang off to the end of his tether and shivered all over—wouldn't let us come near him.

We decided that Ántonia should ride Dude home, and I would walk. As she rode along slowly, her bare legs swinging against the pony's sides, she kept shouting back to me about how astonished everybody would be. I followed with the spade over my shoulder, dragging my snake. Her exultation was contagious. The great land had never looked to me so big and free. If the red grass were full of rattlers, I was equal to them all. Nevertheless, I stole furtive glances behind me now and then to see that no avenging mate, older and bigger than my quarry, was racing up from the rear.

The sun had set when we reached our garden and went down the draw toward the house. Otto Fuchs was the first one we met. He was sitting on the edge of the cattle-pond, having a quiet pipe before supper. Ántonia called him to come quick and look. He did not say anything for a minute, but scratched his head and turned the snake over with his boot.

"Where did you run onto that beauty, Jim?"

"Up at the dog-town," I answered laconically.

"Kill him yourself? How come you to have a weepon?"

"We'd been up to Russian Peter's, to borrow a spade for Ambrosch."

Otto shook the ashes out of his pipe and squatted down to count the rattles. "It was just luck you had a tool," he said cautiously. "Gosh! I wouldn't want to do any business with that fellow myself, unless I had a fence-post along. Your grandmother's snake-cane wouldn't more than tickle him. He could stand right up and talk to you, he could. Did he fight hard?"

Ántonia broke in: "He fight something awful! He is all over Jimmy's boots. I scream for him to run, but he just hit and hit that snake like he was crazy."

Otto winked at me. After Ántonia rode on he said: "Got him in the head first crack, didn't you? That was just as well."

We hung him up to the windmill, and when I went down to the kitchen, I found Ántonia standing in the middle of the floor, telling the story with a great deal of color.

Subsequent experiences with rattlesnakes taught me that my first encounter was fortunate in circumstance. My big rattler was old, and had led too easy a life; there was not much fight in him. He had probably lived there for years, with a fat prairie-dog for breakfast whenever he felt like it, a sheltered home, even an owl-feather bed, perhaps, and he had forgot that the world doesn't owe rattlers a living. A snake of his size, in fighting trim, would be more than any boy could handle. So in reality it was a mock adventure; the game was fixed for me by chance, as it probably was for many a dragon-slayer. I had been adequately armed by Russian Peter; the snake was old and lazy; and I had Ántonia beside me, to appreciate and admire.

That snake hung on our corral fence for several days; some of the neighbors came to see it and agreed that it was the biggest rattler ever killed in those parts. This was enough for Ántonia. She liked me better from that time on, and she never took a supercilious air with me again. I had killed a big snake—I was now a big fellow.

VIII

WHILE THE AUTUMN COLOR was growing pale on the grass and cornfields, things went badly with our friends the Russians. Peter told his troubles to Mr. Shimerda: he was unable to meet a note which fell due on the first of November; had to pay an exorbitant bonus on renewing it, and to give a mortgage on his pigs and horses and even his milk cow. His creditor was Wick Cutter, the merciless Black Hawk moneylender, a man of evil name throughout the county, of whom I shall have more to say later. Peter could give no very clear account of his transactions with Cutter. He only knew that he had first borrowed two hundred dollars, then another hundred, then fifty—that each time a bonus was added to the principal, and the debt grew faster than any crop he planted. Now everything was plastered with mortgages.

Soon after Peter renewed his note, Pavel strained himself lifting timbers for a new barn, and fell over among the shavings with such a gush of blood from the lungs that his fellow workmen thought he would die on the spot. They hauled him home and put him into his bed, and there he lay, very ill indeed. Misfortune seemed to settle like an evil bird on the roof of the log house, and to flap its wings there, warning human beings away. The Russians had such bad luck that people were afraid of them and liked to put them out of mind.

One afternoon Ántonia and her father came over to our house to get buttermilk, and lingered, as they usually did, until the sun was low. Just as they were leaving, Russian Peter drove up. Pavel was very bad, he said, and wanted to talk to Mr. Shimerda and his daughter; he had come to fetch them. When Ántonia and her father got into the wagon, I entreated Grandmother to let me go with them: I would gladly go without my supper, I would sleep in the Shimerdas' barn and run home in the morning. My plan must have seemed very foolish to her, but she was often large-minded about humoring the desires of other people. She asked Peter to wait a moment, and when she came back from the kitchen she brought a bag of sandwiches and doughnuts for us.

Mr. Shimerda and Peter were on the front seat; Ántonia and I sat in the straw behind and ate our lunch as we bumped along. After the sun sank, a cold wind sprang up and moaned over the prairie. If this turn in the weather had come sooner, I should not have got away. We burrowed down in the straw and curled up close together, watching the angry red die out of the west and the stars begin to shine in the clear, windy sky. Peter kept sighing and groaning. Tony whispered to me that he was afraid Pavel would never get well. We lay still and did not talk. Up there the stars grew magnificently bright. Though we had come from such different parts of the world, in both of us there was some dusky superstition that those shining groups have their influence upon what is and what is not to be. Perhaps Russian Peter, come from farther away than any of us, had brought from his land, too, some such belief.

The little house on the hillside was so much the color of the night that we could not see it as we came up the draw. The ruddy windows guided us—the light from the kitchen stove, for there was no lamp burning.

We entered softly. The man in the wide bed seemed to be asleep. Tony and I sat down on the bench by the wall and leaned our arms on the table in front of us. The firelight flickered on the hewn logs that supported the thatch overhead. Pavel made a rasping sound when he breathed, and he kept moaning. We waited. The wind shook the doors and windows impatiently, then swept on again, singing through the big spaces. Each gust, as it bore down, rattled the panes, and swelled off like the others. They made me think of defeated armies, retreating; or of ghosts who were trying desperately to get in for shelter, and then went moaning on. Presently, in one of those sobbing intervals between the blasts, the coyotes tuned up with their whining howl; one, two, three, then all together—to tell us that winter was coming. This sound brought an answer from the bed—a long complaining cry—as if Pavel were having bad dreams or were waking to some old misery. Peter listened, but did not stir. He was sitting on the floor by the kitchen stove. The coyotes broke out again: yap, yap, yap—then the high whine. Pavel called for something and struggled up on his elbow.

"He is scared of the wolves," Ántonia whispered to me. "In his country there are very many, and they eat men and women." We slid closer together along the bench.

I could not take my eyes off the man in the bed. His shirt was hanging open, and his emaciated chest, covered with yellow bristle, rose and fell horribly. He began to cough. Peter shuffled to his feet, caught up the teakettle and mixed him some hot water and whiskey. The sharp smell of spirits went through the room.

Pavel snatched the cup and drank, then made Peter give him the bottle and slipped it under his pillow, grinning disagreeably, as if he had outwitted someone. His eyes followed Peter about the room with a contemptuous, unfriendly expression. It seemed to me that he despised him for being so simple and docile.

Presently Pavel began to talk to Mr. Shimerda, scarcely above a whisper. He was telling a long story, and as he went on, Ántonia took my hand under the table and held it tight. She leaned forward and strained her ears to hear him. He grew more and more excited, and kept pointing all around his bed, as if there were things there and he wanted Mr. Shimerda to see them.

"It's wolves, Jimmy," Ántonia whispered. "It's awful, what he says!"

The sick man raged and shook his fist. He seemed to be cursing people who had wronged him. Mr. Shimerda caught him by the shoulders, but could hardly hold him in bed. At last he was shut off by a coughing fit which fairly choked him. He pulled a cloth from under his pillow and held it to his mouth. Quickly it was covered with bright red spots—I thought I had never seen any blood so bright. When he lay down and turned his face to the wall, all the rage had gone out of him. He lay patiently fighting for breath, like a child with croup. Ántonia's father uncovered one of his long bony legs and rubbed it rhythmically. From our bench we could see what a hollow case his body was. His spine and shoulder-blades stood out like the bones under the hide of a dead steer left in the fields. That sharp backbone must have hurt him when he lay on it.

Gradually, relief came to all of us. Whatever it was, the worst was over. Mr. Shimerda signed to us that Pavel was asleep. Without a word Peter got up and lit his lantern. He was going out to get his team to drive us home. Mr. Shimerda went with him. We sat and watched the long bowed back under the blue sheet, scarcely daring to breathe.

On the way home, when we were lying in the straw, under the jolting and rattling Ántonia told me as much of the story as she could. What she did not tell me then, she told later; we talked of nothing else for days afterward.

When Pavel and Peter were young men, living at home in Russia, they were asked to be groomsmen for a friend who was to marry the belle of another village. It was in the dead of winter and the groom's party went over to the wedding in sledges. Peter and Pavel drove in the groom's sledge, and six sledges followed with all his relatives and friends.

After the ceremony at the church, the party went to a dinner given by the parents of the bride. The dinner lasted all afternoon; then it became a supper and continued far into the night. There was much dancing and drinking. At midnight the parents of the bride said goodbye to her and blessed her. The groom took her up in his arms and carried her out to his sledge and tucked her under the blankets. He sprang in beside her, and Pavel and Peter (our Pavel and Peter!) took the front seat. Pavel drove. The party set out with singing and the jingle of sleigh bells, the groom's sledge going first. All the drivers were more or less the worse for merrymaking, and the groom was absorbed in his bride.

The wolves were bad that winter, and everyone knew it, yet when they heard the first wolf-cry, the drivers were not much alarmed. They had too much good food and drink inside them. The first howls were taken up and echoed and with quickening repetitions. The wolves were coming together. There was no moon, but the starlight was clear on the snow. A black drove came up over the hill behind the wedding party. The wolves ran like streaks of shadow; they looked no bigger than dogs, but there were hundreds of them.

Something happened to the hindmost sledge: the driver lost control—he was probably very drunk—the horses left the road, the sledge was caught in a clump of trees, and overturned. The occupants rolled out over the snow, and the fleetest of the wolves sprang upon them. The shrieks that followed made everybody sober. The drivers stood up and lashed their horses. The groom had the best team and his sledge was lightest—all the others carried from six to a dozen people.

Another driver lost control. The screams of the horses were more terrible to hear than the cries of the men and women. Nothing seemed to check the wolves. It was hard to tell what was happening in the rear; the people who were falling behind shrieked as piteously as those who were already lost. The little bride hid her face on the groom's shoulder and sobbed. Pavel sat still and watched his horses. The road was clear and white, and the groom's three blacks went like the wind. It was only necessary to be calm and to guide them carefully.

At length, as they breasted a long hill, Peter rose cautiously and looked back. "There are only three sledges left," he whispered.

"And the wolves?" Pavel asked.

"Enough! Enough for all of us."

Pavel reached the brow of the hill, but only two sledges followed him down the other side. In that moment on the hilltop, they saw behind them a whirling black group on the snow. Presently the groom screamed. He saw his father's sledge overturned, with his mother and sisters. He sprang up as if he meant to jump, but the girl shrieked and held him back. It was even then too late. The black ground-shadows were already crowding over the heap in the road, and one horse ran out across the fields, his harness hanging to him, wolves at his heels. But the groom's movement had given Pavel an idea.

They were within a few miles of their village now. The only sledge left out of six was not very far behind them, and Pavel's middle horse was failing. Beside a frozen pond something happened to the other sledge; Peter saw it plainly. Three big wolves got abreast of the horses, and the horses went crazy. They tried to jump over each other, got tangled up in the harness, and overturned the sledge.

When the shrieking behind them died away, Pavel realized that he was alone upon the familiar road. "They still come?" he asked Peter.

"Yes."

"How many?"

"Twenty, thirty—enough."

Now his middle horse was being almost dragged by the other two. Pavel gave Peter the reins and stepped carefully into the back of the sledge. He called to the groom that they must lighten—and pointed to the bride. The young man cursed him and held her tighter. Pavel tried to drag her away. In the struggle, the groom rose. Pavel knocked him over the side of the sledge and threw the girl after him. He said he never remembered exactly how he did it, or what happened afterward. Peter, crouching in the front seat, saw nothing. The first thing either of them noticed was a new sound that broke into the clear air, louder than they had ever heard it before—the bell of the monastery of their own village, ringing for early prayers.

Pavel and Peter drove into the village alone, and they had been alone ever since. They were run out of their village. Pavel's own mother would not look at him. They went away to strange towns, but when people learned where they came from, they were always asked if they knew the two men who had fed the bride to the wolves. Wherever they went, the story followed them. It took them five years to save money enough to come to America. They worked in Chicago, Des Moines, Fort Wayne, but they were always unfortunate. When Pavel's health grew so bad, they decided to try farming.

Pavel died a few days after he unburdened his mind to Mr. Shimerda, and was buried in the Norwegian graveyard. Peter sold off everything, and left the country—went to be cook in a railway construction camp where gangs of Russians were employed.

At his sale we bought Peter's wheelbarrow and some of his harness. During the auction he went about with his head down, and never lifted his eyes. He seemed not to care about anything. The Black Hawk moneylender who held mortgages on Peter's livestock was there, and he bought in the sale notes at about fifty cents on the dollar. Everyone said Peter kissed the cow before she was led away by her new owner. I did not see him do it, but this I know: after all his furniture and his cook-stove and pots and pans had been hauled off by the purchasers, when his house was stripped and bare, he sat down on the floor with his clasp-knife and ate all the melons that he had put away for winter. When Mr. Shimerda and Krajiek drove up in their wagon to take Peter to the train, they found him with a dripping beard, surrounded by heaps of melon rinds.

The loss of his two friends had a depressing effect upon old Mr. Shimerda. When he was out hunting, he used to go into the empty log house and sit there, brooding. This cabin was his hermitage until the winter snows penned him in his cave. For Ántonia and me, the story of the wedding party was never at an end. We did not tell Pavel's secret to anyone, but guarded it jealously—as if the wolves of the Ukraine had gathered that night long ago, and the wedding party been sacrificed, to give us a painful and peculiar pleasure. At night, before I went to sleep, I often found myself in a sledge drawn by three horses, dashing through a country that looked something like Nebraska and something like Virginia.

IX

THE FIRST SNOWFALL came early in December. I remember how the world looked from our sitting-room window as I dressed behind the stove that morning: the low sky was like a sheet of metal; the blond cornfields had faded out into ghostliness at last; the little pond was frozen under its stiff willow bushes. Big white flakes were whirling over everything and disappearing in the red grass.

Beyond the pond, on the slope that climbed to the cornfield, there was, faintly marked in the grass, a great circle where the Indians used to ride. Jake and Otto were sure that when they galloped round that ring the Indians tortured prisoners, bound to a stake in the center; but Grandfather thought they merely ran races or trained horses there. Whenever one looked at this slope against the setting sun, the circle showed like a pattern in the grass; and this morning, when the first light spray of snow lay over it, it came out with wonderful distinctness, like strokes of Chinese white on canvas. The old figure stirred me as it had never done before and seemed a good omen for the winter.

As soon as the snow had packed hard, I began to drive about the country in a clumsy sleigh that Otto Fuchs made for me by fastening a wooden goods-box on bobs. Fuchs had been apprenticed to a cabinet-maker in the old country and was very handy with tools. He would have done a better job if I hadn't hurried him. My first trip was to the post office, and the next day I went over to take Yulka and Ántonia for a sleigh ride.

It was a bright, cold day. I piled straw and buffalo robes into the box, and took two hot bricks wrapped in old blankets. When I got to the Shimerdas I did not go up to the house but sat in my sleigh at the bottom of the draw and called. Ántonia and Yulka came running out, wearing little rabbit-skin hats their father had made for them. They had heard about my sledge from Ambrosch and knew why I had come. They tumbled in beside me and we set off toward the north, along a road that happened to be broken.

The sky was brilliantly blue, and the sunlight on the glittering white stretches of prairie was almost blinding. As Ántonia said, the whole world was changed by the snow; we kept looking in vain for familiar landmarks. The deep arroyo through which Squaw Creek wound was now only a cleft between snowdrifts—very blue when one looked down into it. The treetops that had been gold all the autumn were dwarfed and twisted, as if they would never have any life in them again. The few little cedars, which were so dull and dingy before, now stood out a strong, dusky green. The wind had the burning taste of fresh snow; my throat and nostrils smarted as if someone had opened a hartshorn bottle. The cold stung, and at the same time delighted one. My horse's breath rose like steam, and whenever we stopped he smoked all over. The cornfields got back a little of their color under the dazzling light, and stood the palest possible gold in the sun and snow. All about us the snow was crusted in shallow terraces, with tracings like ripple-marks at the edges, curly waves that were the actual impression of the stinging lash in the wind.

The girls had on cotton dresses under their shawls; they kept shivering beneath the buffalo robes and hugging each other for warmth. But they were so glad to get away from their ugly cave and their mother's scolding that they begged me to go on and on, as far as Russian Peter's house. The great fresh open, after the stupefying warmth indoors, made them behave like wild things. They laughed and shouted, and said they never wanted to go home again. Couldn't we settle down and live in Russian Peter's house, Yulka asked, and couldn't I go to town and buy things for us to keep house with?

All the way to Russian Peter's we were extravagantly happy, but when we turned back—it must have been about four o'clock—the east wind grew stronger and began to howl; the sun lost its heartening power and the sky became gray and somber. I took off my long woollen comforter and wound it around Yulka's throat. She got so cold that we made her hide her head under the buffalo robe. Ántonia and I sat erect, but I held the reins clumsily, and my eyes were blinded by the wind a good deal of the time. It was growing dark when we got to their house, but I refused to go in with them and get warm. I knew my hands would ache terribly if I went near a fire. Yulka forgot to give me back my comforter, and I had to drive home directly against the wind. The next day I came down with an attack of quinsy, which kept me in the house for nearly two weeks.

The basement kitchen seemed heavenly safe and warm in those days—like a tight little boat in a winter sea. The men were out in the fields all day, husking corn, and when they came in at noon, with long caps pulled down over their ears and their feet in red-lined overshoes, I used to think they were like Arctic explorers. In the afternoons, when

Grandmother sat upstairs darning, or making husking-gloves, I read *The Swiss Family Robinson* aloud to her, and I felt that the Swiss family had no advantages over us in the way of an adventurous life. I was convinced that man's strongest antagonist is the cold. I admired the cheerful zest with which Grandmother went about keeping us warm and comfortable and well-fed. She often reminded me, when she was preparing for the return of the hungry men, that this country was not like Virginia; and that here a cook had, as she said, "very little to do with." On Sundays she gave us as much chicken as we could eat, and on other days we had ham or bacon or sausage meat. She baked either pies or cake for us every day, unless, for a change, she made my favorite pudding, striped with currants and boiled in a bag.

Next to getting warm and keeping warm, dinner and supper were the most interesting things we had to think about. Our lives centered around warmth and food and the return of the men at nightfall. I used to wonder, when they came in tired from the fields, their feet numb and their hands cracked and sore, how they could do all the chores so conscientiously: feed and water and bed the horses, milk the cows, and look after the pigs. When supper was over, it took them a long while to get the cold out of their bones. While Grandmother and I washed the dishes and Grandfather read his paper upstairs, Jake and Otto sat on the long bench behind the stove, "easing" their inside boots, or rubbing mutton tallow into their cracked hands.

Every Saturday night we popped corn or made taffy, and Otto Fuchs used to sing, "For I Am a Cowboy and Know I've Done Wrong," or, "Bury Me Not on the Lone Prairee." He had a good baritone voice and always led the singing when we went to church services at the sod schoolhouse.

I can still see those two men sitting on the bench; Otto's close-clipped head and Jake's shaggy hair slicked flat in front by a wet comb. I can see the sag of their tired shoulders against the whitewashed wall. What good fellows they were, how much they knew, and how many things they had kept faith with!

Fuchs had been a cowboy, a stage-driver, a bartender, a miner; had wandered all over that great western country and done hard work everywhere, though, as Grandmother said, he had nothing to show for it. Jake was duller than Otto. He could scarcely read, wrote even his name with difficulty, and he had a violent temper which sometimes made him behave like a crazy man—tore him all to pieces and actually made him ill. But he was so soft-hearted that anyone could impose upon him. If he, as he said, "forgot himself" and swore before Grandmother, he went about depressed and shamefaced all day. They were both of them jovial about the cold in winter and the heat in summer, always ready to work overtime and to meet emergencies. It was a matter of pride with them not to spare themselves. Yet they were the sort of men who never get on, somehow, or do anything but work hard for a dollar or two a day.

On those bitter, starlit nights, as we sat around the old stove that fed us and warmed us and kept us cheerful, we could hear the coyotes howling down by the corrals, and their hungry, wintry cry used to remind the boys of wonderful animal stories; about gray wolves and bears in the Rockies, wildcats and panthers in the Virginia mountains. Sometimes Fuchs could be persuaded to talk about the outlaws and desperate characters he had known. I remember one funny story about himself that made Grandmother, who was working her bread on the bread-board, laugh until she wiped her eyes with her bare arm, her hands being floury. It was like this:

When Otto left Austria to come to America, he was asked by one of his relatives to look after a woman who was crossing on the same boat, to join her husband in Chicago. The woman started off with two children, but it was clear that her family might grow larger on the journey. Fuchs said he "got on fine with the kids," and liked the mother, though she played a sorry trick on him. In midocean she proceeded to have not one baby, but three! This event made Fuchs the object of undeserved notoriety, since he was traveling with her. The steerage stewardess was indignant with him, the doctor regarded him with suspicion. The first-cabin passengers, who made up a purse for the woman, took an embarrassing interest in Otto, and often enquired of him about his charge. When the triplets were taken ashore at New York, he had, as he said, "to carry some of them." The trip to Chicago was even worse than the ocean voyage. On the train it was very difficult to get milk for the babies and to keep their bottles clean. The mother did her best, but no woman, out of her natural resources, could feed three babies. The husband, in Chicago, was working in a furniture factory for modest wages, and when he met his family at the station he was rather crushed by the size of it. He, too, seemed to consider Fuchs in some fashion to blame. "I was sure glad," Otto concluded, "that he didn't take his hard feeling out on that poor woman; but he had a sullen eye for me, all right! Now, did you ever hear of a young feller's having such hard luck, Mrs. Burden?"

Grandmother told him she was sure the Lord had remembered these things to his credit, and had helped him out of many a scrape when he didn't realize that he was being protected by Providence.

X

For several weeks after my sleigh ride, we heard nothing from the Shimerdas. My sore throat kept me indoors, and Grandmother had a cold which made the housework heavy for her. When Sunday came she was glad to have a day of rest. One night at supper Fuchs told us he had seen Mr. Shimerda out hunting.

"He's made himself a rabbit-skin cap, Jim, and a rabbit-skin collar that he buttons on outside his coat. They ain't got but one overcoat among 'em over there, and they take turns wearing it. They seem awful scared of cold, and stick in that hole in the bank like badgers."

"All but the crazy boy," Jake put in. "He never wears the coat. Krajiek says he's turrible strong and can stand anything. I guess rabbits must be getting scarce in this locality. Ambrosch come along by the cornfield yesterday where I was at work and showed me three prairie dogs he'd shot. He asked me if they was good to eat. I spit and made a face and took on, to scare him, but he just looked like he was smarter'n me and put 'em back in his sack and walked off."

Grandmother looked up in alarm and spoke to Grandfather. "Josiah, you don't suppose Krajiek would let them poor creatures eat prairie dogs, do you?"

"You had better go over and see our neighbors tomorrow, Emmaline," he replied gravely.

Fuchs put in a cheerful word and said prairie dogs were clean beasts and ought to be good for food, but their family connections were against them. I asked what he meant, and he grinned and said they belonged to the rat family.

When I went downstairs in the morning, I found Grandmother and Jake packing a hamper basket in the kitchen.

"Now, Jake," Grandmother was saying, "if you can find that old rooster that got his comb froze, just give his neck a twist, and we'll take him along. There's no good reason why Mrs. Shimerda couldn't have got hens from her neighbors last fall and had a henhouse going by now. I reckon she was confused and didn't know where to begin. I've come strange to a new country myself, but I never forgot hens are a good thing to have, no matter what you don't have.

"Just as you say, ma'm," said Jake, "but I hate to think of Krajiek getting a leg of that old rooster." He tramped out through the long cellar and dropped the heavy door behind him.

After breakfast Grandmother and Jake and I bundled ourselves up and climbed into the cold front wagon-seat. As we approached the Shimerdas', we heard the frosty whine of the pump and saw Ántonia, her head tied up and her cotton dress blown about her, throwing all her weight on the pump-handle as it went up and down. She heard our wagon, looked back over her shoulder, and, catching up her pail of water, started at a run for the hole in the bank.

Jake helped Grandmother to the ground, saying he would bring the provisions after he had blanketed his horses. We went slowly up the icy path toward the door sunk in the drawside. Blue puffs of smoke came from the stovepipe that stuck out through the grass and snow, but the wind whisked them roughly away.

Mrs. Shimerda opened the door before we knocked and seized Grandmother's hand. She did not say "How do!" as usual, but at once began to cry, talking very fast in her own language, pointing to her feet which were tied up in rags, and looking about accusingly at everyone.

The old man was sitting on a stump behind the stove, crouching over as if he were trying to hide from us. Yulka was on the floor at his feet, her kitten in her lap. She peeped out at me and smiled, but, glancing up at her mother, hid again. Ántonia was washing pans and dishes in a dark corner. The crazy boy lay under the only window, stretched on a gunny-sack stuffed with straw. As soon as we entered, he threw a grain-sack over the crack at the bottom of the door. The air in the cave was stifling, and it was very dark, too. A lighted lantern, hung over the stove, threw out a feeble yellow glimmer.

Mrs. Shimerda snatched off the covers of two barrels behind the door, and made us look into them. In one there were some potatoes that had been frozen and were rotting, in the other was a little pile of flour. Grandmother murmured something in embarrassment, but the Bohemian woman laughed scornfully, a kind of whinny-laugh, and, catching up an empty coffee pot from the shelf, shook it at us with a look positively vindictive.

Grandmother went on talking in her polite Virginia way, not admitting their stark need or her own remissness, until Jake arrived with the hamper, as if in direct answer to Mrs. Shimerda's reproaches. Then the poor woman broke down. She dropped on the floor beside her crazy son, hid her face on her knees, and sat crying bitterly. Grandmother paid no heed to her, but called Ántonia to come and help empty the basket.

Tony left her corner reluctantly. I had never seen her crushed like this before.

"You not mind my poor *mamenka,* Mrs. Burden. She is so sad," she whispered, as she wiped her wet hands on her skirt and took the things Grandmother handed her.

The crazy boy, seeing the food, began to make soft, gurgling noises and stroked his stomach. Jake came in again, this time with a sack of potatoes. Grandmother looked about in perplexity.

"Haven't you got any sort of cave or cellar outside, Ántonia? This is no place to keep vegetables. How did your potatoes get frozen?"

"We get from Mr. Bushy, at the post office—what he throw out. We got no potatoes, Mrs. Burden," Tony admitted mournfully.

When Jake went out, Marek crawled along the floor and stuffed up the door-crack again. Then, quietly as a shadow, Mr. Shimerda came out from behind the stove. He stood brushing his hand over his smooth gray hair, as if he were trying to clear away a fog about his head. He was clean and neat as usual, with his green neckcloth and his coral pin. He took Grandmother's arm and led her behind the stove, to the back of the room. In the rear wall was another little cave; a round hole, not much bigger than an oil barrel, scooped out in the black earth. When I got up on one of the stools and peered into it, I saw some quilts and a pile of straw. The old man held the lantern. "Yulka," he said in a low, despairing voice, "Yulka; my Ántonia!"

Grandmother drew back. 'You mean they sleep in there—your girls?' He bowed his head.

Tony slipped under his arm. "It is very cold on the floor, and this is warm like the badger hole. I like for sleep there," she insisted eagerly. "My *mamenka* have nice bed, with pillows from our own geese in Bohemie. See, Jim?" She pointed to the narrow bunk which Krajiek had built against the wall for himself before the Shimerdas came.

Grandmother sighed. "Sure enough, where *would* you sleep, dear! I don't doubt you're warm there. You'll have a better house after while, Ántonia, and then you will forget these hard times."

Mr. Shimerda made Grandmother sit down on the only chair and pointed his wife to a stool beside her. Standing before them with his hand on Ántonia's shoulder, he talked in a low tone, and his daughter translated. He wanted us to know that they were not beggars in the old country; he made good wages, and his family were respected there. He left Bohemia with more than a thousand dollars in savings, after their passage money was paid. He had in some way lost on exchange in New York, and the railway fare to Nebraska was more than they had expected.

By the time they paid Krajiek for the land, and bought his horses and oxen and some old farm machinery, they had very little money left. He wished Grandmother to know, however, that he still had some money. If they could get through until spring came, they would buy a cow and chickens and plant a garden, and would then do very well. Ambrosch and Ántonia were both old enough to work in the fields, and they were willing to work. But the snow and the bitter weather had disheartened them all.

Ántonia explained that her father meant to build a new house for them in the spring; he and Ambrosch had already split the logs for it, but the logs were all buried in the snow, along the creek where they had been felled.

While Grandmother encouraged and gave them advice, I sat down on the floor with Yulka and let her show me her kitten. Marek slid cautiously toward us and began to exhibit his webbed fingers. I knew he wanted to make his queer noises for me—to bark like a dog or whinny like a horse—but he did not dare in the presence of his elders. Marek was always trying to be agreeable, poor fellow, as if he had it on his mind that he must make up for his deficiencies.

Mrs. Shimerda grew more calm and reasonable before our visit was over, and, while Ántonia translated, put in a word now and then on her own account. The woman had a quick ear, and caught up phrases whenever she heard English spoken. As we rose to go, she opened her wooden chest and brought out a bag made of bed-ticking, about as long as a flour sack and half as wide, stuffed full of something. At sight of it, the crazy boy began to smack his lips. When Mrs. Shimerda opened the bag and stirred the contents with her hand, it gave out a salty, earthy smell, very pungent, even among the other odors of that cave. She measured a teacup full, tied it up in a bit of sacking, and presented it ceremoniously to Grandmother.

"For cook," she announced. "Little now; be very much when cook," spreading out her hands as if to indicate that the pint would swell to a gallon. "Very good. You no have in this country. All things for eat better in my country."

"Maybe so, Mrs. Shimerda," Grandmother said dryly. "I can't say but I prefer our bread to yours, myself."

Ántonia undertook to explain. "This very good, Mrs. Burden"—she clasped her hands as if she could not express how good—"it make very much when you cook, like what my mama say. Cook with rabbit, cook with chicken, in the gravy—oh, so good!"

All the way home Grandmother and Jake talked about how easily good Christian people could forget they were their brothers' keepers.

"I will say, Jake, some of our brothers and sisters are hard to keep. Where's a body to begin, with these people? They're wanting in everything, and most of all in horse sense. Nobody can give 'em that, I guess. Jimmy, here, is about as able to take over a homestead as they are. Do you reckon that boy Ambrosch has any real push in him?"

"He's a worker, all right, ma'm, and he's got some ketch-on about him; but he's a mean one. Folks can be mean enough to get on in this world; and then, ag'in, they can be too mean."

That night, while Grandmother was getting supper, we opened the package Mrs. Shimerda had given her. It was full of little brown chips that looked like the shavings of some root. They were as light as feathers, and the most noticeable thing about them was their penetrating, earthy odor. We could not determine whether they were animal or vegetable.

"They might be dried meat from some queer beast, Jim. They ain't dried fish, and they never grew on stalk or vine. I'm afraid of 'em. Anyhow, I shouldn't want to eat anything that had been shut up for months with old clothes and goose pillows."

She threw the package into the stove, but I bit off a corner of one of the chips I held in my hand, and chewed it tentatively. I never forgot the strange taste; though it was many years before I knew that those little brown shavings, which the Shimerdas had brought so far and treasured so jealously, were dried mushrooms. They had been gathered, probably, in some deep Bohemian forest. . . .

XI

During the week before Christmas, Jake was the most important person of our household, for he was to go to town and do all our Christmas shopping. But on the twenty-first of December, the snow began to fall. The flakes came down so thickly that from the sitting-room windows I could not see beyond the windmill—its frame looked dim and gray, unsubstantial like a shadow. The snow did not stop falling all day, or during the night that followed. The cold was not severe, but the storm was quiet and resistless. The men could not go farther than the barns and corral. They sat about the house most of the day as if it were Sunday—greasing their boots, mending their suspenders, plaiting whip-lashes.

On the morning of the twenty-second, Grandfather announced at breakfast that it would be impossible to go to Black Hawk for Christmas purchases. Jake was sure he could get through on horseback, and bring home our things in saddlebags; but Grandfather told him the roads would be obliterated, and a newcomer in the country would be lost ten times over. Anyway, he would never allow one of his horses to be put to such a strain.

We decided to have a country Christmas, without any help from town. I had wanted to get some picture books for Yulka and Ántonia; even Yulka was able to read a little now. Grandmother took me into the ice-cold storeroom, where she had some bolts of gingham and sheeting. She cut squares of cotton cloth and we sewed them together into a book. We bound it between pasteboards, which I covered with brilliant calico, representing scenes from a circus. For two days I sat at the dining-room table, pasting this book full of pictures for Yulka. We had files of those good old family magazines which used to publish colored lithographs of popular paintings, and I was allowed to use some of these. I took "Napoleon Announcing the Divorce to Josephine" for my frontispiece. On the white pages I grouped Sunday-school cards and advertising cards which I had brought from my "old country." Fuchs got out the old candle-molds and made tallow candles. Grandmother hunted up her fancy cake-cutters and baked gingerbread men and roosters, which we decorated with burnt sugar and red cinnamon drops.

On the day before Christmas, Jake packed the things we were sending to the Shimerdas in his saddlebags and set off on Grandfather's gray gelding. When he mounted his horse at the door, I saw that he had a hatchet slung to his belt, and he gave Grandmother a meaning look which told me he was planning a surprise for me. That afternoon I watched long and eagerly from the sitting-room window. At last I saw a dark spot moving on the west hill, beside the half-buried cornfield, where the sky was taking on a coppery flush from the sun that did not quite break through. I put on my cap and ran out to meet Jake. When I got to the pond, I could see that he was bringing in a little cedar tree across his pommel. He used to help my father cut Christmas trees for me in Virginia, and he had not forgotten how much I liked them.

By the time we had placed the cold, fresh-smelling little tree in a corner of the sitting-room, it was already Christmas Eve. After supper we all gathered there, and even Grandfather, reading his paper by the table, looked up with friendly interest now and then. The cedar was about five feet high and very shapely. We hung it with the gingerbread animals, strings of popcorn, and bits of candle which Fuchs had fitted into pasteboard sockets. Its real splendors, however, came from the most unlikely place in the world—from Otto's cowboy trunk. I had never seen anything in that trunk but old boots and spurs and pistols, and a fascinating mixture of yellow leather thongs, cartridges, and shoemaker's wax. From under the lining he now produced a collection of brilliantly colored paper figures, several inches high and stiff enough to stand alone. They had been sent to him year after year, by his old mother in Austria. There was a bleeding heart, in tufts of paper lace; there was the three kings, gorgeously apparelled, and the ox and the ass and the shepherds; there was the Baby in the manger, and a group of angels, singing; there were camels and leopards, held by the black slaves of the three kings. Our tree became the talking tree of the fairy tale; legends and stories nestled like birds in its branches. Grandmother said it reminded her of the Tree of Knowledge. We put sheets of cotton wool under it for a snow-field, and Jake's pocket-mirror for a frozen lake.

I can see them now, exactly as they looked, working about the table in the lamplight: Jake with his heavy features, so rudely molded that his face seemed, somehow, unfinished; Otto with his half-ear and the savage scar that made his upper lip curl so ferociously under his twisted moustache. As I remember them, what unprotected faces they were; their very roughness and violence made them defenseless. These boys had no practiced manner behind which they could retreat and hold people at a distance. They had only their hard fists to batter at the world with. Otto was already one of those drifting, case-hardened laborers who never marry or have children of their own. Yet he was so fond of children!

XII

On Christmas morning, when I got down to the kitchen, the men were just coming in from their morning chores—the horses and pigs always had their breakfast before we did. Jake and Otto shouted "Merry Christmas!" to me and winked at each other when they saw the waffle-irons on the stove. Grandfather came down, wearing a white shirt and his Sunday coat. Morning prayers were longer than usual. He read the chapters from Saint Matthew about the birth of Christ, and as we listened, it all seemed like something that had happened lately, and near at hand. In his prayer he thanked the Lord for the first Christmas, and for all that it had meant to the world ever since. He gave thanks for our food and comfort, and prayed for the poor and destitute in great cities, where the struggle for life was harder than it was here with us. Grandfather's prayers were often very interesting. He had the gift of simple and moving expression. Because he talked so little, his words had a peculiar force; they were not worn dull from constant use. His prayers reflected what he was thinking about at the time, and it was chiefly through them that we got to know his feelings and his views about things.

After we sat down to our waffles and sausage, Jake told us how pleased the Shimerdas had been with their presents; even Ambrosch was friendly and went to the creek with him to cut the Christmas tree. It was a soft gray day outside, with heavy clouds working across the sky, and occasional squalls of snow. There were always odd jobs to be done about the barn on holidays, and the men were busy until afternoon. Then Jake and I played dominoes, while Otto wrote a long letter home to his mother. He always wrote to her on Christmas Day, he said, no matter where he was, and no matter how long it had been since his last letter. All afternoon he sat in the dining room. He would write for a while, then sit idle, his clenched fist lying on the table, his eyes following the pattern of the oilcloth. He spoke and wrote his own language so seldom that it came to him awkwardly. His effort to remember entirely absorbed him.

At about four o'clock a visitor appeared: Mr. Shimerda, wearing his rabbit-skin cap and collar, and new mittens his wife had knitted. He had come to thank us for the presents, and for all Grandmother's kindness to his family. Jake and Otto joined us from the basement and we sat about the stove, enjoying the deepening grey of the winter afternoon and the atmosphere of comfort and security in my grandfather's house. This feeling seemed completely to take possession of Mr. Shimerda. I suppose, in the crowded clutter of their cave, the old man had come to believe that peace and order had vanished from the earth, or existed only in the old world he had left so far behind. He sat still and passive, his head resting against the back of the wooden rocking chair, his hands relaxed upon the arms. His face had a look of weariness and pleasure, like that of sick people when they feel relief from pain. Grandmother insisted on his drinking a glass of Virginia apple brandy after his long walk in the cold, and when a faint flush came up in his cheeks, his features might have been cut out of a shell, they were so transparent. He said almost nothing, and smiled rarely; but as he rested there we all had a sense of his utter content.

As it grew dark, I asked whether I might light the Christmas tree before the lamp was brought. When the candle-ends sent up their conical yellow flames, all the colored figures from Austria stood out clear and full of meaning against the green boughs. Mr. Shimerda rose, crossed himself, and quietly knelt down before the tree, his head sunk forward. His long body formed a letter *S*. I saw Grandmother look apprehensively at Grandfather. He was rather narrow in religious matters, and sometimes spoke out and hurt people's feelings. There had been nothing strange about the tree before, but now, with some one kneeling before it—images, candles . . . Grandfather merely put his fingertips to his brow and bowed his venerable head, thus Protestantizing the atmosphere.

We persuaded our guest to stay for supper with us. He needed little urging. As we sat down to the table, it occurred to me that he liked to look at us, and that our faces were open books to him. When his deep-seeing eyes rested on me, I felt as if he were looking far ahead into the future for me, down the road I would have to travel.

At nine o'clock Mr. Shimerda lighted one of our lanterns and put on his overcoat and fur collar. He stood in the little entry hall, the lantern and his fur cap under his arm, shaking hands with us. When he took Grandmother's hand, he bent over it as he always did, and said slowly, "Good wo-man!" He made the sign of the cross over me, put on his cap and went off in the dark. As we turned back to the sitting-room, Grandfather looked at me searchingly. "The prayers of all good people are good," he said quietly.

XIII

THE WEEK FOLLOWING Christmas brought in a thaw, and by New Year's Day all the world about us was a broth of gray slush, and the guttered slope between the windmill and the barn was running black water. The soft black earth stood out in patches along the roadsides. I resumed all my chores, carried in the cobs and wood and water, and spent the afternoons at the barn, watching Jake shell corn with a hand-sheller.

One morning, during this interval of fine weather, Ántonia and her mother rode over on one of their shaggy old horses to pay us a visit. It was the first time Mrs. Shimerda had been to our house, and she ran about examining our carpets and curtains and furniture, all the while commenting upon them to her daughter in an envious, complaining tone. In the kitchen she caught up an iron pot that stood on the back of the stove and said: "You got many, Shimerdas no got." I thought it weak-minded of Grandmother to give the pot to her.

After dinner, when she was helping to wash the dishes, she said, tossing her head: "You got many things for cook. If I got all things like you, I make much better."

She was a conceited, boastful old thing, and even misfortune could not humble her. I was so annoyed that I felt coldly even toward Ántonia and listened unsympathetically when she told me her father was not well.

"My papa sad for the old country. He not look good. He never make music any more. At home he play violin all the time, for weddings and for dance. Here never. When I beg him for play, he shake his head no. Some days he take his violin out of his box and make with his fingers on the strings, like this, but never he make the music. He don't like this kawn-tree."

"People who don't like this country ought to stay at home," I said severely. "We don't make them come here."

"He not want to come, nev-er!" she burst out. "My *mamenka* make him come. All the time she says, 'America big country; much money, much land for my boys, much husband for my girls.' My papa, he cry for leave his old friends what make music with him. He love very much the man what play the long horn like this"—she indicated a slide trombone. "They go to school together and are friends from boys. But my mama, she want Ambrosch for be rich, with many cattle."

"Your mama," I said angrily, "wants other people's things."

"Your grandfather is rich," she retorted fiercely. "Why he not help my papa? Ambrosch be rich, too, after while, and he pay back. He is very smart boy. For Ambrosch my mama come here."

Ambrosch was considered the important person in the family. Mrs. Shimerda and Ántonia always deferred to him, though he was often surly with them and contemptuous toward his father. Ambrosch and his mother had everything their own way. Though Ántonia loved her father more than she did anyone else, she stood in awe of her elder brother.

After I watched Ántonia and her mother go over the hill on their miserable horse, carrying our iron pot with them, I turned to Grandmother, who had taken up her darning, and said I hoped that snooping old woman wouldn't come to see us any more.

Grandmother chuckled and drove her bright needle across a hole in Otto's sock. "She's not old, Jim, though I expect she seems old to you. No, I wouldn't mourn if she never came again. But, you see, a body never knows what traits poverty might bring out in 'em. It makes a woman grasping to see her children want for things. Now read me a chapter in *The Prince of the House of David*. Let's forget the Bohemians."

We had three weeks of this mild, open weather. The cattle in the corral ate corn almost as fast as the men could shell it for them, and we hoped they would be ready for an early market. One morning the two big bulls, Gladstone and Brigham Young, thought spring had come, and they began to tease and butt at each other across the barbed wire that separated them. Soon they got angry. They bellowed and pawed up the soft earth with their hoofs, rolling their eyes and tossing their heads. Each withdrew to a far corner of his own corral, and then they made for each other at a gallop. Thud, thud, we could hear the impact of their great heads, and their bellowing shook the pans on the kitchen shelves. Had they not been dehorned, they would have torn each other to pieces. Pretty soon the fat steers took it up and began butting and horning each other. Clearly, the affair had to be stopped. We all stood by and watched admiringly while Fuchs rode into the corral with a pitchfork and prodded the bulls again and again, finally driving them apart.

The big storm of the winter began on my eleventh birthday, the twentieth of January. When I went down to breakfast that morning, Jake and Otto came in white as snowmen, beating their hands and stamping their feet. They began to laugh boisterously when they saw me, calling:

"You've got a birthday present this time, Jim, and no mistake. They was a full-grown blizzard ordered for you."

All day the storm went on. The snow did not fall this time, it simply spilled out of heaven, like thousands of feather-beds being emptied. That afternoon the kitchen was a carpenter-shop; the men brought in their tools and made two great wooden shovels with long handles. Neither Grandmother nor I could go out in the storm, so Jake fed the chickens and brought in a pitiful contribution of eggs.

Next day our men had to shovel until noon to reach the barn—and the snow was still falling! There had not been such a storm in the ten years my grandfather had lived in Nebraska. He said at dinner that we would not try to reach the cattle—they were fat enough to go without their corn for a day or two; but tomorrow we must feed them and thaw out their water-tap so that they could drink. We could not so much as see the corrals, but we knew the steers were over there, huddled together under the north bank. Our ferocious bulls, subdued enough by this time, were probably warming each other's backs. "This'll take the bile out of 'em!" Fuchs remarked gleefully.

At noon that day the hens had not been heard from. After dinner Jake and Otto, their damp clothes now dried on them, stretched their stiff arms and plunged again into the drifts. They made a tunnel through the snow to the henhouse, with walls so solid that Grandmother and I could walk back and forth in it. We found the chickens asleep; perhaps they thought night had come to stay. One old rooster was stirring about, pecking at the solid lump of ice in their water-tin. When we flashed the lantern in their eyes, the hens set up a great cackling and flew about clumsily, scattering down-feathers. The mottled, pin-headed guinea hens, always resentful of captivity, ran screeching out into the tunnel and tried to poke their ugly, painted faces through the snow walls. By five o'clock the chores were done—just when it was time to begin them all over again! That was a strange, unnatural sort of day.

XIV

ON THE MORNING of the twenty-second I wakened with a start. Before I opened my eyes, I seemed to know that something had happened. I heard excited voices in the kitchen—Grandmother's was so shrill that I knew she must be almost beside herself. I looked forward to any new crisis with delight. What could it be, I wondered, as I hurried into my clothes. Perhaps the barn had burned; perhaps the cattle had frozen to death; perhaps a neighbor was lost in the storm.

Down in the kitchen Grandfather was standing before the stove with his hands behind him. Jake and Otto had taken off their boots and were rubbing their woollen socks. Their clothes and boots were steaming, and they both looked exhausted. On the bench behind the stove lay a man, covered up with a blanket. Grandmother motioned me to the dining room. I obeyed reluctantly. I watched her as she came and went, carrying dishes. Her lips were tightly compressed and she kept whispering to herself: "Oh, dear Savior! Lord, Thou knowest!"

Presently Grandfather came in and spoke to me: "Jimmy, we will not have prayers this morning, because we have a great deal to do. Old Mr. Shimerda is dead, and his family are in great distress. Ambrosch came over here in the middle of the night, and Jake and Otto went back with him. The boys have had a hard night, and you must not bother them with questions. That is Ambrosch, asleep on the bench. Come in to breakfast, boys."

After Jake and Otto had swallowed their first cup of coffee, they began to talk excitedly, disregarding Grandmother's warning glances. I held my tongue, but I listened with all my ears.

"No, sir," Fuchs said in answer to a question from Grandfather, "nobody heard the gun go off. Ambrosch was out with the ox-team, trying to break a road, and the women-folks was shut up tight in their cave. When Ambrosch come in, it was dark and he didn't see nothing, but the oxen acted kind of queer. One of 'em ripped around and got away from him—bolted clean out of the stable. His hands is blistered where the rope run through. He got a lantern and went back and found the old man, just as we seen him."

"Poor soul, poor soul!" Grandmother groaned. "I'd like to think he never done it. He was always considerate and unwishful to give trouble. How could he forget himself and bring this on us!"

"I don't think he was out of his head for a minute, Mrs. Burden," Fuchs declared. "He done everything natural. You know he was always sort of fixy, and fixy he was to the last. He shaved after dinner, and washed hisself all over after the girls had done the dishes. Ántonia heated the water for him. Then he put on a clean shirt and clean socks, and after he was dressed he kissed her and the little one and took his gun and said he was going out to hunt rabbits. He must have gone right down to the barn and done it then. He layed down on that bunk bed, close to the ox stalls, where he always slept. When we found him, everything was decent except"—Fuchs wrinkled his brow and hesitated—"except what he couldn't nowise foresee. His coat was hung on a peg, and his boots was under the bed. He'd took off that silk neckcloth he always wore, and folded it smooth and stuck his pin through it. He turned back his shirt at the neck and rolled up his sleeves."

"I don't see how he could do it!" Grandmother kept saying.

Otto misunderstood her. "Why, ma'm, it was simple enough; he pulled the trigger with his big toe. He layed over on his side and put the end of the barrel in his mouth, then he drew up one foot and felt for the trigger. He found it all right!"

"Maybe he did," said Jake grimly. "There's something mighty queer about it."

"Now what do you mean, Jake?" Grandmother asked sharply.

"Well, ma'm, I found Krajiek's axe under the manger, and I picks it up and carries it over to the corpse, and I take my oath it just fit the gash in the front of the old man's face. That there Krajiek had been sneakin' round, pale and quiet, and when he seen me examinin' the axe, he begun whimperin', 'My God, man, don't do that!' 'I reckon I'm a-goin' to look into this,' says I. Then he begun to squeal like a rat and run about wringin' his hands. 'They'll hang me!' says he. 'My God, they'll hang me sure!' "

Fuchs spoke up impatiently. "Krajiek's gone silly, Jake, and so have you. The old man wouldn't have made all them preparations for Krajiek to murder him, would he? It don't hang together. The gun was right beside him when Ambrosch found him."

"Krajiek could 'a' put it there, couldn't he?" Jake demanded.

Grandmother broke in excitedly: "See here, Jake Marpole, don't you go trying to add murder to suicide. We're deep enough in trouble. Otto reads you too many of them detective stories."

"It will be easy to decide all that, Emmaline," said Grandfather quietly. "If he shot himself in the way they think, the gash will be torn from the inside outward."

"Just so it is, Mr. Burden," Otto affirmed. "I seen bunches of hair and stuff sticking to the poles and straw along the roof. They was blown up there by gunshot, no question."

Grandmother told Grandfather she meant to go over to the Shimerdas' with him.

"There is nothing you can do," he said doubtfully. "The body can't be touched until we get the coroner here from Black Hawk, and that will be a matter of several days, this weather."

"Well, I can take them some victuals, anyway, and say a word of comfort to them poor little girls. The oldest one was his darling, and was like a right hand to him. He might have thought of her. He's left her alone in a hard world." She glanced distrustfully at Ambrosch, who was now eating his breakfast at the kitchen table.

Fuchs, although he had been up in the cold nearly all night, was going to make the long ride to Black Hawk to fetch the priest and the coroner. On the gray gelding, our best horse, he would try to pick his way across the country with no roads to guide him.

"Don't you worry about me, Mrs. Burden," he said cheerfully, as he put on a second pair of socks. "I've got a good nose for directions, and I never did need much sleep. It's the gray I'm worried about. I'll save him what I can, but it'll strain him, as sure as I'm telling you!"

"This is no time to be over-considerate of animals, Otto; do the best you can for yourself. Stop at the Widow Steavens's for dinner. She's a good woman, and she'll do well by you."

After Fuchs rode away, I was left with Ambrosch. I saw a side of him I had not seen before. He was deeply, even slavishly, devout. He did not say a word all morning, but sat with his rosary in his hands, praying, now silently, now aloud. He never looked away from his beads, nor lifted his hands except to cross himself. Several times the poor boy fell asleep where he sat, wakened with a start, and began to pray again.

No wagon could be got to the Shimerdas' until a road was broken, and that would be a day's job. Grandfather came from the barn on one of our big black horses, and Jake lifted Grandmother up behind him. She wore her black hood and was bundled up in shawls. Grandfather tucked his bushy white beard inside his overcoat. They looked very biblical as they set off, I thought. Jake and Ambrosch followed them, riding the other black and my pony, carrying bundles of clothes that we had got together for Mrs. Shimerda. I watched them go past the pond and over the hill by the drifted cornfield. Then, for the first time, I realized that I was alone in the house.

I felt a considerable extension of power and authority, and was anxious to acquit myself creditably. I carried in cobs and wood from the long cellar, and filled both the stoves. I remembered that in the hurry and excitement of the morning nobody had thought of the chickens, and the eggs had not been gathered. Going out through the tunnel, I gave the hens their corn, emptied the ice from their drinking-pan, and filled it with water. After the cat had had his milk, I could think of nothing else to do, and I sat down to get warm. The quiet was delightful, and the ticking clock was the most pleasant of companions. I got *Robinson Crusoe* and tried to read, but his life on the island seemed dull compared with ours. Presently, as I looked with satisfaction about our comfortable sitting-room, it flashed upon me that if Mr. Shimerda's soul were lingering about in this world at all, it would be here, in our house, which had been more to his liking than any other in the neighborhood. I remembered his contented face when he was with us on Christmas Day. If he could have lived with us, this terrible thing would never have happened.

I knew it was homesickness that had killed Mr. Shimerda, and I wondered whether his released spirit would not eventually find its way back to his own country. I thought of how far it was to Chicago, and then to Virginia, to Baltimore—and then the great wintry ocean. No, he would not at once set out upon that long journey. Surely, his exhausted spirit, so tired of cold and crowding and the struggle with the ever-falling snow, was resting now in this quiet house.

I was not frightened, but I made no noise. I did not wish to disturb him. I went softly down to the kitchen which, tucked away so snugly underground, always seemed to me the heart and center of the house. There, on the bench behind the stove, I thought and thought about Mr. Shimerda. Outside I could hear the wind singing over hundreds of miles of snow. It was as if I had let the old man in out of the tormenting winter, and were sitting there with him. I went over all that Ántonia had ever told me about his life before he came to this country, how he used to play the fiddle at weddings and dances. I thought about the friends he had mourned to leave, the trombone player, the great forest full of game—belonging, as Ántonia said, to the "nobles"—from which she and her mother used to steal wood on moonlight nights. There was a white hart that lived in that forest, and if anyone killed it, he would be hanged, she said. Such vivid pictures came to me that they might have been Mr. Shimerda's memories, not yet faded out from the air in which they had haunted him.

It had begun to grow dark when my household returned, and Grandmother was so tired that she went at once to bed. Jake and I got supper, and while we were washing the dishes he told me in loud whispers about the state of things over at the Shimerdas'. Nobody could touch the body until the coroner came. If anyone did, something terrible would happen, apparently. The dead man was frozen through, "just as stiff as a dressed turkey you hang out to freeze," Jake said. The horses and oxen would not go into the barn until he was frozen so hard that there was no longer any smell of blood. They were stabled there now, with the dead man, because there was no other place to keep them. A lighted lantern was kept hanging over Mr. Shimerda's head. Ántonia and Ambrosch and the mother took turns going down to pray beside him. The crazy boy went with them, because he did not feel the cold. I believed he felt cold as much as anyone else, but he liked to be thought insensible to it. He was always coveting distinction, poor Marek!

Ambrosch, Jake said, showed more human feeling than he would have supposed him capable of; but he was chiefly concerned about getting a priest, and about his father's soul, which he believed was in a place of torment and would remain there until his family and the priest had prayed a great deal for him. "As I understand it," Jake concluded, "it will be a matter of years to pray his soul out of Purgatory, and right now he's in torment."

"I don't believe it," I said stoutly. "I almost know it isn't true." I did not, of course, say that I believed he had been in that very kitchen all afternoon, on his way back to his own country. Nevertheless, after I went to bed, this idea of punishment and Purgatory came back on me crushingly. I remembered the account of Dives in torment and shuddered. But Mr. Shimerda had not been rich and selfish: he had only been so unhappy that he could not live any longer.

XV

Otto Fuchs got back from Black Hawk at noon the next day. He reported that the coroner would reach the Shimerdas' sometime that afternoon, but the missionary priest was at the other end of his parish, a hundred miles away, and the trains were not running. Fuchs had got a few hours' sleep at the livery barn in town, but he was afraid the gray gelding had strained himself. Indeed, he was never the same horse afterward. That long trip through the deep snow had taken all the endurance out of him.

Fuchs brought home with him a stranger, a young Bohemian who had taken a homestead near Black Hawk, and who came on his only horse to help his fellow countrymen in their trouble. That was the first time I ever saw Anton Jelinek. He was a strapping young fellow in the early twenties then, handsome, warm-hearted, and full of life, and he came to us like a miracle in the midst of that grim business. I remember exactly how he strode into our kitchen in his felt boots and long wolf-skin coat, his eyes and cheeks bright with the cold. At sight of Grandmother, he snatched off his fur cap, greeting her in a deep, rolling voice which seemed older than he.

"I want to thank you very much, Mrs. Burden, for that you are so kind to poor strangers from my kawntree."

He did not hesitate like a farmer boy, but looked one eagerly in the eye when he spoke. Everything about him was warm and spontaneous. He said he would have come to see the Shimerdas before, but he had hired out to husk corn all the fall, and since winter began he had been going to the school by the mill, to learn English, along with the little children. He told me he had a nice "lady-teacher" and that he liked to go to school.

At dinner Grandfather talked to Jelinek more than he usually did to strangers.

"Will they be much disappointed because we cannot get a priest?" he asked.

Jelinek looked serious.

"Yes, sir, that is very bad for them. Their father has done a great sin"—he looked straight at Grandfather. "Our Lord has said that."

Grandfather seemed to like his frankness.

"We believe that, too, Jelinek. But we believe that Mr. Shimerda's soul will come to its Creator as well off without a priest. We believe that Christ is our only intercessor."

The young man shook his head. "I know how you think. My teacher at the school has explain. But I have seen too much. I believe in prayer for the dead. I have seen too much."

We asked him what he meant.

He glanced around the table. "You want I shall tell you? When I was a little boy like this one, I begin to help the priest at the altar. I make my first communion very young; what the church teach seem plain to me. By 'n' by war times come, when the Prussians fight us. We have very many soldiers in camp near my village, and the cholera break out in that camp, and the men die like flies. All day long our priest go about there to give the Sacrament to dying men, and I go with him to carry the vessels with the Holy Sacrament. Everybody that go near that camp catch the sickness but me and the priest. But we have no sickness, we have no fear, because we carry that blood and that body of Christ, and it preserve us." He paused, looking at Grandfather. "That I know, Mr. Burden, for it happened to myself. All the soldiers know, too. When we walk along the road, the old priest and me, we meet all the time soldiers marching and officers on horse. All those officers, when they see what I carry under the cloth, pull up their horses and kneel down on the ground in the road until we pass. So I feel very bad for my kawntree-man to die without the Sacrament, and to die in a bad way for his soul, and I feel sad for his family."

We had listened attentively. It was impossible not to admire his frank, manly faith.

"I am always glad to meet a young man who thinks seriously about these things," said Grandfather, "and I would never be the one to say you were not in God's care when you were among the soldiers."

After dinner it was decided that young Jelinek should hook our two strong black farm-horses to the scraper and break a road through to the Shimerdas', so that a wagon could go when it was necessary. Fuchs, who was the only cabinetmaker in the neighborhood, was set to work on a coffin.

Jelinek put on his long wolf-skin coat, and when we admired it, he told us that he had shot and skinned the coyotes, and the young man who "batched" with him, Jan Bouska, who had been a fur-worker in Vienna, made the coat. From the windmill I watched Jelinek come out of the barn with the blacks, and work his way up the hillside toward the cornfield. Sometimes he was completely hidden by the clouds of snow that rose about him; then he and the horses would emerge black and shining.

Our heavy carpenter's bench had to be brought from the barn and carried down into the kitchen. Fuchs selected boards from a pile of planks Grandfather had hauled out from town in the fall to make a new floor for the oats-bin. When at last the lumber and tools were assembled, and the doors were closed again and the cold drafts shut out, Grandfather rode away to meet the coroner at the Shimerdas', and Fuchs took off his coat and settled down to work. I sat on his work-table and watched him. He did not touch his tools at first, but figured for a long while on a piece of paper, and measured the planks and made marks on them. While he was thus engaged, he whistled softly to himself, or teasingly pulled at his half-ear. Grandmother moved about quietly, so as not to disturb him. At last he folded his ruler and turned a cheerful face to us.

"The hardest part of my job's done," he announced. "It's the head end of it that comes hard with me, especially when I'm out of practice. The last time I made one of these, Mrs. Burden," he continued, as he sorted and tried his chisels, "was for a fellow in the Black Tiger Mine, up above Silverton, Colorado. The mouth of that mine goes right into the face of the cliff, and they used to put us in a bucket and run us over on a trolley and shoot us into the shaft. The bucket traveled across a box canyon three hundred feet deep and about a third full of water. Two Swedes had fell out of that bucket once, and hit the water, feet down. If you'll believe it, they went to work the next day. You can't kill a Swede. But in my time a little Eyetalian tried the high dive, and it turned out different with him. We was snowed in then, like we are now, and I happened to be the only man in camp that could make a coffin for him. It's a handy thing to know, when you knock about like I've done."

"We'd be hard put to it now, if you didn't know, Otto," Grandmother said.

"Yes, 'm," Fuchs admitted with modest pride. "So few folks does know how to make a good tight box that'll turn water. I sometimes wonder if there'll be anybody about to do it for me. However, I'm not at all particular that way."

All afternoon, wherever one went in the house, one could hear the panting wheeze of the saw or the pleasant purring of the plane. They were such cheerful noises, seeming to promise new things for living people: it was a pity that those freshly planed pine boards were to be put underground so soon. The lumber was hard to work because it was full of frost, and the boards gave off a sweet smell of pine woods, as the heap of yellow shavings grew higher and higher. I wondered why Fuchs had not stuck to cabinetwork, he settled down to it with such ease and content. He handled the tools as if he liked the feel of them; and when he planed, his hands went back and forth over the boards in an eager, beneficent way as if he were blessing them. He broke out now and then into German hymns, as if this occupation brought back old times to him.

At four o'clock Mr. Bushy, the postmaster, with another neighbor who lived east of us, stopped in to get warm. They were on their way to the Shimerdas'. The news of what had happened over there had somehow got abroad through the snow-blocked country. Grandmother gave the visitors sugar-cakes and hot coffee. Before these callers were gone, the brother of the Widow Steavens, who lived on the Black Hawk road, drew up at our door, and after him came the father of the German family, our nearest neighbors on the south. They dismounted and joined us in the dining room. They were all eager for any details about the suicide, and they were greatly concerned as to where Mr. Shimerda would be buried. The nearest Catholic cemetery was at Black Hawk, and it might be weeks before a wagon could get so far. Besides, Mr. Bushy and Grandmother were sure that a man who had killed himself could not be buried in a Catholic graveyard. There was a burying-ground over by the Norwegian church, west of Squaw Creek; perhaps the Norwegians would take Mr. Shimerda in.

After our visitors rode away in single file over the hill, we returned to the kitchen. Grandmother began to make the icing for a chocolate cake, and Otto again filled the house with the exciting, expectant song of the plane. One pleasant thing about this time was that everybody talked more than usual. I had never heard the postmaster say anything but "Only papers, today," or, "I've got a sackful of mail for ye," until this afternoon. Grandmother always talked, dear woman: to herself or to the Lord, if there was no one else to listen; but Grandfather was naturally taciturn, and Jake and Otto were often so tired after supper that I used to feel as if I were surrounded by a wall of silence. Now everyone seemed eager to talk. That afternoon Fuchs told me story after story: about the Black Tiger Mine, and about violent deaths and casual buryings, and the queer fancies of dying men. You never really knew a man, he said, until you saw him die. Most men were game, and went without a grudge.

The postmaster, going home, stopped to say that Grandfather would bring the coroner back with him to spend the night. The officers of the Norwegian church, he told us, had held a meeting and decided that the Norwegian graveyard could not extend its hospitality to Mr. Shimerda.

Grandmother was indignant. "If these foreigners are so clannish, Mr. Bushy, we'll have to have an American graveyard that will be more liberal-minded. I'll get right after Josiah to start one in the spring. If anything was to happen to me, I don't want the Norwegians holding inquisitions over me to see whether I'm good enough to be laid amongst 'em."

Soon Grandfather returned, bringing with him Anton Jelinek, and that important person, the coroner. He was a mild, flurried old man, a Civil War veteran, with one sleeve hanging empty. He seemed to find this case very perplexing, and said if it had not been for Grandfather he would have sworn out a warrant against Krajiek. "The way he acted, and the way his axe fit the wound, was enough to convict any man."

Although it was perfectly clear that Mr. Shimerda had killed himself, Jake and the coroner thought something ought to be done to Krajiek because he behaved like a guilty man. He was badly frightened, certainly, and perhaps he even felt some stirrings of remorse for his indifference to the old man's misery and loneliness.

At supper the men ate like Vikings, and the chocolate cake, which I had hoped would linger on until tomorrow in a mutilated condition, disappeared on the second round. They talked excitedly about where they should bury Mr. Shimerda; I gathered that the neighbors were all disturbed and shocked about something. It developed that Mrs. Shimerda and Ambrosch wanted the old man buried on the southwest corner of their own land—indeed, under the very stake that marked the corner. Grandfather had explained to Ambrosch that some day, when the country was put under fence and the roads were confined to section lines, two roads would cross exactly on that corner. But Ambrosch only said, "It makes no matter."

Grandfather asked Jelinek whether in the old country there was some superstition to the effect that a suicide must be buried at the crossroads.

Jelinek said he didn't know; he seemed to remember hearing there had once been such a custom in Bohemia. "Mrs. Shimerda is made up her mind," he added. "I try to persuade her, and say it looks bad for her to all the neighbors; but she say so it must be. "There I will bury him, if I dig the grave myself," she say. I have to promise her I help Ambrosch make the grave tomorrow."

Grandfather smoothed his beard and looked judicial. "I don't know whose wish should decide the matter, if not hers. But if she thinks she will live to see the people of this country ride over that old man's head, she is mistaken."

XVI

MR. SHIMERDA lay dead in the barn four days, and on the fifth they buried him. All day Friday Jelinek was off with Ambrosch digging the grave, chopping out the frozen earth with old axes. On Saturday we breakfasted before daylight and got into the wagon with the coffin. Jake and Jelinek went ahead on horseback to cut the body loose from the pool of blood in which it was frozen fast to the ground.

When Grandmother and I went into the Shimerdas' house, we found the women-folk alone; Ambrosch and Marek were at the barn. Mrs. Shimerda sat crouching by the stove, Ántonia was washing dishes. When she saw me, she ran out of her dark corner and threw her arms around me. "Oh, Jimmy," she sobbed, "what you tink for my lovely papa!" It seemed to me that I could feel her heart breaking as she clung to me.

Mrs. Shimerda, sitting on the stump by the stove, kept looking over her shoulder toward the door while the neighbors were arriving. They came on horseback, all except the postmaster, who brought his family in a wagon over the only broken wagon trail. The Widow Steavens rode up from her farm eight miles down the Black Hawk road. The cold drove the women into the cave-house, and it was soon crowded. A fine, sleety snow was beginning to fall, and everyone was afraid of another storm and anxious to have the burial over with.

Grandfather and Jelinek came to tell Mrs. Shimerda that it was time to start. After bundling her mother up in clothes the neighbors had brought, Ántonia put on an old cape from our house and the rabbit-skin hat her father had made for her. Four men carried Mr. Shimerda's box up the hill; Krajiek slunk along behind them. The coffin was too wide for the door, so it was put down on the slope outside. I slipped out from the cave and looked at Mr. Shimerda. He was lying on his side, with his knees drawn up. His body was draped in a black shawl, and his head was bandaged in white muslin, like a mummy's; one of his long, shapely hands lay out on the black cloth; that was all one could see of him.

Mrs. Shimerda came out and placed an open prayer-book against the body, making the sign of the cross on the bandaged head with her fingers. Ambrosch knelt down and made the same gesture, and after him

Ántonia and Marek. Yulka hung back. Her mother pushed her forward, and kept saying something to her over and over. Yulka knelt down, shut her eyes, and put out her hand a little way, but she drew it back and began to cry wildly. She was afraid to touch the bandage. Mrs. Shimerda caught her by the shoulders and pushed her toward the coffin, but Grandmother interfered.

"No, Mrs. Shimerda," she said firmly, "I won't stand by and see that child frightened into spasms. She is too little to understand what you want of her. Let her alone."

At a look from Grandfather, Fuchs and Jelinek placed the lid on the box, and began to nail it down over Mr. Shimerda. I was afraid to look at Ántonia. She put her arms round Yulka and held the little girl close to her.

The coffin was put into the wagon. We drove slowly away, against the fine, icy snow which cut our faces like a sandblast. When we reached the grave, it looked a very little spot in that snow-covered waste. The men took the coffin to the edge of the hole and lowered it with ropes. We stood about watching them, and the powdery snow lay without melting on the caps and shoulders of the men and the shawls of the women. Jelinek spoke in a persuasive tone to Mrs. Shimerda, and then turned to Grandfather.

"She says, Mr. Burden, she is very glad if you can make some prayer for him here in English, for the neighbors to understand."

Grandmother looked anxiously at Grandfather. He took off his hat, and the other men did likewise. I thought his prayer remarkable. I still remember it. He began, "Oh, great and just God, no man among us knows what the sleeper knows, nor is it for us to judge what lies between him and Thee." He prayed that if any man there had been remiss toward the stranger come to a far country, God would forgive him and soften his heart. He recalled the promises to the widow and the fatherless, and asked God to smooth the way before this widow and her children, and to "incline the hearts of men to deal justly with her." In closing, he said we were leaving Mr. Shimerda at "Thy judgment seat, which is also Thy mercy seat."

All the time he was praying, Grandmother watched him through the black fingers of her glove, and when he said "Amen" I thought she looked satisfied with him. She turned to Otto and whispered, "Can't you start a hymn, Fuchs? It would seem less heathenish."

Fuchs glanced about to see if there was general approval of her suggestion, then began, "Jesus, Lover of my Soul," and all the men and women took it up after him. Whenever I have heard the hymn since, it has made me remember that white waste and the little group of people; and the bluish air, full of fine, eddying snow, like long veils flying:

> While the nearer waters roll,
> While the tempest still is high.

Years afterward, when the open-grazing days were over, and the red grass had been ploughed under and under until it had almost disappeared from the prairie; when all the fields were under fence, and the roads no longer ran about like wild things but followed the surveyed section-lines, Mr. Shimerda's grave was still there, with a sagging wire fence around it, and an unpainted wooden cross. As Grandfather had predicted, Mrs. Shimerda never saw the roads going over his head. The road from the north curved a little to the east just there, and the road from the west swung out a little to the south—so that the grave, with its tall red grass that was never mowed, was like a little island; and at twilight, under a new moon or the clear evening star, the dusty roads used to look like soft gray rivers flowing past it. I never came upon the place without emotion, and in all that country it was the spot most dear to me. I loved the dim superstition, the propitiatory intent, that had put the grave there; and still more I loved the spirit that could not carry out the sentence—the error from the surveyed lines, the clemency of the soft earth roads along which the home-coming wagons rattled after sunset. Never a tired driver passed the wooden cross, I am sure, without wishing well to the sleeper.

XVII

WHEN SPRING CAME, after that hard winter, one could not get enough of the nimble air. Every morning I wakened with a fresh consciousness that winter was over. There were none of the signs of spring for which I used to watch in Virginia, no budding woods or blooming gardens. There was only—spring itself; the throb of it, the light restlessness, the vital essence of it everywhere: in the sky, in the swift clouds, in the pale sunshine, and in the warm, high wind—rising suddenly, sinking suddenly, impulsive and playful like a big puppy that pawed you and then lay down to be petted. If I had been tossed down blindfold on that red prairie, I should have known that it was spring.

Everywhere now there was the smell of burning grass. Our neighbors burned off their pasture before the new grass made a start, so that the fresh growth would not be mixed with the dead stand of last year. Those light, swift fires, running about the country, seemed a part of the same kindling that was in the air.

The Shimerdas were in their new log house by then. The neighbors had helped them to build it in March. It stood directly in front of their old cave, which they used as a cellar. The family were now fairly equipped to begin their struggle with the soil. They had four comfortable rooms to live in, a new windmill—bought on credit—a chicken-house and poultry. Mrs. Shimerda had paid Grandfather ten dollars for a milk cow and was to give him fifteen more as soon as they harvested their first crop.

When I rode up to the Shimerdas' one bright windy afternoon in April, Yulka ran out to meet me. It was to her, now, that I gave reading lessons; Ántonia was busy with other things. I tied my pony and went into the kitchen where Mrs. Shimerda was baking bread, chewing poppy seeds as she worked. By this time she could speak enough English to ask me a great many questions about what our men were doing in the fields. She seemed to think that my elders withheld helpful information, and that from me she might get valuable secrets. On this occasion she asked me very craftily when Grandfather expected to begin planting corn. I told her, adding that he thought we should have a dry spring and that the corn would not be held back by too much rain, as it had been last year.

She gave me a shrewd glance. "He not Jesus," she blustered. "He not know about the wet and the dry."

I did not answer her; what was the use? As I sat waiting for the hour when Ambrosch and Ántonia would return from the fields, I watched Mrs. Shimerda at her work. She took from the oven a coffee cake which she wanted to keep warm for supper, and wrapped it in a quilt stuffed with feathers. I have seen her put even a roast goose in this quilt to keep it hot. When the neighbors were there building the new house, they saw her do this, and the story got abroad that the Shimerdas kept their food in their feather-beds.

When the sun was dropping low, Ántonia came up the big south draw with her team. How much older she had grown in eight months! She had come to us a child, and now she was a tall, strong young girl, although her fifteenth birthday had just slipped by. I ran out and met her as she brought her horses up to the windmill to water them. She wore the boots her father had so thoughtfully taken off before he shot himself, and his old fur cap. Her outgrown cotton dress switched about her calves, over the boot-tops. She kept her sleeves rolled up all day, and her arms and throat were burned as brown as a sailor's. Her neck came up strongly out of her shoulders, like the bole of a tree out of the turf. One sees that draft-horse neck among the peasant women in all old countries.

She greeted me gaily, and began at once to tell me how much ploughing she had done that day. Ambrosch, she said, was on the north quarter, breaking sod with the oxen.

"Jim, you ask Jake how much he ploughed today. I don't want that Jake get more done in one day than me. I want we have very much corn this fall."

While the horses drew in the water, and nosed each other, and then drank again, Ántonia sat down on the windmill step and rested her head on her hand.

"You see the big prairie fire from your place last night? I hope your grandpa ain't lose no stacks?"

"No, we didn't. I came to ask you something, Tony. Grandmother wants to know if you can't go to the term of school that begins next week over at the sod schoolhouse. She says there's a good teacher, and you'd learn a lot."

Ántonia stood up, lifting and dropping her shoulders as if they were stiff. "I ain't got time to learn. I can work like mans now. My mother can't say no more how Ambrosch do all and nobody to help him. I can work as much as him. School is all right for little boys. I help make this land one good farm."

She clucked to her team and started for the barn. I walked beside her, feeling vexed. Was she going to grow up boastful like her mother, I wondered? Before we reached the stable, I felt something tense in her silence, and glancing up I saw that she was crying. She turned her face from me and looked off at the red streak of dying light, over the dark prairie.

I climbed up into the loft and threw down the hay for her, while she unharnessed her team. We walked slowly back toward the house. Ambrosch had come in from the north quarter and was watering his oxen at the tank.

Ántonia took my hand. "Sometime you will tell me all those nice things you learn at the school, won't you, Jimmy?" she asked with a sudden rush of feeling in her voice. "My father, he went much to school. He know a great deal; how to make the fine cloth like what you not got here. He play horn and violin, and he read so many books that the priests in Bohemie come to talk to him. You won't forget my father, Jim?"

"No," I said, "I will never forget him."

Mrs. Shimerda asked me to stay for supper. After Ambrosch and Ántonia had washed the field dust from their hands and faces at the washbasin by the kitchen door, we sat down at the oilcloth-covered table. Mrs. Shimerda ladled meal mush out of an iron pot and poured milk on it. After the mush we had fresh bread and sorghum molasses, and coffee with the cake that had been kept warm in the feathers. Ántonia and Ambrosch were talking in Bohemian, disputing about which of them had done more ploughing that day. Mrs. Shimerda egged them on, chuckling while she gobbled her food.

Presently Ambrosch said sullenly in English: "You take them ox tomorrow and try the sod plough. Then you not be so smart."

His sister laughed. "Don't be mad. I know it's awful hard work for break sod. I milk the cow for you tomorrow, if you want."

Mrs. Shimerda turned quickly to me. "That cow not give so much milk like what your grandpa say. If he make talk about fifteen dollars, I send him back the cow."

"He doesn't talk about the fifteen dollars," I exclaimed indignantly. "He doesn't find fault with people."

"He say I break his saw when we build, and I never," grumbled Ambrosch.

I knew he had broken the saw, and then hid it and lied about it. I began to wish I had not stayed for supper. Everything was disagreeable to me. Ántonia ate so noisily now, like a man, and she yawned often at the table and kept stretching her arms over her head, as if they ached. Grandmother had said, "Heavy field work'll spoil that girl. She'll lose all her nice ways and get rough ones." She had lost them already.

After supper I rode home through the sad, soft spring twilight. Since winter I had seen very little of Ántonia. She was out in the fields from sunup until sundown. If I rode over to see her where she was ploughing, she stopped at the end of a row to chat for a moment, then gripped her plough-handles, clucked to her team, and waded on down the furrow, making me feel that she was now grown up and had no time for me. On Sundays she helped her mother make garden or sewed all day. Grandfather was pleased with Ántonia. When we complained of her, he only smiled and said, "She will help some fellow get ahead in the world."

Nowadays Tony could talk of nothing but the prices of things, or how much she could lift and endure. She was too proud of her strength. I knew, too, that Ambrosch put upon her some chores a girl ought not to do, and that the farmhands around the country joked in a nasty way about it. Whenever I saw her come up the furrow, shouting to her beasts, sunburned, sweaty, her dress open at the neck, and her throat and chest dust-plastered, I used to think of the tone in which poor Mr. Shimerda, who could say so little, yet managed to say so much when he exclaimed, "My Án-tonia!"

XVIII

After I began to go to the country school, I saw less of the Bohemians. We were sixteen pupils at the sod schoolhouse, and we all came on horseback and brought our dinner. My schoolmates were none of them very interesting, but I somehow felt that, by making comrades of them, I was getting even with Ántonia for her indifference. Since the father's death, Ambrosch was more than ever the head of the house, and he seemed to direct the feelings as well as the fortunes of his women-folk. Ántonia often quoted his opinions to me, and she let me see that she admired him, while she thought of me only as a little boy. Before the spring was over, there was a distinct coldness between us and the Shimerdas. It came about in this way.

One Sunday I rode over there with Jake to get a horse-collar which Ambrosch had borrowed from him and had not returned. It was a beautiful blue morning. The buffalo-peas were blooming in pink and purple masses along the roadside, and the larks, perched on last year's dried sunflower stalks, were singing straight at the sun, their heads thrown back and their yellow breasts a-quiver. The wind blew about us in warm, sweet gusts. We rode slowly, with a pleasant sense of Sunday indolence.

We found the Shimerdas working just as if it were a weekday. Marek was cleaning out the stable, and Ántonia and her mother were making garden, off across the pond in the draw-head. Ambrosch was up on the windmill tower, oiling the wheel. He came down, not very cordially. When Jake asked for the collar, he grunted and scratched his head. The collar belonged to Grandfather, of course, and Jake, feeling responsible for it, flared up.

"Now, don't you say you haven't got it, Ambrosch, because I know you have, and if you ain't a-going to look for it, I will."

Ambrosch shrugged his shoulders and sauntered down the hill toward the stable. I could see that it was one of his mean days. Presently he returned, carrying a collar that had been badly used—trampled in the dirt and gnawed by rats until the hair was sticking out of it.

"This what you want?" he asked surlily.

Jake jumped off his horse. I saw a wave of red come up under the rough stubble on his face. "That ain't the piece of harness I loaned you, Ambrosch; or, if it is, you've used it shameful. I ain't a-going to carry such a looking thing back to Mr. Burden."

Ambrosch dropped the collar on the ground. "All right," he said coolly, took up his oilcan, and began to climb the mill. Jake caught him by the belt of his trousers and yanked him back. Ambrosch's feet had scarcely touched the ground when he lunged out with a vicious kick at Jake's stomach. Fortunately, Jake was in such a position that he could dodge it. This was not the sort of thing country boys did when they played at fisticuffs, and Jake was furious. He landed Ambrosch a blow on the head—it sounded like the crack of an axe on a cow-pumpkin. Ambrosch dropped over, stunned.

We heard squeals, and looking up saw Ántonia and her mother coming on the run. They did not take the path around the pond, but plunged through the muddy water, without even lifting their skirts. They came on, screaming and clawing the air. By this time Ambrosch had come to his senses and was sputtering with nosebleed.

Jake sprang into his saddle. "Let's get out of this, Jim," he called.

Mrs. Shimerda threw her hands over her head and clutched as if she were going to pull down lightning. "Law, law!" she shrieked after us. "Law for knock my Ambrosch down!"

"I never like you no more, Jake and Jim Burden," Ántonia panted. "No friends anymore!"

Jake stopped and turned his horse for a second. "Well, you're a damned ungrateful lot, the whole pack of you," he shouted back. "I guess the Burdens can get along without you. You've been a sight of trouble to them, anyhow!"

We rode away, feeling so outraged that the fine morning was spoiled for us. I hadn't a word to say, and poor Jake was white as paper and trembling all over. It made him sick to get so angry.

"They ain't the same, Jimmy," he kept saying in a hurt tone. "These foreigners ain't the same. You can't trust 'em to be fair. It's dirty to kick a feller. You heard how the women turned on you—and after all we went through on account of 'em last winter! They ain't to be trusted. I don't want to see you get too thick with any of 'em."

"I'll never be friends with them again, Jake," I declared hotly. "I believe they are all like Krajiek and Ambrosch underneath."

Grandfather heard our story with a twinkle in his eye. He advised Jake to ride to town tomorrow, go to a justice of the peace, tell him he had knocked young Shimerda down, and pay his fine. Then if Mrs. Shimerda was inclined to make trouble—her son was still under age—she would be forestalled. Jake said he might as well take the wagon and haul to market the pig he had been fattening. On Monday, about an hour after Jake had started, we saw Mrs. Shimerda and her Ambrosch proudly driving by, looking neither to the right nor left. As they rattled out of sight down the Black Hawk road, Grandfather chuckled, saying he had rather expected she would follow the matter up.

Jake paid his fine with a ten-dollar bill Grandfather had given him for that purpose. But when the Shimerdas found that Jake sold his pig in town that day, Ambrosch worked it out in his shrewd head that Jake had to sell his pig to pay his fine. This theory afforded the Shimerdas great satisfaction, apparently. For weeks afterward, whenever Jake and I met Ántonia on her way to the post office, or going along the road with her work-team, she would clap her hands and call to us in a spiteful, crowing voice:

"Jake-y, Jake-y, sell the pig and pay the slap!"

Otto pretended not to be surprised at Ántonia's behavior. He only lifted his brows and said, "You can't tell me anything new about a Czech; I'm an Austrian."

Grandfather was never a party to what Jake called our feud with the Shimerdas. Ambrosch and Ántonia always greeted him respectfully, and he asked them about their affairs and gave them advice as usual. He thought the future looked hopeful for them. Ambrosch was a far-seeing fellow; he soon realized that his oxen were too heavy for any work except breaking sod, and he succeeded in selling them to a newly arrived German. With the money he bought another team of horses, which Grandfather selected for him. Marek was strong, and Ambrosch worked him hard; but he could never teach him to cultivate corn, I remember. The one idea that had ever got through poor Marek's thick head was that all exertion was meritorious. He always bore down on the handles of the cultivator and drove the blades so deep into the earth that the horses were soon exhausted.

In June, Ambrosch went to work at Mr. Bushy's for a week, and took Marek with him at full wages. Mrs. Shimerda then drove the second cultivator; she and Ántonia worked in the fields all day and did the chores at night. While the two women were running the place alone, one of the new horses got colic and gave them a terrible fright.

Ántonia had gone down to the barn one night to see that all was well before she went to bed, and she noticed that one of the roans was swollen about the middle and stood with its head hanging. She mounted another horse, without waiting to saddle him, and hammered on our door just as we were going to bed. Grandfather answered her knock. He did not send one of his men, but rode back with her himself, taking a syringe and an old piece of carpet he kept for hot applications when our horses were sick. He found Mrs. Shimerda sitting by the horse with her lantern, groaning and wringing her hands. It took but a few moments to release the gases pent up in the poor beast, and the two women heard the rush of wind and saw the roan visibly diminish in girth.

"If I lose that horse, Mr. Burden," Ántonia exclaimed, "I never stay here till Ambrosch come home! I go drown myself in the pond before morning."

When Ambrosch came back from Mr. Bushy's, we learned that he had given Marek's wages to the priest at Black Hawk, for Masses for their father's soul. Grandmother thought Ántonia needed shoes more than Mr. Shimerda needed prayers, but Grandfather said tolerantly, "If he can spare six dollars, pinched as he is, it shows he believes what he professes."

It was Grandfather who brought about a reconciliation with the Shimerdas. One morning he told us that the small grain was coming on so well, he thought he would begin to cut his wheat on the first of July. He would need more men, and if it were agreeable to everyone he would engage Ambrosch for the reaping and threshing, as the Shimerdas had no small grain of their own.

"I think, Emmaline," he concluded, "I will ask Ántonia to come over and help you in the kitchen. She will be glad to earn something, and it will be a good time to end misunderstandings. I may as well ride over this morning and make arrangements. Do you want to go with me, Jim?" His tone told me that he had already decided for me.

After breakfast we set off together. When Mrs. Shimerda saw us coming, she ran from her door down into the draw behind the stable, as if she did not want to meet us. Grandfather smiled to himself while he tied his horse, and we followed her.

Behind the barn we came upon a funny sight. The cow had evidently been grazing somewhere in the draw. Mrs. Shimerda had run to the animal, pulled up the lariat pin, and, when we came upon her, she was trying to hide the cow in an old cave in the bank. As the hole was narrow and dark, the cow held back, and the old woman was slapping and pushing at her hind quarters, trying to spank her into the draw-side.

Grandfather ignored her singular occupation and greeted her politely. "Good morning, Mrs. Shimerda. Can you tell me where I will find Ambrosch? Which field?"

"He with the sod corn." She pointed toward the north, still standing in front of the cow as if she hoped to conceal it.

"His sod corn will be good for fodder this winter," said Grandfather encouragingly. "And where is Ántonia?"

"She go with." Mrs. Shimerda kept wiggling her bare feet about nervously in the dust.

"Very well. I will ride up there. I want them to come over and help me cut my oats and wheat next month. I will pay them wages. Good morning. By the way, Mrs. Shimerda," he said as he turned up the path, "I think we may as well call it square about the cow."

She started and clutched the rope tighter. Seeing that she did not understand, Grandfather turned back. "You need not pay me anything more; no more money. The cow is yours."

"Pay no more, keep cow?" she asked in a bewildered tone, her narrow eyes snapping at us in the sunlight.

"Exactly. Pay no more, keep cow." He nodded.

Mrs. Shimerda dropped the rope, ran after us, and, crouching down beside Grandfather, she took his hand and kissed it. I doubt if he had ever been so much embarrassed before. I was a little startled, too. Somehow, that seemed to bring the Old World very close.

We rode away laughing, and Grandfather said: "I expect she thought we had come to take the cow away for certain, Jim. I wonder if she wouldn't have scratched a little if we'd laid hold of that lariat rope!"

Our neighbors seemed glad to make peace with us. The next Sunday Mrs. Shimerda came over and brought Jake a pair of socks she had knitted. She presented them with an air of great magnanimity, saying, "Now you not come any more for knock my Ambrosch down?"

Jake laughed sheepishly. "I don't want to have no trouble with Ambrosch. If he'll let me alone, I'll let him alone."

"If he slap you, we ain't got no pig for pay the fine," she said insinuatingly.

Jake was not at all disconcerted. "Have the last word, ma'm," he said cheerfully. "It's a lady's privilege."

XIX

JULY CAME ON with that breathless, brilliant heat which makes the plains of Kansas and Nebraska the best corn country in the world. It seemed as if we could hear the corn growing in the night; under the stars one caught a faint crackling in the dewy, heavy-odored cornfields where the feathered stalks stood so juicy and green. If all the great plain from the Missouri to the Rocky Mountains had been under glass, and the heat regulated by a thermometer, it could not have been better for the yellow tassels that were ripening and fertilizing the silk day by day. The cornfields were far apart in those times, with miles of wild grazing land between. It took a clear, meditative eye like my grandfather's to foresee that they would enlarge and multiply until they would be, not the Shimerdas' cornfields, or Mr. Bushy's, but the world's cornfields; that their yield would be one of the great economic facts, like the wheat crop of Russia, which underlie all the activities of men, in peace or war.

The burning sun of those few weeks, with occasional rains at night, secured the corn. After the milky ears were once formed, we had little to fear from dry weather. The men were working so hard in the wheat-fields that they did not notice the heat—though I was kept busy carrying water for them—and Grandmother and Ántonia had so much to do in the kitchen that they could not have told whether one day was hotter than another. Each morning, while the dew was still on the grass, Ántonia went with me up to the garden to get early vegetables for dinner. Grandmother made her wear a sunbonnet, but as soon as we reached the garden she threw it on the grass and let her hair fly in the breeze. I remember how, as we bent over the pea-vines, beads of perspiration used to gather on her upper lip like a little moustache.

"Oh, better I like to work out-of-doors than in a house!" she used to sing joyfully. "I not care that your grandmother say it makes me like a man. I like to be like a man." She would toss her head and ask me to feel the muscles swell in her brown arm.

We were glad to have her in the house. She was so gay and responsive that one did not mind her heavy, running step, or her clattery way with pans. Grandmother was in high spirits during the weeks that Ántonia worked for us.

All the nights were close and hot during that harvest season. The harvesters slept in the hayloft because it was cooler there than in the house. I used to lie in my bed by the open window, watching the heat lightning play softly along the horizon, or looking up at the gaunt frame of the windmill against the blue night sky. One night there was a beautiful electric storm, though not enough rain fell to damage the cut grain. The men went down to the barn immediately after supper, and when the dishes were washed, Ántonia and I climbed up on the slanting roof of the chicken-house to watch the clouds. The thunder was loud and metallic, like the rattle of sheet iron, and the lightning broke in great zigzags across the heavens, making everything stand out and come close to us for a moment. Half the sky was checkered with black thunder-heads, but all the west was luminous and clear: in the lightning flashes it looked like deep blue water, with the sheen of moonlight on it; and the mottled part of the sky was like marble pavement, like the quay of some splendid sea-coast city, doomed to destruction. Great warm splashes of rain fell on our upturned faces. One black cloud, no bigger than a little boat, drifted out into the clear space unattended, and kept moving westward. All about us we could hear the felty beat of the raindrops on the soft dust of the farmyard. Grandmother came to the door and said it was late, and we would get wet out there.

"In a minute we come," Ántonia called back to her. "I like your grandmother, and all things here," she sighed. "I wish my papa live to see this summer. I wish no winter ever come again."

"It will be summer a long while yet," I reassured her. "Why aren't you always nice like this, Tony?"

"How nice?"

"Why, just like this; like yourself. Why do you all the time try to be like Ambrosch?"

She put her arms under her head and lay back, looking up at the sky. "If I live here, like you, that is different. Things will be easy for you. But they will be hard for us."

Book Two

The Hired Girls

I

I HAD BEEN LIVING with my grandfather for nearly three years when he decided to move to Black Hawk. He and Grandmother were getting old for the heavy work of a farm, and as I was now thirteen they thought I ought to be going to school. Accordingly our homestead was rented to "that good woman, the Widow Steavens," and her bachelor brother, and we bought Preacher White's house, at the north end of Black Hawk. This was the first town house one passed driving in from the farm, a landmark which told country people their long ride was over.

We were to move to Black Hawk in March, and as soon as Grandfather had fixed the date he let Jake and Otto know of his intention. Otto said he would not be likely to find another place that suited him so well—that he was tired of farming and thought he would go back to what he called the "wild West." Jake Marpole, lured by Otto's stories of adventure, decided to go with him. We did our best to dissuade Jake. He was so handicapped by illiteracy and by his trusting disposition that he would be an easy prey to sharpers. Grandmother begged him to stay among kindly, Christian people, where he was known; but there was no reasoning with him. He wanted to be a prospector. He thought a silver mine was waiting for him in Colorado.

Jake and Otto served us to the last. They moved us into town, put down the carpets in our new house, made shelves and cupboards for Grandmother's kitchen, and seemed loath to leave us. But at last they went, without warning. Those two fellows had been faithful to us through sun and storm, had given us things that cannot be bought in any market in the world. With me they had been like older brothers, had restrained their speech and manners out of care for me and given me so much good comradeship. Now they got on the westbound train one morning, in their Sunday clothes, with their oilcloth valises—and I never saw them again. Months afterward we got a card from Otto, saying that Jake had been down with mountain fever, but now they were both working in the Yankee Girl Mine, and were doing well. I wrote to them at that address, but my letter was returned to me, "Unclaimed." After that we never heard from them.

Black Hawk, the new world in which we had come to live, was a clean, well-planted little prairie town, with white fences and good green yards about the dwellings, wide, dusty streets, and shapely little trees growing along the wooden sidewalks. In the center of the town there were two rows of new brick "store" buildings, a brick schoolhouse, the court-house, and four white churches. Our own house looked down over the town, and from our upstairs windows we could see the winding line of the river bluffs, two miles south of us. That river was to be my compensation for the lost freedom of the farming country.

We came to Black Hawk in March, and by the end of April we felt like town people. Grandfather was a deacon in the new Baptist Church, Grandmother was busy with church suppers and missionary societies, and I was quite another boy, or thought I was. Suddenly put down among boys of my own age, I found I had a great deal to learn. Before the spring term of school was over, I could fight, play "keeps," tease the little girls, and use forbidden words as well as any boy in my class. I was restrained from utter savagery only by the fact that Mrs. Harling, our nearest neighbor, kept an eye on me, and if my behavior went beyond certain bounds I was not permitted to come into her yard or to play with her jolly children.

We saw more of our country neighbors now than when we lived on the farm. Our house was a convenient stopping-place for them. We had a big barn where the farmers could put up their teams, and their women-folk more often accompanied them, now that they could stay with us for dinner, and rest and set their bonnets right before they went shopping. The more our house was like a country hotel, the better I liked it. I was glad, when I came home from school at noon, to see a farm-wagon standing in the backyard, and I was always ready to run downtown to get beefsteak or baker's bread for unexpected company. All through that first spring and summer I kept hoping that Ambrosch would bring Ántonia and Yulka to see our new house. I wanted to show them our red plush furniture, and the trumpet-blowing cherubs the German paper-hanger had put on our parlor ceiling.

When Ambrosch came to town, however, he came alone, and though he put his horses in our barn, he would never stay for dinner, or tell us anything about his mother and sisters. If we ran out and questioned him as he was slipping through the yard, he would merely work his shoulders about in his coat and say, "They all right, I guess."

Mrs. Steavens, who now lived on our farm, grew as fond of Ántonia as we had been, and always brought us news of her. All through the wheat season, she told us, Ambrosch hired his sister out like a man, and she went from farm to farm, binding sheaves or working with the threshers. The farmers liked her and were kind to her; said they would rather have her for a hand than Ambrosch. When fall came she was to husk corn for the neighbors until Christmas, as she had done the year before; but Grandmother saved her from this by getting her a place to work with our neighbors, the Harlings.

II

Grandmother often said that if she had to live in town, she thanked God she lived next to the Harlings. They had been farming people, like ourselves, and their place was like a little farm, with a big barn and a garden, and an orchard and grazing lots—even a windmill. The Harlings were Norwegians, and Mrs. Harling had lived in Christiania until she was ten years old. Her husband was born in Minnesota. He was a grain merchant and cattle buyer, and was generally considered the most enterprising businessman in our country. He controlled a line of grain elevators in the little towns along the railroad to the west of us, and was away from home a great deal. In his absence his wife was the head of the household.

Mrs. Harling was short and square and sturdy-looking, like her house. Every inch of her was charged with an energy that made itself felt the moment she entered a room. Her face was rosy and solid, with bright, twinkling eyes and a stubborn little chin. She was quick to anger, quick to laughter, and jolly from the depths of her soul. How well I remember her laugh; it had in it the same sudden recognition that flashed into her eyes, was a burst of humor, short and intelligent. Her rapid footsteps shook her own floors, and she routed lassitude and indifference wherever she came. She could not be negative or perfunctory about anything. Her enthusiasm, and her violent likes and dislikes, asserted themselves in all the everyday occupations of life. Wash day was interesting, never dreary, at the Harlings'. Preserving-time was a prolonged festival, and house-cleaning was like a revolution. When Mrs. Harling made garden that spring, we could feel the stir of her undertaking through the willow hedge that separated our place from hers.

Three of the Harling children were near me in age. Charley, the only son—they had lost an older boy—was sixteen; Julia, who was known as the musical one, was fourteen when I was; and Sally, the tomboy with short hair, was a year younger. She was nearly as strong as I, and uncannily clever at all boys' sports. Sally was a wild thing, with sun-burned yellow hair, bobbed about her ears, and a brown skin, for she never wore a hat. She raced all over town on one roller skate, often cheated at "keeps," but was such a quick shot one couldn't catch her at it.

The grown-up daughter, Frances, was a very important person in our world. She was her father's chief clerk, and virtually managed his Black Hawk office during his frequent absences. Because of her unusual business ability, he was stern and exacting with her. He paid her a good salary, but she had few holidays and never got away from her responsibilities. Even on Sundays she went to the office to open the mail and read the markets. With Charley, who was not interested in business, but was already preparing for Annapolis, Mr. Harling was very indulgent: bought him guns and tools and electric batteries, and never asked what he did with them.

Frances was dark, like her father, and quite as tall. In winter she wore a sealskin coat and cap, and she and Mr. Harling used to walk home together in the evening, talking about grain-cars and cattle, like two men. Sometimes she came over to see Grandfather after supper, and her visits flattered him. More than once they put their wits together to rescue some unfortunate farmer from the clutches of Wick Cutter, the Black Hawk moneylender. Grandfather said Frances Harling was as good a judge of credits as any banker in the county. The two or three men who had tried to take advantage of her in a deal acquired celebrity by their defeat. She knew every farmer for miles about: how much land he had under cultivation, how many cattle he was feeding, what his liabilities were. Her interest in these people was more than a business interest. She carried them all in her mind as if they were characters in a book or a play.

When Frances drove out into the country on business, she would go miles out of her way to call on some of the old people, or to see the women who seldom got to town. She was quick at understanding the grandmothers who spoke no English, and the most reticent and distrustful of them would tell her their story without realizing they were doing so. She went to country funerals and weddings in all weathers. A farmer's daughter who was to be married could count on a wedding present from Frances Harling.

In August the Harlings' Danish cook had to leave them. Grandmother entreated them to try Ántonia. She cornered Ambrosch the next time he came to town, and pointed out to him that any connection with Christian Harling would strengthen his credit and be of advantage to him. One Sunday Mrs. Harling took the long ride out to the Shimerdas' with Frances. She said she wanted to see "what the girl came from" and to have a clear understanding with her mother. I was in our yard when they came driving home, just before sunset. They laughed and waved to me as they passed, and I could see they were in great good humor. After supper, when Grandfather set off to church, Grandmother and I took my short cut through the willow hedge and went over to hear about the visit to the Shimerdas'.

We found Mrs. Harling with Charley and Sally on the front porch, resting after her hard drive. Julia was in the hammock—she was fond of repose—and Frances was at the piano, playing without a light and talking to her mother through the open window.

Mrs. Harling laughed when she saw us coming. "I expect you left your dishes on the table tonight, Mrs. Burden," she called. Frances shut the piano and came out to join us.

They had liked Ántonia from their first glimpse of her; felt they knew exactly what kind of girl she was. As for Mrs. Shimerda, they found her very amusing. Mrs. Harling chuckled whenever she spoke of her. "I expect I am more at home with that sort of bird than you are, Mrs. Burden. They're a pair, Ambrosch and that old woman!"

They had had a long argument with Ambrosch about Ántonia's allowance for clothes and pocket money. It was his plan that every cent of his sister's wages should be paid over to him each month, and he would provide her with such clothing as he thought necessary. When Mrs. Harling told him firmly that she would keep fifty dollars a year for Ántonia's own use, he declared they wanted to take his sister to town and dress her up and make a fool of her. Mrs. Harling gave us a lively account of Ambrosch's behavior throughout the interview: how he kept jumping up and putting on his cap as if he were through with the whole business, and how his mother tweaked his coat-tail and prompted him in Bohemian. Mrs. Harling finally agreed to pay three dollars a week for Ántonia's services—good wages in those days—and to keep her in shoes. There had been hot dispute about the shoes, Mrs. Shimerda finally saying persuasively that she would send Mrs. Harling three fat geese every year to "make even." Ambrosch was to bring his sister to town next Saturday.

"She'll be awkward and rough at first, like enough," Grandmother said anxiously, "but unless she's been spoiled by the hard life she's led, she has it in her to be a real helpful girl."

Mrs. Harling laughed her quick, decided laugh. "Oh, I'm not worrying, Mrs. Burden! I can bring something out of that girl. She's barely seventeen, not too old to learn new ways. She's good-looking, too!" she added warmly.

Frances turned to Grandmother. "Oh, yes, Mrs. Burden, you didn't tell us that! She was working in the garden when we got there, barefoot and ragged. But she has such fine brown legs and arms, and splendid color in her cheeks—like those big dark red plums."

We were pleased at this praise. Grandmother spoke feelingly. "When she first came to this country, Frances, and had that genteel old man to watch over her, she was as pretty a girl as ever I saw. But, dear me, what a life she's led, out in the fields with those rough threshers! Things would have been very different with poor Ántonia if her father had lived."

The Harlings begged us to tell them about Mr. Shimerda's death and the big snowstorm. By the time we saw Grandfather coming home from church, we had told them pretty much all we knew of the Shimerdas.

"The girl will be happy here, and she'll forget those things," said Mrs. Harling confidently, as we rose to take our leave.

III

On Saturday Ambrosch drove up to the back gate, and Ántonia jumped down from the wagon and ran into our kitchen just as she used to do. She was wearing shoes and stockings, and was breathless and excited. She gave me a playful shake by the shoulders. "You ain't forget about me, Jim?"

Grandmother kissed her. "God bless you, child! Now you've come, you must try to do right and be a credit to us."

Ántonia looked eagerly about the house and admired everything. "Maybe I be the kind of girl you like better; now I come to town," she suggested hopefully.

How good it was to have Ántonia near us again, to see her every day and almost every night! Her greatest fault, Mrs. Harling found, was that she so often stopped her work and fell to playing with the children. She would race about the orchard with us, or take sides in our hay-fights in the barn, or be the old bear that came down from the mountain and carried off Nina. Tony learned English so quickly that by the time school began she could speak as well as any of us.

I was jealous of Tony's admiration for Charley Harling. Because he was always first in his classes at school, and could mend the water-pipes or the doorbell and take the clock to pieces, she seemed to think him a sort of prince. Nothing that Charley wanted was too much trouble for her. She loved to put up lunches for him when he went hunting, to mend his ball-gloves and sew buttons on his shooting-coat, baked the kind of nut-cake he liked, and fed his setter dog when he was away on trips with his father. Ántonia had made herself cloth working-slippers out of Mr. Harling's old coats, and in these she went padding about after Charley, fairly panting with eagerness to please him.

Next to Charley, I think she loved Nina best. Nina was only six, and she was rather more complex than the other children. She was fanciful, had all sorts of unspoken preferences, and was easily offended. At the slightest disappointment or displeasure, her velvety brown eyes filled with tears, and she would lift her chin and walk silently away. If we ran after her and tried to appease her, it did no good. She walked on unmollified. I used to think that no eyes in the world could grow so large or hold so many tears as Nina's. Mrs. Harling and Ántonia invariably took her part. We were never given a chance to explain. The charge was simply: "You have made Nina cry. Now, Jimmy can go home, and Sally must get her arithmetic." I liked Nina, too; she was so quaint and unexpected, and her eyes were lovely; but I often wanted to shake her.

We had jolly evenings at the Harlings' when the father was away. If he was at home, the children had to go to bed early, or they came over to my house to play. Mr. Harling not only demanded a quiet house, he demanded all his wife's attention. He used to take her away to their room in the west ell, and talk over his business with her all evening. Though we did not realize it then, Mrs. Harling was our audience when we played, and we always looked to her for suggestions. Nothing flattered one like her quick laugh.

Mr. Harling had a desk in his bedroom, and his own easy-chair by the window, in which no one else ever sat. On the nights when he was at home, I could see his shadow on the blind, and it seemed to me an arrogant shadow. Mrs. Harling paid no heed to anyone else if he was there. Before he went to bed she always got him a lunch of smoked salmon or anchovies and beer. He kept an alcohol lamp in his room, and a French coffee-pot, and his wife made coffee for him at any hour of the night he happened to want it.

Most Black Hawk fathers had no personal habits outside their domestic ones; they paid the bills, pushed the baby-carriage after office hours, moved the sprinkler about over the lawn, and took the family driving on Sunday. Mr. Harling, therefore, seemed to me autocratic and imperial in his ways. He walked, talked, put on his gloves, shook hands, like a man who felt that he had power. He was not tall, but he carried his head so haughtily that he looked a commanding figure, and there was something daring and challenging in his eyes. I used to imagine that the "nobles" of whom Ántonia was always talking probably looked very much like Christian Harling, wore caped overcoats like his, and just such a glittering diamond upon the little finger.

Except when the father was at home, the Harling house was never quiet. Mrs. Harling and Nina and Ántonia made as much noise as a houseful of children, and there was usually somebody at the piano. Julia was the only one who was held down to regular hours of practicing, but they all played. When Frances came home at noon, she played until dinner was ready. When Sally got back from school, she sat down in her hat and coat and drummed the plantation melodies that Negro minstrel troupes brought to town. Even Nina played the Swedish Wedding March.

Mrs. Harling had studied the piano under a good teacher, and somehow she managed to practice every day. I soon learned that if I were sent over on an errand and found Mrs. Harling at the piano, I must sit down and wait quietly until she turned to me. I can see her at this moment: her short, square person planted firmly on the stool, her little fat hands moving quickly and neatly over the keys, her eyes fixed on the music with intelligent concentration.

IV

I won't have none of your weevily wheat, and I won't have
none of your barley,
But I'll take a measure of fine white flour, to make a cake
for Charley.

WE WERE SINGING rhymes to tease Ántonia while she was beating up one of Charley's favorite cakes in her big mixing-bowl.

It was a crisp autumn evening, just cold enough to make one glad to quit playing tag in the yard and retreat into the kitchen. We had begun to roll popcorn balls with syrup when we heard a knock at the back door, and Tony dropped her spoon and went to open it.

A plump, fair-skinned girl was standing in the doorway. She looked demure and pretty, and made a graceful picture in her blue cashmere dress and little blue hat, with a plaid shawl drawn neatly about her shoulders and a clumsy pocket-book in her hand.

"Hello, Tony. Don't you know me?" she asked in a smooth, low voice, looking in at us archly.

Ántonia gasped and stepped back.

"Why, it's Lena! Of course I didn't know you, so dressed up!"

Lena Lingard laughed, as if this pleased her. I had not recognized her for a moment, either. I had never seen her before with a hat on her head—or with shoes and stockings on her feet, for that matter. And here she was, brushed and smoothed and dressed like a town girl, smiling at us with perfect composure.

"Hello, Jim," she said carelessly as she walked into the kitchen and looked about her. "I've come to town to work, too, Tony."

"Have you, now? Well, ain't that funny!" Ántonia stood ill at ease, and didn't seem to know just what to do with her visitor.

The door was open into the dining room, where Mrs. Harling sat crocheting and Frances was reading. Frances asked Lena to come in and join them.

"You are Lena Lingard, aren't you? I've been to see your mother, but you were off herding cattle that day. Mama, this is Chris Lingard's oldest girl."

Mrs. Harling dropped her worsted and examined the visitor with quick, keen eyes. Lena was not at all disconcerted. She sat down in the chair Frances pointed out, carefully arranging her pocket-book and gray cotton gloves on her lap. We followed with our popcorn, but Ántonia hung back—said she had to get her cake into the oven.

"So you have come to town," said Mrs. Harling, her eyes still fixed on Lena. "Where are you working?"

"For Mrs. Thomas, the dressmaker. She is going to teach me to sew. She says I have quite a knack. I'm through with the farm. There ain't any end to the work on a farm, and always so much trouble happens. I'm going to be a dressmaker."

"Well, there have to be dressmakers. It's a good trade. But I wouldn't run down the farm, if I were you," said Mrs. Harling rather severely. "How is your mother?"

"Oh, mother's never very well; she has too much to do. She'd get away from the farm, too, if she could. She was willing for me to come. After I learn to do sewing, I can make money and help her."

"See that you don't forget to," said Mrs. Harling sceptically, as she took up her crocheting again and sent the hook in and out with nimble fingers.

"No, 'm, I won't," said Lena blandly. She took a few grains of the popcorn we pressed upon her, eating them discreetly and taking care not to get her fingers sticky.

Frances drew her chair up nearer to the visitor. "I thought you were going to be married, Lena," she said teasingly. "Didn't I hear that Nick Svendsen was rushing you pretty hard?"

Lena looked up with her curiously innocent smile. "He did go with me quite a while. But his father made a fuss about it and said he wouldn't give Nick any land if he married me, so he's going to marry Annie Iverson. I wouldn't like to be her; Nick's awful sullen, and he'll take it out on her. He ain't spoke to his father since he promised."

Frances laughed. "And how do you feel about it?"

"I don't want to marry Nick, or any other man," Lena murmured. "I've seen a good deal of married life, and I don't care for it. I want to be so I can help my mother and the children at home, and not have to ask lief of anybody."

"That's right," said Frances. "And Mrs. Thomas thinks you can learn dressmaking?"

"Yes, 'm. I've always liked to sew, but I never had much to do with.

Mrs. Thomas makes lovely things for all the town ladies. Did you know Mrs. Gardener is having a purple velvet made? The velvet came from Omaha. My, but it's lovely!" Lena sighed softly and stroked her cashmere folds. "Tony knows I never did like out-of-door work," she added.

Mrs. Harling glanced at her. "I expect you'll learn to sew all right, Lena, if you'll only keep your head and not go gadding about to dances all the time and neglect your work, the way some country girls do."

"Yes, 'm. Tiny Soderball is coming to town, too. She's going to work at the Boys' Home Hotel. She'll see lots of strangers," Lena added wistfully.

"Too many, like enough," said Mrs. Harling. "I don't think a hotel is a good place for a girl; though I guess Mrs. Gardener keeps an eye on her waitresses."

Lena's candid eyes, that always looked a little sleepy under their long lashes, kept straying about the cheerful rooms with naïve admiration. Presently she drew on her cotton gloves. "I guess I must be leaving," she said irresolutely.

Frances told her to come again, whenever she was lonesome or wanted advice about anything. Lena replied that she didn't believe she would ever get lonesome in Black Hawk.

She lingered at the kitchen door and begged Ántonia to come and see her often. "I've got a room of my own at Mrs. Thomas's, with a carpet."

Tony shuffled uneasily in her cloth slippers. "I'll come sometime, but Mrs. Harling don't like to have me run much," she said evasively.

"You can do what you please when you go out, can't you?" Lena asked in a guarded whisper. "Ain't you crazy about town, Tony? I don't care what anybody says, I'm done with the farm!" She glanced back over her shoulder toward the dining room, where Mrs. Harling sat.

When Lena was gone, Frances asked Ántonia why she hadn't been a little more cordial to her.

"I didn't know if your mother would like her coming here," said Ántonia, looking troubled. "She was kind of talked about, out there."

"Yes, I know. But mother won't hold it against her if she behaves well here. You needn't say anything about that to the children. I guess Jim has heard all that gossip?"

When I nodded, she pulled my hair and told me I knew too much, anyhow. We were good friends, Frances and I.

I ran home to tell Grandmother that Lena Lingard had come to town. We were glad of it, for she had a hard life on the farm.

Lena lived in the Norwegian settlement west of Squaw Creek, and she used to herd her father's cattle in the open country between his place and the Shimerdas'. Whenever we rode over in that direction we saw her out among her cattle, bareheaded and barefooted, scantily dressed in tattered clothing, always knitting as she watched her herd. Before I knew Lena, I thought of her as something wild, that always lived on the prairie, because I had never seen her under a roof. Her yellow hair was burned to a ruddy thatch on her head; but her legs and arms, curiously enough, in spite of constant exposure to the sun, kept a miraculous whiteness which somehow made her seem more undressed than other girls who went scantily clad. The first time I stopped to talk to her, I was astonished at her soft voice and easy, gentle ways. The girls out there usually got rough and mannish after they went to herding. But Lena asked Jake and me to get off our horses and stay awhile, and behaved exactly as if she were in a house and were accustomed to having visitors. She was not embarrassed by her ragged clothes, and treated us as if we were old acquaintances. Even then I noticed the unusual color of her eyes—a shade of deep violet—and their soft, confiding expression.

Chris Lingard was not a very successful farmer, and he had a large family. Lena was always knitting stockings for little brothers and sisters, and even the Norwegian women, who disapproved of her, admitted that she was a good daughter to her mother. As Tony said, she had been talked about. She was accused of making Ole Benson lose the little sense he had—and that at an age when she should still have been in pinafores.

Ole lived in a leaky dugout somewhere at the edge of the settlement. He was fat and lazy and discouraged, and bad luck had become a habit with him. After he had had every other kind of misfortune, his wife, "Crazy Mary," tried to set a neighbor's barn on fire, and was sent to the asylum at Lincoln. She was kept there for a few months, then escaped and walked all the way home, nearly two hundred miles, traveling by night and hiding in barns and haystacks by day. When she got back to the Norwegian settlement, her poor feet were as hard as hoofs. She promised to be good, and was allowed to stay at home—though everyone realized she was as crazy as ever, and she still ran about barefooted through the snow, telling her domestic troubles to her neighbors.

Not long after Mary came back from the asylum, I heard a young Dane, who was helping us to thresh, tell Jake and Otto that Chris Lingard's oldest girl had put Ole Benson out of his head, until he had no more sense than his crazy wife. When Ole was cultivating his corn that summer, he used to get discouraged in the field, tie up his team, and wander off to wherever Lena Lingard was herding. There he would sit down on the draw-side and help her watch her cattle. All the settlement was talking about it. The Norwegian preacher's wife went to Lena and told her she ought not to allow this; she begged Lena to come to church on Sundays. Lena said she hadn't a dress in the world any less ragged than the one on her back. Then the minister's wife went through her old trunks and found some things she had worn before her marriage.

The next Sunday Lena appeared at church, a little late, with her hair done up neatly on her head, like a young woman, wearing shoes and stockings, and the new dress, which she had made over for herself very becomingly. The congregation stared at her. Until that morning no one—unless it were Ole—had realized how pretty she was, or that she was growing up. The swelling lines of her figure had been hidden under the shapeless rags she wore in the fields. After the last hymn had been sung, and the congregation was dismissed, Ole slipped out to the hitch-bar and lifted Lena on her horse. That, in itself, was shocking; a married man was not expected to do such things. But it was nothing to the scene that followed. Crazy Mary darted out from the group of women at the church door, and ran down the road after Lena, shouting horrible threats.

"Look out, you Lena Lingard, look out! I'll come over with a corn-knife one day and trim some of that shape off you. Then you won't sail round so fine, making eyes at the men! . . ."

The Norwegian women didn't know where to look. They were formal housewives, most of them, with a severe sense of decorum. But Lena Lingard only laughed her lazy, good-natured laugh and rode on, gazing back over her shoulder at Ole's infuriated wife.

The time came, however, when Lena didn't laugh. More than once Crazy Mary chased her across the prairie and round and round the Shimerdas' cornfield. Lena never told her father; perhaps she was ashamed; perhaps she was more afraid of his anger than of the corn-knife. I was at the Shimerdas' one afternoon when Lena came bounding through the red grass as fast as her white legs could carry her. She ran straight into the house and hid in Ántonia's feather-bed. Mary was not far behind: she came right up to the door and made us feel how sharp her blade was, showing us very graphically just what she meant to do to Lena. Mrs. Shimerda, leaning out of the window, enjoyed the situation keenly, and was sorry when Ántonia sent Mary away, mollified by an apronful of bottle-tomatoes. Lena came out from Tony's room behind the kitchen, very pink from the heat of the feathers, but otherwise calm. She begged Ántonia and me to go with her, and help get her cattle together; they were scattered and might be gorging themselves in somebody's cornfield.

"Maybe you lose a steer and learn not to make somethings with your eyes at married men," Mrs. Shimerda told her hectoringly.

Lena only smiled her sleepy smile. "I never made anything to him with my eyes. I can't help it if he hangs around, and I can't order him off. It ain't my prairie."

V

After Lena came to Black Hawk, I often met her downtown, where she would be matching sewing silk or buying "findings" for Mrs. Thomas. If I happened to walk home with her, she told me all about the dresses she was helping to make, or about what she saw and heard when she was with Tiny Soderball at the hotel on Saturday nights.

The Boys' Home was the best hotel on our branch of the Burlington, and all the commercial travelers in that territory tried to get into Black Hawk for Sunday. They used to assemble in the parlor after supper on Saturday nights. Marshall Field's man, Anson Kirkpatrick, played the piano and sang all the latest sentimental songs. After Tiny had helped the cook wash the dishes, she and Lena sat on the other side of the double doors between the parlor and the dining room, listening to the music and giggling at the jokes and stories. Lena often said she hoped I would be a traveling man when I grew up. They had a gay life of it—nothing to do but ride about on trains all day and go to theaters when they were in big cities. Behind the hotel there was an old store building, where the salesmen opened their big trunks and spread out their samples on the counters. The Black Hawk merchants went to look at these things and order goods, and Mrs. Thomas, though she was "retail trade," was permitted to see them and to "get ideas." They were all generous, these traveling men; they gave Tiny Soderball handkerchiefs and gloves and ribbons and striped stockings, and so many bottles of perfume and cakes of scented soap that she bestowed some of them on Lena.

One afternoon in the week before Christmas, I came upon Lena and her funny, square-headed little brother Chris, standing before the drugstore, gazing in at the wax dolls and blocks and Noah's Arks arranged in the frosty show window. The boy had come to town with a neighbor to do his Christmas shopping, for he had money of his own this year. He was only twelve, but that winter he had got the job of sweeping out the Norwegian church and making the fire in it every Sunday morning. A cold job it must have been, too!

We went into Duckford's dry-goods store, and Chris unwrapped all his presents and showed them to me—something for each of the six younger than himself, even a rubber pig for the baby. Lena had given him one of Tiny Soderball's bottles of perfume for his mother, and he thought he would get some handkerchiefs to go with it. They were cheap, and he hadn't much money left. We found a tableful of handkerchiefs spread out for view at Duckford's. Chris wanted those with initial letters in the corner, because he had never seen any before. He studied them seriously, while Lena looked over his shoulder, telling him she thought the red letters would hold their color best. He seemed so perplexed that I thought perhaps he hadn't enough money, after all. Presently he said gravely:

"Sister, you know mother's name is Berthe. I don't know if I ought to get *B* for Berthe, or *M* for Mother."

Lena patted his bristly head. "I'd get the *B*, Chrissy. It will please her for you to think about her name. Nobody ever calls her by it now."

That satisfied him. His face cleared at once, and he took three reds and three blues. When the neighbor came in to say that it was time to start, Lena wound Chris's comforter about his neck and turned up his jacket collar—he had no overcoat—and we watched him climb into the wagon and start on his long, cold drive. As we walked together up the windy street, Lena wiped her eyes with the back of her woollen glove. "I get awful homesick for them, all the same," she murmured, as if she were answering some remembered reproach.

VI

Winter comes down savagely over a little town on the prairie. The wind that sweeps in from the open country strips away all the leafy screens that hide one yard from another in summer, and the houses seem to draw closer together. The roofs, that looked so far away across the green treetops, now stare you in the face, and they are so much uglier than when their angles were softened by vines and shrubs.

In the morning, when I was fighting my way to school against the wind, I couldn't see anything but the road in front of me; but in the late afternoon, when I was coming home, the town looked bleak and desolate to me. The pale, cold light of the winter sunset did not beautify—it was like the light of truth itself. When the smoky clouds hung low in the west and the red sun went down behind them, leaving a pink flush on the snowy roofs and the blue drifts, then the wind sprang up afresh, with a kind of bitter song, as if it said: "This is reality, whether you like it or not. All those frivolities of summer, the light and shadow, the living mask of green that trembled over everything, they were lies, and this is what was underneath. This is the truth." It was as if we were being punished for loving the loveliness of summer.

If I loitered on the playground after school, or went to the post office for the mail and lingered to hear the gossip about the cigar-stand, it would be growing dark by the time I came home. The sun was gone; the frozen streets stretched long and blue before me; the lights were shining pale in kitchen windows, and I could smell the suppers cooking as I passed. Few people were abroad, and each one of them was hurrying toward a fire. The glowing stoves in the houses were like magnets. When one passed an old man, one could see nothing of his face but a red nose sticking out between a frosted beard and a long plush cap. The young men capered along with their hands in their pockets, and sometimes tried a slide on the icy sidewalk. The children, in their bright hoods and comforters, never walked, but always ran from the moment they left their door, beating their mittens against their sides. When I got as far as the Methodist Church, I was about halfway home. I can remember how glad I was when there happened to be a light in the church, and the painted glass window shone out at us as we came along the frozen street. In the winter bleakness a hunger for color came over people, like the Laplander's craving for fats and sugar. Without knowing why, we used to linger on the sidewalk outside the church when the lamps were lighted early for choir practice or prayer-meeting, shivering and talking until our feet were like lumps of ice. The crude reds and greens and blues of that colored glass held us there.

On winter nights, the lights in the Harlings' windows drew me like the painted glass. Inside that warm, roomy house there was color, too. After supper I used to catch up my cap, stick my hands in my pockets, and dive through the willow hedge as if witches were after me. Of course, if Mr. Harling was at home, if his shadow stood out on the blind of the west room, I did not go in but turned and walked home by the long way, through the street, wondering what book I should read as I sat down with the two old people.

Such disappointments only gave greater zest to the nights when we acted charades, or had a costume ball in the back parlor, with Sally always dressed like a boy. Frances taught us to dance that winter, and she said, from the first lesson, that Ántonia would make the best dancer among us. On Saturday nights, Mrs. Harling used to play the old operas for us—*Martha, Norma, Rigoletto*—telling us the story while she played. Every Saturday night was like a party. The parlor, the back parlor, and the dining room were warm and brightly lighted, with comfortable chairs and sofas, and gay pictures on the walls. One always felt at ease there. Ántonia brought her sewing and sat with us—she was already beginning to make pretty clothes for herself. After the long winter evenings on the prairie, with Ambrosch's sullen silences and her mother's complaints, the Harlings' house seemed, as she said, "like heaven" to her. She was never too tired to make taffy or chocolate cookies for us. If Sally whispered in her ear, or Charley gave her three winks, Tony would rush into the kitchen and build a fire in the range on which she had already cooked three meals that day.

While we sat in the kitchen waiting for the cookies to bake or the taffy to cool, Nina used to coax Ántonia to tell her stories—about the calf that broke its leg, or how Yulka saved her little turkeys from drowning in the freshet, or about old Christmases and weddings in Bohemia. Nina interpreted the stories about the crêche fancifully, and in spite of our derision she cherished a belief that Christ was born in Bohemia a short time before the Shimerdas left that country. We all liked Tony's stories. Her voice had a peculiarly engaging quality; it was deep, a little husky, and one always heard the breath vibrating behind it. Everything she said seemed to come right out of her heart.

One evening when we were picking out kernels for walnut taffy, Tony told us a new story.

"Mrs. Harling, did you ever hear about what happened up in the Norwegian settlement last summer, when I was threshing there? We were at Iversons', and I was driving one of the grain-wagons."

Mrs. Harling came out and sat down among us. "Could you throw the wheat into the bin yourself, Tony?" She knew what heavy work it was.

"Yes, ma'm, I did. I could shovel just as fast as that fat Andern boy that drove the other wagon. One day it was just awful hot. When we got back to the field from dinner, we took things kind of easy. The men put in the horses and got the machine going, and Ole Iverson was up on the deck, cutting bands. I was sitting against a straw-stack, trying to get some shade. My wagon wasn't going out first, and somehow I felt the heat awful that day. The sun was so hot like it was going to burn the world up. After a while I see a man coming across the stubble, and when he got close I see it was a tramp. His toes stuck out of his shoes, and he hadn't shaved for a long while, and his eyes was awful red and wild, like he had some sickness. He comes right up and begins to talk like he knows me already. He says: 'The ponds in this country is done got so low a man couldn't drowned himself in one of 'em.'

"I told him nobody wanted to drownd themselves, but if we didn't have rain soon we'd have to pump water for the cattle.

" 'Oh, cattle,' he says, 'you'll all take care of your cattle! Ain't you got no beer here?' I told him he'd have to go to the Bohemians for beer; the Norwegians didn't have none when they threshed. 'My God!' he says, 'so it's Norwegians now, is it? I thought this was Americy.'

"Then he goes up to the machine and yells out to Ole Iverson, 'Hello, partner, let me up there. I can cut bands, and I'm tired of trampin'. I won't go no farther.'

"I tried to make signs to Ole, 'cause I thought that man was crazy and might get the machine stopped up. But Ole, he was glad to get down out of the sun and chaff—it gets down your neck and sticks to you something awful when it's hot like that. So Ole jumped down and crawled under one of the wagons for shade, and the tramp got on the machine. He cut bands all right for a few minutes, and then, Mrs. Harling, he waved his hand to me and jumped head-first right into the threshing machine after the wheat.

"I begun to scream, and the men run to stop the horses, but the belt had sucked him down, and by the time they got her stopped, he was all beat and cut to pieces. He was wedged in so tight it was a hard job to get him out, and the machine ain't never worked right since."

"Was he clear dead, Tony?" we cried.

"Was he dead? Well, I guess so! There, now, Nina's all upset. We won't talk about it. Don't you cry, Nina. No old tramp won't get you while Tony's here."

Mrs. Harling spoke up sternly. "Stop crying, Nina, or I'll always send you upstairs when Ántonia tells us about the country. Did they never find out where he came from, Ántonia?"

"Never, ma'm. He hadn't been seen nowhere except in a little town they call Conway. He tried to get beer there, but there wasn't any saloon. Maybe he came in on a freight, but the brakeman hadn't seen him. They couldn't find no letters nor nothing on him; nothing but an old penknife in his pocket and the wishbone of a chicken wrapped up in a piece of paper, and some poetry."

"Some poetry?" we exclaimed.

"I remember," said Frances. "It was 'The Old Oaken Bucket,' cut out of a newspaper and nearly worn out. Ole Iverson brought it into the office and showed it to me."

"Now, wasn't that strange, Miss Frances?" Tony asked thoughtfully. "What would anybody want to kill themselves in summer for? In threshing time, too! It's nice everywhere then."

"So it is. Ántonia," said Mrs. Harling heartily. "Maybe I'll go home and help you thresh next summer. Isn't that taffy nearly ready to eat? I've been smelling it a long while."

There was a basic harmony between Ántonia and her mistress. They had strong, independent natures, both of them. They knew what they liked, and were not always trying to imitate other people. They loved children and animals and music, and rough play and digging in the earth. They liked to prepare rich, hearty food and to see people eat it, to make up soft white beds and to see youngsters asleep in them. They ridiculed conceited people and were quick to help unfortunate ones. Deep down in each of them there was a kind of hearty joviality, a relish of life, not over-delicate, but very invigorating. I never tried to define it, but I was distinctly conscious of it. I could not imagine Ántonia's living for a week in any other house in Black Hawk than the Harlings'.

VII

Winter lies too long in country towns—hangs on until it is stale and shabby, old and sullen. On the farm the weather was the great fact, and men's affairs went on underneath it, as the streams creep under the ice. But in Black Hawk the scene of human life was spread out shrunken and pinched, frozen down to the bare stalk.

Through January and February I went to the river with the Harlings on clear nights, and we skated up to the big island and made bonfires on the frozen sand. But by March the ice was rough and choppy, and the snow on the river bluffs was gray and mournful-looking. I was tired of school, tired of winter clothes, of the rutted streets, of the dirty drifts and the piles of cinders that had lain in the yards so long. There was only one break in the dreary monotony of that month: when Blind d'Arnault, the Negro pianist, came to town. He gave a concert at the Opera House on Monday night, and he and his manager spent Saturday and Sunday at our comfortable hotel. Mrs. Harling had known d'Arnault for years. She told Ántonia she had better go to see Tiny that Saturday evening, as there would certainly be music at the Boys' Home.

Saturday night after supper I ran downtown to the hotel and slipped quietly into the parlor. The chairs and sofas were already occupied, and the air smelled pleasantly of cigar smoke. The parlor had once been two rooms, and the floor was swaybacked where the partition had been cut away. The wind from without made waves in the long carpet. A coal stove glowed at either end of the room, and the grand piano in the middle stood open.

There was an atmosphere of unusual freedom about the house that night, for Mrs. Gardener had gone to Omaha for a week. Johnnie had been having drinks with the guests until he was rather absentminded. It was Mrs. Gardener who ran the business and looked after everything. Her husband stood at the desk and welcomed incoming travelers. He was a popular fellow, but no manager.

Mrs. Gardener was admittedly the best-dressed woman in Black Hawk, drove the best horse, and had a smart trap and a little white-and-gold sleigh. She seemed indifferent to her possessions, was not half so solicitous about them as her friends were. She was tall, dark, severe, with something Indianlike in the rigid immobility of her face. Her manner was cold, and she talked little. Guests felt that they were receiving, not conferring, a favor when they stayed at her house. Even the smartest traveling men were flattered when Mrs. Gardener stopped to chat with them for a moment. The patrons of the hotel were divided into two classes: those who had seen Mrs. Gardener's diamonds, and those who had not.

When I stole into the parlor, Anson Kirkpatrick, Marshall Field's man, was at the piano, playing airs from a musical comedy then running in Chicago. He was a dapper little Irishman, very vain, homely as a monkey, with friends everywhere, and a sweetheart in every port, like a sailor. I did not know all the men who were sitting about, but I recognized a furniture salesman from Kansas City, a drug man, and Willy O'Reilly, who traveled for a jewelry house and sold musical instruments. The talk was all about good and bad hotels, actors and actresses and musical prodigies. I learned that Mrs. Gardener had gone to Omaha to hear Booth and Barrett, who were to play there next week, and that Mary Anderson was having a great success in *A Winter's Tale,* in London.

The door from the office opened, and Johnnie Gardener came in, directing Blind d' Arnault—he would never consent to be led. He was a heavy, bulky mulatto, on short legs, and he came tapping the floor in front of him with his gold-headed cane. His yellow face was lifted in the light, with a show of white teeth, all grinning, and his shrunken, papery eyelids lay motionless over his blind eyes.

"Good evening, gentlemen. No ladies here? Good evening, gentlemen. We going to have a little music? Some of you gentlemen going to play for me this evening?" It was the soft, amiable Negro voice, like those I remembered from early childhood, with the note of docile subservience in it. He had the Negro head, too; almost no head at all; nothing behind the ears but folds of neck under close-clipped wool. He would have been repulsive if his face had not been so kindly and happy. It was the happiest face I had seen since I left Virginia.

He felt his way directly to the piano. The moment he sat down, I noticed the nervous infirmity of which Mrs. Harling had told me. When he was sitting, or standing still, he swayed back and forth incessantly, like a rocking toy. At the piano, he swayed in time to the music, and when he was not playing, his body kept up this motion, like an empty mill grinding on. He found the pedals and tried them, ran his yellow hands up and down the keys a few times, tinkling off scales, then turned to the company.

"She seems all right, gentlemen. Nothing happened to her since the last time I was here. Mrs. Gardener, she always has this piano tuned up before I come. Now gentlemen, I expect you've all got grand voices. Seems like we might have some good old plantation songs tonight."

The men gathered round him, as he began to play "My Old Kentucky Home." They sang one Negro melody after another, while the mulatto sat rocking himself, his head thrown back, his yellow face lifted, his shrivelled eyelids never fluttering.

He was born in the far South, on the d'Arnault plantation, where the spirit if not the fact of slavery persisted. When he was three weeks old, he had an illness which left him totally blind. As soon as he was old enough to sit up alone and toddle about, another affliction, the nervous motion of his body, became apparent. His mother, a buxom young Negro wench who was laundress for the d'Arnaults, concluded that her blind baby was "not right" in his head, and she was ashamed of him. She loved him devotedly, but he was so ugly, with his sunken eyes and his "fidgets," that she hid him away from people. All the dainties she brought down from the big house were for the blind child, and she beat and cuffed her other children whenever she found them teasing him or trying to get his chicken-bone away from him. He began to talk early, remembered everything he heard, and his mammy said he "wasn't all wrong." She named him Samson, because he was blind, but on the plantation he was known as "yellow Martha's simple child." He was docile and obedient, but when he was six years old he began to run away from home, always taking the same direction. He felt his way through the lilacs, along the boxwood hedge, up to the south wing of the Big House, where Miss Nellie d'Arnault practiced the piano every morning. This angered his mother more than anything else he could have done; she was so ashamed of his ugliness that she couldn't bear to have white folks see him. Whenever she caught him slipping away from the cabin, she whipped him unmercifully, and told him what dreadful things old Mr. d'Arnault would do to him if he ever found him near the Big House. But the next time Samson had a chance, he ran away again. If Miss d'Arnault stopped practicing for a moment and went toward the window, she saw this hideous little pickaninny, dressed in an old piece of sacking, standing in the open space between the hollyhock rows, his body rocking automatically, his blind face lifted to the sun and wearing an expression of idiotic rapture. Often she was tempted to tell Martha that the child must be kept at home, but somehow the memory of his foolish, happy face deterred her. She remembered that his sense of hearing was nearly all he had—though it did not occur to her that he might have more of it than other children.

One day Samson was standing thus while Miss Nellie was playing her lesson to her music teacher. The windows were open. He heard them get up from the piano, talk a little while, and then leave the room. He heard the door close after them. He crept up to the front windows and stuck his head in: there was no one there. He could always detect the presence of anyone in a room. He put one foot over the windowsill and straddled it.

His mother had told him over and over how his master would give him to the big mastiff if he ever found him "meddling." Samson had got too near the mastiff's kennel once, and had felt his terrible breath in his face. He thought about that, but he pulled in his other foot.

Through the dark he found his way to the Thing, to its mouth. He touched it softly, and it answered softly, kindly. He shivered and stood still. Then he began to feel it all over, ran his fingertips along the slippery sides, embraced the carved legs, tried to get some conception of its shape and size, of the space it occupied in primeval night. It was cold and hard, and like nothing else in his black universe. He went back to its mouth, began at one end of the keyboard and felt his way down into the mellow thunder, as far as he could go. He seemed to know that it must be done with the fingers, not with the fists or the feet. He approached this highly artificial instrument through a mere instinct, and coupled himself to it, as if he knew it was to piece him out and make a whole creature of him. After he had tried over all the sounds, he began to finger out passages from things Miss Nellie had been practicing, passages that were already his, that lay under the bone of his pinched, conical little skull, definite as animal desires.

The door opened; Miss Nellie and her music-master stood behind it, but blind Samson, who was so sensitive to presences, did not know they were there. He was feeling out the pattern that lay all ready-made on the big and little keys. When he paused for a moment, because the sound was wrong and he wanted another, Miss Nellie spoke softly. He whirled about in a spasm of terror, leaped forward in the dark, struck his head on the open window, and fell screaming and bleeding to the floor. He had what his mother called a fit. The doctor came and gave him opium.

When Samson was well again, his young mistress led him back to the piano. Several teachers experimented with him. They found he had absolute pitch, and a remarkable memory. As a very young child he could repeat, after a fashion, any composition that was played for him. No matter how many wrong notes he struck, he never lost the intention of a passage, he brought the substance of it across by irregular and astonishing means. He wore his teachers out. He could never learn like other people, never acquired any finish. He was always a Negro prodigy who played barbarously and wonderfully. As piano-playing, it was perhaps abominable, but as music it was something real, vitalized by a sense of rhythm that was stronger than his other physical senses—that not only filled his dark mind, but worried his body incessantly. To hear him, to watch him, was to see a Negro enjoying himself as only a Negro can. It was as if all the agreeable sensations possible to creatures of flesh and blood were heaped up on those black-and-white keys, and he were gloating over them and trickling them through his yellow fingers.

In the middle of a crashing waltz, d'Arnault suddenly began to play softly, and, turning to one of the men who stood behind him, whispered, "Somebody dancing in there." He jerked his bullet-head toward the dining room. "I hear little feet—girls, I 'spect."

Anson Kirkpatrick mounted a chair and peeped over the transom. Springing down, he wrenched open the doors and ran out into the dining room. Tiny and Lena, Ántonia and Mary Dusak, were waltzing in the middle of the floor. They separated and fled toward the kitchen, giggling.

Kirkpatrick caught Tiny by the elbows. "What's the matter with you girls? Dancing out here by yourselves, when there's a roomful of lonesome men on the other side of the partition! Introduce me to your friends, Tiny."

The girls, still laughing, were trying to escape. Tiny looked alarmed. "Mrs. Gardener wouldn't like it," she protested. "She'd be awful mad if you was to come out here and dance with us."

"Mrs. Gardener's in Omaha, girl. Now, you're Lena, are you?—and you're Tony and you're Mary. Have I got you all straight?"

O'Reilly and the others began to pile the chairs on the tables. Johnnie Gardener ran in from the office.

"Easy, boys, easy!" he entreated them. "You'll wake the cook, and there'll be the devil to pay for me. She won't hear the music, but she'll be down the minute anything's moved in the dining room."

"Oh, what do you care, Johnnie? Fire the cook and wire Molly to bring another. Come along, nobody'll tell tales."

Johnnie shook his head. " 'S a fact, boys," he said confidentially. "If I take a drink in Black Hawk, Molly knows it in Omaha!"

His guests laughed and slapped him on the shoulder. "Oh, we'll make it all right with Molly. Get your back up, Johnnie."

Molly was Mrs. Gardener's name, of course. "Molly Bawn" was painted in large blue letters on the glossy white sides of the hotel bus, and "Molly" was engraved inside Johnnie's ring and on his watch-case—doubtless on his heart, too. He was an affectionate little man, and he thought his wife a wonderful woman; he knew that without her he would hardly be more than a clerk in some other man's hotel.

At a word from Kirkpatrick, d'Arnault spread himself out over the piano, and began to draw the dance music out of it, while the perspiration shone on his short wool and on his uplifted face. He looked like some glistening African god of pleasure, full of strong, savage blood. Whenever the dancers paused to change partners or to catch breath, he would boom out softly, "Who's that goin' back on me? One of these city gentlemen, I bet! Now, you girls, you ain't goin' to let that floor get cold?"

Ántonia seemed frightened at first, and kept looking questioningly at Lena and Tiny over Willy O'Reilly's shoulder. Tiny Soderball was trim and slender, with lively little feet and pretty ankles—she wore her dresses very short. She was quicker in speech, lighter in movement and manner than the other girls. Mary Dusak was broad and brown of countenance, slightly marked by smallpox, but handsome for all that. She had beautiful chestnut hair, coils of it; her forehead was low and smooth, and her commanding dark eyes regarded the world indifferently and fearlessly. She looked bold and resourceful and unscrupulous, and she was all of these. They were handsome girls, had the fresh color of their country upbringing, and in their eyes that brilliancy which is called—by no metaphor, alas!—"the light of youth."

D'Arnault played until his manager came and shut the piano. Before he left us, he showed us his gold watch which struck the hours, and a topaz ring, given him by some Russian nobleman who delighted in Negro melodies, and had heard d'Arnault play in New Orleans. At last he tapped his way upstairs, after bowing to everybody, docile and happy. I walked home with Ántonia. We were so excited that we dreaded to go to bed. We lingered a long while at the Harlings' gate, whispering in the cold until the restlessness was slowly chilled out of us.

VIII

The Harling children and I were never happier, never felt more contented and secure, than in the weeks of spring which broke that long winter. We were out all day in the thin sunshine, helping Mrs. Harling and Tony break the ground and plant the garden, dig around the orchard trees, tie up vines and clip the hedges. Every morning, before I was up, I could hear Tony singing in the garden rows. After the apple and cherry trees broke into bloom, we ran about under them, hunting for the new nests the birds were building, throwing clods at each other, and playing hide-and-seek with Nina. Yet the summer which was to change everything was coming nearer every day. When boys and girls are growing up, life can't stand still, not even in the quietest of country towns; and they have to grow up, whether they will or no. That is what their elders are always forgetting.

It must have been in June, for Mrs. Harling and Ántonia were preserving cherries, when I stopped one morning to tell them that a dancing pavilion had come to town. I had seen two drays hauling the canvas and painted poles up from the depot.

That afternoon three cheerful-looking Italians strolled about Black Hawk, looking at everything, and with them was a dark, stout woman who wore a long gold watch-chain about her neck and carried a black lace parasol. They seemed especially interested in children and vacant lots. When I overtook them and stopped to say a word, I found them affable and confiding. They told me they worked in Kansas City in the winter, and in summer they went out among the farming towns with their tent and taught dancing. When business fell off in one place, they moved on to another.

The dancing pavilion was put up near the Danish laundry, on a vacant lot surrounded by tall, arched cottonwood trees. It was very much like a merry-go-round tent, with open sides and gay flags flying from the poles. Before the week was over, all the ambitious mothers were sending their children to the afternoon dancing class. At three o'clock one met little girls in white dresses and little boys in the round-collared shirts of the time, hurrying along the sidewalk on their way to the tent. Mrs. Vanni received them at the entrance, always dressed in lavender with a great deal of black lace, her important watch-chain lying on her bosom. She wore her hair on the top of her head, built up in a black tower, with red coral combs. When she smiled, she showed two rows of strong, crooked yellow teeth. She taught the little children herself, and her husband, the harpist, taught the older ones.

Often the mothers brought their fancy-work and sat on the shady side of the tent during the lesson. The popcorn man wheeled his glass wagon under the big cottonwood by the door, and lounged in the sun, sure of a good trade when the dancing was over. Mr. Jensen, the Danish laundryman, used to bring a chair from his porch and sit out in the grass plot. Some ragged little boys from the depot sold pop and iced lemonade under a white umbrella at the corner and made faces at the spruce youngsters who came to dance. That vacant lot soon became the most cheerful place in town. Even on the hottest afternoons the cottonwoods made a rustling shade, and the air smelled of popcorn and melted butter, and Bouncing Bets wilting in the sun. Those hardy flowers had run away from the laundryman's garden, and the grass in the middle of the lot was pink with them.

The Vannis kept exemplary order, and closed every evening at the hour suggested by the city council. When Mrs. Vanni gave the signal, and the harp struck up "Home, Sweet Home," all Black Hawk knew it was ten o'clock. You could set your watch by that tune as confidently as by the roundhouse whistle.

At last there was something to do in those long, empty summer evenings, when the married people sat like images on their front porches, and the boys and girls tramped and tramped the board sidewalks—northward to the edge of the open prairie, south to the depot, then back again to the post office, the ice cream parlor, the butcher shop. Now there was a place where the girls could wear their new dresses, and where one could laugh aloud without being reproved by the ensuing silence. That silence seemed to ooze out of the ground, to hang under the foliage of the black maple trees with the bats and shadows. Now it was broken by lighthearted sounds. First the deep purring of Mr. Vanni's harp came in silvery ripples through the blackness of the dusty-smelling night; then the violins fell in—one of them was almost like a flute. They called so archly, so seductively, that our feet hurried toward the tent of themselves. Why hadn't we had a tent before?

Dancing became popular now, just as roller skating had been the summer before. The Progressive Euchre Club arranged with the Vannis for the exclusive use of the floor on Tuesday and Friday nights. At other times anyone could dance who paid his money and was orderly; the railroad men, the roundhouse mechanics, the delivery boys, the iceman, the farmhands who lived near enough to ride into town after their day's work was over.

I never missed a Saturday night dance. The tent was open until midnight then. The country boys came in from farms eight and ten miles away, and all the country girls were on the floor—Ántonia and Lena and Tiny, and the Danish laundry girls and their friends. I was not the only boy who found these dances gayer than the others. The young men who belonged to the Progressive Euchre Club used to drop in late and risk a tiff with their sweethearts and general condemnation for a waltz with "the hired girls."

IX

THERE WAS A curious social situation in Black Hawk. All the young men felt the attraction of the fine, well-set-up country girls who had come to town to earn a living, and, in nearly every case, to help the father struggle out of debt, or to make it possible for the younger children of the family to go to school.

Those girls had grown up in the first bitter-hard times, and had got little schooling themselves. But the younger brothers and sisters, for whom they made such sacrifices and who have had "advantages," never seem to me, when I meet them now, half as interesting or as well educated. The older girls, who helped to break up the wild sod, learned so much from life, from poverty, from their mothers and grandmothers; they had all, like Ántonia, been early awakened and made observant by coming at a tender age from an old country to a new.

I can remember a score of these country girls who were in service in Black Hawk during the few years I lived there, and I can remember something unusual and engaging about each of them. Physically they were almost a race apart, and out-of-door work had given them a vigor which, when they got over their first shyness on coming to town, developed into a positive carriage and freedom of movement, and made them conspicuous among Black Hawk women.

That was before the day of high-school athletics. Girls who had to walk more than half a mile to school were pitied. There was not a tennis court in the town; physical exercise was thought rather inelegant for the daughters of well-to-do families. Some of the high-school girls were jolly and pretty, but they stayed indoors in winter because of the cold, and in summer because of the heat. When one danced with them, their bodies never moved inside their clothes; their muscles seemed to ask but one thing—not to be disturbed. I remember those girls merely as faces in the schoolroom, gay and rosy, or listless and dull, cut off below the shoulders, like cherubs, by the ink-smeared tops of the high desks that were surely put there to make us round-shouldered and hollow-chested.

The daughters of Black Hawk merchants had a confident, unenquiring belief that they were "refined," and that the country girls, who "worked out," were not. The American farmers in our county were quite as hard-pressed as their neighbors from other countries. All alike had come to Nebraska with little capital and no knowledge of the soil they must subdue. All had borrowed money on their land. But no matter in what straits the Pennsylvanian or Virginian found himself, he would not let his daughters go out into service. Unless his girls could teach a country school, they sat at home in poverty.

The Bohemian and Scandinavian girls could not get positions as teachers, because they had had no opportunity to learn the language. Determined to help in the struggle to clear the homestead from debt, they had no alternative but to go into service. Some of them, after they came to town, remained as serious and as discreet in behavior as they had been when they ploughed and herded on their father's farm. Others, like the three Bohemian Marys, tried to make up for the years of youth they had lost. But every one of them did what she had set out to do, and sent home those hard-earned dollars. The girls I knew were always helping to pay for ploughs and reapers, brood-sows, or steers to fatten.

One result of this family solidarity was that the foreign farmers in our county were the first to become prosperous. After the fathers were out of debt, the daughters married the sons of neighbors—usually of like nationality—and the girls who once worked in Black Hawk kitchens are today managing big farms and fine families of their own; their children are better off than the children of the town women they used to serve.

I thought the attitude of the town people toward these girls very stupid. If I told my schoolmates that Lena Lingard's grandfather was a clergyman, and much respected in Norway, they looked at me blankly. What did it matter? All foreigners were ignorant people who couldn't speak English. There was not a man in Black Hawk who had the intelligence or cultivation, much less the personal distinction, of Ántonia's father. Yet people saw no difference between her and the three Marys; they were all Bohemians, all "hired girls."

I always knew I should live long enough to see my country girls come into their own, and I have. Today the best that a harassed Black Hawk merchant can hope for is to sell provisions and farm machinery and automobiles to the rich farms where that first crop of stalwart Bohemian and Scandinavian girls are now the mistresses.

The Black Hawk boys looked forward to marrying Black Hawk girls, and living in a brand-new little house with best chairs that must not be sat upon, and hand-painted china that must not be used. But sometimes a young fellow would look up from his ledger, or out through the grating of his father's bank, and let his eyes follow Lena Lingard, as she passed the window with her slow, undulating walk, or Tiny Soderball, tripping by in her short skirt and striped stockings.

The country girls were considered a menace to the social order. Their beauty shone out too boldly against a conventional background. But anxious mothers need have felt no alarm. They mistook the mettle of their sons. The respect for respectability was stronger than any desire in Black Hawk youth.

Our young man of position was like the son of a royal house; the boy who swept out his office or drove his delivery wagon might frolic with the jolly country girls, but he himself must sit all evening in a plush parlor where conversation dragged so perceptibly that the father often came in and made blundering efforts to warm up the atmosphere. On his way home from his dull call, he would perhaps meet Tony and Lena, coming along the sidewalk whispering to each other, or the three Bohemian Marys in their long plush coats and caps, comporting themselves with a dignity that only made their eventful histories the more piquant. If he went to the hotel to see a traveling man on business, there was Tiny, arching her shoulders at him like a kitten. If he went into the laundry to get his collars, there were the four Danish girls, smiling up from their ironing-boards, with their white throats and their pink cheeks.

The three Marys were the heroines of a cycle of scandalous stories, which the old men were fond of relating as they sat about the cigar-stand in the drugstore. Mary Dusak had been housekeeper for a bachelor rancher from Boston, and after several years in his service she was forced to retire from the world for a short time. Later she came back to town to take the place of her friend, Mary Svoboda, who was similarly embarrassed. The three Marys were considered as dangerous as high explosives to have about the kitchen, yet they were such good cooks and such admirable housekeepers that they never had to look for a place.

The Vannis' tent brought the town boys and the country girls together on neutral ground. Sylvester Lovett, who was cashier in his father's bank, always found his way to the tent on Saturday night. He took all the dances Lena Lingard would give him, and even grew bold enough to walk home with her. If his sisters or their friends happened to be among the onlookers on "popular nights," Sylvester stood back in the shadow under the cottonwood trees, smoking and watching Lena with a harassed expression. Several times I stumbled upon him there in the dark, and I felt rather sorry for him. He reminded me of Ole Benson, who used to sit on the draw-side and watch Lena herd her cattle. Later in the summer, when Lena went home for a week to visit her mother,

I heard from Ántonia that young Lovett drove all the way out there to see her, and took her buggy-riding. In my ingenuousness I hoped that Sylvester would marry Lena, and thus give all the country girls a better position in the town.

Sylvester dallied about Lena until he began to make mistakes in his work—had to stay at the bank until after dark to make his books balance. He was daft about her, and everyone knew it. To escape from his predicament he ran away with a widow six years older than himself, who owned a half-section. This remedy worked, apparently. He never looked at Lena again, nor lifted his eyes as he ceremoniously tipped his hat when he happened to meet her on the sidewalk.

So that was what they were like, I thought, these white-handed, high-collared clerks and bookkeepers! I used to glare at young Lovett from a distance and only wished I had some way of showing my contempt for him.

X

It was at the Vannis' tent that Ántonia was discovered. Hitherto she had been looked upon more as a ward of the Harlings than as one of the "hired girls." She had lived in their house and yard and garden; her thoughts never seemed to stray outside that little kingdom. But after the tent came to town she began to go about with Tiny and Lena and their friends. The Vannis often said that Ántonia was the best dancer of them all. I sometimes heard murmurs in the crowd outside the pavilion that Mrs. Harling would soon have her hands full with that girl. The young men began to joke with each other about "the Harlings' Tony" as they did about "the Marshalls' Anna" or "the Gardeners' Tiny."

Ántonia talked and thought of nothing but the tent. She hummed the dance tunes all day. When supper was late, she hurried with her dishes, dropped and smashed them in her excitement. At the first call of the music, she became irresponsible. If she hadn't time to dress, she merely flung off her apron and shot out of the kitchen door. Sometimes I went with her; the moment the lighted tent came into view she would break into a run, like a boy. There were always partners waiting for her; she began to dance before she got her breath.

Ántonia's success at the tent had its consequences. The iceman lingered too long now, when he came into the covered porch to fill the refrigerator. The delivery boys hung about the kitchen when they brought the groceries. Young farmers who were in town for Saturday came tramping through the yard to the back door to engage dances, or to invite Tony to parties and picnics. Lena and Norwegian Anna dropped in to help her with her work, so that she could get away early. The boys who brought her home after the dances sometimes laughed at the back gate and wakened Mr. Harling from his first sleep. A crisis was inevitable.

One Saturday night Mr. Harling had gone down to the cellar for beer. As he came up the stairs in the dark, he heard scuffling on the back porch, and then the sound of a vigorous slap. He looked out through the side door in time to see a pair of long legs vaulting over the picket fence. Ántonia was standing there, angry and excited. Young Harry

Paine, who was to marry his employer's daughter on Monday, had come to the tent with a crowd of friends and danced all evening. Afterward, he begged Ántonia to let him walk home with her. She said she supposed he was a nice young man, as he was one of Miss Frances's friends, and she didn't mind. On the back porch he tried to kiss her, and when she protested—because he was going to be married on Monday—he caught her and kissed her until she got one hand free and slapped him.

Mr. Harling put his beer bottles down on the table. "This is what I've been expecting, Ántonia. You've been going with girls who have a reputation for being free and easy, and now you've got the same reputation. I won't have this and that fellow tramping about my backyard all the time. This is the end of it, tonight. It stops, short. You can quit going to these dances, or you can hunt another place. Think it over."

The next morning when Mrs. Harling and Frances tried to reason with Ántonia, they found her agitated but determined. "Stop going to the tent?" she panted. "I wouldn't think of it for a minute! My own father couldn't make me stop! Mr. Harling ain't my boss outside my work. I won't give up my friends, either. The boys I go with are nice fellows. I thought Mr. Paine was all right, too, because he used to come here. I guess I gave him a red face for his wedding, all right!" she blazed out indignantly.

"You'll have to do one thing or the other, Ántonia," Mrs. Harling told her decidedly. "I can't go back on what Mr. Harling has said. This is his house."

"Then I'll just leave, Mrs. Harling. Lena's been wanting me to get a place closer to her for a long while. Mary Svoboda's going away from the Cutters' to work at the hotel, and I can have her place."

Mrs. Harling rose from her chair. "Ántonia, if you go to the Cutters' to work, you cannot come back to this house again. You know what that man is. It will be the ruin of you."

Tony snatched up the teakettle and began to pour boiling water over the glasses, laughing excitedly. "Oh, I can take care of myself! I'm a lot stronger than Cutter is. They pay four dollars there, and there's no children. The work's nothing; I can have every evening, and be out a lot in the afternoons."

"I thought you liked children. Tony, what's come over you?"

"I don't know, something has." Ántonia tossed her head and set her jaw. "A girl like me has got to take her good times when she can. Maybe there won't be any tent next year. I guess I want to have my fling, like the other girls."

Mrs. Harling gave a short, harsh laugh. "If you go to work for the

Cutters, you're likely to have a fling that you won't get up from in a hurry."

Frances said when she told Grandmother and me about this scene that every pan and plate and cup on the shelves trembled when her mother walked out of the kitchen. Mrs. Harling declared bitterly that she wished she had never let herself get fond of Ántonia.

XI

WICK CUTTER was the moneylender who had fleeced poor Russian Peter. When a farmer once got into the habit of going to Cutter, it was like gambling or the lottery; in an hour of discouragement he went back.

Cutter's first name was Wycliffe, and he liked to talk about his pious bringing-up. He contributed regularly to the Protestant churches, "for sentiment's sake," as he said with a flourish of the hand. He came from a town in Iowa where there were a great many Swedes, and could speak a little Swedish, which gave him a great advantage with the early Scandinavian settlers.

In every frontier settlement there are men who have come there to escape restraint. Cutter was one of the "fast set" of Black Hawk businessmen. He was an inveterate gambler, though a poor loser. When we saw a light burning in his office late at night, we knew that a game of poker was going on. Cutter boasted that he never drank anything stronger than sherry, and he said he got his start in life by saving the money that other young men spent for cigars. He was full of moral maxims for boys. When he came to our house on business, he quoted *Poor Richard's Almanack* to me, and told me he was delighted to find a town boy who could milk a cow. He was particularly affable to Grandmother, and whenever they met he would begin at once to talk about "the good old times" and simple living. I detested his pink, bald head, and his yellow whiskers, always soft and glistening. It was said he brushed them every night, as a woman does her hair. His white teeth looked factory-made. His skin was red and rough, as if from perpetual sunburn; he often went away to hot springs to take mud baths. He was notoriously dissolute with women. Two Swedish girls who had lived in his house were the worse for the experience. One of them he had taken to Omaha and established in the business for which he had fitted her. He still visited her.

Cutter lived in a state of perpetual warfare with his wife, and yet, apparently, they never thought of separating. They dwelt in a fussy, scrollwork house, painted white and buried in thick evergreens, with a fussy white fence and barn. Cutter thought he knew a great deal about horses, and usually had a colt which he was training for the track. On Sunday mornings one could see him out at the fairgrounds, speeding around the race course in his trotting-buggy, wearing yellow gloves and a black-and-white-check traveling cap, his whiskers blowing back in the breeze. If there were any boys about, Cutter would offer one of them a quarter to hold the stopwatch, and then drive off, saying he had no change and would "fix it up next time." No one could cut his lawn or wash his buggy to suit him. He was so fastidious and prim about his place that a boy would go to a good deal of trouble to throw a dead cat into his backyard, or to dump a sackful of tin cans in his alley. It was a peculiar combination of old-maidishness and licentiousness that made Cutter seem so despicable.

He had certainly met his match when he married Mrs. Cutter. She was a terrifying-looking person: almost a giantess in height, raw-boned, with iron-gray hair, a face always flushed, and prominent, hysterical eyes. When she meant to be entertaining and agreeable, she nodded her head incessantly and snapped her eyes at one. Her teeth were long and curved, like a horse's; people said babies always cried if she smiled at them. Her face had a kind of fascination for me: it was the very color and shape of anger. There was a gleam of something akin to insanity in her full, intense eyes. She was formal in manner, and made calls in rustling, steel-gray brocades and a tall bonnet with bristling aigrettes.

Mrs. Cutter painted china so assiduously that even her washbowls and pitchers, and her husband's shaving mug, were covered with violets and lilies. Once, when Cutter was exhibiting some of his wife's china to a caller, he dropped a piece. Mrs. Cutter put her handkerchief to her lips as if she were going to faint and said grandly: "Mr. Cutter, you have broken all the Commandments—spare the finger-bowls!"

They quarreled from the moment Cutter came into the house until they went to bed at night, and their hired girls reported these scenes to the town at large. Mrs. Cutter had several times cut paragraphs about unfaithful husbands out of the newspapers and mailed them to Cutter in a disguised handwriting. Cutter would come home at noon, find the mutilated journal in the paper-rack, and triumphantly fit the clipping into the space from which it had been cut. Those two could quarrel all morning about whether he ought to put on his heavy or his light underwear, and all evening about whether he had taken cold or not.

The Cutters had major as well as minor subjects for dispute. The chief of these was the question of inheritance: Mrs. Cutter told her husband it was plainly his fault they had no children. He insisted that Mrs. Cutter had purposely remained childless, with the determination to outlive him and to share his property with her "people," whom he detested. To this she would reply that unless he changed his mode of life, she would certainly outlive him. After listening to her insinuations about his physical soundness, Cutter would resume his dumbbell practice for a month, or rise daily at the hour when his wife most liked to sleep, dress noisily, and drive out to the track with his trotting-horse.

Once when they had quarreled about household expenses, Mrs. Cutter put on her brocade and went among their friends soliciting orders for painted china, saying that Mr. Cutter had compelled her "to live by her brush." Cutter wasn't shamed as she had expected; he was delighted!

Cutter often threatened to chop down the cedar trees which half-buried the house. His wife declared she would leave him if she were stripped of the "privacy" which she felt these trees afforded her. That was his opportunity, surely; but he never cut down the trees. The Cutters seemed to find their relations to each other interesting and stimulating, and certainly the rest of us found them so. Wick Cutter was different from any other rascal I have ever known, but I have found Mrs. Cutters all over the world: sometimes founding new religions, sometimes being forcibly fed—easily recognizable, even when superficially tamed.

XII

After Ántonia went to live with the Cutters, she seemed to care about nothing but picnics and parties and having a good time. When she was not going to a dance, she sewed until midnight. Her new clothes were the subject of caustic comment. Under Lena's direction she copied Mrs. Gardener's new party dress and Mrs. Smith's street costume so ingeniously in cheap materials that those ladies were greatly annoyed, and Mrs. Cutter, who was jealous of them, was secretly pleased.

Tony wore gloves now, and high-heeled shoes and feathered bonnets, and she went downtown nearly every afternoon with Tiny and Lena and the Marshalls' Norwegian Anna. We high-school boys used to linger on the playground at the afternoon recess to watch them as they came tripping down the hill along the board sidewalk, two and two. They were growing prettier every day, but as they passed us, I used to think with pride that Ántonia, like Snow White in the fairy tale, was still "fairest of them all."

Being a senior now, I got away from school early. Sometimes I overtook the girls downtown and coaxed them into the ice cream parlor, where they would sit chattering and laughing, telling me all the news from the country.

I remember how angry Tiny Soderball made me one afternoon. She declared she had heard Grandmother was going to make a Baptist preacher of me. "I guess you'll have to stop dancing and wear a white necktie then. Won't he look funny, girls?"

Lena laughed. "You'll have to hurry up, Jim. If you're going to be a preacher, I want you to marry me. You must promise to marry us all, and then baptize the babies."

Norwegian Anna, always dignified, looked at her reprovingly.

"Baptists don't believe in christening babies, do they, Jim?"

I told her I didn't know what they believed, and didn't care, and that I certainly wasn't going to be a preacher.

"That's too bad," Tiny simpered. She was in a teasing mood. "You'd make such a good one. You're so studious. Maybe you'd like to be a professor. You used to teach Tony, didn't you?"

Ántonia broke in. "I've set my heart on Jim being a doctor. You'd be good with sick people, Jim. Your grandmother's trained you up so nice. My papa always said you were an awful smart boy."

I said I was going to be whatever I pleased. "Won't you be surprised, Miss Tiny, if I turn out to be a regular devil of a fellow?"

They laughed until a glance from Norwegian Anna checked them; the high-school principal had just come into the front part of the shop to buy bread for supper. Anna knew the whisper was going about that I was a sly one. People said there must be something queer about a boy who showed no interest in girls of his own age, but who could be lively enough when he was with Tony and Lena or the three Marys.

The enthusiasm for the dance, which the Vannis had kindled, did not at once die out. After the tent left town, the Euchre Club became the Owl Club, and gave dances in the Masonic Hall once a week. I was invited to join, but declined. I was moody and restless that winter, and tired of the people I saw every day. Charley Harling was already at Annapolis, while I was still sitting in Black Hawk, answering to my name at roll-call every morning, rising from my desk at the sound of a bell and marching out like the grammar-school children. Mrs. Harling was a little cool toward me, because I continued to champion Ántonia. What was there for me to do after supper? Usually I had learned next day's lessons by the time I left the school building, and I couldn't sit still and read forever.

In the evening I used to prowl about, hunting for diversion. There lay the familiar streets, frozen with snow or liquid with mud. They led to the houses of good people who were putting the babies to bed, or simply sitting still before the parlor stove, digesting their supper. Black Hawk had two saloons. One of them was admitted, even by the church people, to be as respectable as a saloon could be. Handsome Anton Jelinek, who had rented his homestead and come to town, was the proprietor. In his saloon there were long tables where the Bohemian and German farmers could eat the lunches they brought from home while they drank their beer. Jelinek kept rye bread on hand and smoked fish and strong imported cheeses to please the foreign palate. I liked to drop into his barroom and listen to the talk. But one day he overtook me on the street and clapped me on the shoulder.

"Jim," he said, "I am good friends with you and I always like to see you. But you know how the church people think about saloons. Your grandpa has always treated me fine, and I don't like to have you come into my place, because I know he don't like it, and it puts me in bad with him."

So I was shut out of that.

One could hang about the drugstore, and listen to the old men who sat there every evening, talking politics and telling raw stories. One could go to the cigar factory and chat with the old German who raised canaries for sale, and look at his stuffed birds. But whatever you began with him, the talk went back to taxidermy. There was the depot, of course; I often went down to see the night train come in, and afterward sat awhile with the disconsolate telegrapher who was always hoping to be transferred to Omaha or Denver, "where there was some life." He was sure to bring out his pictures of actresses and dancers. He got them with cigarette coupons, and nearly smoked himself to death to possess these desired forms and faces. For a change, one could talk to the station agent; but he was another malcontent—spent all his spare time writing letters to officials requesting a transfer. He wanted to get back to Wyoming where he could go trout fishing on Sundays. He used to say there was nothing in life for him but trout streams, ever since he'd lost his twins.

These were the distractions I had to choose from. There were no other lights burning downtown after nine o'clock. On starlight nights I used to pace up and down those long, cold streets, scowling at the little sleeping houses on either side, with their storm windows and covered back porches. They were flimsy shelters, most of them poorly built of light wood, with spindle porch-posts horribly mutilated by the turning-lathe. Yet for all their frailness, how much jealousy and envy and unhappiness some of them managed to contain! The life that went on in them seemed to me made up of evasions and negations: shifts to save cooking, to save washing and cleaning, devices to propitiate the tongue of gossip. This guarded mode of existence was like living under a tyranny. People's speech, their voices, their very glances, became furtive and repressed. Every individual taste, every natural appetite, was bridled by caution. The people asleep in those houses, I thought, tried to live like the mice in their own kitchens; to make no noise, to leave no trace, to slip over the surface of things in the dark. The growing piles of ashes and cinders in the backyards were the only evidence that the wasteful, consuming process of life went on at all. On Tuesday nights the Owl Club danced; then there was a little stir in the streets, and here and there one could see a lighted window until midnight. But the next night all was dark again.

After I refused to join "the Owls," as they were called, I made a bold resolve to go to the Saturday night dances at Firemen's Hall. I knew it would be useless to acquaint my elders with any such plan. Grandfather didn't approve of dancing, anyway; he would only say that if I wanted to dance I could go to the Masonic Hall, among "the people we knew." It was just my point that I saw altogether too much of the people we knew.

My bedroom was on the ground floor, and as I studied there, I had a stove in it. I used to retire to my room early on Saturday night, change my shirt and collar, and put on my Sunday coat. I waited until all was quiet and the old people were asleep, then raised my window, climbed out, and went softly through the yard. The first time I deceived my grandparents I felt rather shabby, perhaps even the second time, but I soon ceased to think about it.

The dance at the Firemen's Hall was the one thing I looked forward to all the week. There I met the same people I used to see at the Vannis' tent. Sometimes there were Bohemians from Wilber, or German boys who came down on the afternoon freight from Bismarck. Tony and Lena and Tiny were always there, and the three Bohemian Marys, and the Danish laundry girls.

The four Danish girls lived with the laundryman and his wife in their house behind the laundry, with a big garden where the clothes were hung out to dry. The laundryman was a kind, wise old fellow, who paid his girls well, looked out for them, and gave them a good home. He told me once that his own daughter died just as she was getting old enough to help her mother, and that he had been "trying to make up for it ever since." On summer afternoons he used to sit for hours on the sidewalk in front of his laundry, his newspaper lying on his knee, watching his girls through the big open window while they ironed and talked in Danish. The clouds of white dust that blew up the street, the gusts of hot wind that withered his vegetable garden, never disturbed his calm. His droll expression seemed to say that he had found the secret of contentment. Morning and evening he drove about in his spring wagon, distributing freshly ironed clothes and collecting bags of linen that cried out for his suds and sunny drying-lines. His girls never looked so pretty at the dances as they did standing by the ironing board, or over the tubs, washing the fine pieces, their white arms and throats bare, their cheeks bright as the brightest wild roses, their gold hair moist with the steam or the heat and curling in little damp spirals about their ears. They had not learned much English, and were not so ambitious as Tony or Lena; but they were kind, simple girls and they were always happy. When one danced with them, one smelled their clean, freshly ironed clothes that had been put away with rosemary leaves from Mr. Jensen's garden.

There were never girls enough to go round at those dances, but everyone wanted a turn with Tony and Lena.

Lena moved without exertion, rather indolently, and her hand often accented the rhythm softly on her partner's shoulder. She smiled if one spoke to her, but seldom answered. The music seemed to put her into a soft, waking dream, and her violet-colored eyes looked sleepily and confidingly at one from under her long lashes. When she sighed she exhaled a heavy perfume of sachet powder. To dance "Home, Sweet Home" with Lena was like coming in with the tide. She danced every dance like a waltz, and it was always the same waltz—the waltz of coming home to something, of inevitable, fated return. After a while one got restless under it, as one does under the heat of a soft, sultry summer day.

When you spun out into the floor with Tony, you didn't return to anything. You set out every time upon a new adventure. I liked to schottische with her; she had so much spring and variety, and was always putting in new steps and slides. She taught me to dance against and around the hard-and-fast beat of the music. If, instead of going to the end of the railroad, old Mr. Shimerda had stayed in New York and picked up a living with his fiddle, how different Ántonia's life might have been!

Ántonia often went to the dances with Larry Donovan, a passenger conductor who was a kind of professional ladies' man, as we said. I remember how admiringly all the boys looked at her the night she first wore her velveteen dress, made like Mrs. Gardener's black velvet. She was lovely to see, with her eyes shining, and her lips always a little parted when she danced. That constant, dark color in her cheeks never changed.

One evening when Donovan was out on his run, Ántonia came to the hall with Norwegian Anna and her young man, and that night I took her home. When we were in the Cutters' yard, sheltered by the evergreens, I told her she must kiss me good night.

"Why, sure, Jim." A moment later she drew her face away and whispered indignantly, "Why, Jim! You know you ain't right to kiss me like that. I'll tell your grandmother on you!"

"Lena Lingard lets me kiss her," I retorted, "and I'm not half as fond of her as I am of you."

"Lena does?" Tony gasped. "If she's up to any of her nonsense with you, I'll scratch her eyes out!" She took my arm again and we walked out of the gate and up and down the sidewalk. "Now, don't you go and be a fool like some of these town boys. You're not going to sit around here and whittle store-boxes and tell stories all your life. You are going away to school and make something of yourself. I'm just awful proud of you. You won't go and get mixed up with the Swedes, will you?"

"I don't care anything about any of them but you," I said. "And you'll always treat me like a kid, I suppose."

She laughed and threw her arms around me. "I expect I will, but you're a kid I'm awful fond of, anyhow! You can like me all you want to, but if I see you hanging round with Lena much, I'll go to your grandmother, as sure as your name's Jim Burden! Lena's all right, only—well, you know yourself she's soft that way. She can't help it. It's natural to her."

If she was proud of me, I was so proud of her that I carried my head high as I emerged from the dark cedars and shut the Cutters' gate softly behind me. Her warm, sweet face, her kind arms, and the true heart in her: she was, oh, she was still my Ántonia! I looked with contempt at the dark, silent little houses about me as I walked home, and thought of the stupid young men who were asleep in some of them. I knew where the real women were, though I was only a boy; and I would not be afraid of them, either!

I hated to enter the still house when I went home from the dances, and it was long before I could get to sleep. Toward morning I used to have pleasant dreams: sometimes Tony and I were out in the country, sliding down straw-stacks as we used to do, climbing up the yellow mountains over and over, and slipping down the smooth sides into soft piles of chaff.

One dream I dreamed a great many times, and it was always the same. I was in a harvest-field full of shocks, and I was lying against one of them. Lena Lingard came across the stubble barefoot, in a short skirt, with a curved reaping-hook in her hand, and she was flushed like the dawn, with a kind of luminous rosiness all about her. She sat down beside me, turned to me with a soft sigh and said, "Now they are all gone, and I can kiss you as much as I like."

I used to wish I could have this flattering dream about Ántonia, but I never did.

XIII

I NOTICED one afternoon that Grandmother had been crying. Her feet seemed to drag as she moved about the house, and I got up from the table where I was studying and went to her, asking if she didn't feel well, and if I couldn't help her with her work.

"No, thank you, Jim. I'm troubled, but I guess I'm well enough. Getting a little rusty in the bones, maybe," she added bitterly.

I stood hesitating. "What are you fretting about, Grandmother? Has Grandfather lost any money?"

"No, it ain't money. I wish it was. But I've heard things. You must 'a' known it would come back to me sometime." She dropped into a chair, and, covering her face with her apron, began to cry. "Jim," she said, "I was never one that claimed old folks could bring up their grandchildren. But it came about so; there wasn't any other way for you, it seemed like."

I put my arms around her. I couldn't bear to see her cry.

"What is it, Grandmother? Is it the Firemen's dances?"

She nodded.

"I'm sorry I sneaked off like that. But there's nothing wrong about the dances, and I haven't done anything wrong. I like all those country girls, and I like to dance with them. That's all there is to it."

"But it ain't right to deceive us, son, and it brings blame on us. People say you are growing up to be a bad boy, and that ain't just to us."

"I don't care what they say about me, but if it hurts you, that settles it. I won't go to the Firemen's Hall again."

I kept my promise, of course, but I found the spring months dull enough. I sat at home with the old people in the evenings now, reading Latin that was not in our high-school course. I had made up my mind to do a lot of college requirement work in the summer, and to enter the freshman class at the university without conditions in the fall. I wanted to get away as soon as possible.

Disapprobation hurt me, I found—even that of people whom I did not admire. As the spring came on, I grew more and more lonely, and fell back on the telegrapher and the cigar-maker and his canaries for companionship. I remember I took a melancholy pleasure in hanging a May basket for Nina Harling that spring. I bought the flowers from an old German woman who always had more window plants than anyone else, and spent an afternoon trimming a little workbasket. When dusk came on, and the new moon hung in the sky, I went quietly to the Harlings' front door with my offering, rang the bell, and then ran away as was the custom. Through the willow hedge I could hear Nina's cries of delight, and I felt comforted.

On those warm, soft spring evenings I often lingered downtown to walk home with Frances, and talked to her about my plans and about the reading I was doing. One evening she said she thought Mrs. Harling was not seriously offended with me.

"Mama is as broad-minded as mothers ever are, I guess. But you know she was hurt about Ántonia, and she can't understand why you like to be with Tiny and Lena better than with the girls of your own set."

"Can you?" I asked bluntly.

Frances laughed. "Yes, I think I can. You knew them in the country, and you like to take sides. In some ways you're older than boys of your age. It will be all right with Mama after you pass your college examinations and she sees you're in earnest."

"If you were a boy," I persisted, "you wouldn't belong to the Owl Club, either. You'd be just like me."

She shook her head. "I would and I wouldn't. I expect I know the country girls better than you do. You always put a kind of glamour over them. The trouble with you, Jim, is that you're romantic. Mama's going to your commencement. She asked me the other day if I knew what your oration is to be about. She wants you to do well."

I thought my oration very good. It stated with fervor a great many things I had lately discovered. Mrs. Harling came to the Opera House to hear the commencement exercises, and I looked at her most of the time while I made my speech. Her keen, intelligent eyes never left my face. Afterward she came back to the dressing room where we stood, with our diplomas in our hands, walked up to me, and said heartily: "You surprised me, Jim. I didn't believe you could do as well as that. You didn't get that speech out of books." Among my graduation presents there was a silk umbrella from Mrs. Harling, with my name on the handle.

I walked home from the Opera House alone. As I passed the Methodist church, I saw three white figures ahead of me, pacing up and down under the arching maple trees, where the moonlight filtered through the lush June foliage. They hurried toward me; they were waiting for me—Lena and Tony and Anna Hansen.

"Oh, Jim, it was splendid!" Tony was breathing hard, as she always did when her feelings outran her language. "There ain't a lawyer in Black Hawk could make a speech like that. I just stopped your grandpa and said so to him. He won't tell you, but he told us he was awful surprised himself, didn't he, girls?"

Lena sidled up to me and said teasingly, "What made you so solemn? I thought you were scared. I was sure you'd forget."

Anna spoke wistfully.

"It must make you very happy, Jim, to have fine thoughts like that in your mind all the time, and to have words to put them in. I always wanted to go to school, you know."

"Oh, I just sat there and wished my papa could hear you! Jim,"—Ántonia took hold of my coat lapels—"there was something in your speech that made me think so about my papa!"

"I thought about your papa when I wrote my speech, Tony," I said. "I dedicated it to him."

She threw her arms around me, and her dear face was all wet with tears.

I stood watching their white dresses glimmer smaller and smaller down the sidewalk as they went away. I have had no other success that pulled at my heartstrings like that one.

XIV

THE DAY AFTER commencement I moved my books and desk upstairs, to an empty room where I should be undisturbed, and I fell to studying in earnest. I worked off a year's trigonometry that summer, and began Virgil alone. Morning after morning I used to pace up and down my sunny little room, looking off at the distant river bluffs and the roll of the blond pastures between, scanning the *Aeneid* aloud and committing long passages to memory. Sometimes in the evening Mrs. Harling called to me as I passed her gate and asked me to come in and let her play for me. She was lonely for Charley, she said, and liked to have a boy about. Whenever my grandparents had misgivings, and began to wonder whether I was not too young to go off to college alone, Mrs. Harling took up my cause vigorously. Grandfather had such respect for her judgment that I knew he would not go against her.

I had only one holiday that summer. It was in July. I met Ántonia downtown on Saturday afternoon, and learned that she and Tiny and Lena were going to the river next day with Anna Hansen—the elder was all in bloom now, and Anna wanted to make elderblow wine.

"Anna's to drive us down in the Marshalls' delivery wagon, and we'll take a nice lunch and have a picnic. Just us; nobody else. Couldn't you happen along, Jim? It would be like old times."

I considered a moment. "Maybe I can, if I won't be in the way."

On Sunday morning I rose early and got out of Black Hawk while the dew was still heavy on the long meadow grasses. It was the high season for summer flowers. The pink bee-bush stood tall along the sandy roadsides, and the cone-flowers and rose mallow grew everywhere. Across the wire fence, in the long grass, I saw a clump of flaming orange-colored milkweed, rare in that part of the state. I left the road and went around through a stretch of pasture that was always cropped short in summer, where the gaillardia came up year after year and matted over the ground with the deep, velvety red that is in Bokhara carpets. The country was empty and solitary except for the larks that Sunday morning, and it seemed to lift itself up to me and to come very close.

The river was running strong for midsummer; heavy rains to the west of us had kept it full. I crossed the bridge and went upstream along the wooded shore to a pleasant dressing room I knew among the dogwood bushes, all overgrown with wild grapevines. I began to undress for a swim. The girls would not be along yet. For the first time it occurred to me that I should be homesick for that river after I left it. The sandbars, with their clean white beaches and their little groves of willows and cottonwood seedlings, were a sort of No Man's Land, little newly created worlds that belonged to the Black Hawk boys. Charley Harling and I had hunted through these woods, fished from the fallen logs, until I knew every inch of the river shores and had a friendly feeling for every bar and shallow.

After my swim, while I was playing about indolently in the water, I heard the sound of hoofs and wheels on the bridge. I struck downstream and shouted, as the open spring wagon came into view on the middle span. They stopped the horse, and the two girls in the bottom of the cart stood up, steadying themselves by the shoulders of the two in front, so that they could see me better. They were charming up there, huddled together in the cart and peering down at me like curious deer when they come out of the thicket to drink. I found bottom near the bridge and stood up, waving to them.

"How pretty you look!" I called.

"So do you!" they shouted altogether, and broke into peals of laughter. Anna Hansen shook the reins and they drove on, while I zigzagged back to my inlet and clambered up behind an overhanging elm. I dried myself in the sun, and dressed slowly, reluctant to leave that green enclosure where the sunlight flickered so bright through the grapevine leaves and the woodpecker hammered away in the crooked elm that trailed out over the water. As I went along the road back to the bridge, I kept picking off little pieces of scaly chalk from the dried water gullies, and breaking them up in my hands.

When I came upon the Marshall's delivery horse, tied in the shade, the girls had already taken their baskets and gone down the east road which wound through the sand and scrub. I could hear them calling to each other. The elder bushes did not grow back in the shady ravines between the bluffs, but in the hot, sandy bottoms along the stream, where their roots were always in moisture and their tops in the sun. The blossoms were unusually luxuriant and beautiful that summer.

I followed a cattle path through the thick underbrush until I came to a slope that fell away abruptly to the water's edge. A great chunk of the shore had been bitten out by some spring freshet, and the scar was masked by elder bushes, growing down to the water in flowery terraces.

I did not touch them. I was overcome by content and drowsiness and by the warm silence about me. There was no sound but the high, singsong buzz of wild bees and the sunny gurgle of the water underneath. I peeped over the edge of the bank to see the little stream that made the noise; it flowed along perfectly clear over the sand and gravel, cut off from the muddy main current by a long sandbar. Down there, on the lower shelf of the bank, I saw Ántonia, seated alone under the pagodalike elders. She looked up when she heard me, and smiled, but I saw that she had been crying. I slid down into the soft sand beside her and asked her what was the matter.

"It makes me homesick, Jimmy, this flower, this smell," she said softly. "We have this flower very much at home, in the old country. It always grew in our yard and my papa had a green bench and a table under the bushes. In summer, when they were in bloom, he used to sit there with his friend that played the trombone. When I was little I used to go down there to hear them talk—beautiful talk, like what I never hear in this country."

"What did they talk about?" I asked her.

She sighed and shook her head. "Oh, I don't know! About music, and the woods, and about God, and when they were young." She turned to me suddenly and looked into my eyes. "You think, Jimmy, that maybe my father's spirit can go back to those old places?"

I told her about the feeling of her father's presence I had on that winter day when my grandparents had gone over to see his dead body and I was left alone in the house. I said I felt sure then that he was on his way back to his own country, and that even now, when I passed his grave, I always thought of him as being among the woods and fields that were so dear to him.

Ántonia had the most trusting, responsive eyes in the world; love and credulousness seemed to look out of them with open faces.

"Why didn't you ever tell me that before? It makes me feel more sure for him." After a while she said: "You know, Jim, my father was different from my mother. He did not have to marry my mother, and all his brothers quarreled with him because he did. I used to hear the old people at home whisper about it. They said he could have paid my mother money, and not married her. But he was older than she was, and he was too kind to treat her like that. He lived in his mother's house, and she was a poor girl come in to do the work. After my father married her, my grandmother never let my mother come into her house again. When I went to my grandmother's funeral was the only time I was ever in my grandmother's house. Don't that seem strange?"

While she talked, I lay back in the hot sand and looked up at the blue sky between the flat bouquets of elder. I could hear the bees humming and singing, but they stayed up in the sun above the flowers and did not come down into the shadow of the leaves. Ántonia seemed to me that day exactly like the little girl who used to come to our house with Mr. Shimerda.

"Some day, Tony, I am going over to your country, and I am going to the little town where you lived. Do you remember all about it?"

"Jim," she said earnestly, "if I was put down there in the middle of the night, I could find my way all over that little town; and along the river to the next town, where my grandmother lived. My feet remember all the little paths through the woods, and where the big roots stick out to trip you. I ain't never forgot my own country."

There was a crackling in the branches above us, and Lena Lingard peered down over the edge of the bank.

"You lazy things!" she cried. "All this elder, and you two lying there! Didn't you hear us calling you?" Almost as flushed as she had been in my dream, she leaned over the edge of the bank and began to demolish our flowery pagoda. I had never seen her so energetic; she was panting with zeal, and the perspiration stood in drops on her short, yielding upper lip. I sprang to my feet and ran up the bank.

It was noon now, and so hot that the dogwoods and scrub-oaks began to turn up the silvery underside of their leaves, and all the foliage looked soft and wilted. I carried the lunch basket to the top of one of the chalk bluffs, where even on the calmest days there was always a breeze. The flat-topped, twisted little oaks threw light shadows on the grass. Below us we could see the windings of the river, and Black Hawk, grouped among its trees, and, beyond, the rolling country, swelling gently until it met the sky. We could recognize familiar farmhouses and windmills. Each of the girls pointed out to me the direction in which her father's farm lay, and told me how many acres were in wheat that year and how many in corn.

"My old folks," said Tiny Soderball, "have put in twenty acres of rye. They get it ground at the mill, and it makes nice bread. It seems like my mother ain't been so homesick, ever since Father's raised rye flour for her."

"It must have been a trial for our mothers," said Lena, "coming out here and having to do everything different. My mother had always lived in town. She says she started behind in farm work and never has caught up."

"Yes, a new country's hard on the old ones, sometimes," said Anna thoughtfully. "My grandmother's getting feeble now, and her mind wanders. She's forgot about this country, and thinks she's at home in Norway. She keeps asking mother to take her down to the waterside and the fish market. She craves fish all the time. Whenever I go home I take her canned salmon and mackerel."

"Mercy, it's hot!" Lena yawned. She was supine under a little oak, resting after the fury of her elder-hunting, and had taken off the high-heeled slippers she had been silly enough to wear. "Come here, Jim. You never got the sand out of your hair." She began to draw her fingers slowly through my hair.

Ántonia pushed her away. "You'll never get it out like that," she said sharply. She gave my head a rough tousling and finished me off with something like a box on the ear. "Lena, you oughtn't to try to wear those slippers anymore. They're too small for your feet. You'd better give them to me for Yulka."

"All right," said Lena goodnaturedly, tucking her white stockings under her skirt. "You get all Yulka's things, don't you? I wish Father didn't have such bad luck with his farm machinery; then I could buy more things for my sisters. I'm going to get Mary a new coat this fall, if the sulky plough's never paid for!"

Tiny asked her why she didn't wait until after Christmas, when coats would be cheaper. "What do you think of poor me," she added, "with six at home, younger than I am? And they all think I'm rich, because when I go back to the country I'm dressed so fine!" She shrugged her shoulders. "But, you know, my weakness is playthings. I like to buy them playthings better than what they need."

"I know how that is," said Anna. "When we first came here, and I was little, we were too poor to buy toys. I never got over the loss of a doll somebody gave me before we left Norway. A boy on the boat broke her, and I still hate him for it."

"I guess after you got here you had plenty of live dolls to nurse, like me!" Lena remarked cynically.

"Yes, the babies came along pretty fast, to be sure. But I never minded. I was fond of them all. The youngest one, that we didn't any of us want, is the one we love best now."

Lena sighed. "Oh, the babies are all right; if only they don't come in winter. Ours nearly always did. I don't see how mother stood it. I tell you what, girls"—she sat up with sudden energy—"I'm going to get my mother out of that old sod house where she's lived so many years. The men will never do it. Johnnie, that's my oldest brother, he's wanting to get married now, and build a house for his girl instead of his mother.

Mrs. Thomas says she thinks I can move to some other town pretty soon, and go into business for myself. If I don't get into business, I'll maybe marry a rich gambler."

"That would be a poor way to get on," said Anna sarcastically. "I wish I could teach school, like Selma Kronn. Just think! She'll be the first Scandinavian girl to get a position in the high school. We ought to be proud of her."

Selma was a studious girl, who had not much tolerance for giddy things like Tiny and Lena; but they always spoke of her with admiration.

Tiny moved about restlessly, fanning herself with her straw hat. "If I was smart like her, I'd be at my books day and night. But she was born smart—and look how her father's trained her! He was something high up in the old country."

"So was my mother's father," murmured Lena, "but that's all the good it does us! My father's father was smart, too, but he was wild. He married a Lapp. I guess that's what's the matter with me; they say Lapp blood will out."

"A real Lapp, Lena?" I exclaimed. "The kind that wear skins?"

"I don't know if she wore skins, but she was a Lapp all right, and his folks felt dreadful about it. He was sent up north on some government job he had, and fell in with her. He would marry her."

"But I thought Lapland women were fat and ugly, and had squint eyes like Chinese?" I objected.

"I don't know, maybe. There must be something mighty taking about the Lapp girls, though; Mother says the Norwegians up north are always afraid their boys will run after them."

In the afternoon, when the heat was less oppressive, we had a lively game of Pussy Wants a Corner on the flat bluff-top, with the little trees for bases. Lena was Pussy so often that she finally said she wouldn't play anymore. We threw ourselves down on the grass, out of breath.

"Jim," Ántonia said dreamily, "I want you to tell the girls about how the Spanish first came here, like you and Charley Harling used to talk about. I've tried to tell them, but I leave out so much."

They sat under a little oak. Tony resting against the trunk and the other girls leaning against her and each other, and listened to the little I was able to tell them about Coronado and his search for the Seven Golden Cities. At school we were taught that he had not got so far north as Nebraska, but had given up his quest and turned back somewhere in Kansas. But Charley Harling and I had a strong belief that he had been along this very river. A farmer in the country north of ours, when he was breaking sod, had turned up a metal stirrup of fine workmanship, and a sword with a Spanish inscription on the blade. He lent these relics to Mr. Harling, who brought them home with him. Charley and I scoured them, and they were on exhibition in the Harling office all summer. Father Kelly, the priest, had found the name of the Spanish maker on the sword and an abbreviation that stood for the city of Cordova.

"And that I saw with my own eyes," Ántonia put in triumphantly. "So Jim and Charley were right, and the teachers were wrong!"

The girls began to wonder among themselves. Why had the Spaniards come so far? What must this country have been like, then? Why had Coronado never gone back to Spain, to his riches and his castles and his king? I couldn't tell them. I only knew the schoolbooks said he "died in the wilderness, of a broken heart."

"More than him has done that," said Ántonia sadly, and the girls murmured assent.

We sat looking off across the country, watching the sun go down. The curly grass about us was on fire now. The bark of the oaks turned red as copper. There was a shimmer of gold on the brown river. Out in the stream the sandbars glittered like glass, and the light trembled in the willow thickets as if little flames were leaping among them. The breeze sank to stillness. In the ravine a ringdove mourned plaintively, and somewhere off in the bushes an owl hooted. The girls sat listless, leaning against each other. The long fingers of the sun touched their foreheads.

Presently we saw a curious thing: there were no clouds; the sun was going down in a limpid, gold-washed sky. Just as the lower edge of the red disk rested on the high fields against the horizon, a great black figure suddenly appeared on the face of the sun. We sprang to our feet, straining our eyes toward it. In a moment we realized what it was. On some upland farm, a plough had been left standing in the field. The sun was sinking just behind it. Magnified across the distance by the horizontal light, it stood out against the sun, was exactly contained within the circle of the disk; the handles, the tongue, the share—black against the molten red. There it was, heroic in size, a picture writing on the sun.

Even while we whispered about it, our vision disappeared; the ball dropped and dropped until the red tip went beneath the earth. The fields below us were dark, the sky was growing pale, and that forgotten plough had sunk back to its own littleness somewhere on the prairie.

XV

LATE IN AUGUST the Cutters went to Omaha for a few days, leaving Ántonia in charge of the house. Since the scandal about the Swedish girl, Wick Cutter could never get his wife to stir out of Black Hawk without him.

The day after the Cutters left, Ántonia came over to see us. Grandmother noticed that she seemed troubled and distracted. "You've got something on your mind, Ántonia," she said anxiously.

"Yes, Mrs. Burden. I couldn't sleep much last night." She hesitated, and then told us how strangely Mr. Cutter had behaved before he went away. He put all the silver in a basket and placed it under her bed, and with it a box of papers which he told her were valuable. He made her promise that she would not sleep away from the house, or be out late in the evening, while he was gone. He strictly forbade her to ask any of the girls she knew to stay with her at night. She would be perfectly safe, he said, as he had just put a new Yale lock on the front door.

Cutter had been so insistent in regard to these details that now she felt uncomfortable about staying there alone. She hadn't liked the way he kept coming into the kitchen to instruct her, or the way he looked at her. "I feel as if he is up to some of his tricks again, and is going to try to scare me, somehow."

Grandmother was apprehensive at once. "I don't think it's right for you to stay there, feeling that way. I suppose it wouldn't be right for you to leave the place alone, either, after giving your word. Maybe Jim would be willing to go over there and sleep, and you could come here nights. I'd feel safer, knowing you were under my own roof. I guess Jim could take care of their silver and old usury notes as well as you could."

Ántonia turned to me eagerly. "Oh, would you, Jim? I'd make up my bed nice and fresh for you. It's a real cool room, and the bed's right next the window. I was afraid to leave the window open last night."

I liked my own room, and I didn't like the Cutters' house under any circumstances; but Tony looked so troubled that I consented to try this arrangement. I found that I slept there as well as anywhere, and when I got home in the morning, Tony had a good breakfast waiting for me.

After prayers she sat down at the table with us, and it was like old times in the country.

The third night I spent at the Cutters' I awoke suddenly with the impression that I had heard a door open and shut. Everything was still, however, and I must have gone to sleep again immediately.

The next thing I knew, I felt someone sit down on the edge of the bed. I was only half awake, but I decided that he might take the Cutters' silver, whoever he was. Perhaps if I did not move, he would find it and get out without troubling me. I held my breath and lay absolutely still. A hand closed softly on my shoulder, and at the same moment I felt something hair and cologne-scented brushing my face. If the room had suddenly been flooded with electric light, I couldn't have seen more clearly the detestable bearded countenance that I knew was bending over me. I caught a handful of whiskers and pulled, shouting something. The hand that held my shoulder was instantly at my throat. The man became insane; he stood over me, choking me with one fist and beating me in the face with the other, hissing and chuckling and letting out a flood of abuse.

"So this is what she's up to when I'm away, is it? Where is she, you nasty whelp, where is she? Under the bed, are you, hussy? I know your tricks! Wait till I get at you! I'll fix this rat you've got in here. He's caught, all right!"

So long as Cutter had me by the throat, there was no chance for me at all. I got hold of his thumb and bent it back, until he let go with a yell. In a bound, I was on my feet, and easily sent him sprawling to the floor. Then I made a dive for the open window, struck the wire screen, knocked it out, and tumbled after it into the yard.

Suddenly I found myself running across the north end of Black Hawk in my nightshirt, just as one sometimes finds oneself behaving in bad dreams. When I got home, I climbed in at the kitchen window. I was covered with blood from my nose and lip, but I was too sick to do anything about it. I found a shawl and an overcoat on the hat-rack, lay down on the parlor sofa, and in spite of my hurts, went to sleep.

Grandmother found me there in the morning. Her cry of fright awakened me. Truly, I was a battered object. As she helped me to my room, I caught a glimpse of myself in the mirror. My lip was cut and stood out like a snout. My nose looked like a big blue plum, and one eye was swollen shut and hideously discolored. Grandmother said we must have the doctor at once, but I implored her, as I had never begged for anything before, not to send for him. I could stand anything, I told her, so long as nobody saw me or knew what had happened to me. I entreated her not to let Grandfather, even, come into my room. She seemed to understand, though I was too faint and miserable to go into explanations. When she took off my nightshirt, she found such bruises on my chest and shoulders that she began to cry. She spent the whole morning bathing and poulticing me, and rubbing me with arnica. I heard Ántonia sobbing outside my door, but I asked Grandmother to send her away. I felt that I never wanted to see her again. I hated her almost as much as I hated Cutter. She had let me in for all this disgustingness. Grandmother kept saying how thankful we ought to be that I had been there instead of Ántonia. But I lay with my disfigured face to the wall and felt no particular gratitude. My one concern was that Grandmother should keep everyone away from me. If the story once got abroad, I would never hear the last of it. I could well imagine what the old men down at the drugstore would do with such a theme.

While Grandmother was trying to make me comfortable, Grandfather went to the depot and learned that Wick Cutter had come home on the night express from the east, and had left again on the six o'clock train for Denver that morning. The agent said his face was striped with court-plaster, and he carried his left hand in a sling. He looked so used up that the agent asked him what had happened to him since ten o'clock the night before; whereat Cutter began to swear at him and said he would have him discharged for incivility.

That afternoon, while I was asleep, Ántonia took Grandmother with her, and went over to the Cutters' to pack her trunk. They found the place locked up, and they had to break the window to get into Ántonia's bedroom. There everything was in shocking disorder. Her clothes had been taken out of her closet, thrown into the middle of the room, and trampled and torn. My own garments had been treated so badly that I never saw them again; Grandmother burned them in the Cutters' kitchen range.

While Ántonia was packing her trunk and putting her room in order, to leave it, the front doorbell rang violently. There stood Mrs. Cutter—locked out, for she had no key to the new lock—her head trembling with rage. "I advised her to control herself, or she would have a stroke," Grandmother said afterward.

Grandmother would not let her see Ántonia at all, but made her sit down in the parlor while she related to her just what had occurred the night before. Ántonia was frightened, and was going home to stay for a while, she told Mrs. Cutter; it would be useless to interrogate the girl, for she knew nothing of what had happened.

Then Mrs. Cutter told her story. She and her husband had started home from Omaha together the morning before. They had to stop over several hours at Waymore Junction to catch the Black Hawk train. During the wait, Cutter left her at the depot and went to the Waymore bank to attend to some business. When he returned, he told her that he would have to stay overnight there, but she could go on home. He bought her ticket and put her on the train. She saw him slip a twenty-dollar bill into her handbag with her ticket. That bill, she said, should have aroused her suspicions at once—but did not.

The trains are never called at little junction towns; everybody knows when they come in. Mr. Cutter showed his wife's ticket to the conductor, and settled her in her seat before the train moved off. It was not until nearly nightfall that she discovered she was on the express bound for Kansas City, that her ticket was made out to that point, and that Cutter must have planned it so. The conductor told her the Black Hawk train was due at Waymore twelve minutes after the Kansas City train left. She saw at once that her husband had played this trick in order to get back to Black Hawk without her. She had no choice but to go on to Kansas City and take the first fast train for home.

Cutter could have got home a day earlier than his wife by any one of a dozen simpler devices; he could have left her in the Omaha hotel, and said he was going on to Chicago for a few days. But apparently it was part of his fun to outrage her feelings as much as possible.

"Mr. Cutter will pay for this, Mrs. Burden. He will pay!" Mrs. Cutter avouched, nodding her horselike head and rolling her eyes.

Grandmother said she hadn't a doubt of it.

Certainly Cutter liked to have his wife think him a devil. In some way he depended upon the excitement he could arouse in her hysterical nature. Perhaps he got the feeling of being a rake more from his wife's rage and amazement than from any experiences of his own. His zest in debauchery might wane, but never Mrs. Cutter's belief in it. The reckoning with his wife at the end of an escapade was something he counted on—like the last powerful liqueur after a long dinner. The one excitement he really couldn't do without was quarreling with Mrs. Cutter!

Book Three

Lena Lingard

I

At the university I had the good fortune to come immediately under the influence of a brilliant and inspiring young scholar. Gaston Cleric had arrived in Lincoln only a few weeks earlier than I, to begin his work as head of the Latin Department. He came west at the suggestion of his physicians, his health having been enfeebled by a long illness in Italy. When I took my entrance examinations, he was my examiner, and my course was arranged under his supervision.

I did not go home for my first summer vacation but stayed in Lincoln, working off a year's Greek, which had been my only condition on entering the freshman class. Cleric's doctor advised against his going back to New England, and, except for a few weeks in Colorado, he, too, was in Lincoln all that summer. We played tennis, read, and took long walks together. I shall always look back on that time of mental awakening as one of the happiest in my life. Gaston Cleric introduced me to the world of ideas; when one first enters that world everything else fades for a time, and all that went before is as if it had not been. Yet I found curious survivals; some of the figures of my old life seemed to be waiting for me in the new.

In those days there were many serious young men among the students who had come up to the university from the farms and the little towns scattered over the thinly settled state. Some of those boys came straight from the cornfields with only a summer's wages in their pockets, hung on through the four years, shabby and underfed, and completed the course by really heroic self-sacrifice. Our instructors were oddly assorted: wandering pioneer schoolteachers, stranded ministers of the Gospel, a few enthusiastic young men just out of graduate schools. There was an atmosphere of endeavor, of expectancy and bright hopefulness about the young college that had lifted its head from the prairie only a few years before.

Our personal life was as free as that of our instructors. There were no college dormitories; we lived where we could and as we could. I took rooms with an old couple, early settlers in Lincoln, who had married off their children and now lived quietly in their house at the edge of town, near the open country. The house was inconveniently situated for students, and on that account I got two rooms for the price of one. My bedroom, originally a linen closet, was unheated and was barely large enough to contain my cot-bed, but it enabled me to call the other room my study. The dresser, and the great walnut wardrobe which held all my clothes, even my hats and shoes, I had pushed out of the way, and I considered them nonexistent, as children eliminate incongruous objects when they are playing house. I worked at a commodious green-topped table placed directly in front of the west window which looked out over the prairie. In the corner at my right were all my books, in shelves I had made and painted myself. On the blank wall at my left the dark, old-fashioned wallpaper was covered by a large map of ancient Rome, the work of some German scholar. Cleric had ordered it for me when he was sending for books from abroad. Over the bookcase hung a photograph of the Tragic Theatre at Pompeii, which he had given me from his collection.

When I sat at work I half-faced a deep, upholstered chair which stood at the end of my table, its high back against the wall. I had bought it with great care. My instructor sometimes looked in upon me when he was out for an evening tramp, and I noticed that he was more likely to linger and become talkative if I had a comfortable chair for him to sit in, and if he found a bottle of Bénédictine and plenty of the kind of cigarettes he liked at his elbow. He was, I had discovered, parsimonious about small expenditures—a trait absolutely inconsistent with his general character. Sometimes when he came he was silent and moody, and after a few sarcastic remarks went away again, to tramp the streets of Lincoln, which were almost as quiet and oppressively domestic as those of Black Hawk. Again, he would sit until nearly midnight, talking about Latin and English poetry, or telling me about his long stay in Italy.

I can give no idea of the peculiar charm and vividness of his talk. In a crowd he was nearly always silent. Even for his classroom he had no platitudes, no stock of professorial anecdotes. When he was tired, his lectures were clouded, obscure, elliptical; but when he was interested they were wonderful. I believe that Gaston Cleric narrowly missed being a great poet, and I have sometimes thought that his bursts of imaginative talk were fatal to his poetic gift. He squandered too much in the heat of personal communication. How often I have seen him draw his dark brows together, fix his eyes upon some object on the wall or a figure in the carpet, and then flash into the lamplight the very image that was in his brain. He could bring the drama of antique life before one out of the shadows—white figures against blue backgrounds. I shall never forget his face as it looked one night when he told me about the solitary day he spent among the sea temples at Paestum: the soft wind blowing through the roofless columns, the birds flying low over the flowering marsh grasses, the changing lights on the silver, cloud-hung mountains. He had willfully stayed the short summer night there, wrapped in his coat and rug, watching the constellations on their path down the sky until "the bride of old Tithonus" rose out of the sea and the mountains stood sharp in the dawn. It was there he caught the fever which held him back on the eve of his departure for Greece and of which he lay ill so long in Naples. He was still, indeed, doing penance for it.

I remember vividly another evening, when something led us to talk of Dante's veneration for Virgil. Cleric went through canto after canto of the *Commedia*, repeating the discourse between Dante and his "sweet teacher," while his cigarette burned itself out unheeded between his long fingers. I can hear him now, speaking the lines of the poet Statius, who spoke for Dante: "I was famous on earth with the name which endures longest and honors most. The seeds of my ardor were the sparks from that divine flame whereby more than a thousand have kindled; I speak of the *Aeneid*, mother to me and nurse to me in poetry."

Although I admired scholarship so much in Cleric, I was not deceived about myself; I knew that I should never be a scholar. I could never lose myself for long among impersonal things. Mental excitement was apt to send me with a rush back to my own naked land and the figures scattered upon it. While I was in the very act of yearning toward the new forms that Cleric brought up before me, my mind plunged away from me, and I suddenly found myself thinking of the places and people of my own infinitesimal past. They stood out strengthened and simplified now, like the image of the plough against the sun. They were all I had for an answer to the new appeal. I begrudged the room that Jake and Otto and Russian Peter took up in my memory, which I wanted to crowd with other things. But whenever my consciousness was quickened, all those early friends were quickened within it, and in some strange way they accompanied me through all my new experiences. They were so much alive in me that I scarcely stopped to wonder whether they were alive anywhere else, or how.

II

ONE MARCH EVENING in my sophomore year I was sitting alone in my room after supper. There had been a warm thaw all day, with mushy yards and little streams of dark water gurgling cheerfully into the streets out of old snowbanks. My window was open, and the earthy wind blowing through made me indolent. On the edge of the prairie, where the sun had gone down, the sky was turquoise blue, like a lake, with gold light throbbing in it. Higher up, in the utter clarity of the western slope, the evening star hung like a lamp suspended by silver chains—like the lamp engraved upon the title-page of old Latin texts, which is always appearing in new heavens, and waking new desires in men. It reminded me, at any rate, to shut my window and light my wick in answer. I did so regretfully, and the dim objects in the room emerged from the shadows and took their place about me with the helpfulness which custom breeds.

I propped my book open and stared listlessly at the page of the *Georgics* where tomorrow's lesson began. It opened with the melancholy reflection that, in the lives of mortals, the best days are the first to flee. *"Optima dies . . . prima fugit."* I turned back to the beginning of the third book, which we had read in class that morning. *"Primus ego in patriam mecum . . . deducam Musas"*—"for I shall be the first, if I live, to bring the Muse into my country." Cleric had explained to us that *patria* here meant, not a nation or even a province, but the little rural neighborhood on the Mincio where the poet was born. This was not a boast, but a hope, at once bold and devoutly humble, that he might bring the Muse (but lately come to Italy from her cloudy Grecian mountains), not to the capital, the *palatia Romana,* but to his own little "country"; to his father's fields, "sloping down to the river and to the old beech trees with broken tops."

Cleric said he thought Virgil, when he was dying at Brindisi, must have remembered that passage. After he had faced the bitter fact that he was to leave the *Aeneid* unfinished, and had decreed that the great canvas, crowded with figures of gods and men, should be burned rather than survive him unperfected, then his mind must have gone back to the perfect utterance of the *Georgics,* where the pen was fitted to the matter as the plough is to the furrow; and he must have said to himself, with the thankfulness of a good man, "I was the first to bring the Muse into my country."

We left the classroom quietly, conscious that we had been brushed by the wing of a great feeling, though perhaps I alone knew Cleric intimately enough to guess what that feeling was. In the evening, as I sat staring at my book, the fervor of his voice stirred through the quantities on the page before me. I was wondering whether that particular rocky strip of New England coast about which he had so often told me was Cleric's *patria*. Before I had got far with my reading, I was disturbed by a knock. I hurried to the door and when I opened it saw a woman standing in the dark hall.

"I expect you hardly know me, Jim."

The voice seemed familiar, but I did not recognize her until she stepped into the light of my doorway and I beheld—Lena Lingard! She was so quietly conventionalized by city clothes that I might have passed her on the street without seeing her. Her black suit fitted her figure smoothly, and a black lace hat, with pale-blue forget-me-nots, sat demurely on her yellow hair.

I led her toward Cleric's chair, the only comfortable one I had, questioning her confusedly.

She was not disconcerted by my embarrassment. She looked about her with the naïve curiosity I remembered so well. "You are quite comfortable here, aren't you? I live in Lincoln now, too, Jim. I'm in business for myself. I have a dressmaking shop in the Raleigh Block, out on O Street. I've made a real good start."

"But, Lena, when did you come?"

"Oh, I've been here all winter. Didn't your grandmother ever write you? I've thought about looking you up lots of times. But we've all heard what a studious young man you've got to be, and I felt bashful. I didn't know whether you'd be glad to see me." She laughed her mellow, easy laugh, that was either very artless or very comprehending, one never quite knew which. "You seem the same, though—except you're a young man, now, of course. Do you think I've changed?"

"Maybe you're prettier—though you were always pretty enough. Perhaps it's your clothes that make a difference."

"You like my new suit? I have to dress pretty well in my business."

She took off her jacket and sat more at ease in her blouse, of some soft, flimsy silk. She was already at home in my place, had slipped quietly into it, as she did into everything. She told me her business was going well, and she had saved a little money.

"This summer I'm going to build the house for Mother I've talked about so long. I won't be able to pay up on it at first, but I want her to have it before she is too old to enjoy it. Next summer I'll take her down new furniture and carpets, so she'll have something to look forward to all winter."

I watched Lena sitting there so smooth and sunny and well-cared-for, and thought of how she used to run barefoot over the prairie until after the snow began to fly, and how Crazy Mary chased her round and round the cornfields. It seemed to me wonderful that she should have got on so well in the world. Certainly she had no one but herself to thank for it.

"You must feel proud of yourself, Lena," I said heartily. "Look at me; I've never earned a dollar, and I don't know that I'll ever be able to."

"Tony says you're going to be richer than Mr. Harling some day. She's always bragging about you, you know."

"Tell me, how *is* Tony?"

"She's fine. She works for Mrs. Gardener at the hotel now. She's housekeeper. Mrs. Gardener's health isn't what it was, and she can't see after everything like she used to. She has great confidence in Tony. Tony's made it up with the Harlings, too. Little Nina is so fond of her that Mrs. Harling kind of overlooked things."

"Is she still going with Larry Donovan?"

"Oh, that's on, worse than ever! I guess they're engaged. Tony talks about him like he was president of the railroad. Everybody laughs about it, because she was never a girl to be soft. She won't hear a word against him. She's so sort of innocent."

I said I didn't like Larry, and never would.

Lena's face dimpled. "Some of us could tell her things, but it wouldn't do any good. She'd always believe him. That's Ántonia's failing, you know; if she once likes people, she won't hear anything against them."

"I think I'd better go home and look after Ántonia," I said.

"I think you had." Lena looked up at me in frank amusement. "It's a good thing the Harlings are friendly with her again. Larry's afraid of them. They ship so much grain, they have influence with the railroad people. What are you studying?" She leaned her elbows on the table and drew my book toward her. I caught a faint odor of violet sachet. "So that's Latin, is it? It looks hard. You do go to the theater sometimes, though, for I've seen you there. Don't you just love a good play, Jim? I can't stay at home in the evening if there's one in town. I'd be willing to work like a slave; it seems to me, to live in a place where there are theaters."

"Let's go to a show together sometime. You are going to let me come to see you, aren't you?"

"Would you like to? I'd be ever so pleased. I'm never busy after six o'clock, and I let my sewing girls go at half-past five. I board, to save time, but sometimes I cook a chop for myself, and I'd be glad to cook one for you. Well"—she began to put on her white gloves—"it's been awful good to see you, Jim."

"You needn't hurry, need you? You've hardly told me anything yet."

"We can talk when you come to see me. I expect you don't often have lady visitors. The old woman downstairs didn't want to let me come up very much. I told her I was from your home town, and had promised your grandmother to come and see you. How surprised Mrs. Burden would be!" Lena laughed softly as she rose.

When I caught up my hat, she shook her head. "No, I don't want you to go with me. I'm to meet some Swedes at the drugstore. You wouldn't care for them. I wanted to see your room so I could write Tony all about it, but I must tell her how I left you right here with your books. She's always so afraid someone will run off with you!" Lena slipped her silk sleeves into the jacket I held for her, smoothed it over her person, and buttoned it slowly. I walked with her to the door. "Come and see me sometimes when you're lonesome. But maybe you have all the friends you want. Have you?" She turned her soft cheek to me. "Have you?" she whispered teasingly in my ear. In a moment I watched her fade down the dusky stairway.

When I turned back to my room the place seemed much pleasanter than before. Lena had left something warm and friendly in the lamplight. How I loved to hear her laugh again! It was so soft and unexcited and appreciative—gave a favorable interpretation to everything. When I closed my eyes I could hear them all laughing—the Danish laundry girls and the three Bohemian Marys. Lena had brought them all back to me. It came over me, as it had never done before, the relation between girls like those and the poetry of Virgil. If there were no girls like them in the world, there would be no poetry. I understood that clearly, for the first time. This revelation seemed to me inestimably precious. I clung to it as if it might suddenly vanish.

As I sat down to my book at last, my old dream about Lena coming across the harvest-field in her short skirt seemed to me like the memory of an actual experience. It floated before me on the page like a picture, and underneath it stood the mournful line: *"Optima dies . . . prima fugit."*

III

In Lincoln the best part of the theatrical season came late, when the good companies stopped off there for one-night stands, after their long runs in New York and Chicago. That spring Lena went with me to see Joseph Jefferson in *Rip Van Winkle*, and to a war play called *Shenandoah*. She was inflexible about paying for her own seat; said she was in business now, and she wouldn't have a schoolboy spending his money on her. I liked to watch a play with Lena; everything was wonderful to her, and everything was true. It was like going to revival meetings with someone who was always being converted. She handed her feelings over to the actors with a kind of fatalistic resignation. Accessories of costume and scene meant much more to her than to me. She sat entranced through *Robin Hood* and hung upon the lips of the contralto who sang, "Oh, Promise Me!"

Toward the end of April, the billboards, which I watched anxiously in those days, bloomed out one morning with gleaming white posters on which two names were impressively printed in blue Gothic letters: the name of an actress of whom I had often heard, and the name *Camille*.

I called at the Raleigh Block for Lena on Saturday evening, and we walked down to the theater. The weather was warm and sultry and put us both in a holiday humor. We arrived early, because Lena liked to watch the people come in. There was a note on the program, saying that the "incidental music" would be from the opera *Traviata*, which was made from the same story as the play. We had neither of us read the play, and we did not know what it was about—though I seemed to remember having heard it was a piece in which great actresses shone. *The Count of Monte Cristo*, which I had seen James O'Neill play that winter, was by the only Alexander Dumas I knew. This play, I saw, was by his son, and I expected a family resemblance. A couple of jackrabbits, run in off the prairie, could not have been more innocent of what awaited them than were Lena and I.

Our excitement began with the rise of the curtain, when the moody Varville, seated before the fire, interrogated Nanine. Decidedly, there was a new tang about this dialogue. I had never heard in the theater lines that were alive, that presupposed and took for granted, like those which passed between Varville and Marguerite in the brief encounter before her friends entered. This introduced the most brilliant, worldly, the most enchantingly gay scene I had ever looked upon. I had never seen champagne bottles opened on the stage before—indeed, I had never seen them opened anywhere. The memory of that supper makes me hungry now; the sight of it then, when I had only a students' boarding-house dinner behind me, was delicate torment. I seem to remember gilded chairs and tables (arranged hurriedly by footmen in white gloves and stockings), linen of dazzling whiteness, glittering glass, silver dishes, a great bowl of fruit, and the reddest of roses. The room was invaded by beautiful women and dashing young men, laughing and talking together. The men were dressed more or less after the period in which the play was written; the women were not. I saw no inconsistency. Their talk seemed to open to one the brilliant world in which they lived; every sentence made one older and wiser, every pleasantry enlarged one's horizon. One could experience excess and satiety without the inconvenience of learning what to do with one's hands in a drawing-room! When the characters all spoke at once and I missed some of the phrases they flashed at each other, I was in misery. I strained my ears and eyes to catch every exclamation.

The actress who played Marguerite was even then old-fashioned, though historic. She had been a member of Daly's famous New York company, and afterward a "star" under his direction. She was a woman who could not be taught, it is said, though she had a crude natural force which carried with people whose feelings were accessible and whose taste was not squeamish. She was already old, with a ravaged countenance and a physique curiously hard and stiff. She moved with difficulty—I think she was lame—I seem to remember some story about a malady of the spine. Her Armand was disproportionately young and slight, a handsome youth, perplexed in the extreme. But what did it matter? I believed devoutly in her power to fascinate him, in her dazzling loveliness. I believed her young, ardent, reckless, disillusioned, under sentence, feverish, avid of pleasure. I wanted to cross the footlights and help the slim-waisted Armand in the frilled shirt to convince her that there was still loyalty and devotion in the world. Her sudden illness, when the gaiety was at its height, her pallor, the handkerchief she crushed against her lips, the cough she smothered under the laughter while Gaston kept playing the piano lightly—it all wrung my heart. But not so much as her cynicism in the long dialogue with her lover which followed. How far was I from questioning her unbelief! While the charmingly sincere young man pleaded with her—accompanied by the orchestra in the old

Traviata duet, *"misterioso, misterios'altero!"*—she maintained her bitter scepticism, and the curtain fell on her dancing recklessly with the others, after Armand had been sent away with his flower.

Between the acts we had no time to forget. The orchestra kept sawing away at the *Traviata* music, so joyous and sad, so thin and far away, so clap-trap and yet so heart-breaking. After the second act I left Lena in tearful contemplation of the ceiling, and went out into the lobby to smoke. As I walked about there I congratulated myself that I had not brought some Lincoln girl who would talk during the waits about the junior dances, or whether the cadets would camp at Plattsmouth. Lena was at least a woman, and I was a man.

Through the scene between Marguerite and the elder Duval, Lena wept unceasingly, and I sat helpless to prevent the closing of that chapter of idyllic love, dreading the return of the young man whose ineffable happiness was only to be the measure of his fall.

I suppose no woman could have been further in person, voice, and temperament from Dumas's appealing heroine than the veteran actress who first acquainted me with her. Her conception of the character was as heavy and uncompromising as her diction; she bore hard on the idea and on the consonants. At all times she was highly tragic, devoured by remorse. Lightness of stress or behavior was far from her. Her voice was heavy and deep: "Ar-r-r-mound!" she would begin, as if she were summoning him to the bar of Judgment. But the lines were enough. She had only to utter them. They created the character in spite of her.

The heartless world which Marguerite reentered with Varville had never been so glittering and reckless as on the night when it gathered in Olympe's salon for the fourth act. There were chandeliers hung from the ceiling, I remember, many servants in livery, gaming tables where the men played with piles of gold, and a staircase down which the guests made their entrance. After all the others had gathered round the card tables and young Duval had been warned by Prudence, Marguerite descended the staircase with Varville: such a cloak, such a fan, such jewels—and her face! One knew at a glance how it was with her. When Armand, with the terrible words, "Look, all of you, I owe this woman nothing!" flung the gold and bank notes at the half-swooning Marguerite, Lena cowered beside me and covered her face with her hands.

The curtain rose on the bedroom scene. By this time there wasn't a nerve in me that hadn't been twisted. Nanine alone could have made me cry. I loved Nanine tenderly; and Gaston, how one clung to that good fellow! The New Year's presents were not too much; nothing could be too much now. I wept unrestrainedly. Even the handkerchief in my breast-pocket, worn for elegance and not at all for use, was wet through by the time that moribund woman sank for the last time into the arms of her lover.

When we reached the door of the theater, the streets were shining with rain. I had prudently brought along Mrs. Harling's useful commencement present, and I took Lena home under its shelter. After leaving her, I walked slowly out into the country part of the town where I lived. The lilacs were all blooming in the yards, and the smell of them after the rain, of the new leaves and the blossoms together, blew into my face with a sort of bitter sweetness. I tramped through the puddles and under the showery trees, mourning for Marguerite Gauthier as if she had died only yesterday, sighing with the spirit of 1840, which had sighed so much, and which had reached me only that night, across long years and several languages, through the person of an infirm old actress. The idea is one that no circumstances can frustrate. Wherever and whenever that piece is put on, it is April.

IV

How well I remember the stiff little parlor where I used to wait for Lena: the hard horsehair furniture, bought at some auction sale, the long mirror, the fashion-plates on the wall. If I sat down even for a moment, I was sure to find threads and bits of colored silk clinging to my clothes after I went away. Lena's success puzzled me. She was so easygoing, had none of the push and self-assertiveness that get people ahead in business. She had come to Lincoln, a country girl, with no introductions except to some cousins of Mrs. Thomas who lived there, and she was already making clothes for the women of "the young married set." Evidently she had great natural aptitude for her work. She knew, as she said, "what people looked well in." She never tired of poring over fashion books. Sometimes in the evening I would find her alone in her workroom, draping folds of satin on a wire figure, with a quite blissful expression of countenance. I couldn't help thinking that the years when Lena literally hadn't enough clothes to cover herself might have something to do with her untiring interest in dressing the human figure. Her clients said that Lena "had style," and overlooked her habitual inaccuracies. She never, I discovered, finished anything by the time she had promised, and she frequently spent more money on materials than her customer had authorized. Once, when I arrived at six o'clock, Lena was ushering out a fidgety mother and her awkward, overgrown daughter. The woman detained Lena at the door to say apologetically:

"You'll try to keep it under fifty for me, won't you, Miss Lingard? You see, she's really too young to come to an expensive dressmaker, but I knew you could do more with her than anybody else."

"Oh, that will be all right, Mrs. Herron. I think we'll manage to get a good effect," Lena replied blandly.

I thought her manner with her customers very good, and wondered where she had learned such self-possession.

Sometimes after my morning classes were over, I used to encounter Lena downtown, in her velvet suit and a little black hat, with a veil tied smoothly over her face, looking as fresh as the spring morning. Maybe she would be carrying home a bunch of jonquils or a hyacinth plant.

When we passed a candy store her footsteps would hesitate and linger. "Don't let me go in," she would murmur. "Get me by if you can." She was very fond of sweets, and was afraid of growing too plump.

We had delightful Sunday breakfasts together at Lena's. At the back of her long workroom was a bay window, large enough to hold a box-couch and a reading table. We breakfasted in this recess, after drawing the curtains that shut out the long room, with cutting tables and wire women and sheet-draped garments on the walls. The sunlight poured in, making everything on the table shine and glitter and the flame of the alcohol lamp disappear altogether. Lena's curly black water spaniel, Prince, breakfasted with us. He sat beside her on the couch and behaved very well until the Polish violin teacher across the hall began to practice, when Prince would growl and sniff the air with disgust. Lena's landlord, old Colonel Raleigh, had given her the dog, and at first she was not at all pleased. She had spent too much of her life taking care of animals to have much sentiment about them. But Prince was a knowing little beast, and she grew fond of him. After breakfast I made him do his lessons; play dead dog, shake hands, stand up like a soldier. We used to put my cadet cap on his head—I had to take military drill at the university—and give him a yard-measure to hold with his front leg. His gravity made us laugh immoderately.

Lena's talk always amused me. Ántonia had never talked like the people about her. Even after she learned to speak English readily, there was always something impulsive and foreign in her speech. But Lena had picked up all the conventional expressions she heard at Mrs. Thomas's dressmaking shop. Those formal phrases, the very flower of small-town proprieties, and the flat commonplaces, nearly all hypocritical in their origin, became very funny, very engaging, when they were uttered in Lena's soft voice, with her caressing intonation and arch naïveté. Nothing could be more diverting than to hear Lena, who was almost as candid as Nature, call a leg a "limb" or a house a "home."

We used to linger a long while over our coffee in that sunny corner. Lena was never so pretty as in the morning; she wakened fresh with the world every day, and her eyes had a deeper color then, like the blue flowers that are never so blue as when they first open. I could sit idle all through a Sunday morning and look at her. Ole Benson's behavior was now no mystery to me.

"There was never any harm in Ole," she said once. "People needn't have troubled themselves. He just liked to come over and sit on the draw-side and forget about his bad luck. I liked to have him. Any company's welcome when you're off with cattle all the time."

"But wasn't he always glum?" I asked. "People said he never talked at all."

"Sure he talked, in Norwegian. He'd been a sailor on an English boat and had seen lots of queer places. He had wonderful tattoos. We used to sit and look at them for hours; there wasn't much to look at out there. He was like a picture book. He had a ship and a strawberry girl on one arm, and on the other a girl standing before a little house, with a fence and gate and all, waiting for her sweetheart. Farther up his arm, her sailor had come back and was kissing her. 'The Sailor's Return,' he called it."

I admitted it was no wonder Ole liked to look at a pretty girl once in a while, with such a fright at home.

"You know," Lena said confidentially, "he married Mary because he thought she was strong-minded and would keep him straight. He never could keep straight on shore. The last time he landed in Liverpool he'd been out on a two years' voyage. He was paid off one morning, and by the next he hadn't a cent left, and his watch and compass were gone. He'd got with some women, and they'd taken everything. He worked his way to this country on a little passenger boat. Mary was a stewardess, and she tried to convert him on the way over. He thought she was just the one to keep him steady. Poor Ole! He used to bring me candy from town, hidden in his feedbag. He couldn't refuse anything to a girl. He'd have given away his tattoos long ago, if he could. He's one of the people I'm sorriest for."

If I happened to spend an evening with Lena and stayed late, the Polish violin teacher across the hall used to come out and watch me descend the stairs, muttering so threateningly that it would have been easy to fall into a quarrel with him. Lena had told him once that she liked to hear him practice, so he always left his door open, and watched who came and went.

There was a coolness between the Pole and Lena's landlord on her account. Old Colonel Raleigh had come to Lincoln from Kentucky and invested an inherited fortune in real estate, at the time of inflated prices. Now he sat day after day in his office in the Raleigh Block, trying to discover where his money had gone and how he could get some of it back. He was a widower, and found very little congenial companionship in this casual western city. Lena's good looks and gentle manners appealed to him. He said her voice reminded him of Southern voices, and he found as many opportunities of hearing it as possible. He painted and papered her rooms for her that spring, and put in a porcelain bathtub in place of the tin one that had satisfied the former tenant. While these repairs were being made, the old gentleman often dropped in to consult Lena's preferences. She told me with amusement how Ordinsky, the Pole, had presented himself at her door one evening, and said that if the landlord was annoying her by his attentions, he would promptly put a stop to it.

"I don't exactly know what to do about him," she said, shaking her head. "He's so sort of wild all the time. I wouldn't like to have him say anything rough to that nice old man. The colonel is long-winded, but then I expect he's lonesome. I don't think he cares much for Ordinsky, either. He said once that if I had any complaints to make of my neighbors, I mustn't hesitate."

One Saturday evening when I was having supper with Lena, we heard a knock at her parlor door, and there stood the Pole, coatless, in a dress shirt and collar. Prince dropped on his paws and began to growl like a mastiff, while the visitor apologized, saying that he could not possibly come in thus attired, but he begged Lena to lend him some safety pins.

"Oh, you'll have to come in, Mr. Ordinsky, and let me see what's the matter." She closed the door behind him. "Jim, won't you make Prince behave?"

I rapped Prince on the nose, while Ordinsky explained that he had not had his dress clothes on for a long time, and tonight, when he was going to play for a concert, his waistcoat had split down the back. He thought he could pin it together until he got it to a tailor.

Lena took him by the elbow and turned him round. She laughed when she saw the long gap in the satin. "You could never pin that, Mr. Ordinsky. You've kept it folded too long, and the goods is all gone along the crease. Take it off. I can put a new piece of lining-silk in there for you in ten minutes." She disappeared into her workroom with the vest, leaving me to confront the Pole, who stood against the door like a wooden figure. He folded his arms and glared at me with his excitable, slanting brown eyes. His head was the shape of a chocolate drop and was covered with dry, straw-colored hair that fuzzed up about his pointed crown. He had never done more than mutter at me as I passed him, and I was surprised when he now addressed me.

"Miss Lingard," he said haughtily, "is a young woman for whom I have the utmost, the utmost respect."

"So have I," I said coldly.

He paid no heed to my remark, but began to do rapid finger-exercises on his shirt sleeves, as he stood with tightly folded arms.

"Kindness of heart," he went on, staring at the ceiling, "sentiment, are not understood in a place like this. The noblest qualities are ridiculed.

Grinning college boys, ignorant and conceited, what do they know of delicacy!"

I controlled my features and tried to speak seriously.

"If you mean me, Mr. Ordinsky, I have known Miss Lingard a long time, and I think I appreciate her kindness. We come from the same town, and we grew up together."

His gaze traveled slowly down from the ceiling and rested on me. "Am I to understand that you have this young woman's interests at heart? That you do not wish to compromise her?"

"That's a word we don't use much here, Mr. Ordinsky. A girl who makes her own living can ask a college boy to supper without being talked about. We take some things for granted."

"Then I have misjudged you, and I ask your pardon"—he bowed gravely. "Miss Lingard," he went on, "is an absolutely trustful heart. She has not learned the hard lessons of life. As for you and me, *noblesse oblige*"—he watched me narrowly.

Lena returned with the vest. "Come in and let us look at you as you go out, Mr. Ordinsky. I've never seen you in your dress suit," she said as she opened the door for him.

A few moments later he reappeared with his violin case—a heavy muffler about his neck and thick woollen gloves on his bony hands. Lena spoke encouragingly to him, and he went off with such an important professional air that we fell to laughing as soon as we had shut the door. "Poor fellow," Lena said indulgently, "he takes everything so hard."

After that Ordinsky was friendly to me and behaved as if there were some deep understanding between us. He wrote a furious article, attacking the musical taste of the town, and asked me to do him a great service by taking it to the editor of the morning paper. If the editor refused to print it, I was to tell him that he would be answerable to Ordinsky "in person." He declared that he would never retract one word, and that he was quite prepared to lose all his pupils. In spite of the fact that nobody ever mentioned his article to him after it appeared—full of typographical errors which he thought intentional—he got a certain satisfaction from believing that the citizens of Lincoln had meekly accepted the epithet "coarse barbarians." "You see how it is," he said to me, "where there is no chivalry, there is no *amour-propre.*" When I met him on his rounds now, I thought he carried his head more disdainfully than ever, and strode up the steps of front porches and rang doorbells with more assurance. He told Lena he would never forget how I had stood by him when he was "under fire."

All this time, of course, I was drifting. Lena had broken up my serious mood. I wasn't interested in my classes. I played with Lena and Prince, I played with the Pole, I went buggy-riding with the old colonel, who had taken a fancy to me and used to talk to me about Lena and the "great beauties" he had known in his youth. We were all three in love with Lena.

Before the first of June, Gaston Cleric was offered an instructorship at Harvard College, and accepted it. He suggested that I should follow him in the fall, and complete my course at Harvard. He had found out about Lena—not from me—and he talked to me seriously.

"You won't do anything here now. You should either quit school and go to work, or change your college and begin again in earnest. You won't recover yourself while you are playing about with this handsome Norwegian. Yes, I've seen her with you at the theater. She's very pretty, and perfectly irresponsible, I should judge."

Cleric wrote my grandfather that he would like to take me east with him. To my astonishment, Grandfather replied that I might go if I wished. I was both glad and sorry on the day when the letter came. I stayed in my room all evening and thought things over. I even tried to persuade myself that I was standing in Lena's way—it is so necessary to be a little noble!—and that if she had not me to play with, she would probably marry and secure her future.

The next evening I went to call on Lena. I found her propped up on the couch in her bay window, with her foot in a big slipper. An awkward little Russian girl whom she had taken into her workroom had dropped a flat-iron on Lena's toe. On the table beside her there was a basket of early summer flowers which the Pole had left after he heard of the accident. He always managed to know what went on in Lena's apartment.

Lena was telling me some amusing piece of gossip about one of her clients, when I interrupted her and picked up the flower basket.

"This old chap will be proposing to you some day, Lena."

"Oh, he has—often!" she murmured.

"What! After you've refused him?"

"He doesn't mind that. It seems to cheer him to mention the subject. Old men are like that, you know. It makes them feel important to think they're in love with somebody."

"The colonel would marry you in a minute. I hope you won't marry some old fellow; not even a rich one."

Lena shifted her pillows and looked up at me in surprise.

"Why, I'm not going to marry anybody. Didn't you know that?"

"Nonsense, Lena. That's what girls say, but you know better. Every handsome girl like you marries, of course."

She shook her head. "Not me."

"But why not? What makes you say that?" I persisted.

Lena laughed.

"Well, it's mainly because I don't want a husband. Men are all right for friends, but as soon as you marry them they turn into cranky old fathers, even the wild ones. They begin to tell you what's sensible and what's foolish, and want you to stick at home all the time. I prefer to be foolish when I feel like it, and be accountable to nobody."

"But you'll be lonesome. You'll get tired of this sort of life, and you'll want a family."

"Not me. I like to be lonesome. When I went to work for Mrs. Thomas I was nineteen years old, and I had never slept a night in my life when there weren't three in the bed. I never had a minute to myself except when I was off with the cattle."

Usually, when Lena referred to her life in the country at all, she dismissed it with a single remark, humorous or mildly cynical. But tonight her mind seemed to dwell on those early years. She told me she couldn't remember a time when she was so little that she wasn't lugging a heavy baby about, helping to wash for babies, trying to keep their little chapped hands and faces clean. She remembered home as a place where there were always too many children, a cross man and work piling up around a sick woman.

"It wasn't Mother's fault. She would have made us comfortable if she could. But that was no life for a girl! After I began to herd and milk, I could never get the smell of the cattle off me. The few underclothes I had I kept in a cracker-box. On Saturday nights, after everybody was in bed, then I could take a bath if I wasn't too tired. I could make two trips to the windmill to carry water, and heat it in the wash-boiler on the stove. While the water was heating, I could bring in a washtub out of the cave, and take my bath in the kitchen. Then I could put on a clean nightgown and get into bed with two others, who likely hadn't had a bath unless I'd given it to them. You can't tell me anything about family life. I've had plenty to last me."

"But it's not all like that," I objected.

"Near enough. It's all being under somebody's thumb. What's on your mind, Jim? Are you afraid I'll want you to marry me some day?"

Then I told her I was going away.

"What makes you want to go away, Jim? Haven't I been nice to you?"

"You've been just awfully good to me, Lena," I blurted. "I don't think about much else. I never shall think about much else while I'm with you. I'll never settle down and grind if I stay here. You know that."

I dropped down beside her and sat looking at the floor. I seemed to have forgotten all my reasonable explanations.

Lena drew close to me, and the little hesitation in her voice that had hurt me was not there when she spoke again.

"I oughtn't to have begun it, ought I?" she murmured. "I oughtn't to have gone to see you that first time. But I did want to. I guess I've always been a little foolish about you. I don't know what first put it into my head, unless it was Ántonia, always telling me I mustn't be up to any of my nonsense with you. I let you alone for a long while, though, didn't I?"

She was a sweet creature to those she loved, that Lena Lingard!

At last she sent me away with her soft, slow, renunciatory kiss.

"You aren't sorry I came to see you that time?" she whispered. "It seemed so natural. I used to think I'd like to be your first sweetheart. You were such a funny kid!"

She always kissed one as if she were sadly and wisely sending one away forever.

We said many goodbyes before I left Lincoln, but she never tried to hinder me or hold me back. "You are going, but you haven't gone yet, have you?" she used to say.

My Lincoln chapter closed abruptly. I went home to my grandparents for a few weeks, and afterward visited my relatives in Virginia until I joined Cleric in Boston. I was then nineteen years old.

BOOK FOUR

The Pioneer Woman's Story

I

TWO YEARS after I left Lincoln, I completed my academic course at Harvard. Before I entered the Law School I went home for the summer vacation. On the night of my arrival, Mrs. Harling and Frances and Sally came over to greet me. Everything seemed just as it used to be. My grandparents looked very little older. Frances Harling was married now, and she and her husband managed the Harling interests in Black Hawk. When we gathered in Grandmother's parlor, I could hardly believe that I had been away at all. One subject, however, we avoided all evening.

When I was walking home with Frances, after we had left Mrs. Harling at her gate, she said simply, "You know, of course, about poor Ántonia."

Poor Ántonia! Everyone would be saying that now, I thought bitterly. I replied that Grandmother had written me how Ántonia went away to marry Larry Donovan at some place where he was working; that he had deserted her, and that there was now a baby. This was all I knew.

"He never married her," Frances said. "I haven't seen her since she came back. She lives at home, on the farm, and almost never comes to town. She brought the baby in to show it to Mama once. I'm afraid she's settled down to be Ambrosch's drudge for good."

I tried to shut Ántonia out of my mind. I was bitterly disappointed in her. I could not forgive her for becoming an object of pity, while Lena Lingard, for whom people had always foretold trouble, was now the leading dressmaker of Lincoln, much respected in Black Hawk. Lena gave her heart away when she felt like it, but she kept her head for her business and had got on in the world.

Just then it was the fashion to speak indulgently of Lena and severely of Tiny Soderball, who had quietly gone west to try her fortune the year before. A Black Hawk boy, just back from Seattle, brought the news that Tiny had not gone to the coast on a venture, as she had allowed people to think, but with very definite plans. One of the roving promoters that used to stop at Mrs. Gardener's hotel owned idle property along the waterfront in Seattle, and he had offered to set Tiny up in business in one of his empty buildings. She was now conducting a sailors' lodging-house. This, everyone said, would be the end of Tiny. Even if she had begun by running a decent place, she couldn't keep it up; all sailors' boarding-houses were alike.

When I thought about it, I discovered that I had never known Tiny as well as I knew the other girls. I remembered her tripping briskly about the dining room on her high heels, carrying a big trayful of dishes, glancing rather pertly at the spruce traveling men, and contemptuously at the scrubby ones—who were so afraid of her that they didn't dare to ask for two kinds of pie. Now it occurred to me that perhaps the sailors, too, might be afraid of Tiny. How astonished we should have been, as we sat talking about her on Frances Harling's front porch, if we could have known what her future was really to be!

This is what actually happened to Tiny: While she was running her lodging-house in Seattle, gold was discovered in Alaska. Miners and sailors came back from the north with wonderful stories and pouches of gold. Tiny saw it and weighed it in her hands. That daring, which nobody had ever suspected in her, awoke. She sold her business and set out for Circle City, in company with a carpenter and his wife whom she had persuaded to go along with her. They reached Skaguay in a snow-storm, went in dog-sledges over the Chilkoot Pass, and shot the Yukon in flatboats. They reached Circle City on the very day when some Siwash Indians came into the settlement with the report that there had been a rich gold strike farther up the river, on a certain Klondike Creek. Two days later Tiny and her friends, and nearly everyone else in Circle City, started for the Klondike fields on the last steamer that went up the Yukon before it froze for the winter. That boatload of people founded Dawson City. Within a few weeks there were fifteen hundred homeless men in camp. Tiny and the carpenter's wife began to cook for them, in a tent. The miners gave her a building lot, and the carpenter put up a log hotel for her. There she sometimes fed 150 men a day. Miners came in on snowshoes from their placer claims twenty miles away to buy fresh bread from her, and paid for it in gold.

That winter Tiny kept in her hotel a Swede whose legs had been frozen one night in a storm when he was trying to find his way back to his cabin. The poor fellow thought it great good fortune to be cared for by a woman, and a woman who spoke his own tongue. When he was told that his feet must be amputated, he said he hoped he would not get well; what could a workingman do in this hard world without feet? He did, in fact, die from the operation, but not before he had deeded Tiny Soderball his claim on Hunker Creek. Tiny sold her hotel, invested half her money in Dawson building lots, and with the rest she developed her claim. She went off into the wilds and lived on the claim. She bought other claims from discouraged miners, traded or sold them on percentages.

After nearly ten years in the Klondike, Tiny returned, with a considerable fortune, to live in San Francisco. I met her in Salt Lake City in 1908. She was a thin, hard-faced woman, very well-dressed, very reserved in manner. Curiously enough, she reminded me of Mrs. Gardener, for whom she had worked in Black Hawk so long ago. She told me about some of the desperate chances she had taken in the gold country, but the thrill of them was quite gone. She said frankly that nothing interested her much now but making money. The only two human beings of whom she spoke with any feeling were the Swede, Johnson, who had given her his claim, and Lena Lingard. She had persuaded Lena to come to San Francisco and go into business there.

"Lincoln was never any place for her," Tiny remarked. "In a town of that size Lena would always be gossiped about. Frisco's the right field for her. She has a fine class of trade. Oh, she's just the same as she always was! She's careless, but she's level-headed. She's the only person I know who never gets any older. It's fine for me to have her there; somebody who enjoys things like that. She keeps an eye on me and won't let me be shabby. When she thinks I need a new dress, she makes it and sends it home—with a bill that's long enough, I can tell you!"

Tiny limped slightly when she walked. The claim on Hunker Creek took toll from its possessors. Tiny had been caught in a sudden turn of weather, like poor Johnson. She lost three toes from one of those pretty little feet that used to trip about Black Hawk in pointed slippers and striped stockings. Tiny mentioned this mutilation quite casually—didn't seem sensitive about it. She was satisfied with her success, but not elated. She was like someone in whom the faculty of becoming interested is worn out.

II

SOON AFTER I got home that summer, I persuaded my grandparents to have their photographs taken, and one morning I went into the photographer's shop to arrange for sittings. While I was waiting for him to come out of his developing-room, I walked about trying to recognize the likenesses on his walls: girls in commencement dresses, country brides and grooms holding hands, family groups of three generations. I noticed, in a heavy frame, one of those depressing "crayon enlargements" often seen in farmhouse parlors, the subject being a round-eyed baby in short dresses. The photographer came out and gave a constrained, apologetic laugh.

"That's Tony Shimerda's baby. You remember her; she used to be the Harling's Tony. Too bad! She seems proud of the baby, though; wouldn't hear to a cheap frame for the picture. I expect her brother will be in for it Saturday."

I went away feeling that I must see Ántonia again. Another girl would have kept her baby out of sight, but Tony, of course, must have its picture on exhibition at the town photographer's, in a great gilt frame. How like her! I could forgive her, I told myself, if she hadn't thrown herself away on such a cheap sort of fellow.

Larry Donovan was a passenger conductor, one of those train-crew aristocrats who are always afraid that someone may ask them to put up a car-window, and who, if requested to perform such a menial service, silently point to the button that calls the porter. Larry wore this air of official aloofness even on the street, where there were no car windows to compromise his dignity. At the end of his run he stepped indifferently from the train along with the passengers, his street hat on his head and his conductor's cap in an alligator-skin bag, went directly into the station and changed his clothes. It was a matter of the utmost importance to him never to be seen in his blue trousers away from his train. He was usually cold and distant with men, but with all women he had a silent, grave familiarity, a special handshake, accompanied by a significant, deliberate look. He took women, married or single, into his confidence, walked them up and down in the moonlight, telling them what a mistake he had made by not entering the office branch of the service, and how much better fitted he was to fill the post of general passenger agent in Denver than the roughshod man who then bore that title. His unappreciated worth was the tender secret Larry shared with his sweethearts, and he was always able to make some foolish heart ache over it.

As I drew near home that morning, I saw Mrs. Harling out in her yard, digging round her mountain-ash tree. It was a dry summer, and she had now no boy to help her. Charley was off in his battleship, cruising somewhere on the Caribbean sea. I turned in at the gate—it was with a feeling of pleasure that I opened and shut that gate in those days; I liked the feel of it under my hand. I took the spade away from Mrs. Harling, and while I loosened the earth around the tree, she sat down on the steps and talked about the oriole family that had a nest in its branches.

"Mrs. Harling," I said presently, "I wish I could find out exactly how Ántonia's marriage fell through."

"Why don't you go out and see your grandfather's tenant, the Widow Steavens? She knows more about it than anybody else. She helped Ántonia get ready to be married, and she was there when Ántonia came back. She took care of her when the baby was born. She could tell you everything. Besides, the Widow Steavens is a good talker, and she has a remarkable memory."

III

On the first or second day of August I got a horse and cart and set out for the high country, to visit the Widow Steavens. The wheat harvest was over, and here and there along the horizon I could see black puffs of smoke from the steam threshing-machines. The old pasture land was now being broken up into wheat-fields and cornfields, the red grass was disappearing, and the whole face of the country was changing. There were wooden houses where the old sod dwellings used to be, and little orchards, and big red barns; all this meant happy children, contented women, and men who saw their lives coming to a fortunate issue. The windy springs and the blazing summers, one after another, had enriched and mellowed that flat tableland; all the human effort that had gone into it was coming back in long, sweeping lines of fertility. The changes seemed beautiful and harmonious to me; it was like watching the growth of a great man or of a great idea. I recognized every tree and sandbank and rugged draw. I found that I remembered the conformation of the land as one remembers the modeling of human faces.

When I drew up to our old windmill, the Widow Steavens came out to meet me. She was brown as an Indian woman, tall, and very strong. When I was little, her massive head had always seemed to me like a Roman senator's. I told her at once why I had come.

"You'll stay the night with us, Jimmy? I'll talk to you after supper. I can take more interest when my work is off my mind. You've no prejudice against hot biscuit for supper? Some have, these days."

While I was putting my horse away, I heard a rooster squawking. I looked at my watch and sighed; it was three o'clock, and I knew that I must eat him at six.

After supper Mrs. Steavens and I went upstairs to the old sitting-room, while her grave, silent brother remained in the basement to read his farm papers. All the windows were open. The white summer moon was shining outside, the windmill was pumping lazily in the light breeze. My hostess put the lamp on a stand in the corner, and turned it low because of the heat. She sat down in her favorite rocking chair and settled a little stool comfortably under her tired feet. "I'm troubled with calluses, Jim; getting old," she sighed cheerfully. She crossed her hands in her lap and sat as if she were at a meeting of some kind.

"Now, it's about that dear Ántonia you want to know? Well, you've come to the right person. I've watched her like she'd been my own daughter.

"When she came home to do her sewing that summer before she was to be married, she was over here about every day. They've never had a sewing-machine at the Shimerdas', and she made all her things here. I taught her hemstitching, and I helped her to cut and fit. She used to sit there at that machine by the window, pedaling the life out of it—she was so strong—and always singing them queer Bohemian songs, like she was the happiest thing in the world.

" 'Ántonia,' I used to say, 'don't run that machine so fast. You won't hasten the day none that way.'

"Then she'd laugh and slow down for a little, but she'd soon forget and begin to pedal and sing again. I never saw a girl work harder to go to housekeeping right and well-prepared. Lovely table linen the Harlings had given her, and Lena Lingard had sent her nice things from Lincoln. We hemstitched all the tablecloths and pillowcases, and some of the sheets. Old Mrs. Shimerda knit yards and yards of lace for her underclothes. Tony told me just how she meant to have everything in her house. She'd even bought silver spoons and forks, and kept them in her trunk. She was always coaxing brother to go to the post office. Her young man did write her real often, from the different towns along his run.

"The first thing that troubled her was when he wrote that his run had been changed, and they would likely have to live in Denver. 'I'm a country girl,' she said, 'and I doubt if I'll be able to manage so well for him in a city. I was counting on keeping chickens, and maybe a cow.' She soon cheered up, though.

"At last she got the letter telling her when to come. She was shaken by it; she broke the seal and read it in this room. I suspected then that she'd begun to get faint-hearted, waiting; though she'd never let me see it.

"Then there was a great time of packing. It was in March, if I remember rightly, and a terrible muddy, raw spell, with the roads bad for hauling her things to town. And here let me say, Ambrosch did the right thing. He went to Black Hawk and bought her a set of plated silver in a purple velvet box, good enough for her station. He gave her three hundred dollars in money; I saw the check. He'd collected her wages all those first years she worked out, and it was but right. I shook him by the hand in this room. 'You're behaving like a man, Ambrosch,' I said, 'and I'm glad to see it, son.'

" 'Twas a cold, raw day he drove her and her three trunks into Black Hawk to take the night train for Denver—the boxes had been shipped before. He stopped the wagon here, and she ran in to tell me goodbye. She threw her arms around me and kissed me, and thanked me for all I'd done for her. She was so happy she was crying and laughing at the same time, and her red cheeks was all wet with rain.

" 'You're surely handsome enough for any man,' I said, looking her over.

"She laughed kind of flighty like, and whispered, 'Goodbye, dear house!' and then ran out to the wagon. I expect she meant that for you and your grandmother, as much as for me, so I'm particular to tell you. This house had always been a refuge to her.

"Well, in a few days we had a letter saying she got to Denver safe, and he was there to meet her. They were to be married in a few days. He was trying to get his promotion before he married, she said. I didn't like that, but I said nothing. The next week Yulka got a postal card, saying she was 'well and happy.' After that we heard nothing. A month went by, and old Mrs. Shimerda began to get fretful. Ambrosch was as sulky with me as if I'd picked out the man and arranged the match.

"One night brother William came in and said that on his way back from the fields he had passed a livery team from town, driving fast out the west road. There was a trunk on the front seat with the driver, and another behind. In the back seat there was a woman all bundled up; but for all her veils, he thought 'twas Ántonia Shimerda, or Ántonia Donovan, as her name ought now to be.

"The next morning I got brother to drive me over. I can walk still, but my feet ain't what they used to be, and I try to save myself. The lines outside the Shimerdas' house was full of washing, though it was the middle of the week. As we got nearer, I saw a sight that made my heart sink—all those underclothes we'd put so much work on, out there swinging in the wind. Yulka came bringing a dishpanful of wrung clothes, but she darted back into the house like she was loath to see us. When I went in, Ántonia was standing over the tubs, just finishing up a big washing. Mrs. Shimerda was going about her work, talking and scolding to herself. She didn't so much as raise her eyes. Tony wiped her hand on her apron and held it out to me, looking at me steady but mournful. When I took her in my arms she drew away. 'Don't, Mrs. Steavens,' she says, 'you'll make me cry, and I don't want to.'

"I whispered and asked her to come out-of-doors with me. I knew she couldn't talk free before her mother. She went out with me, bareheaded, and we walked up toward the garden.

" 'I'm not married, Mrs. Steavens,' she says to me very quiet and natural-like, 'and I ought to be.'

" 'Oh, my child,' says I, 'what's happened to you? Don't be afraid to tell me!'

"She sat down on the draw-side, out of sight of the house. 'He's run away from me,' she said. 'I don't know if he ever meant to marry me.'

" 'You mean he's thrown up his job and quit the country?' says I.

" 'He didn't have any job. He'd been fired; blacklisted for knocking down fares. I didn't know. I thought he hadn't been treated right. He was sick when I got there. He'd just come out of the hospital. He lived with me till my money gave out, and afterward I found he hadn't really been hunting work at all. Then he just didn't come back. One nice fellow at the station told me, when I kept going to look for him, to give it up. He said he was afraid Larry'd gone bad and wouldn't come back any more. I guess he's gone to Old Mexico. The conductors get rich down there, collecting half-fares off the natives and robbing the company. He was always talking about fellows who had got ahead that way.'

"I asked her, of course, why she didn't insist on a civil marriage at once—that would have given her some hold on him. She leaned her head on her hands, poor child, and said, 'I just don't know, Mrs. Steavens. I guess my patience was wore out, waiting so long. I thought if he saw how well I could do for him, he'd want to stay with me.'

"Jimmy, I sat right down on that bank beside her and made lament. I cried like a young thing. I couldn't help it. I was just about heartbroke. It was one of them lovely warm May days, and the wind was blowing and the colts jumping around in the pastures; but I felt bowed with despair. My Ántonia, that had so much good in her, had come home disgraced. And that Lena Lingard, that was always a bad one, say what you will, had turned out so well, and was coming home here every summer in her silks and her satins, and doing so much for her mother. I give credit where credit is due, but you know well enough, Jim Burden, there is a great difference in the principles of those two girls. And here it was the good one that had come to grief! I was poor comfort to her. I marveled at her calm. As we went back to the house, she stopped to feel of her clothes to see if they was drying well, and seemed to take pride in their whiteness—she said she'd been living in a brick block, where she didn't have proper conveniences to wash them.

"The next time I saw Ántonia, she was out in the fields ploughing corn. All that spring and summer she did the work of a man on the farm; it seemed to be an understood thing. Ambrosch didn't get any other hand to help him. Poor Marek had got violent and been sent away to an institution a good while back. We never even saw any of Tony's pretty dresses. She didn't take them out of her trunks. She was quiet and steady. Folks respected her industry and tried to treat her as if nothing had happened. They talked, to be sure, but not like they would if she'd put on airs. She was so crushed and quiet that nobody seemed to want to humble her. She never went anywhere. All that summer she never once came to see me. At first I was hurt, but I got to feel that it was because this house reminded her of too much. I went over there when I could, but the times when she was in from the fields were the times when I was busiest here. She talked about the grain and the weather as if she'd never had another interest, and if I went over at night she always looked dead weary. She was afflicted with toothache; one tooth after another ulcerated, and she went about with her face swollen half the time. She wouldn't go to Black Hawk to a dentist for fear of meeting people she knew. Ambrosch had got over his good spell long ago, and was always surly. Once I told him he ought not to let Ántonia work so hard and pull herself down. He said, 'If you put that in her head, you better stay home.' And after that I did.

"Ántonia worked on through harvest and threshing, though she was too modest to go out threshing for the neighbors, like when she was young and free. I didn't see much of her until late that fall when she begun to herd Ambrosch's cattle in the open ground north of here, up toward the big dog-town. Sometimes she used to bring them over the west hill, there, and I would run to meet her and walk north a piece with her. She had thirty cattle in her bunch; it had been dry, and the pasture was short, or she wouldn't have brought them so far.

It was a fine open fall, and she liked to be alone. While the steers grazed, she used to sit on them grassy banks along the draws and sun herself for hours. Sometimes I slipped up to visit with her, when she hadn't gone too far.

" 'It does seem like I ought to make lace, or knit like Lena used to,' she said one day, 'but if I start to work, I look around and forget to go on. It seems such a little while ago when Jim Burden and I was playing all over this country. Up here I can pick out the very places where my father used to stand. Sometimes I feel like I'm not going to live very long, so I'm just enjoying every day of this fall.'

"After the winter begun she wore a man's long overcoat and boots, and a man's felt hat with a wide brim. I used to watch her coming and going, and I could see that her steps were getting heavier. One day in December, the snow began to fall. Late in the afternoon I saw Ántonia driving her cattle homeward across the hill. The snow was flying round her and she bent to face it, looking more lonesome-like to me than usual. 'Deary me,' I says to myself, 'the girl's stayed out too late. It'll be dark before she gets them cattle put into the corral.' I seemed to sense she'd been feeling too miserable to get up and drive them.

"That very night, it happened. She got her cattle home, turned them into the corral, and went into the house, into her room behind the kitchen, and shut the door. There, without calling to anybody, without a groan, she lay down on the bed and bore her child.

"I was lifting supper when old Mrs. Shimerda came running down the basement stairs, out of breath and screeching:

" 'Baby come, baby come!' she says. 'Ambrosch much like devil!'

"Brother William is surely a patient man. He was just ready to sit down to a hot supper after a long day in the fields. Without a word he rose and went down to the barn and hooked up his team. He got us over there as quick as it was humanly possible. I went right in, and began to do for Ántonia; but she laid there with her eyes shut and took no account of me. The old woman got a tubful of warm water to wash the baby. I overlooked what she was doing and I said out loud: 'Mrs. Shimerda, don't you put that strong yellow soap near that baby. You'll blister its little skin.' I was indignant.

" 'Mrs. Steavens,' Ántonia said from the bed, 'if you'll look in the top tray of my trunk, you'll see some fine soap.' That was the first word she spoke.

"After I'd dressed the baby, I took it out to show it to Ambrosch. He was muttering behind the stove and wouldn't look at it.

" 'You'd better put it out in the rain-barrel," he says.

" 'Now, see here, Ambrosch,' says I, 'there's a law in this land, don't forget that. I stand here a witness that this baby has come into the world sound and strong, and I intend to keep an eye on what befalls it.' I pride myself I cowed him.

"Well, I expect you're not much interested in babies, but Ántonia's got on fine. She loved it from the first as dearly as if she'd had a ring on her finger, and was never ashamed of it. It's a year and eight months old now, and no baby was ever better cared for. Ántonia is a natural-born mother. I wish she could marry and raise a family, but I don't know as there's much chance now."

* * *

I slept that night in the room I used to have when I was a little boy, with the summer wind blowing in at the windows, bringing the smell of the ripe fields. I lay awake and watched the moonlight shining over the barn and the stacks and the pond, and the windmill making its old dark shadow against the blue sky.

IV

THE NEXT AFTERNOON I walked over to the Shimerdas'. Yulka showed me the baby and told me that Ántonia was shocking wheat on the southwest quarter. I went down across the fields, and Tony saw me from a long way off. She stood still by her shocks, leaning on her pitchfork, watching me as I came. We met like the people in the old song, in silence, if not in tears. Her warm hand clasped mine.

"I thought you'd come, Jim. I heard you were at Mrs. Steavens's last night. I've been looking for you all day."

She was thinner than I had ever seen her, and looked as Mrs. Steavens said, "worked down," but there was a new kind of strength in the gravity of her face, and her color still gave her that look of deep-seated health and ardor. Still? Why, it flashed across me that though so much had happened in her life and in mine, she was barely twenty-four years old.

Ántonia stuck her fork in the ground, and instinctively we walked toward that unploughed patch at the crossing of the roads as the fittest place to talk to each other. We sat down outside the sagging wire fence that shut Mr. Shimerda's plot off from the rest of the world. The tall red grass had never been cut there. It had died down in winter and come up again in the spring until it was as thick and shrubby as some tropical garden-grass. I found myself telling her everything: why I had decided to study law and to go into the law office of one of my mother's relatives in New York City; about Gaston Cleric's death from pneumonia last winter, and the difference it had made in my life. She wanted to know about my friends, and my way of living, and my dearest hopes.

"Of course it means you are going away from us for good," she said with a sigh. "But that don't mean I'll lose you. Look at my papa here; he's been dead all these years, and yet he is more real to me than almost anybody else. He never goes out of my life. I talk to him and consult him all the time. The older I grow, the better I know him and the more I understand him."

She asked me whether I had learned to like big cities. "I'd always be miserable in a city. I'd die of lonesomeness. I like to be where I know every stack and tree, and where all the ground is friendly. I want to live and die here. Father Kelly says everybody's put into this world for something, and I know what I've got to do. I'm going to see that my little girl has a better chance than ever I had. I'm going to take care of that girl, Jim."

I told her I knew she would. "Do you know, Ántonia, since I've been away, I think of you more often than of anyone else in this part of the world. I'd have liked to have you for a sweetheart, or a wife, or my mother or my sister—anything that a woman can be to a man. The idea of you is a part of my mind; you influence my likes and dislikes, all my tastes, hundreds of times when I don't realize it. You really are a part of me."

She turned her bright, believing eyes to me, and the tears came up in them slowly, "How can it be like that, when you know so many people, and when I've disappointed you so? Ain't it wonderful, Jim, how much people can mean to each other? I'm so glad we had each other when we were little. I can't wait till my little girl's old enough to tell her about all the things we used to do. You'll always remember me when you think about old times, won't you? And I guess everybody thinks about old times, even the happiest people."

As we walked homeward across the fields, the sun dropped and lay like a great golden globe in the low west. While it hung there, the moon rose in the east, as big as a cartwheel, pale silver and streaked with rose color, thin as a bubble or a ghost-moon. For five, perhaps ten minutes, the two luminaries confronted each other across the level land, resting on opposite edges of the world.

In that singular light every little tree and shock of wheat, every sunflower stalk and clump of snow-on-the-mountain, drew itself up high and pointed; the very clods and furrows in the fields seemed to stand up sharply. I felt the old pull of the earth, the solemn magic that comes out of those fields at nightfall. I wished I could be a little boy again, and that my way could end there.

We reached the edge of the field, where our ways parted. I took her hands and held them against my breast, feeling once more how strong and warm and good they were, those brown hands, and remembering how many kind things they had done for me. I held them now a long while, over my heart. About us it was growing darker and darker, and I had to look hard to see her face, which I meant always to carry with me; the closest, realest face, under all the shadows of women's faces, at the very bottom of my memory.

"I'll come back," I said earnestly, through the soft, intrusive darkness.

"Perhaps you will"—I felt rather than saw her smile. "But even if you don't, you're here, like my father. So I won't be lonesome."

As I went back alone over that familiar road, I could almost believe that a boy and girl ran along beside me, as our shadows used to do, laughing and whispering to each other in the grass.

BOOK FIVE

Cuzak's Boys

I

I TOLD Ántonia I would come back, but life intervened, and it was twenty years before I kept my promise. I heard of her from time to time; that she married, very soon after I last saw her, a young Bohemian, a cousin of Anton Jelinek; that they were poor, and had a large family. Once when I was abroad I went into Bohemia, and from Prague I sent Ántonia some photographs of her native village. Months afterward came a letter from her, telling me the names and ages of her many children, but little else; signed, "Your old friend, Ántonia Cuzak." When I met Tiny Soderball in Salt Lake, she told me that Ántonia had not "done very well"; that her husband was not a man of much force, and she had had a hard life. Perhaps it was cowardice that kept me away so long. My business took me west several times every year, and it was always in the back of my mind that I would stop in Nebraska some day and go to see Ántonia. But I kept putting it off until the next trip. I did not want to find her aged and broken; I really dreaded it. In the course of twenty crowded years one parts with many illusions. I did not wish to lose the early ones. Some memories are realities, and are better than anything that can ever happen to one again.

I owe it to Lena Lingard that I went to see Ántonia at last. I was in San Francisco two summers ago when both Lena and Tiny Soderball were in town. Tiny lives in a house of her own, and Lena's shop is in an apartment house just around the corner. It interested me, after so many years, to see the two women together. Tiny audits Lena's accounts occasionally, and invests her money for her; and Lena, apparently, takes care that Tiny doesn't grow too miserly. "If there's anything I can't stand," she said to me in Tiny's presence, "it's a shabby rich woman." Tiny smiled grimly and assured me that Lena would never be either shabby or rich. "And I don't want to be," the other agreed complacently.

Lena gave me a cheerful account of Ántonia and urged me to make her a visit.

"You really ought to go, Jim. It would be such a satisfaction to her. Never mind what Tiny says. There's nothing the matter with Cuzak. You'd like him. He isn't a hustler, but a rough man would never have suited Tony. Tony has nice children—ten or eleven of them by this time, I guess. I shouldn't care for a family of that size myself, but somehow it's just right for Tony. She'd love to show them to you."

On my way East I broke my journey at Hastings, in Nebraska, and set off with an open buggy and a fairly good livery team to find the Cuzak farm. At a little past midday, I knew I must be nearing my destination. Set back on a swell of land at my right, I saw a wide farmhouse, with a red barn and an ash grove, and cattle-yards in front that sloped down to the high-road. I drew up my horses and was wondering whether I should drive in here, when I heard low voices. Ahead of me, in a plum thicket beside the road, I saw two boys bending over a dead dog. The little one, not more than four or five, was on his knees, his hands folded, and his close-clipped, bare head drooping forward in deep dejection. The other stood beside him, a hand on his shoulder, and was comforting him in a language I had not heard for a long while. When I stopped my horses opposite them, the older boy took his brother by the hand and came toward me. He, too, looked grave. This was evidently a sad afternoon for them.

"Are you Mrs. Cuzak's boys?" I asked.

The younger one did not look up; he was submerged in his own feelings, but his brother met me with intelligent gray eyes. "Yes, sir."

"Does she live up there on the hill? I am going to see her. Get in and ride up with me."

He glanced at his reluctant little brother. "I guess we'd better walk. But we'll open the gate for you."

I drove along the side road and they followed slowly behind. When I pulled up at the windmill, another boy, barefooted and curly-headed, ran out of the barn to tie my team for me. He was a handsome one, this chap, fair-skinned and freckled, with red cheeks and a ruddy pelt as thick as a lamb's wool, growing down on his neck in little tufts. He tied my team with two flourishes of his hands, and nodded when I asked him if his mother was at home. As he glanced at me, his face dimpled with a seizure of irrelevant merriment, and he shot up the windmill tower with a lightness that struck me as disdainful. I knew he was peering down at me as I walked toward the house.

Ducks and geese ran quacking across my path. White cats were sunning themselves among yellow pumpkins on the porch steps. I looked through the wire screen into a big, light kitchen with a white floor. I saw a long table, rows of wooden chairs against the wall, and a shining range in one corner. Two girls were washing dishes at the sink, laughing and chattering, and a little one, in a short pinafore, sat on a stool playing with a rag baby. When I asked for their mother, one of the girls dropped her towel, ran across the floor with noiseless bare feet, and disappeared. The older one, who wore shoes and stockings, came to the door to admit me. She was a buxom girl with dark hair and eyes, calm and self-possessed.

"Won't you come in? Mother will be here in a minute."

Before I could sit down in the chair she offered me, the miracle happened; one of those quiet moments that clutch the heart, and take more courage than the noisy, excited passages in life. Ántonia came in and stood before me: a stalwart, brown woman, flat-chested, her curly brown hair a little grizzled. It was a shock, of course. It always is, to meet people after long years, especially if they have lived as much and as hard as this woman had. We stood looking at each other. The eyes that peered anxiously at me were—simply Ántonia's eyes. I had seen no others like them since I looked into them last, though I had looked at so many thousands of human faces. As I confronted her, the changes grew less apparent to me, her identity stronger. She was there, in the full vigor of her personality, battered but not diminished, looking at me, speaking to me in the husky, breathy voice I remembered so well.

"My husband's not at home, sir. Can I do anything?"

"Don't you remember me, Ántonia? Have I changed so much?"

She frowned into the slanting sunlight that made her brown hair look redder than it was. Suddenly her eyes widened, her whole face seemed to grow broader. She caught her breath and put out two hard-worked hands.

"Why, it's Jim! Anna, Yulka, it's Jim Burden!" She had no sooner caught my hands than she looked alarmed. "What's happened? Is anybody dead?"

I patted her arm.

"No. I didn't come to a funeral this time. I got off the train at Hastings and drove down to see you and your family."

She dropped my hand and began rushing about. "Anton, Yulka, Nina, where are you all? Run, Anna, and hunt for the boys. They're off looking for that dog, somewhere. And call Leo. Where is that Leo?" She pulled them out of corners and came bringing them like a mother cat bringing in her kittens. "You don't have to go right off, Jim? My oldest boy's not here. He's gone with Papa to the street fair at Wilber. I won't let you go! You've got to stay and see Rudolph and our papa." She looked at me imploringly, panting with excitement.

While I reassured her and told her there would be plenty of time, the barefooted boys from outside were slipping into the kitchen and gathering about her.

"Now, tell me their names, and how old they are."

As she told them off in turn, she made several mistakes about ages, and they roared with laughter. When she came to my light-footed friend of the windmill, she said, "This is Leo, and he's old enough to be better than he is."

He ran up to her and butted her playfully with his curly head, like a little ram, but his voice was quite desperate. "You've forgot! You always forget mine. It's mean! Please tell him, Mother!" He clenched his fists in vexation and looked up at her impetuously.

She wound her forefinger in his yellow fleece and pulled it, watching him. "Well, how old are you?"

"I'm twelve," he panted, looking not at me but at her; "I'm twelve years old, and I was born on Easter Day!"

She nodded to me. "It's true. He was an Easter baby."

The children all looked at me, as if they expected me to exhibit astonishment or delight at this information. Clearly, they were proud of each other, and of being so many. When they had all been introduced, Anna, the eldest daughter, who had met me at the door, scattered them gently, and came bringing a white apron which she tied round her mother's waist.

"Now, Mother, sit down and talk to Mr. Burden. We'll finish the dishes quietly and not disturb you."

Ántonia looked about, quite distracted. "Yes, child, but why don't we take him into the parlor, now that we've got a nice parlor for company?"

The daughter laughed indulgently and took my hat from me. "Well, you're here, now, Mother, and if you talk here, Yulka and I can listen, too. You can show him the parlor afterwhile." She smiled at me, and went back to the dishes, with her sister. The little girl with the rag doll found a place on the bottom step of an enclosed back stairway, and sat with her toes curled up, looking out at us expectantly.

"She's Nina, after Nina Harling," Ántonia explained. "Ain't her eyes like Nina's? I declare, Jim, I loved you children almost as much as I love my own. These children know all about you and Charley and Sally, like as if they'd grown up with you. I can't think of what I want to say, you've got me so stirred up. And then, I've forgot my English so. I don't often talk it any more. I tell the children I used to speak real well." She said they always spoke Bohemian at home. The little ones could not speak English at all—didn't learn it until they went to school.

"I can't believe it's you, sitting here, in my own kitchen. You wouldn't have known me, would you, Jim? You've kept so young, yourself. But it's easier for a man. I can't see how my Anton looks any older than the day I married him. His teeth have kept so nice. I haven't got many left. But I feel just as young as I used to, and I can do as much work. Oh, we don't have to work so hard now! We've got plenty to help us, Papa and me. And how many have you got, Jim?"

When I told her I had no children, she seemed embarrassed. "Oh, ain't that too bad! Maybe you could take one of my bad ones, now? That Leo; he's the worst of all." She leaned toward me with a smile. "And I love him the best," she whispered.

"Mother!" the two girls murmured reproachfully from the dishes.

Ántonia threw up her head and laughed. "I can't help it. You know I do. Maybe it's because he came on Easter Day, I don't know. And he's never out of mischief one minute!"

I was thinking, as I watched her, how little it mattered—about her teeth, for instance. I know so many women who have kept all the things that she had lost, but whose inner glow has faded. Whatever else was gone, Ántonia had not lost the fire of life. Her skin, so brown and hardened, had not that look of flabbiness, as if the sap beneath it had been secretly drawn away.

While we were talking, the little boy whom they called Jan came in and sat down on the step beside Nina, under the hood of the stairway. He wore a funny long gingham apron, like a smock, over his trousers, and his hair was clipped so short that his head looked white and naked. He watched us out of his big, sorrowful gray eyes.

"He wants to tell you about the dog, mother. They found it dead," Anna said, as she passed us on her way to the cupboard.

Ántonia beckoned the boy to her. He stood by her chair, leaning his elbows on her knees and twisting her apron strings in his slender fingers, while he told her his story softly in Bohemian, and the tears brimmed over and hung on his long lashes. His mother listened, spoke soothingly to him, and in a whisper promised him something that made him give her a quick, teary smile. He slipped away and whispered his secret to Nina, sitting close to her and talking behind his hand.

When Anna finished her work and had washed her hands, she came and stood behind her mother's chair. "Why don't we show Mr. Burden our new fruit cave?" she asked.

We started off across the yard with the children at our heels. The boys were standing by the windmill, talking about the dog; some of them ran ahead to open the cellar door. When we descended, they all came down after us, and seemed quite as proud of the cave as the girls were.

Ambrosch, the thoughtful-looking one who had directed me down by the plum bushes, called my attention to the stout brick walls and the cement floor. "Yes, it is a good way from the house," he admitted. "But, you see, in winter there are nearly always some of us around to come out and get things."

Anna and Yulka showed me three small barrels; one full of dill pickles, one full of chopped pickles, and one full of pickled watermelon rinds.

"You wouldn't believe, Jim, what it takes to feed them all!" their mother exclaimed. "You ought to see the bread we bake on Wednesdays and Saturdays! It's no wonder their poor papa can't get rich, he has to buy so much sugar for us to preserve with. We have our own wheat ground for flour—but then there's that much less to sell."

Nina and Jan, and a little girl named Lucie, kept shyly pointing out to me the shelves of glass jars. They said nothing, but, glancing at me, traced on the glass with their fingertips the outline of the cherries and strawberries and crabapples within, trying by a blissful expression of countenance to give me some idea of their deliciousness.

"Show him the spiced plums, mother. Americans don't have those," said one of the older boys. "Mother uses them to make *kolaches,"* he added.

Leo, in a low voice, tossed off some scornful remark in Bohemian.

I turned to him. "You think I don't know what *kolaches* are, eh? You're mistaken, young man. I've eaten your mother's *kolaches* long before that Easter Day when you were born."

"Always too fresh, Leo," Ambrosch remarked with a shrug.

Leo dived behind his mother and grinned out at me.

We turned to leave the cave; Ántonia and I went up the stairs first, and the children waited. We were standing outside talking, when they all came running up the steps together, big and little, tow heads and gold heads and brown, and flashing little naked legs; a veritable explosion of life out of the dark cave into the sunlight. It made me dizzy for a moment.

The boys escorted us to the front of the house, which I hadn't yet seen; in farmhouses, somehow, life comes and goes by the back door. The roof was so steep that the eaves were not much above the forest of tall hollyhocks, now brown and in seed. Through July, Ántonia said, the house was buried in them; the Bohemians, I remembered, always planted hollyhocks. The front yard was enclosed by a thorny locust hedge, and at the gate grew two silvery, mothlike trees of the mimosa family. From here one looked down over the cattle-yards, with their two long ponds, and over a wide stretch of stubble which they told me was a rye field in summer.

At some distance behind the house were an ash grove and two orchards: a cherry orchard, with gooseberry and currant bushes between the rows, and an apple orchard, sheltered by a high hedge from the hot winds. The older children turned back when we reached the hedge, but Jan and Nina and Lucie crept through it by a hole known only to themselves and hid under the low-branching mulberry bushes.

As we walked through the apple orchard, grown up in tall bluegrass, Ántonia kept stopping to tell me about one tree and another. "I love them as if they were people," she said, rubbing her hand over the bark. "There wasn't a tree here when we first came. We planted every one, and used to carry water for them, too—after we'd been working in the fields all day. Anton, he was a city man, and he used to get discouraged. But I couldn't feel so tired that I wouldn't fret about these trees when there was a dry time. They were on my mind like children. Many a night after he was asleep I've got up and come out and carried water to the poor things. And now, you see, we have the good of them. My man worked in the orange groves in Florida, and he knows all about grafting. There ain't one of our neighbors has an orchard that bears like ours."

In the middle of the orchard we came upon a grape arbor, with seats built along the sides and a warped plank table. The three children were waiting for us there. They looked up at me bashfully and made some request of their mother.

"They want me to tell you how the teacher has the school picnic here every year. These don't go to school yet, so they think it's all like the picnic."

After I had admired the arbor sufficiently, the youngsters ran away to an open place where there was a rough jungle of French pinks, and squatted down among them, crawling about and measuring with a string.

"Jan wants to bury his dog there," Ántonia explained. "I had to tell him he could. He's kind of like Nina Harling; you remember how hard she used to take little things? He has funny notions, like her."

We sat down and watched them. Ántonia leaned her elbows on the table. There was the deepest peace in that orchard. It was surrounded by a triple enclosure: the wire fence, then the hedge of thorny locusts, then the mulberry hedge which kept out the hot winds of summer and held fast to the protecting snows of winter. The hedges were so tall that we could see nothing but the blue sky above them, neither the barn roof nor the windmill. The afternoon sun poured down on us through the drying grape leaves. The orchard seemed full of sun, like a cup, and we could smell the ripe apples on the trees. The crabs hung on the branches as thick as beads on a string, purple-red, with a thin silvery glaze over them. Some hens and ducks had crept through the hedge and were pecking at the fallen apples. The drakes were handsome fellows, with pinkish gray bodies, their heads and necks covered with iridescent green feathers which grew close and full, changing to blue like a peacock's neck. Ántonia said they always reminded her of soldiers—some uniform she had seen in the old country, when she was a child.

"Are there any quail left now?" I asked. I reminded her how she used to go hunting with me the last summer before we moved to town. "You weren't a bad shot, Tony. Do you remember how you used to want to run away and go for ducks with Charley Harling and me?"

"I know, but I'm afraid to look at a gun now." She picked up one of the drakes and ruffled his green capote with her fingers. "Ever since I've had children, I don't like to kill anything. It makes me kind of faint to wring an old goose's neck. Ain't that strange, Jim?"

"I don't know. The young queen of Italy said the same thing once, to a friend of mine. She used to be a great huntswoman, but now she feels as you do, and only shoots clay pigeons."

"Then I'm sure she's a good mother," Ántonia said warmly.

She told me how she and her husband had come out to this new country when the farm land was cheap and could be had on easy payments. The first ten years were a hard struggle. Her husband knew very little about farming and often grew discouraged. "We'd never have got through if I hadn't been so strong. I've always had good health, thank God, and I was able to help him in the fields until right up to the time before my babies came. Our children were good about taking care of each other. Martha, the one you saw when she was a baby, was such a help to me, and she trained Anna to be just like her. My Martha's married now, and has a baby of her own. Think of that, Jim!

"No, I never got down-hearted. Anton's a good man, and I loved my children and always believed they would turn out well. I belong on a farm. I'm never lonesome here like I used to be in town. You remember what sad spells I used to have, when I didn't know what was the matter with me? I've never had them out here. And I don't mind work a bit, if I don't have to put up with sadness." She leaned her chin on her hand and looked down through the orchard, where the sunlight was growing more and more golden.

"You ought never to have gone to town, Tony," I said, wondering at her.

She turned to me eagerly.

"Oh, I'm glad I went! I'd never have known anything about cooking or housekeeping if I hadn't. I learned nice ways at the Harlings', and I've been able to bring my children up so much better. Don't you think they are pretty well-behaved for country children? If it hadn't been for what Mrs. Harling taught me, I expect I'd have brought them up like wild rabbits. No, I'm glad I had a chance to learn; but I'm thankful none of my daughters will ever have to work out. The trouble with me was, Jim, I never could believe harm of anybody I loved."

While we were talking, Ántonia assured me that she could keep me for the night. "We've plenty of room. Two of the boys sleep in the haymow till cold weather comes, but there's no need for it. Leo always begs to sleep there, and Ambrosch goes along to look after him."

I told her I would like to sleep in the haymow, with the boys.

"You can do just as you want to. The chest is full of clean blankets, put away for winter. Now I must go, or my girls will be doing all the work, and I want to cook your supper myself."

As we went toward the house, we met Ambrosch and Anton, starting off with their milking-pails to hunt the cows. I joined them, and Leo accompanied us at some distance, running ahead and starting up at us out of clumps of ironweed, calling, "I'm a jackrabbit," or, "I'm a big bull-snake."

I walked between the two older boys—straight, well-made fellows, with good heads and clear eyes. They talked about their school and the new teacher, told me about the crops and the harvest, and how many steers they would feed that winter. They were easy and confidential with me, as if I were an old friend of the family—and not too old. I felt like a boy in their company, and all manner of forgotten interests revived in me. It seemed, after all, so natural to be walking along a barbed-wire fence beside the sunset, toward a red pond, and to see my shadow moving along at my right, over the close-cropped grass.

"Has Mother shown you the pictures you sent her from the old country?" Ambrosch asked. "We've had them framed and they're hung up in the parlor. She was so glad to get them. I don't believe I ever saw her so pleased about anything." There was a note of simple gratitude in his voice that made me wish I had given more occasion for it.

I put my hand on his shoulder. "Your mother, you know, was very much loved by all of us. She was a beautiful girl."

"Oh, we know!" They both spoke together—seemed a little surprised that I should think it necessary to mention this. "Everybody liked her, didn't they? The Harlings and your grandmother, and all the town people."

"Sometimes," I ventured, "it doesn't occur to boys that their mother was ever young and pretty."

"Oh, we know!" they said again, warmly. "She's not very old now," Ambrosch added. "Not much older than you."

"Well," I said, "if you weren't nice to her, I think I'd take a club and go for the whole lot of you. I couldn't stand it if you boys were inconsiderate, or thought of her as if she were just somebody who looked after you. You see I was very much in love with your mother once, and I know there's nobody like her."

The boys laughed and seemed pleased and embarrassed.

"She never told us that," said Anton. "But she's always talked lots about you, and about what good times you used to have. She has a picture of you that she cut out of the Chicago paper once, and Leo says he recognized you when you drove up to the windmill. You can't tell about Leo, though; sometimes he likes to be smart."

We brought the cows home to the corner nearest the barn, and the boys milked them while night came on. Everything was as it should be: the strong smell of sunflowers and ironweed in the dew, the clear blue and gold of the sky, the evening star, the purr of the milk into the pails, the grunts and squeals of the pigs fighting over their supper. I began to feel the loneliness of the farm boy at evening, when the chores seem everlastingly the same, and the world so far away.

What a tableful we were at supper: two long rows of restless heads in the lamplight, and so many eyes fastened excitedly upon Ántonia as she sat at the head of the table, filling the plates and starting the dishes on their way. The children were seated according to a system: a little one next an older one, who was to watch over his behavior and to see that he got his food. Anna and Yulka left their chairs from time to time to bring fresh plates of *kolaches* and pitchers of milk.

After supper we went into the parlor, so that Yulka and Leo could play for me. Ántonia went first, carrying the lamp. There were not nearly chairs enough to go round, so the younger children sat down on the bare floor. Little Lucie whispered to me that they were going to have a parlor carpet if they got ninety cents for their wheat. Leo, with a good deal of fussing, got out his violin. It was old Mr. Shimerda's instrument, which Ántonia had always kept, and it was too big for him. But he played very well for a self-taught boy. Poor Yulka's efforts were not so successful. While they were playing, little Nina got up from her corner, came out into the middle of the floor, and began to do a pretty little dance on the boards with her bare feet. No one paid the least attention to her, and when she was through she stole back and sat down by her brother.

Ántonia spoke to Leo in Bohemian. He frowned and wrinkled up his face. He seemed to be trying to pout, but his attempt only brought out dimples in unusual places. After twisting and screwing the keys, he played some Bohemian airs, without the organ to hold him back, and that went better. The boy was so restless that I had not had a chance to look at his face before. My first impression was right; he really was faunlike. He hadn't much head behind his ears, and his tawny fleece grew down thick to the back of his neck. His eyes were not frank and wide apart like those of the other boys, but were deep-set, gold-green in color, and seemed sensitive to the light. His mother said he got hurt oftener than all the others put together. He was always trying to ride the colts before they were broken, teasing the turkey gobbler, seeing just how much red the bull would stand for, or how sharp the new axe was.

After the concert was over, Ántonia brought out a big boxful of photographs: she and Anton in their wedding clothes, holding hands; her brother Ambrosch and his very fat wife, who had a farm of her own, and who bossed her husband, I was delighted to hear; the three Bohemian Marys and their large families.

"You wouldn't believe how steady those girls have turned out," Ántonia remarked. "Mary Svoboda's the best butter maker in all this country, and a fine manager. Her children will have a grand chance."

As Ántonia turned over the pictures the young Cuzaks stood behind her chair, looking over her shoulder with interested faces. Nina and Jan, after trying to see round the taller ones, quietly brought a chair, climbed up on it, and stood close together, looking. The little boy forgot his shyness and grinned delightedly when familiar faces came into view. In the group about Ántonia I was conscious of a kind of physical harmony. They leaned this way and that, and were not afraid to touch each other. They contemplated the photographs with pleased recognition, looked at some admiringly, as if these characters in their mother's girlhood had been remarkable people. The little children, who could not speak English, murmured comments to each other in their rich old language.

Ántonia held out a photograph of Lena that had come from San Francisco last Christmas. "Does she still look like that? She hasn't been home for six years now." Yes, it was exactly like Lena, I told her; a comely woman, a trifle too plump, in a hat a trifle too large, but with the old lazy eyes, and the old dimpled ingenuousness still lurking at the corners of her mouth.

There was a picture of Frances Harling in a befrogged riding costume that I remembered well. "Isn't she fine!" the girls murmured. They all assented. One could see that Frances had come down as a heroine in the family legend. Only Leo was unmoved.

"And there's Mr. Harling, in his grand fur coat. He was awfully rich, wasn't he, Mother?"

"He wasn't any Rockefeller," put in Master Leo, in a very low tone, which reminded me of the way in which Mrs. Shimerda had once said that my grandfather "wasn't Jesus." His habitual scepticism was like a direct inheritance from that old woman.

"None of your smart speeches," said Ambrosch severely.

Leo poked out a supple red tongue at him, but a moment later broke into a giggle at a tintype of two men, uncomfortably seated, with an awkward-looking boy in baggy clothes standing between them: Jake and Otto and I! We had it taken, I remembered, when we went to Black Hawk on the first Fourth of July I spent in Nebraska. I was glad to see Jake's grin again, and Otto's ferocious moustaches. The young Cuzaks knew all about them.

"He made Grandfather's coffin, didn't he?" Anton asked.

"Wasn't they good fellows, Jim?" Ántonia's eyes filled. "To this day I'm ashamed because I quarreled with Jake that way. I was saucy and impertinent to him, Leo, like you are with people sometimes, and I wish somebody had made me behave."

"We aren't through with you, yet," they warned me. They produced a photograph taken just before I went away to college: a tall youth in striped trousers and a straw hat, trying to look easy and jaunty.

"Tell us, Mr. Burden," said Charley, "about the rattler you killed at the dog-town. How long was he? Sometimes Mother says six feet and sometimes she says five."

These children seemed to be upon very much the same terms with Ántonia as the Harling children had been so many years before. They seemed to feel the same pride in her, and to look to her for stories and entertainment as we used to do.

It was eleven o'clock when I at last took my bag and some blankets and started for the barn with the boys. Their mother came to the door with us, and we tarried for a moment to look out at the white slope of the corral and the two ponds asleep in the moonlight, and the long sweep of the pasture under the star-sprinkled sky.

The boys told me to choose my own place in the hay-mow, and I lay down before a big window, left open in warm weather, that looked out into the stars. Ambrosch and Leo cuddled up in a hay-cave, back under the eaves, and lay giggling and whispering. They tickled each other and tossed and tumbled in the hay; and then, all at once, as if they had been shot, they were still. There was hardly a minute between giggles and bland slumber.

I lay awake for a long while, until the slow-moving moon passed my window on its way up the heavens. I was thinking about Ántonia and her children; about Anna's solicitude for her, Ambrosch's grave affection, Leo's jealous, animal little love. That moment, when they all came tumbling out of the cave into the light, was a sight any man might have come far to see. Ántonia had always been one to leave images in the mind that did not fade—that grew stronger with time. In my memory there was a succession of such pictures, fixed there like the old woodcuts of one's first primer: Ántonia kicking her bare legs against the sides of my pony when we came home in triumph with our snake; Ántonia in her black shawl and fur cap, as she stood by her father's grave in the snowstorm; Ántonia coming in with her work team along the evening skyline. She lent herself to immemorial human attitudes which we recognize by instinct as universal and true. I had not been mistaken. She was a battered woman now, not a lovely girl; but she still had that something which fires the imagination, could still stop one's breath for a moment by a look or gesture that somehow revealed the meaning in common things. She had only to stand in the orchard, to put her hand on a little crab tree and look up at the apples, to make you feel the goodness of planting and tending and harvesting at last. All the strong things of her heart came out in her body, that had been so tireless in serving generous emotions.

It was no wonder that her sons stood tall and straight. She was a rich mine of life, like the founders of early races.

II

When I awoke in the morning, long bands of sunshine were coming in at the window and reaching back under the eaves where the two boys lay. Leo was wide awake and was tickling his brother's leg with a dried cone-flower he had pulled out of the hay. Ambrosch kicked at him and turned over. I closed my eyes and pretended to be asleep. Leo lay on his back, elevated one foot, and began exercising his toes. He picked up dried flowers with his toes and brandished them in the belt of sunlight. After he had amused himself thus for some time, he rose on one elbow and began to look at me, cautiously, then critically, blinking his eyes in the light. His expression was droll; it dismissed me lightly. "This old fellow is no different from other people. He doesn't know my secret." He seemed conscious of possessing a keener power of enjoyment than other people; his quick recognitions made him frantically impatient of deliberate judgments. He always knew what he wanted without thinking.

After dressing in the hay, I washed my face in cold water at the windmill. Breakfast was ready when I entered the kitchen, and Yulka was baking griddle-cakes. The three older boys set off for the fields early. Leo and Yulka were to drive to town to meet their father, who would return from Wilber on the noon train.

"We'll only have a lunch at noon," Ántonia said, "and cook the geese for supper, when our papa will be here. I wish my Martha could come down to see you. They have a Ford car now, and she don't seem so far away from me as she used to. But her husband's crazy about his farm and about having everything just right, and they almost never get away except on Sundays. He's a handsome boy, and he'll be rich some day. Everything he takes hold of turns out well. When they bring that baby in here, and unwrap him, he looks like a little prince; Martha takes care of him so beautiful. I'm reconciled to her being away from me now, but at first I cried like I was putting her into her coffin."

We were alone in the kitchen, except for Anna, who was pouring cream into the churn. She looked up at me. "Yes, she did. We were just ashamed of Mother. She went round crying, when Martha was so happy, and the rest of us were all glad. Joe certainly was patient with you, Mother."

Ántonia nodded and smiled at herself. "I know it was silly, but I couldn't help it. I wanted her right here. She'd never been away from me a night since she was born. If Anton had made trouble about her when she was a baby, or wanted me to leave her with my mother, I wouldn't have married him. I couldn't. But he always loved her like she was his own."

"I didn't even know Martha wasn't my full sister until after she was engaged to Joe," Anna told me.

Toward the middle of the afternoon, the wagon drove in, with the father and the eldest son. I was smoking in the orchard, and as I went out to meet them, Ántonia came running down from the house and hugged the two men as if they had been away for months.

"Papa," interested me, from my first glimpse of him. He was shorter than his older sons; a crumpled little man, with run-over boot-heels, and he carried one shoulder higher than the other. But he moved very quickly, and there was an air of jaunty liveliness about him. He had a strong, ruddy color, thick black hair, a little grizzled, a curly moustache, and red lips. His smile showed the strong teeth of which his wife was so proud, and as he saw me his lively, quizzical eyes told me that he knew all about me. He looked like a humorous philosopher who had hitched up one shoulder under the burdens of life, and gone on his way having a good time when he could. He advanced to meet me and gave me a hard hand, burned red on the back and heavily coated with hair. He wore his Sunday clothes, very thick and hot for the weather, an unstarched white shirt, and a blue necktie with big white dots, like a little boy's, tied in a flowing bow. Cuzak began at once to talk about his holiday—from politeness he spoke in English.

"Mama, I wish you had see the lady dance on the slack-wire in the street at night. They throw a bright light on her and she float through the air something beautiful, like a bird! They have a dancing bear, like in the old country, and two-three merry-go-around, and people in balloons, and what you call the big wheel, Rudolph?"

"A Ferris wheel," Rudolph entered the conversation in a deep baritone voice. He was six foot two, and had a chest like a young blacksmith. "We went to the big dance in the hall behind the saloon last night, Mother, and I danced with all the girls, and so did Father. I never saw so many pretty girls. It was a Bohunk crowd, for sure. We didn't hear a word of English on the street, except from the show people, did we, Papa?"

Cuzak nodded. "And very many send word to you, Ántonia. You will excuse"—turning to me—"if I tell her." While we walked toward the house he related incidents and delivered messages in the tongue he spoke fluently, and I dropped a little behind, curious to know what their relations had become—or remained. The two seemed to be on terms of easy friendliness, touched with humor. Clearly, she was the impulse, and he the corrective. As they went up the hill he kept glancing at her sidewise, to see whether she got his point, or how she received it. I noticed later that he always looked at people sidewise, as a work-horse does at its yoke-mate. Even when he sat opposite me in the kitchen, talking, he would turn his head a little toward the clock or the stove and look at me from the side, but with frankness and good nature. This trick did not suggest duplicity or secretiveness, but merely long habit, as with the horse.

He had brought a tintype of himself and Rudolph for Ántonia's collection, and several paper bags of candy for the children. He looked a little disappointed when his wife showed him a big box of candy I had got in Denver—she hadn't let the children touch it the night before. He put his candy away in the cupboard, "for when she rains," and glanced at the box, chuckling. "I guess you must have hear about how my family ain't so small," he said.

Cuzak sat down behind the stove and watched his women folk and the little children with equal amusement. He thought they were nice, and he thought they were funny, evidently. He had been off dancing with the girls and forgetting that he was an old fellow, and now his family rather surprised him; he seemed to think it a joke that all these children should belong to him. As the younger ones slipped up to him in his retreat, he kept taking things out of his pockets; penny dolls, a wooden clown, a balloon pig that was inflated by a whistle. He beckoned to the little boy they called Jan, whispered to him, and presented him with a paper snake, gently, so as not to startle him. Looking over the boy's head he said to me, "This one is bashful. He gets left."

Cuzak had brought home with him a roll of illustrated Bohemian papers. He opened them and began to tell his wife the news, much of which seemed to relate to one person. I heard the name Vasakova, Vasakova, repeated several times with lively interest, and presently I asked him whether he were talking about the singer, Maria Vasak.

"You know? You have heard, maybe?" he asked incredulously. When I assured him that I had heard her, he pointed out her picture and told me that Vasak had broken her leg, climbing in the Austrian Alps, and would not be able to fill her engagements. He seemed delighted to find that I had heard her sing in London and in Vienna—got out his pipe and lit it to enjoy our talk the better. She came from his part of Prague. His father used to mend her shoes for her when she was a student. Cuzak questioned me about her looks, her popularity, her voice; but he particularly wanted to know whether I had noticed her tiny feet, and whether I thought she had saved much money. She was extravagant, of course, but he hoped she wouldn't squander everything and have nothing left when she was old. As a young man, working in Wienn, he had seen a good many artists who were old and poor, making one glass of beer last all evening, and "it was not very nice, that."

When the boys came in from milking and feeding, the long table was laid, and two brown geese, stuffed with apples, were put down sizzling before Ántonia. She began to carve, and Rudolph, who sat next to his mother, started the plates on their way. When everybody was served, he looked across the table at me.

"Have you been to Black Hawk lately, Mr. Burden? Then I wonder if you've heard about the Cutters?"

No, I had heard nothing at all about them.

"Then you must tell him, son, though it's a terrible thing to talk about at supper. Now, all you children be quiet, Rudolph is going to tell about the murder."

"Hurrah! The murder!" the children murmured, looking pleased and interested.

Rudolph told his story in great detail, with occasional promptings from his mother or father.

Wick Cutter and his wife had gone on living in the house that Ántonia and I knew so well, and in the way we knew so well. They grew to be very old people. He shriveled up, Ántonia said, until he looked like a little old yellow monkey, for his beard and his fringe of hair never changed color. Mrs. Cutter remained flushed and wild-eyed as we had known her, but as the years passed she became afflicted with a shaking palsy which made her nervous nod continuous instead of occasional. Her hands were so uncertain that she could no longer disfigure china, poor woman! As the couple grew older, they quarreled more and more often about the ultimate disposition of their "property." A new law was passed in the state, securing the surviving wife a third of her husband's estate under all conditions. Cutter was tormented by the fear that Mrs. Cutter would live longer than he, and that eventually her "people," whom he had always hated so violently, would inherit. Their quarrels on this subject passed the boundary of the close-growing cedars, and were heard in the street by whoever wished to loiter and listen.

One morning, two years ago, Cutter went into the hardware store and bought a pistol, saying he was going to shoot a dog, and adding that he "thought he would take a shot at an old cat while he was about it." (Here the children interrupted Rudolph's narrative by smothered giggles.)

Cutter went out behind the hardware store, put up a target, practiced for an hour or so, and then went home. At six o'clock that evening, when several men were passing the Cutter house on their way home to supper, they heard a pistol shot. They paused and were looking doubtfully at one another, when another shot came crashing through an upstairs window. They ran into the house and found Wick Cutter lying on a sofa in his upstairs bedroom, with his throat torn open, bleeding on a roll of sheets he had placed beside his head.

"Walk in, gentlemen," he said weakly. "I am alive, you see, and competent. You are witnesses that I have survived my wife. You will find her in her own room. Please make your examination at once, so that there will be no mistake."

One of the neighbors telephoned for a doctor, while the others went into Mrs. Cutter's room. She was lying on her bed, in her nightgown and wrapper, shot through the heart. Her husband must have come in while she was taking her afternoon nap and shot her, holding the revolver near her breast. Her nightgown was burned from the powder.

The horrified neighbors rushed back to Cutter. He opened his eyes and said distinctly, "Mrs. Cutter is quite dead, gentlemen, and I am conscious. My affairs are in order." Then, Rudolph said, "he let go and died."

On his desk the coroner found a letter, dated at five o'clock that afternoon. It stated that he had just shot his wife; that any will she might secretly have made would be invalid, as he survived her. He meant to shoot himself at six o'clock and would, if he had strength, fire a shot through the window in the hope that passersby might come in and see him "before life was extinct," as he wrote.

"Now, would you have thought that man had such a cruel heart?" Ántonia turned to me after the story was told. "To go and do that poor woman out of any comfort she might have from his money after he was gone!"

"Did you ever hear of anybody else that killed himself for spite, Mr. Burden?" asked Rudolph.

I admitted that I hadn't. Every lawyer learns over and over how strong a motive hate can be, but in my collection of legal anecdotes I had nothing to match this one. When I asked how much the estate amounted to, Rudolph said it was a little over a hundred thousand dollars.

Cuzak gave me a twinkling, sidelong glance. "The lawyers, they got a good deal of it, sure," he said merrily.

A hundred thousand dollars: so that was the fortune that had been scraped together by such hard dealing, and that Cutter himself had died for in the end!

After supper Cuzak and I took a stroll in the orchard and sat down by the windmill to smoke. He told me his story as if it were my business to know it.

His father was a shoemaker, his uncle a furrier, and he, being a younger son, was apprenticed to the latter's trade. You never got anywhere working for your relatives, he said, so when he was a journeyman he went to Vienna and worked in a big fur shop, earning good money. But a young fellow who liked a good time didn't save anything in Vienna; there were too many pleasant ways of spending every night what he'd made in the day. After three years there, he came to New York. He was badly advised and went to work on furs during a strike, when the factories were offering big wages. The strikers won, and Cuzak was blacklisted. As he had a few hundred dollars ahead, he decided to go to Florida and raise oranges. He had always thought he would like to raise oranges! The second year a hard frost killed his young grove, and he fell ill with malaria. He came to Nebraska to visit his cousin, Anton Jelinek, and to look about. When he began to look about, he saw Ántonia, and she was exactly the kind of girl he had always been hunting for. They were married at once, though he had to borrow money from his cousin to buy the wedding ring.

"It was a pretty hard job, breaking up this place and making the first crops grow," he said, pushing back his hat and scratching his grizzled hair. "Sometimes I git awful sore on this place and want to quit, but my wife she always say we better stick it out. The babies come along pretty fast, so it look like it be hard to move, anyhow. I guess she was right, all right. We got this place clear now. We pay only twenty dollars an acre then, and I been offered a hundred. We bought another quarter ten years ago, and we got it most paid for. We got plenty boys; we can work a lot of land. Yes, she is a good wife for a poor man. She ain't always so strict with me, neither. Sometimes maybe I drink a little too much beer in town, and when I come home she don't say nothing. She don't ask me no questions. We always get along fine, her and me, like at first.

The children don't make trouble between us, like sometimes happens." He lit another pipe and pulled on it contentedly.

I found Cuzak a most companionable fellow. He asked me a great many questions about my trip through Bohemia, about Vienna and the Ringstrasse and the theaters.

"Gee! I like to go back there once, when the boys is big enough to farm the place. Sometimes when I read the papers from the old country, I pretty near run away," he confessed with a little laugh. "I never did think how I would be a settled man like this."

He was still, as Ántonia said, a city man. He liked theaters and lighted streets and music and a game of dominoes after the day's work was over. His sociability was stronger than his acquisitive instinct. He liked to live day by day and night by night, sharing in the excitement of the crowd. Yet his wife had managed to hold him here on a farm, in one of the loneliest countries in the world.

I could see the little chap, sitting here every evening by the windmill, nursing his pipe and listening to the silence; the wheeze of the pump, the grunting of the pigs, an occasional squawking when the hens were disturbed by a rat. It did rather seem to me that Cuzak had been made the instrument of Ántonia's special mission. This was a fine life, certainly, but it wasn't the kind of life he had wanted to live. I wondered whether the life that was right for one was ever right for two!

I asked Cuzak if he didn't find it hard to do without the gay company he had always been used to. He knocked out his pipe against an upright, sighed, and dropped it into his pocket.

"At first I near go crazy with lonesomeness," he said frankly, "but my woman is got such a warm heart. She always make it as good for me as she could. Now it ain't so bad; I can begin to have some fun with my boys, already!"

As we walked toward the house, Cuzak cocked his hat jauntily over one ear and looked up at the moon. "Gee!" he said in a hushed voice, as if he had just wakened up. "It don't seem like I am away from there twenty-six year!"

III

After dinner the next day I said goodbye and drove back to Hastings to take the train for Black Hawk. Ántonia and her children gathered round my buggy before I started, and even the little ones looked up at me with friendly faces. Leo and Ambrosch ran ahead to open the lane gate. When I reached the bottom of the hill, I glanced back. The group was still there by the windmill. Ántonia was waving her apron.

At the gate Ambrosch lingered beside my buggy, resting his arm on the wheel rim. Leo slipped through the fence and ran off into the pasture.

"That's like him," his brother said with a shrug. "He's a crazy kid. Maybe he's sorry to have you go, and maybe he's jealous. He's jealous of anybody Mother makes a fuss over, even the priest."

I found I hated to leave this boy, with his pleasant voice and his fine head and eyes. He looked very manly as he stood there without a hat, the wind rippling his shirt about his brown neck and shoulders.

"Don't forget that you and Rudolph are going hunting with me up on the Niobrara next summer," I said. "Your father's agreed to let you off after harvest."

He smiled. "I won't likely forget. I've never had such a nice thing offered to me before. I don't know what makes you so nice to us boys," he added, blushing.

"Oh, yes, you do!" I said, gathering up my reins.

He made no answer to this, except to smile at me with unabashed pleasure and affection as I drove away.

My day in Black Hawk was disappointing. Most of my old friends were dead or had moved away. Strange children, who meant nothing to me, were playing in the Harling's big yard when I passed; the mountain-ash had been cut down, and only a sprouting stump was left of the tall Lombardy poplar that used to guard the gate. I hurried on. The rest of the morning I spent with Anton Jelinek, under a shady cottonwood tree in the yard behind his saloon. While I was having my midday dinner at the hotel, I met one of the old lawyers who was still in practice, and he took me up to his office and talked over the Cutter case with me. After that, I scarcely knew how to put in the time until the night express was due.

I took a long walk north of the town, out into the pastures where the land was so rough that it had never been ploughed up, and the long red grass of early times still grew shaggy over the draws and hillocks. Out there I felt at home again. Overhead the sky was that indescribable blue of autumn: bright and shadowless, hard as enamel. To the south I could see the dun-shaded river bluffs that used to look so big to me, and all about stretched drying cornfields, of the pale-gold color I remembered so well. Russian thistles were blowing across the uplands and piling against the wire fences like barricades. Along the cattle-paths the plumes of goldenrod were already fading into sun-warmed velvet, gray with gold threads in it. I had escaped from the curious depression that hangs over little towns, and my mind was full of pleasant things—trips I meant to take with the Cuzak boys, in the Bad Lands and up on the Stinking Water. There were enough Cuzaks to play with for a long while yet. Even after the boys grew up, there would always be Cuzak himself! I meant to tramp along a few miles of lighted streets with Cuzak.

As I wandered over those rough pastures, I had the good luck to stumble upon a bit of the first road that went from Black Hawk out to the north country; to my grandfather's farm, then on to the Shimerdas' and to the Norwegian settlement. Everywhere else it had been ploughed under when the highways were surveyed; this half-mile or so within the pasture fence was all that was left of that old road which used to run like a wild thing across the open prairie, clinging to the high places and circling and doubling like a rabbit before the hounds.

On the level land the tracks had almost disappeared—were mere shadings in the grass, and a stranger would not have noticed them. But wherever the road had crossed a draw, it was easy to find. The rains had made channels of the wheel ruts and washed them so deeply that the sod had never healed over them. They looked like gashes torn by a grizzly's claws, on the slopes where the farm wagons used to lurch up out of the hollows with a pull that brought curling muscles on the smooth hips of the horses. I sat down and watched the haystacks turn rosy in the slanting sunlight.

This was the road over which Ántonia and I came on that night when we got off the train at Black Hawk and were bedded down in the straw, wondering children, being taken we knew not whither. I had only to close my eyes to hear the rumbling of the wagons in the dark, and to be again overcome by that obliterating strangeness. The feelings of that night were so near that I could reach out and touch them with my hand. I had the sense of coming home to myself, and of having found out what a little circle man's experience is. For Ántonia and for me, this had been the road of Destiny—had taken us to those early accidents of fortune which predetermined for us all that we can ever be. Now I understood that the same road was to bring us together again. Whatever we had missed, we possessed together the precious, the incommunicable past.

THE TROLL GARDEN

CONTENTS

"We must not look at Goblin men,
We must not buy their fruits;
Who knows upon what soil they fed
Their hungry, thirsty roots?"

—Christina Rossetti,
"Goblin Market"

Flavia and Her Artists

As THE TRAIN neared Tarrytown, Imogen Willard began to wonder why she had consented to be one of Flavia's house party at all. She had not felt enthusiastic about it since leaving the city, and was experiencing a prolonged ebb of purpose, a current of chilling indecision, under which she vainly sought for the motive which had induced her to accept Flavia's invitation.

Perhaps it was a vague curiosity to see Flavia's husband, who had been the magician of her childhood and the hero of innumerable Arabian fairy tales. Perhaps it was a desire to see M. Roux, whom Flavia had announced as the especial attraction of the occasion. Perhaps it was a wish to study that remarkable woman in her own setting.

Imogen admitted a mild curiosity concerning Flavia. She was in the habit of taking people rather seriously, but somehow found it impossible to take Flavia so, because of the very vehemence and insistence with which Flavia demanded it. Submerged in her studies, Imogen had, of late years, seen very little of Flavia; but Flavia, in her hurried visits to New York, between her excursions from studio to studio—her luncheons with this lady who had to play at a matinee, and her dinners with that singer who had an evening concert—had seen enough of her friend's handsome daughter to conceive for her an inclination of such violence and assurance as only Flavia could afford. The fact that Imogen had shown rather marked capacity in certain esoteric lines of scholarship, and had decided to specialize in a well-sounding branch of philology at the Ecole des Chartes, had fairly placed her in that category of "interesting people" whom Flavia considered her natural affinities, and lawful prey.

When Imogen stepped upon the station platform she was immediately appropriated by her hostess, whose commanding figure and assurance of attire she had recognized from a distance. She was hurried into a high tilbury and Flavia, taking the driver's cushion beside her, gathered up the reins with an experienced hand.

"My dear girl," she remarked, as she turned the horses up the street,

"I was afraid the train might be late. M. Roux insisted upon coming up by boat and did not arrive until after seven."

"To think of M. Roux's being in this part of the world at all, and subject to the vicissitudes of river boats! Why in the world did he come over?" queried Imogen with lively interest. "He is the sort of man who must dissolve and become a shadow outside of Paris."

"Oh, we have a houseful of the most interesting people," said Flavia, professionally. "We have actually managed to get Ivan Schemetzkin. He was ill in California at the close of his concert tour, you know, and he is recuperating with us, after his wearing journey from the coast. Then there is Jules Martel, the painter; Signor Donati, the tenor; Professor Schotte, who has dug up Assyria, you know; Restzhoff, the Russian chemist; Alcée Buisson, the philologist; Frank Wellington, the novelist; and Will Maidenwood, the editor of *Woman*. Then there is my second cousin, Jemima Broadwood, who made such a hit in Pinero's comedy last winter, and Frau Lichtenfeld. *Have* you read her?"

Imogen confessed her utter ignorance of Frau Lichtenfeld, and Flavia went on.

"Well, she is a most remarkable person; one of those advanced German women, a militant iconoclast, and this drive will not be long enough to permit of my telling you her history. Such a story! Her novels were the talk of all Germany when I was there last, and several of them have been suppressed—an honor in Germany, I understand. *At Whose Door* has been translated. I am so unfortunate as not to read German."

"I'm all excitement at the prospect of meeting Miss Broadwood," said Imogen. "I've seen her in nearly everything she does. Her stage personality is delightful. She always reminds me of a nice, clean, pink-and-white boy who has just had his cold bath, and come down all aglow for a run before breakfast."

"Yes, but isn't it unfortunate that she will limit herself to those minor comedy parts that are so little appreciated in this country? One ought to be satisfied with nothing less than the best, ought one?" The peculiar, breathy tone in which Flavia always uttered that word "best," the most worn in her vocabulary, always jarred on Imogen and always made her obdurate.

"I don't at all agree with you," she said reservedly. "I thought everyone admitted that the most remarkable thing about Miss Broadwood is her admirable sense of fitness, which is rare enough in her profession."

Flavia could not endure being contradicted; she always seemed to regard it in the light of a defeat, and usually colored unbecomingly. Now she changed the subject.

"Look, my dear," she cried, "there is Frau Lichtenfeld now, coming to meet us. Doesn't she look as if she had just escaped out of Valhalla? She is actually over six feet."

Imogen saw a woman of immense stature, in a very short skirt and a broad, flapping sun hat, striding down the hillside at a long, swinging gait. The refugee from Valhalla approached, panting. Her heavy Teutonic features were scarlet from the rigor of her exercise, and her hair, under her flapping sun hat, was tightly befrizzled about her brow. She fixed her sharp little eyes upon Imogen and extended both her hands.

"So this is the little friend?" she cried, in a rolling baritone.

Imogen was quite as tall as her hostess; but everything, she reflected, is comparative. After the introduction Flavia apologized.

"I wish I could ask you to drive up with us, Frau Lichtenfeld."

"Ah, no!" cried the giantess, drooping her head in humorous caricature of a time-honored pose of the heroines of sentimental romances. "It has never been my fate to be fitted into corners. I have never known the sweet privileges of the tiny."

Laughing, Flavia started the ponies, and the colossal woman, standing in the middle of the dusty road, took off her wide hat and waved them a farewell which, in scope of gesture, recalled the salute of a plumed cavalier.

When they arrived at the house, Imogen looked about her with keen curiosity, for this was veritably the work of Flavia's hands, the materialization of hopes long deferred. They passed directly into a large, square hall with a gallery on three sides, studio fashion. This opened at one end into a Dutch breakfast room, beyond which was the large dining room. At the other end of the hall was the music room. There was a smoking room, which one entered through the library behind the staircase. On the second floor there was the same general arrangement: a square hall and, opening from it, the guest chambers, or, as Miss Broadwood termed them, the "cages."

When Imogen went to her room, the guests had begun to return from their various afternoon excursions. Boys were gliding through the halls with ice water, covered trays, and flowers, colliding with maids and valets who carried shoes and other articles of wearing apparel. Yet, all this was done in response to inaudible bells, on felt soles, and in hushed voices, so that there was very little confusion about it.

Flavia had at last built her house and hewn out her seven pillars; there could be no doubt now that the asylum for talent, the sanatorium of the arts, so long projected, was an accomplished fact. Her ambition had long ago outgrown the dimensions of her house on Prairie Avenue; besides, she had bitterly complained that in Chicago traditions were against her. Her project had been delayed by Arthur's doggedly standing out for the Michigan woods, but Flavia knew well enough that certain of the *rares aves*—"the best"—could not be lured so far away from the seaport, so she declared herself for the historic Hudson and knew no retreat. The establishing of a New York office had at length overthrown Arthur's last valid objection to quitting the lake country for three months of the year; and Arthur could be wearied into anything, as those who knew him knew.

Flavia's house was the mirror of her exultation; it was a temple to the gods of Victory, a sort of triumphal arch. In her earlier days she had swallowed experiences that would have unmanned one of less torrential enthusiasm or blind pertinacity. But, of late years, her determination had told; she saw less and less of those mysterious persons with mysterious obstacles in their path and mysterious grievances against the world, who had once frequented her house on Prairie Avenue. In the stead of this multitude of the unarrived, she had now the few, the select, "the best." Of all that band of indigent retainers who had once fed at her board like the suitors in the halls of Penelope, only Alcée Buisson still retained his right of entrée. He alone had remembered that ambition hath a knapsack at his back, wherein he puts alms to oblivion, and he alone had been considerate enough to do what Flavia had expected of him, and give his name a current value in the world. Then, as Miss Broadwood put it, "he was her first real one"—and Flavia, like Mohammed, could remember her first believer.

The "House of Song," as Miss Broadwood had called it, was the outcome of Flavia's more exalted strategies. A woman who made less a point of sympathizing with their delicate organisms might have sought to plunge these phosphorescent pieces into the tepid bath of domestic life; but Flavia's discernment was deeper. This must be a refuge where the shrinking soul, the sensitive brain, should be unconstrained, where the caprice of fancy should outweigh the civil code if necessary. She considered that this much Arthur owed her; for she, in her turn, had made concessions. Flavia had, indeed, quite an equipment of epigrams to the effect that our century creates the iron genii which evolve its fairy tales: but the fact that her husband's name was annually painted upon some ten thousand threshing machines in reality contributed very little to her happiness.

Arthur Hamilton was born and had spent his boyhood in the West Indies, and physically he had never lost the brand of the tropics. His father, after inventing the machine which bore his name, had returned to the States to patent and manufacture it. After leaving college, Arthur had spent five years ranching in the West and traveling abroad. Upon his father's death he had returned to Chicago and, to the astonishment of all his friends, had taken up the business—without any demonstration of enthusiasm, but with quiet perseverance, marked ability, and amazing industry. Why or how a self-sufficient, rather ascetic man of thirty, indifferent in manner, wholly negative in all other personal relations, should have doggedly wooed and finally married Flavia Malcolm was a problem that had vexed older heads than Imogen's.

While Imogen was dressing she heard a knock at her door, and a young woman entered whom she at once recognized as Jemima Broadwood—"Jimmy" Broadwood she was called by people in her own profession. While there was something unmistakably professional in her frank savoir-faire, Jimmy's was one of those faces to which the rouge never seems to stick. Her eyes were keen and gray as a windy April sky, and so far from having been seared by calcium lights, you might have fancied they had never looked on anything less bucolic than growing fields and country fairs. She wore her thick, brown hair short and parted at the side; and, rather than hinting at freakishness, this seemed admirably in keeping with her fresh, boyish countenance. She extended to Imogen a large, well-shaped hand which it was a pleasure to clasp.

"Ah! You are Miss Willard, and I see I need not introduce myself. Flavia said you were kind enough to express a wish to meet me, and I preferred to meet you alone. Do you mind if I smoke?"

"Why, certainly not," said Imogen, somewhat disconcerted and looking hurriedly about for matches.

"There, be calm, I'm always prepared," said Miss Broadwood, checking Imogen's flurry with a soothing gesture, and producing an oddly fashioned silver match-case from some mysterious recess in her dinner gown. She sat down in a deep chair, crossed her patent-leather Oxfords, and lit her cigarette. "This matchbox," she went on meditatively, "once belonged to a Prussian officer. He shot himself in his bathtub, and I bought it at the sale of his effects."

Imogen had not yet found any suitable reply to make to this rather irrelevant confidence, when Miss Broadwood turned to her cordially: "I'm awfully glad you've come, Miss Willard, though I've not quite decided why you did it. I wanted very much to meet you. Flavia gave me your thesis to read."

"Why, how funny!" ejaculated Imogen.

"On the contrary," remarked Miss Broadwood. "I thought it decidedly lacked humor."

"I meant," stammered Imogen, beginning to feel very much like Alice in Wonderland, "I meant that I thought it rather strange Mrs. Hamilton should fancy you would be interested."

Miss Broadwood laughed heartily. "Now, don't let my rudeness frighten you. Really, I found it very interesting, and no end impressive. You see, most people in my profession are good for absolutely nothing else, and therefore, they have a deep and abiding conviction that in some other line they might have shone. Strange to say, scholarship is the object of our envious and particular admiration. Anything in type impresses us greatly; that's why so many of us marry authors or newspapermen and lead miserable lives." Miss Broadwood saw that she had rather disconcerted Imogen, and blithely tacked in another direction. "You see," she went on, tossing aside her half-consumed cigarette, "some years ago Flavia would not have deemed me worthy to open the pages of your thesis—nor to be one of her house party of the chosen, for that matter. I've Pinero to thank for both pleasures. It all depends on the class of business I'm playing whether I'm in favor or not. Flavia is my second cousin, you know, so I can say whatever disagreeable things I choose with perfect good grace. I'm quite desperate for someone to laugh with, so I'm going to fasten myself upon you—for, of course, one can't expect any of these gypsy-dago people to see anything funny. I don't intend you shall lose the humor of the situation. What do you think of Flavia's infirmary for the arts, anyway?"

"Well, it's rather too soon for me to have any opinion at all," said Imogen, as she again turned to her dressing. "So far, you are the only one of the artists I've met."

"One of them?" echoed Miss Broadwood. "One of the *artists*? My offense may be rank, my dear, but I really don't deserve that. Come, now, whatever badges of my tribe I may bear upon me, just let me divest you of any notion that I take myself seriously."

Imogen turned from the mirror in blank astonishment and sat down on the arm of a chair, facing her visitor. "I can't fathom you at all, Miss Broadwood," she said frankly. "Why shouldn't you take yourself seriously? What's the use of beating about the bush? Surely you know that you are one of the few players on this side of the water who have at all the spirit of natural or ingenuous comedy?"

"Thank you, my dear. Now we are quite even about the thesis, aren't we? Oh, did you mean it? Well, you *are* a clever girl. But you see it doesn't do to permit oneself to look at it in that light. If we do, we always go to pieces and waste our substance astarring as the unhappy daughter of the Capulets. But there, I hear Flavia coming to take you down; and just remember I'm not one of them—the artists, I mean."

Flavia conducted Imogen and Miss Broadwood downstairs. As they reached the lower hall they heard voices from the music room, and dim figures were lurking in the shadows under the gallery, but their hostess led straight to the smoking room. The June evening was chilly, and a fire had been lighted in the fireplace. Through the deepening dusk, the firelight flickered upon the pipes and curious weapons on the wall and threw an orange glow over the Turkish hangings. One side of the smoking room was entirely of glass, separating it from the conservatory, which was flooded with white light from the electric bulbs. There was about the darkened room some suggestion of certain chambers in the *Arabian Nights,* opening on a court of palms. Perhaps it was partially this memory-evoking suggestion that caused Imogen to start so violently when she saw dimly, in a blur of shadow, the figure of a man, who sat smoking in a low, deep chair before the fire. He was long, and thin, and brown. His long, nerveless hands drooped from the arms of his chair. A brown mustache shaded his mouth, and his eyes were sleepy and apathetic. When Imogen entered he rose indolently and gave her his hand, his manner barely courteous.

"I am glad you arrived promptly, Miss Willard," he said with an indifferent drawl. "Flavia was afraid you might be late. You had a pleasant ride up, I hope?"

"Oh, very, thank you, Mr. Hamilton," she replied, feeling that he did not particularly care whether she replied at all.

Flavia explained that she had not yet had time to dress for dinner, as she had been attending to Mr. Will Maidenwood, who had become faint after hurting his finger in an obdurate window, and immediately excused herself. As she left, Hamilton turned to Miss Broadwood with a rather spiritless smile.

"Well, Jimmy," he remarked, "I brought up a piano box full of fireworks for the boys. How do you suppose we'll manage to keep them until the Fourth?"

"We can't, unless we steel ourselves to deny there are any on the premises," said Miss Broadwood, seating herself on a low stool by Hamilton's chair and leaning back against the mantel. "Have you seen Helen, and has she told you the tragedy of the tooth?"

"She met me at the station, with her tooth wrapped up in tissue paper. I had tea with her an hour ago. Better sit down, Miss Willard"; he rose and pushed a chair toward Imogen, who was standing peering into the conservatory. "We are scheduled to dine at seven, but they seldom get around before eight."

By this time Imogen had made out that here the plural pronoun, third person, always referred to the artists. As Hamilton's manner did not spur one to cordial intercourse, and as his attention seemed directed to Miss Broadwood, insofar as it could be said to be directed to anyone, she sat down facing the conservatory and watched him, unable to decide in how far he was identical with the man who had first met Flavia Malcolm in her mother's house, twelve years ago. Did he at all remember having known her as a little girl, and why did his indifference hurt her so, after all these years? Had some remnant of her childish affection for him gone on living, somewhere down in the sealed caves of her consciousness, and had she really expected to find it possible to be fond of him again? Suddenly she saw a light in the man's sleepy eyes, an unmistakable expression of interest and pleasure that fairly startled her. She turned quickly in the direction of his glance, and saw Flavia, just entering, dressed for dinner and lit by the effulgence of her most radiant manner. Most people considered Flavia handsome, and there was no gainsaying that she carried her five-and-thirty years splendidly. Her figure had never grown matronly, and her face was of the sort that does not show wear. Its blond tints were as fresh and enduring as enamel—and quite as hard. Its usual expression was one of tense, often strained, animation, which compressed her lips nervously. A perfect scream of animation, Miss Broadwood had called it, created and maintained by sheer, indomitable force of will. Flavia's appearance on any scene whatever made a ripple, caused a certain agitation and recognition and, among impressionable people, a certain uneasiness. For all her sparkling assurance of manner, Flavia was certainly always ill at ease and, even more certainly, anxious. She seemed not convinced of the established order of material things, seemed always trying to conceal her feeling that walls might crumble, chasms open, or the fabric of her life fly to the winds in irretrievable entanglement. At least this was the impression Imogen got from that note in Flavia which was so manifestly false.

Hamilton's keen, quick, satisfied glance at his wife had recalled to Imogen all her inventory of speculations about them. She looked at him with compassionate surprise. As a child she had never permitted herself to believe that Hamilton cared at all for the woman who had taken him away from her; and since she had begun to think about them again, it had never occurred to her that anyone could become attached to Flavia in that deeply personal and exclusive sense. It seemed quite as irrational as trying to possess oneself of Broadway at noon.

When they went out to dinner Imogen realized the completeness of Flavia's triumph. They were people of one name, mostly, like kings—people whose names stirred the imagination like a romance or a melody. With the notable exception of M. Roux, Imogen had seen most of them before, either in concert halls or lecture rooms; but they looked noticeably older and dimmer than she remembered them.

Opposite her sat Schemetzkin, the Russian pianist, a short, corpulent man, with an apoplectic face and purplish skin, his thick, iron-gray hair tossed back from his forehead. Next to the German giantess sat the Italian tenor—the tiniest of men—pale, with soft, light hair, much in disorder, very red lips, and fingers yellowed by cigarettes. Frau Lichtenfeld shone in a gown of emerald green, fitting so closely as to enhance her natural floridness. However, to do the good lady justice, let her attire be never so modest, it gave an effect of barbaric splendor. At her left sat Herr Schotte, the Assyriologist, whose features were effectually concealed by the convergence of his hair and beard, and whose glasses were continually falling into his plate. This gentleman had removed more tons of earth in the course of his explorations than had any of his confreres, and his vigorous attack upon his food seemed to suggest the strenuous nature of his accustomed toil. His eyes were small and deeply set, and his forehead bulged fiercely above his eyes in a bony ridge. His heavy brows completed the leonine suggestion of his face. Even to Imogen, who knew something of his work and greatly respected it, he was entirely too reminiscent of the Stone Age to be altogether an agreeable dinner companion. He seemed, indeed, to have absorbed something of the savagery of those early types of life which he continually studied.

Frank Wellington, the young Kansas man who had been two years out of Harvard and had published three historical novels, sat next to Mr. Will Maidenwood, who was still pale from his recent sufferings and carried his hand bandaged. They took little part in the general conversation but, like the lion and the unicorn, were always at it, discussing, every time they met, whether there were or were not passages in Mr. Wellington's works which should be eliminated, out of consideration for the Young Person. Wellington had fallen into the hands of a great American syndicate which most effectually befriended struggling authors whose struggles were in the right direction, and which had guaranteed to make him famous before he was thirty. Feeling the security of his position he stoutly defended those passages which jarred upon the sensitive nerves of the young editor of *Woman*. Maidenwood, in the smoothest of voices, urged the necessity of the author's recognizing certain restrictions at the outset, and Miss Broadwood, who joined the argument quite without invitation or encouragement, seconded him with pointed and malicious remarks which caused the young editor manifest discomfort. Restzhoff, the chemist, demanded the attention of the entire company for his exposition of his devices for manufacturing ice cream from vegetable oils and for administering drugs in bonbons.

Flavia, always noticeably restless at dinner, was somewhat apathetic toward the advocate of peptonized chocolate and was plainly concerned about the sudden departure of M. Roux, who had announced that it would be necessary for him to leave tomorrow. M. Emile Roux, who sat at Flavia's right, was a man in middle life and quite bald, clearly without personal vanity, though his publishers preferred to circulate only those of his portraits taken in his ambrosial youth. Imogen was considerably shocked at his unlikeness to the slender, black-stocked Rolla he had looked at twenty. He had declined into the florid, settled heaviness of indifference and approaching age. There was, however, a certain look of durability and solidity about him; the look of a man who has earned the right to be fat and bald, and even silent at dinner if he chooses.

Throughout the discussion between Wellington and Will Maidenwood, though they invited his participation, he remained silent, betraying no sign either of interest or contempt. Since his arrival he had directed most of his conversation to Hamilton, who had never read one of his twelve great novels. This perplexed and troubled Flavia. On the night of his arrival Jules Martel had enthusiastically declared, "There are schools and schools, manners and manners; but Roux is Roux, and Paris sets its watches by his clock." Flavia had already repeated this remark to Imogen. It haunted her, and each time she quoted it she was impressed anew.

Flavia shifted the conversation uneasily, evidently exasperated and excited by her repeated failures to draw the novelist out. "Monsieur Roux," she began abruptly, with her most animated smile, "I remember so well a statement I read some years ago in your *Mes Etudes des Femmes* to the effect that you had never met a really intellectual woman. May I ask, without being impertinent, whether that assertion still represents your experience?"

"I meant, madam," said the novelist conservatively, "intellectual in a sense very special, as we say of men in whom the purely intellectual functions seem almost independent."

"And you still think a woman so constituted a mythical personage?" persisted Flavia, nodding her head encouragingly.

"Une Méduse, madam, who, if she were discovered, would transmute us all into stone," said the novelist, bowing gravely. "If she existed at all," he added deliberately, "it was my business to find her, and she has cost me many a vain pilgrimage. Like Rudel of Tripoli, I have crossed seas and penetrated deserts to seek her out. I have, indeed, encountered women of learning whose industry I have been compelled to respect; many who have possessed beauty and charm and perplexing cleverness; a few with remarkable information and a sort of fatal facility."

"And Mrs. Browning, George Eliot, and your own Mme. Dudevant?" queried Flavia with that fervid enthusiasm with which she could, on occasion, utter things simply incomprehensible for their banality—at her feats of this sort Miss Broadwood was wont to sit breathless with admiration.

"Madam, while the intellect was undeniably present in the performances of those women, it was only the stick of the rocket. Although this woman has eluded me I have studied her conditions and perturbances as astronomers conjecture the orbits of planets they have never seen. If she exists, she is probably neither an artist nor a woman with a mission, but an obscure personage, with imperative intellectual needs, who absorbs rather than produces."

Flavia, still nodding nervously, fixed a strained glance of interrogation upon M. Roux. "Then you think she would be a woman whose first necessity would be to know, whose instincts would be satisfied only with the best, who could draw from others; appreciative, merely?"

The novelist lifted his dull eyes to his interlocutress with an untranslatable smile and a slight inclination of his shoulders. "Exactly so; you are really remarkable, madam," he added, in a tone of cold astonishment.

After dinner the guests took their coffee in the music room, where Schemetzkin sat down at the piano to drum ragtime, and give his celebrated imitation of the boarding-school girl's execution of Chopin. He flatly refused to play anything more serious, and would practice only in the morning, when he had the music room to himself. Hamilton and M. Roux repaired to the smoking room to discuss the necessity of extending the tax on manufactured articles in France—one of those conversations which particularly exasperated Flavia.

After Schemetzkin had grimaced and tortured the keyboard with malicious vulgarities for half an hour, Signor Donati, to put an end to his torture, consented to sing, and Flavia and Imogen went to fetch Arthur to play his accompaniments. Hamilton rose with an annoyed look and placed his cigarette on the mantel. "Why yes, Flavia, I'll accompany him, provided he sings something with a melody, Italian arias or ballads, and provided the recital is not interminable."

"You will join us, M. Roux?"

"Thank you, but I have some letters to write," replied the novelist, bowing.

As Flavia had remarked to Imogen, "Arthur really played accompaniments remarkably well." To hear him recalled vividly the days of her childhood, when he always used to spend his business vacations at her mother's home in Maine. He had possessed for her that almost hypnotic influence which young men sometimes exert upon little girls. It was a sort of phantom love affair, subjective and fanciful, a precocity of instinct, like that tender and maternal concern which some little girls feel for their dolls. Yet this childish infatuation is capable of all the depressions and exaltations of love itself; it has its bitter jealousies, cruel disappointments, its exacting caprices.

Summer after summer she had awaited his coming and wept at his departure, indifferent to the gayer young men who had called her their sweetheart and laughed at everything she said. Although Hamilton never said so, she had been always quite sure that he was fond of her. When he pulled her up the river to hunt for fairy knolls shut about by low, hanging willows, he was often silent for an hour at a time, yet she never felt he was bored or was neglecting her. He would lie in the sand smoking, his eyes half-closed, watching her play, and she was always conscious that she was entertaining him. Sometimes he would take a copy of *Alice in Wonderland* in his pocket, and no one could read it as he could, laughing at her with his dark eyes, when anything amused him. No one else could laugh so, with just their eyes, and without moving a muscle of their face. Though he usually smiled at passages that seemed not at all funny to the child, she always laughed gleefully, because he was so seldom moved to mirth that any such demonstration delighted her and she took the credit of it entirely to herself. Her own inclination had been for serious stories, with sad endings, like "The Little Mermaid," which he had once told her in an unguarded moment when she had a cold, and was put to bed early on her birthday night and cried because she could not have her party. But he highly disapproved of this preference, and had called it a morbid taste, and always shook his finger at her when she asked for the story. When she had been particularly good, or particularly neglected by other people, then he would sometimes melt and tell her the story, and never laugh at her if she enjoyed the "sad ending" even to tears. When Flavia had taken him away and he came no more, she wept inconsolably for the space of two weeks and refused to learn her lessons. Then she found the story of the Little Mermaid herself, and forgot him.

Imogen had discovered at dinner that he could still smile at one secretly, out of his eyes, and that he had the old manner of outwardly seeming bored, but letting you know that he was not. She was intensely curious about his exact state of feeling toward his wife, and more curious still to catch a sense of his final adjustment to the conditions of life in general. This, she could not help feeling, she might get again—if she could have him alone for an hour, in some place where there was a little river and a sandy cove bordered by drooping willows, and a blue sky seen through white sycamore boughs.

That evening, before retiring, Flavia entered her husband's room, where he sat in his smoking jacket, in one of his favorite low chairs.

"I suppose it's a grave responsibility to bring an ardent, serious young thing like Imogen here among all these fascinating personages," she remarked reflectively. "But, after all, one can never tell. These grave, silent girls have their own charm, even for facile people."

"Oh, so that is your plan?" queried her husband dryly. "I was wondering why you got her up here. She doesn't seem to mix well with the faciles. At least, so it struck me."

Flavia paid no heed to this jeering remark, but repeated, "No, after all, it may not be a bad thing."

"Then do consign her to that shaken reed, the tenor," said her husband yawning. "I remember she used to have a taste for the pathetic."

"And then," remarked Flavia coquettishly, "after all, I owe her mother a return in kind. She was not afraid to trifle with destiny."

But Hamilton was asleep in his chair.

Next morning Imogen found only Miss Broadwood in the breakfast room.

"Good morning, my dear girl, whatever are you doing up so early? They never breakfast before eleven. Most of them take their coffee in their room. Take this place by me."

Miss Broadwood looked particularly fresh and encouraging in her blue serge walking skirt, her open jacket displaying an expanse of stiff, white shirt bosom dotted with some almost imperceptible figure, and a dark-blue-and-white necktie, neatly knotted under her wide, rolling collar. She wore a white rosebud in the lapel of her coat, and decidedly she seemed more than ever like a nice, clean boy on his holiday. Imogen was just hoping that they would breakfast alone when Miss Broadwood exclaimed, "Ah, there comes Arthur with the children. That's the reward or early rising in this house; you never get to see the youngsters at any other time."

Hamilton entered, followed by two dark, handsome little boys. The girl, who was very tiny, blonde like her mother, and exceedingly frail, he carried in his arms. The boys came up and said good morning with an ease and cheerfulness uncommon, even in well-bred children, but the little girl hid her face on her father's shoulder.

"She's a shy little lady," he explained as he put her gently down in her chair. "I'm afraid she's like her father; she can't seem to get used to meeting people. And you, Miss Willard, did you dream of the White Rabbit or the Little Mermaid?"

"Oh, I dreamed of them all! All the personages of that buried civilization," cried Imogen, delighted that his estranged manner of the night before had entirely vanished and feeling that, somehow, the old confidential relations had been restored during the night.

"Come, William," said Miss Broadwood, turning to the younger of the two boys, "and what did you dream about?"

"We dreamed," said William gravely—he was the more assertive of the two and always spoke for both—"we dreamed that there were fireworks hidden in the basement of the carriage house; lots and lots of fireworks."

His elder brother looked up at him with apprehensive astonishment, while Miss Broadwood hastily put her napkin to her lips and Hamilton dropped his eyes. "If little boys dream things, they are so apt not to come true," he reflected sadly. This shook even the redoubtable William, and he glanced nervously at his brother. "But do things vanish just because they have been dreamed?" he objected.

"Generally that is the very best reason for their vanishing," said Arthur gravely.

"But, Father, people can't help what they dream," remonstrated Edward gently.

"Oh, come! You're making these children talk like a Maeterlinck dialogue," laughed Miss Broadwood.

Flavia presently entered, a book in her hand, and bade them all good morning. "Come, little people, which story shall it be this morning?" she asked winningly. Greatly excited, the children followed her into the garden. "She does then, sometimes," murmured Imogen as they left the breakfast room.

"Oh, yes, to be sure," said Miss Broadwood cheerfully. "She reads a story to them every morning in the most picturesque part of the garden. The mother of the Gracchi, you know. She does so long, she says, for the time when they will be intellectual companions for her. What do you say to a walk over the hills?"

As they left the house they met Frau Lichtenfeld and the bushy Herr Schotte—the professor cut an astonishing figure in golf stockings—returning from a walk and engaged in an animated conversation on the tendencies of German fiction.

"Aren't they the most attractive little children!" exclaimed Imogen as they wound down the road toward the river.

"Yes, and you must not fail to tell Flavia that you think so. She will look at you in a sort of startled way and say, 'Yes, aren't they?' and maybe she will go off and hunt them up and have tea with them, to fully appreciate them. She is awfully afraid of missing anything good, is Flavia. The way those youngsters manage to conceal their guilty presence in the House of Song is a wonder."

"But don't any of the artist-folk fancy children?" asked Imogen.

"Yes, they just fancy them and no more. The chemist remarked the other day that children are like certain salts which need not be actualized because the formulae are quite sufficient for practical purposes. I don't see how even Flavia can endure to have that man about."

"I have always been rather curious to know what Arthur thinks of it all," remarked Imogen cautiously.

"Thinks of it!" ejaculated Miss Broadwood. "Why, my dear, what would any man think of having his house turned into an hotel, habited by freaks who discharge his servants, borrow his money, and insult his neighbors? This place is shunned like a lazaretto!"

"Well, then, why does he—why does he—" persisted Imogen.

"Bah!" interrupted Miss Broadwood impatiently. "Why did he in the first place? That's the question."

"Marry her, you mean?" said Imogen coloring.

"Exactly so," said Miss Broadwood sharply, as she snapped the lid of her matchbox.

"I suppose that is a question rather beyond us, and certainly one which we cannot discuss," said Imogen. "But his toleration on this one point puzzles me, quite apart from other complications."

"Toleration? Why this point, as you call it, simply *is* Flavia. Who could conceive of her without it? I don't know where it's all going to end, I'm sure, and I'm equally sure that, if it were not for Arthur, I shouldn't care," declared Miss Broadwood, drawing her shoulders together.

"But will it end at all, now?"

"Such an absurd state of things can't go on indefinitely. A man isn't going to see his wife make a guy of herself forever, is he? Chaos has already begun in the servants' quarters. There are six different languages spoken there now. You see, it's all on an entirely false basis. Flavia hasn't the slightest notion of what these people are really like, their good and their bad alike escape her. They, on the other hand, can't imagine what she is driving at. Now, Arthur is worse off than either faction; he is not in the fairy story in that he sees these people exactly as they are, *but* he is utterly unable to see Flavia as they see her. There you have the situation. Why can't he see her as we do? My dear, that has kept me awake o' nights. This man who has thought so much and lived so much, who is naturally a critic, really takes Flavia at very nearly her own estimate. But now I am entering upon a wilderness. From a brief acquaintance with her you can know nothing of the icy fastnesses of Flavia's self-esteem. It's like St. Peter's; you can't realize its magnitude at once. You have to grow into a sense of it by living under its shadow. It has perplexed even Emile Roux, that merciless dissector of egoism. She has puzzled him the more because he saw at a glance what some of them do not perceive at once, and what will be mercifully concealed from Arthur until the trump sounds: namely, that all Flavia's artists have done or ever will do means exactly as much to her as a symphony means to an oyster; that there is no bridge by which the significance of any work of art could be conveyed to her."

"Then, in the name of goodness, why does she bother?" gasped Imogen. "She is pretty, wealthy, well-established; why should she bother?"

"That's what M. Roux has kept asking himself. I can't pretend to analyze it. She reads papers on the Literary Landmarks of Paris, the Loves of the Poets, and that sort of thing, to clubs out in Chicago. To Flavia it is more necessary to be called clever than to breathe. I would give a good deal to know that glum Frenchman's diagnosis. He has been watching her out of those fishy eyes of his as a biologist watches a hemisphereless frog."

For several days after M. Roux's departure Flavia gave an embarrassing share of her attention to Imogen. Embarrassing, because Imogen had the feeling of being energetically and futilely explored, she knew not for what. She felt herself under the globe of an air pump, expected to yield up something. When she confined the conversation to matters of general interest, Flavia conveyed to her with some pique that her one endeavor in life had been to fit herself to converse with her friends upon those things which vitally interested them. "One has no right to accept their best from people unless one gives, isn't it so? I want to be able to give—!" she declared vaguely. Yet whenever Imogen strove to pay her tithes and plunged bravely into her plans for study next winter, Flavia grew absent-minded and interrupted her by amazing generalizations or by such embarrassing questions as "And these grim studies really have charm for you; you are quite buried in them; they make other things seem light and ephemeral?"

"I rather feel as though I had got in here under false pretenses," Imogen confided to Miss Broadwood. "I'm sure I don't know what it is that she wants of me."

"Ah," chuckled Jemima, "you are not equal to these heart to heart talks with Flavia. You utterly fail to communicate to her the atmosphere of that untroubled joy in which you dwell. You must remember that she gets no feeling out of things herself, and she demands that you impart yours to her by some process of psychic transmission. I once met a blind girl, blind from birth, who could discuss the peculiarities of the Barbizon school with just Flavia's glibness and enthusiasm. Ordinarily Flavia knows how to get what she wants from people, and her memory is wonderful. One evening I heard her giving Frau Lichtenfeld some random impressions about *Hedda Gabler* which she extracted from me five years ago; giving them with an impassioned conviction of which I was never guilty. But I have known other people who could appropriate your stories and opinions; Flavia is infinitely more subtle than that; she can soak up the very thrash and drift of your daydreams, and take the very thrills off your back, as it were."

After some days of unsuccessful effort, Flavia withdrew herself, and Imogen found Hamilton ready to catch her when she was tossed afield. He seemed only to have been awaiting this crisis, and at once their old intimacy reestablished itself as a thing inevitable and beautifully prepared for. She convinced herself that she had not been mistaken in him, despite all the doubts that had come up in later years, and this renewal of faith set more than one question thumping in her brain. "How did he, how can he?" she kept repeating with a tinge of her childish resentment. "What right had he to waste anything so fine?"

When Imogen and Arthur were returning from a walk before luncheon one morning about a week after M. Roux's departure, they noticed an absorbed group before one of the hall windows. Herr Schotte and Restzhoff sat on the window seat with a newspaper between them, while Wellington, Schemetzkin, and Will Maidenwood looked over their shoulders. They seemed intensely interested, Herr Schotte occasionally pounding his knees with his fists in ebullitions of barbaric glee. When

Imogen entered the hall, however, the men were all sauntering toward the breakfast room and the paper was lying innocently on the divan. During luncheon the personnel of that window group were unwontedly animated and agreeable—all save Schemetzkin, whose stare was blanker than ever, as though Roux's mantle of insulting indifference had fallen upon him, in addition to his own oblivious self-absorption. Will Maidenwood seemed embarrassed and annoyed; the chemist employed himself with making polite speeches to Hamilton. Flavia did not come down to lunch—and there was a malicious gleam under Herr Schotte's eyebrows. Frank Wellington announced nervously that an imperative letter from his protecting syndicate summoned him to the city.

After luncheon the men went to the golf links, and Imogen, at the first opportunity, possessed herself of the newspaper which had been left on the divan. One of the first things that caught her eye was an article headed "Roux on Tuft Hunters: The Advanced American Woman as He Sees Her—Aggressive, Superficial, and Insincere." The entire interview was nothing more nor less than a satiric characterization of Flavia, aquiver with irritation and vitriolic malice. No one could mistake it; it was done with all his deftness of portraiture. Imogen had not finished the article when she heard a footstep, and clutching the paper she started precipitately toward the stairway as Arthur entered. He put out his hand, looking critically at her distressed face.

"Wait a moment, Miss Willard," he said peremptorily, "I want to see whether we can find what it was that so interested our friends this morning. Give me the paper, please."

Imogen grew quite white as he opened the journal. She reached forward and crumpled it with her hands. "Please don't, please don't," she pleaded. "It's something I don't want you to see. Oh, why will you? It's just something low and despicable that you can't notice."

Arthur had gently loosed her hands, and he pointed her to a chair. He lit a cigar and read the article through without comment. When he had finished it he walked to the fireplace, struck a match, and tossed the flaming journal between the brass andirons.

"You are right," he remarked as he came back, dusting his hands with his handkerchief. "It's quite impossible to comment. There are extremes of blackguardism for which we have no name. The only thing necessary is to see that Flavia gets no wind of this. This seems to be my cue to act; poor girl."

Imogen looked at him tearfully; she could only murmur, "Oh, why did you read it!"

Hamilton laughed spiritlessly. "Come, don't you worry about it. You always took other people's troubles too seriously. When you were little and all the world was gay and everybody happy, you must needs get the Little Mermaid's troubles to grieve over. Come with me into the music room. You remember the musical setting I once made you for the Lay of the Jabberwock? I was trying it over the other night, long after you were in bed, and I decided it was quite as fine as the Erl-King music. How I wish I could give you some of the cake that Alice ate and make you a little girl again. Then, when you had got through the glass door into the little garden, you could call to me, perhaps, and tell me all the fine things that were going on there. What a pity it is that you ever grew up!" he added, laughing; and Imogen, too, was thinking just that.

At dinner that evening, Flavia, with fatal persistence, insisted upon turning the conversation to M. Roux. She had been reading one of his novels and had remembered anew that Paris set its watches by his clock. Imogen surmised that she was tortured by a feeling that she had not sufficiently appreciated him while she had had him. When she first mentioned his name she was answered only by the pall of silence that fell over the company. Then everyone began to talk at once, as though to correct a false position. They spoke of him with a fervid, defiant admiration, with the sort of hot praise that covers a double purpose. Imogen fancied she could see that they felt a kind of relief at what the man had done, even those who despised him for doing it; that they felt a spiteful hate against Flavia, as though she had tricked them, and a certain contempt for themselves that they had been beguiled. She was reminded of the fury of the crowd in the fairy tale, when once the child had called out that the king was in his night clothes. Surely these people knew no more about Flavia than they had known before, but the mere fact that the thing had been said altered the situation. Flavia, meanwhile, sat chattering amiably, pathetically unconscious of her nakedness.

Hamilton lounged, fingering the stem of his wineglass, gazing down the table at one face after another and studying the various degrees of self-consciousness they exhibited. Imogen's eyes followed his, fearfully. When a lull came in the spasmodic flow of conversation, Arthur, leaning back in his chair, remarked deliberately, "As for M. Roux, his very profession places him in that class of men whom society has never been able to accept unconditionally because it has never been able to assume that they have any ordered notion of taste. He and his ilk remain, with the mountebanks and snake charmers, people indispensable to our civilization, but wholly unreclaimed by it; people whom we receive, but whose invitations we do not accept."

Fortunately for Flavia, this mine was not exploded until just before the coffee was brought. Her laughter was pitiful to hear; it echoed through the silent room as in a vault, while she made some tremulously light remark about her husband's drollery, grim as a jest from the dying. No one responded and she sat nodding her head like a mechanical toy and smiling her white, set smile through her teeth, until Alcée Buisson and Frau Lichtenfeld came to her support.

After dinner the guests retired immediately to their rooms, and Imogen went upstairs on tiptoe, feeling the echo of breakage and the dust of crumbling in the air. She wondered whether Flavia's habitual note of uneasiness were not, in a manner, prophetic, and a sort of unconscious premonition, after all. She sat down to write a letter, but she found herself so nervous, her head so hot and her hands so cold, that she soon abandoned the effort. Just as she was about to seek Miss Broadwood, Flavia entered and embraced her hysterically.

"My dearest girl," she began, "was there ever such an unfortunate and incomprehensible speech made before? Of course it is scarcely necessary to explain to you poor Arthur's lack of tact, and that he meant nothing. But they! Can they be expected to understand? He will feel wretchedly about it when he realizes what he has done, but in the meantime? And M. Roux, of all men! When we were so fortunate as to get him, and he made himself so unreservedly agreeable, and I fancied that, in his way, Arthur quite admired him. My dear, you have no idea what that speech has done. Schemetzkin and Herr Schotte have already sent me word that they must leave us tomorrow. Such a thing from a host!" Flavia paused, choked by tears of vexation and despair.

Imogen was thoroughly disconcerted; this was the first time she had ever seen Flavia betray any personal emotion which was indubitably genuine. She replied with what consolation she could. "Need they take it personally at all? It was a mere observation upon a class of people—"

"Which he knows nothing whatever about, and with whom he has no sympathy," interrupted Flavia. "Ah, my dear, you could not be *expected* to understand. You can't realize, knowing Arthur as you do, his entire lack of any aesthetic sense whatever. He is absolutely *nil,* stone deaf and stark blind, on that side. He doesn't mean to be brutal, it is just the brutality of utter ignorance. They always feel it—they are so sensitive to unsympathetic influences, you know; they know it the moment they come into the house. I have spent my life apologizing for him and struggling to conceal it; but in spite of me, he wounds them; his very attitude, even in silence, offends them. Heavens! Do I not know? Is it not perpetually and forever wounding me? But there has never been anything so dreadful as this—never! If I could conceive of any possible motive, even!"

"But, surely, Mrs. Hamilton, it was, after all, a mere expression of opinion, such as we are any of us likely to venture upon any subject whatever. It was neither more personal nor more extravagant than many of M. Roux's remarks."

"But, Imogen, certainly M. Roux has the right. It is a part of his art, and that is altogether another matter. Oh, this is not the only instance!" continued Flavia passionately. "I've always had that narrow, bigoted prejudice to contend with. It has always held me back. But this—!"

"I think you mistake his attitude," replied Imogen, feeling a flush that made her ears tingle. "That is, I fancy he is more appreciative than he seems. A man can't be very demonstrative about those things—not if he is a real man. I should not think you would care much about saving the feelings of people who are too narrow to admit of any other point of view than their own." She stopped, finding herself in the impossible position of attempting to explain Hamilton to his wife; a task which, if once begun, would necessitate an entire course of enlightenment which she doubted Flavia's ability to receive, and which she could offer only with very poor grace.

"That's just where it stings most"—here Flavia began pacing the floor—"it is just because they have all shown such tolerance and have treated Arthur with such unfailing consideration that I can find no reasonable pretext for his rancor. How can he fail to see the value of such friendships on the children's account, if for nothing else! What an advantage for them to grow up among such associations! Even though he cares nothing about these things himself he might realize that. Is there nothing I could say by way of explanation? To them, I mean? If someone were to explain to them how unfortunately limited he is in these things—"

"I'm afraid I cannot advise you," said Imogen decidedly, "but that, at least, seems to me impossible."

Flavia took her hand and glanced at her affectionately, nodding nervously. "Of course, dear girl, I can't ask you to be quite frank with me. Poor child, you are trembling and your hands are icy. Poor Arthur! But you must not judge him by this altogether; think how much he misses in life. What a cruel shock you've had. I'll send you some sherry. Good night, my dear."

When Flavia shut the door Imogen burst into a fit of nervous weeping.

Next morning she awoke after a troubled and restless night. At eight o'clock Miss Broadwood entered in a red-and-white-striped bathrobe.

"Up, up, and see the great doom's image!" she cried, her eyes sparkling with excitement. "The hall is full of trunks, they are packing. What bolt has fallen? It's you, *ma chérie,* you've brought Ulysses home again and the slaughter has begun!" She blew a cloud of smoke triumphantly from her lips and threw herself into a chair beside the bed.

Imogen, rising on her elbow, plunged excitedly into the story of the Roux interview, which Miss Broadwood heard with the keenest interest, frequently interrupting her with exclamations of delight. When Imogen reached the dramatic scene which terminated in the destruction of the newspaper, Miss Broadwood rose and took a turn about the room, violently switching the tasseled cords of her bathrobe.

"Stop a moment," she cried. "You mean to tell me that he had such a heaven-sent means to bring her to her senses and didn't use it—that he held such a weapon and threw it away?"

"Use it?" cried Imogen unsteadily. "Of course he didn't! He bared his back to the tormentor, signed himself over to punishment in that speech he made at dinner, which everyone understands but Flavia. She was here for an hour last night and disregarded every limit of taste in her maledictions."

"My dear!" cried Miss Broadwood, catching her hand in inordinate delight at the situation. "Do you see what he has done? There'll be no end to it. Why he has sacrificed himself to spare the very vanity that devours him, put rancors in the vessels of his peace, and his eternal jewel given to the common enemy of man, to make them kings, the seed of Banquo kings! He is magnificent!"

"Isn't he always that?" cried Imogen hotly. "He's like a pillar of sanity and law in this house of shams and swollen vanities, where people stalk about with a sort of madhouse dignity, each one fancying himself a king or a pope. If you could have heard that woman talk of him! Why, she thinks him stupid, bigoted, blinded by middle-class prejudices. She talked about his having no aesthetic sense and insisted that her artists had always shown him tolerance. I don't know why it should get on my nerves so, I'm sure, but her stupidity and assurance are enough to drive one to the brink of collapse."

"Yes, as opposed to his singular fineness, they are calculated to do just that," said Miss Broadwood gravely, wisely ignoring Imogen's tears. "But what has been is nothing to what will be. Just wait until Flavia's black swans have flown! You ought not to try to stick it out; that would only make it harder for everyone. Suppose you let me telephone your mother to wire you to come home by the evening train?"

"Anything, rather than have her come at me like that again. It puts me in a perfectly impossible position, and he *is* so fine!"

"Of course it does," said Miss Broadwood sympathetically, "and there is no good to be got from facing it. I will stay because such things interest me, and Frau Lichtenfeld will stay because she has no money to get away, and Buisson will stay because he feels somewhat responsible. These complications are interesting enough to cold-blooded folk like myself who have an eye for the dramatic element, but they are distracting and demoralizing to young people with any serious purpose in life."

Miss Broadwood's counsel was all the more generous seeing that, for her, the most interesting element of this denouement would be eliminated by Imogen's departure. "If she goes now, she'll get over it," soliloquized Miss Broadwood. "If she stays, she'll be wrung for him and the hurt may go deep enough to last. I haven't the heart to see her spoiling things for herself." She telephoned Mrs. Willard and helped Imogen to pack. She even took it upon herself to break the news of Imogen's going to Arthur, who remarked, as he rolled a cigarette in his nerveless fingers:

"Right enough, too. What should she do here with old cynics like you and me, Jimmy? Seeing that she is brim full of dates and formulae and other positivisms, and is so girt about with illusions that she still casts a shadow in the sun. You've been very tender of her, haven't you? I've watched you. And to think it may all be gone when we see her next. 'The common fate of all things rare,' you know. What a good fellow you are, anyway, Jimmy," he added, putting his hands affectionately on her shoulders.

Arthur went with them to the station. Flavia was so prostrated by the concerted action of her guests that she was able to see Imogen only for a moment in her darkened sleeping chamber, where she kissed her hysterically, without lifting her head, bandaged in aromatic vinegar. On the way to the station both Arthur and Imogen threw the burden of keeping up appearances entirely upon Miss Broadwood, who blithely rose to the occasion. When Hamilton carried Imogen's bag into the car, Miss Broadwood detained her for a moment, whispering as she gave her a large, warm handclasp, "I'll come to see you when I get back to town; and, in the meantime, if you meet any of our artists, tell them you have left Caius Marius among the ruins of Carthage."

The Sculptor's Funeral

A GROUP of the townspeople stood on the station siding of a little Kansas town, awaiting the coming of the night train, which was already twenty minutes overdue. The snow had fallen thick over everything; in the pale starlight the line of bluffs across the wide, white meadows south of the town made soft, smoke-colored curves against the clear sky. The men on the siding stood first on one foot and then on the other, their hands thrust deep into their trousers pockets, their overcoats open, their shoulders screwed up with the cold; and they glanced from time to time toward the southeast, where the railroad track wound along the river shore. They conversed in low tones and moved about restlessly, seeming uncertain as to what was expected of them. There was but one of the company who looked as though he knew exactly why he was there, and he kept conspicuously apart: walking to the far end of the platform, returning to the station door, then pacing up the track again, his chin sunk in the high collar of his overcoat, his burly shoulders drooping forward, his gait heavy and dogged. Presently he was approached by a tall, spare, grizzled man clad in a faded Grand Army suit, who shuffled out from the group and advanced with a certain deference, craning his neck forward until his back made the angle of a jackknife three-quarters open.

"I reckon she's agoin' to be pretty late ag'in tonight, Jim," he remarked in a squeaky falsetto. "S'pose it's the snow?"

"I don't know," responded the other man with a shade of annoyance, speaking from out an astonishing cataract of red beard that grew fiercely and thickly in all directions.

The spare man shifted the quill toothpick he was chewing to the other side of his mouth. "It ain't likely that anybody from the East will come with the corpse, I s'pose," he went on reflectively.

"I don't know," responded the other, more curtly than before.

"It's too bad he didn't belong to some lodge or other. I like an order funeral myself. They seem more appropriate for people of some repytation," the spare man continued, with an ingratiating concession in his shrill voice, as he carefully placed his toothpick in his vest pocket. He always carried the flag at the GAR funerals in the town.

The heavy man turned on his heel, without replying, and walked up the siding. The spare man shuffled back to the uneasy group. "Jim's ez full ez a tick, ez ushel," he commented commiseratingly.

Just then a distant whistle sounded, and there was a shuffling of feet on the platform. A number of lanky boys of all ages appeared as suddenly and slimily as eels wakened by the crack of thunder; some came from the waiting room, where they had been warming themselves by the red stove, or half-asleep on the slat benches; others uncoiled themselves from baggage trucks or slid out of express wagons. Two clambered down from the driver's seat of a hearse that stood backed up against the siding. They straightened their stooping shoulders and lifted their heads, and a flash of momentary animation kindled their dull eyes at that cold, vibrant scream, the worldwide call for men. It stirred them like the note of a trumpet, just as it had often stirred the man who was coming home tonight, in his boyhood.

The night express shot, red as a rocket, from out the eastward marsh lands and wound along the river shore under the long lines of shivering poplars that sentineled the meadows, the escaping steam hanging in gray masses against the pale sky and blotting out the Milky Way. In a moment the red glare from the headlight streamed up the snow-covered track before the siding and glittered on the wet, black rails. The burly man with the disheveled red beard walked swiftly up the platform toward the approaching train, uncovering his head as he went. The group of men behind him hesitated, glanced questioningly at one another, and awkwardly followed his example. The train stopped, and the crowd shuffled up to the express car just as the door was thrown open, the spare man in the GAR suit thrusting his head forward with curiosity. The express messenger appeared in the doorway, accompanied by a young man in a long ulster and traveling cap.

"Are Mr. Merrick's friends here?" inquired the young man.

The group on the platform swayed and shuffled uneasily. Philip Phelps, the banker, responded with dignity: "We have come to take charge of the body. Mr. Merrick's father is very feeble and can't be about."

"Send the agent out here," growled the express messenger, "and tell the operator to lend a hand."

The coffin was got out of its rough box and down on the snowy platform. The townspeople drew back enough to make room for it and then formed a close semicircle about it, looking curiously at the palm leaf which lay across the black cover. No one said anything. The baggage man stood by his truck, waiting to get at the trunks. The engine panted heavily, and the fireman dodged in and out among the wheels with his yellow torch and long oilcan, snapping the spindle boxes. The young Bostonian, one of the dead sculptor's pupils who had come with the body, looked about him helplessly. He turned to the banker, the only one of that black, uneasy, stoop-shouldered group who seemed enough of an individual to be addressed.

"None of Mr. Merrick's brothers are here?" he asked uncertainly.

The man with the red beard for the first time stepped up and joined the group. "No, they have not come yet; the family is scattered. The body will be taken directly to the house." He stooped and took hold of one of the handles of the coffin.

"Take the long hill road up, Thompson—it will be easier on the horses," called the liveryman as the undertaker snapped the door of the hearse and prepared to mount to the driver's seat.

Laird, the red-bearded lawyer, turned again to the stranger: "We didn't know whether there would be anyone with him or not," he explained. "It's a long walk, so you'd better go up in the hack." He pointed to a single, battered conveyance, but the young man replied stiffly: "Thank you, but I think I will go up with the hearse. If you don't object," turning to the undertaker, "I'll ride with you."

They clambered up over the wheels and drove off in the starlight up the long, white hill toward the town. The lamps in the still village were shining from under the low, snow-burdened roofs; and beyond, on every side, the plains reached out into emptiness, peaceful and wide as the soft sky itself, and wrapped in a tangible, white silence.

When the hearse backed up to a wooden sidewalk before a naked, weatherbeaten frame house, the same composite, ill-defined group that had stood upon the station siding was huddled about the gate. The front yard was an icy swamp, and a couple of warped planks, extending from the sidewalk to the door, made a sort of rickety footbridge. The gate hung on one hinge and was opened wide with difficulty. Steavens, the young stranger, noticed that something black was tied to the knob of the front door.

The grating sound made by the casket, as it was drawn from the hearse, was answered by a scream from the house; the front door was wrenched open, and a tall, corpulent woman rushed out bareheaded into the snow and flung herself upon the coffin, shrieking: "My boy, my boy! And this is how you've come home to me!"

As Steavens turned away and closed his eyes with a shudder of unutterable repulsion, another woman, also tall, but flat and angular, dressed entirely in black, darted out of the house and caught Mrs. Merrick by the shoulders, crying sharply: "Come, come, Mother; you mustn't go on like this!" Her tone changed to one of obsequious solemnity as she turned to the banker: "The parlor is ready, Mr. Phelps."

The bearers carried the coffin along the narrow boards, while the undertaker ran ahead with the coffin-rests. They bore it into a large, unheated room that smelled of dampness and disuse and furniture polish, and set it down under a hanging lamp ornamented with jingling glass prisms and before a "Rogers group" of John Alden and Priscilla, wreathed with smilax. Henry Steavens stared about him with the sickening conviction that there had been some horrible mistake, and that he had somehow arrived at the wrong destination. He looked painfully about over the clover-green Brussels, the fat plush upholstery, among the hand-painted china plaques and panels, and vases, for some mark of identification, for something that might once conceivably have belonged to Harvey Merrick. It was not until he recognized his friend in the crayon portrait of a little boy in kilts and curls hanging above the piano that he felt willing to let any of these people approach the coffin.

"Take the lid off, Mr. Thompson; let me see my boy's face," wailed the elder woman between her sobs. This time Steavens looked fearfully, almost beseechingly into her face, red and swollen under its masses of strong, black, shiny hair. He flushed, dropped his eyes, and then, almost incredulously, looked again. There was a kind of power about her face—a kind of brutal handsomeness, even, but it was scarred and furrowed by violence, and so colored and coarsened by fiercer passions that grief seemed never to have laid a gentle finger there. The long nose was distended and knobbed at the end, and there were deep lines on either side of it; her heavy, black brows almost met across her forehead; her teeth were large and square and set far apart—teeth that could tear. She filled the room; the men were obliterated, seemed tossed about like twigs in an angry water, and even Steavens felt himself being drawn into the whirlpool.

The daughter—the tall, rawboned woman in crepe, with a mourning comb in her hair which curiously lengthened her long face—sat stiffly upon the sofa, her hands, conspicuous for their large knuckles, folded in her lap, her mouth and eyes drawn down, solemnly awaiting the opening of the coffin. Near the door stood a mulatto woman, evidently a servant in the house, with a timid bearing and an emaciated face pitifully sad and gentle. She was weeping silently, the corner of her calico apron lifted to her eyes, occasionally suppressing a long, quivering sob. Steavens walked over and stood beside her.

Feeble steps were heard on the stairs, and an old man, tall and frail, odorous of pipe smoke, with shaggy, unkept gray hair and a dingy beard, tobacco stained about the mouth, entered uncertainly. He went slowly up to the coffin and stood, rolling a blue cotton handkerchief between his hands, seeming so pained and embarrassed by his wife's orgy of grief that he had no consciousness of anything else.

"There, there, Annie, dear, don't take on so," he quavered timidly, putting out a shaking hand and awkwardly patting her elbow. She turned with a cry and sank upon his shoulder with such violence that he tottered a little. He did not even glance toward the coffin, but continued to look at her with a dull, frightened, appealing expression, as a spaniel looks at the whip. His sunken cheeks slowly reddened and burned with miserable shame. When his wife rushed from the room her daughter strode after her with set lips. The servant stole up to the coffin, bent over it for a moment, and then slipped away to the kitchen, leaving Steavens, the lawyer, and the father to themselves. The old man stood trembling and looking down at his dead son's face. The sculptor's splendid head seemed even more noble in its rigid stillness than in life. The dark hair had crept down upon the wide forehead; the face seemed strangely long, but in it there was not that beautiful and chaste repose which we expect to find in the faces of the dead. The brows were so drawn that there were two deep lines above the beaked nose, and the chin was thrust forward defiantly. It was as though the strain of life had been so sharp and bitter that death could not at once wholly relax the tension and smooth the countenance into perfect peace—as though he were still guarding something precious and holy, which might even yet be wrested from him.

The old man's lips were working under his stained beard. He turned to the lawyer with timid deference: "Phelps and the rest are comin' back to set up with Harve, ain't they?" he asked. "Thank 'ee, Jim, thank 'ee." He brushed the hair back gently from his son's forehead. "He was a good boy, Jim; always a good boy. He was ez gentle ez a child and the kindest of 'em all—only we didn't none of us ever onderstand him." The tears trickled slowly down his beard and dropped upon the sculptor's coat.

"Martin, Martin. Oh, Martin! come here," his wife wailed from the top of the stairs. The old man started timorously: "Yes, Annie, I'm coming." He turned away, hesitated, stood for a moment in miserable indecision; then he reached back and patted the dead man's hair softly, and stumbled from the room.

"Poor old man, I didn't think he had any tears left. Seems as if his eyes would have gone dry long ago. At his age nothing cuts very deep," remarked the lawyer.

Something in his tone made Steavens glance up. While the mother had been in the room the young man had scarcely seen anyone else; but now, from the moment he first glanced into Jim Laird's florid face and bloodshot eyes, he knew that he had found what he had been heartsick at not finding before—the feeling, the understanding, that must exist in someone, even here.

The man was red as his beard, with features swollen and blurred by dissipation, and a hot, blazing blue eye. His face was strained—that of a man who is controlling himself with difficulty—and he kept plucking at his beard with a sort of fierce resentment. Steavens, sitting by the window, watched him turn down the glaring lamp, still its jangling pendants with an angry gesture, and then stand with his hands locked behind him, staring down into the master's face. He could not help wondering what link there could have been between the porcelain vessel and so sooty a lump of potter's clay.

From the kitchen an uproar was sounding; when the dining-room door opened the import of it was clear. The mother was abusing the maid for having forgotten to make the dressing for the chicken salad which had been prepared for the watchers. Steavens had never heard anything in the least like it; it was injured, emotional, dramatic abuse, unique and masterly in its excruciating cruelty, as violent and unrestrained as had been her grief of twenty minutes before. With a shudder of disgust the lawyer went into the dining room and closed the door into the kitchen.

"Poor Roxy's getting it now," he remarked when he came back. "The Merricks took her out of the poorhouse years ago; and if her loyalty would let her, I guess the poor old thing could tell tales that would curdle your blood. She's the mulatto woman who was standing in here a while ago, with her apron to her eyes. The old woman is a fury; there never was anybody like her for demonstrative piety and ingenious cruelty. She made Harvey's life a hell for him when he lived at home; he was so sick ashamed of it. I never could see how he kept himself so sweet."

"He was wonderful," said Steavens slowly, "wonderful; but until tonight I have never known how wonderful."

"That is the true and eternal wonder of it, anyway; that it can come even from such a dung heap as this," the lawyer cried, with a sweeping gesture which seemed to indicate much more than the four walls within which they stood.

"I think I'll see whether I can get a little air. The room is so close I am beginning to feel rather faint," murmured Steavens, struggling with one of the windows. The sash was stuck, however, and would not yield, so he sat down dejectedly and began pulling at his collar. The lawyer came over, loosened the sash with one blow of his red fist, and sent the window up a few inches. Steavens thanked him, but the nausea which had been gradually climbing into his throat for the last half-hour left him with but one desire—a desperate feeling that he must get away from this place with what was left of Harvey Merrick. Oh, he comprehended well enough now the quiet bitterness of the smile that he had seen so often on his master's lips!

He remembered that once, when Merrick returned from a visit home, he brought with him a singularly feeling and suggestive bas-relief of a thin, faded old woman, sitting and sewing something pinned to her knee; while a full-lipped, full-blooded little urchin, his trousers held up by a single gallows, stood beside her, impatiently twitching her gown to call her attention to a butterfly he had caught. Steavens, impressed by the tender and delicate modeling of the thin, tired face, had asked him if it were his mother. He remembered the dull flush that had burned up in the sculptor's face.

The lawyer was sitting in a rocking chair beside the coffin, his head thrown back and his eyes closed. Steavens looked at him earnestly, puzzled at the line of the chin, and wondering why a man should conceal a feature of such distinction under that disfiguring shock of beard. Suddenly, as though he felt the young sculptor's keen glance, he opened his eyes.

"Was he always a good deal of an oyster?" he asked abruptly. "He was terribly shy as a boy."

"Yes, he was an oyster, since you put it so," rejoined Steavens. "Although he could be very fond of people, he always gave one the impression of being detached. He disliked violent emotion; he was reflective, and rather distrustful of himself—except, of course, as regarded his work. He was surefooted enough there. He distrusted men pretty thoroughly and women even more, yet somehow without believing ill of them. He was determined, indeed, to believe the best, but he seemed afraid to investigate."

"A burnt dog dreads the fire," said the lawyer grimly, and closed his eyes.

Steavens went on and on, reconstructing that whole miserable boyhood. All this raw, biting ugliness had been the portion of the man whose tastes were refined beyond the limits of the reasonable—whose mind was an exhaustless gallery of beautiful impressions, and so sensitive that the mere shadow of a poplar leaf flickering against a sunny wall would be etched and held there forever. Surely, if ever a man had the magic word in his fingertips, it was Merrick. Whatever he touched, he revealed its holiest secret—liberated it from enchantment and restored it to its pristine loveliness, like the Arabian prince who fought the enchantress spell for spell. Upon whatever he had come in contact with, he had left a beautiful record of the experience—a sort of ethereal signature; a scent, a sound, a color that was his own.

Steavens understood now the real tragedy of his master's life: neither love nor wine, as many had conjectured, but a blow which had fallen earlier and cut deeper than these could have done—a shame not his, and yet so unescapably his, to hide in his heart from his very boyhood. And without—the frontier warfare; the yearning of a boy, cast ashore upon a desert of newness and ugliness and sordidness, for all that is chastened and old, and noble with traditions.

At eleven o'clock the tall, flat woman in black crepe entered, announced that the watchers were arriving, and asked them "to step into the dining room." As Steavens rose, the lawyer said dryly: "You go on—it'll be a good experience for you, doubtless; as for me, I'm not equal to that crowd tonight; I've had twenty years of them."

As Steavens closed the door after him he glanced back at the lawyer, sitting by the coffin in the dim light, with his chin resting on his hand.

The same misty group that had stood before the door of the express car shuffled into the dining room. In the light of the kerosene lamp they separated and became individuals. The minister, a pale, feeble-looking man with white hair and blond chin-whiskers, took his seat beside a small side table and placed his Bible upon it. The Grand Army man sat down behind the stove and tilted his chair back comfortably against the wall, fishing his quill toothpick from his waistcoat pocket. The two bankers, Phelps and Elder, sat off in a corner behind the dinner table, where they could finish their discussion of the new usury law and its effect on chattel security loans. The real estate agent, an old man with a smiling, hypocritical face, soon joined them. The coal-and-lumber dealer and the cattle shipper sat on opposite sides of the hard coal-burner, their feet on the nickelwork. Steavens took a book from his pocket and began to read. The talk around him ranged through various topics of local interest while the house was quieting down. When it was clear that the members of the family were in bed, the Grand Army man hitched his shoulders and, untangling his long legs, caught his heels on the rounds of his chair.

"S'pose there'll be a will, Phelps?" he queried in his weak falsetto.

The banker laughed disagreeably and began trimming his nails with a pearl-handled pocketknife.

"There'll scarcely be any need for one, will there?" he queried in his turn.

The restless Grand Army man shifted his position again, getting his knees still nearer his chin. "Why, the ole man says Harve's done right well lately," he chirped.

The other banker spoke up. "I reckon he means by that Harve ain't asked him to mortgage any more farms lately, so as he could go on with his education."

"Seems like my mind don't reach back to a time when Harve wasn't bein' edycated," tittered the Grand Army man.

There was a general chuckle. The minister took out his handkerchief and blew his nose sonorously. Banker Phelps closed his knife with a snap. "It's too bad the old man's sons didn't turn out better," he remarked with reflective authority. "They never hung together. He spent money enough on Harve to stock a dozen cattle farms and he might as well have poured it into Sand Creek. If Harve had stayed at home and helped nurse what little they had, and gone into stock on the old man's bottom farm, they might all have been well fixed. But the old man had to trust everything to tenants and was cheated right and left."

"Harve never could have handled stock none," interposed the cattleman. "He hadn't it in him to be sharp. Do you remember when he bought Sander's mules for eight-year-olds, when everybody in town knew that Sander's father-in-law give 'em to his wife for a wedding present eighteen years before, an' they was full-grown mules then."

Everyone chuckled, and the Grand Army man rubbed his knees with a spasm of childish delight.

"Harve never was much account for anything practical, and he shore was never fond of work," began the coal-and-lumber dealer. "I mind the last time he was home; the day he left, when the old man was out to the barn helpin' his hand hitch up to take Harve to the train, and Cal Moots was patchin' up the fence, Harve, he come out on the step and sings out, in his ladylike voice: "Cal Moots, Cal Moots! Please come cord my trunk."

"That's Harve for you," approved the Grand Army man gleefully. "I kin hear him howlin' yet when he was a big feller in long pants and his mother used to whale him with a rawhide in the barn for lettin' the cows git foundered in the cornfield when he was drivin' 'em home from pasture. He killed a cow of mine that-a-way onc't—a pure Jersey and the best milker I had, an' the ole man had to put up for her. Harve, he was watchin' the sun set acros't the marshes when the anamile got away; he argued that sunset was oncommon fine."

"Where the old man made his mistake was in sending the boy East to school," said Phelps, stroking his goatee and speaking in a deliberate, judicial tone. "There was where he got his head full of traipsing to Paris and all such folly. What Harve needed, of all people, was a course in some first-class Kansas City business college."

The letters were swimming before Steavens's eyes. Was it possible that these men did not understand, that the palm on the coffin meant nothing to them? The very name of their town would have remained forever buried in the postal guide had it not been now and again mentioned in the world in connection with Harvey Merrick's. He remembered what his master had said to him on the day of his death, after the congestion of both lungs had shut off any probability of recovery, and the sculptor had asked his pupil to send his body home. "It's not a pleasant place to be lying while the world is moving and doing and bettering," he had said with a feeble smile, "but it rather seems as though we ought to go back to the place we came from in the end. The townspeople will come in for a look at me; and after they have had their say I shan't have much to fear from the judgment of God. The wings of the Victory, in there"—with a weak gesture toward his studio—"will not shelter me."

The cattleman took up the comment. "Forty's young for a Merrick to cash in; they usually hang on pretty well. Probably he helped it along with whisky."

"His mother's people were not long-lived, and Harvey never had a robust constitution," said the minister mildly. He would have liked to say more. He had been the boy's Sunday-school teacher, and had been fond of him; but he felt that he was not in a position to speak. His own sons had turned out badly, and it was not a year since one of them had made his last trip home in the express car, shot in a gambling house in the Black Hills.

"Nevertheless, there is no disputin' that Harve frequently looked upon the wine when it was red, also variegated, and it shore made an oncommon fool of him," moralized the cattleman.

Just then the door leading into the parlor rattled loudly, and everyone started involuntarily, looking relieved when only Jim Laird came out. His red face was convulsed with anger, and the Grand Army man ducked his head when he saw the spark in his blue, bloodshot eye. They were all afraid of Jim; he was a drunkard, but he could twist the law to suit his client's needs as no other man in all western Kansas could do; and there were many who tried. The lawyer closed the door gently behind him, leaned back against it and folded his arms, cocking his head a little to one side. When he assumed this attitude in the courtroom, ears were always pricked up, as it usually foretold a flood of withering sarcasm.

"I've been with you gentlemen before," he began in a dry, even tone, "when you've sat by the coffins of boys born and raised in this town; and, if I remember rightly, you were never any too well satisfied when you checked them up. What's the matter, anyhow? Why is it that reputable young men are as scarce as millionaires in Sand City? It might almost seem to a stranger that there was some way something the matter with your progressive town. Why did Ruben Sayer, the brightest young lawyer you ever turned out, after he had come home from the university as straight as a die, take to drinking and forge a check and shoot himself? Why did Bill Merrit's son die of the shakes in a saloon in Omaha? Why was Mr. Thomas's son, here, shot in a gambling house? Why did young Adams burn his mill to beat the insurance companies and go to the pen?"

The lawyer paused and unfolded his arms, laying one clenched fist quietly on the table. "I'll tell you why. Because you drummed nothing but money and knavery into their ears from the time they wore knickerbockers; because you carped away at them as you've been carping here tonight, holding our friends Phelps and Elder up to them for their models, as our grandfathers held up George Washington and John Adams. But the boys, worse luck, were young and raw at the business you put them to; and how could they match coppers with such artists as Phelps and Elder? You wanted them to be successful rascals; they were only unsuccessful ones—that's all the difference. There was only one boy ever raised in this borderland between ruffianism and civilization who didn't come to grief, and you hated Harvey Merrick more for winning out than you hated all the other boys who got under the wheels. Lord, Lord, how you did hate him! Phelps, here, is fond of saying that he could buy and sell us all out any time he's a mind to; but he knew Harve wouldn't have given a tinker's damn for his bank and all his cattle farms put together; and a lack of appreciation, that way, goes hard with Phelps.

"Old Nimrod, here, thinks Harve drank too much; and this from such as Nimrod and me!

"Brother Elder says Harve was too free with the old man's money—fell short in filial consideration, maybe. Well, we can all remember the very tone in which brother Elder swore his own father was a liar, in the county court; and we all know that the old man came out of that partnership with his son as bare as a sheared lamb. But maybe I'm getting personal, and I'd better be driving ahead at what I want to say."

The lawyer paused a moment, squared his heavy shoulders, and went on: "Harvey Merrick and I went to school together, back East. We were dead in earnest, and we wanted you all to be proud of us some day. We meant to be great men. Even I, and I haven't lost my sense of humor, gentlemen, I meant to be a great man. I came back here to practice, and I found you didn't in the least want me to be a great man. You wanted me to be a shrewd lawyer—oh, yes! Our veteran here wanted me to get him an increase of pension, because he had dyspepsia; Phelps wanted a new county survey that would put the widow Wilson's little bottom farm inside his south line; Elder wanted to lend money at 5 percent a month and get it collected; old Stark here wanted to wheedle old women up in Vermont into investing their annuities in real estate mortgages that are not worth the paper they are written on. Oh, you needed me hard enough, and you'll go on needing me; and that's why I'm not afraid to plug the truth home to you this once.

"Well, I came back here and became the damned shyster you wanted me to be. You pretend to have some sort of respect for me; and yet you'll stand up and throw mud at Harvey Merrick, whose soul you couldn't dirty and whose hands you couldn't tie. Oh, you're a discriminating lot of Christians! There have been times when the sight of Harvey's name in some Eastern paper has made me hang my head like a whipped dog; and, again, times when I liked to think of him off there in the world, away from all this hog wallow, doing his great work and climbing the big, clean upgrade he'd set for himself.

"And we? Now that we've fought and lied and sweated and stolen, and hated as only the disappointed strugglers in a bitter, dead little Western town know how to do, what have we got to show for it? Harvey Merrick wouldn't have given one sunset over your marshes for all you've got put together, and you know it. It's not for me to say why, in the inscrutable wisdom of God, a genius should ever have been called from this place of hatred and bitter waters; but I want this Boston man to know that the drivel he's been hearing here tonight is the only tribute any truly great man could ever have from such a lot of sick, side-tracked, burnt-dog, land-poor sharks as the here-present financiers of Sand City—upon which town may God have mercy!"

The lawyer thrust out his hand to Steavens as he passed him, caught up his overcoat in the hall, and had left the house before the Grand Army man had had time to lift his ducked head and crane his long neck about at his fellows.

Next day Jim Laird was drunk and unable to attend the funeral services. Steavens called twice at his office, but was compelled to start East without seeing him. He had a presentiment that he would hear from him again, and left his address on the lawyer's table; but if Laird found it, he never acknowledged it. The thing in him that Harvey Merrick had loved must have gone underground with Harvey Merrick's coffin; for it never spoke again, and Jim got the cold he died of driving across the Colorado mountains to defend one of Phelps's sons, who had got into trouble out there by cutting government timber.

The Garden Lodge

WHEN CAROLINE NOBLE'S friends learned that Raymond d'Esquerré was to spend a month at her place on the Sound before he sailed to fill his engagement for the London opera season, they considered it another striking instance of the perversity of things. That the month was May, and the most mild and florescent of all the blue-and-white Mays the middle coast had known in years, but added to their sense of wrong. D'Esquerré, they learned, was ensconced in the lodge in the apple orchard, just beyond Caroline's glorious garden, and report went that at almost any hour the sound of the tenor's voice and of Caroline's crashing accompaniment could be heard floating through the open windows, out among the snowy apple boughs. The Sound, steel-blue and dotted with white sails, was splendidly seen from the windows of the lodge. The garden to the left and the orchard to the right had never been so riotous with spring, and had burst into impassioned bloom, as if to accommodate Caroline, though she was certainly the last woman to whom the witchery of Freya could be attributed; the last woman, as her friends affirmed, to at all adequately appreciate and make the most of such a setting for the great tenor.

Of course, they admitted, Caroline was musical—well, she ought to be!—but in that, as in everything, she was paramountly cool-headed, slow of impulse, and disgustingly practical; in that, as in everything else, she had herself so provokingly well in hand. Of course, it would be she, always mistress of herself in any situation, she, who would never be lifted one inch from the ground by it, and who would go on superintending her gardeners and workmen as usual—it would be she who got him. Perhaps some of them suspected that this was exactly why she did get him, and it but nettled them the more.

Caroline's coolness, her capableness, her general success especially exasperated people because they felt that, for the most part, she had made herself what she was; that she had cold-bloodedly set about complying with the demands of life and making her position comfortable and masterful. That was why, everyone said, she had married Howard Noble.

Women who did not get through life so well as Caroline, who could not make such good terms either with fortune or their husbands, who did not find their health so unfailingly good, or hold their looks so well, or manage their children so easily, or give such distinction to all they did, were fond of stamping Caroline as a materialist, and called her hard.

The impression of cold calculation, of having a definite policy, which Caroline gave, was far from a false one; but there was this to be said for her—that there were extenuating circumstances which her friends could not know.

If Caroline held determinedly to the middle course, if she was apt to regard with distrust everything which inclined toward extravagance, it was not because she was unacquainted with other standards than her own, or had never seen another side of life. She had grown up in Brooklyn, in a shabby little house under the vacillating administration of her father, a music teacher who usually neglected his duties to write orchestral compositions for which the world seemed to have no especial need. His spirit was warped by bitter vindictiveness and puerile self-commiseration, and he spent his days in scorn of the labor that brought him bread and in pitiful devotion to the labor that brought him only disappointment, writing interminable scores which demanded of the orchestra everything under heaven except melody.

It was not a cheerful home for a girl to grow up in. The mother, who idolized her husband as the music lord of the future, was left to a lifelong battle with broom and dustpan, to never-ending conciliatory overtures to the butcher and grocer, to the making of her own gowns and of Caroline's, and to the delicate task of mollifying Auguste's neglected pupils.

The son, Heinrich, a painter, Caroline's only brother, had inherited all his father's vindictive sensitiveness without his capacity for slavish application. His little studio on the third floor had been much frequented by young men as unsuccessful as himself, who met there to give themselves over to contemptuous derision of this or that artist whose industry and stupidity had won him recognition. Heinrich, when he worked at all, did newspaper sketches at twenty-five dollars a week. He was too indolent and vacillating to set himself seriously to his art, too irascible and poignantly self-conscious to make a living, too much addicted to lying late in bed, to the incontinent reading of poetry, and to the use of chloral to be anything very positive except painful. At twenty-six he shot himself in a frenzy, and the whole wretched affair had effectually shattered his mother's health and brought on the decline of which she died. Caroline had been fond of him, but she felt a certain relief when he no longer wandered about the little house, commenting ironically upon its shabbiness, a Turkish cap on his head and a cigarette hanging from between his long, tremulous fingers.

After her mother's death Caroline assumed the management of that bankrupt establishment. The funeral expenses were unpaid, and Auguste's pupils had been frightened away by the shock of successive disasters and the general atmosphere of wretchedness that pervaded the house. Auguste himself was writing a symphonic poem, Icarus, dedicated to the memory of his son. Caroline was barely twenty when she was called upon to face this tangle of difficulties, but she reviewed the situation candidly. The house had served its time at the shrine of idealism; vague, distressing, unsatisfied yearnings had brought it low enough. Her mother, thirty years before, had eloped and left Germany with her music teacher, to give herself over to lifelong, drudging bondage at the kitchen range. Ever since Caroline could remember, the law in the house had been a sort of mystic worship of things distant, intangible and unattainable. The family had lived in successive ebullitions of generous enthusiasm, in talk of masters and masterpieces, only to come down to the cold facts in the case, to boiled mutton and to the necessity of turning the dining-room carpet. All these emotional pyrotechnics had ended in petty jealousies, in neglected duties, and in cowardly fear of the little grocer on the corner.

From her childhood she had hated it, that humiliating and uncertain existence, with its glib tongue and empty pockets, its poetic ideals and sordid realities, its indolence and poverty tricked out in paper roses. Even as a little girl, when vague dreams beset her, when she wanted to lie late in bed and commune with visions, or to leap and sing because the sooty little trees along the street were putting out their first pale leaves in the sunshine, she would clench her hands and go to help her mother sponge the spots from her father's waistcoat or press Heinrich's trousers. Her mother never permitted the slightest question concerning anything Auguste or Heinrich saw fit to do, but from the time Caroline could reason at all she could not help thinking that many things went wrong at home. She knew, for example, that her father's pupils ought not to be kept waiting half an hour while he discussed Schopenhauer with some bearded socialist over a dish of herrings and a spotted tablecloth. She knew that Heinrich ought not to give a dinner on Heine's birthday, when the laundress had not been paid for a month and when he frequently had to ask his mother for carfare. Certainly Caroline had served her apprenticeship to idealism and to all the embarrassing inconsistencies which it sometimes entails, and she decided to deny herself this diffuse, ineffectual answer to the sharp questions of life.

When she came into the control of herself and the house she refused to proceed any further with her musical education. Her father, who had intended to make a concert pianist of her, set this down as another item in his long list of disappointments and his grievances against the world. She was young and pretty, and she had worn turned gowns and soiled gloves and improvised hats all her life. She wanted the luxury of being like other people, of being honest from her hat to her boots, of having nothing to hide, not even in the matter of stockings, and she was willing to work for it. She rented a little studio away from that house of misfortune and began to give lessons. She managed well and was the sort of girl people liked to help. The bills were paid and Auguste went on composing, growing indignant only when she refused to insist that her pupils should study his compositions for the piano. She began to get engagements in New York to play accompaniments at song recitals. She dressed well, made herself agreeable, and gave herself a chance. She never permitted herself to look further than a step ahead, and set herself with all the strength of her will to see things as they are and meet them squarely in the broad day. There were two things she feared even more than poverty: the part of one that sets up an idol and the part of one that bows down and worships it.

When Caroline was twenty-four she married Howard Noble, then a widower of forty, who had been for ten years a power in Wall Street. Then, for the first time, she had paused to take breath. It took a substantialness as unquestionable as his; his money, his position, his energy, the big vigor of his robust person, to satisfy her that she was entirely safe. Then she relaxed a little, feeling that there was a barrier to be counted upon between her and that world of visions and quagmires and failure.

Caroline had been married for six years when Raymond d'Esquerré came to stay with them. He came chiefly because Caroline was what she was; because he, too, felt occasionally the need of getting out of Klingsor's garden, of dropping down somewhere for a time near a quiet nature, a cool head, a strong hand. The hours he had spent in the garden lodge were hours of such concentrated study as, in his fevered life, he seldom got in anywhere. She had, as he told Noble, a fine appreciation of the seriousness of work.

One evening two weeks after d'Esquerré had sailed, Caroline was in the library giving her husband an account of the work she had laid out for the gardeners. She superintended the care of the grounds herself. Her garden, indeed, had become quite a part of her; a sort of beautiful adjunct, like gowns or jewels. It was a famous spot, and Noble was very proud of it.

"What do you think, Caroline, of having the garden lodge torn down and putting a new summer house there at the end of the arbor; a big rustic affair where you could have tea served in midsummer?" he asked.

"The lodge?" repeated Caroline looking at him quickly. "Why, that seems almost a shame, doesn't it, after d'Esquerré has used it?"

Noble put down his book with a smile of amusement.

"Are you going to be sentimental about it? Why, I'd sacrifice the whole place to see that come to pass. But I don't believe you could do it for an hour together."

"I don't believe so, either," said his wife, smiling.

Noble took up his book again and Caroline went into the music room to practice. She was not ready to have the lodge torn down. She had gone there for a quiet hour every day during the two weeks since d'Esquerré had left them. It was the sheerest sentiment she had ever permitted herself. She was ashamed of it, but she was childishly unwilling to let it go.

Caroline went to bed soon after her husband, but she was not able to sleep. The night was close and warm, presaging storm. The wind had fallen, and the water slept, fixed and motionless as the sand. She rose and thrust her feet into slippers and, putting a dressing gown over her shoulders, opened the door of her husband's room; he was sleeping soundly. She went into the hall and down the stairs; then, leaving the house through a side door, stepped into the vine-covered arbor that led to the garden lodge. The scent of the June roses was heavy in the still air, and the stones that paved the path felt pleasantly cool through the thin soles of her slippers. Heat-lightning flashed continuously from the bank of clouds that had gathered over the sea, but the shore was flooded with moonlight and, beyond, the rim of the Sound lay smooth and shining. Caroline had the key of the lodge, and the door creaked as she opened it. She stepped into the long, low room radiant with the moonlight which streamed through the bow window and lay in a silvery pool along the waxed floor. Even that part of the room which lay in the shadow was vaguely illuminated; the piano, the tall candlesticks, the picture frames and white casts standing out as clearly in the half-light as did the sycamores and black poplars of the garden against the still, expectant night sky. Caroline sat down to think it all over. She had come here to do just that every day of the two weeks since d'Esquerré's departure, but, far from ever having reached a conclusion, she had succeeded only in losing her way in a maze of memories—sometimes bewilderingly confused, sometimes too acutely distinct—where there was neither path, nor clue, nor any hope of finality. She had, she realized, defeated a lifelong regimen; completely confounded herself by falling unaware and incontinently into that luxury of reverie which, even as a little girl, she had so determinedly denied herself; she had been developing with alarming celerity that part of one which sets up an idol and that part of one which bows down and worships it.

It was a mistake, she felt, ever to have asked d'Esquerré to come at all. She had an angry feeling that she had done it rather in self-defiance, to rid herself finally of that instinctive fear of him which had always troubled and perplexed her. She knew that she had reckoned with herself before he came; but she had been equal to so much that she had never really doubted she would be equal to this. She had come to believe, indeed almost arrogantly, in her own malleability and endurance; she had done so much with herself that she had come to think that there was nothing which she could not do—like swimmers, overbold, who reckon upon their strength and their power to hoard it, forgetting the ever-changing moods of their adversary, the sea.

And d'Esquerré was a man to reckon with. Caroline did not deceive herself now upon that score. She admitted it humbly enough, and since she had said goodbye to him she had not been free for a moment from the sense of his formidable power. It formed the undercurrent of her consciousness; whatever she might be doing or thinking, it went on, involuntarily, like her breathing, sometimes welling up until suddenly she found herself suffocating. There was a moment of this tonight, and Caroline rose and stood shuddering, looking about her in the blue duskiness of the silent room. She had not been here at night before, and the spirit of the place seemed more troubled and insistent than ever it had in the quiet of the afternoons. Caroline brushed her hair back from her damp forehead and went over to the bow window. After raising it she sat down upon the low seat. Leaning her head against the sill, and loosening her nightgown at the throat, she half-closed her eyes and looked off into the troubled night, watching the play of the heat-lightning upon the massing clouds between the pointed tops of the poplars.

Yes, she knew, she knew well enough, of what absurdities this spell was woven; she mocked, even while she winced. His power, she knew, lay not so much in anything that he actually had—though he had so much—or in anything that he actually was, but in what he suggested, in what he seemed picturesque enough to have or be—and that was just anything that one chose to believe or to desire. His appeal was all the more persuasive and alluring in that it was to the imagination alone, in that it was as indefinite and impersonal as those cults of idealism which so have their way with women. What he had was that, in his mere personality, he quickened and in a measure gratified that something without which—to women—life is no better than sawdust, and to the desire for which most of their mistakes and tragedies and astonishingly poor bargains are due.

D'Esquerré had become the center of a movement, and the Metropolitan had become the temple of a cult. When he could be induced to cross the Atlantic, the opera season in New York was successful; when he could not, the management lost money; so much everyone knew. It was understood, too, that his superb art had disproportionately little to do with his peculiar position. Women swayed the balance this way or that; the opera, the orchestra, even his own glorious art, achieved at such a cost, were but the accessories of himself; like the scenery and costumes and even the soprano, they all went to produce atmosphere, were the mere mechanics of the beautiful illusion.

Caroline understood all this; tonight was not the first time that she had put it to herself so. She had seen the same feeling in other people, watched for it in her friends, studied it in the house night after night when he sang, candidly putting herself among a thousand others.

D'Esquerré's arrival in the early winter was the signal for a feminine hegira toward New York. On the nights when he sang women flocked to the Metropolitan from mansions and hotels, from typewriter desks, schoolrooms, shops, and fitting rooms. They were of all conditions and complexions: women of the world who accepted him knowingly, as they sometimes took champagne for its agreeable effect; sisters of charity and overworked shopgirls, who received him devoutly; withered women who had taken doctorate degrees and who worshipped furtively through prism spectacles; business women and women of affairs, the Amazons who dwelt afar from men in the stony fastnesses of apartment houses. They all entered into the same romance; dreamed, in terms as various as the hues of fantasy, the same dream; drew the same quick breath when he stepped upon the stage; and, at his exit, felt the same dull pain of shouldering the pack again.

There were the maimed, even; those who came on crutches, who were pitted by smallpox or grotesquely painted by cruel birth stains. These, too, entered with him into enchantment. Stout matrons became slender girls again; worn spinsters felt their cheeks flush with the tenderness of their lost youth. Young and old, however hideous, however fair, they yielded up their heat—whether quick or latent—sat hungering for the mystic bread wherewith he fed them at this eucharist of sentiment.

Sometimes, when the house was crowded from the orchestra to the last row of the gallery, when the air was charged with this ecstasy of fancy, he himself was the victim of the burning reflection of his power. They acted upon him in turn; he felt their fervent and despairing appeal to him; it stirred him as the spring drives the sap up into an old tree; he, too, burst into bloom. For the moment he, too, believed again, desired again, he knew not what, but something.

But it was not in these exalted moments that Caroline had learned to fear him most. It was in the quiet, tired reserve, the dullness, even, that kept him company between these outbursts that she found that exhausting drain upon her sympathies which was the very pith and substance of their alliance. It was the tacit admission of disappointment under all this glamor of success—the helplessness of the enchanter to at all enchant himself—that awoke in her an illogical, womanish desire to in some way compensate, to make it up to him.

She had observed drastically to herself that it was her eighteenth year he awoke in her—those hard years she had spent in turning gowns and placating tradesmen, and which she had never had time to live. After all, she reflected, it was better to allow one's self a little youth—to dance a little at the carnival and to live these things when they are natural and lovely, not to have them coming back on one and demanding arrears when they are humiliating and impossible. She went over tonight all the catalogue of her self-deprivations; recalled how, in the light of her father's example, she had even refused to humor her innocent taste for improvising at the piano; how, when she began to teach, after her mother's death, she had struck out one little indulgence after another, reducing her life to a relentless routine, unvarying as clockwork. It seemed to her that ever since d'Esquerré first came into the house she had been haunted by an imploring little girlish ghost that followed her about, wringing its hands and entreating for an hour of life.

The storm had held off unconscionably long; the air within the lodge was stifling, and without the garden waited, breathless. Everything seemed pervaded by a poignant distress, the hush of feverish, intolerable expectation. The still earth, the heavy flowers, even the growing darkness breathed the exhaustion of protracted waiting. Caroline felt that she ought to go; that it was wrong to stay; that the hour and the place were as treacherous as her own reflections. She rose and began to pace the floor, stepping softly, as though in fear of awakening someone, her figure, in its thin drapery, diaphanously vague and white. Still unable to shake off the obsession of the intense stillness, she sat down at the piano and began to run over the first act of the *Walküre,* the last of his roles they had practiced together, playing listlessly and absently at first, but with gradually increasing seriousness. Perhaps it was the still heat of the summer night, perhaps it was the heavy odors from the garden that came in through the open windows; but as she played there grew and grew the feeling that he was there, beside her, standing in his accustomed place. In the duet at the end of the first act she heard him clearly: *"Thou art the Spring for which I sighed in Winter's cold embraces."* Once as he sang it, he had put his arm about her, his one hand under her heart, while with the other he took her right from the keyboard, holding her as he always held Sieglinde when he drew her toward the window. She had been wonderfully the mistress of herself at the time, neither repellent nor acquiescent. She remembered that she had rather exulted, then, in her self-control—which he had seemed to take for granted, though there was perhaps the whisper of a question from the hand under her heart. *"Thou art the Spring for which I sighed in Winter's cold embraces."* Caroline lifted her hands quickly from the keyboard, and she bowed her head in them, sobbing.

The storm broke and the rain beat in, spattering her nightdress until she rose and lowered the windows. She dropped upon the couch and began fighting over again the battles of other days, while the ghosts of the slain rose as from a sowing of dragon's teeth. The shadows of things, always so scorned and flouted, bore down upon her merciless and triumphant. It was not enough; this happy, useful, well-ordered life was not enough. It did not satisfy, it was not even real. No, the other things, the shadows—they were the realities. Her father, poor Heinrich, even her mother, who had been able to sustain her poor romance and keep her little illusions amid the tasks of a scullion, were nearer happiness than she. Her sure foundation was but made ground, after all, and the people in Klingsor's garden were more fortunate, however barren the sands from which they conjured their paradise.

The lodge was still and silent; her fit of weeping over, Caroline made no sound, and within the room, as without in the garden, was the blackness of storm. Only now and then a flash of lightning showed a woman's slender figure rigid on the couch, her face buried in her hands.

Toward morning, when the occasional rumbling of thunder was heard no more and the beat of the raindrops upon the orchard leaves was steadier, she fell asleep and did not waken until the first red streaks of dawn shone through the twisted boughs of the apple trees. There was a moment between world and world, when, neither asleep nor awake, she felt her dream grow thin, melting away from her, felt the warmth under her heart growing cold. Something seemed to slip from the clinging hold of her arms, and she groaned protestingly through her parted lips, following it a little way with fluttering hands. Then her eyes opened wide and she sprang up and sat holding dizzily to the cushions of the couch, staring down at her bare, cold feet, at her laboring breast, rising and falling under her open nightdress.

The dream was gone, but the feverish reality of it still pervaded her and she held it as the vibrating string holds a tone. In the last hour the shadows had had their way with Caroline. They had shown her the nothingness of time and space, of system and discipline, of closed doors and broad waters. Shuddering, she thought of the Arabian fairy tale in which the genie brought the princess of China to the sleeping prince of Damascus and carried her through the air back to her palace at dawn. Caroline closed her eyes and dropped her elbows weakly upon her knees, her shoulders sinking together. The horror was that it had not come from without, but from within. The dream was no blind chance; it was the expression of something she had kept so close a prisoner that she had never seen it herself; it was the wail from the donjon deeps when the watch slept. Only as the outcome of such a night of sorcery could the thing have been loosed to straighten its limbs and measure itself with her; so heavy were the chains upon it, so many a fathom deep, it was crushed down into darkness. The fact that d'Esquerré happened to be on the other side of the world meant nothing; had he been here, beside her, it could scarcely have hurt her self-respect so much. As it was, she was without even the extenuation of an outer impulse, and she could scarcely have despised herself more had she come to him here in the night three weeks ago and thrown herself down upon the stone slab at the door there.

Caroline rose unsteadily and crept guiltily from the lodge and along the path under the arbor, terrified lest the servants should be stirring, trembling with the chill air, while the wet shrubbery, brushing against her, drenched her nightdress until it clung about her limbs.

At breakfast her husband looked across the table at her with concern. "It seems to me that you are looking rather fagged, Caroline. It was a beastly night to sleep. Why don't you go up to the mountains until this hot weather is over? By the way, were you in earnest about letting the lodge stand?"

Caroline laughed quietly. "No, I find I was not very serious. I haven't sentiment enough to forego a summer house. Will you tell Baker to come tomorrow to talk it over with me? If we are to have a house party, I should like to put him to work on it at once."

Noble gave her a glance, half-humorous, half-vexed. "Do you know I am rather disappointed?" he said. "I had almost hoped that, just for once, you know, you would be a little bit foolish."

"Not now that I've slept over it," replied Caroline, and they both rose from the table, laughing.

"A Death in the Desert"

EVERETT HILGARDE was conscious that the man in the seat across the aisle was looking at him intently. He was a large, florid man, wore a conspicuous diamond solitaire upon his third finger, and Everett judged him to be a traveling salesman of some sort. He had the air of an adaptable fellow who had been about the world and who could keep cool and clean under almost any circumstances.

The "High Line Flyer," as this train was derisively called among railroad men, was jerking along through the hot afternoon over the monotonous country between Holdridge and Cheyenne. Besides the blond man and himself the only occupants of the car were two dusty, bedraggled-looking girls who had been to the Exposition at Chicago, and who were earnestly discussing the cost of their first trip out of Colorado. The four uncomfortable passengers were covered with a sediment of fine, yellow dust which clung to their hair and eyebrows like gold powder. It blew up in clouds from the bleak, lifeless country through which they passed, until they were one color with the sagebrush and sandhills. The gray-and-yellow desert was varied only by occasional ruins of deserted towns, and the little red boxes of station houses, where the spindling trees and sickly vines in the blue-grass yards made little green reserves fenced off in that confusing wilderness of sand.

As the slanting rays of the sun beat in stronger and stronger through the car windows, the blond gentleman asked the ladies' permission to remove his coat, and sat in his lavender-striped shirt sleeves, with a black silk handkerchief tucked carefully about his collar. He had seemed interested in Everett since they had boarded the train at Holdridge, and kept glancing at him curiously and then looking reflectively out of the window, as though he were trying to recall something. But wherever Everett went someone was almost sure to look at him with that curious interest, and it had ceased to embarrass or annoy him. Presently the stranger, seeming satisfied with his observation, leaned back in his seat, half-closed his eyes, and began softly to whistle the "Spring Song" from *Proserpine*, the cantata that a dozen years before had made its young composer famous in a night. Everett had heard that air on guitars in Old Mexico, on mandolins at college glees, on cottage organs in New England hamlets, and only two weeks ago he had heard it played on sleighbells at a variety theater in Denver. There was literally no way of escaping his brother's precocity. Adriance could live on the other side of the Atlantic, where his youthful indiscretions were forgotten in his mature achievements, but his brother had never been able to outrun *Proserpine,* and here he found it again in the Colorado sand hills. Not that Everett was exactly ashamed of *Proserpine;* only a man of genius could have written it, but it was the sort of thing that a man of genius outgrows as soon as he can.

Everett unbent a trifle and smiled at his neighbor across the aisle. Immediately the large man rose and, coming over, dropped into the seat facing Hilgarde, extending his card.

"Dusty ride, isn't it? I don't mind it myself; I'm used to it. Born and bred in de briar patch, like Br'er Rabbit. I've been trying to place you for a long time; I think I must have met you before."

"Thank you," said Everett, taking the card; "my name is Hilgarde. You've probably met my brother, Adriance; people often mistake me for him."

The traveling man brought his hand down upon his knee with such vehemence that the solitaire blazed.

"So I was right after all, and if you're not Adriance Hilgarde, you're his double. I thought I couldn't be mistaken. Seen him? Well, I guess! I never missed one of his recitals at the Auditorium, and he played the piano score of *Proserpine* through to us once at the Chicago Press Club. I used to be on the *Commercial* there before I began to travel for the publishing department of the concern. So you're Hilgarde's brother, and here I've run into you at the jumping-off place. Sounds like a newspaper yarn, doesn't it?"

The traveling man laughed and offered Everett a cigar, and plied him with questions on the only subject that people ever seemed to care to talk to Everett about. At length the salesman and the two girls alighted at a Colorado way station, and Everett went on to Cheyenne alone.

The train pulled into Cheyenne at nine o'clock, late by a matter of four hours or so; but no one seemed particularly concerned at its tardiness except the station agent, who grumbled at being kept in the office overtime on a summer night. When Everett alighted from the train he walked down the platform and stopped at the track crossing, uncertain as to what direction he should take to reach a hotel. A phaeton stood near the crossing, and a woman held the reins. She was dressed in white, and her figure was clearly silhouetted against the cushions, though it was too dark to see her face. Everett had scarcely noticed her, when the switch engine came puffing up from the opposite direction, and the headlight threw a strong glare of light on his face. Suddenly the woman in the phaeton uttered a low cry and dropped the reins. Everett started forward and caught the horse's head, but the animal only lifted its ears and whisked its tail in impatient surprise. The woman sat perfectly still, her head sunk between her shoulders and her handkerchief pressed to her face. Another woman came out of the depot and hurried toward the phaeton, crying, "Katharine, dear, what is the matter?"

Everett hesitated a moment in painful embarrassment, then lifted his hat and passed on. He was accustomed to sudden recognitions in the most impossible places, especially by women, but this cry out of the night had shaken him.

While Everett was breakfasting the next morning, the headwaiter leaned over his chair to murmur that there was a gentleman waiting to see him in the parlor. Everett finished his coffee and went in the direction indicated, where he found his visitor restlessly pacing the floor. His whole manner betrayed a high degree of agitation, though his physique was not that of a man whose nerves lie near the surface. He was something below medium height, square-shouldered and solidly built. His thick, closely cut hair was beginning to show gray about the ears, and his bronzed face was heavily lined. His square brown hands were locked behind him, and he held his shoulders like a man conscious of responsibilities; yet, as he turned to greet Everett, there was an incongruous diffidence in his address.

"Good morning, Mr. Hilgarde," he said, extending his hand; "I found your name on the hotel register. My name is Gaylord. I'm afraid my sister startled you at the station last night, Mr. Hilgarde, and I've come around to apologize."

"Ah! The young lady in the phaeton? I'm sure I didn't know whether I had anything to do with her alarm or not. If I did, it is I who owe the apology."

The man colored a little under the dark brown of his face.

"Oh, it's nothing you could help, sir, I fully understand that. You see, my sister used to be a pupil of your brother's, and it seems you favor him; and when the switch engine threw a light on your face it startled her."

Everett wheeled about in his chair. "Oh! *Katharine* Gaylord! Is it possible! Now it's you who have given me a turn. Why, I used to know her when I was a boy. What on earth —"

"Is she doing here?" said Gaylord, grimly filling out the pause. "You've got at the heart of the matter. You knew my sister had been in bad health for a long time?"

"No, I had never heard a word of that. The last I knew of her she was singing in London. My brother and I correspond infrequently and seldom get beyond family matters. I am deeply sorry to hear this. There are more reasons why I am concerned than I can tell you."

The lines in Charley Gaylord's brow relaxed a little.

"What I'm trying to say, Mr. Hilgarde, is that she wants to see you. I hate to ask you, but she's so set on it. We live several miles out of town, but my rig's below, and I can take you out anytime you can go."

"I can go now, and it will give me real pleasure to do so," said Everett, quickly. "I'll get my hat and be with you in a moment."

When he came downstairs Everett found a cart at the door, and Charley Gaylord drew a long sigh of relief as he gathered up the reins and settled back into his own element.

"You see, I think I'd better tell you something about my sister before you see her, and I don't know just where to begin. She traveled in Europe with your brother and his wife, and sang at a lot of his concerts; but I don't know just how much you know about her."

"Very little, except that my brother always thought her the most gifted of his pupils, and that when I knew her she was very young and very beautiful and turned my head sadly for a while."

Everett saw that Gaylord's mind was quite engrossed by his grief. He was wrought up to the point where his reserve and sense of proportion had quite left him, and his trouble was the one vital thing in the world. "That's the whole thing," he went on, flicking his horses with the whip.

"She was a great woman, as you say, and she didn't come of a great family. She had to fight her own way from the first. She got to Chicago, and then to New York, and then to Europe, where she went up like lightning, and got a taste for it all; and now she's dying here like a rat in a hole, out of her own world, and she can't fall back into ours. We've grown apart, some way—miles and miles apart—and I'm afraid she's fearfully unhappy."

"It's a very tragic story that you are telling me, Gaylord," said Everett. They were well out into the country now, spinning along over the dusty plains of red grass, with the ragged-blue outline of the mountains before them.

"Tragic!" cried Gaylord, starting up in his seat. "My God, man, nobody will ever know how tragic. It's a tragedy I live with and eat with and sleep with, until I've lost my grip on everything. You see she had made a good bit of money, but she spent it all going to health resorts. It's her lungs, you know. I've got money enough to send her anywhere, but the doctors all say it's no use. She hasn't the ghost of a chance. It's just getting through the days now. I had no notion she was half so bad before she came to me. She just wrote that she was all run down. Now that she's here, I think she'd be happier anywhere under the sun, but she won't leave. She says it's easier to let go of life here, and that to go East would be dying twice. There was a time when I was a brakeman with a run out of Bird City, Iowa, and she was a little thing I could carry on my shoulder, when I could get her everything on earth she wanted, and she hadn't a wish my eighty dollars a month didn't cover; and now, when I've got a little property together, I can't buy her a night's sleep!"

Everett saw that, whatever Charley Gaylord's present status in the world might be, he had brought the brakeman's heart up the ladder with him, and the brakeman's frank avowal of sentiment. Presently Gaylord went on:

"You can understand how she has outgrown her family. We're all a pretty common sort, railroaders from away back. My father was a conductor. He died when we were kids. Maggie, my other sister, who lives with me, was a telegraph operator here while I was getting my grip on things. We had no education to speak of. I have to hire a stenographer because I can't spell straight—the Almighty couldn't teach me to spell. The things that make up life to Kate are all Greek to me, and there's scarcely a point where we touch any more, except in our recollections of the old times when we were all young and happy together, and Kate sang in a church choir in Bird City. But I believe, Mr. Hilgarde, that if she can see just one person like you, who knows about the things and people she's interested in, it will give her about the only comfort she can have now."

The reins slackened in Charley Gaylord's hand as they drew up before a showily painted house with many gables and a round tower. "Here we are," he said, turning to Everett, "and I guess we understand each other."

They were met at the door by a thin, colorless woman, whom Gaylord introduced as "my sister, Maggie." She asked her brother to show Mr. Hilgarde into the music room, where Katharine wished to see him alone.

When Everett entered the music room he gave a little start of surprise, feeling that he had stepped from the glaring Wyoming sunlight into some New York studio that he had always known. He wondered which it was of those countless studios, high up under the roofs, over banks and shops and wholesale houses, that this room resembled, and he looked incredulously out of the window at the gray plain that ended in the great upheaval of the Rockies.

The haunting air of familiarity about the room perplexed him. Was it a copy of some particular studio he knew, or was it merely the studio atmosphere that seemed so individual and poignantly reminiscent here in Wyoming? He sat down in a reading chair and looked keenly about him. Suddenly his eye fell upon a large photograph of his brother above the piano. Then it all became clear to him: this was veritably his brother's room. If it were not an exact copy of one of the many studios that Adriance had fitted up in various parts of the world, wearying of them and leaving almost before the renovator's varnish had dried, it was at least in the same tone. In every detail Adriance's taste was so manifest that the room seemed to exhale his personality.

Among the photographs on the wall there was one of Katharine Gaylord, taken in the days when Everett had known her, and when the flash of her eye or the flutter of her skirt was enough to set his boyish heart in a tumult. Even now, he stood before the portrait with a certain degree of embarrassment. It was the face of a woman already old in her first youth, thoroughly sophisticated and a trifle hard, and it told of what her brother had called her fight. The camaraderie of her frank, confident eyes was qualified by the deep lines about her mouth and the curve of the lips, which was both sad and cynical. Certainly she had more good will than confidence toward the world, and the bravado of her smile could not conceal the shadow of an unrest that was almost discontent. The chief charm of the woman, as Everett had known her, lay in her superb figure and in her eyes, which possessed a warm, life-giving quality like the sunlight, eyes which glowed with a sort of perpetual *salutat* to the world. Her head Everett remembered as peculiarly well-shaped and proudly poised. There had been always a little of the imperatrix about her, and her pose in the photograph revived all his old impressions of her unattachedness, of how absolutely and valiantly she stood alone.

Everett was still standing before the picture, his hands behind him and his head inclined, when he heard the door open. A very tall woman advanced toward him, holding out her hand. As she started to speak, she coughed slightly; then, laughing, said, in a low, rich voice, a trifle husky: "You see I make the traditional Camille entrance—with the cough. How good of you to come, Mr. Hilgarde."

Everett was acutely conscious that while addressing him she was not looking at him at all, and, as he assured her of his pleasure in coming, he was glad to have an opportunity to collect himself. He had not reckoned upon the ravages of a long illness. The long, loose folds of her white gown had been especially designed to conceal the sharp outlines of her emaciated body, but the stamp of her disease was there; simple and ugly and obtrusive, a pitiless fact that could not be disguised or evaded. The splendid shoulders were stooped, there was a swaying unevenness in her gait, her arms seemed disproportionately long, and her hands were transparently white and cold to the touch. The changes in her face were less obvious; the proud carriage of the head, the warm, clear eyes, even the delicate flush of color in her cheeks, all defiantly remained, though they were all in a lower key—older, sadder, softer.

She sat down upon the divan and began nervously to arrange the pillows. "I know I'm not an inspiring object to look upon, but you must be quite frank and sensible about that and get used to it at once, for we've no time to lose. And if I'm a trifle irritable you won't mind?—for I'm more than usually nervous."

"Don't bother with me this morning, if you are tired," urged Everett. "I can come quite as well tomorrow."

"Gracious, no!" she protested, with a flash of that quick, keen humor that he remembered as a part of her. "It's solitude that I'm tired to death of—solitude and the wrong kind of people. You see, the minister, not content with reading the prayers for the sick, called on me this morning. He happened to be riding by on his bicycle and felt it his duty to stop. Of course, he disapproves of my profession, and I think he takes it for granted that I have a dark past. The funniest feature of his conversation is that he is always excusing my own vocation to me—condoning it, you know—and trying to patch up my peace with my conscience by suggesting possible noble uses for what he kindly calls my talent."

Everett laughed. "Oh! I'm afraid I'm not the person to call after such a serious gentleman—I can't sustain the situation. At my best I don't reach higher than low comedy. Have you decided to which one of the noble uses you will devote yourself?"

Katharine lifted her hands in a gesture of renunciation and exclaimed: "I'm not equal to any of them, not even the least noble. I didn't study that method."

She laughed and went on nervously: "The parson's not so bad. His English never offends me, and he has read Gibbon's *Decline and Fall*, all five volumes, and that's something. Then, he has been to New York, and that's a great deal. But how we are losing time! Do tell me about New York; Charley says you're just on from there. How does it look and taste and smell just now? I think a whiff of the Jersey ferry would be as flagons of cod-liver oil to me. Who conspicuously walks the Rialto now, and what does he or she wear? Are the trees still green in Madison

Square, or have they grown brown and dusty? Does the chaste Diana on the Garden Theatre still keep her vestal vows through all the exasperating changes of weather? Who has your brother's old studio now, and what misguided aspirants practice their scales in the rookeries about Carnegie Hall? What do people go to see at the theaters, and what do they eat and drink there in the world nowadays? You see, I'm homesick for it all, from the Battery to Riverside. Oh, let me die in Harlem!" She was interrupted by a violent attack of coughing, and Everett, embarrassed by her discomfort, plunged into gossip about the professional people he had met in town during the summer and the musical outlook for the winter. He was diagraming with his pencil, on the back of an old envelope he found in his pocket, some new mechanical device to be used at the Metropolitan in the production of the *Rheingold*, when he became conscious that she was looking at him intently, and that he was talking to the four walls.

Katharine was lying back among the pillows, watching him through half-closed eyes, as a painter looks at a picture. He finished his explanation vaguely enough and put the envelope back in his pocket. As he did so she said, quietly: "How wonderfully like Adriance you are!" and he felt as though a crisis of some sort had been met and tided over.

He laughed, looking up at her with a touch of pride in his eyes that made them seem quite boyish. "Yes, isn't it absurd? It's almost as awkward as looking like Napoleon—but, after all, there are some advantages. It has made some of his friends like me, and I hope it will make you."

Katharine smiled and gave him a quick, meaning glance from under her lashes. "Oh, it did that long ago. What a haughty, reserved youth you were then, and how you used to stare at people and then blush and look cross if they paid you back in your own coin. Do you remember that night when you took me home from a rehearsal and scarcely spoke a word to me?"

"It was the silence of admiration," protested Everett, "very crude and boyish, but very sincere and not a little painful. Perhaps you suspected something of the sort? I remember you saw fit to be very grown-up and worldly."

"I believe I suspected a pose; the one that college boys usually affect with singers—'an earthen vessel in love with a star,' you know. But it rather surprised me in you, for you must have seen a good deal of your brother's pupils. Or had you an omnivorous capacity, and elasticity that always met the occasion?"

"Don't ask a man to confess the follies of his youth," said Everett, smiling a little sadly. "I am sensitive about some of them even now. But

I was not so sophisticated as you imagined. I saw my brother's pupils come and go, but that was about all. Sometimes I was called on to play accompaniments, or to fill out a vacancy at a rehearsal, or to order a carriage for an infuriated soprano who had thrown up her part. But they never spent any time on me, unless it was to notice the resemblance you speak of."

"Yes," observed Katharine, thoughtfully, "I noticed it then, too; but it has grown as you have grown older. That is rather strange, when you have lived such different lives. It's not merely an ordinary family likeness of feature, you know, but a sort of interchangeable individuality, the suggestion of the other man's personality in your face—like an air transposed to another key. But I'm not attempting to define it; it's beyond me, something altogether unusual and a trifle—well, uncanny," she finished, laughing.

"I remember," Everett said seriously, twirling the pencil between his fingers and looking, as he sat with his head thrown back, out under the red window blind which was raised just a little, and as it swung back and forth in the wind revealed the glaring panorama of the desert—a blinding stretch of yellow, flat as the sea in dead calm, splotched here and there with deep purple shadows; and, beyond, the ragged-blue outline of the mountains and the peaks of snow, white as the white clouds—"I remember, when I was a little fellow I used to be very sensitive about it. I don't think it exactly displeased me, or that I would have had it otherwise if I could, but it seemed to me like a birthmark, or something not to be lightly spoken of. People were naturally always fonder of Ad than of me, and I used to feel the chill of reflected light pretty often. It came into even my relations with my mother. Ad went abroad to study when he was absurdly young, you know, and mother was all broken up over it. She did her whole duty by each of us, but it was sort of generally understood among us that she'd have made burnt offerings of us all for Ad any day. I was a little fellow then, and when she sat alone on the porch in the summer dusk she used sometimes to call me to her and turn my face up in the light that streamed out through the shutters and kiss me, and then I always knew she was thinking of Adriance."

"Poor little chap," said Katharine, and her tone was a trifle huskier than usual. "How fond people have always been of Adriance! Now tell me the latest news of him. I haven't heard, except through the press, for a year or more. He was in Algeria then, in the valley of the Chelif, riding horseback night and day in an Arabian costume, and in his usual enthusiastic fashion he had quite made up his mind to adopt the Mohammedan faith and become as nearly as Arab as possible. How many countries and faiths has he adopted, I wonder? Probably he was playing Arab to himself all the time. I remember he was a sixteenth-century duke in Florence once for weeks together."

"Oh, that's Adriance," chuckled Everett. "He is himself barely long enough to write checks and be measured for his clothes. I didn't hear from him while he was an Arab; I missed that."

"He was writing an Algerian suite for the piano then; it must be in the publisher's hands by this time. I have been too ill to answer his letter, and have lost touch with him."

Everett drew a letter from his pocket. "This came about a month ago. It's chiefly about his new opera, which is to be brought out in London next winter. Read it at your leisure."

"I think I shall keep it as a hostage, so that I may be sure you will come again. Now I want you to play for me. Whatever you like; but if there is anything new in the world, in mercy let me hear it. For nine months I have heard nothing but 'The Baggage Coach Ahead' and 'She Is My Baby's Mother.' "

He sat down at the piano, and Katharine sat near him, absorbed in his remarkable physical likeness to his brother and trying to discover in just what it consisted. She told herself that it was very much as though a sculptor's finished work had been rudely copied in wood. He was of a larger build than Adriance, and his shoulders were broad and heavy, while those of his brother were slender and rather girlish. His face was of the same oval mold, but it was gray and darkened about the mouth by continual shaving. His eyes were of the same inconstant April color, but they were reflective and rather dull; while Adriance's were always points of highlight, and always meaning another thing than the thing they meant yesterday. But it was hard to see why this earnest man should so continually suggest that lyric, youthful face that was as gay as his was grave. For Adriance, though he was ten years the elder, and though his hair was streaked with silver, had the face of a boy of twenty, so mobile that it told his thoughts before he could put them into words. A contralto, famous for the extravagance of her vocal methods and of her affections, had once said to him that the shepherd boys who sang in the Vale of Tempe must certainly have looked like young Hilgarde; and the comparison had been appropriated by a hundred shyer women who preferred to quote.

As Everett sat smoking on the veranda of the Inter-Ocean House that night, he was a victim to random recollections. His infatuation for Katharine Gaylord, visionary as it was, had been the most serious of his boyish love affairs, and had long disturbed his bachelor dreams. He was painfully timid in everything relating to the emotions, and his hurt had withdrawn him from the society of women. The fact that it was all so done and dead and far behind him, and that the woman had lived her life out since then, gave him an oppressive sense of age and loss. He bethought himself of something he had read about "sitting by the hearth and remembering the faces of women without desire," and felt himself an octogenarian.

He remembered how bitter and morose he had grown during his stay at his brother's studio when Katharine Gaylord was working there, and how he had wounded Adriance on the night of his last concert in New York. He had sat there in the box while his brother and Katharine were called back again and again after the last number, watching the roses go up over the footlights until they were stacked half as high as the piano, brooding, in his sullen boy's heart, upon the pride those two felt in each other's work—spurring each other to their best and beautifully contending in song. The footlights had seemed a hard, glittering line drawn sharply between their life and his; a circle of flame set about those splendid children of genius. He walked back to his hotel alone and sat in his window staring out on Madison Square until long after midnight, resolving to beat no more at doors that he could never enter and realizing more keenly than ever before how far this glorious world of beautiful creations lay from the paths of men like himself. He told himself that he had in common with this woman only the baser uses of life.

Everett's week in Cheyenne stretched to three, and he saw no prospect of release except through the thing he dreaded. The bright, windy days of the Wyoming autumn passed swiftly. Letters and telegrams came urging him to hasten his trip to the coast, but he resolutely postponed his business engagements. The mornings he spent on one of Charley Gaylord's ponies, or fishing in the mountains, and in the evenings he sat in his room writing letters or reading. In the afternoon he was usually at his post of duty. Destiny, he reflected, seems to have very positive notions about the sort of parts we are fitted to play. The scene changes and the compensation varies, but in the end we usually find that we have played the same class of business from first to last. Everett had been a stopgap all his life. He remembered going through a looking glass labyrinth when he was a boy and trying gallery after gallery, only at every turn to bump his nose against his own face—which, indeed, was not his own, but his brother's. No matter what his mission, east or west, by land or sea, he was sure to find himself employed in his brother's business, one of the tributary lives which helped to swell the shining current of Adriance Hilgarde's. It was not the first time that his duty had been to comfort, as best he could, one of the broken things his brother's imperious speed had cast aside and forgotten. He made no attempt to analyze the situation or to state it in exact terms; but he felt Katharine Gaylord's need for him, and he accepted it as a commission from his brother to help this woman to die. Day by day he felt her demands on him grow more imperious, her need for him grow more acute and positive; and day by day he felt that in his peculiar relation to her his own individuality played a smaller and smaller part. His power to minister to her comfort, he saw, lay solely in his link with his brother's life. He understood all that his physical resemblance meant to her. He knew that she sat by him always watching for some common trick of gesture, some familiar play of expression, some illusion of light and shadow, in which he should seem wholly Adriance. He knew that she lived upon this and that her disease fed upon it; that it sent shudders of remembrance through her and that in the exhaustion which followed this turmoil of her dying senses, she slept deep and sweet and dreamed of youth and art and days in a certain old Florentine garden, and not of bitterness and death.

The question which most perplexed him was, "How much shall I know? How much does she wish me to know?" A few days after his first meeting with Katharine Gaylord, he had cabled his brother to write her. He had merely said that she was mortally ill; he could depend on Adriance to say the right thing—that was a part of his gift. Adriance always said not only the right thing, but the opportune, graceful, exquisite thing. His phrases took the color of the moment and the then-present condition, so that they never savored of perfunctory compliment or frequent usage. He always caught the lyric essence of the moment, the poetic suggestion of every situation. Moreover, he usually did the right thing, the opportune, graceful, exquisite thing—except when he did very cruel things—bent upon making people happy when their existence touched his, just as he insisted that his material environment should be beautiful, lavishing upon those near him all the warmth and radiance of his rich nature, all the homage of the poet and troubadour, and, when they were no longer near, forgetting—for that also was a part of Adriance's gift.

Three weeks after Everett had sent his cable, when he made his daily call at the gaily painted ranch house, he found Katharine laughing like a schoolgirl. "Have you ever thought," she said, as he entered the music room, "how much these seances of ours are like Heine's *Florentine Nights,* except that I don't give you an opportunity to monopolize the conversation as Heine did?" She held his hand longer than usual, as she greeted him, and looked searchingly up into his face. "You are the kindest man living; the kindest," she added, softly.

Everett's gray face colored faintly as he drew his hand away, for he felt that this time she was looking at him and not at a whimsical caricature of his brother. "Why, what have I done now?" he asked, lamely. "I can't remember having sent you any stale candy or champagne since yesterday."

She drew a letter with a foreign postmark from between the leaves of a book and held it out, smiling. "You got him to write it. Don't say you didn't, for it came direct, you see, and the last address I gave him was a place in Florida. This deed shall be remembered of you when I am with the just in Paradise. But one thing you did not ask him to do, for you didn't know about it. He has sent me his latest work, the new sonata, the most ambitious thing he has ever done, and you are to play it for me directly, though it looks horribly intricate. But first for the letter; I think you would better read it aloud to me."

Everett sat down in a low chair facing the window seat in which she reclined with a barricade of pillows behind her. He opened the letter, his lashes half-veiling his kind eyes, and saw to his satisfaction that it was a long one—wonderfully tactful and tender, even for Adriance, who was tender with his valet and his stable boy, with his old gondolier and the beggar-women who prayed to the saints for him.

The letter was from Granada, written in the Alhambra, as he sat by the fountain of the Patio di Lindaraxa. The air was heavy with the warm fragrance of the South and full of the sound of splashing, running water, as it had been in a certain old garden in Florence, long ago. The sky was one great turquoise, heated until it glowed. The wonderful Moorish arches threw graceful blue shadows all about him. He had sketched an outline of them on the margin of his notepaper. The subtleties of Arabic decoration had cast an unholy spell over him, and the brutal exaggerations of Gothic art were a bad dream, easily forgotten. The Alhambra itself had, from the first, seemed perfectly familiar to him, and he knew that he must have trod that court, sleek and brown and obsequious, centuries before Ferdinand rode into Andalusia. The letter was full of confidences about his work, and delicate allusions to their old happy days of study and comradeship, and of her own work, still so warmly remembered and appreciatively discussed everywhere he went.

As Everett folded the letter he felt that Adriance had divined the thing needed and had risen to it in his own wonderful way. The letter was consistently egotistical and seemed to him even a trifle patronizing, yet it was just what she had wanted. A strong realization of his brother's charm and intensity and power came over him; he felt the breath of that whirlwind of flame in which Adriance passed, consuming all in his path, and himself even more resolutely than he consumed others. Then he looked down at this white, burnt-out brand that lay before him. "Like him, isn't it?" she said, quietly.

"I think I can scarcely answer his letter, but when you see him next you can do that for me. I want you to tell him many things for me, yet they can all be summed up in this: I want him to grow wholly into his best and greatest self, even at the cost of the dear boyishness that is half his charm to you and me. Do you understand me?"

"I know perfectly well what you mean," answered Everett, thoughtfully. "I have often felt so about him myself. And yet it's difficult to prescribe for those fellows; so little makes, so little mars."

Katharine raised herself upon her elbow, and her face flushed with feverish earnestness. "Ah, but it is the waste of himself that I mean; his lashing himself out on stupid and uncomprehending people until they take him at their own estimate. He can kindle marble, strike fire from putty, but is it worth what it costs him?"

"Come, come," expostulated Everett, alarmed at her excitement. "Where is the new sonata? Let him speak for himself."

He sat down at the piano and began playing the first movement, which was indeed the voice of Adriance, his proper speech. The sonata was the most ambitious work he had done up to that time and marked the transition from his purely lyric vein to a deeper and nobler style. Everett played intelligently and with that sympathetic comprehension which seems peculiar to a certain lovable class of men who never accomplish anything in particular. When he had finished he turned to Katharine.

"How he has grown!" she cried. "What the three last years have done for him! He used to write only the tragedies of passion; but this is the tragedy of the soul, the shadow coexistent with the soul. This is the tragedy of effort and failure, the thing Keats called hell. This is my tragedy, as I lie here spent by the racecourse, listening to the feet of the runners as they pass me. Ah, God! The swift feet of the runners!"

She turned her face away and covered it with her straining hands. Everett crossed over to her quickly and knelt beside her. In all the days he had known her she had never before, beyond an occasional ironical jest, given voice to the bitterness of her own defeat. Her courage had become a point of pride with him, and to see it going sickened him.

"Don't do it," he gasped. "I can't stand it, I really can't, I feel it too much. We mustn't speak of that; it's too tragic and too vast."

When she turned her face back to him there was a ghost of the old, brave, cynical smile on it, more bitter than the tears she could not shed. "No, I won't be so ungenerous; I will save that for the watches of the night when I have no better company. Now you may mix me another drink of some sort. Formerly, when it was not *if* I should ever sing Brunnhilde, but quite simply when I *should* sing Brunnhilde, I was always starving myself and thinking what I might drink and what I might not. But broken music boxes may drink whatsoever they list, and no one cares whether they lose their figure. Run over that theme at the beginning again. That, at least, is not new. It was running in his head when we were in Venice years ago, and he used to drum it on his glass at the dinner table. He had just begun to work it out when the late autumn came on, and the paleness of the Adriatic oppressed him, and he decided to go to Florence for the winter, and lost touch with the theme during his illness. Do you remember those frightful days? All the people who have loved him are not strong enough to save him from himself! When I got word from Florence that he had been ill I was in Nice filling a concert engagement. His wife was hurrying to him from Paris, but I reached him first. I arrived at dusk, in a terrific storm. They had taken an old palace there for the winter, and I found him in the library—a long, dark room full of old Latin books and heavy furniture and bronzes. He was sitting by a wood fire at one end of the room, looking, oh, so worn and pale!—as he always does when he is ill, you know. Ah, it is so good that you *do* know! Even his red smoking jacket lent no color to his face. His first words were not to tell me how ill he had been, but that that morning he had been well enough to put the last strokes to the score of his *Souvenirs d'Automne.* He was as I most like to remember him: so calm and happy and tired, not gay, as he usually is, but just contented and tired with that heavenly tiredness that comes after a good work done at last. Outside, the rain poured down in torrents, and the wind moaned for the pain of all the world and sobbed in the branches of the shivering olives and about the walls of that desolated old palace. How that night comes back to me! There were no lights in the room, only the wood fire which glowed upon the hard features of the bronze Dante, like the reflection of purgatorial flames, and threw long black shadows about us; beyond us it scarcely penetrated the gloom at all. Adriance sat staring at the fire with the weariness of all his life in his eyes, and of all the other lives that must aspire and suffer to make up one such life as his. Somehow the wind with all its world-pain had got into the room, and the cold rain was in our eyes, and the wave came up in both of us at once—that awful, vague, universal pain, that cold fear of life and death and God and hope—and we were like two clinging together on a spar in midocean after the shipwreck of everything. Then we heard the front door open with a great gust of wind that shook even the walls, and the servants came running with lights, announcing that Madam had returned, *'and in the book we read no more that night.'* "

She gave the old line with a certain bitter humor, and with the hard, bright smile in which of old she had wrapped her weakness as in a glittering garment. That ironical smile, worn like a mask through so many years, had gradually changed even the lines of her face completely, and when she looked in the mirror she saw not herself, but the scathing critic, the amused observer and satirist of herself. Everett dropped his head upon his hand and sat looking at the rug. "How much you have cared!" he said.

"Ah, yes, I cared," she replied, closing her eyes with a long-drawn sigh of relief; and lying perfectly still, she went on: "You can't imagine what a comfort it is to have you know how I cared, what a relief it is to be able to tell it to someone. I used to want to shriek it out to the world in the long nights when I could not sleep. It seemed to me that I could not die with it. It demanded some sort of expression. And now that you know, you would scarcely believe how much less sharp the anguish of it is."

Everett continued to look helplessly at the floor. "I was not sure how much you wanted me to know," he said.

"Oh, I intended you should know from the first time I looked into your face, when you came that day with Charley. I flatter myself that I have been able to conceal it when I chose, though I suppose women always think that. The more observing ones may have seen, but discerning people are usually discreet and often kind, for we usually bleed a little before we begin to discern. But I wanted you to know; you are so like him that it is almost like telling him himself. At least, I feel now that he will know some day, and then I will be quite sacred from his compassion, for we none of us dare pity the dead. Since it was what my life has chiefly meant, I should like him to know. On the whole I am not ashamed of it. I have fought a good fight."

"And has he never known at all?" asked Everett, in a thick voice.

"Oh! Never at all in the way that you mean. Of course, he is accustomed to looking into the eyes of women and finding love there; when he doesn't find it there he thinks he must have been guilty of some discourtesy and is miserable about it. He has a genuine fondness for everyone who is not stupid or gloomy, or old or preternaturally ugly. Granted youth and cheerfulness, and a moderate amount of wit and some tact, and Adriance will always be glad to see you coming around the corner. I shared with the rest; shared the smiles and the gallantries and the droll little sermons. It was quite like a Sunday-school picnic; we wore our best clothes and a smile and took our turns. It was his kindness that was hardest. I have pretty well used my life up at standing punishment."

"Don't; you'll make me hate him," groaned Everett.

Katharine laughed and began to play nervously with her fan. "It wasn't in the slightest degree his fault; that is the most grotesque part of it. Why, it had really begun before I ever met him. I fought my way to him, and I drank my doom greedily enough."

Everett rose and stood hesitating. "I think I must go. You ought to be quiet, and I don't think I can hear any more just now."

She put out her hand and took his playfully. "You've put in three weeks at this sort of thing, haven't you? Well, it may never be to your glory in this world, perhaps, but it's been the mercy of heaven to me, and it ought to square accounts for a much worse life than yours will ever be."

Everett knelt beside her, saying, brokenly: "I stayed because I wanted to be with you, that's all. I have never cared about other women since I met you in New York when I was a lad. You are a part of my destiny, and I could not leave you if I would."

She put her hands on his shoulders and shook her head. "No, no; don't tell me that. I have seen enough of tragedy, God knows. Don't show me any more just as the curtain is going down. No, no, it was only a boy's fancy, and your divine pity and my utter pitiableness have recalled it for a moment. One does not love the dying, dear friend. If some fancy of that sort had been left over from boyhood, this would rid you of it, and that were well. Now go, and you will come again tomorrow, as long as there are tomorrows, will you not?" She took his hand with a smile that lifted the mask from her soul, that was both courage and despair, and full of infinite loyalty and tenderness, as she said softly:

> Forever and forever, farewell, Cassius;
> If we do meet again, why, we shall smile;
> If not, why then, this parting was well made.

The courage in her eyes was like the clear light of a star to him as he went out.

On the night of Adriance Hilgarde's opening concert in Paris Everett sat by the bed in the ranch house in Wyoming, watching over the last battle that we have with the flesh before we are done with it and free of it forever. At times it seemed that the serene soul of her must have left already and found some refuge from the storm, and only the tenacious animal life were left to do battle with death. She labored under a delusion at once pitiful and merciful, thinking that she was in the Pullman on her way to New York, going back to her life and her work. When she aroused from her stupor it was only to ask the porter to waken her half an hour out of Jersey City, or to remonstrate with him about the delays and the roughness of the road. At midnight Everett and the nurse were left alone with her. Poor Charley Gaylord had lain down on a couch outside the door. Everett sat looking at the sputtering night lamp until it made his eyes ache. His head dropped forward on the foot of the bed, and he sank into a heavy, distressful slumber. He was dreaming of Adriance's concert in Paris, and of Adriance, the troubadour, smiling and debonair, with his boyish face and the touch of silver gray in his hair. He heard the applause and he saw the roses going up over the footlights until they were stacked half as high as the piano, and the petals fell and scattered, making crimson splotches on the floor. Down this crimson pathway came Adriance with his youthful step, leading his prima donna by the hand; a dark woman this time, with Spanish eyes.

The nurse touched him on the shoulder; he started and awoke. She screened the lamp with her hand. Everett saw that Katharine was awake and conscious, and struggling a little. He lifted her gently on his arm and began to fan her. She laid her hands lightly on his hair and looked into his face with eyes that seemed never to have wept or doubted. "Ah, dear Adriance, dear, dear," she whispered.

Everett went to call her brother, but when they came back the madness of art was over for Katharine.

Two days later Everett was pacing the station siding, waiting for the westbound train. Charley Gaylord walked beside him, but the two men had nothing to say to each other. Everett's bags were piled on the truck, and his step was hurried and his eyes were full of impatience, as he gazed again and again up the track, watching for the train. Gaylord's impatience was not less than his own; these two, who had grown so close, had now become painful and impossible to each other, and longed for the wrench of farewell.

As the train pulled in Everett wrung Gaylord's hand among the crowd of alighting passengers. The people of a German opera company, en route to the coast, rushed by them in frantic haste to snatch their breakfast during the stop. Everett heard an exclamation in a broad German dialect, and a massive woman whose figure persistently escaped from her stays in the most improbable places rushed up to him, her blond hair disordered by the wind, and glowing with joyful surprise she caught his coat sleeve with her tightly gloved hands.

"Herr Gott, Adriance, *lieber Freund,"* she cried, emotionally.

Everett quickly withdrew his arm and lifted his hat, blushing. "Pardon me, madam, but I see that you have mistaken me for Adriance Hilgarde. I am his brother," he said quietly, and turning from the crestfallen singer, he hurried into the car.

The Marriage of Phaedra

THE SEQUENCE of events was such that MacMaster did not make his pilgrimage to Hugh Treffinger's studio until three years after that painter's death. MacMaster was himself a painter, an American of the Gallicized type, who spent his winters in New York, his summers in Paris, and no inconsiderable amount of time on the broad waters between. He had often contemplated stopping in London on one of his return trips in the late autumn, but he had always deferred leaving Paris until the prick of necessity drove him home by the quickest and shortest route.

Treffinger was a comparatively young man at the time of his death, and there had seemed no occasion for haste until haste was of no avail. Then, possibly, though there had been some correspondence between them, MacMaster felt certain qualms about meeting in the flesh a man who in the flesh was so diversely reported. His intercourse with Treffinger's work had been so deep and satisfying, so apart from other appreciations, that he rather dreaded a critical juncture of any sort. He had always felt himself singularly inept in personal relations, and in this case he had avoided the issue until it was no longer to be feared or hoped for. There still remained, however, Treffinger's great unfinished picture, the *Marriage of Phaedra,* which had never left his studio, and of which MacMaster's friends had now and again brought report that it was the painter's most characteristic production.

The young man arrived in London in the evening, and the next morning went out to Kensington to find Treffinger's studio. It lay in one of the perplexing bystreets off Holland Road, and the number he found on a door set in a high garden wall, the top of which was covered with broken green glass and over which a budding lilac bush nodded. Treffinger's plate was still there, and a card requesting visitors to ring for the attendant. In response to MacMaster's ring, the door was opened by a cleanly built little man, clad in a shooting jacket and trousers that had been made for an ampler figure. He had a fresh complexion, eyes of that common uncertain shade of gray, and was closely shaven except for the incipient muttonchops on his ruddy cheeks. He bore himself in a manner strikingly capable, and there was a sort of trimness and alertness about him, despite the too-generous shoulders of his coat. In one hand he held a bulldog pipe, and in the other a copy of *Sporting Life.* While MacMaster was explaining the purpose of his call he noticed that the man surveyed him critically, though not impertinently. He was admitted into a little tank of a lodge made of whitewashed stone, the back door and windows opening upon a garden. A visitor's book and a pile of catalogues lay on a deal table, together with a bottle of ink and some rusty pens. The wall was ornamented with photographs and colored prints of racing favorites.

"The studio is h'only open to the public on Saturdays and Sundays," explained the man—he referred to himself as "Jymes"—"but of course we make exceptions in the case of pynters. Lydy Elling Treffinger 'erself is on the Continent, but Sir 'Ugh's orders was that pynters was to 'ave the run of the place." He selected a key from his pocket and threw open the door into the studio which, like the lodge, was built against the wall of the garden.

MacMaster entered a long, narrow room, built of smoothed planks, painted a light green, cold and damp even on that fine May morning. The room was utterly bare of furniture—unless a stepladder, a model throne, and a rack laden with large leather portfolios could be accounted such—and was windowless, without other openings than the door and the skylight, under which hung the unfinished picture itself. MacMaster had never seen so many of Treffinger's paintings together. He knew the painter had married a woman with money and had been able to keep such of his pictures as he wished. These, with all of his replicas and studies, he had left as a sort of common legacy to the younger men of the school he had originated.

As soon as he was left alone MacMaster sat down on the edge of the model throne before the unfinished picture. Here indeed was what he had come for; it rather paralyzed his receptivity for the moment, but gradually the thing found its way to him.

At one o'clock he was standing before the collection of studies done for *Boccaccio's Garden* when he heard a voice at his elbow.

"Pardon, sir, but I was just about to lock up and go to lunch. Are you lookin' for the figure study of Boccaccio 'imself?" James queried respectfully. "Lydy Elling Treffinger give it to Mr. Rossiter to take down to Oxford for some lectures he's been agiving there."

"Did he never paint out his studies, then?" asked MacMaster with perplexity. "Here are two completed ones for this picture. Why did he keep them?"

"I don't know as I could say as to that, sir," replied James, smiling indulgently, "but that was 'is way. That is to say, 'e pynted out very frequent, but 'e always made two studies to stand; one in watercolors and one in oils, before 'e went at the final picture—to say nothink of all the pose studies 'e made in pencil before he begun on the composition proper at all. He was that particular. You see, 'e wasn't so keen for the final effect as for the proper pyntin' of 'is pictures. 'E used to say they ought to be well made, the same as any other h'article of trade. I can lay my 'and on the pose studies for you, sir." He rummaged in one of the portfolios and produced half a dozen drawings. "These three," he continued, "was discarded; these two was the pose he finally accepted; this one without alteration, as it were.

"That's in Paris, as I remember," James continued reflectively. "It went with the *Saint Cecilia* into the Baron H——'s collection. Could you tell me, sir, 'as 'e it still? I don't like to lose account of them, but some 'as changed 'ands since Sir 'Ugh's death."

"H——'s collection is still intact, I believe," replied MacMaster. "You were with Treffinger long?"

"From my boyhood, sir," replied James with gravity. "I was a stable boy when 'e took me."

"You were his man, then?"

"That's it, sir. Nobody else ever done anything around the studio. I always mixed 'is colors and 'e taught me to do a share of the varnishin'; 'e said as 'ow there wasn't a 'ouse in England as could do it proper. You ayn't looked at the *Marriage* yet, sir?" he asked abruptly, glancing doubtfully at MacMaster, and indicating with his thumb the picture under the north light.

"Not very closely. I prefer to begin with something simpler; that's rather appalling, at first glance," replied MacMaster.

"Well may you say that, sir," said James warmly. "That one regular killed Sir 'Ugh; it regular broke 'im up, and nothink will ever convince me as 'ow it didn't bring on 'is second stroke."

When MacMaster walked back to High Street to take his bus his mind was divided between two exultant convictions. He felt that he had not only found Treffinger's greatest picture, but that, in James, he had discovered a kind of cryptic index to the painter's personality—a clue which, if tactfully followed, might lead to much.

Several days after his first visit to the studio, MacMaster wrote to Lady

Mary Percy, telling her that he would be in London for some time and asking her if he might call. Lady Mary was an only sister of Lady Ellen Treffinger, the painter's widow, and MacMaster had known her during one winter he spent at Nice. He had known her, indeed, very well, and Lady Mary, who was astonishingly frank and communicative upon all subjects, had been no less so upon the matter of her sister's unfortunate marriage.

In her reply to his note Lady Mary named an afternoon when she would be alone. She was as good as her word, and when MacMaster arrived he found the drawing room empty. Lady Mary entered shortly after he was announced. She was a tall woman, thin and stiffly jointed, and her body stood out under the folds of her gown with the rigor of cast iron. This rather metallic suggestion was further carried out in her heavily knuckled hands, her stiff gray hair, and her long, bold-featured face, which was saved from freakishness only by her alert eyes.

"Really," said Lady Mary, taking a seat beside him and giving him a sort of military inspection through her nose glasses, "really, I had begun to fear that I had lost you altogether. It's four years since I saw you at Nice, isn't it? I was in Paris last winter, but I heard nothing from you."

"I was in New York then."

"It occurred to me that you might be. And why are you in London?"

"Can you ask?" replied MacMaster gallantly.

Lady Mary smiled ironically. "But for what else, incidentally?"

"Well, incidentally, I came to see Treffinger's studio and his unfinished picture. Since I've been here, I've decided to stay the summer. I'm even thinking of attempting to do a biography of him."

"So that is what brought you to London?"

"Not exactly. I had really no intention of anything so serious when I came. It's his last picture, I fancy, that has rather thrust it upon me. The notion has settled down on me like a thing destined."

"You'll not be offended if I question the clemency of such a destiny," remarked Lady Mary dryly. "Isn't there rather a surplus of books on that subject already?"

"Such as they are. Oh, I've read them all"—here MacMaster faced Lady Mary triumphantly. "He has quite escaped your amiable critics," he added, smiling.

"I know well enough what you think, and I daresay we are not much on art," said Lady Mary with tolerant good humor. "We leave that to peoples who have no physique. Treffinger made a stir for a time, but it seems that we are not capable of a sustained appreciation of such extraordinary methods. In the end we go back to the pictures we find agreeable and unperplexing. He was regarded as an experiment, I fancy; and now it seems that he was rather an unsuccessful one. If you've come to us in a missionary spirit, we'll tolerate you politely, but we'll laugh in our sleeve, I warn you."

"That really doesn't daunt me, Lady Mary," declared MacMaster blandly. "As I told you, I'm a man with a mission."

Lady Mary laughed her hoarse, baritone laugh. "Bravo! And you've come to me for inspiration for your panegyric?"

MacMaster smiled with some embarrassment. "Not altogether for that purpose. But I want to consult you, Lady Mary, about the advisability of troubling Lady Ellen Treffinger in the matter. It seems scarcely legitimate to go on without asking her to give some sort of grace to my proceedings, yet I feared the whole subject might be painful to her. I shall rely wholly upon your discretion."

"I think she would prefer to be consulted," replied Lady Mary judicially. "I can't understand how she endures to have the wretched affair continually raked up, but she does. She seems to feel a sort of moral responsibility. Ellen has always been singularly conscientious about this matter, insofar as her light goes—which rather puzzles me, as hers is not exactly a magnanimous nature. She is certainly trying to do what she believes to be the right thing. I shall write to her, and you can see her when she returns from Italy."

"I want very much to meet her. She is, I hope, quite recovered in every way," queried MacMaster, hesitatingly.

"No, I can't say that she is. She has remained in much the same condition she sank to before his death. He trampled over pretty much whatever there was in her, I fancy. Women don't recover from wounds of that sort—at least, not women of Ellen's grain. They go on bleeding inwardly."

"You, at any rate, have not grown more reconciled," MacMaster ventured.

"Oh, I give him his dues. He was a colorist, I grant you; but that is a vague and unsatisfactory quality to marry to; Lady Ellen Treffinger found it so."

"But, my dear Lady Mary," expostulated MacMaster, "and just repress me if I'm becoming too personal—but it must, in the first place, have been a marriage of choice on her part as well as on his."

Lady Mary poised her glasses on her large forefinger and assumed an attitude suggestive of the clinical lecture room as she replied. "Ellen, my dear boy, is an essentially romantic person. She is quiet about it, but she runs deep. I never knew how deep until I came against her on the issue of that marriage. She was always discontented as a girl; she found things dull and prosaic, and the ardor of his courtship was agreeable to her. He met her during her first season in town. She is handsome, and there were plenty of other men, but I grant you your scowling brigand was the most picturesque of the lot. In his courtship, as in everything else, he was theatrical to the point of being ridiculous, but Ellen's sense of humor is not her strongest quality. He had the charm of celebrity, the air of a man who could storm his way through anything to get what he wanted. That sort of vehemence is particularly effective with women like Ellen, who can be warmed only by reflected heat, and she couldn't at all stand out against it. He convinced her of his necessity; and that done, all's done."

"I can't help thinking that, even on such a basis, the marriage should have turned out better," MacMaster remarked reflectively.

"The marriage," Lady Mary continued with a shrug, "was made on the basis of a mutual misunderstanding. Ellen, in the nature of the case, believed that she was doing something quite out of the ordinary in accepting him, and expected concessions which, apparently, it never occurred to him to make. After his marriage he relapsed into his old habits of incessant work, broken by violent and often brutal relaxations. He insulted her friends and foisted his own upon her—many of them well calculated to arouse aversion in any well-bred girl. He had Ghillini constantly at the house—a homeless vagabond, whose conversation was impossible. I don't say, mind you, that he had not grievances on his side. He had probably overrated the girl's possibilities, and he let her see that he was disappointed in her. Only a large and generous nature could have borne with him, and Ellen's is not that. She could not at all understand that odious strain of plebeian pride which plumes itself upon not having risen above its sources."

As MacMaster drove back to his hotel he reflected that Lady Mary Percy had probably had good cause for dissatisfaction with her brother-in-law. Treffinger was, indeed, the last man who should have married into the Percy family. The son of a small tobacconist, he had grown up a sign-painter's apprentice; idle, lawless, and practically letterless until he had drifted into the night classes of the Albert League, where Ghillini sometimes lectured. From the moment he came under the eye and influence of that erratic Italian, then a political exile, his life had swerved sharply from its old channel. This man had been at once incentive and guide, friend and master, to his pupil. He had taken the raw clay out of the London streets and molded it anew. Seemingly he had divined at once where the boy's possibilities lay, and had thrown aside every canon of orthodox instruction in the training of him. Under him Treffinger acquired his superficial, yet facile, knowledge of the classics; had steeped himself in the monkish Latin and medieval romances which later gave his work so naive and remote a quality. That was the beginning of the wattle fences, the cobble pave, the brown roof beams, the cunningly wrought fabrics that gave to his pictures such a richness of decorative effect.

As he had told Lady Mary Percy, MacMaster had found the imperative inspiration of his purpose in Treffinger's unfinished picture, the *Marriage of Phaedra.* He had always believed that the key to Treffinger's individuality lay in his singular education; in the *Roman de la Rose,* in Boccaccio, and Amadis, those works which had literally transcribed themselves upon the blank soul of the London street boy, and through which he had been born into the world of spiritual things. Treffinger had been a man who lived after his imagination; and his mind, his ideals and, as MacMaster believed, even his personal ethics, had to the last been colored by the trend of his early training. There was in him alike the freshness and spontaneity, the frank brutality and the religious mysticism, which lay well back of the fifteenth century. In the *Marriage of Phaedra* MacMaster found the ultimate expression of this spirit, the final word as to Treffinger's point of view.

As in all Treffinger's classical subjects, the conception was wholly medieval. This Phaedra, just turning from her husband and maidens to greet her husband's son, giving him her first fearsome glance from under her half-lifted veil, was no daughter of Minos. The daughter of *heathenesse* and the early church she was; doomed to torturing visions and scourgings, and the wrangling of soul with flesh. The venerable Theseus might have been victorious Charlemagne, and Phaedra's maidens belonged rather in the train of Blanche of Castile than at the Cretan court. In the earlier studies Hippolytus had been done with a more pagan suggestion; but in each successive drawing the glorious figure had been deflowered of something of its serene unconsciousness, until, in the canvas under the skylight, he appeared a very Christian knight. This male figure, and the face of Phaedra, painted with such magical preservation of tone under the heavy shadow of the veil, were plainly Treffinger's highest achievements of craftsmanship. By what labor he had reached the seemingly inevitable composition of the picture—with its twenty figures, its plenitude of light and air, its restful distances seen through white porticoes—countless studies bore witness.

From James's attitude toward the picture MacMaster could well conjecture what the painter's had been. This picture was always uppermost in James's mind; its custodianship formed, in his eyes, his occupation. He was manifestly apprehensive when visitors—not many came nowadays—lingered near it. "It was the *Marriage* as killed 'im," he would often say, "and for the matter 'o that, it did like to 'av been the death of all of us."

By the end of his second week in London MacMaster had begun the notes for his study of Hugh Treffinger and his work. When his researches led him occasionally to visit the studios of Treffinger's friends and erstwhile disciples, he found their Treffinger manner fading as the ring of Treffinger's personality died out in them. One by one they were stealing back into the fold of national British art; the hand that had wound them up was still. MacMaster despaired of them and confined himself more and more exclusively to the studio, to such of Treffinger's letters as were available—they were for the most part singularly negative and colorless—and to his interrogation of Treffinger's man.

He could not himself have traced the successive steps by which he was gradually admitted into James's confidence. Certainly most of his adroit strategies to that end failed humiliatingly, and whatever it was that built up an understanding between them must have been instinctive and intuitive on both sides. When at last James became anecdotal, personal, there was that in every word he let fall which put breath and blood into MacMaster's book. James had so long been steeped in that penetrating personality that he fairly exuded it. Many of his very phrases, mannerisms, and opinions were impressions that he had taken on like wet plaster in his daily contact with Treffinger. Inwardly he was lined with cast-off epitheliums, as outwardly he was clad in the painter's discarded coats. If the painter's letters were formal and perfunctory, if his expressions to his friends had been extravagant, contradictory, and often apparently insincere—still, MacMaster felt himself not entirely without authentic sources. It was James who possessed Treffinger's legend; it was with James that he had laid aside his pose. Only in his studio, alone, and face to face with his work, as it seemed, had the man invariably been himself. James had known him in the one attitude in which he was entirely honest; their relation had fallen well within the painter's only indubitable integrity. James's report of Treffinger was distorted by no hallucination of artistic insight, colored by no interpretation of his own. He merely held what he had heard and seen; his mind was a sort of camera obscura. His very limitations made him the more literal and minutely accurate.

One morning, when MacMaster was seated before the *Marriage of Phaedra,* James entered on his usual round of dusting.

"I've 'eard from Lydy Elling by the post, sir," he remarked, "an' she's give h'orders to 'ave the 'ouse put in readiness. I doubt she'll be 'ere by Thursday or Friday next."

"She spends most of her time abroad?" queried MacMaster; on the subject of Lady Treffinger James consistently maintained a very delicate reserve.

"Well, you could 'ardly say she does that, sir. She finds the 'ouse a bit dull, I daresay, so durin' the season she stops mostly with Lydy Mary Percy, at Grosvenor Square. Lydy Mary's a h'only sister." After a few moments he continued, speaking in jerks governed by the rigor of his dusting: "H'only this morning I come upon this scarf-pin," exhibiting a very striking instance of that article, "an' I recalled as 'ow Sir 'Ugh give it me when 'e was acourting of Lydy Elling. Blowed if I ever see a man go in for a 'oman like 'im! 'E was that gone, sir. 'E never went in on anythink so 'ard before nor since, till 'e went in on the *Marriage* there—though 'e mostly went in on things pretty keen; 'ad the measles when 'e was thirty, strong as cholera, an' come close to dyin' of 'em. 'E wasn't strong for Lydy Elling's set; they was a bit too stiff for 'im. A free an' easy gentleman, 'e was; 'e liked 'is dinner with a few friends an' them jolly, but 'e wasn't much on what you might call big affairs. But once 'e went in for Lydy Elling 'e broke 'imself to new paces. He give away 'is rings an' pins, an' the tylor's man an' the 'aberdasher's man was at 'is rooms continual. 'E got 'imself put up for a club in Piccadilly; 'e starved 'imself thin, an' worrited 'imself white, an' ironed 'imself out, an' drawed 'imself tight as a bow string. It was a good job 'e come a winner, or I don't know w'at'd 'a been to pay."

The next week, in consequence of an invitation from Lady Ellen Treffinger, MacMaster went one afternoon to take tea with her. He was shown into the garden that lay between the residence and the studio, where the tea table was set under a gnarled pear tree. Lady Ellen rose as he approached—he was astonished to note how tall she was—and greeted him graciously, saying that she already knew him through her sister. MacMaster felt a certain satisfaction in her: in her reassuring poise and repose, in the charming modulations of her voice and the indolent reserve of her full, almond eyes. He was even delighted to find her face so inscrutable, though it chilled his own warmth and made the open frankness he had wished to permit himself impossible. It was a long face, narrow at the chin, very delicately featured, yet steeled by an impassive mask of self-control. It was behind just such finely cut, close-sealed faces, MacMaster reflected, that nature sometimes hid astonishing secrets. But in spite of this suggestion of hardness he felt that the unerring taste that Treffinger had always shown in larger matters had not deserted him when he came to the choosing of a wife, and he admitted that he could not himself have selected a woman who looked more as Treffinger's wife should look.

While he was explaining the purpose of his frequent visits to the studio she heard him with courteous interest. "I have read, I think, everything that has been published on Sir Hugh Treffinger's work, and it seems to me that there is much left to be said," he concluded.

"I believe they are rather inadequate," she remarked vaguely. She hesitated a moment, absently fingering the ribbons of her gown, then continued, without raising her eyes; "I hope you will not think me too exacting if I ask to see the proofs of such chapters of your work as have to do with Sir Hugh's personal life. I have always asked that privilege."

MacMaster hastily assured her as to this, adding, "I mean to touch on only such facts in his personal life as have to do directly with his work—such as his monkish education under Ghillini."

"I see your meaning, I think," said Lady Ellen, looking at him with wide, uncomprehending eyes.

When MacMaster stopped at the studio on leaving the house he stood for some time before Treffinger's one portrait of himself: that brigand of a picture, with its full throat and square head, the short upper lip blackened by the close-clipped mustache, the wiry hair tossed down over the forehead, the strong white teeth set hard on a short pipestem. He could well understand what manifold tortures the mere grain of the man's strong red and brown flesh might have inflicted upon a woman like Lady Ellen. He could conjecture, too, Treffinger's impotent revolt against that very repose which had so dazzled him when it first defied his daring—and how once possessed of it, his first instinct had been to crush it, since he could not melt it.

Toward the close of the season Lady Ellen Treffinger left town. MacMaster's work was progressing rapidly, and he and James wore away the days in their peculiar relation, which by this time had much of friendliness. Excepting for the regular visits of a Jewish picture dealer, there were few intrusions upon their solitude. Occasionally a party of Americans rang at the little door in the garden wall, but usually they departed speedily for the Moorish hall and tinkling fountain of the great show studio of London, not far away.

This Jew, an Austrian by birth, who had a large business in Melbourne, Australia, was a man of considerable discrimination, and at once selected the *Marriage of Phaedra* as the object of his especial interest. When, upon his first visit, Lichtenstein had declared the picture one of the things done for time, MacMaster had rather warmed toward him and had talked to him very freely. Later, however, the man's repulsive personality and innate vulgarity so wore upon him that, the more genuine the Jew's appreciation, the more he resented it and the more base he somehow felt it to be. It annoyed him to see Lichtenstein walking up and down before the picture, shaking his head and blinking his watery eyes over his nose glasses, ejaculating: "Dot is a chem, a chem! It is wordt to gome den dousant miles for such a bainting, eh? To make Eurobe abbreciate such a work of ardt it is necessary to take it away while she is napping. She has never abbreciated until she has lost, but," knowingly, "she will buy back."

James had, from the first, felt such a distrust of the man that he would never leave him alone in the studio for a moment. When Lichtenstein insisted upon having Lady Ellen Treffinger's address James rose to the point of insolence. "It ayn't no use to give it, noway. Lydy Treffinger never has nothink to do with dealers." MacMaster quietly repented his rash confidences, fearing that he might indirectly cause Lady Ellen annoyance from this merciless speculator, and he recalled with chagrin that Lichtenstein had extorted from him, little by little, pretty much the entire plan of his book, and especially the place in it which the *Marriage of Phaedra* was to occupy.

By this time the first chapters of MacMaster's book were in the hands of his publisher, and his visits to the studio were necessarily less frequent. The greater part of his time was now employed with the engravers who were to reproduce such of Treffinger's pictures as he intended to use as illustrations.

He returned to his hotel late one evening after a long and vexing day at the engravers to find James in his room, seated on his steamer trunk by the window, with the outline of a great square draped in sheets resting against his knee.

"Why, James, what's up?" he cried in astonishment, glancing inquiringly at the sheeted object.

"Ayn't you seen the pypers, sir?" jerked out the man.

"No, now I think of it, I haven't even looked at a paper. I've been at the engravers' plant all day. I haven't seen anything."

James drew a copy of the *Times* from his pocket and handed it to him, pointing with a tragic finger to a paragraph in the social column. It was merely the announcement of Lady Ellen Treffinger's engagement to Captain Alexander Gresham.

"Well, what of it, my man? That surely is her privilege."

James took the paper, turned to another page, and silently pointed to a paragraph in the art notes which stated that Lady Treffinger had presented to the X—— gallery the entire collection of paintings and sketches now in her late husband's studio, with the exception of his unfinished picture, the *Marriage of Phaedra,* which she had sold for a large sum to an Australian dealer who had come to London purposely to secure some of Treffinger's paintings.

MacMaster pursed up his lips and sat down, his overcoat still on. "Well, James, this is something of a—something of a jolt, eh? It never occurred to me she'd really do it."

"Lord, you don't know 'er, sir," said James bitterly, still staring at the floor in an attitude of abandoned dejection.

MacMaster started up in a flash of enlightenment, "What on earth have you got there, James? It's not—surely it's not—"

"Yes, it is, sir," broke in the man excitedly. "It's the *Marriage* itself. It ayn't agoing to H'Australia, no'ow!"

"But man, what are you going to do with it? It's Lichtenstein's property now, as it seems."

"It ayn't, sir, that it ayn't. No, by Gawd, it ayn't!" shouted James, breaking into a choking fury. He controlled himself with an effort and added supplicatingly: "Oh, sir, you ayn't agoing to see it go to H'Australia, w'ere they send convic's?" He unpinned and flung aside the sheets as though to let *Phaedra* plead for herself.

MacMaster sat down again and looked sadly at the doomed masterpiece. The notion of James having carried it across London that night rather appealed to his fancy. There was certainly a flavor about such a highhanded proceeding. "However did you get it here?" he queried.

"I got a four-wheeler and come over direct, sir. Good job I 'appened to 'ave the chaynge about me."

"You came up High Street, up Piccadilly, through the Haymarket and Trafalgar Square, and into the Strand?" queried MacMaster with a relish.

"Yes, sir. Of course, sir," assented James with surprise.

MacMaster laughed delightedly. "It was a beautiful idea, James, but I'm afraid we can't carry it any further."

"I was thinkin' as 'ow it would be a rare chance to get you to take the *Marriage* over to Paris for a year or two, sir, until the thing blows over?" suggested James blandly.

"I'm afraid that's out of the question, James. I haven't the right stuff in me for a pirate, or even a vulgar smuggler, I'm afraid." MacMaster found it surprisingly difficult to say this, and he busied himself with the lamp as he said it. He heard James's hand fall heavily on the trunk top, and he discovered that he very much disliked sinking in the man's estimation.

"Well, sir," remarked James in a more formal tone, after a protracted silence, "then there's nothink for it but as 'ow I'll 'ave to make way with it myself."

"And how about your character, James? The evidence would be heavy against you, and even if Lady Treffinger didn't prosecute you'd be done for."

"Blow my character!—your pardon, sir," cried James, starting to his feet. "W'at do I want of a character? I'll chuck the 'ole thing, and damned lively, too. The shop's to be sold out, an' my place is gone any'ow. I'm agoing to enlist, or try the gold fields. I've lived too long with h'artists; I'd never give satisfaction in livery now. You know 'ow it is yourself, sir; there ayn't no life like it, no'ow."

For a moment MacMaster was almost equal to abetting James in his theft. He reflected that pictures had been whitewashed, or hidden in the crypts of churches, or under the floors of palaces from meaner motives, and to save them from a fate less ignominious. But presently, with a sigh, he shook his head.

"No, James, it won't do at all. It has been tried over and over again, ever since the world has been agoing and pictures amaking. It was tried in Florence and in Venice, but the pictures were always carried away in the end. You see, the difficulty is that, although Treffinger told you what was not to be done with the picture, he did not say definitely what was to be done with it. Do you think Lady Treffinger really understands that he did not want it to be sold?"

"Well, sir, it was like this, sir," said James, resuming his seat on the trunk and again resting the picture against his knee. "My memory is as clear as glass about it. After Sir 'Ugh got up from 'is first stroke, 'e took a fresh start at the *Marriage*. Before that 'e 'ad been working at it only at night for a while back; the *Legend* was the big picture then, an' was under the north light w'ere 'e worked of a morning. But one day 'e bid me take the *Legend* down an' put the *Marriage* in its place, an' 'e says, dashin' on 'is jacket, 'Jymes, this is a start for the finish, this time.'

"From that on 'e worked at the night picture in the mornin'—a thing contrary to 'is custom. The *Marriage* went wrong, and wrong—an' Sir 'Ugh agettin' seedier an' seedier every day. 'E tried models an' models, an' smudged an' pynted out on account of 'er face goin' wrong in the shadow. Sometimes 'e layed it on the colors, an' swore at me an' things in general. He got that discouraged about 'imself that on 'is low days 'e used to say to me: 'Jymes, remember one thing; if anythink 'appens to me, the *Marriage* is not to go out of 'ere unfinished. It's worth the lot of 'em, my boy, an' it's not agoing to go shabby for lack of pains.' 'E said things to that effect repeated.

"He was workin' at the picture the last day, before 'e went to 'is club. 'E kept the carriage waitin' near an hour while 'e put on a stroke an' then drawed back for to look at it, an' then put on another, careful like. After 'e 'ad 'is gloves on, 'e come back an' took away the brushes I was startin' to clean, an' put in another touch or two. 'It's acomin' Jymes,' 'e says, 'by gad if it ayn't.' An' with that 'e goes out. It was cruel sudden, w'at come after.

"That night I was lookin' to 'is clothes at the 'ouse when they brought 'im 'ome. He was conscious, but w'en I ran downstairs for to 'elp lift 'im up, I knowed 'e was a finished man. After we got 'im into bed 'e kept lookin' restless at me and then at Lydy Elling and ajerkin' of 'is 'and. Finally 'e quite raised it an' shot 'is thumb out toward the wall. 'He wants water; ring, Jymes,' says Lydy Elling, placid. But I knowed 'e was pointin' to the shop.

" 'Lydy Treffinger,' says I, bold, 'he's pointin' to the studio. He means about the *Marriage;* 'e told me today as 'ow 'e never wanted it sold unfinished. Is that it, Sir 'Ugh?'

"He smiled an' nodded slight an' closed 'is eyes. 'Thank you, Jymes,' says Lydy Elling, placid. Then 'e opened 'is eyes an' looked long and 'ard at Lydy Elling.

" 'Of course I'll try to do as you'd wish about the picture, 'Ugh, if that's w'at's troublin' you,' she says quiet. With that 'e closed 'is eyes and 'e never opened 'em. He died unconscious at four that mornin'.

"You see, sir, Lydy Elling was always cruel 'ard on the *Marriage.* From the first it went wrong, an' Sir 'Ugh was out of temper pretty constant. She came into the studio one day and looked at the picture an' asked 'im why 'e didn't throw it up an' quit aworriting 'imself. He answered sharp, an' with that she said as 'ow she didn't see w'at there was to make such a row about, no'ow. She spoke 'er mind about that picture, free; an' Sir 'Ugh swore 'ot an' let a 'andful of brushes fly at 'is study, an' Lydy Elling picked up 'er skirts careful an' chill, an' drifted out of the studio with 'er eyes calm and 'er chin 'igh. If there was one thing Lydy Elling 'ad no comprehension of, it was the usefulness of swearin'. So the *Marriage* was a sore thing between 'em. She is uncommon calm, but uncommon bitter, is Lydy Elling. She's never come anear the studio since that day she went out 'oldin up of 'er skirts. W'en 'er friends goes over she excuses 'erself along o' the strain. Strain—Gawd!" James ground his wrath short in his teeth.

"I'll tell you what I'll do, James, and it's our only hope. I'll see Lady Ellen tomorrow. The *Times* says she returned today. You take the picture back to its place, and I'll do what I can for it. If anything is done to save it, it must be done through Lady Ellen Treffinger herself; that much is clear. I can't think that she fully understands the situation. If she did, you know, she really couldn't have any motive —" He stopped suddenly. Somehow, in the dusky lamplight, her small, close-sealed face came ominously back to him. He rubbed his forehead and knitted his brows thoughtfully. After a moment he shook his head and went on: "I am positive that nothing can be gained by highhanded methods, James. Captain Gresham is one of the most popular men in London, and his friends would tear up Treffinger's bones if he were annoyed by any scandal of our making—and this scheme you propose would inevitably result in scandal. Lady Ellen has, of course, every legal right to sell the picture. Treffinger made considerable inroads upon her estate, and, as she is about to marry a man without income, she doubtless feels that she has a right to replenish her patrimony."

He found James amenable, though doggedly skeptical. He went down into the street, called a carriage, and saw James and his burden into it. Standing in the doorway, he watched the carriage roll away through the drizzling mist, weave in and out among the wet, black vehicles and darting cab lights, until it was swallowed up in the glare and confusion of the Strand. "It is rather a fine touch of irony," he reflected, "that he, who is so out of it, should be the one to really care. Poor Treffinger," he murmured as, with a rather spiritless smile, he turned back into his hotel, "Poor Treffinger; *sic transit gloria.*"

The next afternoon MacMaster kept his promise. When he arrived at Lady Mary Percy's house he saw preparations for a function of some sort, but he went resolutely up the steps, telling the footman that his business was urgent. Lady Ellen came down alone, excusing her sister. She was dressed for receiving, and MacMaster had never seen one so beautiful. The color in her cheeks sent a softening glow over her small, delicately cut features.

MacMaster apologized for his intrusion and came unflinchingly to the object of his call. He had come, he said, not only to offer her his warmest congratulations, but to express his regret that a great work of art was to leave England.

Lady Treffinger looked at him in wide-eyed astonishment. Surely, she said, she had been careful to select the best of the pictures for the X—— gallery, in accordance with Sir Hugh Treffinger's wishes.

"And did he—pardon me, Lady Treffinger, but in mercy set my mind at rest—did he or did he not express any definite wish concerning this one picture, which to me seems worth all the others, unfinished as it is?"

Lady Treffinger paled perceptibly, but it was not the pallor of confusion. When she spoke there was a sharp tremor in her smooth voice, the edge of a resentment that tore her like pain. "I think his man has some such impression, but I believe it to be utterly unfounded. I cannot find that he ever expressed any wish concerning the disposition of the picture to any of his friends. Unfortunately, Sir Hugh was not always discreet in his remarks to his servants."

"Captain Gresham, Lady Ellingham, and Miss Ellingham," announced a servant, appearing at the door.

There was a murmur in the hall, and MacMaster greeted the smiling Captain and his aunt as he bowed himself out.

To all intents and purposes the *Marriage of Phaedra* was already entombed in a vague continent in the Pacific, somewhere on the other side of the world.

A Wagner Matinee

I RECEIVED one morning a letter, written in pale ink on glassy, blue-lined notepaper, and bearing the postmark of a little Nebraska village. This communication, worn and rubbed, looking as though it had been carried for some days in a coat pocket that was none too clean, was from my Uncle Howard and informed me that his wife had been left a small legacy by a bachelor relative who had recently died, and that it would be necessary for her to go to Boston to attend to the settling of the estate. He requested me to meet her at the station and render her whatever services might be necessary. On examining the date indicated as that of her arrival I found it no later than tomorrow. He had characteristically delayed writing until, had I been away from home for a day, I must have missed my aunt altogether.

The name of my Aunt Georgiana opened before me a gulf of recollection so wide and deep that, as the letter dropped from my hand, I felt suddenly a stranger to all the present conditions of my existence, wholly ill at ease and out of place amid the familiar surroundings of my study. I became, in short, the gangling farm boy my aunt had known, scourged with chilblains and bashfulness, my hands cracked and sore from the corn husking. I sat again before her parlor organ, fumbling the scales with my stiff, red hands, while she, beside me, made canvas mittens for the huskers.

The next morning, after preparing my landlady somewhat, I set out for the station. When the train arrived I had some difficulty in finding my aunt. She was the last of the passengers to alight, and it was not until I got her into the carriage that she seemed really to recognize me. She had come all the way in a day coach; her linen duster had become black with soot and her black bonnet gray with dust during the journey. When we arrived at my boardinghouse the landlady put her to bed at once and I did not see her again until the next morning.

Whatever shock Mrs. Springer experienced at my aunt's appearance she considerately concealed. As for myself, I saw my aunt's misshapen figure with that feeling of awe and respect with which we behold explorers who have left their ears and fingers north of Franz Josef Land, or their health somewhere along the Upper Congo. My Aunt Georgiana had been a music teacher at the Boston Conservatory, somewhere back in the latter sixties. One summer, while visiting in the little village among the Green Mountains where her ancestors had dwelt for generations, she had kindled the callow fancy of the most idle and shiftless of all the village lads, and had conceived for this Howard Carpenter one of those extravagant passions which a handsome country boy of twenty-one sometimes inspires in an angular, spectacled woman of thirty. When she returned to her duties in Boston Howard followed her, and the upshot of this inexplicable infatuation was that she eloped with him, eluding the reproaches of her family and the criticisms of her friends by going with him to the Nebraska frontier. Carpenter, who, of course, had no money, had taken a homestead in Red Willow County, fifty miles from the railroad. There they had measured off their quarter section themselves by driving across the prairie in a wagon, to the wheel of which they had tied a red cotton handkerchief, and counting off its revolutions. They built a dugout in the red hillside, one of those cave dwellings whose inmates so often reverted to primitive conditions. Their water they got from the lagoons where the buffalo drank, and their slender stock of provisions was always at the mercy of bands of roving Indians. For thirty years my aunt had not been further than fifty miles from the homestead.

But Mrs. Springer knew nothing of all this, and must have been considerably shocked at what was left of my kinswoman. Beneath the soiled linen duster which, on her arrival, was the most conspicuous feature of her costume, she wore a black stuff dress, whose ornamentation showed that she had surrendered herself unquestioningly into the hands of a country dressmaker. My poor aunt's figure, however, would have presented astonishing difficulties to any dressmaker. Originally stooped, her shoulders were now almost bent together over her sunken chest. She wore no stays, and her gown, which trailed unevenly behind, rose in a sort of peak over her abdomen. She wore ill-fitting false teeth, and her skin was as yellow as a Mongolian's from constant exposure to a pitiless wind and to the alkaline water which hardens the most transparent cuticle into a sort of flexible leather.

I owed to this woman most of the good that ever came my way in my boyhood and had a reverential affection for her. During the years when I was riding herd for my uncle, my aunt, after cooking the three meals—the first of which was ready at six o'clock in the morning—and putting the six children to bed, would often stand until midnight at her ironing board, with me at the kitchen table beside her, hearing me recite

Latin declensions and conjugations, gently shaking me when my drowsy head sank down over a page of irregular verbs. It was to her, at her ironing or mending, that I read my first Shakespeare, and her old textbook on mythology was the first that ever came into my empty hands. She taught me my scales and exercises, too—on the little parlor organ, which her husband had bought her after fifteen years, during which she had not so much as seen any instrument, but an accordion that belonged to one of the Norwegian farmhands. She would sit beside me by the hour, darning and counting while I struggled with the "Joyous Farmer" but she seldom talked to me about music, and I understood why. She was a pious woman; she had the consolations of religion and, to her at least, her martyrdom was not wholly sordid. Once when I had been doggedly beating out some easy passages from an old score of *Euryanthe* I had found among her music books, she came up to me and, putting her hands over my eyes, gently drew my head back upon her shoulder, saying tremulously, "Don't love it so well, Clark, or it may be taken from you. Oh, dear boy, pray that whatever your sacrifice may be, it be not that."

When my aunt appeared on the morning after her arrival she was still in a semisomnambulant state. She seemed not to realize that she was in the city where she had spent her youth, the place longed for hungrily half a lifetime. She had been so wretchedly train-sick throughout the journey that she had no recollection of anything but her discomfort, and, to all intents and purposes, there were but a few hours of nightmare between the farm in Red Willow County and my study on Newbury Street. I had planned a little pleasure for her that afternoon, to repay her for some of the glorious moments she had given me when we used to milk together in the straw-thatched cowshed and she, because I was more than usually tired, or because her husband had spoken sharply to me, would tell me of the splendid performance of the *Huguenots* she had seen in Paris, in her youth.

At two o'clock the Symphony Orchestra was to give a Wagner program, and I intended to take my aunt; though, as I conversed with her I grew doubtful about her enjoyment of it. Indeed, for her own sake, I could only wish her taste for such things quite dead, and the long struggle mercifully ended at last. I suggested our visiting the Conservatory and the Common before lunch, but she seemed altogether too timid to wish to venture out. She questioned me absently about various changes in the city, but she was chiefly concerned that she had forgotten to leave instructions about feeding half-skimmed milk to a certain weakling calf, "old Maggie's calf, you know, Clark," she explained, evidently having forgotten how long I had been away. She was further troubled because she had neglected to tell her daughter about the freshly opened kit of mackerel in the cellar, which would spoil if it were not used directly.

I asked her whether she had ever heard any of the Wagnerian operas and found that she had not, though she was perfectly familiar with their respective situations, and had once possessed the piano score of *The Flying Dutchman.* I began to think it would have been best to get her back to Red Willow County without waking her, and regretted having suggested the concert.

From the time we entered the concert hall, however, she was a trifle less passive and inert, and for the first time seemed to perceive her surroundings. I had felt some trepidation lest she might become aware of the absurdities of her attire, or might experience some painful embarrassment at stepping suddenly into the world to which she had been dead for a quarter of a century. But, again, I found how superficially I had judged her. She sat looking about her with eyes as impersonal, almost as stony, as those with which the granite Rameses in a museum watches the froth and fret that ebbs and flows about his pedestal—separated from it by the lonely stretch of centuries. I have seen this same aloofness in old miners who drift into the Brown Hotel at Denver, their pockets full of bullion, their linen soiled, their haggard faces unshaven; standing in the thronged corridors as solitary as though they were still in a frozen camp on the Yukon, conscious that certain experiences have isolated them from their fellows by a gulf no haberdasher could bridge.

We sat at the extreme left of the first balcony, facing the arc of our own and the balcony above us, veritable hanging gardens, brilliant as tulip beds. The matinee audience was made up chiefly of women. One lost the contour of faces and figures—indeed, any effect of line whatever—and there was only the color of bodices past counting, the shimmer of fabrics soft and firm, silky and sheer: red, mauve, pink, blue, lilac, purple, ecru, rose, yellow, cream, and white, all the colors that an impressionist finds in a sunlit landscape, with here and there the dead shadow of a frock coat. My Aunt Georgiana regarded them as though they had been so many daubs of tube-paint on a palette.

When the musicians came out and took their places, she gave a little stir of anticipation and looked with quickening interest down over the rail at that invariable grouping, perhaps the first wholly familiar thing that had greeted her eye since she had left old Maggie and her weakling calf. I could feel how all those details sank into her soul, for I had not forgotten how they had sunk into mine when I came fresh from plowing forever and forever between green aisles of corn, where, as in a treadmill, one might walk from daybreak to dusk without perceiving a shadow of change. The clean profiles of the musicians, the gloss of their linen, the dull black of their coats, the beloved shapes of the instruments, the patches of yellow light thrown by the green-shaded lamps on the smooth, varnished bellies of the cellos and the bass viols in the rear, the restless, wind-tossed forest of fiddle necks and bows—I recalled how, in the first orchestra I had ever heard, those long bow strokes seemed to draw the heart out of me, as a conjurer's stick reels out yards of paper ribbon from a hat.

The first number was the *Tannhauser* overture. When the horns drew out the first strain of the "Pilgrim's Chorus" my Aunt Georgiana clutched my coat sleeve. Then it was I first realized that for her this broke a silence of thirty years; the inconceivable silence of the plains. With the battle between the two motives, with the frenzy of the Venusberg theme and its ripping of strings, there came to me an overwhelming sense of the waste and wear we are so powerless to combat; and I saw again the tall, naked house on the prairie, black and grim as a wooden fortress; the black pond where I had learned to swim, its margin pitted with sun-dried cattle tracks; the rain-gullied clay banks about the naked house; the four dwarf ash seedlings where the dishcloths were always hung to dry before the kitchen door. The world there was the flat world of the ancients; to the east, a cornfield that stretched to daybreak; to the west, a corral that reached to sunset; between, the conquests of peace, dearer bought than those of war.

The overture closed; my aunt released my coat sleeve, but she said nothing. She sat staring at the orchestra through a dullness of thirty years, through the films made little by little by each of the 365 days in every one of them. What, I wondered, did she get from it? She had been a good pianist in her day I knew, and her musical education had been broader than that of most music teachers of a quarter of a century ago. She had often told me of Mozart's operas and Meyerbeer's, and I could remember hearing her sing, years ago, certain melodies of Verdi's. When I had fallen ill with a fever in her house she used to sit by my cot in the evening—when the cool, night wind blew in through the faded mosquito netting tacked over the window, and I lay watching a certain bright star that burned red above the cornfield—and sing "Home to our mountains, O, let us return!" in a way fit to break the heart of a Vermont boy near dead of homesickness already.

I watched her closely through the prelude to *Tristan and Isolde*, trying vainly to conjecture what that seething turmoil of strings and winds might mean to her, but she sat mutely staring at the violin bows that drove obliquely downward, like the pelting streaks of rain in a summer shower. Had this music any message for her? Had she enough left to at all comprehend this power which had kindled the world since she had left it? I was in a fever of curiosity, but Aunt Georgiana sat silent upon her peak in Darien. She preserved this utter immobility throughout the number from *The Flying Dutchman*, though her fingers worked mechanically upon her black dress, as though, of themselves, they were recalling the piano score they had once played. Poor old hands! They had been stretched and twisted into mere tentacles to hold and lift and knead with, the palms unduly swollen, the fingers bent and knotted—on one of them a thin, worn band that had once been a wedding ring. As I pressed and gently quieted one of those groping hands, I remembered with quivering eyelids their services for me in other days.

Soon after the tenor began the "Prize Song," I heard a quick drawn breath and turned to my aunt. Her eyes were closed, but the tears were glistening on her cheeks, and I think, in a moment more, they were in my eyes as well. It never really died, then—the soul that can suffer so excruciatingly and so interminably; it withers to the outward eye only, like that strange moss which can lie on a dusty shelf half a century and yet, if placed in water, grows green again. She wept so throughout the development and elaboration of the melody.

During the intermission before the second half of the concert, I questioned my aunt and found that the "Prize Song" was not new to her. Some years before there had drifted to the farm in Red Willow County a young German, a tramp cowpuncher, who had sung the chorus at Bayreuth when he was a boy, along with the other peasant boys and girls. Of a Sunday morning he used to sit on his gingham-sheeted bed in the hands' bedroom which opened off the kitchen, cleaning the leather of his boots and saddle, singing the "Prize Song," while my aunt went about her work in the kitchen. She had hovered about him until she had prevailed upon him to join the country church, though his sole fitness for this step, insofar as I could gather, lay in his boyish face and his possession of this divine melody. Shortly afterward he had gone to town on the Fourth of July, been drunk for several days, lost his money at a faro table, ridden a saddled Texan steer on a bet, and disappeared with a fractured collarbone. All this my aunt told me huskily, wanderingly, as though she were talking in the weak lapses of illness.

"Well, we have come to better things than the old *Trovatore* at any rate, Aunt Georgie?" I queried, with a well-meant effort at jocularity.

Her lip quivered and she hastily put her handkerchief up to her mouth. From behind it she murmured, "And you have been hearing this ever since you left me, Clark?" Her question was the gentlest and saddest of reproaches.

The second half of the program consisted of four numbers from the *Ring* and closed with Siegfried's funeral march. My aunt wept quietly, but almost continuously, as a shallow vessel overflows in a rainstorm. From time to time her dim eyes looked up at the lights which studded the ceiling, burning softly under their dull glass globes; doubtless they were stars in truth to her. I was still perplexed as to what measure of musical comprehension was left to her, she who had heard nothing but the singing of gospel hymns at Methodist services in the square frame schoolhouse on Section Thirteen for so many years. I was wholly unable to gauge how much of it had been dissolved in soapsuds, or worked into bread, or milked into the bottom of a pail.

The deluge of sound poured on and on; I never knew what she found in the shining current of it; I never knew how far it bore her, or past what happy islands. From the trembling of her face I could well believe that before the last numbers she had been carried out where the myriad graves are, into the gray, nameless burying grounds of the sea—or into some world of death vaster yet, where, from the beginning of the world, hope has lain down with hope and dream with dream and, renouncing, slept.

The concert was over; the people filed out of the hall chattering and laughing, glad to relax and find the living level again, but my kinswoman made no effort to rise. The harpist slipped its green felt cover over his instrument; the flute players shook the water from their mouthpieces; the men of the orchestra went out one by one, leaving the stage to the chairs and music stands, empty as a winter cornfield.

I spoke to my aunt. She burst into tears and sobbed pleadingly. "I don't want to go, Clark, I don't want to go!"

I understood. For her, just outside the door of the concert hall lay the black pond with the cattle-tracked bluffs; the tall, unpainted house, with weather-curled boards, naked as a tower; the crook-backed ash seedlings where the dishcloths hung to dry; the gaunt, molting turkeys picking up refuse about the kitchen door.

Paul's Case

It was Paul's afternoon to appear before the faculty of the Pittsburgh High School to account for his various misdemeanors. He had been suspended a week ago, and his father had called at the principal's office and confessed his perplexity about his son. Paul entered the faculty room suave and smiling. His clothes were a trifle outgrown, and the tan velvet on the collar of his open overcoat was frayed and worn; but for all that there was something of the dandy about him, and he wore an opal pin in his neatly knotted black four-in-hand, and a red carnation in his buttonhole. This latter adornment the faculty somehow felt was not properly significant of the contrite spirit befitting a boy under the ban of suspension.

Paul was tall for his age and very thin, with high, cramped shoulders and a narrow chest. His eyes were remarkable for a certain hysterical brilliancy, and he continually used them in a conscious, theatrical sort of way, peculiarly offensive in a boy. The pupils were abnormally large, as though he were addicted to belladonna, but there was a glassy glitter about them which that drug does not produce.

When questioned by the principal as to why he was there Paul stated, politely enough, that he wanted to come back to school. This was a lie, but Paul was quite accustomed to lying—found it, indeed, indispensable for overcoming friction. His teachers were asked to state their respective charges against him, which they did with such a rancor and aggrievedness as evinced that this was not a usual case. Disorder and impertinence were among the offenses named, yet each of his instructors felt that it was scarcely possible to put into words the real cause of the trouble, which lay in a sort of hysterically defiant manner of the boy's, in the contempt which they all knew he felt for them and which he seemingly made not the least effort to conceal. Once, when he had been making a synopsis of a paragraph at the blackboard, his English teacher had stepped to his side and attempted to guide his hand. Paul had started back with a shudder and thrust his hands violently behind him. The astonished woman could scarcely have been more hurt and embarrassed had he struck at her. The insult was so involuntary and definitely personal as to be unforgettable. In one way and another he had made all his teachers, men and women alike, conscious of the same feeling of physical aversion. In one class he habitually sat with his hand shading his eyes; in another he always looked out of the window during the recitation; in another he made a running commentary on the lecture, with humorous intention.

His teachers felt this afternoon that his whole attitude was symbolized by his shrug and his flippantly red carnation flower, and they fell upon him without mercy, his English teacher leading the pack. He stood through it smiling, his pale lips parted over his white teeth. (His lips were continually twitching, and he had a habit of raising his eyebrows that was contemptuous and irritating to the last degree.) Older boys than Paul had broken down and shed tears under that baptism of fire, but his set smile did not once desert him, and his only sign of discomfort was the nervous trembling of the fingers that toyed with the buttons of his overcoat, and an occasional jerking of the other hand that held his hat. Paul was always smiling, always glancing about him, seeming to feel that people might be watching him and trying to detect something. This conscious expression, since it was as far as possible from boyish mirthfulness, was usually attributed to insolence or "smartness."

As the inquisition proceeded, one of his instructors repeated an impertinent remark of the boy's, and the principal asked him whether he thought that a courteous speech to have made a woman. Paul shrugged his shoulders slightly and his eyebrows twitched.

"I don't know," he replied. "I didn't mean to be polite or impolite, either. I guess it's a sort of way I have of saying things regardless."

The principal, who was a sympathetic man, asked him whether he didn't think that a way it would be well to get rid of. Paul grinned and said he guessed so. When he was told that he could go, he bowed gracefully and went out. His bow was but a repetition of the scandalous red carnation.

His teachers were in despair, and his drawing master voiced the feeling of them all when he declared there was something about the boy which none of them understood. He added: "I don't really believe that smile of his comes altogether from insolence; there's something sort of haunted about it. The boy is not strong, for one thing. I happen to know that he was born in Colorado, only a few months before his mother died out there of a long illness. There is something wrong about the fellow."

The drawing master had come to realize that, in looking at Paul, one saw only his white teeth and the forced animation of his eyes. One warm afternoon the boy had gone to sleep at his drawing board, and his master had noted with amazement what a white, blue-veined face it was: drawn and wrinkled like an old man's about the eyes, the lips twitching even in his sleep and stiff with a nervous tension that drew them back from his teeth.

His teachers left the building dissatisfied and unhappy, humiliated to have felt so vindictive toward a mere boy, to have uttered this feeling in cutting terms, and to have set each other on, as it were, in the gruesome game of intemperate reproach. Some of them remembered having seen a miserable street cat set at bay by a ring of tormentors.

As for Paul, he ran down the hill whistling the "Soldiers' Chorus" from *Faust*, looking wildly behind him now and then to see whether some of his teachers were not there to writhe under his lightheartedness. As it was now late in the afternoon and Paul was on duty that evening as usher at Carnegie Hall, he decided that he would not go home to supper. When he reached the concert hall the doors were not yet open and, as it was chilly outside, he decided to go up into the picture gallery—always deserted at this hour—where there were some of Raffelli's gay studies of Paris streets and an airy blue Venetian scene or two that always exhilarated him. He was delighted to find no one in the gallery but the old guard, who sat in one corner, a newspaper on his knee, a black patch over one eye and the other closed. Paul possessed himself of the place and walked confidently up and down, whistling under his breath. After a while he sat down before a blue Rico and lost himself. When he bethought him to look at his watch, it was after seven o'clock, and he rose with a start and ran downstairs, making a face at Augustus, peering out from the cast room, and an evil gesture at the Venus de Milo as he passed her on the stairway.

When Paul reached the ushers' dressing room half a dozen boys were there already, and he began excitedly to tumble into his uniform. It was one of the few that at all approached fitting, and Paul thought it very becoming—though he knew that the tight, straight coat accentuated his narrow chest, about which he was exceedingly sensitive. He was always considerably excited while he dressed, twanging all over to the tuning of the strings and the preliminary flourishes of the horns in the music room; but tonight he seemed quite beside himself, and he teased and plagued the boys until, telling him that he was crazy, they put him down on the floor and sat on him.

Somewhat calmed by his suppression, Paul dashed out to the front of the house to seat the early comers. He was a model usher; gracious and smiling he ran up and down the aisles; nothing was too much trouble for him; he carried messages and brought programs as though it were his greatest pleasure in life, and all the people in his section thought him a charming boy, feeling that he remembered and admired them. As the house filled, he grew more and more vivacious and animated, and the color came to his cheeks and lips. It was very much as though this were a great reception and Paul were the host. Just as the musicians came out to take their places, his English teacher arrived with checks for the seats which a prominent manufacturer had taken for the season. She betrayed some embarrassment when she handed Paul the tickets, and a hauteur which subsequently made her feel very foolish. Paul was startled for a moment, and had the feeling of wanting to put her out; what business had she here among all these fine people and gay colors? He looked her over and decided that she was not appropriately dressed and must be a fool to sit downstairs in such togs. The tickets had probably been sent her out of kindness, he reflected as he put down a seat for her, and she had about as much right to sit there as he had.

When the symphony began Paul sank into one of the rear seats with a long sigh of relief and lost himself as he had done before the Rico. It was not that symphonies, as such, meant anything in particular to Paul, but the first sigh of the instruments seemed to free some hilarious and potent spirit within him—something that struggled there like the genie in the bottle found by the Arab fisherman. He felt a sudden zest of life; the lights danced before his eyes and the concert hall blazed into unimaginable splendor. When the soprano soloist came on Paul forgot even the nastiness of his teacher's being there and gave himself up to the peculiar stimulus such personages always had for him. The soloist chanced to be a German woman, by no means in her first youth, and the mother of many children; but she wore an elaborate gown and a tiara, and above all she had that indefinable air of achievement, that world-shine upon her, which, in Paul's eyes, made her a veritable queen of Romance.

After a concert was over Paul was always irritable and wretched until he got to sleep, and tonight he was even more than usually restless. He had the feeling of not being able to let down, of its being impossible to give up this delicious excitement which was the only thing that could be called living at all. During the last number he withdrew and, after hastily changing his clothes in the dressing room, slipped out to the side door where the soprano's carriage stood. Here he began pacing rapidly up and down the walk, waiting to see her come out.

Over yonder, the Schenley, in its vacant stretch, loomed big and square through the fine rain, the windows of its twelve stories glowing like those of a lighted cardboard house under a Christmas tree. All the actors and singers of the better class stayed there when they were in the city, and a number of the big manufacturers of the place lived there in the winter. Paul had often hung about the hotel, watching the people go in and out, longing to enter and leave schoolmasters and dull care behind him forever.

At last the singer came out, accompanied by the conductor, who helped her into her carriage and closed the door with a cordial *auf wiedersehen*—which set Paul to wondering whether she were not an old sweetheart of his. Paul followed the carriage over to the hotel, walking so rapidly as not to be far from the entrance when the singer alighted, and disappeared behind the swinging glass doors that were opened by a Negro in a tall hat and a long coat. In the moment that the door was ajar it seemed to Paul that he, too, entered. He seemed to feel himself go after her up the steps, into the warm, lighted building, into an exotic, tropical world of shiny, glistening surfaces and basking ease. He reflected upon the mysterious dishes that were brought into the dining room, the green bottles in buckets of ice, as he had seen them in the supper party pictures of the *Sunday World* supplement. A quick gust of wind brought the rain down with sudden vehemence, and Paul was startled to find that he was still outside in the slush of the gravel driveway; that his boots were letting in the water and his scanty overcoat was clinging wet about him; that the lights in front of the concert hall were out and that the rain was driving in sheets between him and the orange glow of the windows above him. There it was, what he wanted—tangibly before him, like the fairy world of a Christmas pantomime—but mocking spirits stood guard at the doors, and, as the rain beat in his face, Paul wondered whether he were destined always to shiver in the black night outside, looking up at it.

He turned and walked reluctantly toward the car tracks. The end had to come sometime: his father in his nightclothes at the top of the stairs, explanations that did not explain, hastily improvised fictions that were forever tripping him up, his upstairs room and its horrible yellow wallpaper, the creaking bureau with the greasy plush collarbox, and over his painted wooden bed the pictures of George Washington and John Calvin, and the framed motto, "Feed My Lambs," which had been worked in red worsted by his mother.

Half an hour later Paul alighted from the Negley Avenue car and went slowly down one of the side streets off the main thoroughfare. It was a highly respectable street, where all the houses were exactly alike, and where businessmen of moderate means begot and reared large families of children, all of whom went to Sabbath school and learned the shorter catechism and were interested in arithmetic; all of whom were as exactly alike as their homes, and of a piece with the monotony in which they lived. Paul never went up Cordelia Street without a shudder of loathing. His home was next to the house of the Cumberland minister. He approached it tonight with the nerveless sense of defeat, the hopeless feeling of sinking back forever into ugliness and commonness that he had always had when he came home. The moment he turned into Cordelia Street he felt the waters close above his head. After each of these orgies of living he experienced all the physical depression which follows a debauch: the loathing of respectable beds, of common food, of a house penetrated by kitchen odors; a shuddering repulsion for the flavorless, colorless mass of everyday existence; a morbid desire for cool things and soft lights and fresh flowers.

The nearer he approached the house, the more absolutely unequal Paul felt to the sight of it all: his ugly sleeping chamber; the cold bathroom with the grimy zinc tub, the cracked mirror, the dripping spiggots; his father, at the top of the stairs, his hairy legs sticking out from his nightshirt, his feet thrust into carpet slippers. He was so much later than usual that there would certainly be inquiries and reproaches. Paul stopped short before the door. He felt that he could not be accosted by his father tonight, that he could not toss again on that miserable bed. He would not go in. He would tell his father that he had no carfare and it was raining so hard he had gone home with one of the boys and stayed all night.

Meanwhile, he was wet and cold. He went around to the back of the house and tried one of the basement windows, found it open, raised it cautiously, and scrambled down the cellar wall to the floor. There he stood, holding his breath, terrified by the noise he had made; but the floor above him was silent, and there was no creak on the stairs. He found a soapbox, and carried it over to the soft ring of light that streamed from the furnace door, and sat down. He was horribly afraid of rats, so he did not try to sleep but sat looking distrustfully at the dark, still terrified lest he might have awakened his father. In such reactions, after one of the experiences which made days and nights out of the dreary blanks of the calendar, when his senses were deadened, Paul's head was always singularly clear. Suppose his father had heard him getting in at the window and had come down and shot him for a burglar? Then, again, suppose his father had come down, pistol in hand, and he had cried out in time to save himself, and his father had been horrified to think how nearly he had killed him? Then, again, suppose a day should come when his father would remember that night, and wish there had been no warning cry to stay his hand? With this last supposition Paul entertained himself until daybreak.

The following Sunday was fine; the sodden November chill was broken by the last flash of autumnal summer. In the morning Paul had to go to church and Sabbath school, as always. On seasonable Sunday afternoons the burghers of Cordelia Street always sat out on their front stoops and talked to their neighbors on the next stoop, or called to those across the street in neighborly fashion. The men usually sat on gay cushions placed upon the steps that led down to the sidewalk, while the women, in their Sunday "waists," sat in rockers on the cramped porches, pretending to be greatly at their ease. The children played in the streets; there were so many of them that the place resembled the recreation grounds of a kindergarten. The men on the steps—all in their shirt sleeves, their vests unbuttoned—sat with their legs well apart, their stomachs comfortably protruding, and talked of the prices of things or told anecdotes of the sagacity of their various chiefs and overlords. They occasionally looked over the multitude of squabbling children, listened affectionately to their high-pitched, nasal voices, smiling to see their own proclivities reproduced in their offspring, and interspersed their legends of the iron kings with remarks about their sons' progress at school, their grades in arithmetic, and the amounts they had saved in their toy banks.

On this last Sunday of November Paul sat all the afternoon on the lowest step of his stoop, staring into the street, while his sisters, in their rockers, were talking to the minister's daughters next door about how many shirtwaists they had made in the last week and how many waffles someone had eaten at the last church supper. When the weather was warm, and his father was in a particularly jovial frame of mind, the girls made lemonade, which was always brought out in a red-glass pitcher, ornamented with forget-me-nots in blue enamel. This the girls thought very fine, and the neighbors always joked about the suspicious color of the pitcher.

Today Paul's father sat on the top step, talking to a young man who shifted a restless baby from knee to knee. He happened to be the young man who was daily held up to Paul as a model, and after whom it was his father's dearest hope that he would pattern. This young man was of a ruddy complexion, with a compressed, red mouth and faded, near-sighted eyes, over which he wore thick spectacles with gold bows that curved about his ears. He was clerk to one of the magnates of a great steel corporation, and was looked upon in Cordelia Street as a young man with a future. There was a story that, some five years ago—he was now barely twenty-six—he had been a trifle dissipated, but in order to curb his appetites and save the loss of time and strength that a sowing of wild oats might have entailed, he had taken his chief's advice, oft reiterated to his employees, and at twenty-one had married the first woman whom he could persuade to share his fortunes. She happened to be an angular schoolmistress, much older than he, who also wore thick glasses, and who had now borne him four children, all nearsighted, like herself.

The young man was relating how his chief, now cruising in the Mediterranean, kept in touch with all the details of the business, arranging his office hours on his yacht just as though he were at home, and "knocking off work enough to keep two stenographers busy." His father told, in turn, the plan his corporation was considering, of putting in an electric railway plant in Cairo. Paul snapped his teeth; he had an awful apprehension that they might spoil it all before he got there. Yet he rather liked to hear these legends of the iron kings that were told and retold on Sundays and holidays; these stories of palaces in Venice, yachts on the Mediterranean, and high play at Monte Carlo appealed to his fancy, and he was interested in the triumphs of these cash boys who had become famous, though he had no mind for the cash-boy stage.

After supper was over and he had helped to dry the dishes, Paul nervously asked his father whether he could go to George's to get some help in his geometry, and still more nervously asked for carfare. This latter request he had to repeat, as his father, on principle, did not like to hear requests for money, whether much or little. He asked Paul whether he could not go to some boy who lived nearer, and told him that he ought not to leave his schoolwork until Sunday; but he gave him the dime. He was not a poor man, but he had a worthy ambition to come up in the world. His only reason for allowing Paul to usher was that he thought a boy ought to be earning a little.

Paul bounded upstairs, scrubbed the greasy odor of the dishwater from his hands with the ill-smelling soap he hated, and then shook over his fingers a few drops of violet water from the bottle he kept hidden in his drawer. He left the house with his geometry conspicuously under his arm, and the moment he got out of Cordelia Street and boarded a downtown car, he shook off the lethargy of two deadening days and began to live again.

The leading juvenile of the permanent stock company which played at one of the downtown theaters was an acquaintance of Paul's, and the boy had been invited to drop in at the Sunday-night rehearsals whenever he could. For more than a year Paul had spent every available moment loitering about Charley Edwards's dressing room. He had won a place among Edwards's following not only because the young actor, who could not afford to employ a dresser, often found him useful, but because he recognized in Paul something akin to what churchmen term "vocation."

It was at the theater and at Carnegie Hall that Paul really lived; the rest was but a sleep and a forgetting. This was Paul's fairy tale, and it had for him all the allurement of a secret love. The moment he inhaled the gassy, painty, dusty odor behind the scenes, he breathed like a prisoner set free and felt within him the possibility of doing or saying splendid, brilliant, poetic things. The moment the cracked orchestra beat out the overture from *Martha,* or jerked at the serenade from *Rigoletto,* all stupid and ugly things slid from him, and his senses were deliciously yet delicately fired.

Perhaps it was because, in Paul's world, the natural nearly always wore the guise of ugliness that a certain element of artificiality seemed to him necessary in beauty. Perhaps it was because his experience of life elsewhere was so full of Sabbath-school picnics, petty economies, wholesome advice as to how to succeed in life, and the inescapable odors of cooking that he found this existence so alluring, these smartly clad men and women so attractive, that he was so moved by these starry apple orchards that bloomed perennially under the limelight.

It would be difficult to put it strongly enough how convincingly the stage entrance of that theater was for Paul the actual portal of Romance. Certainly none of the company ever suspected it, least of all Charley Edwards. It was very like the old stories that used to float about London of fabulously rich Jews, who had subterranean halls there, with palms, and fountains, and soft lamps and richly appareled women who never saw the disenchanting light of London day. So, in the midst of that smoke-palled city, enamored of figures and grimy toil, Paul had his secret temple, his wishing carpet, his bit of blue-and-white Mediterranean shore bathed in perpetual sunshine.

Several of Paul's teachers had a theory that his imagination had been perverted by garish fiction, but the truth was that he scarcely ever read at all. The books at home were not such as would either tempt or corrupt a youthful mind, and as for reading the novels that some of his friends urged upon him—well, he got what he wanted much more quickly from music: any sort of music, from an orchestra to a barrel organ. He needed only the spark, the indescribable thrill that made his imagination master of his senses, and he could make plots and pictures enough of his own. It was equally true that he was not stage-struck—not, at any rate, in the usual acceptation of that expression. He had no desire to become an actor, any more than he had to become a musician. He felt no necessity to do any of these things; what he wanted was to see, to be in the atmosphere, float on the wave of it, to be carried out, blue league after blue league, away from everything.

After a night behind the scenes Paul found the schoolroom more than ever repulsive: the bare floors and naked walls; the prosy men who never wore frock coats or violets in their buttonholes; the women with their dull gowns, shrill voices, and pitiful seriousness about prepositions that govern the dative. He could not bear to have the other pupils think, for a moment, that he took these people seriously; he must convey to them that he considered it all trivial, and was there only by way of a jest, anyway. He had autographed pictures of all the members of the stock company which he showed his classmates, telling them the most incredible stories of his familiarity with these people, of his acquaintance with the soloists who came to Carnegie Hall, his suppers with them and the flowers he sent them. When these stories lost their effect, and his audience grew listless, he became desperate and would bid all the boys good-bye, announcing that he was going to travel for a while, going to Naples, to Venice, to Egypt. Then, next Monday, he would slip back, conscious and nervously smiling; his sister was ill, and he should have to defer his voyage until spring.

Matters went steadily worse with Paul at school. In the itch to let his instructors know how heartily he despised them and their homilies, and how thoroughly he was appreciated elsewhere, he mentioned once or twice that he had no time to fool with theorems; adding—with a twitch of the eyebrows and a touch of that nervous bravado which so perplexed them—that he was helping the people down at the stock company; they were old friends of his.

The upshot of the matter was that the principal went to Paul's father, and Paul was taken out of school and put to work. The manager at Carnegie Hall was told to get another usher in his stead; the doorkeeper at the theater was warned not to admit him to the house; and Charley Edwards remorsefully promised the boy's father not to see him again.

The members of the stock company were vastly amused when some of Paul's stories reached them—especially the women. They were hard-working women, most of them supporting indigent husbands or brothers, and they laughed rather bitterly at having stirred the boy to such fervid and florid inventions. They agreed with the faculty and with his father that Paul's was a bad case.

The eastbound train was plowing through a January snowstorm; the dull dawn was beginning to show gray when the engine whistled a mile out of Newark. Paul started up from the seat where he had lain curled in uneasy slumber, rubbed the breath-misted window glass with his hand, and peered out. The snow was whirling in curling eddies above the white bottom lands, and the drifts lay already deep in the fields and along the fences, while here and there the long, dead grass and dried weed stalks protruded black above it. Lights shone from the scattered houses, and a gang of laborers who stood beside the track waved their lanterns.

Paul had slept very little, and he felt grimy and uncomfortable. He had made the all-night journey in a day coach, partly because he was ashamed, dressed as he was, to go into a Pullman, and partly because he was afraid of being seen there by some Pittsburgh businessman, who might have noticed him in Denny & Carson's office. When the whistle awoke him, he clutched quickly at his breast pocket, glancing about him with an uncertain smile. But the little, clay-bespattered Italians were still sleeping, the slatternly women across the aisle were in open-mouthed oblivion, and even the crumby, crying babies were for the nonce stilled. Paul settled back to struggle with his impatience as best he could.

When he arrived at the Jersey City station he hurried through his breakfast, manifestly ill at ease and keeping a sharp eye about him. After he reached the Twenty-third Street station, he consulted a cabman and had himself driven to a men's-furnishings establishment that was just opening for the day. He spent upward of two hours there, buying with endless reconsidering and great care. His new street suit he put on in the fitting room; the frock coat and dress clothes he had bundled into the cab with his linen. Then he drove to a hatter's and a shoe house. His next errand was at Tiffany's, where he selected his silver and a new scarf pin. He would not wait to have his silver marked, he said. Lastly, he stopped at a trunk shop on Broadway and had his purchases packed into various traveling bags.

It was a little after one o'clock when he drove up to the Waldorf and, after settling with the cabman, went into the office. He registered from Washington; said his mother and father had been abroad, and that he had come down to await the arrival of their steamer. He told his story plausibly and had no trouble, since he volunteered to pay for them in advance, in engaging his rooms; a sleeping room, sitting room, and bath.

Not once but a hundred times Paul had planned this entry into New

York. He had gone over every detail of it with Charley Edwards, and in his scrapbook at home there were pages of description about New York hotels, cut from the Sunday papers.

When he was shown to his sitting room on the eighth floor he saw at a glance that everything was as it should be; there was but one detail in his mental picture that the place did not realize, so he rang for the bellboy and sent him down for flowers. He moved about nervously until the boy returned, putting away his new linen and fingering it delightedly as he did so. When the flowers came he put them hastily into water, and then tumbled into a hot bath. Presently he came out of his white bathroom, resplendent in his new silk underwear, and playing with the tassels of his red robe. The snow was whirling so fiercely outside his windows that he could scarcely see across the street; but within, the air was deliciously soft and fragrant. He put the violets and jonquils on the taboret beside the couch and threw himself down, with a long sigh, covering himself with a Roman blanket. He was thoroughly tired; he had been in such haste, he had stood up to such a strain, covered so much ground in the last twenty-four hours, that he wanted to think how it had all come about. Lulled by the sound of the wind, the warm air, and the cool fragrance of the flowers, he sank into deep, drowsy retrospection.

It had been wonderfully simple; when they had shut him out of the theater and concert hall, when they had taken away his bone, the whole thing was virtually determined. The rest was a mere matter of opportunity. The only thing that at all surprised him was his own courage—for he realized well enough that he had always been tormented by fear, a sort of apprehensive dread that, of late years, as the meshes of the lies he had told closed about him, had been pulling the muscles of his body tighter and tighter. Until now he could not remember the time when he had not been dreading something. Even when he was a little boy it was always there—behind him, or before, or on either side. There had always been the shadowed corner, the dark place into which he dared not look, but from which something seemed always to be watching him—and Paul had done things that were not pretty to watch, he knew.

But now he had a curious sense of relief, as though he had at last thrown down the gauntlet to the thing in the corner.

Yet it was but a day since he had been sulking in the traces; but yesterday afternoon that he had been sent to the bank with Denny & Carson's deposit, as usual—but this time he was instructed to leave the book to be balanced. There was above two thousand dollars in checks, and nearly a thousand in the bank notes which he had taken from the book and quietly transferred to his pocket. At the bank he had made out a new deposit slip. His nerves had been steady enough to permit of his returning to the office, where he had finished his work and asked for a full day's holiday tomorrow, Saturday, giving a perfectly reasonable pretext. The bankbook, he knew, would not be returned before Monday or Tuesday, and his father would be out of town for the next week. From the time he slipped the bank notes into his pocket until he boarded the night train for New York, he had not known a moment's hesitation. It was not the first time Paul had steered through treacherous waters.

How astonishingly easy it had all been; here he was, the thing done; and this time there would be no awakening, no figure at the top of the stairs. He watched the snowflakes whirling by his window until he fell asleep.

When he awoke, it was three o'clock in the afternoon. He bounded up with a start; half of one of his precious days gone already! He spent more than an hour in dressing, watching every stage of his toilet carefully in the mirror. Everything was quite perfect; he was exactly the kind of boy he had always wanted to be.

When he went downstairs Paul took a carriage and drove up Fifth Avenue toward the Park. The snow had somewhat abated; carriages and tradesmen's wagons were hurrying soundlessly to and fro in the winter twilight; boys in woolen mufflers were shoveling off the doorsteps; the avenue stages made fine spots of color against the white street. Here and there on the corners were stands with whole flower gardens blooming under glass cases, against the sides of which the snowflakes stuck and melted; violets, roses, carnations, lilies of the valley—somehow vastly more lovely and alluring that they blossomed thus unnaturally in the snow. The Park itself was a wonderful stage winterpiece.

When he returned, the pause of the twilight had ceased and the tune of the streets had changed. The snow was falling faster, lights streamed from the hotels that reared their dozen stories fearlessly up into the storm, defying the raging Atlantic winds. A long, black stream of carriages poured down the avenue, intersected here and there by other streams, tending horizontally. There were a score of cabs about the entrance of his hotel, and his driver had to wait. Boys in livery were running in and out of the awning stretched across the sidewalk, up and down the red velvet carpet laid from the door to the street. Above, about, within it all was the rumble and roar, the hurry and toss of thousands of human beings as hot for pleasure as himself, and on every side of him towered the glaring affirmation of the omnipotence of wealth.

The boy set his teeth and drew his shoulders together in a spasm of realization; the plot of all dramas, the text of all romances, the nerve-stuff of all sensations was whirling about him like the snowflakes. He burnt like a faggot in a tempest.

When Paul went down to dinner the music of the orchestra came floating up the elevator shaft to greet him. His head whirled as he stepped into the thronged corridor, and he sank back into one of the chairs against the wall to get his breath. The lights, the chatter, the perfumes, the bewildering medley of color—he had, for a moment, the feeling of not being able to stand it. But only for a moment; these were his own people, he told himself. He went slowly about the corridors, through the writing rooms, smoking rooms, reception rooms, as though he were exploring the chambers of an enchanted palace, built and peopled for him alone.

When he reached the dining room he sat down at a table near a window. The flowers, the white linen, the many-colored wineglasses, the gay toilettes of the women, the low popping of corks, the undulating repetitions of the *Blue Danube* from the orchestra all flooded Paul's dream with bewildering radiance. When the roseate tinge of his champagne was added—that cold, precious, bubbling stuff that creamed and foamed in his glass—Paul wondered that there were honest men in the world at all. This was what all the world was fighting for, he reflected; this was what all the struggle was about. He doubted the reality of his past. Had he ever known a place called Cordelia Street, a place where fagged-looking businessmen got on the early car? Mere rivets in a machine they seemed to Paul—sickening men, with combings of children's hair always hanging to their coats, and the smell of cooking in their clothes. Cordelia Street—Ah, that belonged to another time and country! Had he not always been thus, had he not sat here night after night, from as far back as he could remember, looking pensively over just such shimmering textures and slowly twirling the stem of a glass like this one between his thumb and middle finger? He rather thought he had.

He was not in the least abashed or lonely. He had no especial desire to meet or to know any of these people; all he demanded was the right to look on and conjecture, to watch the pageant. The mere stage properties were all he contended for. Nor was he lonely later in the evening, in his loge at the Metropolitan. He was now entirely rid of his nervous misgivings, of his forced aggressiveness, of the imperative desire to show himself different from his surroundings. He felt now that his surroundings explained him. Nobody questioned the purple;

he had only to wear it passively. He had only to glance down at his attire to reassure himself that here it would be impossible for anyone to humiliate him.

He found it hard to leave his beautiful sitting room to go to bed that night, and sat long watching the raging storm from his turret window. When he went to sleep, it was with the lights turned on in his bedroom; partly because of his old timidity, and partly so that, if he should wake in the night, there would be no wretched moment of doubt, no horrible suspicion of yellow wallpaper, or of Washington and Calvin above his bed.

Sunday morning the city was practically snowbound. Paul breakfasted late, and in the afternoon he fell in with a wild San Francisco boy, a freshman at Yale, who said he had run down for a "little flyer" over Sunday. The young man offered to show Paul the night side of the town, and the two boys went out together after dinner, not returning to the hotel until seven o'clock the next morning. They had started out in the confiding warmth of a champagne friendship, but their parting in the elevator was singularly cool. The freshman pulled himself together to make his train, and Paul went to bed. He awoke at two o'clock in the afternoon, very thirsty and dizzy, and rang for ice water, coffee, and the Pittsburgh papers.

On the part of the hotel management, Paul excited no suspicion. There was this to be said for him, that he wore his spoils with dignity and in no way made himself conspicuous. Even under the glow of his wine he was never boisterous, though he found the stuff like a magician's wand for wonder-building. His chief greediness lay in his ears and eyes, and his excesses were not offensive ones. His dearest pleasures were the gray winter twilights in his sitting room, his quiet enjoyment of his flowers, his clothes, his wide divan, his cigarette, and his sense of power. He could not remember a time when he had felt so at peace with himself. The mere release from the necessity of petty lying, lying every day and every day, restored his self-respect. He had never lied for pleasure, even at school, but to be noticed and admired, to assert his difference from other Cordelia Street boys; and he felt a good deal more manly, more honest, even, now that he had no need for boastful pretensions, now that he could, as his actor friends used to say, "dress the part." It was characteristic that remorse did not occur to him. His golden days went by without a shadow, and he made each as perfect as he could.

On the eighth day after his arrival in New York he found the whole affair exploited in the Pittsburgh papers, exploited with a wealth of detail which indicated that local news of a sensational nature was at a low ebb.

The firm of Denny & Carson announced that the boy's father had refunded the full amount of the theft and that they had no intention of prosecuting. The Cumberland minister had been interviewed, and expressed his hope of yet reclaiming the motherless lad, and his Sabbath-school teacher declared that she would spare no effort to that end. The rumor had reached Pittsburgh that the boy had been seen in a New York hotel, and his father had gone East to find him and bring him home.

Paul had just come in to dress for dinner; he sank into a chair, weak to the knees, and clasped his head in his hands. It was to be worse than jail, even; the tepid waters of Cordelia Street were to close over him finally and forever. The gray monotony stretched before him in hopeless, unrelieved years; Sabbath school, Young People's Meeting, the yellow-papered room, the damp dishtowels; it all rushed back upon him with a sickening vividness. He had the old feeling that the orchestra had suddenly stopped, the sinking sensation that the play was over. The sweat broke out on his face, and he sprang to his feet, looked about him with his white, conscious smile, and winked at himself in the mirror. With something of the childish belief in miracles with which he had so often gone to class, all his lessons unlearned, Paul dressed and dashed whistling down the corridor to the elevator.

He had no sooner entered the dining room and caught the measure of the music than his remembrance was lightened by his old elastic power of claiming the moment, mounting with it, and finding it all-sufficient. The glare and glitter about him, the mere scenic accessories had again, and for the last time, their old potency. He would show himself that he was game, he would finish the thing splendidly. He doubted, more than ever, the existence of Cordelia Street, and for the first time he drank his wine recklessly. Was he not, after all, one of those fortunate beings born to the purple? Was he not still himself and in his own place? He drummed a nervous accompaniment to the Pagliacci music and looked about him, telling himself over and over that it had paid.

He reflected drowsily, to the swell of the music and the chill sweetness of his wine, that he might have done it more wisely. He might have caught an outbound steamer and been well out of their clutches before now. But the other side of the world had seemed too far away and too uncertain then; he could not have waited for it; his need had been too sharp. If he had to choose over again, he would do the same thing tomorrow. He looked affectionately about the dining room, now gilded with a soft mist. Ah, it had paid indeed!

Paul was awakened next morning by a painful throbbing in his head and feet. He had thrown himself across the bed without undressing, and had slept with his shoes on. His limbs and hands were lead heavy, and his tongue and throat were parched and burnt. There came upon him one of those fateful attacks of clearheadedness that never occurred except when he was physically exhausted and his nerve[illegible]ung loose. He lay still, closed his eyes, and let the tide of things w[illegible]er him.

His father was in New York, "stopping at some join[illegible]her," he told himself. The memory of successive summers on the fr[illegible]oop fell upon him like a weight of black water. He had not a hundred dollars left; and he knew now, more than ever, that money was everything, the wall that stood between all he loathed and all he wanted. The thing was winding itself up; he had thought of that on his first glorious day in New York, and had even provided a way to snap the thread. It lay on his dressing table now; he had got it out last night when he came blindly up from dinner, but the shiny metal hurt his eyes, and he disliked the looks of it.

He rose and moved about with a painful effort, succumbing now and again to attacks of nausea. It was the old depression exaggerated; all the world had become Cordelia Street. Yet somehow he was not afraid of anything, was absolutely calm; perhaps because he had looked into the dark corner at last and knew. It was bad enough, what he saw there, but somehow not so bad as his long fear of it had been. He saw everything clearly now. He had a feeling that he had made the best of it, that he had lived the sort of life he was meant to live, and for half an hour he sat staring at the revolver. But he told himself that was not the way, so he went downstairs and took a cab to the ferry.

When Paul arrived in Newark he got off the train and took another cab, directing the driver to follow the Pennsylvania tracks out of the town. The snow lay heavy on the roadways and had drifted deep in the open fields. Only here and there the dead grass or dried weed stalks projected, singularly black, above it. Once well into the country, Paul dismissed the carriage and walked, floundering along the tracks, his mind a medley of irrelevant things. He seemed to hold in his brain an actual picture of everything he had seen that morning. He remembered every feature of both his drivers, of the toothless old woman from whom he had bought the red flowers in his coat, the agent from whom he had got his ticket, and all of his fellow passengers on the ferry. His mind, unable to cope with vital matters near at hand, worked feverishly and deftly at sorting and grouping these images. They made for him a part of the ugliness of the world, of the ache in his head, and the bitter burning on his tongue. He stooped and put a handful of snow into his mouth as he walked, but that, too, seemed hot. When he reached a little hillside, where the tracks ran through a cut some twenty feet below him, he stopped and sat down.

The carnations in his coat were drooping with the cold, he noticed, their red glory all over. It occurred to him that all the flowers he had seen in the glass cases that first night must have gone the same way, long before this. It was only one splendid breath they had, in spite of their brave mockery at the winter outside the glass; and it was a losing game in the end, it seemed, this revolt against the homilies by which the world is run. Paul took one of the blossoms carefully from his coat and scooped a little hole in the snow, where he covered it up. Then he dozed awhile, from his weak condition, seemingly insensible to the cold.

The sound of an approaching train awoke him, and he started to his feet, remembering only his resolution, and afraid lest he should be too late. He stood watching the approaching locomotive, his teeth chattering, his lips drawn away from them in a frightened smile; once or twice he glanced nervously sidewise, as though he were being watched. When the right moment came, he jumped. As he fell, the folly of his haste occurred to him with merciless clearness, the vastness of what he had left undone. There flashed through his brain, clearer than ever before, the blue of Adriatic water, the yellow of Algerian sands.

He felt something strike his chest, and that his body was being thrown swiftly through the air, on and on, immeasurably far and fast, while his limbs were gently relaxed. Then, because the picture-making mechanism was crushed, the disturbing visions flashed into black, and Paul dropped back into the immense design of things.

SELECTED SHORT STORIES

CONTENTS

[illegible]
the two young men who were talking at the corner.
"Well," remarked the elder of the two, "I guess [illegible]

The Burglar's Christmas

TWO VERY shabby-looking young men stood at the corner of Prairie Avenue and Eightieth Street, looking despondently at the carriages that whirled by. It was Christmas Eve, and the streets were full of vehicles; florists' wagons, grocers' carts, and carriages. The streets were in that half-liquid, half-congealed condition peculiar to the streets of Chicago at that season of the year. The swift wheels that spun by sometimes threw the slush of mud and snow over the two young men who were talking on the corner.

"Well," remarked the elder of the two, "I guess we are at our rope's end, sure enough. How do you feel?"

"Pretty shaky. The wind's sharp tonight. If I had had anything to eat I mightn't mind it so much. There is simply no show. I'm sick of the whole business. Looks like there's nothing for it but the lake."

"Oh, nonsense, I thought you had more grit. Got anything left you can hock?"

"Nothing but my beard, and I am afraid they wouldn't find it worth a pawn ticket," said the younger man ruefully, rubbing the week's growth of stubble on his face.

"Got any folks anywhere? Now's your time to strike 'em if you have."

"Never mind if I have, they're out of the question."

"Well, you'll be out of it before many hours if you don't make a move of some sort. A man's got to eat. See here, I am going down to Longtin's saloon. I used to play the banjo in there, and I'll bone him for some of his free-lunch stuff. You'd better come along; perhaps they'll fill an order for two."

"How far down is it?"

"Well, it's clear downtown, of course, 'way down on Michigan Avenue."

"Thanks, I guess I'll loaf around here. I don't feel equal to the walk, and the cars—well, the cars are crowded." His features drew themselves into what might have been a smile under happier circumstances.

"No, you never did like streetcars, you're too aristocratic. See here,

Crawford, I don't like leaving you here. You ain't good company for yourself tonight."

"Crawford? Oh yes, that's the last one. There have been so many I forget them."

"Have you got a real name, anyway?"

"Oh yes, but it's one of the ones I've forgotten. Don't you worry about me. You go along and get your free lunch. I think I had a row in Longtin's place once. I'd better not show myself there again." As he spoke the young man nodded and turned slowly up the avenue.

He was miserable enough to want to be quite alone. Even the crowd that jostled by him annoyed him. He wanted to think about himself. He had avoided this final reckoning with himself for a year now. He had laughed it off and drunk it off. But now, when all those artificial devices which are employed to turn our thoughts into other channels and shield us from ourselves had failed him, it must come. Hunger is a powerful incentive to introspection.

It is a tragic hour, that hour when we are finally driven to reckon with ourselves, when every avenue of mental distraction has been cut off and our own life and all its ineffaceable failures closes about us like the walls of that old torture chamber of the Inquisition. Tonight, as this man stood stranded in the streets of the city, his hour came. It was not the first time he had been hungry and desperate and alone. But always before there had been some outlook, some chance ahead, some pleasure yet untasted that seemed worth the effort, some face that he fancied was, or would be, dear. But it was not so tonight. The unyielding conviction was upon him that he had failed in everything, had outlived everything. It had been near him for a long time, that Pale Specter. He had caught its shadow at the bottom of his glass many a time, at the head of his bed when he was sleepless at night, in the twilight shadows when some great sunset broke upon him. It had made life hateful to him when he awoke in the morning before now. But now it settled slowly over him, like night, the endless Northern nights that bid the sun a long farewell. It rose up before him like granite. From this brilliant city with its glad bustle of Yuletide he was shut off as completely as though he were a creature of another species. His days seemed numbered and done, sealed over like the little coral cells at the bottom of the sea. Involuntarily he drew that cold air through his lungs slowly, as though he were tasting it for the last time.

Yet he was but four and twenty, this man—he looked even younger—and he had a father someplace down East who had been very proud of him once. Well, he had taken his life into his own hands, and this was what he had made of it. That was all there was to be said. He could remember the hopeful things they used to say about him at college in the old days, before he had cut away and begun to live by his wits, and he found courage to smile at them now. They had read him wrongly. He knew now that he never had the essentials of success, only the superficial agility that is often mistaken for it. He was tow without the tinder, and he had burnt himself out at other people's fires. He had helped other people to make it win, but he himself—he had never touched an enterprise that had not failed eventually. Or, if it survived his connection with it, it left him behind.

His last venture had been with some ten-cent specialty company, a little lower than all the others, that had gone to pieces in Buffalo, and he had worked his way to Chicago by boat. When the boat made up its crew for the outward voyage, he was dispensed with as usual. He was used to that. The reason for it? Oh, there are so many reasons for failure! His was a very common one.

As he stood there in the wet under the street light he drew up his reckoning with the world and decided that it had treated him as well as he deserved. He had overdrawn his account once too often. There had been a day when he thought otherwise—when he had said he was unjustly handled, that his failure was merely the lack of proper adjustment between himself and other men, that someday he would be recognized and it would all come right. But he knew better than that now, and he was still man enough to bear no grudge against anyone—man or woman.

Tonight was his birthday, too. There seemed something particularly amusing in that. He turned up a limp little coat collar to try to keep a little of the wet chill from his throat and instinctively began to remember all the birthday parties he used to have. He was so cold and empty that his mind seemed unable to grapple with any serious question. He kept thinking about gingerbread and frosted cakes like a child. He could remember the splendid birthday parties his mother used to give him, when all the other little boys in the block came in their Sunday clothes and creaking shoes, with their ears still red from their mother's towel, and the pink and white birthday cake, and the stuffed olives and all the dishes of which he had been particularly fond, and how he would eat and eat and then go to bed and dream of Santa Claus. And in the morning he would awaken and eat again, until by night the family doctor arrived with his castor oil, and poor William used to dolefully say that it was altogether too much to have your birthday and Christmas all at once. He could remember, too, the royal birthday suppers he had given at college, and the stag dinners, and the toasts, and the music, and the good fellows who had wished him happiness and really meant what they said.

And since then there were other birthday suppers that he could not remember so clearly; the memory of them was heavy and flat, like cigarette smoke that has been shut in a room all night, like champagne that has been a day opened, a song that has been too often sung, an acute sensation that has been overstrained. They seemed tawdry and garish, discordant to him now. He rather wished he could forget them altogether.

Whichever way his mind now turned there was one thought that it could not escape, and that was the idea of food. He caught the scent of a cigar suddenly, and felt a sharp pain in the pit of his abdomen and a sudden moisture in his mouth. His cold hands clenched angrily, and for a moment he felt that bitter hatred of wealth, of ease, of everything that is well fed and well housed that is common to starving men. At any rate he had a right to eat! He had demanded great things from the world once: fame and wealth and admiration. Now it was simply bread—and he would have it! He looked about him quickly and felt the blood begin to stir in his veins. In all his straits he had never stolen anything, his tastes were above it. But tonight there would be no tomorrow. He was amused at the way in which the idea excited him. Was it possible there was yet one more experience that would distract him, one thing that had power to excite his jaded interest? Good! He had failed at everything else, now he would see what his chances would be as a common thief. It would be amusing to watch the beautiful consistency of his destiny work itself out even in that role. It would be interesting to add another study to his gallery of futile attempts, and then label them all: "The failure as a journalist," "The failure as a lecturer," "The failure as a businessman," "The failure as a thief," and so on, like the titles under the pictures of the Dance of Death. It was time that Childe Roland came to the dark tower.

A girl hastened by him with her arms full of packages. She walked quickly and nervously, keeping well within the shadow, as if she were not accustomed to carrying bundles and did not care to meet any of her friends. As she crossed the muddy street, she made an effort to lift her skirt a little, and as she did so one of the packages slipped unnoticed from beneath her arm. He caught it up and overtook her. "Excuse me, but I think you dropped something."

She started, "Oh yes, thank you, I would rather have lost anything than that."

The young man turned angrily upon himself. The package must have contained something of value. Why had he not kept it? Was this the sort of thief he would make? He ground his teeth together. There is nothing more maddening than to have morally consented to crime and then lack the nerve force to carry it out.

A carriage drove up to the house before which he stood. Several richly dressed women alighted and went in. It was a new house, and must have been built since he was in Chicago last. The front door was open and he could see down the hallway and up the staircase. The servant had left the door and gone with the guests. The first floor was brilliantly lighted, but the windows upstairs were dark. It looked very easy, just to slip upstairs to the darkened chambers where the jewels and trinkets of the fashionable occupants were kept.

Still burning with impatience against himself he entered quickly. Instinctively he removed his mud-stained hat as he passed quickly and quietly up the staircase. It struck him as being a rather superfluous courtesy in a burglar, but he had done it before he had thought. His way was clear enough, he met no one on the stairway or in the upper hall. The gas was lit in the upper hall. He passed the first chamber door through sheer cowardice. The second he entered quickly, thinking of something else lest his courage should fail him, and closed the door behind him. The light from the hall shone into the room through the transom. The apartment was finished richly enough to justify his expectations. He went at once to the dressing case. A number of rings and small trinkets lay in a silver tray. These he put hastily in his pocket. He opened the upper drawer and found, as he expected, several leather cases. In the first he opened was a lady's watch, in the second a pair of old-fashioned bracelets; he seemed to dimly remember having seen bracelets like them before, somewhere. The third case was heavier, the spring was much worn, and it opened easily. It held a cup of some kind. He held it up to the light and then his strained nerves gave way and he uttered a sharp exclamation. It was the silver mug he used to drink from when he was a little boy.

The door opened, and a woman stood in the doorway facing him. She was a tall woman, with white hair, in evening dress. The light from the hall streamed in upon him, but she was not afraid. She stood looking at him a moment, then she threw out her hand and went quickly toward him.

"Willie, Willie! Is it you?"

He struggled to loose her arms from him, to keep her lips from his cheek. "Mother—you must not! You do not understand! Oh, my God, this is worst of all!" Hunger, weakness, cold, shame, all came back to him, and shook his self-control completely. Physically he was too weak to stand a shock like this. Why could it not have been an ordinary discovery, arrest, the station house and all the rest of it. Anything but this! A hard dry sob broke from him. Again he strove to disengage himself.

"Who is it says I shall not kiss my son? Oh, my boy, we have waited so long for this! You have been so long in coming, even I almost gave you up."

Her lips upon his cheek burnt him like fire. He put his hand to his throat, and spoke thickly and incoherently: "You do not understand. I did not know you were here. I came here to rob—it is the first time—I swear it—but I am a common thief. My pockets are full of your jewels now. Can't you hear me? I am a common thief!"

"Hush, my boy, those are ugly words. How could you rob your own house? How could you take what is your own? They are all yours, my son, as wholly yours as my great love—and you can't doubt that, Will, do you?"

That soft voice, the warmth and fragrance of her person stole through his chill, empty veins like a gentle stimulant. He felt as though all his strength were leaving him and even consciousness. He held fast to her and bowed his head on her strong shoulder, and groaned aloud.

"O, Mother, life is hard, hard!"

She said nothing, but held him closer. And Oh, the strength of those white arms that held him! Oh, the assurance of safety in that warm bosom that rose and fell under his cheek! For a moment they stood so, silently. Then they heard a heavy step upon the stair. She led him to a chair and went out and closed the door. At the top of the staircase she met a tall, broad-shouldered man, with iron-gray hair, and a face alert and stern. Her eyes were shining and her cheeks on fire, her whole face was one expression of intense determination.

"James, it is William in there, come home. You must keep him at any cost. If he goes this time, I go with him. Oh, James, be easy with him, he has suffered so." She broke from a command to an entreaty, and laid her hand on his shoulder. He looked questioningly at her a moment, then went in the room and quietly shut the door.

She stood leaning against the wall, clasping her temples with her hands and listening to the low indistinct sound of the voices within. Her own lips moved silently. She waited a long time, scarcely breathing. At last the door opened, and her husband came out. He stopped to say in a shaken voice, "You go to him now, he will stay. I will go to my room. I will see him again in the morning."

She put her arm about his neck, "Oh, James, I thank you, I thank you! This is the night he came so long ago, you remember? I gave him to you then, and now you give him back to me!"

"Don't, Helen," he muttered. "He is my son, I have never forgotten that. I failed with him. I don't like to fail, it cuts my pride. Take him and make a man of him." He passed on down the hall.

She flew into the room where the young man sat with his head bowed upon his knee. She dropped to her knees beside him. Ah, it was so good to him to feel those arms again!

"He is so glad, Willie, so glad! He may not show it, but he is as happy as I. He never was demonstrative with either of us, you know."

"Oh my God, he was good enough," groaned the man. "I told him everything, and he was good enough. I don't see how either of you can look at me, speak to me, touch me." He shivered under her clasp again as when she had first touched him, and tried weakly to throw her off.

But she whispered softly, "This is my right, my son."

Presently, when he was calmer, she rose. "Now, come with me into the library, and I will have your dinner brought there."

As they went downstairs she remarked apologetically, "I will not call Ellen tonight; she has a number of guests to attend to. She is a big girl now, you know, and came out last winter. Besides, I want you all to myself tonight."

When the dinner came, and it came very soon, he fell upon it savagely. As he ate she told him all that had transpired during the years of his absence, and how his father's business had brought them there. "I was glad when we came. I thought you would drift West. I seemed a good deal nearer to you here."

There was a gentle unobtrusive sadness in her tone that was too soft for a reproach.

"Have you everything you want? It is a comfort to see you eat."

He smiled grimly. "It is certainly a comfort to me. I have not indulged in this frivolous habit for some thirty-five hours."

She caught his hand and pressed it sharply, uttering a quick remonstrance.

"Don't say that! I know, but I can't hear you say it—it's too terrible! My boy, food has choked me many a time when I have thought of the possibility of that. Now take the old lounging chair by the fire, and if you are too tired to talk, we will just sit and rest together."

He sank into the depths of the big leather chair with the lions' heads on the arms, where he had sat so often in the days when his feet did not touch the floor and he was half afraid of the grim monsters cut in the polished wood. That chair seemed to speak to him of things long forgotten. It was like the touch of an old familiar friend. He felt a sudden yearning tenderness for the happy little boy who had sat there and dreamed of the big world so long ago. Alas, he had been dead many a summer, that little boy!

He sat looking up at the magnificent woman beside him. He had almost forgotten how handsome she was; how lustrous and sad were the eyes that set under that serene brow, how impetuous and wayward the mouth even now, how superb the white throat and shoulders! Ah, the wit and grace and fineness of this woman! He remembered how proud he had been of her as a boy when she came to see him at school. Then in the deep red coals of the grate he saw the faces of other women who had come since then into his vexed, disordered life. Laughing faces, with eyes artificially bright, eyes without depth or meaning, features without the stamp of high sensibilities. And he had left this face for such as those!

He sighed restlessly and laid his hand on hers. There seemed refuge and protection in the touch of her, as in the old days when he was afraid of the dark. He had been in the dark so long now, his confidence was so thoroughly shaken, and he was bitterly afraid of the night and of himself.

"Ah, Mother, you make other things seem so false. You must feel that I owe you an explanation, but I can't make any, even to myself. Ah, but we make poor exchanges in life. I can't make out the riddle of it all. Yet there are things I ought to tell you before I accept your confidence like this."

"I'd rather you wouldn't, Will. Listen: Between you and me there can be no secrets. We are more alike than other people. Dear boy, I know all about it. I am a woman, and circumstances were different with me, but we are of one blood. I have lived all your life before you. You have never had an impulse that I have not known, you have never touched a brink that my feet have not trod. This is your birthday night. Twenty-four years ago I foresaw all this. I was a young woman then and I had hot battles of my own, and I felt your likeness to me. You were not like other babies. From the hour you were born you were restless and discontented, as I had been before you. You used to brace your strong little limbs against mine and try to throw me off as you did tonight. Tonight you have come back to me, just as you always did after you ran away to swim in the river that was forbidden you, the river you loved because it was forbidden. You are tired and sleepy, just as you used to be then, only a little older and a little paler and a little more foolish. I never asked you where you had been then, nor will I now. You have come back to me, that's all in all to me. I know your every possibility and limitation, as a composer knows his instrument."

He found no answer that was worthy to give to talk like this. He had not found life easy since he had lived by his wits. He had come to know poverty at close quarters. He had known what it was to be gay with an empty pocket, to wear violets in his buttonhole when he had not breakfasted, and all the hateful shams of the poverty of idleness. He had been a reporter on a big metropolitan daily, where men grind out their brains on paper until they have not one idea left—and still grind on. He had worked in a real estate office, where ignorant men were swindled. He had sung in a comic opera chorus, and played Harris in an *Uncle Tom's Cabin* company, and edited a socialist weekly. He had been dogged by debt and hunger and grinding poverty, until to sit here by a warm fire without concern as to how it would be paid for seemed unnatural.

He looked up at her questioningly. "I wonder if you know how much you pardon?"

"Oh, my poor boy, much or little, what does it matter? Have you wandered so far and paid such a bitter price for knowledge and not yet learned that love has nothing to do with pardon or forgiveness, that it only loves, and loves—and loves? They have not taught you well, the women of your world." She leaned over and kissed him, as no woman had kissed him since he left her.

He drew a long sigh of rich content. The old life, with all its bitterness and useless antagonism and flimsy sophistries, its brief delights that were always tinged with fear and distrust and unfaith, that whole miserable, futile, swindled world of Bohemia seemed immeasurably distant and far away, like a dream that is over and done. And as the chimes rang joyfully outside and sleep pressed heavily upon his eyelids, he wondered dimly if the Author of this sad little riddle of ours were not able to solve it after all, and if the Potter would not finally mete out his all comprehensive justice, such as none but he could have, to his Things of Clay, which are made in his own patterns, weak or strong, for his own ends; and if some day we will not awaken and find that all evil is a dream, a mental distortion that will pass when the dawn shall break.

Eric Hermannson's Soul

I

It was a great night at the Lone Star schoolhouse—a night when the Spirit was present with power and when God was very near to man. So it seemed to Asa Skinner, servant of God and Free Gospeller. The schoolhouse was crowded with the saved and sanctified, robust men and women, trembling and quailing before the power of some mysterious psychic force. Here and there among this cowering, sweating multitude crouched some poor wretch who had felt the pangs of an awakened conscience but had not yet experienced that complete divestment of reason, that frenzy born of a convulsion of the mind, which, in the parlance of the Free Gospellers, is termed "the Light." On the floor before the mourners' bench lay the unconscious figure of a man in whom outraged Nature had sought her last resort. This "trance" state is the highest evidence of grace among the Free Gospellers and indicates a close walking with God.

Before the desk stood Asa Skinner, shouting of the mercy and vengeance of God, and in his eyes shone a terrible earnestness, an almost prophetic flame. Asa was a converted train gambler who used to run between Omaha and Denver. He was a man made for the extremes of life; from the most debauched of men he had become the most ascetic. His was a bestial face, a face that bore the stamp of Nature's eternal injustice. The forehead was low, projecting over the eyes, and the sandy hair was plastered down over it and then brushed back at an abrupt right angle. The chin was heavy, the nostrils were low and wide, and the lower lip hung loosely except in his moments of spasmodic earnestness, when it shut like a steel trap. Yet about those coarse features there were deep, rugged furrows, the scars of many a hand-to-hand struggle with the weakness of the flesh, and about that drooping lip were sharp, strenuous lines that had conquered it and taught it to pray. Over those seamed cheeks there was a certain pallor, a grayness caught from many a vigil. It was as though, after Nature had done her worst with that face, some fine chisel had gone over it, chastening and almost transfiguring it. Tonight, as his muscles twitched with emotion, and the perspiration dropped from his hair and chin, there was a certain convincing power in the man. For Asa Skinner was a man possessed of a belief, of that sentiment of the sublime before which all inequalities are leveled, that transport of conviction which seems superior to all laws of condition, under which debauchees have become martyrs, which made a tinker an artist and a camel-driver the founder of an empire. This was with Asa Skinner tonight, as he stood proclaiming the vengeance of God.

It might have occurred to an impartial observer that Asa Skinner's God was indeed a vengeful God if he could reserve vengeance for those of his creatures who were packed into the Lone Star schoolhouse that night: poor exiles of all nations; men from the South and the North; peasants from almost every country of Europe, most of them from the mountainous, night-bound coast of Norway; honest men for the most part, but men with whom the world had dealt hardly—the failures of all countries, men sobered by toil and saddened by exile, who had been driven to fight for the dominion of an untoward soil, to sow where others should gather, the advance guard of a mighty civilization to be.

Never had Asa Skinner spoken more earnestly than now. He felt that the Lord had this night a special work for him to do. Tonight Eric Hermannson, the wildest lad on all the Divide, sat in his audience with a fiddle on his knee, just as he had dropped in on his way to play for some dance. The violin is an object of particular abhorrence to the Free Gospellers. Their antagonism to the church organ is bitter enough, but the fiddle they regard as a very incarnation of evil desires, singing forever of worldly pleasures and inseparably associated with all forbidden things.

Eric Hermannson had long been the object of the prayers of the revivalists. His mother had felt the power of the Spirit weeks ago, and special prayer-meetings had been held at her house for her son. But Eric had only gone his ways laughing, the ways of youth, which are short enough at best, and none too flowery on the Divide. He slipped away from the prayer-meetings to meet the Campbell boys in Genereau's saloon, or hug the plump little French girls at Chevalier's dances, and sometimes, of a summer night, he even went across the dewy cornfields and through the wild-plum thicket to play the fiddle for Lena Hanson, whose name was a reproach through all the Divide country, where the women are usually too plain and too busy and too tired to depart from the ways of virtue. On such occasions Lena, attired in a pink wrapper and silk stockings and tiny pink slippers, would sing to him, accompanying herself on a battered guitar. It gave him a delicious sense of freedom and experience to be with a woman who, no matter how, had lived in big cities and knew the ways of town folk, who had never worked in the fields and had kept her hands white and soft, her throat fair and tender, who had heard great singers in Denver and Salt Lake, and who knew the strange language of flattery and idleness and mirth.

Yet, careless as he seemed, the frantic prayers of his mother were not altogether without their effect upon Eric. For days he had been fleeing before them as a criminal from his pursuers, and over his pleasures had fallen the shadow of something dark and terrible that dogged his steps. The harder he danced, the louder he sang, the more was he conscious that this phantom was gaining upon him, that in time it would track him down. One Sunday afternoon, late in the fall, when he had been drinking beer with Lena Hanson and listening to a song which made his cheeks burn, a rattlesnake had crawled out of the side of the sod house and thrust its ugly head in under the screen door. He was not afraid of snakes, but he knew enough of Gospellism to feel the significance of the reptile lying coiled there upon her doorstep. His lips were cold when he kissed Lena goodbye, and he went there no more.

The final barrier between Eric and his mother's faith was his violin, and to that he clung as a man sometimes will cling to his dearest sin, to the weakness more precious to him than all his strength. In the great world beauty comes to men in many guises, and art in a hundred forms, but for Eric there was only his violin. It stood, to him, for all the manifestations of art; it was his only bridge into the kingdom of the soul.

It was to Eric Hermannson that the evangelist directed his impassioned pleading that night.

"Saul, Saul, why persecutest thou me? Is there a Saul here tonight who has stopped his ears to that gentle pleading, who has thrust a spear into that bleeding side? Think of it, my brother; you are offered this wonderful love and you prefer the worm that dieth not and the fire which will not be quenched. What right have you to lose one of God's precious souls? *Saul, Saul, why persecutest thou me?"*

A great joy dawned in Asa Skinner's pale face, for he saw that Eric Hermannson was swaying to and fro in his seat. The minister fell upon his knees and threw his long arms over his head.

"O my brothers! I feel it coming, the blessing we have prayed for. I tell you the Spirit is coming! Just a little more prayer, brothers, a little more zeal, and he will be here. I can feel his cooling wing upon my brow. Glory be to God forever and ever, amen!"

The whole congregation groaned under the pressure of this spiritual panic. Shouts and hallelujahs went up from every lip. Another figure fell prostrate upon the floor. From the mourners' bench rose a chant of terror and rapture:

"Eating honey and drinking wine,
Glory to the bleeding Lamb!
I am my Lord's and he is mine,
Glory to the bleeding Lamb!"

The hymn was sung in a dozen dialects and voiced all the vague yearning of these hungry lives, of these people who had starved all the passions so long, only to fall victims to the basest of them all, fear.

A groan of ultimate anguish rose from Eric Hermannson's bowed head, and the sound like the groan of a great tree when it falls in the forest.

The minister rose suddenly to his feet and threw back his head, crying in a loud voice:

"Lazarus, come forth! Eric Hermannson, you are lost, going down at sea. In the name of God, and Jesus Christ his Son, I throw you the life line. Take hold! Almighty God, my soul for his!" The minister threw his arms out and lifted his quivering face.

Eric Hermannson rose to his feet; his lips were set and the lightning was in his eyes. He took his violin by the neck and crushed it to splinters across his knee, and to Asa Skinner the sound was like the shackles of sin broken audibly asunder.

II

For more than two years Eric Hermannson kept the austere faith to which he had sworn himself, kept it until a girl from the East came to spend a week on the Nebraska Divide. She was a girl of other manners and conditions, and there were greater distances between her life and Eric's than all the miles which separated Rattlesnake Creek from New York City. Indeed, she had no business to be in the West at all; but ah! across what leagues of land and sea, by what improbable chances, do the unrelenting gods bring to us our fate!

It was in a year of financial depression that Wyllis Elliot came to Nebraska to buy cheap land and revisit the country where he had spent a year of his youth. When he had graduated from Harvard it was still customary for moneyed gentlemen to send their scapegrace sons to rough it on ranches in the wilds of Nebraska or Dakota, or to consign them to a living death in the sagebrush of the Black Hills. These young men did not always return to the ways of civilized life. But Wyllis Elliot had not married a half-breed, nor been shot in a cowpunchers' brawl, nor wrecked by bad whisky, nor appropriated by a smirched adventuress. He had been saved from these things by a girl, his sister, who had been very near to his life ever since the days when they read fairy tales together and dreamed the dreams that never come true. On this, his first visit to his father's ranch since he left it six years before, he brought her with him. She had been laid up half the winter from a sprain received while skating, and had had too much time for reflection during those months. She was restless and filled with a desire to see something of the wild country of which her brother had told her so much. She was to be married the next winter, and Wyllis understood her when she begged him to take her with him on this long, aimless jaunt across the continent, to taste the last of their freedom together. It comes to all women of her type—that desire to taste the unknown which allures and terrifies, to run one's whole soul's length out to the wind—just once.

It had been an uneventful journey. Wyllis somehow understood that strain of gypsy blood in his sister, and he knew where to take her. They had slept in sod houses on the Platte River, made the acquaintance of the personnel of a third-rate opera company on the train to Deadwood, dined in a camp of railroad constructors at the world's end beyond New Castle, gone through the Black Hills on horseback, fished for trout in Dome Lake, watched a dance at Cripple Creek, where the lost souls who hide in the hills gathered for their besotted revelry. And now, last of all, before the return to thraldom, there was this little shack, anchored on the windy crest of the Divide, a little black dot against the flaming sunsets, a scented sea of cornland bathed in opalescent air and blinding sunlight.

Margaret Elliot was one of those women of whom there are so many in this day, when old order, passing, giveth place to new: beautiful, talented, critical, unsatisfied, tired of the world at twenty-four. For the moment the life and people of the Divide interested her. She was there but a week; perhaps had she stayed longer, that inexorable ennui which travels faster even than the *Vestibule Limited* would have overtaken her. The week she tarried there was the week that Eric Hermannson was helping Jerry Lockhart thresh; a week earlier or a week later, and there would have been no story to write.

It was on Thursday and they were to leave on Saturday. Wyllis and his sister were sitting on the wide piazza of the ranchhouse, staring out into the afternoon sunlight and protesting against the gusts of hot wind that blew up from the sandy riverbottom twenty miles to the southward.

The young man pulled his cap lower over his eyes and remarked:

"The wind is the real thing; you don't strike it anywhere else. You remember we had a touch of it in Algiers and I told you it came from Kansas. It's the keynote of this country."

Wyllis touched her hand that lay on the hammock and continued gently:

"I hope it's paid you, Sis. Roughing it's dangerous business; it takes the taste out of things."

She shut her fingers firmly over the brown hand that was so like her own.

"Paid? Why, Wyllis, I haven't been so happy since we were children and were going to discover the ruins of Troy together some day. Do you know, I believe I could just stay on here forever and let the world go on its own gait. It seems as though the tension and strain we used to talk of last winter were gone for good, as though one could never give one's strength out to such petty things anymore."

Wyllis brushed the ashes of his pipe away from the silk handkerchief that was knotted about his neck and stared moodily off at the skyline.

"No, you're mistaken. This would bore you after a while. You can't shake the fever of the other life. I've tried it. There was a time when the gay fellows of Rome could trot down into the Thebaid and burrow into the sandhills and get rid of it. But it's all too complex now. You see, we've made our dissipations so dainty and respectable that they've gone further in than the flesh, and taken hold of the ego proper. You couldn't rest, even here. The war cry would follow you."

"You don't waste words, Wyllis, but you never miss fire. I talk more than you do, without saying half so much. You must have learned the art of silence from these taciturn Norwegians. I think I like silent men."

"Naturally," said Wyllis, "since you have decided to marry the most brilliant talker you know."

Both were silent for a time, listening to the sighing of the hot wind through the parched morning-glory vines. Margaret spoke first.

"Tell me, Wyllis, were many of the Norwegians you used to know as interesting as Eric Hermannson?"

"Who, Siegfried? Well, no. He used to be the flower of the Norwegian youth in my day, and he's rather an exception, even now. He has retrograded, though. The bonds of the soil have tightened on him, I fancy."

"Siegfried? Come, that's rather good, Wyllis. He looks like a dragon-slayer. What is it that makes him so different from the others? I can talk to him; he seems quite like a human being."

"Well," said Wyllis, meditatively, "I don't read Bourget as much as my cultured sister, and I'm not so well up in analysis, but I fancy it's because one keeps cherishing a perfectly unwarranted suspicion that under that big, hulking anatomy of his, he may conceal a soul somewhere. *Nicht wahr?*"

"Something like that," said Margaret, thoughtfully, "except that it's more than a suspicion, and it isn't groundless. He has one, and he makes it known, somehow, without speaking."

"I always have my doubts about loquacious souls," Wyllis remarked, with the unbelieving smile that had grown habitual with him.

Margaret went on, not heeding the interruption. "I knew it from the first, when he told me about the suicide of his cousin, the Bernstein boy. That kind of blunt pathos can't be summoned at will in anybody. The earlier novelists rose to it, sometimes, unconsciously. But last night when I sang for him I was doubly sure. Oh, I haven't told you about that yet! Better light your pipe again. You see, he stumbled in on me in the dark when I was pumping away at that old parlor organ to please Mrs. Lockhart. It's her household fetish and I've forgotten how many pounds of butter she made and sold to buy it. Well, Eric stumbled in, and in some inarticulate manner made me understand that he wanted me to sing for him. I sang just the old things, of course. It's queer to sing familiar things here at the world's end. It makes one think how the hearts of men have carried them around the world, into the waste of Iceland and the jungles of Africa and the islands of the Pacific. I think if one lived here long enough one would quite forget how to be trivial, and would read only the great books that we never get time to read in the world, and would remember only the great music, and the things that are really worthwhile would stand out clearly against that horizon over there. And of course I played the intermezzo from *Cavalleria Rusticana* for him; it goes rather better on an organ than most things do. He shuffled his feet and twisted his big hands up into knots and blurted out that he didn't know there was any music like that in the world. Why, there were tears in his voice, Wyllis! Yes, like Rossetti, I *heard* his tears. Then it dawned upon me that it was probably the first good music he had ever heard in all his life. Think of it, to care for music as he does and never to hear it, never to know that it exists on earth! To long for it as we long for other perfect experiences that never come. I can't tell you what music means to that man. I never saw anyone so susceptible to it. It gave him speech, he became alive. When I had finished the intermezzo, he began telling me about a little crippled brother who died and whom he loved and used to carry everywhere in his arms. He did not wait for encouragement. He took up the story and told it slowly, as if to himself, just sort of rose up and told his own woe to answer Mascagni's. It overcame me."

"Poor devil," said Wyllis, looking at her with mysterious eyes, "and so you've given him a new woe. Now he'll go on wanting Grieg and Schubert the rest of his days and never getting them. That's a girl's philanthropy for you!"

Jerry Lockhart came out of the house screwing his chin over the unusual luxury of a stiff white collar, which his wife insisted upon as a necessary article of toilet while Miss Elliot was at the house. Jerry sat down on the step and smiled his broad, red smile at Margaret.

"Well, I've got the music for your dance, Miss Elliot. Olaf Oleson will bring his accordion and Mollie will play the organ, when she isn't lookin' after the grub, and a little chap from Frenchtown will bring his fiddle—though the French don't mix with the Norwegians much."

"Delightful! Mr. Lockhart, the dance will be the feature of our trip, and it's so nice of you to get it up for us. We'll see the Norwegians in character at last," cried Margaret, cordially.

"See here, Lockhart, I'll settle with you for backing her in this scheme," said Wyllis, sitting up and knocking the ashes out of his pipe. "She's done crazy things enough on this trip, but to talk of dancing all night with a gang of half-mad Norwegians and taking the carriage at four to catch the six o'clock train out of Riverton—well, it's tommy-rot, that's what it is!"

"Wyllis, I leave it to your sovereign power of reason to decide whether it isn't easier to stay up all night than to get up at three in the morning. To get up at three, think what that means! No, sir, I prefer to keep my vigil and then get into a sleeper."

"But what do you want with the Norwegians? I thought you were tired of dancing."

"So I am, with some people. But I want to see a Norwegian dance, and I intend to. Come, Wyllis, you know how seldom it is that one really wants to do anything nowadays. I wonder when I have really wanted to go to a party before. It will be something to remember next month at Newport, when we have to and don't want to. Remember your own theory that contrast is about the only thing that makes life endurable. This is my party and Mr. Lockhart's; your whole duty tomorrow night will consist in being nice to the Norwegian girls. I'll warrant you were adept enough at it once. And you'd better be very nice indeed, for if there are many such young Valkyries as Eric's sister among them, they would simply tie you up in a knot if they suspected you were guying them."

Wyllis groaned and sank back into the hammock to consider his fate, while his sister went on.

"And the guests, Mr. Lockhart, did they accept?"

Lockhart took out his knife and began sharpening it on the sole of his plowshoe.

"Well, I guess we'll have a couple dozen. You see it's pretty hard to get a crowd together here anymore. Most of 'em have gone over to the Free Gospellers, and they'd rather put their feet in the fire than shake 'em to a fiddle."

Margaret made a gesture of impatience. "Those Free Gospellers have just cast an evil spell over this country, haven't they?"

"Well," said Lockhart, cautiously, "I don't just like to pass judgment on any Christian sect, but if you're to know the chosen by their works, the Gospellers can't make a very proud showin', an' that's a fact. They're responsible for a few suicides, and they've sent a good-sized delegation to the state insane asylum, an' I don't see as they've made the rest of us much better than we were before. I had a little herdboy last spring, as square a little Dane as I want to work for me, but after the Gospellers got hold of him and sanctified him, the little beggar used to get down on his knees out on the prairie and pray by the hour and let the cattle get into the corn, an' I had to fire him. That's about the way it goes. Now there's Eric; that chap used to be a hustler and the spryest dancer in all this section—called all the dances. Now he's got no ambition and he's glum as a preacher. I don't suppose we can even get him to come in tomorrow night."

"Eric? Why, he must dance, we can't let him off," said Margaret, quickly. "Why, I intend to dance with him myself!"

"I'm afraid he won't dance. I asked him this morning if he'd help us out and he said, 'I don't dance now, anymore,' " said Lockhart, imitating the labored English of the Norwegian.

" 'The Miller of Hofbau, the Miller of Hofbau, O my Princess!' " chirped Wyllis, cheerfully, from his hammock.

The red on his sister's cheek deepened a little, and she laughed mischievously. "We'll see about that, sir. I'll not admit that I am beaten until I have asked him myself."

Every night Eric rode over to St. Anne, a little village in the heart of the French settlement, for the mail. As the road lay through the most attractive part of the Divide country, on several occasions Margaret Elliot and her brother had accompanied him. Tonight Wyllis had business with Lockhart, and Margaret rode with Eric, mounted on a frisky little mustang that Mrs. Lockhart had broken to the sidesaddle.

Margaret regarded her escort very much as she did the servant who always accompanied her on long rides at home, and the ride to the village was a silent one. She was occupied with thoughts of another world, and Eric was wrestling with more thoughts than had ever been crowded into his head before. He rode with his eyes riveted on that slight figure before him, as though he wished to absorb it through the optic nerves and hold it in his brain forever. He understood the situation perfectly. His brain worked slowly, but he had a keen sense of the values of things. This girl represented an entirely new species of humanity to him, but he knew where to place her. The prophets of old, when an angel first appeared unto them, never doubted its high origin.

Eric was patient under the adverse conditions of his life, but he was not servile. The Norse blood in him had not entirely lost its self-reliance. He came of a proud fisher line, men who were not afraid of anything but the ice and the devil, and he had prospects before him when his father went down off the North Cape in the long Arctic night, and his mother, seized by a violent horror of seafaring life, had followed her brother to America. Eric was eighteen then, handsome as young Siegfried, a giant in stature, with a skin singularly pure and delicate, like a Swede's; hair as yellow as the locks of Tennyson's amorous Prince, and eyes of a fierce, burning blue, whose flash was most dangerous to women. He had in those days a certain pride of bearing, a certain confidence of approach, that usually accompanies physical perfection. It was even said of him then that he was in love with life, and inclined to levity, a vice most unusual on the Divide. But the sad history of those Norwegian exiles, transplanted in an arid soil and under a scorching sun, had repeated itself in his case. Toil and isolation had sobered him, and he grew more and more like the clods among which he labored. It was as though some red-hot instrument had touched for a moment those delicate fibers of the brain which respond to acute pain or pleasure, in which lies the power of exquisite sensation, and had seared them quite away. It is a painful thing to watch the light die out of the eyes of those Norsemen, leaving an expression of impenetrable sadness, quite passive, quite hopeless, a shadow that is never lifted. With some this change comes almost at once, in the first bitterness of homesickness, with others it comes more slowly, according to the time it takes each man's heart to die.

Oh, those poor Northmen of the Divide! They are dead many a year before they are put to rest in the little graveyard on the windy hill where exiles of all nations grow akin.

The peculiar species of hypochondria to which the exiles of his people sooner or later succumb had not developed in Eric until that night at the

Lone Star schoolhouse, when he had broken his violin across his knee. After that, the gloom of his people settled down upon him, and the gospel of maceration began its work. *"If thine eye offend thee, pluck it out,"* et cetera. The pagan smile that once hovered about his lips was gone, and he was one with sorrow. Religion heals a hundred hearts for one that it embitters, but when it destroys, its work is quick and deadly, and where the agony of the cross has been, joy will not come again. This man understood things literally: one must live without pleasure to die without fear; to save the soul it was necessary to starve the soul.

The sun hung low above the cornfields when Margaret and her cavalier left St. Anne. South of the town there is a stretch of road that runs for some three miles through the French settlement, where the prairie is as level as the surface of a lake. There the fields of flax and wheat and rye are bordered by precise rows of slender, tapering Lombard poplars. It was a yellow world that Margaret Elliot saw under the wide light of the setting sun.

The girl gathered up her reins and called back to Eric, "It will be safe to run the horses here, won't it?"

"Yes, I think so, now," he answered, touching his spur to his pony's flank. They were off like the wind. It is an old saying in the West that newcomers always ride a horse or two to death before they get broken in to the country. They are tempted by the great open spaces and try to outride the horizon, to get to the end of something. Margaret galloped over the level road, and Eric, from behind, saw her long veil fluttering in the wind. It had fluttered just so in his dreams last night and the night before. With a sudden inspiration of courage he overtook her and rode beside her, looking intently at her half-averted face. Before, he had only stolen occasional glances at it, seen it in blinding flashes, always with more or less embarrassment, but now he determined to let every line of it sink into his memory. Men of the world would have said that it was an unusual face, nervous, finely cut, with clear, elegant lines that betokened ancestry. Men of letters would have called it a historic face, and would have conjectured at what old passions long asleep, what old sorrows forgotten time out of mind, doing battle together in ages gone, had curved those delicate nostrils, left their unconscious memory in those eyes. But Eric read no meaning in these details. To him this beauty was something more than color and line; it was a flash of white light, in which one cannot distinguish color because all colors are there. To him it was a complete revelation, an embodiment of those dreams of impossible loveliness that linger by a young man's pillow on midsummer nights; yet, because it held something more than the attraction of health and youth and shapeliness, it troubled him, and in its presence he felt as the Goths before the white marbles in the Roman Capitol, not knowing whether they were men or gods. At times he felt like uncovering his head before it, again the fury seized him to break and despoil, to find the clay in this spirit-thing and stamp upon it. Away from her, he longed to strike out with his arms, and take and hold; it maddened him that this woman whom he could break in his hands should be so much stronger than he. But near her, he never questioned this strength; he admitted its potentiality as he admitted the miracles of the Bible; it enervated and conquered him. Tonight, when he rode so close to her that he could have touched her, he knew that he might as well reach out his hand to take a star.

Margaret stirred uneasily under his gaze and turned questioningly in her saddle.

"This wind puts me a little out of breath when we ride fast," she said.

Eric turned his eyes away.

"I want to ask you if I go to New York to work, if I maybe hear music like you sang last night? I been a purty good hand to work," he asked, timidly.

Margaret looked at him with surprise, and then, as she studied the outline of his face, pityingly.

"Well, you might—but you'd lose a good deal else. I shouldn't like you to go to New York—and be poor, you'd be out of atmosphere, some way," she said, slowly. Inwardly she was thinking: *There he would be altogether sordid, impossible—a machine who would carry one's trunks upstairs, perhaps. Here he is every inch a man, rather picturesque; why is it?* "No," she added aloud, "I shouldn't like that."

"Then I not go," said Eric, decidedly.

Margaret turned her face to hide a smile. She was a trifle amused and a trifle annoyed. Suddenly she spoke again.

"But I'll tell you what I do want you to do, Eric. I want you to dance with us tomorrow night and teach me some of the Norwegian dances; they say you know them all. Won't you?"

Eric straightened himself in his saddle and his eyes flashed as they had done in the Lone Star schoolhouse when he broke his violin across his knee.

"Yes, I will," he said, quietly, and he believed that he delivered his soul to hell as he said it.

They had reached the rougher country now, where the road wound through a narrow cut in one of the bluffs along the creek, when a beat of hoofs ahead and the sharp neighing of horses made the ponies start and Eric rose in his stirrups. Then down the gulch in front of them and over the steep clay banks thundered a herd of wild ponies, nimble as monkeys and wild as rabbits, such as horse-traders drive east from the plains of Montana to sell in the farming country. Margaret's pony made a shrill sound, a neigh that was almost a scream, and started up the clay bank to meet them, all the wild blood of the range breaking out in an instant. Margaret called to Eric just as he threw himself out of the saddle and caught her pony's bit. But the wiry little animal had gone mad and was kicking and biting like a devil. Her wild brothers of the range were all about her, neighing, and pawing the earth, and striking her with their forefeet and snapping at her flanks. It was the old liberty of the range that the little beast fought for.

"Drop the reins and hold tight!" Eric called, throwing all his weight upon the bit, struggling under those frantic forefeet that now beat at his breast and now kicked at the wild mustangs that surged and tossed about him. He succeeded in wrenching the pony's head toward him and crowding her withers against the clay bank, so that she could not roll.

"Hold tight, tight!" he shouted again, launching a kick at a snorting animal that reared back against Margaret's saddle. If she should lose her courage and fall now, under those hoofs— He struck out again and again, kicking right and left with all his might. Already the negligent drivers had galloped into the cut, and their long quirts were whistling over the heads of the herd. As suddenly as it had come, the struggling, frantic wave of wild life swept up out of the gulch and on across the open prairie, and with a long despairing whinny of farewell the pony dropped her head and stood trembling in her sweat, shaking the foam and blood from her bit.

Eric stepped close to Margaret's side and laid his hand on her saddle. "You are not hurt?" he asked, hoarsely. As he raised his face in the soft starlight she saw that it was white and drawn and that his lips were working nervously.

"No, no, not at all. But you, you are suffering; they struck you!" she cried in sharp alarm.

He stepped back and drew his hand across his brow.

"No, it is not that," he spoke rapidly now, with his hands clenched at his side. "But if they had hurt you, I would beat their brains out with my hands, I would kill them all. I was never afraid before. You are the only beautiful thing that has ever come close to me. You came like an angel out of the sky. You are like the music you sing, you are like the stars and the snow on the mountains where I played when I was a little boy. You are like all that I wanted once and never had, you are all that they have killed in me. I die for you tonight, tomorrow, for all eternity. I am not a coward; I was afraid because I love you more than Christ who died for me, more than I am afraid of hell, or hope for heaven. I was never afraid before. If you had fallen—oh, my God!" He threw his arms out blindly and dropped his head upon the pony's mane, leaning limply against the animal like a man struck by some sickness. His shoulders rose and fell perceptibly with his labored breathing. The horse stood cowed with exhaustion and fear. Presently Margaret laid her hand on Eric's head and said gently:

"You are better now, shall we go on? Can you get your horse?"

"No, he has gone with the herd. I will lead yours, she is not safe. I will not frighten you again." His voice was still husky, but it was steady now. He took hold of the bit and tramped home in silence.

When they reached the house, Eric stood stolidly by the pony's head until Wyllis came to lift his sister from the saddle.

"The horses were badly frightened, Wyllis. I think I was pretty thoroughly scared myself," she said as she took her brother's arm and went slowly up the hill toward the house. "No, I'm not hurt, thanks to Eric. You must thank him for taking such good care of me. He's a mighty fine fellow. I'll tell you all about it in the morning, dear. I was pretty well shaken up and I'm going right to bed now. Good night."

When she reached the low room in which she slept, she sank upon the bed in her riding dress face downward.

"Oh, I pity him! I pity him!" she murmured, with a long sigh of exhaustion. She must have slept a little. When she rose again, she took from her dress a letter that had been waiting for her at the village post office. It was closely written in a long, angular hand, covering a dozen pages of foreign note paper, and began:

My dearest Margaret:

If I should attempt to say *how like a winter hath thine absence been,* I should incur the risk of being tedious. Really, it takes the sparkle out of everything. Having nothing better to do, and not caring to go anywhere in particular without you, I remained in the city until Jack Courtwell noted my general despondency and brought me down here to his place on the sound to manage some open-air theatricals he is getting up. *As You Like It* is of course the piece selected. Miss Harrison plays Rosalind. I wish you had been here to take the part. Miss Harrison reads her lines well, but she is either a maiden-all-forlorn or a tomboy; insists on reading into the part all sorts of deeper meanings and highly colored suggestions wholly out of harmony with the pastoral setting. Like most of the professionals, she exaggerates the emotional element and quite fails to do justice to Rosalind's facile wit and really brilliant mental qualities. Gerard will do Orlando, but rumor says he is *épris* of your sometime friend, Miss Meredith, and his memory is treacherous and his interest fitful.

My new pictures arrived last week on the *Gascogne.* The Puvis de Chavannes is even more beautiful than I thought it in Paris. A pale dream-maiden sits by a pale dream-cow and a stream of anemic water flows at her feet. The Constant, you will remember, I got because you admired it. It is here in all its florid splendor, the whole dominated by a glowing sensuosity. The drapery of the female figure is as wonderful as you said; the fabric all barbaric pearl and gold, painted with an easy, effortless voluptuousness, and that white, gleaming line of African coast in the background recalls memories of you very precious to me. But it is useless to deny that Constant irritates me. Though I cannot prove the charge against him, his brilliancy always makes me suspect him of cheapness.

Here Margaret stopped and glanced at the remaining pages of this strange love letter. They seemed to be filled chiefly with discussions of pictures and books, and with a slow smile she laid them by.

She rose and began undressing. Before she lay down she went to open the window. With her hand on the sill, she hesitated, feeling suddenly as though some danger were lurking outside, some inordinate desire waiting to spring upon her in the darkness. She stood there for a long time, gazing at the infinite sweep of the sky.

"Oh, it is all so little, so little there," she murmured. "When everything else is so dwarfed, why should one expect love to be great? Why should one try to read highly colored suggestions into a life like that? If only I could find one thing in it all that mattered greatly, one thing that would warm me when I am alone! Will life never give me that one great moment?"

As she raised the window, she heard a sound in the plum bushes outside. It was only the house-dog roused from his sleep, but Margaret started violently and trembled so that she caught the foot of the bed for support. Again she felt herself pursued by some overwhelming longing, some desperate necessity for herself, like the outstretching of helpless, unseen arms in the darkness, and the air seemed heavy with sighs of yearning. She fled to her bed with the words, "I love you more than Christ, who died for me!" ringing in her ears.

III

About midnight the dance at Lockhart's was at its height. Even the old men who had come to "look on" caught the spirit of revelry and stamped the floor with the vigor of old Silenus. Eric took the violin from the Frenchman, and Minna Oleson sat at the organ, and the music grew more and more characteristic—rude, half mournful music, made up of the folksongs of the North, that the villagers sing through the long night in hamlets by the sea, when they are thinking of the sun, and the spring, and the fishermen so long away. To Margaret some of it sounded like Grieg's *Peer Gynt* music. She found something irresistibly infectious in the mirth of these people who were so seldom merry, and she felt almost one of them. Something seemed struggling for freedom in them tonight, something of the joyous childhood of the nations which exile had not killed. The girls were all boisterous with delight. Pleasure came to them but rarely, and when it came, they caught at it wildly and crushed its fluttering wings in their strong brown fingers. They had a hard life enough, most of them. Torrid summers and freezing winters, labor and drudgery and ignorance, were the portion of their girlhood; a short wooing, a hasty, loveless marriage, unlimited maternity, thankless sons, premature age and ugliness were the dower of their womanhood. But what matter? Tonight there was hot liquor in the glass and hot blood in the heart; tonight they danced.

Tonight Eric Hermannson had renewed his youth. He was no longer the big, silent Norwegian who had sat at Margaret's feet and looked hopelessly into her eyes. Tonight he was a man, with a man's rights and a man's power. Tonight he was Siegfried indeed. His hair was yellow as the heavy wheat in the ripe of summer, and his eyes flashed like the blue water between the ice packs in the North Seas. He was not afraid of Margaret tonight, and when he danced with her he held her firmly. She was tired and dragged on his arm a little, but the strength of the man was like an all-pervading fluid, stealing through her veins, awakening under her heart some nameless, unsuspected existence that had slumbered there all these years and that went out through her throbbing fingertips to his that answered. She wondered if the hoydenish blood of some lawless ancestor, long asleep, were calling out in her tonight, some drop of a hotter fluid that the centuries had failed to cool, and why, if this curse were in her, it had not spoken before. But was it a curse, this awakening, this wealth before undiscovered, this music set free? For the first time in her life her heart held something stronger than herself; was not this worthwhile? Then she ceased to wonder. She lost sight of the lights and the faces, and the music was drowned by the beating of her own arteries. She saw only the blue eyes that flashed above her, felt only the warmth of that throbbing hand which held hers and which the blood of his heart fed. Dimly, as in a dream, she saw the drooping shoulders, high white forehead and tight, cynical mouth of the man she was to marry in December. For an hour she had been crowding back the memory of that face with all her strength.

"Let us stop, this is enough," she whispered. His only answer was to tighten the arm behind her. She sighed and let that masterful strength bear her where it would. She forgot that this man was little more than a savage, that they would part at dawn. The blood has no memories, no reflections, no regrets for the past, no consideration of the future.

"Let us go out where it is cooler," she said when the music stopped, thinking, *I am growing faint here, I shall be all right in the open air.* They stepped out into the cool, blue air of the night.

Since the older folk had begun dancing, the young Norwegians had been slipping out in couples to climb the windmill tower into the cooler atmosphere, as is their custom.

"You like to go up?" asked Eric, close to her ear.

She turned and looked at him with suppressed amusement. "How high is it?"

"Forty feet, about. I not let you fall." There was a note of irresistible pleading in his voice, and she felt that he tremendously wished her to go. Well, why not? This was a night of the unusual, when she was not herself at all, but was living an unreality. Tomorrow, yes, in a few hours, there would be the *Vestibule Limited* and the world.

"Well, if you'll take good care of me. I used to be able to climb, when I was a little girl."

Once at the top and seated on the platform, they were silent. Margaret wondered if she would not hunger for that scene all her life, through all the routine of the days to come. Above them stretched the great western sky, serenely blue, even in the night, with its big, burning stars, never so cold and dead and far away as in denser atmospheres. The moon would not be up for twenty minutes yet, and all about the horizon, that wide horizon, which seemed to reach around the world, lingered a pale, white light, as of a universal dawn. The weary wind brought up to them the heavy odors of the cornfields. The music of the dance sounded faintly from below. Eric leaned on his elbow beside her, his legs swinging down on the ladder. His great shoulders looked more than ever like those of the stone Doryphorus, who stands in his perfect, reposeful strength in the Louvre, and had often made her wonder if such men died forever with the youth of Greece.

"How sweet the corn smells at night," said Margaret nervously.

"Yes, like the flowers that grow in paradise, I think."

She was somewhat startled by this reply, and more startled when this taciturn man spoke again.

"You go away tomorrow?"

"Yes, we have stayed longer than we thought to now."

"You not come back anymore?"

"No, I expect not. You see, it is a long trip halfway across the continent."

"You soon forget about this country, I guess." It seemed to him now a little thing to lose his soul for this woman; but that she should utterly forget this night into which he threw all his life and all his eternity—that was a bitter thought.

"No, Eric, I will not forget. You have all been too kind to me for that. And you won't be sorry you danced this one night, will you?"

"I never be sorry. I have not been so happy before. I not be so happy again, ever. You will be happy many nights yet, I only this one. I will dream sometimes, maybe."

The mighty resignation of his tone alarmed and touched her. It was as when some great animal composes itself for death, as when a great ship goes down at sea.

She sighed, but did not answer him. He drew a little closer and looked into her eyes.

"You are not always happy, too?" he asked.

"No, not always, Eric; not very often, I think."

"You have a trouble?"

"Yes, but I cannot put it into words. Perhaps if I could do that, I could cure it."

He clasped his hands together over his heart, as children do when they pray, and said falteringly, "If I own all the world, I give him you."

Margaret felt a sudden moisture in her eyes, and laid her hand on his.

"Thank you, Eric; I believe you would. But perhaps even then I should not be happy. Perhaps I have too much of it already."

She did not take her hand away from him; she did not dare. She sat still and waited for the traditions in which she had always believed to speak and save her. But they were dumb. She belonged to an ultrarefined civilization which tries to cheat Nature with elegant sophistries. Cheat Nature? Bah! One generation may do it, perhaps two; but the third? Can we ever rise above Nature or sink below her? Did she not turn on

Jerusalem as upon Sodom, upon St. Anthony in his desert as upon Nero in his seraglio? Does she not always cry in brutal triumph: "I am here still, at the bottom of things, warming the roots of life; you cannot starve me nor tame me nor thwart me; I made the world, I rule it, and I am its destiny."

This woman, on a windmill tower at the world's end with a giant barbarian, heard that cry tonight, and she was afraid! Ah, the terror and the delight of that moment when first we fear ourselves! Until then we have not lived.

"Come, Eric, let us go down; the moon is up and the music has begun again," she said.

He rose silently and stepped down upon the ladder, putting his arm about her to help her. That arm could have thrown Thor's hammer out in the cornfields yonder, yet it scarcely touched her, and his hand trembled as it had done in the dance. His face was level with hers now and the moonlight fell sharply upon it. All her life she had searched the faces of men for the look that lay in his eyes. She knew that that look had never shone for her before, would never shine for her on earth again, that such love comes to one only in dreams or in impossible places like this, unattainable always. This was Love's self; in a moment it would die. Stung by the agonized appeal that emanated from the man's whole being, she leaned forward and laid her lips on his. Once, twice, and again she heard the deep respirations rattle in his throat while she held them there, and the riotous force under her heart became an engulfing weakness. He drew her up to him until he felt all the resistance go out of her body, until every nerve relaxed and yielded. When she drew her face back from his, it was white with fear.

"Let us go down, oh, my God! Let us go down!" she muttered. And the drunken stars up yonder seemed reeling to some appointed doom as she clung to the rounds of the ladder. All that she was to know of love she had left upon his lips.

"The Devil is loose again," whispered Olaf Oleson, as he saw Eric dancing a moment later, his eye blazing.

But Eric was thinking with an almost savage exultation of the time when he should pay for this. Ah, there would be no quailing then! If ever a soul went fearlessly, proudly down to the gates infernal, his should go. For a moment he fancied he was there already, treading down the tempest of flame, hugging the fiery hurricane to his breast. He wondered whether in ages gone—all the countless years of sinning in which men had sold and lost and flung their souls away—any man had ever so cheated Satan, had ever bartered his soul for so great a price.

It seemed but a little while till dawn.

The carriage was brought to the door and Wyllis Elliot and his sister said goodbye. She could not meet Eric's eyes as she gave him her hand, but as he stood by the horse's head, just as the carriage moved off, she gave him one swift glance that said, "I will not forget." In a moment the carriage was gone.

Eric changed his coat and plunged his head into the water tank and went to the barn to hook up his team. As he led his horses to the door, a shadow fell across his path, and he saw Skinner rising in his stirrups. His rugged face was pale and worn with looking after his wayward flock, with dragging men into the way of salvation.

"Good morning, Eric. There was a dance here last night?" he asked, sternly.

"A dance? Oh, yes, a dance," replied Eric, cheerfully.

"Certainly you did not dance, Eric?"

"Yes, I danced. I danced all the time."

The minister's shoulders drooped, and an expression of profound discouragement settled over his haggard face. There was almost anguish in the yearning he felt for his soul.

"Eric, I didn't look for this from you. I thought God had set his mark on you if he ever had on any man. And it is for things like this that you set your soul back a thousand years from God. O foolish and perverse generation!"

Eric drew himself up to his full height and looked off to where the new day was gilding the corn tassels and flooding the uplands with light. As his nostrils drew in the breath of the dew and the morning, something from the only poetry he had ever read flashed across his mind, and he murmured, half to himself, with dreamy exultation:

" 'And a day shall be as a thousand years, and a thousand years as a day.' "

The Sentimentality of William Tavener

It takes a strong woman to make any sort of success of living in the West, and Hester undoubtedly was that. When people spoke of William Tavener as the most prosperous farmer in McPherson County, they usually added that his wife was a "good manager." She was an executive woman, quick of tongue and something of an imperatrix. The only reason her husband did not consult her about his business was that she did not wait to be consulted.

It would have been quite impossible for one man, within the limited sphere of human action, to follow all Hester's advice, but in the end William usually acted upon some of her suggestions. When she incessantly denounced the "shiftlessness" of letting a new threshing machine stand unprotected in the open, he eventually built a shed for it. When she sniffed contemptuously at his notion of fencing a hog corral with sod walls, he made a spiritless beginning on the structure—merely to "show his temper," as she put it—but in the end he went off quietly to town and bought enough barbed wire to complete the fence. When the first heavy rains came on, and the pigs rooted down the sod wall and made little paths all over it to facilitate their ascent, he heard his wife relate with relish the story of the little pig that built a mud house, to the minister at the dinner table, and William's gravity never relaxed for an instant. Silence, indeed, was William's refuge and his strength.

William set his boys a wholesome example to respect their mother. People who knew him very well suspected that he even admired her. He was a hard man toward his neighbors, and even toward his sons: grasping, determined, and ambitious.

There was an occasional blue day about the house when William went over the store bills, but he never objected to items relating to his wife's gowns or bonnets. So it came about that many of the foolish, unnecessary little things that Hester bought for boys she had charged to her personal account.

One spring night Hester sat in a rocking chair by the sitting room window, darning socks. She rocked violently and sent her long needle vigorously back and forth over her gourd, and it took only a very casual glance to see that she was wrought up over something. William sat on the other side of the table reading his farm paper. If he had noticed his wife's agitation, his calm, clean-shaven face betrayed no sign of concern. He must have noticed the sarcastic turn of her remarks at the supper table, and he must have noticed the moody silence of the older boys as they ate. When supper was but half over little Billy, the youngest, had suddenly pushed back his plate and slipped away from the table, manfully trying to swallow a sob. But William Tavener never heeded ominous forecasts in the domestic horizon, and he never looked for a storm until it broke.

After supper the boys had gone to the pond under the willows in the big cattle corral, to get rid of the dust of plowing. Hester could hear an occasional splash and a laugh ringing clear through the stillness of the night, as she sat by the open window. She sat silent for almost an hour reviewing in her mind many plans of attack. But she was too vigorous a woman to be much of a strategist, and she usually came to her point with directness. At last she cut her thread and suddenly put her darning down, saying emphatically:

"William, I don't think it would hurt you to let the boys go to that circus in town tomorrow."

William continued to read his farm paper, but it was not Hester's custom to wait for an answer. She usually divined his arguments and assailed them one by one before he uttered them.

"You've been short of hands all summer, and you've worked the boys hard, and a man ought use his own flesh and blood as well as he does his hired hands. We're plenty able to afford it, and it's little enough our boys ever spend. I don't see how you can expect 'em to be steady and hard workin' unless you encourage 'em a little. I never could see much harm in circuses, and our boys have never been to one. Oh, I know Jim Howley's boys get drunk an' carry on when they go, but our boys ain't that sort, an' you know it, William. The animals are real instructive, an' our boys don't get to see much out here on the prairie. It was different where we were raised, but the boys have got no advantages here, an' if you don't take care, they'll grow up to be greenhorns."

Hester paused a moment, and William folded up his paper, but vouchsafed no remark. His sisters in Virginia had often said that only a quiet man like William could ever have lived with Hester Perkins. Secretly, William was rather proud of his wife's "gift of speech" and of the fact that she could talk in prayer meeting as fluently as a man. He confined his own efforts in that line to a brief prayer at Covenant meetings.

Hester shook out another sock and went on.

"Nobody was ever hurt by goin' to a circus. Why, law me! I remember I went to one myself once, when I was little. I had most forgot about it. It was over at Pewtown, an' I remember how I had set my heart on going. I don't think I'd ever forgiven my father if he hadn't taken me, though that red clay road was in a frightful way after the rain. I mind they had an elephant and six poll parrots, an' a Rocky Mountain lion, an' a cage of monkeys, an' two camels. My, but they were a sight to me then!"

Hester dropped the black sock and shook her head and smiled at the recollection. She was not expecting anything from William yet, and she was fairly startled when he said gravely, in much the same tone in which he announced the hymns in prayer meeting:

"No, there was only one camel. The other was a dromedary."

She peered around the lamp and looked at him keenly.

"Why, William, how come you to know?"

William folded his paper and answered with some hesitation, "I was there, too."

Hester's interest flashed up. "Well, I never, William! To think of my finding it out after all these years! Why, you couldn't have been much bigger'n our Billy then. It seems queer I never saw you when you was little, to remember about you. But then you Back Creek folks never have anything to do with us Gap people. But how come you to go? Your father was stricter with you than you are with your boys."

"I reckon I shouldn't 'a gone," he said slowly, "but boys will do foolish things. I had done a good deal of fox hunting the winter before, and father let me keep the bounty money. I hired Tom Smith's Tap to weed the corn for me, an' I slipped off unbeknownst to father an' went to the show."

Hester spoke up warmly: "Nonsense, William! It didn't do you no harm, I guess. You was always worked hard enough. It must have been a big sight for a little fellow. That clown must have just tickled you to death."

William crossed his knees and leaned back in his chair.

"I reckon I could tell all that fool's jokes now. Sometimes I can't help thinkin' about 'em in meetin' when the sermon's long. I mind I had on a pair of new boots that hurt me like the mischief, but I forgot all about 'em when that fellow rode the donkey. I recall I had to take them boots off as soon as I got out of sight o' town, and walked home in the mud barefoot."

"O poor little fellow!" Hester ejaculated, drawing her chair nearer and leaning her elbows on the table. "What cruel shoes they did use to make for children. I remember I went up to Back Creek to see the circus wagons go by. They came down from Romney, you know. The circus men stopped at the creek to water the animals, an' the elephant got stubborn an' broke a big limb off the yellow willow tree that grew there by the toll house porch, an' the Scribners were 'fraid as death he'd pull the house down. But this much I saw him do; he waded in the creek an' filled his trunk with water and squirted it in at the window and nearly ruined Ellen Scribner's pink lawn dress that she had just ironed an' laid out on the bed ready to wear to the circus."

"I reckon that must have been a trial to Ellen," chuckled William, "for she was mighty prim in them days."

Hester drew her chair still nearer William's. Since the children had begun growing up, her conversation with her husband had been almost wholly confined to questions of economy and expense. Their relationship had become purely a business one, like that between landlord and tenant. In her desire to indulge her boys she had unconsciously assumed a defensive and almost hostile attitude toward her husband. No debtor ever haggled with his usurer more doggedly than did Hester with her husband in behalf of her sons. The strategic contest had gone on so long that it had almost crowded out the memory of a closer relationship. This exchange of confidences tonight, when common recollections took them unawares and opened their hearts, had all the miracle of romance. They talked on and on; of old neighbors, of old familiar faces in the valley where they had grown up, of long forgotten incidents of their youth—weddings, picnics, sleighing parties, and baptizings. For years they had talked of nothing else but butter and eggs and the prices of things, and now they had as much to say to each other as people who meet after a long separation.

When the clock struck ten, William rose and went over to his walnut secretary and unlocked it. From his red leather wallet he took out a ten-dollar bill and laid it on the table beside Hester.

"Tell the boys not to stay late, an' not to drive the horses hard," he said quietly, and went off to bed.

Hester blew out the lamp and sat still in the dark a long time. She left the bill lying on the table where William had placed it. She had a painful sense of having missed something, or lost something; she felt that somehow the years had cheated her.

The little locust trees that grew by the fence were white with blossoms. Their heavy odor floated in to her on the night wind and recalled a night long ago, when the first whippoorwill of the spring was heard, and the rough, buxom girls of Hawkins Gap had held her laughing and struggling under the locust trees, and searched in her bosom for a lock of her sweetheart's hair, which is supposed to be on every girl's breast when the first whippoorwill sings. Two of those same girls had been her bridesmaids. Hester had been a very happy bride. She rose and went softly into the room where William lay. He was sleeping heavily, but occasionally moved his hand before his face to ward off the flies. Hester went into the parlor and took the piece of mosquito net from the basket of wax apples and pears that her sister had made before she died. One of the boys had brought it all the way from Virginia, packed in a tin pail, since Hester would not risk shipping so precious an ornament by freight. She went back to the bedroom and spread the net over William's head. Then she sat down by the bed and listened to his deep, regular breathing until she heard the boys returning. She went out to meet them and warn them not to waken their father.

"I'll be up early to get your breakfast, boys. Your father says you can go to the show." As she handed the money to the eldest, she felt a sudden throb of allegiance to her husband and said sharply, "And you be careful of that, an' don't waste it. Your father works hard for his money."

The boys looked at each other in astonishment and felt that they had lost a powerful ally.

A Singer's Romance

THE RAIN FELL in torrents and the great stream of people which poured out of the Metropolitan Opera House stagnated about the doors and seemed effectually checked by the black line of bobbing umbrellas on the sidewalk. The entrance was fairly blockaded, and the people who were waiting for carriages formed a solid phalanx, which the more unfortunate operagoers, who had to depend on streetcars no matter what the condition of the weather, tried to break through in vain. There was much shouting of numbers and hurrying of drivers, from whose oilcloth-covered hats the water trickled in tiny streams, quite as though the brims had been curved just to accommodate it. The wind made the management of the hundreds of umbrellas difficult, and they rose and fell and swayed about like toy balloons tugging at their moorings. At the stage entrance there was less congestion, but the confusion was not proportionally small, and Frau Selma Schumann was in no very amiable mood when she was at last told that her carriage awaited her. As she stepped out of the door, the wind caught the black lace mantilla wound about her head and lifted it high in the air in such a ludicrous fashion that the substantial soprano cut a figure much like a malicious Beardsley poster. In her frantic endeavor to replace her sportive headgear, she dropped the little velvet bag in which she carried her jewel case. A young man stationed by the door darted forward and snatched it up from the sidewalk, uncovered his head and returned the bag to her with a low bow. He was a tall man, slender and graceful, and he looked as dark as a Spaniard in the bright light that fell upon him from the doorway. His curling black hair would have been rather long even for a tenor, and he wore a dark mustache. His face had that oval contour, slightly effeminate, which belongs to the Latin races. He wore a long black ulster and held in his hand a wide-brimmed, black felt hat. In his buttonhole was a single red carnation. Frau Schumann took the bag with a radiant smile, quite forgetting her ill humor. "I thank you, sir," she said graciously. But the young man remained standing with bared head, never raising his eyes. "Merci, Monsieur," she ventured again, rather timidly, but his only recognition was to bow even lower than before, and Madame hastened to her carriage to hide her confusion from her maid, who followed close behind. Once in the carriage, Madame permitted herself to smile and to sigh a little in the darkness, and to wonder whether the disagreeable American prima donna, who manufactured gossip about every member of the company, had seen the little episode of the jewel bag. She almost hoped she had.

This signorino's reserve puzzled her more than his persistence. This was the third time she had given him an opportunity to speak, to make himself known, and the third time her timid advance had been met by silence and downcast eyes. She was unable to comprehend it. She had been singing in New York now eight weeks, and since the first week this dark man, clad in black, had followed her like a shadow. When she and Annette walked in the park, they always encountered him on one of the benches. When she went shopping, he sauntered after them on the other side of the street. She continually encountered him in the corridors of her hotel; when she entered the theater he was always stationed near the stage door, and when she came out again, he was still at his post. One evening, just to assure herself, she had gone to the Opera House when she was not in the cast, and, as she had hoped, the dark signor was absent. He had grown so familiar to her that she knew the outline of his head and shoulders a square away, and in the densest crowd her eyes instantly singled him out. She looked for him so constantly that she knew she would miss him if he should not appear. Yet he made no attempt whatever to address her. Once, when he was standing near her in the hotel corridor, she made pointless and incoherent inquiries about directions from the bell boy, in the hope that the young man would volunteer information, which he did not. On another occasion, when she found him smoking a cigarette at the door of the Holland as she went out into a drizzling rain, she had feigned impossible difficulties in raising her umbrella. He did, indeed, raise it for her, and bowing passed quickly down the street. Madame had begun to feel like a very bold and forward woman, and to blush guiltily under the surveillance of her maid. By every doorstep, at every corner, wherever she turned, whenever she looked out of a window, she encountered always the dark signorino, with his picturesque face and Spanish eyes, his broad-brimmed black felt hat set at an angle on his glistening black curls, and the inevitable red carnation in his buttonhole.

When they arrived at the hotel Antoinette went to the office to ask for Madame's mail, and returned to Madame's rooms with a letter which bore the familiar postmark of Monte Carlo. This threw Madame into an honest German rage, refreshing to witness, and she threw herself into a chair and wept audibly. The letter was from her husband, who spent most of his time and her money at the Casino, and who continually sent urgent letters for reenforcement.

"It's too much, 'Toinette, too much," she sobbed. "He says he must have money to pay his doctor. Why I have sent him money enough to pay the doctor bills of the royal family. Here am I singing three and four nights a week—no, I will not do it."

But she ended by sitting down at her desk and writing out a check, with which she enclosed very pointed advice, and directed it to the suave old gentleman at Monte Carlo.

Then she permitted 'Toinette to shake out her hair, and became lost in the contemplation of her own image in the mirror. She had to admit that she had grown a trifle stout, that there were many fine lines about her mouth and eyes, and little wrinkles on her forehead that had defied the arts of massage. Her blonde hair had lost its luster and was somewhat deadened by the heat of the curling iron. She had to hold her chin very high indeed in order not to have two, and there were little puffy places under her eyes that told of her love for pastry and champagne. Above her own face in the glass she saw the reflection of her maid's. Pretty, slender 'Toinette, with her satin-smooth skin and rosy cheeks and little pink ears, her arched brows and long black lashes and her coil of shining black hair. 'Toinette's youth and freshness irritated her tonight. She could not help wondering—but then this man was probably a man of intelligence, quite proof against the charm of mere prettiness. He was probably, she reflected, an artist like herself, a man who revered her art, and art, certainly, does not come at sixteen. Secretly, she wondered what 'Toinette thought of this dark signorino whom she must have noticed by this time. She had great respect for 'Toinette's opinion. 'Toinette was by no means an ordinary ladies' maid, and Madame had grown to regard her as a companion and confidante. She was the child of a French opera singer who had been one of Madame's earliest professional friends and who had come to an evil end and died in a hospital, leaving her young daughter wholly without protection. As the girl had no vocal possibilities, Madame Schumann had generously rescued her from the awful fate of the chorus by taking her into her service.

"You have been contented here, 'Toinette? You like America, you will be a little sorry to leave?" asked Madame as she said good night.

"Oh, yes, Madame, I should be sorry," returned 'Toinette.

"And so shall I," said Madame softly, smiling to herself.

'Toinette lingered a moment at the door; "Madame will have nothing to eat, no refreshment of any kind?"

"No, nothing tonight, 'Toinette."

"Not even the very smallest glass of champagne?"

"No, no, nothing," said Madame impatiently.

'Toinette turned out the light and left her in bed, where she lay awake for a long time, indulging in luxurious dreams.

In the morning she awoke long before it was time for 'Toinette to bring her coffee, and lay still, with her eyes closed, while the early rumble of the city was audible through the open window.

Selma Schumann was a singer without a romance. No one felt the incongruity of this more than she did, yet she had lived to the age of two-and-forty without ever having known an *affaire de coeur.* After her debut in grand opera she had married her former singing teacher, who at once decided that he had already done quite enough for his wife and the world in the placing and training of that wonderful voice, and lived in cheerful idleness, gambling her earnings with the utmost complacency, and when her reproaches grew too cutting, he would respectfully remind her that he had enlarged her upper register four tones, and in so doing had fulfilled the whole duty of man.

Madame had always been industrious and an indefatigable student. She could sing a large repertoire at the shortest notice, and her good nature made her invaluable to managers. She lacked, certainly, that poignant individuality which alone secures great eminence in the world of art, and no one ever went to the opera solely because her name was on the bill. She was known as a thoroughly "competent" artist, and as all singers know, that means a thankless life of underpaid drudgery. Her father had been a professor of etymology in a German university and she had inherited something of his taste for grubbing and had been measurably happy in her work. She practiced incessantly and skimped herself and saved money and dutifully supported her husband, and surely such virtue should bring its own reward. Yet when she saw other women in the company appear in a new tiara of diamonds, or saw them snatch notes from the hands of messenger boys, or take a carriage full of flowers back to the hotel with them, she had felt ill used, and had wondered what that other side of life was like. In short, from the wastes of this humdrum existence which seems so gay to the uninitiated, she had wished for a romance. Under all her laborious habits and thrift and economy there was left enough of the unsatisfied spirit of youth for that.

Since the shadow of the dark signorino had fallen across her path, the routine of her life, hitherto as fixed as that of the planets or of a German housewife, had become less rigid and more variable. She had decided that she owed it to her health to walk frequently in the park, and to sleep later in the morning. She had spent entire afternoons in dreamful idleness, whereas she should have been struggling with the new roles she was to sing in London. She had begun to pay the most scrupulous attention to her toilettes, which she had begun to neglect in the merciless routine of her work. She was visited by many *massageurs,* for she discovered that her figure and skin had been allowed to take care of themselves and had done it ill. She thought with bitter regret that a little less economy and a little more care might have prevented a wrinkle. One great sacrifice she made. She stopped drinking champagne. The sole one of the luxuries of life she had permitted herself was that of the table. She had all her countrywomen's love for good living, and she had indulged herself freely. She had known for a long time that champagne and sweets were bad for her complexion, and that they made her stout, but she had told herself that it was little enough pleasure she had at best.

But since the appearance of the dark signorino, all this had been changed, and it was by no means an easy sacrifice.

Madame waited a long time for her coffee, but 'Toinette did not appear. Then she rose and went into her reception room, but no one was there. In the little music room next door she heard a low murmur of voices. She parted the curtains a little, and saw 'Toinette with both her hands clasped in the hands of the dark signorino.

"But Madame," 'Toinette was saying, "she is so lonely, I cannot find the heart to tell her that I must leave her."

"Ah," murmured the signorino, and his voice was as caressing as Madame had imagined it in her dreams, "she has been like a mother to you, the Madame, she will be glad of your happiness."

When Selma Schumann reached her own room again she threw herself on her bed and wept furiously. Then she dried her eyes and railed at Fortune in deep German polysyllables, gesturing like an enraged Valkyrie.

Then she ordered her breakfast—and a quart of champagne.

The Professor's Commencement

THE PROFESSOR sat at his library table at six o'clock in the morning. He had risen with the sun, which is up betimes in June. An uncut volume of *Huxley's Life and Letters* lay open on the table before him, but he tapped the pages absently with his paper knife and his eyes were fixed unseeingly on the St. Gaudens medallion of Stevenson on the opposite wall. The professor's library testified to the superior quality of his taste in art as well as to his wide and varied scholarship. Only by a miracle of taste could so unpretentious a room have been made so attractive; it was as dainty as a boudoir and as original in color scheme as a painter's studio. The walls were hung with photographs of the works of the best modern painters—Burne-Jones, Rossetti, Corot, and a dozen others. Above the mantel were delicate reproductions in color of some of Fra Angelico's most beautiful paintings. The rugs were exquisite in pattern and color, pieces of weaving that the professor had picked up himself in his wanderings in the Orient. On close inspection, however, the contents of the bookshelves formed the most remarkable feature of the library. The shelves were almost equally apportioned to the accommodation of works on literature and science, suggesting a form of bigamy rarely encountered in society. The collection of works of pure literature was wide enough to include nearly all the major languages of modern Europe, besides the Greek and Roman classics.

To an interpretive observer nearly everything that was to be found in the professor's library was represented in his personality. Occasionally, when he read Hawthorne's "Great Stone Face" with his classes, some clear-sighted student wondered whether the man ever realized how completely he illustrated the allegory in himself. The professor was truly a part of all that he had met, and he had managed to meet most of the good things that the mind of man had desired. In his face there was much of the laborious precision of the scientist and not a little of Fra Angelico and of the lyric poets whose influence had prolonged his youth well into the fifties. His pupils always remembered the professor's face long after they had forgotten the things he had endeavored to teach them. He had the bold, prominent nose and chin of the oldest and most beloved of American actors, and the high, broad forehead which Nature loves to build about her finely adjusted minds. The grave, large outlines of his face were softened by an infinite kindness of mouth and eye. His mouth, indeed, was as sensitive and mobile as that of a young man, and, given certain passages from *Tristan and Isolde* or certain lines from Heine, his eyes would flash out at you like wet cornflowers after a spring shower. His hair was very thick, straight, and silver white. This, with his clear skin, gave him a somewhat actorlike appearance. He was slight of build and exceedingly frail, with delicate, sensitive hands curving back at the finger-ends, with dark purple veins showing prominently on the back. They were exceedingly small, white as a girl's, and well kept as a pianist's.

As the professor sat caressing his Huxley, a lady entered.

"It is half past six, Emerson, and breakfast will be served at seven." Anyone would have recognized her as the professor's older sister, for she was a sort of simplified and expurgated edition of himself, the more alert and masculine character of the two, and the scholar's protecting angel. She wore a white lace cap on her head and a knitted shawl about her shoulders. Though she had been a widow for twenty-five years and more, she was always called Miss Agatha Graves. She scanned her brother critically and having satisfied herself that his linen was immaculate and his white tie a fresh one, she remarked, "You were up early this morning, even for you."

"The roses never have the fragrance that they have in the first sun; they give out their best then," said her brother, nodding toward the window where the garden roses thrust their pink heads close to the screen as though they would not be kept outside. "And I have something on my mind, Agatha," he continued, nervously fingering the sandalwood paper-cutter. "I feel distraught and weary. You know how I shrink from changes of any sort, and this—why, this is the most alarming thing that has ever confronted me. It is absolutely cutting my life off at the stalk, and who knows whether it will bud again?"

Miss Agatha turned sharply about from the window where she had been standing and gravely studied her brother's drooping shoulders and dejected figure.

"There you go at your old tricks, Em," she remonstrated. "I have heard many kinds of ability attributed to you, but to my mind no one has ever put his finger on the right spot. Your real gift is for getting all the possible pain out of life, and extracting needless annoyance from commonplace and trivial things. Here you have buried yourself for the best part of your life in that high school, for motives Quixotic to an absurdity. If you had chosen a university I should not complain, but in that place all your best tools have rusted. Granted that you have done your work a little better than the people about you, it's no great place in which to excel—a city high school where failures in every trade drift to teach the business they cannot make a living by. Now it is time that you do something to justify the faith your friends have always had in you. You owe something to them and to your own name."

"I have builded myself a monument more lasting than brass," quoted the professor softly, balancing the tips of his slender fingers together.

"Nonsense, Emerson!" said Miss Agatha impatiently. "You are a sentimentalist and your vanity is that of a child. As for those slovenly persons with offensive manners whom you call your colleagues, do you fancy they appreciate you? They are as envious as green gourds and their mouths pucker when they pay you compliments. I hope you are not so unsophisticated as to believe all the sentimental twaddle of your old students. When they want recommendations to some school board, or run for a city office and want your vote, they come here and say that you have been the inspiration of their lives, and I believe in my heart that you are goose enough to accept it all."

"As for my confreres," said the professor, smiling, "I have no doubt that each one receives in the bosom of his family exactly the same advice that you are giving me. If there dwell an appreciated man on earth I have never met him. As for the students, I believe I have, to some at least, in a measure supplied a vital element that their environment failed to give them. Whether they realize this or not is of slight importance; it is in the very nature of youth to forget its sources, physical and mental alike. If one labors at all in the garden of youth, it must be free from the passion of seeing things grow, from an innate love of watching the strange processes of the brain under varying influences and limitations. He gets no more thanks than the novelist gets from the character he creates, nor does he deserve them. He has the whole human comedy before him in embryo, the beginning of all passions and all achievements. As I have often told you, this city is a disputed strategic point. It controls a vast manufacturing region given over to sordid and materialistic ideals. Any work that has been done here for esthetics cannot be lost. I suppose we shall win in the end, but the reign of Mammon has been long and oppressive. You remember when I was a boy working in the fields how we used to read Bunyan's *Holy War* at night? Well, I have always felt very much as though I were keeping the Ear Gate of the town of Mansoul, and I know not whether the captains who succeed me be trusty or no."

Miss Agatha was visibly moved, but she shook her head. "Well, I wish you had gone into the church, Emerson. I respect your motives, but there are more tares than wheat in your crop, I suspect."

"My dear girl," said the professor, his eye brightening, "that is the very reason for the sowing. There is a picture by Vedder of the enemy sowing tares at the foot of the cross, and his seeds are golden coins. That is the call to arms; the other side never sleeps; in the theaters, in the newspapers, in the mills and offices and coal fields, by day and by night the enemy sows tares."

As the professor slowly climbed the hill to the high school that morning, he indulged in his favorite fancy, that the old gray-stone building was a fortress set upon the dominant acclivity of that great manufacturing city, a stronghold of knowledge in the heart of Mammon's kingdom, a Pharos to all those drifting, storm-driven lives in the valley below, where mills and factories thronged, blackening the winding shores of the river, which was dotted with coal barges and frantic, puffing little tugs. The high school commanded the heart of the city, which was like that of any other manufacturing town—a scene of bleakness and naked ugliness and of that remorseless desolation which follows upon the fiercest lust of man. The beautiful valley, where long ago two limpid rivers met at the foot of wooded heights, had become a scorched and blackened waste. The river banks were lined with bellowing mills which broke the silence of the night with periodic crashes of sound, filled the valley with heavy carboniferous smoke, and sent the chilled products of their red forges to all parts of the known world—to fashion railways in Siberia, bridges in Australia, and to tear the virgin soil of Africa. To the west, across the river, rose the steep bluffs, faintly etched through the brown smoke, rising five hundred feet, almost as sheer as a precipice, traversed by cranes and inclines and checkered by winding yellow paths like sheep trails which led to the wretched habitations clinging to the face of the cliff, the lairs of the vicious and the poor, miserable rodents of civilization. In the middle of the stream, among the tugs and barges, were the dredging boats, hoisting muck and filth from the clogged channel. It was difficult to believe that this was the shining river which tumbles down the steep hills of the lumbering district, odorous of wet spruce logs and echoing the ring of axes and the song of the raftsmen, come to this black ugliness at last, with not one throb of its woodland passion and bright vehemence left.

For thirty years the professor's classroom had overlooked this scene which caused him unceasing admiration and regret. For thirty years he had cried out against the image set up there as the Hebrew prophets cried out against the pride and blind prosperity of Tyre. Nominally he was a professor of English literature, but his real work had been to try to secure for youth the rights of youth; the right to be generous, to dream, to enjoy; to feel a little the seduction of the old romance, and to yield a little. His students were boys and girls from the factories and offices, destined to return thither, and hypnotized by the glitter of yellow metal. They were practical, provident, unimaginative, and mercenary at sixteen. Often, when some lad was reading aloud in the classroom, the puffing of the engines in the switch yard at the foot of the hill would drown the verse and the young voice entirely, and the professor would murmur sadly to himself: "Not even this respite is left to us; even here the voice of youth is drowned by the voice of the taskmaster that waits for them all impatiently enough."

Never had his duty seemed to call him so urgently as on this morning when he was to lay down his arms. As he entered the building he met the boys carrying palms up into the chapel for class-day exercises, and it occurred to him for the first time that this was his last commencement, a commencement without congratulations and without flowers. When he went into the chapel to drill the seniors on their commencement orations, he was unable to fix his mind upon his work. For thirty years he had heard youth say exactly the same thing in the same place; had heard young men swear fealty to the truth, pay honor to the pursuit of noble pleasures, and pledge themselves "to follow knowledge like a sinking star beyond the utmost bound of human thought." How many, he asked himself, had kept their vows? He could remember the occasion of his own commencement in that same chapel: the story that every senior class still told the juniors, of the professor's humiliation and disgrace when, in attempting to recite "Horatius at the Bridge," he had been unable to recall one word of the poem following

> Then out spake bold Horatius
> The Captain of the gate;

and after some moments of agonizing silence he had shamefacedly left the platform. Even the least receptive of the professor's students realized that he had risen to a much higher plane of scholarship than any of his colleagues, and they delighted to tell this story of the frail, exquisite, little man whom generations of students had called "the bold Horatius."

All the morning the professor was busy putting his desk and bookcases in order, impeded by the painful consciousness that he was doing it for the last time. He made many trips to the window and often lapsed into periods of idleness. The room had been connected in one way and another with most of his intellectual passions, and was as full of sentimental associations for him as the haunts of his courtship days are to a lover. At two o'clock he met his last class, which was just finishing *Sohrab and Rustum,* and he was forced to ask one of the boys to read and interpret the majestic closing lines on the "shorn and parceled Oxus." What the boy's comment was the professor never knew, he felt so close a kinship to that wearied river that he sat stupefied, with his hand shading his eyes and his fingers twitching. When the bell rang announcing the end of the hour he felt a sudden pain clutch his heart; he had a vague hope that the students would gather around his desk to discuss some point that youth loves to discuss, as they often did, but their work was over and they hurried out, eager for their freedom, while the professor sat helplessly watching them.

That evening a banquet was given to the retiring professor in the chapel, but Miss Agatha had to exert all her native power of command to induce him to go. He had come home so melancholy and unnerved that after laying out his dress clothes she literally had to put them on him. When he was in his shirt sleeves and Miss Agatha had carefully brushed his beautiful white hair and arranged his tie, she wheeled him sharply about and retreated to a chair.

"Now, Emerson, say your piece," she commanded.

Plucking up his shirt sleeves and making sure of his cuffs, the professor began valiantly:

> "Lars Porsena of Clusium,
> By the Nine Gods he swore . . ."

It was all Miss Agatha's idea. After the invitations to the banquet were out and she discovered that half-a-dozen of the professor's own classmates and many of his old students were to be present, she divined that it would be a tearful and depressing occasion. Emerson, she knew, was an indifferent speaker when his heart was touched, so she had decided that after a silence of thirty-five years Horatius should be heard from. The idea of correcting his youthful failure in his old age had rather pleased the professor on the whole, and he had set to work to memorize Lord Macaulay's lay, rehearsing in private to Miss Agatha, who had drilled him for that fatal exploit of his commencement night.

After this dress rehearsal the professor's spirits rose, and during the carriage ride he even made several feeble efforts to joke with his sister.

But later in the evening when he sat down at the end of the long table in the dusky chapel, green with palms for commencement week, he fell into deep depression. The guests chattered and boasted and gossiped, but the guest of honor sat silent, staring at the candles. Beside him sat old Fairbrother, of the Greek department, who had come into the faculty in the fifth year of Graves's professorship, and had married a pretty senior girl who had rejected Graves's timid suit. She had been dead this many a year; since his bereavement lonely old Fairbrother had clung to Graves, and now the professor felt a singular sense of support in his presence.

The professor tried to tell himself that now his holiday time had come, and that he had earned it; that now he could take up the work he had looked forward to and prepared for for years, his History of Modern Painting, the Italian section of which was already practically complete. But his heart told him that he had no longer the strength to take up independent work. Now that the current of young life had cut away from him and into a new channel, he felt like a ruin of some extinct civilization, like a harbor from which the sea has receded. He realized that he had been living by external stimulation from the warm young blood about him, and now that it had left him, all his decrepitude was horribly exposed. All those hundreds of thirsty young lives had drunk him dry. He compared himself to one of those gigantic colossi of antique lands, from which each traveler has chipped a bit of stone until only a mutilated torso is left.

He looked reflectively down the long table, picking out the faces of his colleagues here and there, souls that had toiled and wrought and thought with him, that simple, unworldly sect of people he loved. They were still discussing the difficulties of the third conjugation, as they had done there for twenty years. They were cases of arrested development, most of them. Always in contact with immature minds, they had kept the simplicity and many of the callow enthusiasms of youth. Those facts and formulae which interest the rest of the world for but a few years at most, were still the vital facts of life for them. They believed quite sincerely in the supreme importance of quadratic equations, and the rule for the special verbs that govern the dative was a part of their decalogue. And he himself—what had he done with the youth, the strength, the enthusiasm and splendid equipment he had brought there from Harvard thirty years ago? He had come to stay but a little while—five years at the most, until he could save money enough to defray the expense of a course in some German university. But then the battle had claimed him; the desire had come upon him to bring some message of repose and peace to the youth of this work-driven, joyless people, to cry the name of beauty so loud that the roar of the mills could not drown it. Then the reward of his first labors had come in the person of his one and only genius: his restless, incorrigible pupil with the gentle eyes and manner of a girl, at once timid and utterly reckless, who had seen even as Graves saw—who had suffered a little, sung a little, struck the true lyric note, and died wretchedly at three-and-twenty in his master's arms, the victim of a tragedy as old as the world and as grim as Samson, the Israelite's.

He looked about at his comrades and wondered what they had done with their lives. Doubtless they had deceived themselves as he had done. With youth always about them, they had believed themselves of it. Like the monk in the legend they had wandered a little way into the wood to hear the bird's song—the magical song of youth so engrossing and so treacherous—and they had come back to their cloister to find themselves old men, spent warriors who could only chatter on the wall, like grasshoppers, and sigh at the beauty of Helen as she passed.

The toasts were nearly over, but the professor had heard none of the appreciative and enthusiastic things that his students and colleagues had said of him. He read a deeper meaning into this parting than they had done and his thoughts stopped his ears. He heard Miss Agatha clear her throat and caught her meaning glance. Realizing that everyone was waiting for him, he blinked his eyes like a man heavy with sleep and arose.

"How handsome he looks," murmured the woman looking at his fine old face and silver hair. The professor's remarks were as vague as they were brief. After expressing his thanks for the honor done him, he stated that he had still some work to finish among them, which had been too long incomplete. Then with as much of his schoolboy attitude as he could remember, and a smile on his gentle lips, he began his

> "Lars Porsena of Clusium,
> By the Nine Gods he swore
> That the noble house of Tarquin
> Should suffer wrong no more."

A murmur of laughter ran up and down the long table, and Dr. Maitland, the great theologian, who had vainly tried to prompt his stage-struck fellow graduate thirty-five years ago, laughed until his nose glasses fell off and dangled across his black waistcoat. Miss Agatha was highly elated over the success of her idea, but the professor had no heart in what he was doing, and the merriment rather hurt him. Surely this was a time for silence and reflection, if ever such time was. Memories crowded upon him faster than the lines he spoke, and the warm eyes turned upon him, full of pride and affection for their scholar and their "great man," moved him almost beyond endurance.

"—the Consul's brow was sad
And the Consul's speech was low,"

he read, and suited the action marvelously to the word. His eyes wandered to the chapel rostrum. Thirty-five years ago he had stood there repeating those same lines, a young man, resolute and gifted, with the strength of Ulysses and the courage of Hector, with the kingdoms of the earth and the treasures of the ages at his feet, and the singing rose in his heart; a spasm of emotion contracted the old man's vocal cords.

"Outspake the bold Horatius,
The Captain of the gate"

—he faltered; his white hand nervously sought his collar, then the hook on his breast where his glasses usually hung, and at last tremulously for his handkerchief; then with a gesture of utter defeat, the professor sat down. There was a tearful silence; white handkerchiefs fluttered down the table as from a magician's wand, and Miss Agatha was sobbing. Dr. Maitland arose to his feet, his face distorted between laughter and tears. "I ask you all," he cried, "whether Horatius has any need to speak, for has he not kept the bridge these thirty years? God bless him!"

"It's all right, so don't worry about it, Emerson," said Miss Agatha as they got into the carriage. "At least they were appreciative, which is more than I would have believed."

"Ah, Agatha," said the professor, wiping his face wearily with his crumpled handkerchief, "I am a hopeless dunce, and you ought to have known better. If you could make nothing of me at twenty, you showed poor judgment to undertake it at fifty-five. I was not made to shine, for they put a woman's heart in me."

The Treasure of Far Island

Dark brown is the river,
  Golden is the sand;
It flows along forever,
  With trees on either hand.

—Robert Louis Stevenson

I

Far Island is an oval sandbar, half a mile in length and perhaps a hundred yards wide, which lies about two miles up from Empire City in a turbid little Nebraska river. The island is known chiefly to the children who dwell in that region, and generation after generation of them have claimed it—fished there, and pitched their tents under the great arched tree, and built campfires on its level, sandy outskirts. In the middle of the island, which is always above water except in flood time, grow thousands of yellow-green creek willows and cottonwood seedlings, brilliantly green, even when the hottest winds blow, by reason of the surrounding moisture. In the summer months, when the capricious stream is low, the children's empire is extended by many rods, and a long irregular beach of white sand is exposed along the east coast of the island, never out of the water long enough to acquire any vegetation, but dazzling white, ripple marked, and full of possibilities for the imagination. The island is No-Man's-Land; every summer a new chief claims it and it has been called by many names; but it seemed particularly to belong to the two children who christened it Far Island, partially because they were the original discoverers and claimants, but more especially because they were of that favored race whom a New England sage called the true landlords and sealords of the world.

One afternoon, early in June, the Silvery Beaches of Far Island were glistening in the sun like pounded glass, and the same slanting yellow rays that scorched the sand beat upon the windows of the passenger train from the East as it swung into the Republican Valley from the uplands.

Then a young man dressed in a suit of gray tweed changed his seat in order to be on the side of the car next to the river. When he crossed the car several women looked up and smiled, for it was with a movement of boyish abandon and an audible chuckle of delight that he threw himself into the seat to watch for the shining curves of the river as they unwound through the trees. He was sufficiently distinguished in appearance to interest even tired women at the end of a long, sultry day's travel. As the train rumbled over a trestle built above a hollow grown up with sunflowers and ironweed, he sniffed with delight the rank odor, familiar to the prairie-bred man, that is exhaled by such places as evening approaches. "Ha," he murmured under his breath, "there's the white chalk cliff where the Indians used to run the buffalo over Bison Leap—we kids called it—the remote sea wall of the boy world. I'm getting home sure enough. And heavens! There's the island, Far Island, the Ultima Thule; and the arched tree, and Spy Glass Hill, and the Silvery Beaches; my heart's going like a boy's. 'Once on a day he sailed away, over the sea to Skye.' "

He sat bolt upright with his lips tightly closed and his chest swelling, for he was none other than the original discoverer of the island, Douglass Burnham, the playwright—our only playwright, certain critics contend—and, for the first time since he left it a boy, he was coming home. It was only twelve years ago that he had gone away, when Pagie and Temp and Birkner and Shorty Thompson had stood on the station siding and waved him goodbye, while he shut his teeth to keep the tears back; and now the train bore him up the old river valley, through the meadows where he used to hunt for cattails, along the streams where he had paddled his canvas boat, and past the willow-grown island where he had buried the pirate's treasure—a man with a man's work done and the world well in hand. Success had never tasted quite so sweet as it tasted then. The whistle sounded, the brakemen called Empire City, and Douglass crossed to the other side of the car and looked out toward the town, which lay half a mile up from the station on a low range of hills, half hidden by the tall cottonwood trees that still shaded its streets. Down the curve of the track he could see the old railroad "eating house," painted the red Burlington color; on the hill above the town the standpipe towered up from the treetops. Douglass felt the years dropping away from him. The train stopped. Waiting on the platform stood his father and a tall spare man, with a straggling colorless beard, whose dejected stoop and shapeless hat and ill-fitting clothes were in themselves both introduction and biography. The narrow chest, long arms, and skinny neck were not to be mistaken. It was Rhinehold Birkner, old

Rhine who had not been energetic enough to keep up his father's undertaking business, and who now sold sewing machines and parlor organs in a feeble attempt to support an invalid wife and ten children, all colorless and narrow-chested like himself. Douglass sprang from the platform and grasped his father's hand.

"Hello, Father, hello, Rhine, where are the other fellows? Why, that's so, you must be the only one left. Heavens! How we *have* scattered. What a lot of talking we two have got before us."

Probably no event had transpired since Rhine's first baby was born that had meant so much to him as Douglass's return, but he only chuckled, putting his limp, rough hand into the young man's smooth, warm one, and ventured.

"Jest the same old coot, Doug."

"How's Mother, Father?" Douglass asked as he hunted for his checks.

"She's well, son, but she thought she couldn't leave supper to come down to meet you. She has been cooking pretty much all day and worrying for fear the train would be late and your supper would spoil."

"Of course she has. When I am elected to the academy mother will worry about my supper." Douglass felt a trifle nervous and made a dash for the shabby little streetcar which ever since he could remember had been drawn by mules that wore jingling bells on their collars.

A silence settled down over the occupants of the car as the mules trotted off. Douglass felt that his father stood somewhat in awe of him, or at least in awe of that dread Providence which ordered such dark things as that a hard-headed, money-saving real-estate man should be the father of a white-fingered playwright who spent more on his fads in a year than his father had saved by the thrift of a lifetime. All the hundred things Douglass had had to say seemed congested upon his tongue, and though he had a good measure of that cheerful assurance common to young people whom the world has made much of, he felt a strange embarrassment in the presence of this angular gray-whiskered man who used to warm his jacket for him in the hayloft.

His mother was waiting for him under the bittersweet vines on the porch, just where she had always stood to greet him when he came home for his college vacations, and, as Douglass had lived in a world where the emotions are cultivated and not despised, he was not ashamed of the lump that rose in his throat when he took her in his arms. She hurried him out of the dark into the parlor lamplight and looked him over from head to foot to assure herself that he was still the handsomest of men, and then she told him to go into her bedroom to wash his face for supper. She followed him, unable to take her eyes from this splendid creature whom all the world claimed but who was only hers after all. She watched him take off his coat and collar, rejoicing in the freshness of his linen and the whiteness of his skin; even the color of his silk suspenders seemed a matter of importance to her.

"Douglass," she said impressively, "Mrs. Governor gives a reception for you tomorrow night, and I have promised her that you will read some selections from your plays."

This was a matter which was very near Mrs. Burnham's heart. Those dazzling first nights and receptions and author's dinners which happened out in the great world were merely hearsay, but it was a proud day when her son was held in honor by the women of her own town, of her own church; women she had shopped and marketed and gone to sewing circle with, women whose cakes and watermelon pickles won premiums over hers at the county fair.

"Read?" ejaculated Douglass, looking out over the towel and pausing in his brisk rubbing. "Why, Mother, dear, I can't read, not anymore than a John rabbit. Besides, plays aren't meant to be read. Let me give them one of my old stunts; 'The Polish Boy' or 'Regulus to the Carthaginians.' "

"But you must do it, my son; it won't do to disappoint Mrs. Governor. Margie was over this morning to see about it. She has grown into a very pretty girl." When his mother spoke in that tone Douglass acquiesced, just as naturally as he helped himself to her violet water, the same kind, he noticed, that he used to covertly sprinkle on his handkerchief when he was primping for Sunday school after she had gone to church.

"Mrs. Governor still leads the pack, then? What a civilizing influence she has been in this community. Taught most of us all the manners we ever knew. Little Margie has grown up pretty, you say? Well, I should never have thought it. How many boys have I slugged for yelling 'Reddy, go dye your hair green' at her. She was not an indifferent slugger herself and never exactly stood in need of masculine protection. What a wild Indian she was! Game, clear through, though! I never found such a mind in a girl. But *is* she a girl? I somehow always fancied she would grow up a man—and a ripping fine one. Oh, I see you are looking at me hard! No, Mother, the girls don't trouble me much." His eyes met hers laughingly in the glass as he parted his hair. "You spoiled me so outrageously that women tell me frankly I'm a selfish cad and they will have none of me."

His mother handed him his coat with a troubled glance. "I was afraid, my son, that some of those actresses—"

The young man laughed outright. "Oh, never worry about them, Mother. Wait till you've seen them at rehearsals in soiled shirtwaists wearing out their antiques and doing what they call 'resting' their hair. Poor things! They have to work too hard to bother about being attractive."

He went out into the dining room where the table was set for him just as it had always been when he came home on that same eight o'clock train from college. There were all his favorite viands and the old family silver spread on the white cloth with the maidenhair fern pattern, under the soft lamplight. It had been years since he had eaten by the mild light of a kerosene lamp. By his plate stood his own glass that his grandmother had given him with "For a Good Boy" ground on the surface which was dewy from the ice within. The other glasses were unclouded and held only fresh water from the pump, for his mother was very economical about ice and held the most exaggerated views as to the pernicious effects of ice water on the human stomach. Douglass only got it because he was the first dramatist of the country and a great man. When he decided that he would like a cocktail and asked for whiskey, his mother dealt him out a niggardly tablespoonful, saying, "That's as much as you ought to have at your age, Douglass." When he went out into the kitchen to greet the old servant and get some ice for his drink, his mother hurried after him crying with solicitude.

"I'll get the ice for you, Douglass. Don't you go into the refrigerator; you always leave the ice uncovered and it wastes."

Douglass threw up his hands. "Mother, whatever I may do in the world I shall never be clever enough to be trusted with that refrigerator. 'Into all the chambers of the palace mayest thou go, save into this thou shalt not go.' " And now he knew he was at home, indeed, for his father stood chuckling in the doorway, washing his hands from the milking, and the old servant threw her apron over her head to stifle her laughter at this strange reception of a celebrity. The memory of his luxurious rooms in New York, where he lived when he was an artist, faded dim; he was but a boy again in his father's house and must not keep supper waiting.

The next evening Douglass with resignation accompanied his father and mother to the reception given in his honor. The town had advanced somewhat since his day; and he was amused to see his father appear in an apology for a frock coat and a black tie, such as Kentucky politicians wear. Although people wore frock coats nowadays they still walked to receptions, and as Douglass climbed the hill the whole situation struck him as farcical. He dropped his mother's arm and ran up to the porch with his hat in his hand, laughing. "Margie!" he called, intending to dash through the house until he found her. But in the vestibule he bumped up against something large and splendid, then stopped and caught his breath. A woman stood in the dark by the hall lamp with a lighted match in her hand. She was in white and very tall. The match burned but a moment; a moment the light played on her hair, red as Etruscan gold and piled high above the curve of the neck and head; a moment upon the oval chin, the lips curving upward and red as a crimson cactus flower; the deep, gray, fearless eyes; the white shoulders framed about with darkness. Then the match went out, leaving Douglass to wonder whether, like Anchises, he had seen the vision that should forever blind him to the beauty of mortal women.

"I beg your pardon," he stammered, backing toward the door, "I was looking for Miss Van Dyck. Is she—" Perhaps it was a mere breath of stifled laughter, perhaps it was a recognition by some sense more trustworthy than sight and subtler than mind; but there seemed a certain familiarity in the darkness about him, a certain sense of the security and peace which one experiences among dear and intimate things, and with widening eyes he said softly,

"Tell me, is this Margie?"

There was just a murmur of laughter from the tall, white figure. "I was going to be presented to you in the most proper form, and now you've spoiled it all. How are you, Douglass, and did you get a whipping this time? You've played hooky longer than usual. Ten years, isn't it?" She put out her hand in the dark and he took it and drew it through his arm.

"No, I didn't get a whipping, but I may get worse. I wish I'd come back five years ago. I would if I had known," he said promptly.

The reading was just as stupid as he had said it would be, but his audience enjoyed it and he enjoyed his audience. There was the old deacon who had once caught him in his watermelon patch and set the dog on him; the president of the WCTU, with her memorable black lace shawl and cane, who still continued to send him temperance tracts, mindful of the hundredth sheep in the parable; his old Sunday school teacher, a good man of limited information who never read anything but his Bible and *Teacher's Quarterly,* and who had once hung a cheap edition of *Camille* on the church Christmas tree for Douglass, with an inscription on the inside to the effect that the fear of the Lord is the beginning of wisdom. There was the village criminal lawyer, one of those brilliant wrecks sometimes found in small towns, who, when he was so drunk he could not walk, used to lie back in his office chair and read Shakespeare by the hour to a little barefoot boy. Next to him sat the rich banker who used to offer the boys a quarter to hitch up his horse for him, and then drive off, forgetting all about the quarter. Then there were fathers and mothers of Douglass's old clansmen and vassals who were scattered all over the world now. After the reading Douglass spent half an hour chatting with nice tiresome old ladies who reminded him of how much he used to like their teacakes and cookies, and answering labored compliments with genuine feeling. Then he went with a clear conscience and light heart whither his eyes had been wandering ever since he had entered the house.

"Margie, I needn't apologize for not recognizing you, since it was such an involuntary compliment. However did you manage to grow up like this? Was it boarding school that did it? I might have recognized you with your hair down, and oh, I'd know you anywhere when you smile! The teeth are just the same. Do you still crack nuts with them?"

"I haven't tried it for a long time. How remarkably little the years change you, Douglass. I haven't seen you since the night you brought out *The Clover Leaf,* and I heard your curtain speech. Oh, I was very proud of our Pirate Chief!"

Douglass sat down on the piano stool and looked searchingly into her eyes, which met his with laughing frankness.

"What! You were in New York then and didn't let me know? There was a day when you wouldn't have treated me so badly. Didn't you want to see me just a little bit—out of curiosity?"

"Oh, I was visiting some school friends who said it would be atrocious to bother you, and the newspapers were full of interesting details about your being so busy that you ate and got shaved at the theater. Then one's time isn't one's own when one is visiting, you know." She saw the hurt expression on his face and repented, adding gayly, "But I may as well confess that I kept a sharp lookout for you on the street, and when I did meet you you didn't know me."

"And you didn't stop me? That's worse yet. How in heaven's name was I to know you? Accost a goddess and say, 'Oh yes, you used to be a Pirate Chief and wear a butcher knife in your belt.' But I hadn't grown into an Apollo, save the mark! And you knew me well enough. I couldn't have passed you like that in a strange land."

"No, you do your duty by your countrymen, Douglass. You haven't grown haughty. One by one our old townspeople go out to see the world and bring us back tales of your glory. What unpromising specimens have you not dined and wined in New York! Why even old Skin Jackson, when he went to New York to have his eyes treated, you took to the Waldorf and to the Player's Club, where he drank with the immortals. How do you have the courage to do it? *Did* he wear those dreadful gold nugget shirt studs that he dug up in Colorado when we were young?"

"Even the same, Margie, and he scored a hit with them. But you are dodging the point. When and where did you see me in New York?"

"Oh, it was one evening when you were crossing Madison Square. You were probably going to the theater for Flashingham and Miss Grew were with you and you seemed in a hurry." Margie wished now that she had not mentioned the incident. "I remember that was the time I so deeply offended your mother on my return by telling her that Miss Grew had announced her engagement to you. How did it come out? She certainly did announce it."

"Doubtless, but it was entirely a misunderstanding on the lady's part. We never were anything of the sort," said Douglass impatiently. "That is a disgusting habit of Edith's; she announces a new engagement every fortnight as mechanically as the butler announces dinner. About once a month she calls the dear Twelfth Night girls together to a solemn high tea and gently breaks the news of a new engagement, and they kiss and cry over her and say the things they have said a dozen times before and go away tittering. Why, she has been engaged to every society chap in New York and to the whole Milton family, with the possible exception of Sir Henry, and her papa has cabled his blessing all over the known world to her. But it is a waste of time to talk about such nonsense; don't let's," he urged.

"I think it is very interesting; I don't indulge in weekly engagements myself. But there is one thing I want to know, Douglass; I want to know how you did it."

"Did what?"

Margie threw out her hands with an impetuous gesture. "Oh, all of it, all the wonderful things you have done. You remember that night when we lay on the sandbar—"

"The Uttermost Desert," interrupted Douglass softly.

"Yes, the Uttermost Desert, and in the light of the driftwood fire we planned the conquest of the world? Well, other people plan, too, and fight and suffer and fail the world over, and a very few succeed at the bitter end when they are old and it is no longer worthwhile. But you have done it as they used to do it in the fairy tales, without soiling your golden armor, and I can't find one line in your face to tell me that you have suffered or found life bitter to your tongue. How have you cheated fate?"

Douglass looked about him and saw that the guests had thronged about the punchbowl, and his mother, beaming in her new black satin, was relating touching incidents of his infancy to a group of old ladies. He leaned forward, clasped his hands between his knees, and launched into an animated description of how his first play, written at college, had taken the fancy of an old school friend of his father's who had turned manager. The second, a political farce, had put him fairly on his feet. Then followed his historical drama, *Lord Fairfax*, in which he had at first failed completely. He told her of those desperate days in New York when he would draw his blinds and work by lamplight until he was utterly exhausted, of how he fell ill and lost the thread of his play and used to wander about the streets trying to beat it out of the paving stones when the very policemen who jostled him on the crossings knew more about *Lord Fairfax* than he.

As he talked he felt the old sense of power, lost for many years—the power of conveying himself wholly to her in speech, of awakening in her mind every tint and shadow and vague association that was in his at the moment. He quite forgot the beauty of the woman beside him in the exultant realization of comradeship, the egotistic satisfaction of being wholly understood. Suddenly he stopped short.

"Come, Margie, you're not playing fair, you're telling me nothing about yourself. What plays have you been playing? Pirate or enchanted princess or sleeping beauty or Helen of Troy, to the disaster of men?"

Margie sighed as she awoke out of the fairyland. Doug's tales were as wonderful as ever.

"Oh, I stopped playing long ago. I have grown up and you have not. Someone has said that is wherein geniuses are different; they go on playing and never grow up. So you see you're only a case of arrested development, after all."

"I don't believe it, you play still, I can see it in your eyes. And don't say genius to me. People say that to me only when they want to be disagreeable or tell me how they would have written my plays. The word is my bogie. But tell me, are the cattails ripe in the Salt Marshes, and will your mother let you wade if the sun is warm, and do the winds still smell sharp with salt when they blow through the mists at night?"

"Why, Douglass, did the wind always smell salty to you there too? It does to me yet, and you know there isn't a particle of salt there. Why did we ever name them the Salt Marshes?"

"Because they *were* the Salt Marshes and couldn't have had any other name any more than the Far Island could. I went down to those pestiferous Maremma marshes in Italy to see whether they would be as real as our marshes, but they were not real at all; only miles and miles of bog. And do the nightingales still sing in the grove?"

"Yes. Other people call them ring doves—but they still sing there."

"And you still call them nightingales to yourself and laugh at the density of big people?"

"Yes, sometimes."

Later in the evening Douglass found another opportunity, and this time he was fortunate enough to encounter Margie alone as she was crossing the veranda.

"Do you know why I have come home in June, instead of July as I had intended, Margie? Well, sit down and let me tell you. They don't need you in there just now. About a month ago I changed my apartment in New York, and as I was sorting over my traps I came across a box of childish souvenirs. Among them was a faded bit of paper on which a map was drawn with elaborate care. It was the map of an island with curly blue lines all around it to represent water, such as we used always to draw around the continents in our geography class. On the west coast of the island a red sword was sticking upright in the earth. Beneath this scientific drawing was an inscription to the effect that *'whoso should dig twelve paces west of the huge fallen tree, in direct line with the path made by the setting sun on the water on the tenth day of June, should find the great treasure and his heart's desire!'* "

Margie laughed and applauded gently with her hands. "And so you have come to dig for it; some two thousand miles almost. There's a dramatic situation for you. I have my map still, and I've often contemplated going down to Far Island and digging, but it wouldn't have been fair, for the treasure was really yours, after all."

"Well, you are going now, and on the tenth day of June, that's next Friday, for that's what I came home for, and I had to spoil the plans and temper of a manager and all his company to do it."

"Nonsense, there are too many mosquitoes on Far Island and I mind them more than I used to. Besides, there are no good boats like the *Jolly Roger* nowadays."

"We'll go if I have to build another *Jolly Roger*. You can't make me believe you are afraid of mosquitoes. I know too well the mettle of your pasture. Please do, Margie, please." He used his old insidious coaxing tone.

"Douglass, you have made me do dreadful things enough by using that tone of voice to me. I believe you used to hypnotize me. Will you never, never grow up?"

"Never so long as there are pirate's treasures to dig for and you will play with me, Margie. Oh, I wish I had some of the cake that Alice ate in Wonderland and could make you a little girl again."

That night, after the household was asleep, Douglass went out for a walk about the old town, treading the ways he had trod when he was a founder of cities and a leader of hosts. But he saw few of the old landmarks, for the blaze of Etruscan gold was in his eyes, and he felt as a man might feel who in some sleepy humdrum Italian village had unearthed a new marble goddess, as beautiful as she of Milo; and he felt as a boy might feel who had lost all his favorite marbles and his best peashooter and the dog that slept with him, and had found them all again. He tried to follow, step by step, the wonderful friendship of his childhood.

A child's normal attitude toward the world is that of the artist, pure and simple. The rest of us have to do with the solids of this world, whereas only their form and color exist for the painter. So, in every wood and street and building there are things, not seen of older people at all, which make up their whole desirableness or objectionableness to children. There are maps and pictures formed by cracks in the walls of bare and unsightly sleeping chambers which make them beautiful; smooth places on the lawn where the grass is greener than anywhere else and which are good to sit upon; trees which are valuable by reason of the peculiar way in which the branches grow, and certain spots under the scrub willows along the creek which are in a manner sacred, like the sacrificial groves of the Druids, so that a boy is almost afraid to walk there. Then there are certain carpets which are more beautiful than others, because with a very little help from the imagination they become the rose garden of the Thousand and One Nights; and certain couches which are peculiarly adapted for playing Sinbad in his days of ease, after the toilsome voyages were over. A child's standard of value is so entirely his own, and his peculiar part and possessions in the material objects around him are so different from those of his elders, that it may be said his rights are granted by a different lease. To these two children the entire external world, like the people who dwelt in it, had been valued solely for what they suggested to the imagination, and people and places alike were merely stage properties, contributing more or less to the intensity of their inner life.

II

"Green leaves a-floating
Castles of the foam,
Boats of mine a-boating
When will all come home?"

sang Douglass as they pulled from the mill wharf out into the rapid current of the river, which that morning seemed the most beautiful and noble of rivers, an enchanted river flowing peacefully out of Arcady with the Happy Isles somewhere in the distance. The ripples were touched with silver and the sky was as blue as though it had been made today; the cowbells sounded faintly from the meadows along the shore like the bells of fairy cities ringing on the day the prince errant brought home his bride; the meadows that sloped to the water's edge were the greenest in all the world because they were the meadows of the long ago; and the flowers that grew there were the freshest and sweetest of growing things because once, long ago in the golden age, two children had gathered other flowers like them, and the beauties of vanished summers were everywhere. Douglass sat in the end of the boat, his back to the sun and his straw hat tilted back on his head, pulling slowly and feeling that the day was fine rather than seeing it; for his eyes were fixed upon his helmsman in the other end of the boat, who sat with her hat in her lap, shading her face with a white parasol, and her wonderful hair piled high on her head like a helmet of gleaming bronze.

Of all the possessions of their childhood's Wonderland, Far Island had been dearest; it was graven on their hearts as Calais was upon Mary Tudor's. Long before they had set foot upon it, the island was the goal of their loftiest ambitions and most delightful imaginings. They had wondered what trees grew there and what delightful spots were hidden away under the matted grapevines. They had even decided that a race of kindly dwarfs must inhabit it and had built up a civilization and historic annals for these imaginary inhabitants, surrounding the sandbar with all the mystery and enchantment which was attributed to certain islands of the sea by the mariners of Greece. Douglass and Margie had sometimes found it expedient to admit other children into their world, but for the most part these were but hewers of wood and drawers of water, who helped to shift the scenery and construct the balcony and place the king's throne, and were no more in the atmosphere of the play than were the supers who watched Mr. Keane's famous duel with Richmond. Indeed

Douglass frequently selected the younger and more passive boys for his vassals on the principle that they did as they were bid and made no trouble. But there is something of the explorer in the least imaginative of boys, and when Douglass came to the building of his famous boat, the *Jolly Roger,* he found willing hands to help him. Indeed, the sawing and hammering, the shavings and cut fingers and blood blisters fell chiefly to the lot of dazzled lads who claimed no part in the craft, and who gladly trotted and sweated for their board and keep in this fascinating play world which was so much more exhilarating than any they could make for themselves.

"Think of it, Margie, we are really going back to the island after so many years, just you and I, the captain and his mate. Where are the other gallant lads that sailed with us then?"

"Where are the snows of yesteryear?" sighed Margie softly. "It is very sad to grow up."

"Sad for them, yes. But we have never grown up, you know, we have only grown more considerate of our complexions," nodding at the parasol. "What a little mass of freckles you used to be, but I liked you freckled, too. Let me see: old Temp is commanding a regiment in the Philippines, and Bake has a cattle ranch in Wyoming, Mac is a government clerk in Washington, Jim keeps his father's hardware store, poor Ned and Shorty went down in a catboat on the Hudson while they were at college (I went out to hunt for the bodies, you know), and old Rhine is selling sewing machines; he never did get away at all, did he?"

"No, not for any length of time. You know it used to frighten Rhine to go to the next town to see a circus. He went to Arizona once for his lungs, but his family never could tell where he was for he headed all his letters 'Empire City, Nebraska,' from habit."

"Oh, that's delightful, Margie, you must let me use that. Rhine would carry Empire City through Europe with him and never know he was out of it. Have I told you about Pagie? Well, you know Pagie is traveling for a New York tailoring house and I let his people make some clothes for me that I had to give to Flashingham's valet. When he first came to town he tried to be gay, with his fond mother's prayers still about him, a visible nimbus, and the Sunday school boy written all over his open countenance and downy lip and large, white butter teeth. But I know, at heart, he still detested naughty words and whiskey made him sick. One day I was standing at the Hoffman House bar with some fellows, when a slender youth, who looked like a nice girl masquerading as a rake, stepped up and ordered a claret and seltzer. The whine was unmistakable. I turned and said, even before I had looked at him squarely, 'Oh, Pagie! If your mother saw you here!' "

"Poor Pagie! I'll warrant he would rather have had bread and sugar. Do you remember how, at the Sunday school concerts on Children's Day, you and Pagie and Shorty and Temp used to stand in a row behind the flower-wreathed pulpit rail, all in your new round-about suits with large silk bows tied under your collars, your hands behind you, and assure us with sonorous voices that you would come rejoicing bringing in the sheaves? Somehow, even then, I never doubted that you would do it."

The keel grated on the sand and Douglass sprang ashore and gave her his hand.

"Descend, O Miranda, upon your island! Do you know, Margie, it makes me seem fifteen again to feel this sand crunching under my feet. I wonder if I ever again shall feel such a thrill of triumph as I felt when I first leaped upon this sandbar? None of my first nights have given me anything like it. Do you remember *really,* and did you feel the same?"

"Of course I remember, and I knew that you were playing a double role that day, and that you were really the trail-breaker and world-finder inside of the pirate all the while. Here are the same ripple marks on the Silvery Beaches, and here is the great arched tree; let's run for it." She started fleetly across the glittering sand and Douglass fell behind to watch with immoderate joy that splendid, generous body that governed itself so well in the open air. There was a wholesomeness of the sun and soil in her that was utterly lacking in the women among whom he had lived for so long. She had preserved that strength of arm and freedom of limb that had made her so fine a playfellow, and which modern modes of life have well-nigh robbed the world of altogether. Surely, he thought, it was like that that Diana's women sped after the stag down the slopes of Ida, with shouting and bright spear. She caught an overhang branch and swung herself upon the embankment and, leaning against the trunk of a tree, awaited him flushed and panting, her bosom rising and falling with her quick drawn breaths.

"Why did you close the tree behind you, Margie? I have always wanted to see just how Dryads keep house," he exclaimed, brushing away a dried leaf that had fallen on her shoulder.

"Don't strain your inventive powers to make compliments, Douglass; this is your vacation and you are to rest your imagination. See, the willows have scarcely grown at all. I'm sure we shall hear Pagie whimpering over there on the Uttermost Desert where we marooned him, or singing hymns to keep up his courage. Now for the Huge Fallen Tree. Do you suppose the floods have moved it?"

They struck through the dense willow thicket, matted with fragrant wild grapevines which Douglass beat down with his spade, and came upon the great white log, the bleached skeleton of a tree, and found the cross hacked upon it, the rough gashes of the hatchet now worn smooth by the wind and rain and the seething of spring freshets. Near the cross were cut the initials of the entire pirate crew; some of them were cut on gravestones now. The scrub willows had grown over the spot where they had decided the treasure must lie, and together they set to work to break them away. Douglass paused more than once to watch the strong young creature beside him, outlined against the tender green foliage, reaching high and low and snapping the withes where they were weakest. He was still wondering whether it was not all a dream picture, and was half afraid that his man would call him to tell him that some piqued and faded woman was awaiting him at the theater to quarrel about her part.

"Still averse to manual labor, Douglass?" she laughed as she turned to bend a tall sapling. "The most remarkable thing about your enthusiasm was that you had only to sing of the glories of toil to make other people do all the work for you."

"No, Margie, I was thinking very hard indeed—about the Thracian women when they broke the boughs wherewith they flayed unhappy Orpheus."

"Now, Douglass, you'll spoil the play. A sentimental pirate is impossible. Pagie was a sentimental pirate and that was what spoiled him. A little more of this and I will maroon you upon the Uttermost Desert."

Douglass laughed and settled himself back among the green boughs and gazed at her with the abandoned admiration of an artist contemplating a masterpiece.

When they came to the digging of the treasure a little exertion was enough to unearth what had seemed hidden so fabulously deep in olden time. The chest was rotten and fell apart as the spade struck it, but the glass jar was intact, covered with sand and slime. Douglass spread his handkerchief upon the sand and weighted the corners down with pebbles and upon it poured the treasure of Far Island. There was the manuscript written in blood, a confession of fantastic crimes, and the Spaniard's heart in a bottle of alcohol, and Temp's Confederate bank notes, damp and gruesome to the touch, and Pagie's rare tobacco tags, their brilliant colors faded entirely away, and poor Shorty's bars of tinfoil dull and eaten with rust.

"And, Douglass," cried Maggie, "there is your father's silver ring that was made from a nugget; he whipped you for burying it. You remember it was given to a Christian knight by an English queen, and when he was slain before Jerusalem a Saracen took it and we killed the Saracen in the desert and cut off his finger to get the ring. It is strange how those wild imaginings of ours seem, in retrospect, realities, things that I actually lived through. I suppose that in cold fact my life was a good deal like that of other little girls who grow up in a village; but whenever I look back on it, it is all exultation and romance—sea fights and splendid galleys and Roman triumphs and brilliant caravans winding through the desert."

"To people who live by imagination at all, that is the only life that goes deep enough to leave memories. We were artists in those days, creating for the day only; making epics sung once and then forgotten, building empires that set with the sun. Nobody worked for money then, and nobody worked for fame, but only for the joy of the doing. Keats said the same thing more elegantly in his May Day Ode, and we were not so unlike those Hellenic poets who were content to sing to the shepherds and forget and be forgotten, 'rich in the simple worship of a day.' "

"Why, Douglass," she cried as she bent her face down to the little glass jar, "it was really our childhood that we buried here, never guessing what a precious thing we were putting under the ground. That was the real treasure of Far Island, and we might dig up the whole island for it but all the king's horses and all the king's men could not bring it back to us. That voyage we made to bury our trinkets, just before you went away to school, seems like unconscious symbolism, and somehow it stands out from all the other good times we knew then as the happiest of all." She looked off where the setting sun hung low above the water.

"Shall I tell you why, Margie? That was the end of our childhood, and there the golden days died in a blaze of glory, passed in music out of sight. That night, after our boat had drifted away from us, when we had to wade down the river hand in hand, we two, and the noises and the coldness of the water frightened us, and there were quicksands and sharp rocks and deep holes to shun, and terrible things lurking in the woods on the shore, you cried in a different way from the way you sometimes cried when you hurt yourself, and I found that I loved you afraid better than I had ever loved you fearless, and in that moment we grew up, and shut the gates of Eden behind us, and our empire was at an end."

"And now we are only kings in exile," sighed Margie softly, "who wander back to look down from the mountaintops upon the happy land we used to rule."

Douglass took her hand gently; "If there is to be any Eden on earth again for us, dear, we must make it with our two hearts."

There was a sudden brightness of tears in her eyes, and she drew away from him. "Ah, Douglass, you are determined to spoil it all. It is you who have grown up and taken on the ways of the world. The play is at an end for me." She tried to rise, but he held her firmly.

"From the moment I looked into your eyes in the vestibule that night we have been parts of the same dream again. Why, Margie, we have more romance behind us than most men and women ever live."

Margie's face grew whiter, but she pushed his hand away and the look in her eyes grew harder. "This is only a new play, Douglass, and you will weary of it tomorrow. I am not so good at playing as I used to be. I am no longer content with the simple worship of a day."

In her touch, in her white face, he divined the greatness of what she had to give. He bit his lip and answered, "I think you owe me more confidence than that, if only for the sake of those days when we trusted each other entirely."

She turned with a quick flash of remorseful tenderness, as she used to do when she hurt him at play. "I only want to keep you from hurting us both, Douglass. We neither of us could go on feeling like this. It's only the dregs of the old enchantment. Things have always come easily to you, I know, for at your birth nature and fortune joined to make you great. But they do not come so to me; I should wake and weep."

"Then weep, my princess, for I will wake you now!"

The fire and fancy that had so bewitched her girlhood that no other man had been able to dim the memory of it came furiously back upon her, with arms that were new and strange and strong, and with tenderness stranger still in this wild fellow of dreams and jests; and all her vows never to grace another of his Roman triumphs were forgotten.

"You are right, Margie; the pirate play is ended and the time has come to divide the prizes, and I choose what I chose fifteen years ago. Out of the spoils of a lifetime of crime and bloodshed I claimed only the captive princess, and I claim her still. I have sought the world over for her, only to find her at last in the land of lost content."

Margie lifted her face from his shoulder, and, after the manner of women of her kind, she played her last card rhapsodically. "And she, O Douglass! The years she has waited have been longer than the waiting of Penelope, and she has woven a thousand webs of dreams by night and torn them asunder by day, and looked out across the Salt Marshes for the night train, and still you did not come. I was only your pensioner like Shorty and Temp and the rest, and I could not play anything alone. You took my world with you when you went and left me only a village of mud huts and loneliness."

As her eyes and then her lips met his in the dying light, he knew that she had caught the spirit of the play, and that she would ford the river by night with him and never be afraid.

The locust chirped in the thicket; the setting sun threw a track of flame across the water; the willows burned with fire and were not consumed; a glory was upon the sand and the river and upon the Silvery Beaches; and these two looked about over God's world and saw that it was good. In the western sky the palaces of crystal and gold were quenched in night, like the cities of old empires; and out of the east rose the same moon that has glorified all the romances of the world—that lighted Paris over the blue Aegean and the feet of young Montague to the Capulets' orchard. The dinner hour in Empire City was long past, but the two upon the island wist naught of these things, for they had become as the gods, who dwell in their golden houses, recking little of the woes and labors of mortals, neither heeding any fall of rain or snow.

The Namesake

Seven of us, students, sat one evening in Hartwell's studio on the Boulevard St. Michel. We were all fellow countrymen, one from New Hampshire, one from Colorado, another from Nevada, several from the farmlands of the Middle West, and I myself from California. Lyon Hartwell, though born abroad, was simply, as everyone knew, "from America." He seemed, almost more than any other one living man, to mean all of it—from ocean to ocean. When he was in Paris, his studio was always open to the seven of us who were there that evening, and we intruded upon his leisure as often as we thought permissible.

Although we were within the terms of the easiest of all intimacies, and although the great sculptor, even when he was more than usually silent, was at all times the most gravely cordial of hosts, yet, on that long remembered evening, as the sunlight died on the burnished brown of the horse chestnuts below the windows, a perceptible dullness yawned through our conversation.

We were, indeed, somewhat low in spirit, for one of our number, Charley Bentley, was leaving us indefinitely, in response to an imperative summons from home. Tomorrow his studio, just across the hall from Hartwell's, was to pass into other hands, and Bentley's luggage was even now piled in discouraged resignation before his door. The various bales and boxes seemed literally to weigh upon us as we sat in his neighbor's hospitable rooms, drearily putting in the time until he should leave us to catch the ten o'clock express for Dieppe.

The day we had got through very comfortably, for Bentley made it the occasion of a somewhat pretentious luncheon at Maxim's. There had been twelve of us at table, and the two young Poles were so thirsty, the Gascon so fabulously entertaining, that it was near upon five o'clock when we put down our liqueur glasses for the last time, and the red, perspiring waiter, having pocketed the reward of his arduous and protracted services, bowed us affably to the door, flourishing his napkin and brushing back the streaks of wet, black hair from his rosy forehead. Our guests having betaken themselves belated to their respective engagements, the rest of us returned with Bentley—only to be confronted by the depressing array before his door. A glance about his denuded room had sufficed to chill the glow of the afternoon, and we fled across the hall in a body and begged Lyon Hartwell to take us in.

Bentley had said very little about it, but we all knew what it meant to him to be called home. Each of us knew what it would mean to himself, and each had felt something of that quickened sense of opportunity which comes at seeing another man in any way counted out of the race. Never had the game seemed so enchanting, the chance to play it such a piece of unmerited, unbelievable good fortune.

It must have been, I think, about the middle of October, for I remember that the sycamores were almost bare in the Luxembourg Gardens that morning, and the terraces about the queens of France were strewn with crackling brown leaves. The fat red roses, out the summer long on the stand of the old flower woman at the corner, had given place to dahlias and purple asters. First glimpses of autumn toilettes flashed from the carriages; wonderful little bonnes nodded at one along the Champs Élysées; and in the Quarter an occasional feather boa, red or black or white, brushed one's coat sleeve in the gay twilight of the early evening. The crisp, sunny autumn air was all day full of the stir of people and carriages and of the cheer of salutations; greetings of the students, returned brown and bearded from their holiday, gossip of people come back from Trouville, from St. Valery, from Dieppe, from all over Brittany and the Norman coast. Everywhere was the joyousness of return, the taking up again of life and work and play.

I had felt ever since early morning that this was the saddest of all possible seasons for saying goodbye to that old, old city of youth, and to that little corner of it on the south shore which since the Dark Ages themselves—yes, and before—has been so peculiarly the land of the young.

I can recall our very postures as we lounged about Hartwell's rooms that evening, with Bentley making occasional hurried trips to his desolated workrooms across the hall—as if haunted by a feeling of having forgotten something—or stopping to poke nervously at his *perroquets*, which he had bequeathed to Hartwell, gilt cage and all. Our host himself sat on the couch, his big, bronzelike shoulders backed up against the window, his shaggy head, beaked nose, and long chin cut clean against the gray light.

Our drowsing interest, in so far as it could be said to be fixed upon anything, was centered upon Hartwell's new figure, which stood on the block ready to be cast in bronze, intended as a monument for some American battlefield. He called it *The Color Sergeant.* It was the figure of a young soldier running, clutching the folds of a flag, the staff of which had been shot away. We had known it in all the stages of its growth, and the splendid action and feeling of the thing had come to have a kind of special significance for the half dozen of us who often gathered at Hartwell's rooms—though, in truth, there was as much to dishearten one as to inflame, in the case of a man who had done so much in a field so amazingly difficult, who had thrown up in bronze all the restless, teeming force of that adventurous wave still climbing westward in our own land across the waters. We recalled his *Scout,* his *Pioneer,* his *Gold Seekers,* and those monuments in which he had invested one and another of the heroes of the Civil War with such convincing dignity and power.

"Where in the world does he get the heat to make an idea like that carry?" Bentley remarked morosely, scowling at the clay figure. "Hang me, Hartwell, if I don't think it's just because you're not really an American at all that you can look at it like that."

The big man shifted uneasily against the window. "Yes," he replied smiling, "perhaps there is something in that. My citizenship was somewhat belated and emotional in its flowering. I've half a mind to tell you about it, Bentley." He rose uncertainly, and, after hesitating a moment, went back into his workroom, where he began fumbling among the litter in the corners.

At the prospect of any sort of personal expression from Hartwell, we glanced questioningly at one another; for although he made us feel that he liked to have us about, we were always held at a distance by a certain diffidence of his. There were rare occasions—when he was in the heat of work or of ideas—when he forgot to be shy, but they were so exceptional that no flattery was quite so seductive as being taken for a moment into Hartwell's confidence. Even in the matter of opinions—the commonest of currency in our circle—he was niggardly and prone to qualify. No man ever guarded his mystery more effectually. There was a singular, intense spell, therefore, about those few evenings when he had broken through this excessive modesty, or shyness, or melancholy, and had, as it were, committed himself.

When Hartwell returned from the back room, he brought with him an unframed canvas which he put on an easel near his clay figure. We drew close about it, for the darkness was rapidly coming on. Despite the dullness of the light, we instantly recognized the boy of Hartwell's *Color Sergeant.* It was the portrait of a very handsome lad in uniform, standing beside a charger impossibly rearing. Not only in his radiant countenance and flashing eyes, but in every line of his young body there was an energy, a gallantry, a joy of life, that arrested and challenged one.

"Yes, that's where I got the notion," Hartwell remarked, wandering back to his seat in the window. "I've wanted to do it for years, but I've never felt quite sure of myself. I was afraid of missing it. He was an uncle of mine, my father's half-brother, and I was named for him. He was killed in one of the big battles of '64, when I was a child. I never saw him—never knew him until he had been dead for twenty years. And then, one night, I came to know him as we sometimes do living persons—intimately, in a single moment."

He paused to knock the ashes out of his short pipe, refilled it, and puffed at it thoughtfully for a few moments with his hands on his knees. Then, settling back heavily among the cushions and looking absently out of the window, he began his story. As he proceeded further and further into the experience which he was trying to convey to us, his voice sank so low and was sometimes so charged with feeling that I almost thought he had forgotten our presence and was remembering aloud. Even Bentley forgot his nervousness in astonishment and sat breathless under the spell of the man's thus breathing his memories out into the dusk.

"It was just fifteen years ago this last spring that I first went home, and Bentley's having to cut away like this brings it all back to me.

"I was born, you know, in Italy. My father was a sculptor, though I dare say you've not heard of him. He was one of those first fellows who went over after Story and Powers—went to Italy for 'Art,' quite simply, to lift from its native bough the willing, iridescent bird. Their story is told, informingly enough, by some of those ingenuous marble things at the Metropolitan. My father came over sometime before the outbreak of the Civil War, and was regarded as a renegade by his family because he did not go home to enter the army. His half-brother, the only child of my grandfather's second marriage, enlisted at fifteen and was killed the next year. I was ten years old when the news of his death reached us. My mother died the following winter, and I was sent away to a Jesuit school, while my father, already ill himself, stayed on at Rome, chipping away at his Indian maidens and marble goddesses, still gloomily seeking the thing for which he had made himself the most unhappy of exiles.

"He died when I was fourteen, but even before that I had been put to work under an Italian sculptor. He had an almost morbid desire that I should carry on his work, under, as he often pointed out to me, conditions so much more auspicious. He left me in the charge of his one intimate friend, an American gentleman in the consulate at Rome, and his instructions were that I was to be educated there and to live there until I was twenty-one. After I was of age, I came to Paris and studied under one master after another until I was nearly thirty. Then, almost for the first time, I was confronted by a duty which was not my pleasure.

"My grandfather's death, at an advanced age, left an invalid maiden sister of my father's quite alone in the world. She had suffered for years from a cerebral disease, a slow decay of the faculties which rendered her almost helpless. I decided to go to America and, if possible, bring her back to Paris, where I seemed on my way toward what my poor father had wished for me.

"On my arrival at my father's birthplace, however, I found that this was not to be thought of. To tear this timid, feeble, shrinking creature, doubly aged by years and illness, from the spot where she had been rooted for a lifetime would have been little short of brutality. To leave her to the care of strangers seemed equally heartless. There was clearly nothing for me to do but to remain and wait for that slow and painless malady to run its course. I was there something over two years.

"My grandfather's home, his father's homestead before him, lay on the high banks of a river in western Pennsylvania. The little town twelve miles down the stream, whither my great-grandfather used to drive his ox-wagon on market days, had become, in two generations, one of the largest manufacturing cities in the world. For hundreds of miles about us the gentle hill slopes were honeycombed with gas wells and coal shafts; oil derricks creaked in every valley and meadow; the brooks were sluggish and discolored with crude petroleum, and the air was impregnated by its searching odor. The great glass and iron manufactories had come up and up the river almost to our very door; their smoky exhalations brooded over us, and their crashing was always in our ears. I was plunged into the very incandescence of human energy. But, though my nerves tingled with the feverish, passionate endeavor which snapped in the very air about me, none of these great arteries seemed to feed me; this tumultuous life did not warm me. On every side were the great muddy rivers, the ragged mountains from which the timber was being ruthlessly torn away, the vast tracts of wild country, and the gulches that were like wounds in the earth; everywhere the glare of that relentless energy which followed me like a searchlight and seemed to scorch and consume me. I could only hide myself in the tangled garden, where the dropping of a leaf or the whistle of a bird was the only incident.

"The Hartwell homestead had been sold away little by little, until all that remained of it was garden and orchard. The house, a square brick structure, stood in the midst of a great garden which sloped toward the river, ending in a grassy bank which fell some forty feet to the water's edge. The garden was now little more than a tangle of neglected shrubbery: damp, rank, and of that intense blue-green peculiar to vegetation in smoky places where the sun shines but rarely, and the mists form early in the evening and hang late in the morning.

"I shall never forget it as I saw it first, when I arrived there in the chill of a backward June. The long, rank grass, thick and soft and falling in billows, was always wet until midday. The gravel walks were bordered with great lilac bushes, mock orange, and bridal wreath. Back of the house was a neglected rose garden, surrounded by a low stone wall over which the long suckers trailed and matted. They had wound their pink, thorny tentacles, layer upon layer, about the lock and the hinges of the rusty iron gate. Even the porches of the house, and the very windows, were damp and heavy with growth: wisteria, clematis, honeysuckle, and trumpet vine. The garden was grown up with trees, especially that part of it which lay above the river. The bark of the old locusts was blackened by the smoke that crept continually up the valley, and their feathery foliage, so merry in its color, seemed peculiarly precious under that somber sky. There were sycamores and copper beeches; gnarled apple trees, too old to bear; and fall pear trees, hung with a sharp, hard fruit in October; all with a leafage singularly rich and luxuriant, and peculiarly vivid in color. The oaks about the house had been old trees when my great-grandfather built his cabin there, more than a century before, and this garden was almost the only spot for miles along the river where any of the original forest growth still survived. The smoke from the mills was fatal to trees of the larger sort, and even these had the look of doomed things—bent a little toward the town and seemed to wait with head inclined before that oncoming, shrieking force.

"About the river, too, there was a strange hush, a tragic submission—it was so leaden and sullen in its color, and it flowed so soundlessly forever past our door.

"I sat there every evening, on the high veranda overlooking it, watching the dim outlines of the steep hills on the other shore, the flicker of the lights on the island, where there was a boathouse, and listening to the call of the boatmen through the mist. The mist came as certainly as night, whitened by moonshine or starshine. The tin water pipes went splash, splash, with it all evening, and the wind, when it rose at all, was little more than a sighing in the heavy grasses.

"At first it was to think of my distant friends and my old life that I used to sit there; but after a while it was simply to watch the days and weeks go by, like the river which seemed to carry them away.

"Within the house I was never at home. Month followed month, and yet I could feel no sense of kinship with anything there. Under the roof where my father and grandfather were born, I remained utterly detached. The somber rooms never spoke to me, the old furniture never seemed tinctured with race. This portrait of my boy uncle was the only thing to which I could draw near, the only link with anything I had ever known before.

"There is a good deal of my father in the face, but it is my father transformed and glorified, his hesitating discontent drowned in a kind of triumph. From my first day in that house, I continually turned to this handsome kinsman of mine, wondering in what terms he had lived and had his hope—what he had found there to look like that, to bound at one, after all those years, so joyously out of the canvas.

"From the timid, clouded old woman over whose life I had come to watch I learned that in the backyard, near the old rose garden, there was a locust tree which my uncle had planted. After his death, while it was still a slender sapling, his mother had a seat built round it, and she used to sit there on summer evenings. His grave was under the apple trees in the old orchard.

"My aunt could tell me little more than this. There were days when she seemed not to remember him at all.

"It was from an old soldier in the village that I learned the boy's story. Lyon was, the old man told me, but fourteen when the first enlistment occurred, but was even then eager to go. He was in the courthouse square every evening to watch the recruits at their drill, and when the home company was ordered off he rode into the city on his pony to see the men board the train and to wave them goodbye. The next year he spent at home with a tutor, but when he was fifteen he held his parents to their promise and went into the army. He was color sergeant of his regiment and fell in a charge upon the breastworks of a fort about a year after his enlistment.

"The veteran showed me an account of this charge which had been written for the village paper by one of my uncle's comrades who had seen his part in the engagement. It seems that as his company were running at full speed across the bottom lands toward the fortified hill, a shell burst over them. This comrade, running beside my uncle, saw the colors waver and sink as if falling, and looked to see that the boy's hand and forearm had been torn away by the exploding shrapnel. The boy, he thought, did not realize the extent of his injury, for he laughed, shouted something which his comrade did not catch, caught the flag in his left hand, and ran on up the hill. They went splendidly up over the breastworks, but just as my uncle, his colors flying, reached the top of the embankment, a second shell carried away his left arm at the armpit, and he fell over the wall with the flag settling about him.

"It was because this story was ever present with me, because I was unable to shake it off, that I began to read such books as my grandfather had collected upon the Civil War. I found that this war was fought largely by boys, that more men enlisted at eighteen than at any other age. When I thought of those battlefields—and I thought of them much in those days—there was always that glory of youth above them, that impetuous, generous passion stirring the long lines on the march, the blue battalions in the plain. The bugle, whenever I have heard it since, has always seemed to me the very golden throat of that boyhood which spent itself so gaily, so incredibly.

"I used often to wonder how it was that this uncle of mine, who seemed to have possessed all the charm and brilliancy allotted to his family and to have lived up its vitality in one splendid hour, had left so little trace in the house where he was born and where he had awaited his destiny. Look as I would, I could find no letters from him, no clothing or books that might have been his. He had been dead but twenty years, and yet nothing seemed to have survived except the tree he had planted. It seemed incredible and cruel that no physical memory of him should linger to be cherished among his kindred—nothing but the dull image in the brain of that aged sister. I used to pace the garden walks in the evening, wondering that no breath of his, no echo of his laugh, of his call to his pony or his whistle to his dogs, should linger about those shaded paths where the pale roses exhaled their dewy, country smell. Sometimes, in the dim starlight, I have thought that I heard on the grasses beside me the stir of a footfall lighter than my own, and under the black arch of the lilacs I have fancied that he bore me company.

"There was, I found, one day in the year for which my old aunt waited, and which stood out from the months that were all of a sameness to her. On the thirtieth of May she insisted that I should bring down the big flag from the attic and run it up upon the tall flagstaff beside Lyon's tree in the garden. Later in the morning she went with me to carry some of the garden flowers to the grave in the orchard—a grave scarcely larger than a child's.

"I had noticed, when I was hunting for the flag in the attic, a leather trunk with my own name stamped upon it, but was unable to find the key. My aunt was all day less apathetic than usual; she seemed to realize more clearly who I was, and to wish me to be with her. I did not have an opportunity to return to the attic until after dinner that evening, when I carried a lamp upstairs and easily forced the lock of the trunk. I found all the things that I had looked for, put away, doubtless, by his mother, and still smelling faintly of lavender and rose leaves: his clothes, his exercise books, his letters from the army, his first boots, his riding whip, some of his toys, even. I took them out and replaced them gently. As I was about to shut the lid, I picked up a copy of the Aeneid, on the flyleaf of which was written in a slanting, boyish hand:

Lyon Hartwell, January 1862.

He had gone to the wars in '63, I remembered.

"My uncle, I gathered, was none too apt at his Latin, for the pages were dog-eared and rubbed and interlined, the margins mottled with pencil sketches—bugles, stacked bayonets, and artillery carriages. In the act of putting the book down, I happened to run over the pages to the end, and on the flyleaf at the back I saw his name again, and a drawing—with his initials and a date—of the federal flag; above it, written in a kind of arch and in the same unformed hand:

Oh, say, can you see by the dawn's early light
What so proudly we hailed at the twilight's
    last gleaming?

It was a stiff, wooden sketch, not unlike a detail from some Egyptian inscription, but, the moment I saw it, wind and color seemed to touch it. I caught up the book, blew out the lamp, and rushed down into the garden.

"I seemed, somehow, at last to have known him, to have been with him in that careless, unconscious moment and to have known him as he was then.

"As I sat there in the rush of this realization, the wind began to rise, stirring the light foliage of the locust over my head and bringing, fresher than before, the woody odor of the pale roses that overran the little neglected garden. Then, as it grew stronger, it brought the sound of something sighing and stirring over my head in the perfumed darkness.

"I thought of that sad one of the Destinies who, as the Greeks believed, watched from birth over those marked for a violent or untimely death. Oh, I could see him, there in the shine of the morning, his book idly on his knee, his flashing eyes looking straight before him, and at his side that grave figure, hidden in her draperies, her eyes following his, but seeing so much farther—seeing what he never saw, that great moment at the end, when he swayed above his comrades on the earthen wall.

"All the while, the bunting I had run up in the morning flapped fold against fold, heaving and tossing softly in the dark—against a sky so black with rain clouds that I could see above me only the blur of something in soft, troubled motion.

"The experience of that night, coming so overwhelmingly to a man so dead, almost rent me in pieces. It was the same feeling that artists know when we, rarely, achieve truth in our work; the feeling of union with some great force, of purpose and security, of being glad that we have lived. For the first time I felt the pull of race and blood and kindred, and felt beating within me things that had not begun with me. It was as if the earth under my feet had grasped and rooted me, and were pouring its essence into me. I sat there until the dawn of morning, and all night long my life seemed to be pouring out of me and running into the ground."

Hartwell drew a long breath that lifted his heavy shoulders, and then let them fall again. He shifted a little and faced more squarely the scattered, silent company before him. The darkness had made us almost invisible to each other, and, except for the occasional red circuit of a cigarette end traveling upward from the arm of a chair, he might have supposed us all asleep.

"And so," Hartwell added thoughtfully, "I naturally feel an interest in fellows who are going home. It's always an experience."

No one said anything, and in a moment there was a loud rap at the door—the concierge, come to take down Bentley's luggage and to announce that the cab was below. Bentley got his hat and coat, enjoined Hartwell to take good care of his *perroquets,* gave each of us a grip of the hand, and went briskly down the long flights of stairs. We followed him into the street, calling our good wishes, and saw him start on his drive across the lighted city to the Gare St. Lazare.

The Profile

THE SUBJECT of discussion at the Impressionists' Club was a picture, *Circe's Swine*, by a young German painter: a grotesque study showing the enchantress among a herd of bestial things, variously diverging from the human type—furry-eared fauns, shaggy-hipped satyrs, apes with pink palms, snuffing jackals, and thick-jowled swine, all with more or less of human intelligence protesting mutely from their hideous lineaments.

"They are all errors, these freakish excesses," declared an old painter of the Second Empire. "Triboulet, Quasimodo, Gwynplaine have no proper place in art. Such art belongs to the Huns and Iroquois, who could only be stirred by laceration and dismemberment. The only effects of horror properly within the province of the artist are psychological. Everything else is a mere matter of the abattoir. The body, as Nature has evolved it, is sanctified by her purpose, in any natural function or attitude decent and comely. But lop away so much as a finger, and you have wounded the creature beyond reparation."

Once launched upon this subject, there was no stopping the old lion, and several of his confreres were relieved when Aaron Dunlap quietly rose and left the room. They felt that this was a subject which might well be distasteful to him.

I

Dunlap was a portrait painter—preferably a painter of women. He had the faculty of transferring personalities to his canvas, rather than of putting conceptions there. He was finely sensitive to the merest prettiness, was tender and indulgent of it, careful never to deflower a pretty woman of her little charm, however commonplace.

Nicer critics always discerned, even in his most radiant portraits, a certain quiet element of sympathy, almost of pity, in the treatment. The sharp, flexible profile of Madame R—— of the Française; the worn, but subtle and all-capricious physiognomy of her great Semitic rival; the plump contours of a shopkeeper's pretty wife—Dunlap treated them with equal respect and fidelity. He accepted each as she was, and could touch even obvious prettiness with dignity. Behind the delicate pleasure manifested in his treatment of a beautiful face, one could divine the sadness of knowledge, and one felt that the painter had yearned to arrest what was so fleeting and to hold it back from the cruelty of the years. At an exhibition of Dunlap's pictures, the old painter of the Second Empire had said, with a sigh, that he ought to get together all his portraits of young women and call them "Les Fiançées," so abloom were they with the confidence of their beautiful secret. Then, with that sensitiveness to style, which comes from long and passionate study of form, the old painter had added reflectively, "And, after all, how sad a thing it is to be young."

Dunlap had come from a country where women are hardly used. He had grown up on a farm in the remote mountains of West Virginia, and his mother had died of pneumonia contracted from taking her place at the washtub too soon after the birth of a child. When a boy, he had been apprenticed to his grandfather, a country cobbler, who, in his drunken rages, used to beat his wife with odd strips of shoe leather. The painter's hands still bore the mark of that apprenticeship, and the suffering of the mountain women he had seen about him in his childhood had left him almost morbidly sensitive.

Just how or why Dunlap had come to Paris, none of his fellow painters had ever learned. When he ran away from his grandfather, he had been sent by a missionary fund to some sectarian college in his own state, after which he had taught a country school for three winters and saved money enough for his passage. He arrived in Paris with something less than a hundred dollars, wholly ignorant of the language, without friends, and, apparently, without especial qualifications for study there.

Perhaps the real reason that he never succumbed to want was that he was never afraid of it. He felt that he could never be really hungry so long as the poplars flickered along the gray quay behind the Louvre, never friendless while the gay buses rolled home across the bridges through the violet twilight and the barge lights winked above the water.

Little by little his stripes were healed, his agony of ignorance alleviated. The city herself taught him whatever was needful for him to know. She repeated with him that fanciful romance which she has played at with youth for centuries, in which her spontaneity is ever young. She gave him of her best, quickened in him a sense of the more slight and feminine fairness in things; trained his hand and eye to the subtleties of the thousand types of subtle beauty in which she abounds; made him, after a delicate and chivalrous fashion, the expiator of his mountain race. He lived in a bright atmosphere of clear vision and happy associations, delighted at having to do with what was fair and exquisitely brief.

Life went on so during the first ten years of his residence in Paris—a happiness which, despite its almost timorous modesty, tempted fate. It was after Dunlap's name had become somewhat the fashion that he chanced one day, in a café on the Boulevard St. Michel, to be of some service to an American who was having trouble about his order. After assisting him, Dunlap had some conversation with the man, a Californian, whose wheatlands comprised acres enough for a principality, and whose enthusiasm was as fresh as a boy's. Several days later, at the Luxembourg, he met him again, standing in a state of abject bewilderment before Manet's *Olympe.* Dunlap again came to his rescue and took him off to lunch, after which they went to the painter's studio. The acquaintance warmed on both sides, and, before they separated, Dunlap was engaged to paint the old gentleman's daughter, agreeing that the sittings should be at the house on the Boulevard de Courcelles, which the family had taken for the winter.

When Dunlap called at the house, he went through one of the most excruciating experiences of his life. He found Mrs. Gilbert and her daughter waiting to receive him. The shock of the introduction over, the strain of desultory conversation began. The only thing that made conversation tolerable—though it added a new element of perplexity—was the girl's seeming unconsciousness, her utter openness and unabashedness. She laughed and spoke, almost with coquetry, of the honor of sitting to him, of having heard that he was fastidious as to his subjects. Dunlap felt that he wanted to rush from the house and escape the situation which confronted him. The conviction kept recurring that it had just happened, had come upon her since last she had passed a mirror—that she would suddenly become conscious of it, and be suffocated with shame. He felt as if someone ought to tell her and lead her away.

"Shall we get to work?" she asked presently, apparently curious and eager to begin. "How do you wish me to sit to you?"

Dunlap murmured something about usually asking his sitters to decide that for themselves.

"Suppose we try a profile, then?" she suggested carelessly, sitting down in a carved wooden chair.

For the first time since he had entered the room, Dunlap felt the pressure about his throat relax. For the first time it was entirely turned from him, and he could not see it at all. What he did see was a girlish profile, unusually firm for a thing so softly colored; oval, flower-tinted, and shadowed by soft, blonde hair that wound about her head and curled and clung about her brow and neck and ears.

Dunlap began setting up his easel, recovering from his first discomfort and grateful to the girl for having solved his difficulty so gracefully. But no sooner was it turned from him than he felt a strong desire to see it again. Perhaps it had been only a delusion, after all; the clear profile before him so absolutely contradicted it. He went behind her chair to experiment with the window shades, and there, as he drew them up and down, he could look unseen. He gazed long and hard, to blunt his curiosity once and for all, and prevent a further temptation to covert glances. It had evidently been caused by a deep burn, as if from a splash of molten metal. It drew the left eye and the corner of the mouth; made of her smile a grinning distortion, like the shameful conception of some despairing medieval imagination. It was as if some grotesque mask, worn for disport, were just slipping sidewise from her face.

When Dunlap crossed to the right again, he found the same clear profile awaiting him, the same curves of twining, silken hair. "What courage," he thought, "what magnificent courage!" His heart ached at the injustice of it; that her very beauty, the alert, girlish figure, the firm, smooth throat and chin, even her delicate hands, should, through an inch or two of seared flesh, seem tainted and false. He felt that in a plain woman it would have been so much less horrible.

Dunlap left the house overcast by a haunting sense of tragedy, and for the rest of the day he was a prey to distressing memories. All that he had tried to forget seemed no longer dim and faraway—like the cruelties of vanished civilizations—but present and painfully near. He thought of his mother and grandmother, of his little sister, who had died from the bite of a copperhead snake, as if they were creatures yet unreleased from suffering.

II

From the first, Virginia's interest in the portrait never wavered; yet, as the sittings progressed, it became evident to Dunlap that her enthusiasm for the picture was but accessory to her interest in him. By her every look and action she asserted her feeling, as a woman, young and handsome and independent, may sometimes do.

As time went on, he was drawn to her by what had once repelled him. Her courageous candor appealed to his chivalry, and he came to love her, not despite the scar, but, in a manner, for its very sake. He had some indefinite feeling that love might heal her, that in time her hurt might disappear, like the deformities imposed by enchantment to test the hardihood of lovers.

He gathered from her attitude, as well as from that of her family, that the thing had never been mentioned to her, never alluded to by word or look. Both her father and mother had made it their first care to shield her. Had she ever, in the streets of some foreign city, heard a brutal allusion to it? He shuddered to think of such a possibility. Was she not living for the moment when she could throw down the mask and point to it and weep, to be comforted for all time? He looked forward to the hour when there would be no lie of unconsciousness between them. The moment must come when she would give him her confidence; perhaps it would be only a whisper, a gesture, a guiding of his hand in the dark; but, however it might come, it was the pledge he awaited.

During the last few weeks before his marriage, the scar, through the mere strength of his anticipation, had ceased to exist for him. He had already entered to the perfect creature which he felt must dwell behind it: the soul of tragic serenity and twofold loveliness.

They went to the south for their honeymoon, through the Midi and along the coast to Italy. Never, by word or sign, did Virginia reveal any consciousness of what he felt must be said once, and only once, between them. She was spirited, adventurous, impassioned; she exacted much, but she gave magnificently. Her interests in the material world were absorbing, and she demanded continual excitement and continual novelty. Granted these, her good spirits were unfailing.

It was during their wedding journey that he discovered her two all-absorbing interests, which were to become intensified as years went on: her passion for dress and her feverish admiration of physical beauty, whether in men or women or children. This touched Dunlap deeply, as it seemed in a manner an admission of a thing she could not speak.

Before their return to Paris, Dunlap had, for the time, quite renounced his hope of completely winning her confidence. He tried to believe his exclusion just; he told himself that it was only a part of her splendid self-respect. He thought of how, from her very childhood, she had been fashioning, day by day, that armor of unconsciousness in which she sheathed her scar. After all, so deep a hurt could, perhaps, be bared to any one rather than the man she loved.

Yet, he felt that their life was enmeshed in falsehood; that he could not live year after year with a woman who shut so deep a part of her nature from him; that since he had married a woman outwardly different from others, he must have that within her which other women did not possess. Until this was granted him, he felt there would be a sacredness lacking in their relation which it peculiarly ought to have. He counted upon the birth of her child to bring this about. It would touch deeper than he could hope to do, and with fingers that could not wound. That would be a tenderness more penetrating, more softening than passion; without pride or caprice; a feeling that would dwell most in the one part of her he had failed to reach. The child, certainly, she could not shut out; whatever hardness or defiant shame it was that held him away from her, her maternity would bring enlightenment—would bring that sad wisdom, that admission of the necessity and destiny to suffer, which is, somehow, so essential in a woman.

Virginia's child was a girl, a sickly baby which cried miserably from the day it was born. The listless, wailing, almost unwilling battle for life that daily went on before his eyes saddened Dunlap profoundly. All his painter's sophistries fell away from him, and more than ever his early destiny seemed closing about him. There was, then, no escaping from the cruelty of physical things—no matter how high and bright the sunshine, how gray and poplar-clad the ways of one's life. The more willing the child seemed to relinquish its feeble hold, the more tenderly he loved it, and the more determinedly he fought to save it.

Virginia, on the contrary, had almost from the first exhibited a marked indifference toward her daughter. She showed plainly that the sight of its wan, aged little face was unpleasant to her; she disliked being clutched by its skeleton fingers, and said its wailing made her head ache. She was always taking Madame de Montebello and her handsome children to drive in the Bois, but she was never to be seen with little Eleanor. If her friends asked to see the child, she usually put them off, saying that she was asleep or in her bath.

When Dunlap once impatiently asked her whether she never intended to permit anyone to see her daughter, she replied coldly: "Certainly, when she has filled out and begins to look like something."

Little Eleanor grew into a shy, awkward child, who slipped about the house like an unwelcome dependent. She was four years old when a cousin of Virginia's came from California to spend a winter in Paris. Virginia had known her only slightly at home, but, as she proved to be a charming girl, and as she was ill-equipped to bear the hardships of a winter in a *pension,* the Dunlaps insisted upon her staying with them.

The cousin's name was also Eleanor—she had been called so after Virginia's mother—and, from the first, the two Eleanors seemed drawn to each other. Miss Vane was studying, and went out to her lectures every day, but whenever she was at home, little Eleanor was with her. The child would sit quietly in her room while she wrote, playing with anything her cousin happened to give her, or would lie for hours on the hearth rug, whispering to her woolly dog. Dunlap felt a weight lifted from his mind. Whenever Eleanor was at home, he knew that the child was happy.

He had long ceased to expect any solicitude for her from Virginia. That had gone with everything else. It was one of so many disappointments that he took it rather as a matter of course, and it seldom occurred to him that it might have been otherwise. For two years he had been living like a man who knows that some reptile has housed itself and hatched its young in his cellar, and who never cautiously puts his foot out of his bed without the dread of touching its coils. The change in his feeling toward his wife kept him in perpetual apprehension; it seemed to threaten everything he held dear, even his self-respect. His life was a continual effort of self-control, and he found it necessary to make frequent trips to London or sketching tours into Brittany to escape from the strain of the repression he put upon himself. Under this state of things, Dunlap aged perceptibly, and his friends made various and usual conjectures. Whether Virginia was conscious of the change in him, he never knew. Her feeling for him had, in its very nature, been as temporary as it was violent; it had abated naturally, and she probably took for granted that the same readjustment had taken place in him. Perhaps she was too much engrossed in other things to notice it at all.

In Dunlap the change seemed never to be finally established but forever painfully working. Whereas he had once seen the scar on his wife's face not at all, he now saw it continually. Inch by inch it had crept over her whole countenance. Yet the scar itself seemed now a trivial thing; he had known for a long time that the burn had gone deeper than the flesh.

Virginia's extravagant fondness for gaiety seemed to increase, and her mania for lavish display, doubtless common enough in the Californian wheat empire, was a discordant note in Paris. Dunlap found himself condemned to an existence which daily did violence to his sense of propriety. His wife gave fêtes, the cost of which was noised abroad by the Associated Press and flaunted in American newspapers. Her vanity, the pageantries of her toilet, made them both ridiculous, he felt. She was a woman now, with a husband and child; she had no longer a pretext for keeping up the pitiful bravado under which she had hidden the smarting pride of her girlhood.

He became more and more convinced that she had been shielded from a realization of her disfigurement only to the end of a shocking perversity. Her costumes, her very jewels, blazed defiance. Her confidence became almost insolent, and her laugh was nothing but a frantic denial of a thing so cruelly obvious. The unconsciousness he had once reverenced now continually tempted his brutality, and when he felt himself reduced to the point of actual vituperation, he fled to Normandy or Languedoc to save himself. He had begun, indeed, to feel strangely out of place in Paris. The ancient comfort of the city, never lacking in the days when he had known cold and hunger, failed him now. A certain sordidness had spread itself over ways and places once singularly perfect and pure.

III

One evening when Virginia refused to allow little Eleanor to go down to the music room to see some pantomine performers who were to entertain their guests, Dunlap, to conceal his displeasure, stepped quickly out upon the balcony and closed the window behind him. He stood for some moments in the cold, clear night air.

"God help me," he groaned. "Some day I shall tell her. I shall hold her and tell her."

When he entered the house again, it was by another window, and his anger had cooled. As he stepped into the hallway, he met Eleanor the elder, going upstairs with the little girl in her arms. For the life of him he could not refrain from appealing for sympathy to her kind, grave eyes. He was so hurt, so sick, that he could have put his face down beside the child's and wept.

"Give her to me, little cousin. She is too heavy for you," he said gently, as they went upstairs together.

He remembered with resentment his wife's perfectly candid and careless jests about his fondness for her cousin. After he had put the little girl down in Eleanor's room, as they leaned together above the child's head in the firelight, he became, for the first time, really aware. A sudden tenderness weakened him. He put out his hand and took hers, which was holding the child's, and murmured: "Thank you, thank you, little cousin."

She started violently and caught her hand away from him, trembling all over. Dunlap left the room, thrice more miserable than he had entered it.

After that evening he noticed that Eleanor avoided meeting him alone. Virginia also noticed it, but upon this point she was consistently silent. One morning, as Dunlap was leaving his wife's dressing room, having been to consult her as to whether she intended going to the ball at the Russian Embassy, she called him back. She was carefully arranging her beautiful hair, which she always dressed herself, and said carelessly, without looking up at him:

"Eleanor has a foolish notion of returning home in March. I wish you would speak to her about it. Her family expect her to stay until June, and her going now would be commented upon."

"I scarcely see how I can interfere," he replied coolly. "She doubtless has her reasons."

"Her reasons are not far to seek, I should say," remarked Virginia, carefully slipping the pins into the yellow coils of her hair. "She is pathetically ingenuous about it. I should think you might improve upon the present state of affairs if you were to treat it—well, say a trifle more lightly. That would put her more at ease, at least."

"What nonsense, Virginia," he exclaimed, laughing unnaturally and closing the door behind him with guarded gentleness.

That evening Dunlap joined his wife in her dressing room, his coat on his arm and his hat in his hand. The maid had gone upstairs to hunt for Virginia's last-year's fur shoes, as the pair warming before the grate would not fit over her new dancing slippers. Virginia was standing before the mirror, carefully surveying the effect of a new gown, which struck her husband as more than usually conspicuous and defiant. He watched her arranging a pink-and-gold butterfly in her hair and held his peace, but when she put on a pink chiffon collar, with a flaring bow which came directly under her left cheek, in spite of himself he shuddered.

"For heaven's sake, Virginia, take that thing off," he cried. "You ought really to be more careful about such extremes. They only emphasize the scar." He was frightened at the brittleness of his own voice; it seemed to whistle dryly in the air like his grandfather's thong.

She caught her breath and wheeled suddenly about, her face crimson and then gray. She opened her lips twice, but no sound escaped them. He saw the muscles of her throat stiffen, and she began to shudder convulsively, like one who has been plunged into icy water. He started toward her, sick with pity; at last, perhaps—but she pointed him steadily to the door, her eyes as hard as shell, and bright and small, like the sleepless eyes of reptiles.

He went to bed with the sick feeling of a man who has tortured an animal, yet with a certain sense of relief and finality which he had not known in years.

When he came down to breakfast in the morning, the butler told him that Madame and her maid had left for Nice by the early train. Mademoiselle Vane had gone out to her lectures. Madame requested that Monsieur take Mademoiselle to the opera in the evening, where the widowed sister of Madame de Montebello would join them; she would come home with them to remain until Madame's return. Dunlap accepted these instructions as a matter of course, and announced that he would not dine at home.

When he entered the hall upon his return that evening, he heard little Eleanor sobbing, and she flew to meet him, with her dress burned, and her hands black. Dunlap smelled the sickening odor of ointments. The nurse followed with explanations. The doctor was upstairs. Mademoiselle Vane always used a little alcohol lamp in making her toilet; tonight, when she touched a match to it, it exploded. Little Eleanor was leaning against her dressing table at the time, and her dress caught fire; Mademoiselle Vane had wrapped the rug about her and extinguished it. When the nurse arrived, Mademoiselle Vane was standing in the middle of the floor, plucking at her scorched hair, her face and arms badly burned. She had bent over the lamp in lighting it, and had received the full force of the explosion in her face. The doctor was unable to discover what the explosive had been, as it was entirely consumed. Mademoiselle always filled the little lamp herself; all the servants knew about it, for Madame had sent the nurse to borrow it on several occasions, when little Eleanor had the earache.

The next morning Dunlap received a telegram from his wife, stating that she would go to St. Petersburg for the remainder of the winter. In May he heard that she had sailed for America, and a year later her attorneys wrote that she had begun action for divorce. Immediately after the decree was granted, Dunlap married Eleanor Vane. He never met or directly heard from Virginia again, though when she returned to Russia and took up her residence in St. Petersburg, the fame of her toilets spread even to Paris.

Society, always prone to crude antitheses, knew of Dunlap only that he had painted many of the most beautiful women of his time, that he had been twice married, and that each of his wives had been disfigured by a scar on the face.

The Willing Muse

I

VARIOUS OPINIONS were held among Kenneth Gray's friends regarding his approaching marriage, but on the whole it was considered a hopeful venture, and, what was with some of us much more to the point, a hopeful indication. From the hour his engagement was an assured relation, he had seemed to gain. There was now a certain intention in his step, an eager, almost confident flash behind his thick glasses, which cheered his friends like indications of recovery after long illness. Even his shoulders seemed to droop less despondently and his head to sit upon them more securely. Those of us who knew him best drew a long sigh of relief that Kenneth had at last managed to get right with the current.

If, on the insecurity of a meager income and a career at its belated dawn, he was to marry at all, we felt that a special indulgence of destiny had allowed him to fix his choice upon Bertha Torrence. If there was anywhere a woman who seemed able to give him what he needed, to play upon him a continual stream of inspiriting confidence, to order the very simple affairs which he had so besottedly bungled, surely Bertha was the woman.

There were certain of his friends in Olympia who held out that it was a mistake for him to marry a woman who followed his own profession; who was, indeed, already much more within the public consciousness than Kenneth himself. To refute such arguments, one had only to ask what was possible between that and a housekeeper. Could anyone conceive of Kenneth's living in daily intercourse with a woman who had no immediate and personal interest in letters, bitten to the bone as he was by his slow, consuming passion?

Perhaps, insofar as I was concerned, my personal satisfaction at Kenneth's projected marriage was not without its alloy of selfishness, and I think more than one of us counted upon carrying lighter hearts to his wedding than we had known in his company for some time. It was not that we did not believe in him. Hadn't it become a fixed habit to believe? But we, perhaps, felt slightly aggrieved that our faith had not wrought for him the miracles we could have hoped. We were, we found, willing enough to place the direct administration, the first responsibility, upon Bertha's firm young shoulders.

With Harrison, the musical critic, and me, Kenneth was an old issue. We had been college classmates of his, out in Olympia, Ohio, and even then no one had questioned his calling and election, unless it was Kenneth himself. But he had taxed us all sorely, the town and the college, and he had continued to tax us long afterward. As Harrison put it, he had kept us all holding our breath for years. There was never such a man for getting people into a fever of interest and determination for him, for making people (even people who had very vague surmises as to the particular eminence toward which he might be headed) fervidly desire to push him and for refusing, on any terms, to be pushed. There was nothing more individual about Kenneth than his inability to be exploited. Coercion and encouragement spent themselves upon him like summer rain.

He was thirty-five when his first book, *Charles de Montpensier,* was published, and the work was, to those who knew its author intimately, a kind of record of his inverse development. It was first conceived and written as a prose drama, then amplified into an historical novel, and had finally been compressed into a psychological study of two hundred pages, in which the action was hushed to a whisper and the teeming pageantry of his background, which he had spent years in developing and which had cost him several laborious summers in France and Italy, was reduced to a shadowy atmosphere, suggestive enough, doubtless, but presenting very little that was appreciable to the eyes of the flesh. The majority of Kenneth's readers, even those baptized into his faith, must have recalled the fable of the mouse and the mountain. As for those of us who had travailed with him, confident as we were of the high order of the ultimate production, we had a baffled feeling that there had been a distressing leakage of power. However, when this study of the High Constable of Bourbon was followed by an exquisite prose idyl, *The Wood of Ronsard,* we began to take heart, and when we learned that a stimulus so reassuring as a determination to marry had hurried this charming bit of romance into the world, we felt that Kenneth had at last entered upon the future that had seemed for so long only a step before him.

Since Gray's arrival in New York, Harrison and I had had more than ever the feeling of having him on our hands. He had been so long accustomed to the respectful calm of Olympia that he was unable to find his way about in a new environment. He was incapable of falling in with any of the prevailing attitudes, and even of civilly tolerating them in other people. Commercialism wounded him, flippancy put him out of countenance, and he clung stubbornly to certain fond, Olympian superstitions regarding his profession. One by one his new acquaintances chilled, offended by his arrogant reception of their genial efforts to put him in the way of things. Even those of us who had known him at his best, and who remembered the summer evenings in his garden at Olympia, found his seriousness and punctilious reservations tedious in the broad glare of short, noisy working days.

Some weeks before the day set for Kenneth's marriage, I learned that it might be necessary for me to go to Paris for a time to take the place of our correspondent there, who had fallen into precarious health, and I called at Bertha's apartment for a serious talk with her. I found her in the high tide of work; but she made a point of accepting interruptions agreeably, just as she made a point of looking astonishingly well, of being indispensable in an appalling number of "circles," and of generally nullifying the traditional reproach attaching to clever women.

"In all loyalty to you both," I remarked, "I feel that I ought to remind you that you are accepting a responsibility."

"His uncertainty, you mean?"

"Oh, I mean all of them—the barriers which are so intangible he cannot climb them and so terrifying he can't jump them, which lie between him and everything."

Bertha looked at me thoughtfully out of her candid blue eyes. "But what he needs is, after all, so little compared with what he has."

"What he has," I admitted, "is inestimably precious; but the problem is to keep it from going back into the ground with him."

She shot a glance of alarm at me from under her blond lashes. "But certainly he is endlessly more capable of doing than any of us. With such depth to draw from, how can he possibly fail?"

"Perhaps it's his succeeding that I fear more than anything. I think the fair way to measure Kenneth is by what he simply can't do."

"The cheap, you mean?" she asked reflectively. "Oh, that he will never do. We may just eliminate that from our discussion. The problem is simply to make him mine his vein, even if, from his fanciful angle of vision, it's at first a losing business."

"Ah, my dear young lady, but it's just his fanciful angle, as you so happily term it, that puts a stop to everything, and I've never quite dared to urge him past his scruples, though I'm not saying I could if I would. If there is anything at all in the whole business, any element of chosenness, of a special call, any such value in individual tone as he fancies, then, the question is, dare one urge him?"

"Nonsense!" snapped Bertha, drawing up her slender shoulders with decision—I had purposely set out to exhaust her patience—"You have all put a halo about him until he daren't move for fear of putting it out. What he needs is simply to keep at it. How much satisfaction do you suppose he gets out of hanging back?"

"The point, it seems to me, my dear Bertha, is not that, but the remarkableness of anyone's having the conviction, the moral force, just now and under the circumstances, to hang back at all. There must be either very much or very little in a man when he refuses to make the most of his vogue and sell out on a rising market. If he would rather bring up a little water out of the well than turn the river across his lands, has one a right to coerce him?" I put my shaft home steadily, and Bertha caught fire with proper spirit.

"All I can say is, that it's a miracle he's as adaptable as he is. I simply can't understand what you meant, you and Harrison, by keeping him out there in Ohio so long."

"But we didn't," I expostulated. "We didn't keep him there. We only did not succeed in getting him away. We, too, had our scruples. He had his old house there, and his garden, his friends, and the peace of God. And then, Olympia isn't a bad sort of place. It kept his feeling fresh, at least, and in fifteen years or so you'll begin to know the value of that. There everything centers about the college, and everyone reads, just as everyone goes to church. It's a part of the decent, comely life of the place. In Olympia there is a deep-seated, old-fashioned respect for the printed page, and Kenneth naturally found himself in the place of official sanctity. The townswomen reverently attended his college lectures, along with their sons and daughters, and, had he been corruptible, he might have established a walled supremacy of personal devotion behind which he could have sheltered himself to the end of his days."

"But he didn't, you see," said Bertha, triumphantly. "Which is proof that he was meant for the open waters. Oh, we shall do fine things, I promise you! I can just fancy the hushed breath of the place for wonder at him. And his rose garden! Will people never have done with his rose garden! I remember you and Harrison told me of it, with an air, before I had met Kenneth at all. I wonder that you didn't keep him down there forever from a pure sense of the picturesque. What sort of days and nights do you imagine he passed in his garden, in his miserably uncertain state? I suppose we should all like well enough to grow roses, if we had nothing else to do."

I felt that Bertha was considerately keeping her eyes from the clock, and I rose to go.

"Well, Bertha, I suppose the only reason we haven't brought him to a worse pass than we have is just the fact that he happens to have been born an anachronism, and such a stubborn one that we leave him pretty much where we found him."

II

After Kenneth's wedding, I left immediately for Paris, and during the next four years I knew of the Grays only what I could sense from Kenneth's labored letters, ever more astonishing in their aridity, and from the parcels I received twice a year by book-post, containing Bertha's latest work. I never picked up an American periodical that Bertha's name was not the first to greet my eye on the advertising pages. She surpassed all legendary accounts of phenomenal productiveness, and I could feel no anxiety for the fortunes of the pair while Bertha's publishers thought her worth such a display of heavy type. There was scarcely a phase of colonial life left untouched by her, and her last, *The Maid of Domremy,* showed that she had fairly crowded herself out of her own field.

The real wonder was that, making so many, she could make them so well—should make them, indeed, rather better and better. Even were one so unreasonable as to consider her gain a loss, there was no denying it. I read her latest, one after another, as they arrived, with growing interest and amazement, wholly unable to justify my first suspicion. There was every evidence that she had absorbed from Kenneth like a water plant, but none that she had used him more violently than a clever woman may properly use her husband. Knowing him as I did, I could never accredit him with having any hand in Bertha's intrepid, wholehearted, unimpeachable conventionality. One could not exactly call her unscrupulous; one could observe only that no predicament embarrassed her—that she went ahead and pulled it off.

When I returned to New York, I found a curious state of feeling prevalent concerning the Grays. Bertha was *la fille du régiment* more than ever. Everyone championed her, everyone went to her teas, everyone was smilingly and conspicuously present in her triumph. Even those who had formerly stood somewhat aloof, now found no courage to dissent. With Bertha herself so gracious, so eager to please, the charge of pettiness, of jealousy, even, could be too easily incurred. She quite floated the sourest and heaviest upon her rising tide.

There was, however, the undertow. I felt it even before I had actually made sure of it—in the peculiar warmth with which people spoke of Kenneth. In him they saw their own grievances magnified until he became symbolic. Publicly every one talked of Bertha; but behind closed doors it was of Kenneth they spoke—*sotto voce* and with a shake of the head. As he had published nothing since his marriage, this smothered feeling had resulted in a new and sumptuous edition of *Montpensier* and *The Wood of Ronsard:* one of those final, votive editions, suggestive of the bust and the catafalque.

I called upon the Grays at the first opportunity. They had moved from their downtown flat into a new apartment house on Eighty-fifth Street. The servant who took my card did not return, but Kenneth himself stumbled into the reception hall, overturning a gilt chair in his haste, and gripped my hands as if he would never let them go. He held onto my arm as he took me to his study, telling me again and again that I couldn't possibly know what pleasure it gave him to see me. When he dropped limply into his desk chair, he seemed really quite overcome with excitement. It was not until I asked him about his wife that he collected himself and began to talk coherently.

"I'm sorry I can't speak to her now," he explained, rapidly twirling a paper cutter between his long fingers. "She won't be free until four o'clock. She will be so pleased that I'm almost tempted to call her at once. But she's so overworked, poor girl, and she will go out so much."

"My dear Kenneth, how does she ever manage it all? She must have nerves of iron."

"Oh, she's wonderful, wonderful!" he exclaimed, brushing his limp hair back from his forehead with a perplexed gesture. "As to how she does it, I really don't know much more than you. It all gets done, somehow." He glanced quickly toward the partition, through which we heard the steady clicking of a typewriter. "I scarcely know what she is up to until her proofs come in. I usually go at those with her." He darted a piercing look at me, and I wondered whether he had got a hint of the malicious stories which found their way about concerning his varied usefulness to Bertha.

"If you'll excuse me for a moment, Philip," he went on, "I'll finish a letter that must go out this afternoon, and then I shall be quite free."

He turned in his revolving chair to a desk littered deep with papers, and began writing hurriedly. I could see that the simplest kind of composition still perplexed and disconcerted him. He stopped, hesitated, bit his nails, then scratched desperately ahead, darting an annoyed glance at the partition as if the sharp, regular click of the machine bewildered him.

He had grown older, I noticed, but it was good to see him again—his limp, straight hair, which always hung down in a triangle over his high forehead; his lean cheek, loose under lip, and long whimsical chin; his faded, serious eyes, which were always peering inquiringly from behind his thick glasses; his long, tremulous fingers, which handled a pen as uncertainly as ever. There was a general looseness of articulation about his gaunt frame that made his every movement seem more or less haphazard.

On the desk lay a heap of letters, the envelopes marked "answered" in Kenneth's small, irregular hand, and all of them, I noticed, addressed to Bertha. In the open drawer at his left were half a dozen manuscript envelopes, addressed to her in as many different hands.

"What on earth!" I gasped. "Does Bertha conduct a literary agency as well?"

Kenneth swung round in his chair, and made a wry face as he glanced at the contents of the drawer. "It's almost as bad as that. Really, it's the most abominable nuisance. But we're the victims of success, as Bertha says. Sometimes a dozen manuscripts come in to her for criticism in one week. She dislikes to hurt anyone's feelings, so one of us usually takes a look at them."

"Bertha's correspondence must be something of a responsibility in itself," I ventured.

"Oh, it is, I assure you. People are most inconsiderate. I'm rather glad, though, when it piles up like this and I can take a hand at it. It gives me an excuse for putting off my own work, and you know how I welcome any pretext," he added, with a flushed, embarrassed smile.

"What are you doing, anyhow? I don't know where you'll ever learn industry if Bertha can't teach you."

"I'm working, I'm working," he insisted, hurriedly crossing out the last sentence of his letter and blotting it carefully. "You know how reprehensibly slow I am. It seems to grow on me. I'm finishing up some studies in the French Renaissance. They'll be ready by next fall, I think." As he spoke, he again glanced hurriedly over the closely written page before him; then, stopping abruptly, he tore the sheet across the middle. "Really, you've quite upset me. Tell me about yourself, Philip. Are you going out to Olympia?"

"That depends upon whether I remain here or decamp immediately for China, which prospect is in the cards. Olympia is greatly changed, Harrison tells me."

Kenneth sighed and sank deeper into his chair, reaching again for the paper cutter. "Ruined completely. Capital and enterprise have broken in even there. They've all sorts of new industries, and the place is black with smoke and thick with noise from sunrise to sunset. I still own my house there, but I seldom go back. I don't know where we're bound for, I'm sure. There must be places, somewhere in the world, where a man can take a book or two and drop behind the procession for an hour; but they seem impossibly far from here."

I could not help smiling at the deeply despondent gaze which he fixed upon the paper cutter. "But the procession itself is the thing we've got to enjoy," I suggested, "the mere sense of speed."

"I suppose so, I suppose so," he reiterated, wiping his forehead with his handkerchief. "The six-day bicycle race seems to be what we've all come to, and doubtless one form of it's as much worthwhile as another. We don't get anywhere, but we go. We certainly go; and that's what we're after. You'll be lucky if you are sent to China. There must be calm there as yet, I imagine."

Our conversation went on fitfully, with interruptions, irrelevant remarks, and much laughter, as talk goes between two persons who have once been frank with each other, and who find that frankness has become impossible. My coming had clearly upset him, and his agitation of manner visibly increased when he spoke of his wife. He wiped his forehead and hands repeatedly, and finally opened a window. He fairly wrested the conversation out of my hands and was continually interrupting and forestalling me, as if he were apprehensive that I might say something he did not wish to hear. He started and leaned forward in his chair whenever I approached a question.

At last we were aware of a sudden slack in the tension; the typewriter had stopped. Kenneth looked at his watch, and disappeared through a door into his wife's study. When he returned, Bertha was beside him, her hand on his shoulder, taller, straighter, younger than I had left her—positively childlike in her freshness and candor.

"Didn't I tell you," she cried, "that we should do fine things?"

III

A few weeks later I was sent to Hong Kong, where I remained for two years. Before my return to America, I was ordered into the interior for eight months, during which time my mail was to be held for me at the consul's office in Canton, the port where I was to take ship for home. Once in the Szechuen province, floods and bad roads delayed me to such an extent that I barely reached Canton on the day my vessel sailed. I hurried onboard with all my letters unread, having had barely time to examine the instructions from my paper.

We were well out at sea when I opened a letter from Harrison in which he gave an account of Kenneth Gray's disappearance. He had, Harrison stated, gone out to Olympia to dispose of his property there which, since the development of the town, had greatly increased in value. He completed his business after a week's stay, and left for New York by the night train, several of his friends accompanying him to the station. Since that night he had not been seen or heard of. Detectives had been at work; hospitals and morgues had been searched without result.

The date of this communication put me beside myself. It had awaited me in Canton for nearly seven months, and Gray had last been seen on the tenth of November, four months before the date of Harrison's letter, which was written as soon as the matter was made public. It was eleven months, then, since Kenneth Gray had been seen in America. During my long voyage I went through an accumulated bulk of American newspapers, but found nothing more reassuring than occasional items to the effect that the mystery surrounding Gray's disappearance remained unsolved. In a literary supplement of comparatively recent date, I came upon a notice to the effect that the new novel by Bertha Torrence Gray, announced for spring publication, would, owing to the excruciating experience through which the young authoress had lately passed, be delayed until the autumn.

I bore my suspense as best I could across ocean and continent. When I arrived in New York, I went from the ferry to the *Messenger* office, and, once there, directly to Harrison's room.

"What's all this," I cried, "about Kenneth Gray? I tell you I saw Gray in Canton ten months ago."

Harrison sprang to his feet and put his finger to his lip.

"Hush! Don't say another word! There are leaky walls about here. Go and attend to your business, and then come back and go to lunch with me. In the meantime, be careful not to discuss Gray with anyone."

Four hours later, when we were sitting in a quiet corner of a café, Harrison dismissed the waiter and turned to me. "Now," he said, leaning across the table, "if you can be sufficiently guarded, you may tell me what you know about our friend."

"Well," I replied, "it would have been, under ordinary circumstances, a commonplace thing enough. On the day before I started for the interior, I was in Canton, making some last purchases to complete my outfit. I stepped out of a shop on one of the crooked streets in the old part of the city, and I saw him as plainly as I see you, being trundled by in a jinrikisha, got up in a helmet and white duck, a fat white umbrella across his knees, peering hopefully out through his glasses. He was so like himself, his look and attitude, his curious chin poked forward, that I simply stood and stared until he had passed me and turned a corner, vanishing like a stereopticon picture traveling across the screen. I hurried to the banks, the big hotels, to the consul's, getting no word of him, but leaving letters for him everywhere. My party started the next day, and I was compelled to leave for an eight-months' nightmare in the interior. I got back to Canton barely in time to catch my steamer, and did not open your letter until we were down the river and losing sight of land. Either I saw Kenneth, or I am a subject for the Society for Psychical Research."

"Just so," said Harrison, peering mysteriously above his coffee cup. "And now forget it. Simply disabuse yourself of any notion that you've seen him since we crossed the ferry with you three years ago. It's your last service to him, probably."

"Speak up," I cried, exasperated. "I've had about all of this I can stand. I came near wiring the story in from San Francisco. I don't know why I didn't."

"Well, here's to whatever withheld you! When a man comes to the pass where he wants to wipe himself off the face of the earth, when it's the last play he can make for his self-respect, the only decent thing is to let him do it. You know the yielding stuff he's made of well enough to appreciate the amount of pressure it must have taken to harden him to such an exit. I'm sure I never supposed he had it in him."

"But what, short of insanity—"

"Insanity? Nonsense! I wonder that people don't do it oftener. The pressure simply got past the bearing-point. His life was going, and going for nothing—worse than nothing. His future was chalked out for him, and whichever way he turned he was confronted by his unescapable destiny. In the light of Bertha's splendid success, he couldn't be churlish or ungracious; he had to play his little part along with the rest of us. And

Bertha, you know, has passed all the limits of nature, not to speak of decorum. They come as certainly as the seasons, her new ones, each cleverer and more damnable than the last. And yet there is nothing that one can actually put one's finger on—not, at least, without saying the word that would lay us open to a charge which as her friends we are none of us willing to incur, and which no one would listen to if it were said.

"I tell you," Harrison continued, "the whole thing sickened him. He had dried up like a stockfish. His brain was beaten into torpidity by the mere hammer of her machine, as by so many tiny mallets. He had lived to help lessen the value of all that he held precious, to disprove all that he wanted to believe. Having ridden to victory under the banners of what he most despised, there was nothing for him but to live in the blaze of her conquest, and that was the very measure of his fall. His usefulness to the world was over when he had done what he did for Bertha. I don't believe he even knew where he stood; the thing had gone so, seemed to answer the purpose so wonderfully well, and there was never anything that one could really put one's finger on—except all of it. It was a trial of faith, and Bertha had won out so beautifully. He had proved the fallacy of his own position. There was nothing left for him to say. I'm sure I don't know whether he had anything left to think."

"Do you remember," I said slowly, "I used to hold that, in the end, Kenneth would be measured by what he didn't do, by what he couldn't do? What a wonder he was at not being able to do it. Surely, if Bertha couldn't convince him, fire and faggots couldn't."

"For, after all," sighed Harrison, as we rose to go, "Bertha is a wonderful woman—a woman of her time and people; and she has managed, in spite of her fatal facility, to be enough sight better than most of us."

Eleanor's House

I

"SHALL YOU, THEN," Harriet ventured, "go to Fortuney?" The girl threw a startled glance toward the corner of the garden where Westfield and Harold were examining a leak in the basin of the little fountain, and Harriet was sorry that she had put the question so directly. Ethel's reply, when it came, seemed a mere emission of breath rather than articulation.

"I think we shall go later. It's very trying for him there, of course. He hasn't been there since." She relapsed into silence—indeed, she had never come very far out of it—and Harriet called to Westfield. She found that she couldn't help resenting Ethel's singular inadeptness at keeping herself in hand.

"Come, Robert. Harold is tired after his journey, and he and Ethel must have much to say to each other."

Both Harold and his wife, however, broke into hurried random remarks with an eagerness which seemed like a protest.

"It is delightful to be near you here at Arques, with only a wall between our gardens," Ethel spurred herself to say. "It will mean so much to Harold. He has so many old associations with you, Mrs. Westfield."

The two men had come back to the tea table, and as the younger one overheard his wife's last remark, his handsome brown face took on the blackness of disapproval.

Ethel glanced at him furtively, but Harriet was unable to detect whether she realized just why or to what extent her remark had been unfortunate. She certainly looked as if she might not be particularly acute, drooping about in her big garden hat and her limp white frock, which had not been very well put on. However, some sense of maladroitness certainly penetrated her vagueness, for she shrank behind the tea table, gathering her scarf about her shoulders as if she were mysteriously blown upon by a chilling current.

The Westfields drew together to take their leave. Harold stepped to his wife's side as they went toward the gate with their guests, and put his hand lightly on her shoulder, at which she waveringly emerged from her eclipse and smiled.

Harriet could not help looking back at them from under her sunshade as they stood there in the gateway; the man with his tense brown face and abstracted smile, the girl drooping, positively swaying in her softness and uncertainty.

When they reached the sunny square of their own garden, Harriet sank into a wicker chair in the deep shadow of the stucco wall and addressed her husband with conviction:

"I know now, my dear, why he wished so much to come. I sensed it yesterday, when I first met her. But now that I've seen them together, it's perfectly clear. He brought her here to keep her away from Fortuney, and he's counting on us to help him."

Westfield, who was carefully examining his rose trees, looked at his wife with interest and frank bewilderment, a form of interrogation with which she was perfectly familiar.

"If there is one thing that's plainer even than his misery," Harriet continued, "it is that she is headed toward Fortuney. They've been married over two years, and he couldn't, I suppose, keep her across the Channel any longer. So he has simply deflected her course, and we are the pretext."

"Certainly," Westfield admitted, as he looked up from his pruning, "one feels something not altogether comfortable with them, but why should it be Fortuney any more than a hundred other things? There are opportunities enough for people who wish to play at crosspurposes."

"Ah! But Fortuney," sighed his wife, "Fortuney's the summing up of all his past. It's Eleanor herself. How could he, Robert, take this poor girl there? It would be cruelty. The figure she'd cut in a place of such distinction!"

"I should think that if he could marry her, he could take her to Fortuney," Westfield maintained bluntly.

"Oh, as to his marrying her! But I suppose we are all to blame for that—all his and Eleanor's old friends. We certainly failed him. We fled at the poor fellow's approach. We simply couldn't face the extent of his bereavement. He seemed a mere fragment of a man dragged out from under the wreckage. They had so grown together that when she died there was nothing in him left whole. We dreaded him, and were glad enough to get him off to India. I even hoped he would marry out there. When the news came that he had, I supposed that would end it, that he would become merely a chapter in natural history. But, you see, he hasn't; he's more widowed than before. He can't do anything well without her. You see, he couldn't even do this."

"This?" repeated Westfield, quitting his gardening abruptly. "Am I to understand that she would have been of assistance in selecting another wife for him?"

Harriet preferred to ignore that his tone implied an enormity. "She would certainly have kept him from getting into such a box as he's in now. She could at least have found him someone who wouldn't lacerate him by her every movement. Oh, that poor, limp, tactless, terrified girl! Have you noticed the exasperating way in which she walks, even? It's as if she were treading pain, forbearing and forgiving, when she but steps to the tea table. There was never a person so haunted by the notion of her own untidy picturesqueness. It wears her thin and consumes her, like her unhappy passion. I know how he feels; he hates the way she likes what she likes, and he hates the way she dislikes what she doesn't like. And, mark my words, she is bent upon Fortuney. That, at least, Robert, he certainly can't permit. At Fortuney, Eleanor is living still. The place is so intensely, so rarely personal. The girl has fixed her eye, made up her mind. It's symbolic to her, too, and she's circling about it; she can't endure to be kept out. Yesterday, when I went to see her, she couldn't wait to begin explaining her husband to me. She seemed to be afraid I might think she hadn't poked into everything."

While his wife grew more and more vehement, Westfield lay back in a garden chair, half succumbing to the drowsy warmth of the afternoon.

"It seems to me," he remarked, with a discreet yawn, "that the poor child is only putting up a good fight against the tormenting suspicion that she hasn't got into anything. She may be just decently trying to conceal her uncertainty."

Harriet looked at him intently for a moment, watching the shadows of the sycamore leaves play across his face, and then laughed indulgently. "The idea of her decently trying to conceal anything amuses me. So that's how much you know of her!" she sighed. "She's taken you in just as she took him. He doubtless thought she wouldn't poke, that she would go on keeping the door of the chamber, breathing faint benedictions and smiling her moonbeam smile as he came and went. But, under all her meekness and air of poetically foregoing, she has a forthcomingness and an outputtingness which all the brutality he's driven to can't discourage. I've known her kind before! You may clip their tendrils every day of your life only to find them renewed and sweetly taking hold the next morning. She'd find the crevices in polished alabaster. Can't you see what she wants?" Mrs. Westfield sat up with flashing eyes. "She wants to be to him what Eleanor was; she sees no reason why she shouldn't be!"

Westfield rubbed the stiff blond hair above his ear in perplexity. "Well, why, in heaven's name, shouldn't she be? He married her. What less can she expect?"

"Oh, Robert!" cried Harriet, as if he had uttered something impious. "But then, you never knew them. Why, Eleanor made him. He is the work of her hands. She saved him from being something terrible."

Westfield smiled ironically.

"Was he, then, in his natural state, so—so very much worse?"

"Oh, he was better than he is now, even then. But he was somehow terribly off the key. He was the most immature thing ever born into the world. Youth was a disease with him; he almost died of it. He was so absorbed in his own waking up, and he so overestimated its importance. He made such a clamor about it and so thrust it upon one that I used to wonder whether he would ever get past the stage of opening packages under the Christmas tree and shouting. I suppose he did know that his experiences were not unique, but I'm sure he felt that the degree of them was peculiarly his.

"When he met Eleanor he lost himself, and that was what he needed. She happened to be born tempered and poised. There never was a time when she wasn't discriminating. She could enjoy all kinds of things and people, but she was never, never mistaken in the kind. The beauty of it was that her distinctions had nothing to do with reason; they were purely shades of feeling.

"Well, you can conjecture what followed. She gave him the one thing which made everything else he had pertinent and dignified. He simply had better fiber than any of us realized, and she saw it. She was infallible in detecting quality.

"Two years after their marriage, I spent six weeks with them at Fortuney, and even then I saw their possibilities, what they would do for each other. And they went on and on. They had all there is—except children. I suppose they were selfish. As Eleanor once said to me, they needed only eternity and each other. But, whatever it was, it was Olympian."

II

Harriet was walking one morning on the green hill that rises, topped by its sprawling feudal ruin, behind Arques-la-Bataille. The sunlight still had the magical golden hue of early day, and the dew shone on the smooth, grassy folds and clefts that mark the outlines of the old fortifications. Below lay the delicately colored town—seen through a grove of glistening white birches—the shining, sinuous curves of the little river, and the green, open stretches of the pleasant Norman country.

As she skirted the base of one of the thick towers on the inner edge of the moat, her sunshade over her shoulder and her white shoes gray with dew, she all but stepped upon a man who lay in a shaded corner within the elbow of the wall and the tower, his straw hat tilted over his eyes.

"Why, Harold Forscythe!" she exclaimed breathlessly.

He sprang to his feet, baring his head in the sun.

"Sit down, do," he urged. "It's quite dry there—the masonry crops out—and the view's delightful."

"You didn't seem to be doing much with the view as I came up." Harriet put down her sunshade and stood looking at him, taking in his careless morning dress, his gray, unshaven face and heavy eyes. "But I shall sit down," she affectionately assured him, "to look at you, since I have so few opportunities. Why haven't you been to see me?"

Forscythe gazed attentively at her canvas shoes, hesitating and thrusting out his lower lip, an impetuous mannerism she had liked in him as a boy. "Perhap—perhaps I haven't quite dared," he suggested.

"Which means," commented Harriet reproachfully, "that you accredit me with a very disagreeable kind of stupidity."

"You? Oh, dear, no! I didn't—I don't. How could you suppose it?" He helped her to her seat on the slant of gray rock, moving about her solicitously but avoiding her eyes.

"Then why do you stand there, hesitating?"

"I was just thinking"—he shot her a nervous glance from under a frown—"whether I ought not to cut away now, on your account. I'm in the devil of a way in the early morning sometimes."

Mrs. Westfield looked at him compassionately as he stood poking the turf with his stick. She wondered how he could have reached eight-and-thirty without growing at all older than he had been in his twenties. And yet, that was just what their happiness had done for them. If it had kept them young, gloriously and resplendently young, it had also kept them from arriving anywhere. It had prolonged his flowering time, but it hadn't mellowed him. Growing older would have meant making concessions. He had never made any, had not even learned how, and was still striking back like a boy.

Harriet pointed to the turf beside her, and he dropped down suddenly.

"I'm really not fit to see anyone this morning. These first hours—" He shrugged his shoulders and began to pull the grass blades swiftly, one at a time.

"Are hard for you?"

He nodded.

"Because they used to be your happiest?" Harriet continued, feeling her way.

"It's queer," he said quietly, "but in the morning I often feel such an absurd certainty of finding her. I suppose one has more vitality at this time of day, a keener sense of things."

"My poor boy! Is it still as hard as that?"

"Did you for a moment suppose that it would ever be any—easier?" he asked, with a short laugh.

"I hoped so. Oh, I hoped so."

Forscythe shook his head. "You know why I haven't been to see you," he brought out abruptly.

Harriet touched his arm. "You ought not to be afraid with me. If I didn't love her as much as you did, at least I never loved anything else so well."

"I know. That's one reason I came here. You were always together when I first knew her, and it's easy to see her beside you. Sometimes I think the image of her—coming down the stairs, crossing the garden, holding out her hand—is growing dimmer, and that terrifies me. Some people and some places give me the feeling of her." He stopped with a jerk, and threw a pebble across the moat, where the sloping bank, softened and made shallower by the slow centuries, was yellow with buttercups.

"But that feeling, Harold, must be more in you than anywhere. There's where she willed it and breathed it and stored it for years."

Harold was looking fixedly at the bare spot under his hand and pulling the grass blades out delicately. When he spoke, his voice fairly startled her with its sound of water working underground.

"It was like that once, but now I lose it sometimes—for weeks together. It's like trying to hold some delicate scent in your nostrils, and heavier odors come in and blur it."

"My poor boy, what can I say to you?" Harriet's eyes were so dim that she could only put out a hand to be sure that he was there. He pressed it and held it a moment.

"You don't have to say anything. Your thinking reaches me. It's extraordinary how we can be trained down, how little we can do with. If she could only have written to me—if there could have been a sign, a shadow on the grass or in the sky, to show that she went on with me, it would have been enough. And now—I wouldn't ask anything but to be left alone with my hurt. It's all that's left me. It's the most precious thing in the world."

"Oh, but that, my dear Harold, is too terrible! She couldn't have endured your doing it," murmured Harriet, overcome.

"Yes, she could. She'd have done it. She'd have kept me alive in her anguish, in her incompleteness."

Mrs. Westfield put out her hand entreatingly to stop him. He had lain beside her on the grass so often in the days of his courtship, of his first tempestuous happiness. It was incredible that he should have changed so little. He hadn't grown older, or wiser, or, in himself, better. He had simply grown more and more to be Eleanor. The misery of his entanglement touched her afresh, and she put her hands to her eyes and murmured, "Oh, that poor little Ethel! How could you do it?"

She heard him bound up, and when she lifted her face he was half the length of the wall away. She called to him, but he waved his hat meaninglessly, and she watched him hurry across the smooth green swell of the hill. Harriet leaned back into the warm angle of masonry and tried to settle into the deep peace of the place, where so many follies and passions had spent themselves and ebbed back into the stillness of the grass. But a sense of pain kept throbbing about her. It seemed to come from the spot where poor Forscythe had lain, and to rise like a miasma between her and the farms and orchards and the graygreen windings of the river. When at last she rose with a sigh, she murmured to herself, "Oh, my poor Eleanor! If you know, I pity you. Wherever you are, I pity you."

III

The silence once broken, Forscythe came often to Mrs. Westfield's garden. He spent whole mornings there, watching her embroider, or walked with her about the ruins on the hilltop or along the streams that wound through the fertile farm country. Though he said little himself, he made it supremely easy for her to talk. He followed her about in grateful silence while she told him, freely and almost lightly, of her girlhood with Eleanor Sanford; of their life at a convent school in Paris; of the copy of *Manon Lescaut* which they kept sewed up in the little pine pillow they had brought from Schenectady; of the adroit machinations by which, on her fête day, under the guardianship of an innocent aunt from Albany, Eleanor had managed to convey all her birthday roses out to Père-la-Chaise and arrange them under de Musset's willow.

Harriet even found a quiet happiness in being with him. She felt that he was making amends—that she could trust him not to renew the terrible experience which had crushed her at their first meeting on the hill. When he spoke of Eleanor at all, it was only to recall the beauty of their companionship, a thing she loved to reflect upon. For if they had been selfish, at least their selfishness had never taken the form of comfortable indolence. They had kept the edge of their zest for action; their affection had never grown stocky and middleaged. How, Harriet often asked herself, could two people have crowded so much into ten circumscribed mortal years? And, of course, the best of it was that all the things they did and the places they went to and the people they knew didn't in the least matter, were only the incidental music of their drama.

The end, when it came, had, by the mercy of heaven, come suddenly. An illness of three days at Fortuney, their own place on the Oise, and it was over. He was flung out into space to find his way alone, to keep fighting about in his circle, forever yearning toward the center.

One morning, when Harold asked her to go for a long walk into the country, Harriet felt from the moment they left the town behind them that he had something serious to say to her. They were having their déjeuner in the garden of a little auberge, sitting at a table beside a yellow clay wall overgrown with wall peaches, when he told her that he was going away.

"I don't know for just how long. Perhaps a week; perhaps two. I'd hate to have you misunderstand. I don't want you to underestimate the good you've done me these last weeks. But, you see, this is a sort of—a sort of tryst," he explained, smiling faintly. "We got stranded once in an absurd little town down on the Mediterranean, not far from Hyères. We liked it and stayed for days, and when we left, Eleanor said we'd go back every year when the grapes were ripe. We never did go back, for that was the last year. But I've been there that same week every autumn. The people there all remember her. It's a little bit of a place."

Harriet looked at him, holding her breath. The black kitten came up and brushed against him, tapping his arm with its paw and mewing to be fed.

"Is that why you go away so much? Ethel has told me. She said there was some business, but I doubted that."

"I'm sorry it has to be so. Of course, I feel despicable—do all the time, for that matter." He wiped his face and hands miserably with his napkin and pushed back his chair. "You see," he went on, beginning to make geometrical figures in the sand with his walking stick, "you see, I can't settle down to anything and I'm so driven. There are times when places pull me—places where things happened, you know. Not big things, but just our own things." He stopped, and then added thoughtfully, "Going to miss her is almost what going to meet her used to be. I get in such a state of impatience."

Harriet couldn't, she simply couldn't, altogether despise him, and it was because, as he said, she did know. They sat in the quiet, sunny little garden, full of dahlias and sunflowers and the hum of bees, and she remembered what Eleanor had told her about this fishing village where they had lived on figs and goat's milk and watched the meager vintage being gathered—how, when they had to leave it, got into their compartment and flashed away along the panoramic Mediterranean shore, she had cried, she who never wept for pain or weariness, Harriet put in fondly. It was not the blue bay and the lavender and the pine hills they were leaving, but some peculiar shade of being together. Yet they were always leaving that. Every day brought colors in the sky, on the sea, in the heart, which could not possibly come just so again. That tomorrow's would be just as beautiful never quite satisfied them. They wanted it all. Yes, whatever they were, those two, they were Olympian.

As they were nearing home in the late afternoon, Forscythe turned suddenly to Harriet. "I shall have to count on you for something while I am away, you know."

"About the business? Oh, yes, I'll understand."

"And you'll do what you can for her, won't you?" he asked shakily. "It's such a hellish existence for her. I'd do anything if I could undo what I've done—anything."

Harriet paused a moment. "It simply can't, you know, go on like this."

"Yes, yes, I know that," he replied abstractedly. "But that's not the worst of it. The worst is that sometimes I feel as if Eleanor wants me to give her up, that she can't stand it any longer and is begging me to let her rest."

Harriet tried to look at him, but he had turned away his face.

IV

Forscythe's absence stretched beyond a fortnight, and no one seemed very definitely informed as to when he might return. Meanwhile, Mrs. Westfield had his wife considerably upon her hands. She could not, indeed, account for the degree to which she seemed responsible. It was always there, groping for her and pulling at her, as she told Westfield. The garden wall was not high enough to shut out entirely the other side—the girl pacing the gravel paths with the meek, bent step which poor Harriet found so exasperating, her wistful eyes peering from under her garden hat, her preposterous skirts trailing behind her like the brier-torn gown of some wandering Griselda.

During the long, dull hours in which they had their tea together, Harriet realized more and more the justice of the girl's position—of her claim, since she apparently had no position that one could well define. The reasonableness of it was all the more trying since Harriet felt so compelled to deny it. They read and walked and talked, and the subject to which they never alluded was always in the air. It was in the girl's long, silent, entreating looks; in her thin hands, nervously clasping and unclasping; in her ceaseless pacing about. Harriet distinctly felt that she was working herself up to something, and she declared to Westfield every morning that, whatever it was, she wouldn't be a party to it.

"I can understand perfectly," she insisted to her husband, "how he did it. He married her to talk to her about Eleanor. Eleanor had been the theme of their courtship. The rest of the world went on attending to its own business and shaking him off, and she stopped and sympathized and let him pour himself out. He didn't see, I suppose, why he shouldn't have just a wife like other men, for it didn't occur to him that he couldn't be just a husband. He thought she'd be content to console; he never dreamed she'd try to heal."

As for Ethel, Harriet had to admit that she, too, could be perfectly accounted for. She had gone into it, doubtless, in the spirit of self-sacrifice, a mood she was romantically fond of permitting herself and humanly unable to live up to. She had married him in one stage of feeling, and had inevitably arrived at another—had come, indeed, to the place where she must be just one thing to him. What she was, or was not, hung on the throw of the dice in a way that savored of trembling captives and barbarous manners, and Harriet had to acknowledge that almost anything might be expected of a woman who had let herself go to such lengths and had yet got nowhere worth mentioning.

"She is certainly going to do something," Harriet declared. "But whatever can she hope to do now? What weapon has she left? How is she, after she's poured herself out so, ever to gather herself up again? What she'll do is the horror. It's sure to be ineffectual, and it's equally sure to have distinctly dramatic aspects."

Harriet was not, however, quite prepared for the issue which confronted her one morning. She sat down shaken and aghast when Ethel, pale and wraithlike, glided somnambulantly into her garden and asked whether Mrs. Westfield would accompany her to Fortuney on the following day.

"But, my dear girl, ought you to go there alone?"

"Without Harold, you mean?" the other inaudibly suggested. "Yes, I think I ought. He has such a dread of going back there, and yet I feel that he'll never be satisfied until he gets among his own things. He would be happier if he took the shock and had done with it. And my going there first might make it easier for him."

Harriet stared. "Don't you think he should be left to decide that for himself?" she reasoned mildly. "He may wish to forget the place in so far as he can."

"He doesn't forget," Ethel replied simply. "He thinks about it all the time. He ought to live there; it's his home. He ought not," she brought out, with a fierce little burst, "to be kept away."

"I don't know that he or anyone else can do much in regard to that," commented Harriet dryly.

"He ought to live there," Ethel repeated automatically; "and it might make it easier for him if I went first."

"How?" gasped Mrs. Westfield.

"It might," she insisted childishly, twisting her handkerchief around her fingers. "We can take an early train and get there in the afternoon. It's but a short drive from the station. I am sure"—she looked pleadingly at Harriet—"I'm sure he'd like it better if you went with me."

Harriet made a clutch at herself and looked pointedly at the ground. "I really don't see how I could, Ethel. It doesn't seem to me a proper thing to do."

Ethel sat straight and still. Her liquid eyes brimmed over and the tears rolled mildly down her cheeks. "I'm sorry it seems wrong to you. Of course you can't go if it does. I shall go alone, then, tomorrow." She rose and stood poised in uncertainty, her hand on the back of the chair.

Harriet moved quickly toward her. The girl's infatuate obstinacy carried a power with it.

"But why, dear child, do you wish me to go with you? What good could that possibly do?"

There was a long silence, trembling and gentle tears. At last Ethel murmured: "I thought, because you were her friend, that would make it better. If you were with me, it couldn't seem quite so—indelicate." Her shoulders shook with a sudden wrench of feeling and she pressed her hands over her face. "You see," she faltered, "I'm so at a loss. I haven't—anyone."

Harriet put an arm firmly about her drooping slenderness. "Well, for this venture, at least, you shall have me. I can't see it, but I'm willing to go—more willing than I am that you should go alone. I must tell Robert and ask him to look up the trains for us."

The girl drew gently away from her and stood in an attitude of deep dejection. "It's difficult for you, too, our being here. We ought never to have come. And I must not take advantage of you. Before letting you go with me, I must tell you the real reason why I am going to Fortuney."

"The real reason?" echoed Harriet.

"Yes. I think he's there now."

"Harold? At Fortuney?"

"Yes. I haven't heard from him for five days. Then it was only a telegram, dated from Pontoise. That's very near Fortuney. Since then I haven't had a word."

"You poor child, how dreadful! Come here and tell me about it." Harriet drew her to a chair, into which she sank limply.

"There's nothing to tell, except what one fears. I've lost sleep until I imagine all sorts of horrible things. If he has been alone there for days, shut up with all those memories, who knows what may have happened to him? I shouldn't, you know, feel like this if he were with—anyone. But this—oh, you are all against me! You none of you understand. You think I am trying to make him—inconstant" (for the first time her voice broke into passionate scorn). "But there's no other way to save him. It's simply killing him. He's been frightfully ill twice, once in London and once before we left India. The London doctors told me that unless he was got out of this state he might do almost anything. They even wanted me to leave him. So, you see, I must do something."

Harriet sat down on the stool beside her and took her hand.

"Why don't you, then, my dear, do it—leave him?"

The girl looked wildly toward the garden wall. "I can't—not now. I might have once, perhaps. Oh," with a burst of trembling, "don't, please don't talk about it. Just help me to save him if you can."

"Had you rather, Ethel, that I went to Fortuney alone?" Harriet suggested hopefully.

The girl shook her head. "No; he'd know I sent you, and he'd think I was afraid. I am, of course, but not in the way he thinks. I've never crossed him in anything, but we can't go on like this any longer. I'll go, and he'll just have to—choose."

Having seen Ethel safely to her own door, Harriet went to her husband, who was at work in the library, and told him to what she had committed herself. Westfield received the intelligence with marked discouragement. He disliked her being drawn more and more into the Forscythes' affairs, which he found very depressing and disconcerting, and he flatly declared that he wanted nothing so much as to get away from all that hysteria next door and finish the summer in Switzerland.

"It's an obsession with her to get to Fortuney," Harriet explained. "To her it somehow means getting into everything she's out of. I really can't have her thinking I'm against her in that definite, petty sort of way. So I've promised to go. Besides, if she is going down there, where all Eleanor's things are—"

"Ah, so it's to keep her out, and not to help her in, that you're going," Westfield deduced.

"I declare to you, I don't know which it is. I'm going for both of them—for her and for Eleanor."

V

Fortuney stood in its cluster of cool green, halfway up the hillside and overlooking the green loop of the river. Harriet remembered, as she approached it, how Eleanor used to say that after the south, it was good to come back and rest her eyes there. Nowhere were skies so gray, streams so clear, or fields so pleasantly interspersed with woodland. The hill on which the house stood overlooked an island where the haymakers were busy cutting a second crop, swinging their bright scythes in the long grass and stopping to hail the heavy lumber barges as they passed slowly up the glassy river.

Ethel insisted upon leaving the carriage by the roadside, so the two women alighted and walked up the long driveway that wound under the linden trees. An old man who was clipping the hedge looked curiously at them as they passed. Except for the snipping of his big shears and occasional halloos from the island, a pale, sunny quiet lay over the place, and their approach, Harriet reflected, certainly savored all too much of a reluctance to break it. She looked at Ethel with all the exasperation of fatigue, and felt that there was something positively stealthy about her soft, driven tread.

The front door was open, but, as they approached, a bent old woman ran out from the garden behind the house, her apron full of gourds, calling to them as she ran. Ethel addressed her without embarrassment: "I am Madame Forscythe. Monsieur is awaiting me. Yes, I know that he is ill. You need not announce me."

The old woman tried to detain her by salutations and questions, tried to explain that she would immediately get rooms ready for Madame and her friend. Why had she not been told?

But Ethel brushed past her, seeming to float over the threshold and up the staircase, while Harriet followed her, protesting. They went through the salon, the library, into Harold's study, straight toward the room which had been Eleanor's.

"Let us wait for him here in his study, please, Ethel," Harriet whispered. "We've no right to steal upon anyone like this."

But Ethel seemed drawn like the victim of mesmerism. The door opening from the study into Eleanor's room was hung with a heavy curtain. She lifted it, and there they paused, noiselessly. It was just as Harriet remembered it; the tapestries, the prie-Dieu, the Louis Seize furniture—absolutely unchanged, except that her own portrait, by Constant, hung where Harold's used to be. Across the foot of the bed, in a tennis shirt and trousers, lay Harold himself, asleep. He was lying on his side, his face turned toward the door and one arm thrown over his head. The habit of being on his guard must have sharpened his senses, for as they looked at him he awoke and sprang up, flushed and disordered.

"Ethel, what on earth—?" he cried hotly.

She was frightened enough now. She trembled from head to foot and pressed her hands tightly over her breast. "You never told me not to come," she panted. "You only said," with a wild burst of reproach, "that you couldn't."

Harold gripped the foot of the bed with both hands and his voice shook with anger. "Please go downstairs and wait in the reception room, while I ask Mrs. Westfield to enlighten me."

Something leaped into Ethel's eyes as she took another step forward into the room and let the curtain fall behind her. "I won't go, Harold, until you go with me," she cried. Drawing up her frail shoulders, she glanced desperately about her—at the room, at her husband, at Harriet, and finally at her, the handsome, disdainful face which glowed out of the canvas. "You have no right to come here secretly," she broke out. "It's shameful to her as well as to me. I'm not afraid of her. She couldn't but loathe you for what you do to me. She couldn't have been so contemptible as you all make her—so jealous!"

Forscythe swung round on his heel, his clenched hands hanging at his side, and, throwing back his head, faced the picture.

"Jealous? Of whom—my God!"

"Harold!" cried Mrs. Westfield entreatingly.

But she was too late. The girl had slipped to the floor as if she had been cut down.

VI

One rainy night, four weeks after her visit to Fortuney, Forscythe stood at Mrs. Westfield's door, his hat in his hand, bidding her good night. Harriet looked worn and troubled, but Forscythe himself was calm.

"I'm so glad you gave me a chance at Fortuney, Harold. I couldn't bear to see it go to strangers. I'll keep it just as it is—as it was; you may be sure of that, and if ever you wish to come back—"

Forscythe spoke up quickly: "I don't think I shall be coming back again, Mrs. Westfield. And please don't hesitate to make any changes. As I've tried to tell you, I don't feel the need of it any longer. She has come back to me as much as she ever can."

"In another person?"

Harold smiled a little and shook his head. "In another way. She lived and died, dear Harriet, and I'm all there is to show for it. That's pitiful enough, but I must do what I can. I shall die very far short of the mark—but she was always generous."

He held out his hand to Mrs. Westfield and took hers resolutely, though she hesitated as if to detain him.

"Tell Ethel I shall go over to see her in the morning before you leave, and thank her for her message," Harriet murmured.

"Please come. She has been seeing to the packing in spite of me, and is quite worn out. She'll be herself again, once I get her back to Surrey, and she's very keen about going to America. Good night, dear lady," he called after him as he crossed the veranda.

Harriet heard him splash down the gravel walk to the gate and then closed the door. She went slowly through the hall and into her husband's study, where she sat quietly down by the wood fire.

Westfield rose from his work and looked at her with concern.

"Why didn't you send that madman home long ago, Harriet? It's past midnight, and you're completely done out. You look like a ghost." He opened a cabinet and poured her a glass of wine.

"I feel like one, dear. I'm beginning to feel my age. I've no spirit to hold it off any longer. I'm going to buy Fortuney and give up to it. It will be pleasant to grow old there in that atmosphere of lovely things past and forgotten."

Westfield sat down on the arm of her chair and drew her head to him. "He is really going to sell it, then? He has come round sure enough, hasn't he?"

"Oh, he melts the heart in me, Robert. He makes me feel so old and lonely, that he and I are left over from another age—a lovely time that's gone. He's giving up everything. He's going to take her home to America after her child is born."

"Her child?"

"Yes. He didn't know until after that dreadful day at Fortuney. She had never told anyone. He says he's so glad—that it will make up to her for everything. Oh, Robert! If only Eleanor had left him children all this wouldn't have been."

"Do you think," Westfield asked after a long silence, "that he is glad?"

"I know it. He's been so gentle and comprehending with her." Harriet stopped to dry the tears on her cheek, and put her head down on her husband's shoulder. "And oh, Robert, I never would have believed that he could be so splendid about it. It's as if he had come up to his possibilities for the first time, through this silly, infatuated girl, while Eleanor, who gave him kingdoms—"

She cried softly on his shoulder for a long while, and then he felt that she was thinking. When at last she looked up, she smiled gratefully into his eyes.

"Well, we'll have Fortuney, dearest. We'll have all that's left of them. He'll never turn back; I feel such a strength in him now. He'll go on doing it and being finer and finer. And do you know, Robert," her lips trembled again, but she still smiled from her misty eyes, "if Eleanor knows, I believe she'll be glad; for—oh, my Eleanor!—she loved him beyond anything, beyond even his love."

On the Gulls' Road

THE AMBASSADOR'S STORY

I

IT OFTEN happens that one or another of my friends stops before a red chalk drawing in my study and asks me where I ever found so lovely a creature. I have never told the story of that picture to anyone, and the beautiful woman on the wall, until yesterday, in all these twenty years has spoken to no one but me. Yesterday a young painter, a countryman of mine, came to consult me on a matter of business, and upon seeing my drawing of Alexandra Ebbling, straightway forgot his errand. He examined the date upon the sketch and asked me, very earnestly, if I could tell him whether the lady were still living. When I answered him, he stepped back from the picture and said slowly, "So long ago? She must have been very young. She was happy?"

"As to that, who can say—about any one of us?" I replied. "Out of all that is supposed to make for happiness, she had very little."

He shrugged his shoulders and turned away to the window, saying as he did so, "Well, there is very little use in troubling about anything, when we can stand here and look at her, and you can tell me that she has been dead all these years, and that she had very little."

We returned to the object of his visit, but when he bade me goodbye at the door his troubled gaze again went back to the drawing, and it was only by turning sharply about that he took his eyes away from her.

I went back to my study fire, and as the rain kept away less impetuous visitors I had a long time in which to think of Mrs. Ebbling. I even got out the little box she gave me, which I had not opened for years, and when Mrs. Hemway brought my tea I had barely time to close the lid and defeat her disapproving gaze.

My young countryman's perplexity, as he looked at Mrs. Ebbling, had recalled to me the delight and pain she gave me when I was of his years. I sat looking at her face and trying to see it through his eyes—freshly, as I saw it first upon the deck of the *Germania,* twenty years ago. Was it her loveliness, I often ask myself, or her loneliness, or her simplicity, or was it merely my own youth? Was her mystery only that of the mysterious north out of which she came? I still feel that she was very different from all the beautiful and brilliant women I have known; as the night is different from the day, or as the sea is different from the land. But this is our story, as it comes back to me.

For two years I had been studying Italian and working in the capacity of clerk to the American legation at Rome, and I was going home to secure my first consular appointment. Upon boarding my steamer at Genoa, I saw my luggage into my cabin and then started for a rapid circuit of the deck. Everything promised well. The boat was thinly peopled, even for a July crossing; the decks were roomy; the day was fine; the sea was blue; I was sure of my appointment, and, best of all, I was coming back to Italy. All these things were in my mind when I stopped sharply before a chaise longue placed sidewise near the stern. Its occupant was a woman, apparently ill, who lay with her eyes closed, and in her open arm was a chubby little red-haired girl, asleep. I can still remember that first glance at Mrs. Ebbling, and how I stopped as a wheel does when the band slips. Her splendid, vigorous body lay still and relaxed under the loose folds of her clothing, her white throat and arms and red-gold hair were drenched with sunlight. Such hair as it was: wayward as some kind of gleaming seaweed that curls and undulates with the tide. A moment gave me her face; the high cheekbones, the thin cheeks, the gentle chin, arching back to a girlish throat, and singular loveliness of the mouth. Even then it flashed through me that the mouth gave the whole face its peculiar beauty and distinction. It was proud and sad and tender, and strangely calm. The curve of the lips could not have been cut more cleanly with the most delicate instrument, and whatever shade of feeling passed over them seemed to partake of their exquisiteness.

But I am anticipating. While I stood stupidly staring (as if, at twenty-five, I had never before beheld a beautiful woman) the whistles broke into a hoarse scream, and the deck under us began to vibrate. The woman opened her eyes, and the little girl struggled into a sitting position, rolled out of her mother's arm, and ran to the deck rail. After putting my chair near the stern, I went forward to see the gangplank up and did not return until we were dragging out to sea at the end of a long towline.

The woman in the chaise longue was still alone. She lay there all day, looking at the sea. The little girl, Carin, played noisily about the deck. Occasionally she returned and struggled up into the chair, plunged her head, round and red as a little pumpkin, against her mother's shoulder in an impetuous embrace, and then struggled down again with a lively flourishing of arms and legs. Her mother took such opportunities to pull up the child's socks or to smooth the fiery little braids; her beautiful hands, rather large and very white, played about the riotous little girl with a quieting tenderness. Carin chattered away in Italian and kept asking for her father, only to be told that he was busy.

When any of the ship's officers passed, they stopped for a word with my neighbor, and I heard the first mate address her as Mrs. Ebbling. When they spoke to her, she smiled appreciatively and answered in low, faltering Italian, but I fancied that she was glad when they passed on and left her to her fixed contemplation of the sea. Her eyes seemed to drink the color of it all day long, and after every interruption they went back to it. There was a kind of pleasure in watching her satisfaction, a kind of excitement in wondering what the water made her remember or forget. She seemed not to wish to talk to anyone, but I knew I should like to hear whatever she might be thinking. One could catch some hint of her thoughts, I imagined, from the shadows that came and went across her lips, like the reflection of light clouds. She had a pile of books beside her, but she did not read, and neither could I. I gave up trying at last, and watched the sea, very conscious of her presence, almost of her thoughts. When the sun dropped low and shone in her face, I rose and asked if she would like me to move her chair. She smiled and thanked me, but said the sun was good for her. Her yellow-hazel eyes followed me for a moment and then went back to the sea.

After the first bugle sounded for dinner, a heavy man in uniform came up the deck and stood beside the chaise longue, looking down at its two occupants with a smile of satisfied possession. The breast of his trim coat was hidden by waves of soft blond beard, as long and heavy as a woman's hair, which blew about his face in glittering profusion. He wore a large turquoise ring upon the thick hand that he rubbed good-humoredly over the little girl's head. To her he spoke Italian, but he and his wife conversed in some Scandinavian tongue. He stood stroking his fine beard until the second bugle blew, then bent stiffly from his hips, like a soldier, and patted his wife's hand as it lay on the arm of her chair. He hurried down the deck, taking stock of the passengers as he went, and stopped before a thin girl with frizzed hair and a lace coat, asking her a facetious question in thick English. They began to talk about Chicago and went below. Later I saw him at the head of his table in the dining room, the befrizzed Chicago lady on his left. They must have got a famous start at luncheon, for by the end of the dinner Ebbling was peeling figs for her and presenting them on the end of a fork.

The doctor confided to me that Ebbling was the chief engineer and the dandy of the boat; but this time he would have to behave himself, for he had brought his sick wife along for the voyage. She had a bad heart valve, he added, and was in a serious way.

After dinner Ebbling disappeared, presumably to his engines, and at ten o'clock, when the stewardess came to put Mrs. Ebbling to bed, I helped her to rise from her chair, and the second mate ran up and supported her down to her cabin. About midnight I found the engineer in the card room, playing with the doctor, an Italian naval officer, and the commodore of a Long Island yacht club. His face was even pinker than it had been at dinner, and his fine beard was full of smoke. I thought a long while about Ebbling and his wife before I went to sleep.

The next morning we tied up at Naples to take on our cargo, and I went on shore for the day. I did not, however, entirely escape the ubiquitous engineer, whom I saw lunching with the Long Island commodore at a hotel in the Santa Lucia. When I returned to the boat in the early evening, the passengers had gone down to dinner, and I found Mrs. Ebbling quite alone upon the deserted deck. I approached her and asked whether she had had a dull day. She looked up smiling and shook her head, as if her Italian had quite failed her. I saw that she was flushed with excitement, and her yellow eyes were shining like two clear topazes.

"Dull? Oh, no! I love to watch Naples from the sea, in this white heat. She has just lain there on her hillside among the vines and laughed for me all day long. I have been able to pick out many of the places I like best."

I felt that she was really going to talk to me at last. She had turned to me frankly, as to an old acquaintance, and seemed not to be hiding from me anything of what she felt. I sat down in a glow of pleasure and excitement and asked her if she knew Naples well.

"Oh, yes! I lived there for a year after I was first married. My husband has a great many friends in Naples. But he was at sea most of the time, so I went about alone. Nothing helps one to know a city like that. I came first by sea, like this. Directly to Naples from Finmark, and I had never been south before." Mrs. Ebbling stopped and looked over my shoulder. Then, with a quick, eager glance at me, she said abruptly: "It was like a baptism of fire. Nothing has ever been quite the same since. Imagine how this bay looked to a Finmark girl. It seemed like the overture to Italy."

I laughed. "And then one goes up the country—song by song and wine by wine."

Mrs. Ebbling sighed. "Ah, yes. It must be fine to follow it. I have never been away from the seaports myself. We live now in Genoa."

The deck steward brought her tray, and I moved forward a little and stood by the rail. When I looked back, she smiled and nodded to let me know that she was not missing anything. I could feel her intentness as keenly as if she were standing beside me.

The sun had disappeared over the high ridge behind the city, and the stone pines stood black and flat against the fires of the afterglow. The lilac haze that hung over the long, lazy slopes of Vesuvius warmed with golden light, and films of blue vapor began to float down toward Baiae. The sky, the sea, and the city between them turned a shimmering violet, fading grayer as the lights began to glow like luminous pearls along the waterfront—the necklace of an irreclaimable queen. Behind me I heard a low exclamation: a slight, stifled sound, but it seemed the perfect vocalization of that weariness with which we at last let go of beauty, after we have held it until the senses are darkened. When I turned to her again, she seemed to have fallen asleep.

That night, as we were moving out to sea and the tail lights of Naples were winking across the widening stretch of black water, I helped Mrs. Ebbling to the foot of the stairway. She drew herself up from her chair with effort and leaned on me wearily. I could have carried her all night without fatigue.

"May I come and talk to you tomorrow?" I asked. She did not reply at once. "Like an old friend?" I added. She gave me her languid hand, and her mouth, set with the exertion of walking, softened altogether. *"Grazia,"* she murmured.

I returned to the deck and joined a group of my countrywomen, who, primed with inexhaustible information, were discussing the baseness of Renaissance art. They were intelligent and alert, and as they leaned forward in their deck chairs under the circle of light, their faces recalled to me Rembrandt's picture of a clinical lecture. I heard them through, against my will, and then went to the stern to smoke and to see the last of the island lights. The sky had clouded over, and a soft, melancholy wind was rushing over the sea. I could not help thinking how disappointed I would be if rain should keep Mrs. Ebbling in her cabin tomorrow. My mind played constantly with her image. At one moment she was very clear and directly in front of me; the next she was far away. Whatever else I thought about, some part of my consciousness was busy with Mrs. Ebbling—hunting for her, finding her, losing her, then groping again. How was it that I was so conscious of whatever she might be feeling—that when she sat still behind me and watched the evening sky, I had had a sense of speed and change, almost of danger, and when she was tired and sighed, I had wished for night and loneliness?

II

Though when we are young we seldom think much about it, there is now and again a golden day when we feel a sudden, arrogant pride in our youth; in the lightness of our feet and the strength of our arms, in the warm fluid that courses so surely within us; when we are conscious of something powerful and mercurial in our breasts, which comes up wave after wave and leaves us irresponsible and free. All the next morning I felt this flow of life, which continually impelled me toward Mrs. Ebbling. After the merest greeting, however, I kept away. I found it pleasant to thwart myself, to measure myself against a current that was sure to carry me with it in the end. I was content to let her watch the sea—the sea that seemed now to have come into me, warm and soft, still and strong. I played shuffleboard with the commodore, who was anxious to keep down his figure, and ran about the deck with the stout legs of the little pumpkin-colored Carin about my neck. It was not until the child was having her afternoon nap below that I at last came up and stood beside her mother.

"You are better today," I exclaimed, looking down at her white gown. She colored unreasonably, and I laughed with a familiarity which she must have accepted as the mere foolish noise of happiness, or it would have seemed impertinent.

We talked at first of a hundred trivial things, and we watched the sea. The coast of Sardinia had lain to our port for some hours and would lie there for hours to come, now advancing in rocky promontories, now retreating behind blue bays. It was the naked south coast of the island, and though our course held very near the shore, not a village or habitation was visible; there was not even a goatherd's hut hidden away among the low, pinkish sandhills: pinkish sandhills and yellow headlands, with dull-colored scrubby bushes massed about their bases and following the dried watercourses. A narrow strip of beach glistened like white paint between the purple sea and the umber rocks, and the whole island lay gleaming in the yellow sunshine and translucent air. Not a wave broke on that fringe of white sand, not the shadow of a cloud played across the bare hills. In the air about us there was no sound but that of a vessel moving rapidly through absolutely still water. She seemed like some great sea-animal, swimming silently, her head well up. The sea before us was so rich and heavy and opaque that it might have been lapis lazuli. It was the blue of legend, simply, the color that satisfies the soul like sleep.

And it was of the sea we talked, for it was the substance of Mrs. Ebbling's story. She seemed always to have been swept along by ocean streams, warm or cold, and to have hovered about the edge of great waters. She was born and had grown up in a little fishing town on the Arctic Ocean. Her father was a doctor, a widower, who lived with his daughter and who divided his time between his books and his fishing rod. Her uncle was skipper on a coasting vessel, and with him she had made many trips along the Norwegian coast. But she was always reading and thinking about the blue seas of the south.

"There was a curious old woman in our village, Dame Ericson, who had been in Italy in her youth. She had gone to Rome to study art, and had copied a great many pictures there. She was well connected, but had little money, and as she grew older and poorer she sold her pictures one by one, until there was scarcely a well-to-do family in our district that did not own one of Dame Ericson's paintings. But she brought home many other strange things: a little orange tree which she cherished until the day of her death, and bits of colored marble, and seashells and pieces of coral, and a thin flask full of water from the Mediterranean. When I was a little girl she used to show me her things and tell me about the south, about the coral fishers, and the pink islands, and the smoking mountains, and the old, underground Naples. I suppose the water in her flask was like any other, but it never seemed so to me. It looked so elastic and alive that I used to think if one unsealed the bottle something penetrating and fruitful might leap out and work an enchantment over Finmark."

Lars Ebbling, I learned, was one of her father's friends. She could remember him from the time when she was a little girl and he a dashing young man who used to come home from the sea and make a stir in the village. After he got his promotion to an Atlantic liner and went south, she did not see him until the summer she was twenty, when he came home to marry her. That was five years ago. The little girl, Carin, was three. From her talk, one might have supposed that Ebbling was proprietor of the Mediterranean and its adjacent lands, and could have kept her away at his pleasure. Her own rights in him she seemed not to consider.

But we wasted very little time on Lars Ebbling. We talked, like two very young persons, of arms and men, of the sea beneath us and the shores it washed. We were carried a little beyond ourselves, for we were in the presence of the things of youth that never change—fleeing past them. Tomorrow they would be gone, and no effort of will or memory could bring them back again. All about us was the sea of great adventure, and below us, caught somewhere in its gleaming meshes, were the bones of nations and navies . . . nations and navies that gave youth its hope and made life something more than a hunger of the bowels. The unpeopled Sardinian coast unfolded gently before us, like something left over out of a world that was gone, a place that might well have had no later news since the corn ships brought the tidings of Actium.

"I shall never go to Sardinia," said Mrs. Ebbling. "It could not possibly be as beautiful as this."

"Neither shall I," I replied.

As I was gong down to dinner that evening, I was stopped by Lars Ebbling, freshly brushed and scented, wearing a white uniform, and polished and glistening as one of his own engines. He smiled at me with his own kind of geniality. "You have been very kind to talk to my wife," he explained. "It is very bad for her this trip that she speaks no English. I am indebted to you."

I told him curtly that he was mistaken, but my acrimony made no impression upon his blandness. I felt that I should certainly strike the fellow if he stood there much longer, running his blue ring up and down his beard. I should probably have hated any man who was Mrs. Ebbling's husband, but Ebbling made me sick.

III

The next day I began my drawing of Mrs. Ebbling. She seemed pleased and a little puzzled when I asked her to sit for me. It occurred to me that she had always been among dull people who took her looks as a matter of course, and that she was not at all sure that she was really beautiful. I can see now her quick, confused look of pleasure. I thought very little about the drawing then, except that the making of it gave me an opportunity to study her face—to look as long as I pleased into her yellow eyes, at the noble lines of her mouth, at her splendid, vigorous hair.

"We have a yellow vine at home," I told her, "that is very like your hair. It seems to be growing while one looks at it, and it twines and tangles about itself and throws out little tendrils in the wind."

"Has it any name?"

"We call it love vine."

How little a thing could disconcert her!

As for me, nothing disconcerted me. I awoke every morning with a sense of speed and joy. At night I loved to hear the swish of the water rushing by. As fast as the pistons could carry us, as fast as the water could bear us, we were going forward to something delightful—to something together. When Mrs. Ebbling told me that she and her husband would be five days in the docks in New York and then return to Genoa, I was not disturbed, for I did not believe her. I came and went, and she sat still all day, watching the water. I heard an American lady say that she watched it like one who is going to die, but even that did not frighten me: I somehow felt that she had promised me to live.

All those long, blue days when I sat beside her talking about Finmark and the sea, she must have known that I loved her. I sat with my hands idle on my knees and let the tide come up in me. It carried me so swiftly that, across the narrow space of deck between us, it must have swayed her, too, a little. I had no wish to disturb or distress her. If a little, a very little of it reached her, I was satisfied. If it drew her softly, but drew her, I wanted no more. Sometimes I could see that even the light pressure of my thoughts made her paler. One still evening, after a long talk, she whispered to me, "You must go and walk now, and—don't think about me." She had been held too long and too closely in my thoughts, and she begged me to release her for a little while. I went out into the bow and put her far away, at the skyline, with the faintest star, and thought of her gently across the water. When I went back to her, she was asleep.

But even in those first days I had my hours of misery. Why, for instance, should she have been born in Finmark, and why should Lars Ebbling have been her only door of escape? Why should she be silently taking leave of the world at the age when I was just beginning it, having had nothing, nothing of whatever is worthwhile?

She never talked about taking leave of things and yet I sometimes felt that she was counting the sunsets. One yellow afternoon, when we were gliding between the shores of Spain and Africa, she spoke of her illness for the first time. I had got some magnolias at Gibraltar, and she wore a bunch of them in her girdle and the rest lay on her lap. She held the cool leaves against her cheek and fingered the white petals. "I can never," she remarked, "get enough of the flowers of the south. They make me breathless, just as they did at first. Because of them I should like to live a long while—almost forever."

I leaned forward and looked at her. "We could live almost forever if we had enough courage. It's of our lives that we die. If we had the courage to change it all, to run away to some blue coast like that over there, we could live on and on, until we were tired."

She smiled tolerantly and looked southward through half-shut eyes. "I am afraid I should never have courage enough to go behind that mountain, at least. Look at it, it looks as if it hid horrible things."

A sea mist, blown in from the Atlantic, began to mask the impassive African coast, and above the fog, the gray mountain peak took on the angry red of the sunset. It burned sullen and threatening until the dark land drew the night about her and settled back into the sea. We watched it sink, while under us, slowly but ever increasing, we felt the throb of the Atlantic come and go, the thrill of the vast, untamed waters of that lugubrious and passionate sea. I drew Mrs. Ebbling's wraps about her and shut the magnolias under her cloak. When I left her, she slipped me one warm, white flower.

IV

From the Straits of Gibraltar we dropped into the abyss, and by morning we were rolling in the trough of a sea that drew us down and held us deep, shaking us gently back and forth until the timbers creaked, and then shooting us out on the crest of a swelling mountain. The water was bright and blue, but so cold that the breath of it penetrated one's bones, as if the chill of the deep underfathoms of the sea were being loosed upon us. There were not more than a dozen people upon the deck that morning, and Mrs. Ebbling was sheltered behind the stern, muffled in a sea jacket, with drops of moisture upon her long lashes and on her hair. When a shower of icy spray beat back over the deck rail, she took it gleefully.

"After all," she insisted, "this is my own kind of water; the kind I was born in. This is first cousin to the Pole waters, and the sea we have left is only a kind of fairy tale. It's like the burnt-out volcanoes; its day is over. This is the real sea now, where the doings of the world go on."

"It is not our reality, at any rate," I answered.

"Oh, yes, it is! These are the waters that carry men to their work, and they will carry you to yours."

I sat down and watched her hair grow more alive and iridescent in the moisture. "You are pleased to take an attitude," I complained.

"No, I don't love realities any more than another, but I admit them, all the same."

"And who are you and I to define the realities?"

"Our minds define them clearly enough, yours and mine, everybody's. Those are the lines we never cross, though we flee from the equator to the Pole. I have never really got out of Finmark, of course. I shall live and die in a fishing town on the Arctic Ocean, and the blue seas and the pink islands are as much a dream as they ever were. All the same, I shall continue to dream them."

The Gulf Stream gave us warm blue days again, but pale, like sad memories. The water had faded, and the thin, tepid sunshine made something tighten about one's heart. The stars watched us coldly, and seemed always to be asking me what I was going to do. The advancing line on the chart, which at first had been mere foolishness, began to mean something, and the wind from the west brought disturbing fears and forebodings. I slept lightly, and all day I was restless and uncertain except when I was with Mrs. Ebbling. She quieted me as she did little Carin, and soothed me without saying anything, as she had done that evening at Naples when we watched the sunset. It seemed to me that every day her eyes grew more tender and her lips more calm. A kind of fortitude seemed to be gathering about her mouth, and I dreaded it. Yet when, in an involuntary glance, I put to her the question that tortured me, her eyes always met mine steadily, deep and gentle and full of reassurance. That I had my word at last happened almost by accident.

On the second night out from shore there was the concert for the Sailors' Orphanage, and Mrs. Ebbling dressed and went down to dinner for the first time, and sat on her husband's right. I was not the only one who was glad to see her. Even the women were pleased. She wore a pale green gown, and she came up out of it regally white and gold. I was so proud that I blushed when anyone spoke of her. After dinner she was standing by her deck chair talking to her husband when people began to go below for the concert. She took up a long cloak and attempted to put it on. The wind blew the light thing about, and Ebbling chatted and smiled his public smile while she struggled with it. Suddenly his roving eye caught sight of the Chicago girl, who was having a similar difficulty with her draperies, and he pranced half the length of the deck to assist her. I had been watching from the rail, and when she was left alone I threw my cigar away and wrapped Mrs. Ebbling up roughly.

"Don't go down," I begged. "Stay up here. I want to talk to you."

She hesitated a moment and looked at me thoughtfully. Then, with a sigh, she sat down. Everyone hurried down to the saloon, and we were absolutely alone at last, behind the shelter of the stern, with the thick darkness all about us and a warm east wind rushing over the sea. I was too sore and angry to think. I leaned toward her, holding the arm of her chair with both hands, and began anywhere.

"You remember those two blue coasts out of Gibraltar? It shall be either one you choose, if you will come with me. I have not much money, but we shall get on somehow. There has got to be an end of this. We are neither one of us cowards, and this is humiliating, intolerable."

She sat looking down at her hands, and I pulled her chair impatiently toward me.

"I felt," she said at last, "that you were going to say something like this. You are sorry for me, and I don't wish to be pitied. You think Ebbling neglects me, but you are mistaken. He has had his disappointments, too. He wants children and a gay, hospitable house, and he is tied to a sick woman who cannot get on with people. He has more to complain of than I have, and yet he bears with me. I am grateful to him, and there is no more to be said."

"Oh, isn't there?" I cried, "and I?"

She laid her hand entreatingly upon my arm. "Ah, you, you! Don't ask me to talk about that. *You —*" Her fingers slipped down my coat sleeve to my hand and pressed it. I caught her two hands and held them, telling her I would never let them go.

"And you meant to leave me day after tomorrow, to say goodbye to me as you will to the other people on this boat? You meant to cut me adrift like this, with my heart on fire and all my life unspent in me?"

She sighed despondently. "I am willing to suffer—whatever I must suffer—to have had you," she answered simply. "I was ill—and so lonely—and it came so quickly and quietly. Ah, don't begrudge it to me! Do not leave me in bitterness. If I have been wrong, forgive me." She bowed her head and pressed my fingers entreatingly. A warm tear splashed on my hand. It occurred to me that she bore my anger as she bore little Carin's importunities, as she bore Ebbling. What a circle of pettiness she had about her! I fell back in my chair and my hands dropped at my side. I felt like a creature with its back broken. I asked her what she wished me to do.

"Don't ask me," she whispered. "There is nothing that we can do. I thought you knew that. You forget that—that I am too ill to begin my life over. Even if there were nothing else in the way, that would be enough. And that is what has made it all possible, our loving each other, I mean. If I were well, we couldn't have had even this much. Don't reproach me. Hasn't it been at all pleasant to you to find me waiting for you every morning, to feel me thinking of you when you went to sleep? Every night I have watched the sea for you, as if it were mine and I had made it, and I have listened to the water rushing by you, full of sleep and youth and hope. And everything you had done or said during the day came back to me, and when I went to sleep it was only to feel you more. You see there was never anyone else; I have never thought of anyone in the dark but you." She spoke pleadingly, and her voice had sunk so low that I could scarcely hear her.

"And yet you will do nothing," I groaned. "You will dare nothing. You will give me nothing."

"Don't say that. When I leave you day after tomorrow, I shall have given you all my life. I can't tell you how, but it is true. There is something in each of us that does not belong to the family or to society, not even to ourselves. Sometimes it is given in marriage, and sometimes it is given in love, but oftener it is never given at all. We have nothing to do with giving or withholding it. It is a wild thing that sings in us once and flies away and never comes back, and mine has flown to you. When one loves like that, it is enough, somehow. The other things can go if they must. That is why I can live without you, and die without you."

I caught her hands and looked into her eyes that shone warm in the darkness. She shivered and whispered in a tone so different from any I ever heard from her before or afterward: "Do you grudge it to me? You are so young and strong, and you have everything before you. I shall have only a little while to want you in—and I could want you forever and not weary." I kissed her hair, her cheeks, her lips, until her head fell forward on my shoulder and she put my face away with her soft, trembling fingers. She took my hand and held it close to her, in both her own. We sat silent, and the moments came and went, bringing us closer and closer, and the wind and water rushed by us, obliterating our tomorrows and all our yesterdays.

The next day Mrs. Ebbling kept her cabin, and I sat stupidly by her chair until dark, with the rugged little girl to keep me company, and an occasional nod from the engineer.

I saw Mrs. Ebbling again only for a few moments, when we were coming into the New York harbor. She wore a street dress and a hat, and these alone would have made her seem far away from me. She was very pale and looked down when she spoke to me, as if she had been guilty of a wrong toward me. I have never been able to remember that interview without heartache and shame, but then I was too desperate to care about anything. I stood like a wooden post and let her approach me, let her speak to me, let her leave me. She came up to me as if it were a hard thing to do, and held out a little package, timidly, and her gloved hand shook as if she were afraid of me.

"I want to give you something," she said. "You will not want it now, so I shall ask you to keep it until you hear from me. You gave me your address a long time ago, when you were making that drawing. Some day I shall write to you and ask you to open this. You must not come to tell me goodbye this morning, but I shall be watching you when you go ashore. Please don't forget that."

I took the little box mechanically and thanked her. I think my eyes must have filled, for she uttered an exclamation of pity, touched my sleeve quickly, and left me. It was one of those strange, low, musical exclamations which meant everything and nothing, like the one that had thrilled me that night at Naples, and it was the last sound I ever heard from her lips.

An hour later I went on shore, one of those who crowded over the gangplank the moment it was lowered. But the next afternoon I wandered back to the docks and went on board the *Germania.* I asked for the engineer, and he came up in his shirt sleeves from the engine room. He was red and disheveled, angry and voluble; his bright eye had a hard glint, and I did not once see his masterful smile. When he heard my inquiry he became profane. Mrs. Ebbling had sailed for Bremen on the *Hohenstauffen* that morning at eleven o'clock. She had decided to return by the northern route and pay a visit to her father in Finmark. She was in no condition to travel alone, he said. He evidently smarted under her extravagance. But who, he asked, with a blow of his fist on the rail, could stand between a woman and her whim? She had always been a willful girl, and she had a doting father behind her. When she set her head with the wind, there was no holding her; she ought to have married the Arctic Ocean. I think Ebbling was still talking when I walked away.

I spent that winter in New York. My consular appointment hung fire (indeed, I did not pursue it with much enthusiasm), and I had a good many idle hours in which to think of Mrs. Ebbling. She had never mentioned the name of her father's village, and somehow I could never quite bring myself to go to the docks when Ebbling's boat was in and ask for news of her. More than once I made up my mind definitely to go to Finmark and take my chance at finding her; the shipping people would know where Ebbling came from. But I never went. I have often wondered why. When my resolve was made and my courage high, when I could almost feel myself approaching her, suddenly everything crumbled under me, and I fell back as I had done that night when I dropped her hands, after telling her, only a moment before, that I would never let them go.

In the twilight of a wet March day, when the gutters were running black outside and the square was liquefying under crusts of dirty snow, the housekeeper brought me a damp letter which bore a blurred foreign postmark. It was from Niels Nannestad, who wrote that it was his sad duty to inform me that his daughter, Alexandra Ebbling, had died on the second day of February, in the twenty-sixth year of her age. Complying with her request, he enclosed a letter which she had written some days before her death.

I at last brought myself to break the seal of the second letter. It read thus:

My Friend:

You may open now the little package I gave you. May I ask you to keep it? I gave it to you because there is no one else who would care about it in just that way. Ever since I left you I have been thinking what it would be like to live a lifetime caring and being cared for like that. It was not the life I was meant to live, and yet, in a way, I have been living it ever since I first knew you.

Of course you understand now why I could not go with you. I would have spoiled your life for you. Besides that, I was ill—and I was too proud to give you the shadow of myself. I had much to give you, if you had come earlier. As it was, I was ashamed. Vanity sometimes saves us when nothing else will, and mine saved you. Thank you for everything. I hold this to my heart, where I once held your hand.

ALEXANDRA

The dusk had thickened into night long before I got up from my chair and took the little box from its place in my desk drawer. I opened it and lifted out a thick coil, cut from where her hair grew thickest and brightest. It was tied firmly at one end, and when it fell over my arm it curled and clung about my sleeve like a living thing set free. How it gleamed, how it still gleams in the firelight! It was warm and softly scented under my lips, and stirred under my breath like seaweed in the tide . . . this, and a withered magnolia flower, and two pink seashells—nothing more. And it was all twenty years ago!

The Joy of Nelly Deane

NELL AND I were almost ready to go on for the last act of *Queen Esther,* and we had for the moment got rid of our three patient dressers, Mrs. Dow, Mrs. Freeze, and Mrs. Spinny. Nell was peering over my shoulder into the little cracked looking glass that Mrs. Dow had taken from its nail on her kitchen wall and brought down to the church under her shawl that morning. When she realized that we were alone, Nell whispered to me in the quick, fierce way she had:

"Say, Peggy, won't you go up and stay with me tonight? Scott Spinny's asked to take me home, and I don't want to walk up with him alone."

"I guess so, if you'll ask my mother."

"Oh, I'll fix her!" Nell laughed, with a toss of her head which meant that she usually got what she wanted, even from people much less tractable than my mother.

In a moment our tiring women were back again. The three old ladies—at least they seemed old to us—fluttered about us, more agitated than we were ourselves. It seemed as though they would never leave off patting Nell and touching her up. They kept trying things this way and that, never able in the end to decide which way was best. They wouldn't hear to her using rouge, and as they powdered her neck and arms, Mrs. Freeze murmured that she hoped we wouldn't get into the habit of using such things. Mrs. Spinny divided her time between pulling up and tucking down the "illusion" that filled in the square neck of Nelly's dress. She didn't like things much low, she said; but after she had pulled it up, she stood back and looked at Nell thoughtfully through her glasses. While the excited girl was reaching for this and that, buttoning a slipper, pinning down a curl, Mrs. Spinny's smile softened more and more until, just before Esther made her entrance, the old lady tiptoed up to her and softly tucked the illusion down as far as it would go.

"She's so pink; it seems a pity not," she whispered apologetically to Mrs. Dow.

Everyone admitted that Nelly was the prettiest girl in Riverbend, and the gayest—oh, the gayest! When she was not singing, she was laughing. When she was not laid up with a broken arm, the outcome of a foolhardy coasting feat, or suspended from school because she ran away at recess to go buggy-riding with Guy Franklin, she was sure to be up to mischief of some sort. Twice she broke through the ice and got soused in the river because she never looked where she skated or cared what happened so long as she went fast enough. After the second of these duckings our three dressers declared that she was trying to be a Baptist despite herself.

Mrs. Spinny and Mrs. Freeze and Mrs. Dow, who were always hovering about Nelly, often whispered to me their hope that she would eventually come into our church and not "go with the Methodists"; her family were Wesleyans. But to me these artless plans of theirs never wholly explained their watchful affection. They had good daughters themselves—except Mrs. Spinny, who had only the sullen Scott—and they loved their plain girls and thanked God for them. But they loved Nelly differently. They were proud of her pretty figure and yellow-brown eyes, which dilated so easily and sparkled with a kind of golden effervescence. They were always making pretty things for her, always coaxing her to come to the sewing circle, where she knotted her thread, and put in the wrong sleeve, and laughed and chattered and said a great many things that she should not have said, and somehow always warmed their hearts. I think they loved her for her unquenchable joy.

All the Baptist ladies liked Nell, even those who criticized her most severely, but the three who were first in fighting the battles of our little church, who held it together by their prayers and the labor of their hands, watched over her as they did over Mrs. Dow's century plant before it blossomed. They looked for her on Sunday morning and smiled at her as she hurried, always a little late, up to the choir. When she rose and stood behind the organ and sang "There Is a Green Hill," one could see Mrs. Dow and Mrs. Freeze settle back in their accustomed seats and look up at her as if she had just come from that hill and had brought them glad tidings.

It was because I sang contralto, or, as we said, alto, in the Baptist choir that Nell and I became friends. She was so gay and grown up, so busy with parties and dances and picnics, that I would scarcely have seen much of her had we not sung together. She liked me better than she did any of the older girls, who tried clumsily to be like her, and I felt almost as solicitous and admiring as did Mrs. Dow and Mrs. Spinny. I think even then I must have loved to see her bloom and glow, and I loved to hear her sing, in "The Ninety and Nine,"

But one was out on the hills away

in her sweet, strong voice. Nell had never had a singing lesson, but she had sung from the time she could talk, and Mrs. Dow used fondly to say that it was singing so much that made her figure so pretty.

After I went into the choir it was found to be easier to get Nelly to choir practice. If I stopped outside her gate on my way to church and coaxed her, she usually laughed, ran in for her hat and jacket, and went along with me. The three old ladies fostered our friendship, and because I was "quiet," they esteemed me a good influence for Nelly. This view was propounded in a sewing-circle discussion and, leaking down to us through our mothers, greatly amused us. Dear old ladies! It was so manifestly for what Nell was that they loved her, and yet they were always looking for "influences" to change her.

The *Queen Esther* performance had cost us three months of hard practice, and it was not easy to keep Nell up to attending the tedious rehearsals. Some of the boys we knew were in the chorus of Assyrian youths, but the solo cast was made up of older people, and Nell found them very poky. We gave the cantata in the Baptist church on Christmas Eve, "to a crowded house," as the Riverbend *Messenger* truly chronicled. The country folk for miles about had come in through a deep snow, and their teams and wagons stood in a long row at the hitch-bars on each side of the church door. It was certainly Nelly's night, for however much the tenor—he was her schoolmaster, and naturally thought poorly of her—might try to eclipse her in his dolorous solos about the rivers of Babylon, there would be no doubt as to whom the people had come to hear—and to see.

After the performance was over, our fathers and mothers came back to the dressing rooms—the little rooms behind the baptistry where the candidates for baptism were robed—to congratulate us, and Nell persuaded my mother to let me go home with her. This arrangement may not have been wholly agreeable to Scott Spinny, who stood glumly waiting at the baptistry door; though I used to think he dogged Nell's steps not so much for any pleasure he got from being with her as for the pleasure of keeping other people away. Dear little Mrs. Spinny was perpetually in a state of humiliation on account of his bad manners, and she tried by a very special tenderness to make up to Nelly for the remissness of her ungracious son.

Scott was a spare, muscular fellow, good-looking, but with a face so set and dark that I used to think it very like the castings he sold. He was taciturn and domineering, and Nell rather liked to provoke him. Her father was so easy with her that she seemed to enjoy being ordered about now and then. That night, when everyone was praising her and telling her how well she sang and how pretty she looked, Scott only said, as we came out of the dressing room:

"Have you got your high shoes on?"

"No; but I've got rubbers on over my low ones. Mother doesn't care."

"Well, you just go back and put 'em on as fast as you can."

Nell made a face at him and ran back, laughing. Her mother, fat, comfortable Mrs. Deane, was immensely amused at this.

"That's right, Scott," she chuckled. "You can do enough more with her than I can. She walks right over me an' Jud."

Scott grinned. If he was proud of Nelly, the last thing he wished to do was to show it. When she came back he began to nag again. "What are you going to do with all those flowers? They'll freeze stiff as pokers."

"Well, there won't none of *your* flowers freeze, Scott Spinny, so there!" Nell snapped. She had the best of him that time, and the Assyrian youths rejoiced. They were most of them high-school boys, and the poorest of them had "chipped in" and sent all the way to Denver for Queen Esther's flowers. There were bouquets from half-a-dozen townspeople, too, but none from Scott. Scott was a prosperous hardware merchant and notoriously penurious, though he saved his face, as the boys said, by giving liberally to the church.

"There's no use freezing the fool things, anyhow. You get me some newspapers, and I'll wrap 'em up." Scott took from his pocket a folded copy of the Riverbend *Messenger* and began laboriously to wrap up one of the bouquets. When we left the church door he bore three large newspaper bundles, carrying them as carefully as if they had been so many newly frosted wedding cakes, and left Nell and me to shift for ourselves as we floundered along the snow-burdened sidewalk.

Although it was after midnight, lights were shining from many of the little wooden houses, and the roofs and shrubbery were so deep in snow that Riverbend looked as if it had been tucked down into a warm bed. The companies of people, all coming from church, tramping this way and that toward their homes and calling "Good night" and "Merry Christmas" as they parted company, all seemed to us very unusual and exciting.

When we got home, Mrs. Deane had a cold supper ready, and Jud Deane had already taken off his shoes and fallen to on his fried chicken and pie. He was so proud of his pretty daughter that he must give her her Christmas presents then and there, and he went into the sleeping chamber behind the dining room and from the depths of his wife's closet brought out a short sealskin jacket and a round cap and made Nelly put them on.

Mrs. Deane, who sat busy between a plate of spice cake and a tray piled with her famous whipped-cream tarts, laughed inordinately at his behavior.

"Ain't he worse than any kid you ever see? He's been running to that closet like a cat shut away from her kittens. I wonder Nell ain't caught on before this. I did think he'd make out now to keep 'em till Christmas morning; but he's never made out to keep anything yet."

That was true enough, and fortunately Jud's inability to keep anything seemed always to present a highly humorous aspect to his wife. Mrs. Deane put her heart into her cooking, and said that so long as a man was a good provider she had no cause to complain. Other people were not so charitable toward Jud's failing. I remember how many strictures were passed upon that little sealskin and how he was censured for his extravagance. But what a public-spirited thing, after all, it was for him to do! How, the winter through, we all enjoyed seeing Nell skating on the river or running about the town with the brown collar turned up about her bright cheeks and her hair blowing out from under the round cap! "No seal," Mrs. Dow said, "would have begrudged it to her. Why should we?" This was at the sewing circle, when the new coat was under grave discussion.

At last Nelly and I got upstairs and undressed, and the pad of Jud's slippered feet about the kitchen premises—where he was carrying up from the cellar things that might freeze—ceased. He called "Good night, daughter" from the foot of the stairs, and the house grew quiet. But one is not a prima donna the first time for nothing, and it seemed as if we could not go to bed. Our light must have burned long after every other in Riverbend was out. The muslin curtains of Nell's bed were drawn back; Mrs. Deane had turned down the white counterpane and taken off the shams and smoothed the pillows for us. But their fair plumpness offered no temptation to two such hot young heads. We could not let go of life even for a little while. We sat and talked in Nell's cozy room, where there was a tiny, white fur rug—the only one in Riverbend—before the bed; and there were white sash curtains, and the prettiest little desk and dressing table I had ever seen. It was a warm, gay little room, flooded all day long with sunlight from east and south windows that had climbing roses all about them in summer. About the dresser were photographs of adoring high-school boys; and one of Guy Franklin, much groomed and barbered, in a dress coat and a boutonniere. I never liked to see that photograph there. The home boys looked properly modest and bashful on the dresser, but he seemed to be staring impudently all the time.

I knew nothing definite against Guy, but in Riverbend all "traveling men" were considered worldly and wicked. He traveled for a Chicago dry-goods firm, and our fathers didn't like him because he put extravagant ideas into our mothers' heads. He had very smooth and flattering ways, and he introduced into our simple community a great variety of perfumes and scented soaps, and he always reminded me of the merchants in Caesar, who brought into Gaul "those things which effeminate the mind," as we translated that delightfully easy passage.

Nell was sitting before the dressing table in her nightgown, holding the new fur coat and rubbing her cheek against it, when I saw a sudden gleam of tears in her eyes. "You know, Peggy," she said in her quick, impetuous way, "this makes me feel bad. I've got a secret from my daddy."

I can see her now, so pink and eager, her brown hair in two springy braids down her back, and her eyes shining with tears and with something even softer and more tremulous.

"I'm engaged, Peggy," she whispered, "really and truly."

She leaned forward, unbuttoning her nightgown, and there on her breast, hung by a little gold chain about her neck, was a diamond ring—Guy Franklin's solitaire; everyone in Riverbend knew it well.

"I'm going to live in Chicago, and take singing lessons, and go to operas, and do all those nice things—oh, everything! I know you don't like him, Peggy, but you know you *are* a kid. You'll see how it is yourself when you grow up. He's so *different* from our boys, and he's just terribly in love with me. And then, Peggy"—flushing all down over her soft shoulders—"I'm awfully fond of him, too. Awfully."

"Are you, Nell, truly?" I whispered. She seemed so changed to me by the warm light in her eyes and that delicate suffusion of color. I felt as I did when I got up early on picnic mornings in summer, and saw the dawn come up in the breathless sky above the river meadows and make all the cornfields golden.

"Sure I do, Peggy; don't look so solemn. It's nothing to look that way about, kid. It's nice." She threw her arms about me suddenly and hugged me.

"I hate to think about your going so far away from us all, Nell."

"Oh, you'll love to come and visit me. Just you wait."

She began breathlessly to go over things Guy Franklin had told her about Chicago, until I seemed to see it all looming up out there under the stars that kept watch over our little sleeping town. We had neither of us ever been to a city, but we knew what it would be like. We heard it throbbing like great engines, and calling to us, that faraway world. Even after we had opened the windows and scurried into bed, we seemed to feel a pulsation across all the miles of snow. The winter silence trembled with it, and the air was full of something new that seemed to break over us in soft waves. In that snug, warm little bed I had a sense of imminent change and danger. I was somehow afraid for Nelly when I heard her breathing so quickly beside me, and I put my arm about her protectingly as we drifted toward sleep.

In the following spring we were both graduated from the Riverbend high school, and I went away to college. My family moved to Denver, and during the next four years I heard very little of Nelly Deane. My life was crowded with new people and new experiences, and I am afraid I held her little in mind. I heard indirectly that Jud Deane had lost what little property he owned in a luckless venture in Cripple Creek, and that he had been able to keep his house in Riverbend only through the clemency of his creditors. Guy Franklin had his route changed and did not go to Riverbend anymore. He married the daughter of a rich cattleman out near Long Pine, and ran a dry-goods store of his own. Mrs. Dow wrote me a long letter about once a year, and in one of these she told me that Nelly was teaching in the sixth grade in the Riverbend school.

> Dear Nelly does not like teaching very well. The children try her, and she is so pretty it seems a pity for her to be tied down to uncongenial employment. Scott is still very attentive, and I have noticed him look up at the window of Nelly's room in a very determined way as he goes home to dinner. Scott continues prosperous; he has made money during these hard times and now owns both our hardware stores. He is close, but a very honorable fellow. Nelly seems to hold off, but I think Mrs. Spinny has hopes. Nothing would please her more. If Scott were more careful about his appearance, it would help. He of course gets black about his business, and Nelly, you know, is very dainty. People do say his mother does his courting for him, she is so eager. If only Scott does not turn out hard and penurious like his father! We must all have our schooling in this life, but I don't want Nelly's to be too severe. She is a dear girl, and keeps her color.

Mrs. Dow's own schooling had been none too easy. Her husband had long been crippled with rheumatism, and was bitter and faultfinding. Her daughters had married poorly, and one of her sons had fallen into evil ways. But her letters were always cheerful, and in one of them she gently remonstrated with me because I "seemed inclined to take a sad view of life."

In the winter vacation of my senior year I stopped on my way home to visit Mrs. Dow. The first thing she told me when I got into her old buckboard at the station was that "Scott had at last prevailed," and that Nelly was to marry him in the spring. As a preliminary step, Nelly was about to join the Baptist church. "Just think, you will be here for her baptizing! How that will please Nell! She is to be immersed tomorrow night."

I met Scott Spinny in the post office that morning and he gave me a hard grip with one black hand. There was something grim and saturnine about his powerful body and bearded face and his strong, cold hands. I wondered what perverse fate had driven him for eight years to dog the footsteps of a girl whose charm was due to qualities naturally distasteful to him. It still seems strange to me that in easygoing Riverbend, where there were so many boys who could have lived contentedly enough with my little grasshopper, it was the pushing ant who must have her and all her careless ways.

By a kind of unformulated etiquette one did not call upon candidates for baptism on the day of the ceremony, so I had my first glimpse of Nelly that evening. The baptistry was a cemented pit directly under the pulpit rostrum, over which we had our stage when we sang *Queen Esther*. I sat through the sermon somewhat nervously. After the minister, in his long, black gown, had gone down into the water and the choir had finished singing, the door from the dressing room opened, and, led by one of the deacons, Nelly came down the steps into the pool. Oh, she looked so little and meek and chastened! Her white cashmere robe clung about her, and her brown hair was brushed straight back and hung in two soft braids from a little head bent humbly. As she stepped down into the water I shivered with the cold of it, and I remembered sharply how much I had loved her. She went down until the water was well above her waist, and stood white and small, with her hands crossed on her breast, while the minister said the words about being buried with Christ in baptism. Then, lying in his arm, she disappeared under the dark water. "It will be like that when she dies," I thought, and a quick pain caught my heart. The choir began to sing "Washed in the Blood of the Lamb" as she rose again, the door behind the baptistry opened, revealing those three dear guardians, Mrs. Dow, Mrs. Freeze, and Mrs. Spinny, and she went up into their arms.

I went to see Nell next day, up in the little room of many memories. Such a sad, sad visit! She seemed changed—a little embarrassed and quietly despairing. We talked of many of the old Riverbend girls and boys, but she did not mention Guy Franklin or Scott Spinny, except to say that her father had got work in Scott's hardware store. She begged me, putting her hands on my shoulders with something of her old impulsiveness, to come and stay a few days with her. But I was afraid—afraid of what she might tell me and of what I might say. When I sat in that room with all her trinkets, the foolish harvest of her girlhood, lying about, and the white curtains and the little white rug, I thought of Scott Spinny with positive terror and could feel his hard grip on my hand again. I made the best excuse I could about having to hurry on to Denver; but she gave me one quick look, and her eyes ceased to plead. I saw that she understood me perfectly. We had known each other so well. Just once, when I got up to go and had trouble with my veil, she laughed her old merry laugh and told me there were some things I would never learn, for all my schooling.

The next day, when Mrs. Dow drove me down to the station to catch the morning train for Denver, I saw Nelly hurrying to school with several books under her arm. She had been working up her lessons at home, I thought. She was never quick at her books, dear Nell.

It was ten years before I again visited Riverbend. I had been in Rome for a long time, and had fallen into bitter homesickness. One morning, sitting among the dahlias and asters that bloom so bravely upon those gigantic heaps of earth-red ruins that were once the palaces of the Caesars, I broke the seal of one of Mrs. Dow's long yearly letters. It brought so much sad news that I resolved then and there to go home to Riverbend, the only place that had ever really been home to me. Mrs. Dow wrote me that her husband, after years of illness, had died in the cold spell last March. "So good and patient toward the last," she wrote, "and so afraid of giving extra trouble." There was another thing she saved until the last. She wrote on and on, dear woman, about new babies and village improvements, as if she could not bear to tell me; and then it came:

> You will be sad to hear that two months ago our dear Nelly left us. It was a terrible blow to us all. I cannot write about it yet, I fear. I

wake up every morning feeling that I ought to go to her. She went three days after her little boy was born. The baby is a fine child and will live, I think, in spite of everything. He and her little girl, now eight years old, whom she named Margaret, after you, have gone to Mrs. Spinny's. She loves them more than if they were her own. It seems as if already they had made her quite young again. I wish you could see Nelly's children.

Ah, that was what I wanted, to see Nelly's children! The wish came aching from my heart along with the bitter homesick tears, along with a quick, torturing recollection that flashed upon me, as I looked about and tried to collect myself, of how we two had sat in our sunny seat in the corner of the old bare schoolroom one September afternoon and learned the names of the seven hills together. In that place, at that moment, after so many years, how it all came back to me—the warm sun on my back, the chattering girl beside me, the curly hair, the laughing yellow eyes, the stubby little finger on the page! I felt as if even then, when we sat in the sun with our heads together, it was all arranged, written out like a story, that at this moment I should be sitting among the crumbling bricks and drying grass, and she should be lying in the place I knew so well, on that green hill far away.

Mrs. Dow sat with her Christmas sewing in the familiar sitting room, where the carpet and the wallpaper and the tablecover had all faded into soft, dull colors, and even the chromo of Hagar and Ishmael had been toned to the sobriety of age. In the bay window the tall wire flowerstand still bore its little terraces of potted plants, and the big fuchsia and the Martha Washington geranium had blossomed for Christmastide. Mrs. Dow herself did not look greatly changed to me. Her hair, thin ever since I could remember it, was now quite white, but her spare, wiry little person had all its old activity, and her eyes gleamed with the old friendliness behind her silver-bowed glasses. Her gray housedress seemed just like those she used to wear when I ran in after school to take her angelfood cake down to the church supper.

The house sat on a hill, and from behind the geraniums I could see pretty much all of Riverbend, tucked down in the soft snow, and the air above was full of big, loose flakes, falling from a gray sky which betokened settled weather. Indoors the hard-coal burner made a tropical temperature, and glowed a warm orange from its isinglass sides. We sat and visited, the two of us, with a great sense of comfort and completeness. I had reached Riverbend only that morning, and Mrs. Dow, who had been haunted by thoughts of shipwreck and suffering upon wintery seas, kept urging me to draw nearer to the fire and suggesting incidental refreshment. We had chattered all through the winter morning and most of the afternoon, taking up one after another of the Riverbend girls and boys, and agreeing that we had reason to be well satisfied with most of them. Finally, after a long pause in which I had listened to the contented ticking of the clock and the crackle of the coal, I put the question I had until then held back:

"And now, Mrs. Dow, tell me about the one we loved best of all. Since I got your letter I've thought of her every day. Tell me all about Scott and Nelly."

The tears flashed behind her glasses, and she smoothed the little pink bag on her knee.

"Well, dear, I'm afraid Scott proved to be a hard man, like his father. But we must remember that Nelly always had Mrs. Spinny. I never saw anything like the love there was between those two. After Nelly lost her own father and mother, she looked to Mrs. Spinny for everything. When Scott was too unreasonable, his mother could 'most always prevail upon him. She never lifted a hand to fight her own battles with Scott's father, but she was never afraid to speak up for Nelly. And then Nelly took great comfort of her little girl. Such a lovely child!"

"Had she been very ill before the little baby came?"

"No, Margaret; I'm afraid 'twas all because they had the wrong doctor. I feel confident that either Dr. Tom or Dr. Jones could have brought her through. But, you see, Scott had offended them both, and they'd stopped trading at his store, so he would have young Dr. Fox, a boy just out of college and a stranger. He got scared and didn't know what to do. Mrs. Spinny felt he wasn't doing right, so she sent for Mrs. Freeze and me. It seemed like Nelly had got discouraged. Scott would move into their big new house before the plastering was dry, and though 'twas summer, she had taken a terrible cold that seemed to have drained her, and she took no interest in fixing the place up. Mrs. Spinny had been down with her back again and wasn't able to help, and things was just anyway. We won't talk about that, Margaret; I think 'twould hurt Mrs. Spinny to have you know. She nearly died of mortification when she sent for us, and blamed her poor back. We did get Nelly fixed up nicely before she died. I prevailed upon Dr. Tom to come in at the last, and it 'most broke his heart. 'Why, Mis' Dow,' he said, 'if you'd only have come and told me how 'twas, I'd have come and carried her right off in my arms.' "

"Oh, Mrs. Dow," I cried, "then it needn't have been?"

Mrs. Dow dropped her needle and clasped her hands quickly. "We mustn't look at it that way, dear," she said tremulously and a little sternly. "We mustn't let ourselves. We must just feel that our Lord wanted her *then,* and took her to Himself. When it was all over, she did look so like a child of God, young and trusting, like she did on her baptizing night, you remember?"

I felt that Mrs. Dow did not want to talk any more about Nelly then, and, indeed, I had little heart to listen; so I told her I would go for a walk, and suggested that I might stop at Mrs. Spinny's to see the children.

Mrs. Dow looked up thoughtfully at the clock. "I doubt if you'll find little Margaret there now. It's half-past four, and she'll have been out of school an hour and more. She'll be most likely coasting on Lupton's Hill. She usually makes for it with her sled the minute she is out of the schoolhouse door. You know, it's the old hill where you all used to slide. If you stop in at the church about six o'clock, you'll likely find Mrs. Spinny there with the baby. I promised to go down and help Mrs. Freeze finish up the tree, and Mrs. Spinny said she'd run in with the baby, if 't wasn't too bitter. She won't leave him alone with the Swede girl. She's like a young woman with her first."

Lupton's Hill was at the other end of town, and when I got there the dusk was thickening, drawing blue shadows over the snowy fields. There were perhaps twenty children creeping up the hill or whizzing down the packed sled track. When I had been watching them for some minutes, I heard a lusty shout, and a little red sled shot past me into the deep snowdrift beyond. The child was quite buried for a moment, then she struggled out and stood dusting the snow from her short coat and red woolen comforter. She wore a brown fur cap, which was too big for her and of an old-fashioned shape, such as girls wore long ago, but I would have known her without the cap. Mrs. Dow had said a beautiful child, and there would not be two like this in Riverbend. She was off before I had time to speak to her, going up the hill at a trot, her sturdy little legs plowing through the trampled snow. When she reached the top she never paused to take breath, but threw herself upon her sled and came down with a whoop that was quenched only by the deep drift at the end.

"Are you Margaret Spinny?" I asked as she struggled out in a cloud of snow.

"Yes, 'm." She approached me with frank curiosity, pulling her little sled behind her. "Are you the strange lady staying at Mrs. Dow's?" I nodded, and she began to look my clothes over with respectful interest.

"Your grandmother is to be at the church at six o'clock, isn't she?"

"Yes, 'm."

"Well, suppose we walk up there now. It's nearly six, and all the other children are going home." She hesitated, and looked up at the faintly gleaming track on the hill slope. "Do you want another slide? Is that it?" I asked.

"Do you mind?" she asked shyly.

"No. I'll wait for you. Take your time; don't run."

Two little boys were still hanging about the slide, and they cheered her as she came down, her comforter streaming in the wind.

"Now," she announced, getting up out of the drift, "I'll show you where the church is."

"Shall I tie your comforter again?"

"No, 'm, thanks. I'm plenty warm." She put her mittened hand confidingly in mine and trudged along beside me.

Mrs. Dow must have heard us tramping up the snowy steps of the church, for she met us at the door. Everyone had gone except the old ladies. A kerosene lamp flickered over the Sunday-school chart, with the lesson-picture of the Wise Men, and the little barrel stove threw out a deep glow over the three white heads that bent above the baby. There the three friends sat, patting him, and smoothing his dress, and playing with his hands, which made theirs look so brown.

"You ain't seen nothing finer in all your travels," said Mrs. Spinny, and they all laughed.

They showed me his full chest and how strong his back was; had me feel the golden fuzz on his head, and made him look at me with his round, bright eyes. He laughed and reared himself in my arms as I took him up and held him close to me. He was so warm and tingling with life, and he had the flush of new beginnings, of the new morning and the new rose. He seemed to have come so lately from his mother's heart! It was as if I held her youth and all her young joy. As I put my cheek down against his, he spied a pink flower in my hat, and making a gleeful sound, he lunged at it with both fists.

"Don't let him spoil it," murmured Mrs. Spinny. "He loves color so—like Nelly."

The Bohemian Girl

I

THE TRANSCONTINENTAL express swung along the windings of the Sand River Valley, and in the rear seat of the observation car a young man sat greatly at his ease, not in the least discomfited by the fierce sunlight which beat in upon his brown face and neck and strong back. There was a look of relaxation and of great passivity about his broad shoulders, which seemed almost too heavy until he stood up and squared them. He wore a pale flannel shirt and a blue silk necktie with loose ends. His trousers were wide and belted at the waist, and his short sackcoat hung open. His heavy shoes had seen good service. His reddish-brown hair, like his clothes, had a foreign cut. He had deep-set, dark blue eyes under heavy reddish eyebrows. His face was kept clean only by close shaving, and even the sharpest razor left a glint of yellow in the smooth brown of his skin. His teeth and the palms of his hands were very white. His head, which looked hard and stubborn, lay indolently in the green cushion of the wicker chair, and as he looked out at the ripe summer country a teasing, not unkindly smile played over his lips. Once, as he basked thus comfortably, a quick light flashed in his eyes, curiously dilating the pupils, and his mouth became a hard, straight line, gradually relaxing into its former smile of rather kindly mockery. He told himself, apparently, that there was no point in getting excited; and he seemed a master hand at taking his ease when he could. Neither the sharp whistle of the locomotive nor the brakeman's call disturbed him. It was not until after the train had stopped that he rose, put on a Panama hat, took from the rack a small valise and a flute case, and stepped deliberately to the station platform. The baggage was already unloaded, and the stranger presented a check for a battered sole-leather steamer trunk.

"Can you keep it here for a day or two?" he asked the agent. "I may send for it, and I may not."

"Depends on whether you like the country, I suppose?" demanded the agent in a challenging tone.

"Just so."

The agent shrugged his shoulders, looked scornfully at the small trunk, which was marked "N.E.," and handed out a claim check without further comment. The stranger watched him as he caught one end of the trunk and dragged it into the express room. The agent's manner seemed to remind him of something amusing. "Doesn't seem to be a very big place," he remarked, looking about.

"It's big enough for us," snapped the agent, as he banged the trunk into a corner.

That remark, apparently, was what Nils Ericson had wanted. He chuckled quietly as he took a leather strap from his pocket and swung his valise around his shoulder. Then he settled his Panama securely on his head, turned up his trousers, tucked the flute case under his arm, and started off across the fields. He gave the town, as he would have said, a wide berth, and cut through a great fenced pasture, emerging, when he rolled under the barbed wire at the farther corner, upon a white dusty road which ran straight up from the river valley to the high prairies, where the ripe wheat stood yellow and the tin roofs and weathercocks were twinkling in the fierce sunlight. By the time Nils had done three miles, the sun was sinking and the farm wagons on their way home from town came rattling by, covering him with dust and making him sneeze. When one of the farmers pulled up and offered to give him a lift, he clambered in willingly. The driver was a thin, grizzled old man with a long lean neck and a foolish sort of beard, like a goat's. "How fur ye goin'?" he asked, as he clucked to his horses and started off.

"Do you go by the Ericson place?"

"Which Ericson?" The old man drew in his reins as if he expected to stop again.

"Preacher Ericson's."

"Oh, the Old Lady Ericson's!" He turned and looked at Nils. "La, me! If you're goin' out there you might 'a' rid out in the automobile. That's a pity, now. The Old Lady Ericson was in town with her auto. You might 'a' heard it snortin' anywhere about the post office er the butcher shop."

"Has she a motor?" asked the stranger absently.

" 'Deed an' she has! She runs into town every night about this time for her mail and meat for supper. Some folks say she's afraid her auto won't get exercise enough, but I say that's jealousy."

"Aren't there any other motors about here?"

"Oh, yes! We have fourteen in all. But nobody else gets around like the Old Lady Ericson. She's out, rain er shine, over the whole county, chargin' into town and out amongst her farms, an' up to her sons' places. Sure you ain't goin' to the wrong place?" He craned his neck and looked at Nils's flute case with eager curiosity. "The old woman ain't got any piany that I knows on. Olaf, he has a grand. His wife's musical; took lessons in Chicago."

"I'm going up there tomorrow," said Nils imperturbably. He saw that the driver took him for a piano tuner.

"Oh, I see!" The old man screwed up his eyes mysteriously. He was a little dashed by the stranger's noncommunicativeness, but he soon broke out again.

"I'm one o' Mis' Ericson's tenants. Look after one of her places. I did own the place myself oncet, but I lost it a while back, in the bad years just after the World's Fair. Just as well, too, I say. Lets you out o' payin' taxes. The Ericsons do own most of the county now. I remember the old preacher's fav'rite text used to be, 'To them that hath shall be given.' They've spread something wonderful—run over this here country like bindweed. But I ain't one that begretches it to 'em. Folks is entitled to what they kin git; and they're hustlers. Olaf, he's in the legislature now, and a likely man fur Congress. Listen, if that ain't the old woman comin' now. Want I should stop her?"

Nils shook his head. He heard the deep chug-chug of a motor vibrating steadily in the clear twilight behind them. The pale lights of the car swam over the hill, and the old man slapped his reins and turned clear out of the road, ducking his head at the first of three angry snorts from behind. The motor was running at a hot, even speed, and passed without turning an inch from its course. The driver was a stalwart woman who sat at ease in the front seat and drove her car bareheaded. She left a cloud of dust and a trail of gasoline behind her. Her tenant threw back his head and sneezed.

"Whew! I sometimes say I'd as lief be *before* Mrs. Ericson as behind her. She does beat all! Nearly seventy, and never lets another soul touch that car. Puts it into commission herself every morning, and keeps it tuned up by the hitch-bar all day. I never stop work for a drink o' water that I don't hear her a-churnin' up the road. I reckon her darter-in-laws never sets down easy nowadays. Never know when she'll pop in. Mis' Otto, she says to me: 'We're so afraid that thing'll blow up and do Ma some injury yet, she's so turrible venturesom.' Says I: 'I wouldn't stew, Mis' Otto; the old lady'll drive that car to the funeral of every darter-in-law she's got.' That was after the old woman had jumped a turrible bad culvert."

The stranger heard vaguely what the old man was saying. Just now he was experiencing something very much like homesickness, and he was wondering what had brought it about. The mention of a name or two, perhaps; the rattle of a wagon along a dusty road; the rank, resinous smell of sunflowers and ironweed, which the night damp brought up from the draws and low places; perhaps, more than all, the dancing lights of the motor that had plunged by. He squared his shoulders with a comfortable sense of strength.

The wagon, as it jolted westward, climbed a pretty steady upgrade. The country, receding from the rough river valley, swelled more and more gently, as if it had been smoothed out by the wind. On one of the last of the rugged ridges, at the end of a branch road, stood a grim square house with a tin roof and double porches. Behind the house stretched a row of broken, wind-racked poplars, and down the hill slope to the left straggled the sheds and stables. The old man stopped his horses where the Ericsons' road branched across a dry sand creek that wound about the foot of the hill.

"That's the old lady's place. Want I should drive in?"

"No, thank you. I'll roll out here. Much obliged to you. Good night."

His passenger stepped down over the front wheel, and the old man drove on reluctantly, looking back as if he would like to see how the stranger would be received.

As Nils was crossing the dry creek he heard the restive tramp of a horse coming toward him down the hill. Instantly he flashed out of the road and stood behind a thicket of wild plum bushes that grew in the sandy bed. Peering through the dusk, he saw a light horse, under tight rein, descending the hill at a sharp walk. The rider was a slender woman—barely visible against the dark hillside—wearing an old-fashioned derby hat and a long riding skirt. She sat lightly in the saddle, with her chin high, and seemed to be looking into the distance. As she passed the plum thicket her horse snuffed the air and shied. She struck him, pulling him in sharply, with an angry exclamation, *"Blázne!"* in Bohemian. Once in the main road, she let him out into a lope, and they soon emerged upon the crest of high land, where they moved along the skyline, silhouetted against the band of faint color that lingered in the west. This horse and rider, with their free, rhythmical gallop, were the only moving things to be seen on the face of the flat country. They seemed, in the last sad light of evening, not to be there accidentally, but as an inevitable detail of the landscape.

Nils watched them until they had shrunk to a mere moving speck against the sky; then he crossed the sand creek and climbed the hill. When he reached the gate the front of the house was dark, but a light was shining from the side windows. The pigs were squealing in the hog corral, and Nils could see a tall boy, who carried two big wooden buckets, moving about among them. Halfway between the barn and the house, the windmill wheezed lazily. Following the path that ran around to the back porch, Nils stopped to look through the screen door into the lamplit kitchen. The kitchen was the largest room in the house; Nils remembered that his older brothers used to give dances there when he was a boy. Beside the stove stood a little girl with two light yellow braids and a broad, flushed face, peering anxiously into a frying pan. In the dining room beyond, a large, broad-shouldered woman was moving about the table. She walked with an active, springy step. Her face was heavy and florid, almost without wrinkles, and her hair was black at seventy. Nils felt proud of her as he watched her deliberate activity—never a momentary hesitation, or a movement that did not tell. He waited until she came out into the kitchen and, brushing the child aside, took her place at the stove. Then he tapped on the screen door and entered.

"It's nobody but Nils, Mother. I expect you weren't looking for me."

Mrs. Ericson turned away from the stove and stood staring at him. "Bring the lamp, Hilda, and let me look."

Nils laughed and unslung his valise. "What's the matter, Mother? Don't you know me?"

Mrs. Ericson put down the lamp. "You must be Nils. You don't look very different, anyway."

"Nor you, Mother. You hold your own. Don't you wear glasses yet?"

"Only to read by. Where's your trunk, Nils?"

"Oh, I left that in town. I thought it might not be convenient for you to have company so near threshing-time."

"Don't be foolish, Nils." Mrs. Ericson turned back to the stove. "I don't thresh now. I hitched the wheat land onto the next farm and have a tenant. Hilda, take some hot water up to the company room, and go call little Eric."

The tow-haired child, who had been standing in mute amazement, took up the tea kettle and withdrew, giving Nils a long, admiring look from the door of the kitchen stairs.

"Who's the youngster?" Nils asked, dropping down on the bench behind the kitchen stove.

"One of your Cousin Henrik's."

"How long has Cousin Henrik been dead?"

"Six years. There are two boys. One stays with Peter and one with Anders. Olaf is their guardeen."

There was a clatter of pails on the porch, and a tall, lanky boy peered wonderingly in through the screen door. He had a fair, gentle face and big gray eyes, and wisps of soft yellow hair hung down under his cap. Nils sprang up and pulled him into the kitchen, hugging him and slapping him on the shoulders. "Well, if it isn't my kid! Look at the size of him! Don't you know me, Eric?"

The boy reddened under his sunburn and freckles, and hung his head. "I guess it's Nils," he said shyly.

"You're a good guesser," laughed Nils giving the lad's hand a swing. To himself he was thinking: "That's why the little girl looked so friendly. He's taught her to like me. He was only six when I went away, and he's remembered for twelve years."

Eric stood fumbling with his cap and smiling. "You look just like I thought you would," he ventured.

"Go wash your hands, Eric," called Mrs. Ericson. "I've got cob corn for supper, Nils. You used to like it. I guess you don't get much of that in the old country. Here's Hilda; she'll take you up to your room. You'll want to get the dust off you before you eat."

Mrs. Ericson went into the dining room to lay another plate, and the little girl came up and nodded to Nils as if to let him know that his room was ready. He put out his hand and she took it, with a startled glance up at his face. Little Eric dropped his towel, threw an arm about Nils and one about Hilda, gave them a clumsy squeeze, and then stumbled out to the porch.

During supper Nils heard exactly how much land each of his eight grown brothers farmed, how their crops were coming on, and how much livestock they were feeding. His mother watched him narrowly as she talked. "You've got better looking, Nils," she remarked abruptly, whereupon he grinned and the children giggled. Eric, although he was eighteen and as tall as Nils, was always accounted a child, being the last of so many sons. His face seemed childlike, too, Nils thought, and he had the open, wandering eyes of a little boy. All the others had been men at his age.

After supper Nils went out to the front porch and sat down on the step to smoke a pipe. Mrs. Ericson drew a rocking chair up near him and began to knit busily. It was one of the few old-world customs she had kept up, for she could not bear to sit with idle hands.

"Where's little Eric, Mother?"

"He's helping Hilda with the dishes. He does it of his own will; I don't like a boy to be too handy about the house."

"He seems like a nice kid."

"He's very obedient."

Nils smiled a little in the dark. It was just as well to shift the line of conversation. "What are you knitting there, Mother?"

"Baby stockings. The boys keep me busy." Mrs. Ericson chuckled and clicked her needles.

"How many grandchildren have you?"

"Only thirty-one now. Olaf lost his three. They were sickly, like their mother."

"I supposed he had a second crop by this time!"

"His second wife has no children. She's too proud. She tears about on horseback all the time. But she'll get caught up with, yet. She sets herself very high, though nobody knows what for. They were low enough Bohemians she came of. I never thought much of Bohemians; always drinking."

Nils puffed away at his pipe in silence, and Mrs. Ericson knitted on. In a few moments she added grimly: "She was down here tonight, just before you came. She'd like to quarrel with me and come between me and Olaf, but I don't give her the chance. I suppose you'll be bringing a wife home some day."

"I don't know. I've never thought much about it."

"Well, perhaps it's best as it is," suggested Mrs. Ericson hopefully. "You'd never be contented tied down to the land. There was roving blood in your father's family, and it's come out in you. I expect your own way of life suits you best." Mrs. Ericson had dropped into a blandly agreeable tone which Nils well remembered. It seemed to amuse him a good deal and his white teeth flashed behind his pipe. His mother's strategies had always diverted him, even when he was a boy—they were so flimsy and patent, so illy proportioned to her vigor and force. "They've been waiting to see which way I'd jump," he reflected. He felt that Mrs. Ericson was pondering his case deeply as she sat clicking her needles.

"I don't suppose you've ever got used to steady work," she went on presently. "Men ain't apt to if they roam around too long. It's a pity you didn't come back the year after the World's Fair. Your father picked up a good bit of land cheap then, in the hard times, and I expect maybe he'd have give you a farm. It's too bad you put off comin' back so long, for I always thought he meant to do something by you."

Nils laughed and shook the ashes out of his pipe. "I'd have missed a lot if I had come back then. But I'm sorry I didn't get back to see father."

"Well, I suppose we have to miss things at one end or the other.

Perhaps you are as well satisfied with your own doings, now, as you'd have been with a farm," said Mrs. Ericson reassuringly.

"Land's a good thing to have," Nils commented, as he lit another match and sheltered it with his hand.

His mother looked sharply at his face until the match burned out. "Only when you stay on it!" she hastened to say.

Eric came round the house by the path just then, and Nils rose, with a yawn. "Mother, if you don't mind, Eric and I will take a little tramp before bedtime. It will make me sleep."

"Very well; only don't stay long. I'll sit up and wait for you. I like to lock up myself."

Nils put his hand on Eric's shoulder, and the two tramped down the hill and across the sand creek into the dusty highroad beyond. Neither spoke. They swung along at an even gait, Nils puffing at his pipe. There was no moon, and the white road and the wide fields lay faint in the starlight. Over everything was darkness and thick silence, and the smell of dust and sunflowers. The brothers followed the road for a mile or more without finding a place to sit down. Finally, Nils perched on a stile over the wire fence, and Eric sat on the lower step.

"I began to think you never would come back, Nils," said the boy softly.

"Didn't I promise you I would?"

"Yes; but people don't bother about promises they make to babies. Did you really know you were going away for good when you went to Chicago with the cattle that time?"

"I thought it very likely, if I could make my way."

"I don't see how you did it, Nils. Not many fellows could." Eric rubbed his shoulder against his brother's knee.

"The hard thing was leaving home—you and father. It was easy enough, once I got beyond Chicago. Of course I got awful homesick; used to cry myself to sleep. But I'd burned my bridges."

"You had always wanted to go, hadn't you?"

"Always. Do you still sleep in our little room? Is that cottonwood still by the window?"

Eric nodded eagerly and smiled up at his brother in the gray darkness.

"You remember how we always said the leaves were whispering when they rustled at night? Well, they always whispered to me about the sea. Sometimes they said names out of the geography books. In a high wind they had a desperate sound, like something trying to tear loose."

"How funny, Nils," said Eric dreamily, resting his chin on his hand. "That tree still talks like that, and 'most always it talks to me about you."

"Sure they did; but he didn't have cholera; and there were plenty of hogs left in the world, weren't there?"

"Well, but, if they weren't his, how could they do him any good?" Eric asked, in astonishment.

"Oh, scat! He could have had lots of fun with other people's hogs. He was a chump, Lou Sandberg. To kill yourself for a pig—think of that, now!" Nils laughed all the way downstairs, and quite embarrassed little Eric, who fell to scrubbing his face and hands at the tin basin. While he was parting his wet hair at the kitchen looking glass, a heavy tread sounded on the stairs. The boy dropped his comb. "Gracious, there's Mother. We must have talked too long." He hurried out to the shed, slipped on his overalls, and disappeared with the milking pails.

Mrs. Ericson came in, wearing a clean white apron, her black hair shining from the application of a wet brush.

"Good morning, Mother. Can't I make the fire for you?"

"No, thank you, Nils. It's no trouble to make a cob fire, and I like to manage the kitchen stove myself." Mrs. Ericson paused with a shovel full of ashes in her hand. "I expect you will be wanting to see your brothers as soon as possible. I'll take you up to Anders's place this morning. He's threshing, and most of our boys are over there."

"Will Olaf be there?"

Mrs. Ericson went on taking out the ashes, and spoke between shovels. "No; Olaf's wheat is all in, put away in his new barn. He got six thousand bushel this year. He's going to town today to get men to finish roofing his barn."

"So Olaf is building a new barn?" Nils asked absently.

"Biggest one in the county, and almost done. You'll likely be here for the barn-raising. He's going to have a supper and a dance as soon as everybody's done threshing. Says it keeps the voters in a good humor. I tell him that's all nonsense; but Olaf has a long head for politics."

"Does Olaf farm all Cousin Henrik's land?"

Mrs. Ericson frowned as she blew into the faint smoke curling up about the cobs. "Yes; he holds it in trust for the children, Hilda and her brothers. He keeps strict account of everything he raises on it, and puts the proceeds out at compound interest for them."

Nils smiled as he watched the little flames shoot up. The door of the back stairs opened, and Hilda emerged, her arms behind her, buttoning up her long gingham apron as she came. He nodded to her gaily, and she twinkled at him out of her little blue eyes, set far apart over her wide cheekbones.

"There, Hilda, you grind the coffee—and just put in an extra handful;

They sat a while longer, watching the stars. At last Eric whispered anxiously: "Hadn't we better go back now? Mother will get tired waiting for us." They rose and took a shortcut home, through the pasture.

II

The next morning Nils woke with the first flood of light that came with dawn. The white-plastered walls of his room reflected the glare that shone through the thin window shades, and he found it impossible to sleep. He dressed hurriedly and slipped down the hall and up the back stairs to the half-story room which he used to share with his little brother. Eric, in a skimpy nightshirt, was sitting on the edge of the bed, rubbing his eyes, his pale yellow hair standing up in tufts all over his head. When he saw Nils, he murmured something confusedly and hustled his long legs into his trousers. "I didn't expect you'd be up so early, Nils," he said, as his head emerged from his blue shirt.

"Oh, you thought I was a dude, did you?" Nils gave him a playful tap which bent the tall boy up like a clasp knife. "See here, I must teach you to box." Nils thrust his hands into his pockets and walked about. "You haven't changed things much up here. Got most of my old traps, haven't you?"

He took down a bent, withered piece of sapling that hung over the dresser. "If this isn't the stick Lou Sandberg killed himself with!"

The boy looked up from his shoe-lacing.

"Yes; you never used to let me play with that. Just how did he do it, Nils? You were with father when he found Lou, weren't you?"

"Yes. Father was going off to preach somewhere, and, as we drove along, Lou's place looked sort of forlorn, and we thought we'd stop and cheer him up. When we found him father said he'd been dead a couple of days. He'd tied a piece of binding twine round his neck, made a noose in each end, fixed the nooses over the ends of a bent stick, and let the stick spring straight; strangled himself."

"What made him kill himself such a silly way?"

The simplicity of the boy's question set Nils laughing. He clapped little Eric on the shoulder. "What made him such a silly as to kill himself at all, I should say!"

"Oh, well! But his hogs had the cholera, and all up and died on him, didn't they?"

wondering what had brought it about. The mention of a name or two, perhaps; the rattle of a wagon along a dusty road; the rank, resinous smell of sunflowers and ironweed, which the night damp brought up from the draws and low places; perhaps, more than all, the dancing lights of the motor that had plunged by. He squared his shoulders with a comfortable sense of strength.

The wagon, as it jolted westward, climbed a pretty steady upgrade. The country, receding from the rough river valley, swelled more and more gently, as if it had been smoothed out by the wind. On one of the last of the rugged ridges, at the end of a branch road, stood a grim square house with a tin roof and double porches. Behind the house stretched a row of broken, wind-racked poplars, and down the hill slope to the left straggled the sheds and stables. The old man stopped his horses where the Ericsons' road branched across a dry sand creek that wound about the foot of the hill.

"That's the old lady's place. Want I should drive in?"

"No, thank you. I'll roll out here. Much obliged to you. Good night."

His passenger stepped down over the front wheel, and the old man drove on reluctantly, looking back as if he would like to see how the stranger would be received.

As Nils was crossing the dry creek he heard the restive tramp of a horse coming toward him down the hill. Instantly he flashed out of the road and stood behind a thicket of wild plum bushes that grew in the sandy bed. Peering through the dusk, he saw a light horse, under tight rein, descending the hill at a sharp walk. The rider was a slender woman—barely visible against the dark hillside—wearing an old-fashioned derby hat and a long riding skirt. She sat lightly in the saddle, with her chin high, and seemed to be looking into the distance. As she passed the plum thicket her horse snuffed the air and shied. She struck him, pulling him in sharply, with an angry exclamation, *"Blázne!"* in Bohemian. Once in the main road, she let him out into a lope, and they soon emerged upon the crest of high land, where they moved along the skyline, silhouetted against the band of faint color that lingered in the west. This horse and rider, with their free, rhythmical gallop, were the only moving things to be seen on the face of the flat country. They seemed, in the last sad light of evening, not to be there accidentally, but as an inevitable detail of the landscape.

Nils watched them until they had shrunk to a mere moving speck against the sky; then he crossed the sand creek and climbed the hill. When he reached the gate the front of the house was dark, but a light places. Sure you ain't goin' to the wrong place?" He craned his neck and looked at Nils's flute case with eager curiosity. "The old woman ain't got any piany that I knows on. Olaf, he has a grand. His wife's musical; took lessons in Chicago."

"I'm going up there tomorrow," said Nils imperturbably. He saw that the driver took him for a piano tuner.

"Oh, I see!" The old man screwed up his eyes mysteriously. He was a little dashed by the stranger's noncommunicativeness, but he soon broke out again.

"I'm one o' Mis' Ericson's tenants. Look after one of her places. I did own the place myself oncet, but I lost it a while back, in the bad years just after the World's Fair. Just as well, too, I say. Lets you out o' payin' taxes. The Ericsons do own most of the county now. I remember the old preacher's fav'rite text used to be, 'To them that hath shall be given.' They've spread something wonderful—run over this here country like bindweed. But I ain't one that begretches it to 'em. Folks is entitled to what they kin git; and they're hustlers. Olaf, he's in the legislature now, and a likely man fur Congress. Listen, if that ain't the old woman comin' now. Want I should stop her?"

Nils shook his head. He heard the deep chug-chug of a motor vibrating steadily in the clear twilight behind them. The pale lights of the car swam over the hill, and the old man slapped his reins and turned clear out of the road, ducking his head at the first of three angry snorts from behind. The motor was running at a hot, even speed, and passed without turning an inch from its course. The driver was a stalwart woman who sat at ease in the front seat and drove her car bareheaded. She left a cloud of dust and a trail of gasoline behind her. Her tenant threw back his head and sneezed.

"Whew! I sometimes say I'd as lief be *before* Mrs. Ericson as behind her. She does beat all! Nearly seventy, and never lets another soul touch that car. Puts it into commission herself every morning, and keeps it tuned up by the hitch-bar all day. I never stop work for a drink o' water that I don't hear her a-churnin' up the road. I reckon her darter-in-laws never sets down easy nowadays. Never know when she'll pop in. Mis' Otto, she says to me: 'We're so afraid that thing'll blow up and do Ma some injury yet, she's so turrible venturesom.' Says I: 'I wouldn't stew, Mis' Otto; the old lady'll drive that car to the funeral of every darter-in-law she's got.' That was after the old woman had jumped a turrible bad culvert."

The stranger heard vaguely what the old man was saying. Just now he was experiencing something very much like homesickness, and he was

I expect your Cousin Nils likes his strong," said Mrs. Ericson, as she went out to the shed.

Nils turned to look at the little girl, who gripped the coffee grinder between her knees and ground so hard that her two braids bobbed and her face flushed under its broad spattering of freckles. He noticed on her middle finger something that had not been there last night, and that had evidently been put on for company: a tiny gold ring with a clumsily set garnet stone. As her hand went round and round he touched the ring with the tip of his finger, smiling.

Hilda glanced toward the shed door through which Mrs. Ericson had disappeared. "My Cousin Clara gave me that," she whispered bashfully. "She's Cousin Olaf's wife."

III

Mrs. Olaf Ericson—Clara Vavrika, as many people still called her—was moving restlessly about her big bare house that morning. Her husband had left for the county town before his wife was out of bed—her lateness in rising was one of the many things the Ericson family had against her. Clara seldom came downstairs before eight o'clock, and this morning she was even later, for she had dressed with unusual care. She put on, however, only a tight-fitting black dress, which people thereabouts thought very plain. She was a tall, dark woman of thirty, with a rather sallow complexion and a touch of dull salmon red in her cheeks, where the blood seemed to burn under her brown skin. Her hair, parted evenly above her low forehead, was so black that there were distinctly blue lights in it. Her black eyebrows were delicate half-moons and her lashes were long and heavy. Her eyes slanted a little, as if she had a strain of Tartar or gypsy blood, and were sometimes full of fiery determination and sometimes dull and opaque. Her expression was never altogether amiable; was often, indeed, distinctly sullen or, when she was animated, sarcastic. She was most attractive in profile, for then one saw to advantage her small, well-shaped head and delicate ears, and felt at once that here was a very positive, if not an altogether pleasing, personality.

The entire management of Mrs. Olaf's household devolved upon her aunt, Johanna Vavrika, a superstitious, doting woman of fifty. When Clara was a little girl her mother died, and Johanna's life had been spent in ungrudging service to her niece. Clara, like many self-willed and discontented persons, was really very apt, without knowing it, to do as other people told her, and to let her destiny be decided for her by intelligences much below her own. It was her Aunt Johanna who had humored and spoiled her in her girlhood, who had got her off to Chicago to study piano, and who had finally persuaded her to marry Olaf Ericson as the best match she would be likely to make in that part of the country. Johanna Vavrika had been deeply scarred by smallpox in the old country. She was short and fat, homely and jolly and sentimental. She was so broad, and took such short steps when she walked, that her brother, Joe Vavrika, always called her his duck. She adored her niece because of her talent, because of her good looks and masterful ways, but most of all because of her selfishness.

Clara's marriage with Olaf Ericson was Johanna's particular triumph. She was inordinately proud of Olaf's position, and she found a sufficiently exciting career in managing Clara's house, in keeping it above the criticism of the Ericsons, in pampering Olaf to keep him from finding fault with his wife, and in concealing from everyone Clara's domestic infelicities. While Clara slept of a morning, Johanna Vavrika was bustling about, seeing that Olaf and the men had their breakfast, and that the cleaning or the butter-making or the washing was properly begun by the two girls in the kitchen. Then, at about eight o'clock, she would take Clara's coffee up to her, and chat with her while she drank it, telling her what was going on in the house. Old Mrs. Ericson frequently said that her daughter-in-law would not know what day of the week it was if Johanna did not tell her every morning. Mrs. Ericson despised and pitied Johanna, but did not wholly dislike her. The one thing she hated in her daughter-in-law above everything else was the way in which Clara could come it over people. It enraged her that the affairs of her son's big, barnlike house went on as well as they did, and she used to feel that in this world we have to wait overlong to see the guilty punished. "Suppose Johanna Vavrika died or got sick?" the old lady used to say to Olaf. "Your wife wouldn't know where to look for her own dishcloth." Olaf only shrugged his shoulders. The fact remained that Johanna did not die, and, although Mrs. Ericson often told her she was looking poorly, she was never ill. She seldom left the house, and she slept in a little room off the kitchen. No Ericson, by night or day, could come prying about there to find fault without her knowing it. Her one weakness was that she was an incurable talker, and she sometimes made trouble without meaning to.

This morning Clara was tying a wine-colored ribbon about her throat when Johanna appeared with her coffee. After putting the tray on a sewing table, she began to make Clara's bed, chattering the while in Bohemian.

"Well, Olaf got off early, and the girls are baking. I'm going down presently to make some poppyseed bread for Olaf. He asked for prune preserves at breakfast, and I told him I was out of them and to bring some prunes and honey and cloves from town."

Clara poured her coffee. "Ugh! I don't see how men can eat so much sweet stuff. In the morning, too!"

Her aunt chuckled knowingly. "Bait a bear with honey, as we say in the old country."

"Was he cross?" her niece asked indifferently.

"Olaf? Oh, no! He was in fine spirits. He's never cross if you know how to take him. I never knew a man to make so little fuss about bills. I gave him a list of things to get a yard long, and he didn't say a word; just folded it up and put it in his pocket."

"I can well believe he didn't say a word," Clara remarked with a shrug. "Some day he'll forget how to talk."

"Oh, but they say he's a grand speaker in the legislature. He knows when to keep quiet. That's why he's got such influence in politics. The people have confidence in him." Johanna beat up a pillow and held it under her fat chin while she slipped on the case. Her niece laughed.

"Maybe we could make people believe we were wise, Aunty, if we held our tongues. Why did you tell Mrs. Ericson that Norman threw me again last Saturday and turned my foot? She's been talking to Olaf."

Johanna fell into great confusion. "Oh, but, my precious, the old lady asked for you, and she's always so angry if I can't give an excuse. Anyhow, she needn't talk; she's always tearing up something with that motor of hers."

When her aunt clattered down to the kitchen, Clara went to dust the parlor. Since there was not much there to dust, this did not take very long. Olaf had built the house new for her before their marriage, but her interest in furnishing it had been short-lived. It went, indeed, little beyond a bathtub and her piano. They had disagreed about almost every other article of furniture, and Clara had said she would rather have her house empty than full of things she didn't want. The house was set in a hillside, and the west windows of the parlor looked out above the kitchen yard thirty feet below. The east windows opened directly into the front yard. At one of the latter, Clara, while she was dusting, heard a low whistle. She did not turn at once, but listened intently as she drew her cloth slowly along the round of a chair. Yes, there it was:

I dreamt that I dwelt in ma-a-arble halls.

She turned and saw Nils Ericson laughing in the sunlight, his hat in his hand, just outside the window. As she crossed the room he leaned against the wire screen. "Aren't you at all surprised to see me, Clara Vavrika?"

"No; I was expecting to see you. Mother Ericson telephoned Olaf last night that you were here."

Nils squinted and gave a long whistle. "Telephoned? That must have been while Eric and I were out walking. Isn't she enterprising? Lift this screen, won't you?"

Clara lifted the screen, and Nils swung his leg across the window sill. As he stepped into the room she said: "You didn't think you were going to get ahead of your mother, did you?"

He threw his hat on the piano. "Oh, I do sometimes. You see, I'm ahead of her now. I'm supposed to be in Anders's wheatfield. But, as we were leaving, Mother ran her car into a soft place beside the road and sank up to the hubs. While they were going for horses to pull her out, I cut away behind the stacks and escaped." Nils chuckled. Clara's dull eyes lit up as she looked at him admiringly.

"You've got them guessing already. I don't know what your mother said to Olaf over the telephone, but he came back looking as if he'd seen a ghost, and he didn't go to bed until a dreadful hour—ten o'clock, I should think. He sat out on the porch in the dark like a graven image. It had been one of his talkative days, too." They both laughed, easily and lightly, like people who have laughed a great deal together; but they remained standing.

"Anders and Otto and Peter looked as if they had seen ghosts, too, over in the threshing field. What's the matter with them all?"

Clara gave him a quick, searching look. "Well, for one thing, they've always been afraid you have the other will."

Nils looked interested. "The other will?"

"Yes. A later one. They knew your father made another, but they never knew what he did with it. They almost tore the old house to pieces looking for it. They always suspected that he carried on a clandestine correspondence with you, for the one thing he would do was to get his own mail himself. So they thought he might have sent the new will to you for safekeeping. The old one, leaving everything to your mother, was made long before you went away, and it's understood among them that it cuts you out—that she will leave all the property to the others.

Your father made the second will to prevent that. I've been hoping you had it. It would be such fun to spring it on them." Clara laughed mirthfully, a thing she did not often do now.

Nils shook his head reprovingly. "Come, now, you're malicious."

"No, I'm not. But I'd like something to happen to stir them all up, just for once. There never was such a family for having nothing ever happen to them but dinner and threshing. I'd almost be willing to die, just to have a funeral. *You* wouldn't stand it for three weeks."

Nils bent over the piano and began pecking at the keys with the finger of one hand. "I wouldn't? My dear young lady, how do you know what I can stand? *You* wouldn't wait to find out."

Clara flushed darkly and frowned. "I didn't believe you would ever come back—" she said defiantly.

"Eric believed I would, and he was only a baby when I went away. However, all's well that ends well, and I haven't come back to be a skeleton at the feast. We mustn't quarrel. Mother will be here with a search warrant pretty soon." He swung round and faced her, thrusting his hands into his coat pockets. "Come, you ought to be glad to see me, if you want something to happen. I'm something, even without a will. We can have a little fun, can't we? I think we can!"

She echoed him, "I think we can!" They both laughed and their eyes sparkled. Clara Vavrika looked ten years younger than when she had put the velvet ribbon about her throat that morning.

"You know, I'm so tickled to see Mother," Nils went on. "I didn't know I was so proud of her. A regular piledriver. How about little pigtails, down at the house? Is Olaf doing the square thing by those children?"

Clara frowned pensively. "Olaf has to do something that looks like the square thing, now that he's a public man!" She glanced drolly at Nils. "But he makes a good commission out of it. On Sundays they all get together here and figure. He lets Peter and Anders put in big bills for the keep of the two boys, and he pays them out of the estate. They are always having what they call accountings. Olaf gets something out of it, too. I don't know just how they do it, but it's entirely a family matter, as they say. And when the Ericsons say that—" Clara lifted her eyebrows.

Just then the angry *honk-honk* of an approaching motor sounded from down the road. Their eyes met and they began to laugh. They laughed as children do when they cannot contain themselves, and cannot explain the cause of their mirth to grown people, but share it perfectly together.

When Clara Vavrika sat down at the piano after he was gone, she felt that she had laughed away a dozen years. She practiced as if the house were burning over her head.

When Nils greeted his mother and climbed into the front seat of the motor beside her, Mrs. Ericson looked grim, but she made no comment upon his truancy until she had turned her car and was retracing her revolutions along the road that ran by Olaf's big pasture. Then she remarked dryly:

"If I were you I wouldn't see too much of Olaf's wife while you are here. She's the kind of woman who can't see much of men without getting herself talked about. She was a good deal talked about before he married her."

"Hasn't Olaf tamed her?" Nils asked indifferently.

Mrs. Ericson shrugged her massive shoulders. "Olaf don't seem to have much luck, when it comes to wives. The first one was meek enough, but she was always ailing. And this one has her own way. He says if he quarreled with her she'd go back to her father, and then he'd lose the Bohemian vote. There are a great many Bohunks in this district. But when you find a man under his wife's thumb you can always be sure there's a soft spot in him somewhere."

Nils thought of his own father, and smiled. "She brought him a good deal of money, didn't she, besides the Bohemian vote?"

Mrs. Ericson sniffed. "Well, she has a fair half section in her own name, but I can't see as that does Olaf much good. She will have a good deal of property some day, if old Vavrika don't marry again. But I don't consider a saloonkeeper's money as good as other people's money."

Nils laughed outright. "Come, Mother, don't let your prejudices carry you that far. Money's money. Old Vavrika's a mighty decent sort of saloonkeeper. Nothing rowdy about him."

Mrs. Ericson spoke up angrily: "Oh, I know you always stood up for them! But hanging around there when you were a boy never did you any good, Nils, nor any of the other boys who went there. There weren't so many after her when she married Olaf, let me tell you. She knew enough to grab her chance."

Nils settled back in his seat. "Of course I liked to go there, Mother, and you were always cross about it. You never took the trouble to find out that it was the one jolly house in this country for a boy to go to. All the rest of you were working yourselves to death, and the houses were mostly a mess, full of babies and washing and flies. Oh, it was all right—I understand that; but you are young only once, and I happened to be young then. Now, Vavrika's was always jolly. He played the violin, and I used to take my flute, and Clara played the piano, and Johanna used to sing Bohemian songs. She always had a big supper for us—herrings and pickles and poppyseed bread, and lots of cake and preserves. Old Joe had been in the army in the old country, and he could tell lots of good stories. I can see him cutting bread, at the head of the table, now. I don't know what I'd have done when I was a kid if it hadn't been for the Vavrikas, really."

"And all the time he was taking money that other people had worked hard in the fields for," Mrs. Ericson observed.

"So do the circuses, Mother, and they're a good thing. People ought to get fun for some of their money. Even father liked old Joe."

"Your father," Mrs. Ericson said grimly, "liked everybody."

As they crossed the sand creek and turned into her own place, Mrs. Ericson observed, "There's Olaf's buggy. He's stopped on his way from town." Nils shook himself and prepared to greet his brother, who was waiting on the porch.

Olaf was a big, heavy Norwegian, slow of speech and movement. His head was large and square, like a block of wood. When Nils, at a distance, tried to remember what his brother looked like, he could recall only his heavy head, high forehead, large nostrils, and pale blue eyes, set far apart. Olaf's features were rudimentary: the thing one noticed was the face itself, wide and flat and pale, devoid of any expression, betraying his fifty years as little as it betrayed anything else, and powerful by reason of its very stolidness. When Olaf shook hands with Nils he looked at him from under his light eyebrows, but Nils felt that no one could ever say what that pale look might mean. The one thing he had always felt in Olaf was a heavy stubbornness, like the unyielding stickiness of wet loam against the plow. He had always found Olaf the most difficult of his brothers.

"How do you do, Nils? Expect to stay with us long?"

"Oh, I may stay forever," Nils answered gaily. "I like this country better than I used to."

"There's been some work put into it since you left," Olaf remarked.

"Exactly. I think it's about ready to live in now—and I'm about ready to settle down." Nils saw his brother lower his big head. ("Exactly like a bull," he thought.) "Mother's been persuading me to slow down now, and go in for farming," he went on lightly.

Olaf made a deep sound in his throat. "Farming ain't learned in a day," he brought out, still looking at the ground.

"Oh, I know! But I pick things up quickly." Nils had not meant to antagonize his brother, and he did not know now why he was doing it.

"Of course," he went on, "I shouldn't expect to make a big success, as you fellows have done. But then, I'm not ambitious. I won't want much. A little land, and some cattle, maybe."

Olaf still stared at the ground, his head down. He wanted to ask Nils what he had been doing all these years, that he didn't have a business somewhere he couldn't afford to leave; why he hadn't more pride than to come back with only a little sole-leather trunk to show for himself, and to present himself as the only failure in the family. He did not ask one of these questions, but he made them all felt distinctly.

"Humph!" Nils thought. "No wonder the man never talks, when he can butt his ideas into you like that without ever saying a word. I suppose he uses that kind of smokeless powder on his wife all the time. But I guess she has her innings." He chuckled, and Olaf looked up. "Never mind me, Olaf. I laugh without knowing why, like little Eric. He's another cheerful dog."

"Eric," said Olaf slowly, "is a spoiled kid. He's just let his mother's best cow go dry because he don't milk her right. I was hoping you'd take him away somewhere and put him into business. If he don't do any good among strangers, he never will." This was a long speech for Olaf, and as he finished it he climbed into his buggy.

Nils shrugged his shoulders. "Same old tricks," he thought. "Hits from behind you every time. What a whale of a man!" He turned and went round to the kitchen, where his mother was scolding little Eric for letting the gasoline get low.

IV

Joe Vavrika's saloon was not in the county seat, where Olaf and Mrs. Ericson did their trading, but in a cheerfuller place, a little Bohemian settlement which lay at the other end of the county, ten level miles north of Olaf's farm. Clara rode up to see her father almost every day. Vavrika's house was, so to speak, in the backyard of his saloon. The garden between the two buildings was enclosed by a high board fence as tight as a partition, and in summer Joe kept beer tables and wooden benches among the gooseberry bushes under his little cherry tree. At one of these tables Nils Ericson was seated in the late afternoon, three days after his return home. Joe had gone in to serve a customer, and Nils was lounging on his elbows, looking rather mournfully into his half-emptied pitcher, when he heard a laugh across the little garden. Clara, in her riding habit, was standing at the back door of the house, under the grapevine trellis that old Joe had grown there long ago. Nils rose.

"Come out and keep your father and me company. We've been gossiping all afternoon. Nobody to bother us but the flies."

She shook her head. "No, I never come out here any more. Olaf doesn't like it. I must live up to my position, you know."

"You mean to tell me you never come out and chat with the boys, as you used to? He *has* tamed you! Who keeps up these flower beds?"

"I come out on Sundays, when father is alone, and read the Bohemian papers to him. But I am never here when the bar is open. What have you two been doing?"

"Talking, as I told you. I've been telling him about my travels. I find I can't talk much at home, not even to Eric."

Clara reached up and poked with her riding-whip at a white moth that was fluttering in the sunlight among the vine leaves. "I suppose you will never tell me about all those things."

"Where can I tell them? Not in Olaf's house, certainly. What's the matter with our talking here?" He pointed persuasively with his hat to the bushes and the green table, where the flies were singing lazily above the empty beer glasses.

Clara shook her head weakly. "No, it wouldn't do. Besides, I am going now."

"I'm on Eric's mare. Would you be angry if I overtook you?"

Clara looked back and laughed. "You might try and see. I can leave you if I don't want you. Eric's mare can't keep up with Norman."

Nils went into the bar and attempted to pay his score. Big Joe, six feet four, with curly yellow hair and mustache, clapped him on the shoulder. "Not a God-damn a your money go in my drawer, you hear? Only next time you bring your flute, te-te-te-te-te-ty." Joe wagged his fingers in imitation of the flute player's position. "My Clara, she come all-a-time Sundays an' play for me. She not like to play at Ericson's place." He shook his yellow curls and laughed. "Not a God-damn a fun at Ericson's. You come a Sunday. You like-a fun. No forget de flute." Joe talked very rapidly and always tumbled over his English. He seldom spoke it to his customers, and had never learned much.

Nils swung himself into the saddle and trotted to the west end of the village, where the houses and gardens scattered into prairie land and the road turned south. Far ahead of him, in the declining light, he saw Clara Vavrika's slender figure, loitering on horseback. He touched his mare with the whip, and shot along the white, level road, under the reddening sky. When he overtook Olaf's wife he saw that she had been crying.

"What's the matter, Clara Vavrika?" he asked kindly.

"Oh, I get blue sometimes. It was awfully jolly living there with Father. I wonder why I ever went away."

Nils spoke in a low, kind tone that he sometimes used with women: "That's what I've been wondering these many years. You were the last girl in the country I'd have picked for a wife for Olaf. What made you do it, Clara?"

"I suppose I really did it to oblige the neighbors"—Clara tossed her head. "People were beginning to wonder."

"To wonder?"

"Yes—why I didn't get married. I suppose I didn't like to keep them in suspense. I've discovered that most girls marry out of consideration for the neighborhood."

Nils bent his head toward her and his white teeth flashed. "I'd have gambled that one girl I knew would say, 'Let the neighborhood be damned.' "

Clara shook her head mournfully. "You see, they have it on you, Nils; that is, if you're a woman. They say you're beginning to go off. That's what makes us get married: we can't stand the laugh."

Nils looked sidewise at her. He had never seen her head droop before. Resignation was the last thing he would have expected of her. "In your case, there wasn't something else?"

"Something else?"

"I mean, you didn't do it to spite somebody? Somebody who didn't come back?"

Clara drew herself up. "Oh, I never thought you'd come back. Not after I stopped writing to you, at least. *That* was all over, long before I married Olaf."

"It never occurred to you, then, that the meanest thing you could do to me was to marry Olaf?"

Clara laughed. "No; I didn't know you were so fond of Olaf."

Nils smoothed his horse's mane with his glove. "You know, Clara Vavrika, you are never going to stick it out. You'll cut away some day, and I've been thinking you might as well cut away with me."

Clara threw up her chin. "Oh, you don't know me as well as you think. I won't cut away. Sometimes, when I'm with Father, I feel like it. But I can hold out as long as the Ericsons can. They've never got the best of me yet, and one can live, so long as one isn't beaten. If I go back to Father, it's all up with Olaf in politics. He knows that, and he never goes much beyond sulking. I've as much wit as the Ericsons. I'll never leave them unless I can show them a thing or two."

"You mean unless you can come it over them?"

"Yes—unless I go away with a man who is cleverer than they are, and who has more money."

Nils whistled. "Dear me, you are demanding a good deal. The Ericsons, take the lot of them, are a bunch to beat. But I should think the excitement of tormenting them would have worn off by this time."

"It has, I'm afraid," Clara admitted mournfully.

"Then why don't you cut away? There are more amusing games than this in the world. When I came home I thought it might amuse me to bully a few quarter-sections out of the Ericsons; but I've almost decided I can get more fun for my money somewhere else."

Clara took in her breath sharply. "Ah, you have got the other will! That was why you came home!"

"No, it wasn't. I came home to see how you were getting on with Olaf."

Clara struck her horse with the whip, and in a bound she was far ahead of him. Nils dropped one word, "Damn!" and whipped after her; but she leaned forward in her saddle and fairly cut the wind. Her long riding skirt rippled in the still air behind her. The sun was just sinking behind the stubble in a vast, clear sky, and the shadows drew across the fields so rapidly that Nils could scarcely keep in sight the dark figure on the road. When he overtook her he caught her horse by the bridle. Norman reared, and Nils was frightened for her; but Clara kept her seat.

"Let me go, Nils Ericson!" she cried. "I hate you more than any of them. You were created to torture me, the whole tribe of you—to make me suffer in every possible way."

She struck her horse again and galloped away from him. Nils set his teeth and looked thoughtful. He rode slowly home along the deserted road, watching the stars come out in the clear violet sky. They flashed softly into the limpid heavens, like jewels let fall into clear water. They were a reproach, he felt, to a sordid world. As he turned across the sand creek, he looked up at the North Star and smiled, as if there were an understanding between them. His mother scolded him for being late for supper.

V

On Sunday afternoon Joe Vavrika, in his shirtsleeves and carpet slippers, was sitting in his garden, smoking a long-tasseled porcelain pipe with a hunting scene painted on the bowl. Clara sat under the cherry tree, reading aloud to him from the weekly Bohemian papers. She had worn a white muslin dress under her riding habit, and the leaves of the cherry tree threw a pattern of sharp shadows over her skirt. The black cat was dozing in the sunlight at her feet, and Joe's dachshund was scratching a hole under the scarlet geraniums and dreaming of badgers. Joe was filling his pipe for the third time since dinner, when he heard a knocking on the fence. He broke into a loud guffaw and unlatched the little door that led into the street. He did not call Nils by name, but caught him by the hand and dragged him in. Clara stiffened and the color deepened under her dark skin. Nils, too, felt a little awkward. He had not seen her since the night when she rode away from him and left him alone on the level road between the fields. Joe dragged him to the wooden bench beside the green table.

"You bring de flute," he cried, tapping the leather case under Nils' arm. "Ah, das-a good! Now we have some liddle fun like old times. I got somet'ing good for you." Joe shook his finger at Nils and winked his blue eye, a bright clear eye, full of fire, though the tiny blood vessels on the ball were always a little distended. "I got somet'ing for you from"—he paused and waved his hand—"Hongarie. You know Hongarie? You wait!" He pushed Nils down on the bench, and went through the back door of his saloon.

Nils looked at Clara, who sat frigidly with her white skirts drawn tight about her. "He didn't tell you he had asked me to come, did he? He wanted a party and proceeded to arrange it. Isn't he fun? Don't be cross; let's give him a good time."

Clara smiled and shook out her skirt. "Isn't that like Father? And he has sat here so meekly all day. Well, I won't pout. I'm glad you came. He doesn't have very many good times now any more. There are so few of his kind left. The second generation are a tame lot."

Joe came back with a flask in one hand and three wine glasses caught by the stems between the fingers of the other. These he placed on the table with an air of ceremony, and going behind Nils, held the flask between him and the sun, squinting into it admiringly. "You know dis, Tokai? A great friend of mine, he bring dis to me, a present out of Hongarie. You know how much it cost, dis wine? Chust so much what it weigh in gold. Nobody but de nobles drink him in Bohemie. Many, many years I save him up, dis Tokai." Joe whipped out his official corkscrew and delicately removed the cork. "De old man die what bring him to me, an' dis wine he lay on his belly in my cellar an' sleep. An' now," carefully pouring out the heavy yellow wine, "an' now he wake up; and maybe he wake us up, too!" He carried one of the glasses to his daughter and presented it with great gallantry.

Clara shook her head, but seeing her father's disappointment, relented. "You taste it first. I don't want so much."

Joe sampled it with a beatific expression, and turned to Nils. "You drink him slow, dis wine. He very soft, but he go down hot. You see!"

After a second glass Nils declared that he couldn't take anymore without getting sleepy. "Now get your fiddle, Vavrika," he said as he opened his flute case.

But Joe settled back in his wooden rocker and wagged his big carpet slipper. "No-no-no-no-no-no-no! No play fiddle now anymore: too much ache in de finger," waving them, "all-a-time rheumatiz. You play de flute, te-tety-te-tety-te. Bohemie songs."

"I've forgotten all the Bohemian songs I used to play with you and Johanna. But here's one that will make Clara pout. You remember how her eyes used to snap when we called her the Bohemian Girl?" Nils lifted his flute and began "When Other Lips and Other Hearts," and Joe hummed the air in a husky baritone, waving his carpet slipper. "Oh-h-h, das-a fine music," he cried, clapping his hands as Nils finished. "Now 'Marble Halls, Marble Halls'! Clara, you sing him."

Clara smiled and leaned back in her chair, beginning softly:

> "I dreamt that I dwelt in ma-a-arble halls,
> With vassals and serfs at my knee,"

and Joe hummed like a big bumblebee.

"There's one more you always played," Clara said quietly: "I remember that best." She locked her hands over her knee and began "The Heart Bowed Down," and sang it through without groping for the words. She was singing with a good deal of warmth when she came to the end of the old song:

> "For memory is the only friend
> That grief can call its own."

Joe flashed out his red silk handkerchief and blew his nose, shaking his head. "No-no-no-no-no-no-no! Too sad, too sad! I not like-a dat. Play quick somet'ing gay now."

Nils put his lips to the instrument, and Joe lay back in his chair, laughing and singing, "Oh, Evelina, Sweet Evelina!" Clara laughed, too. Long ago, when she and Nils went to high school, the model student of their class was a very homely girl in thick spectacles. Her name was Evelina Oleson; she had a long, swinging walk which somehow suggested the measure of that song, and they used mercilessly to sing it at her.

"Dat ugly Oleson girl, she teach in de school," Joe gasped, "an' she still walk chust like dat, yup-a, yup-a, yup-a, chust like a camel she go! Now, Nils, we have some more li'l drink. Oh, yes-yes-yes-yes-yes-yes-*yes!* Dis time you haf to drink, and Clara she haf to, so she show she not jealous. So, we all drink to your girl. You not tell her name, eh? No-no-no, I no make you tell. She pretty, eh? She make good sweetheart? I bet!" Joe winked and lifted his glass. "How soon you get married?"

Nils screwed up his eyes. "That I don't know. When she says."

Joe threw out his chest. "Das-a way boys talks. No way for mans. Mans say, 'You come to de church, an' get a hurry on you.' Das-a way mans talks."

"Maybe Nils hasn't got enough to keep a wife," put in Clara ironically. "How about that, Nils?" she asked him frankly, as if she wanted to know.

Nils looked at her coolly, raising one eyebrow. "Oh, I can keep her, all right."

"The way she wants to be kept?"

"With my wife, I'll decide that," replied Nils calmly. "I'll give her what's good for her."

Clara made a wry face. "You'll give her the strap, I expect, like old Peter Oleson gave his wife."

"When she needs it," said Nils lazily, locking his hands behind his head and squinting up through the leaves of the cherry tree. "Do you remember the time I squeezed the cherries all over your clean dress, and Aunt Johanna boxed my ears for me? My gracious, weren't you mad! You had both hands full of cherries, and I squeezed 'em and made the juice fly all over you. I liked to have fun with you; you'd get so mad."

"We *did* have fun, didn't we? None of the other kids ever had so much fun. We knew how to play."

Nils dropped his elbows on the table and looked steadily across at her. "I've played with lots of girls since, but I haven't found one who was such good fun."

Clara laughed. The late afternoon sun was shining full in her face, and deep in the back of her eyes there shone something fiery, like the yellow drops of Tokai in the brown glass bottle. "Can you still play, or are you only pretending?"

"I can play better than I used to, and harder."

"Don't you ever work, then?" She had not intended to say it. It slipped out because she was confused enough to say just the wrong thing.

"I work between times." Nils's steady gaze still beat upon her. "Don't you worry about my working, Mrs. Ericson. You're getting like all the rest of them." He reached his brown, warm hand across the table and dropped it on Clara's, which was cold as an icicle. "Last call for play, Mrs. Ericson!" Clara shivered, and suddenly her hands and cheeks grew warm. Her fingers lingered in his a moment, and they looked at each other earnestly. Joe Vavrika had put the mouth of the bottle to his lips and was swallowing the last drops of the Tokai, standing. The sun, just about to sink behind his shop, glistened on the bright glass, on his flushed face and curly yellow hair. "Look," Clara whispered; "that's the way I want to grow old."

VI

On the day of Olaf Ericson's barn-raising, his wife, for once in a way, rose early. Johanna Vavrika had been baking cakes and frying and boiling and spicing meats for a week beforehand, but it was not until the day before the party was to take place that Clara showed any interest in it. Then she was seized with one of her fitful spasms of energy, and took the wagon and little Eric and spent the day on Plum Creek, gathering vines and swamp goldenrod to decorate the barn.

By four o'clock in the afternoon buggies and wagons began to arrive at the big unpainted building in front of Olaf's house. When Nils and his mother came at five, there were more than fifty people in the barn, and a great drove of children. On the ground floor stood six long tables, set with the crockery of seven flourishing Ericson families, lent for the occasion. In the middle of each table was a big yellow pumpkin, hollowed out and filled with woodbine. In one corner of the barn, behind a pile of green-and-white-striped watermelons, was a circle of chairs for the old people: the younger guests sat on bushel measures or barbed-wire spools, and the children tumbled about in the haymow. The box stalls Clara had converted into booths. The framework was hidden by goldenrod and sheaves of wheat, and the partitions were covered with wild grapevines full of fruit. At one of these Johanna Vavrika watched over her cooked meats, enough to provision an army; and at the next her kitchen girls had ranged the ice-cream freezers, and Clara was already cutting pies and cakes against the hour of serving. At the third stall, little Hilda, in a bright pink lawn dress, dispensed lemonade throughout the afternoon. Olaf, as a public man, had thought it inadvisable to serve beer in his barn; but Joe Vavrika had come over wilth two demijohns concealed in his buggy, and after his arrival the wagon shed was much frequented by the men.

"Hasn't Cousin Clara fixed things lovely?" little Hilda whispered, when Nils went up to her stall and asked for lemonade.

Nils leaned against the booth, talking to the excited little girl and watching the people. The barn faced the west, and the sun, pouring in at the big doors, filled the whole interior with a golden light, through which filtered fine particles of dust from the haymow, where the children were romping. There was a great chattering from the stall where Johanna Vavrika exhibited to the admiring women her platters heaped with fried chicken, her roasts of beef, boiled tongues, and baked hams with cloves stuck in the crisp brown fat and garnished with tansy and parsley. The older women, having assured themselves that there were twenty kinds of cake, not counting cookies, and three dozen fat pies, repaired to the corner behind the pile of watermelons, put on their white aprons, and fell to their knitting and fancywork. They were a fine company of old women, and a Dutch painter would have loved to find them there together, where the sun made bright patches on the floor and sent long, quivering shafts of gold through the dusky shade up among the rafters. There were fat, rosy old women who looked hot in their best black dresses; spare, alert old women with brown, dark-veined hands; and several of almost heroic frame, not less massive than old Mrs. Ericson herself. Few of them wore glasses, and old Mrs. Svendsen, a Danish woman, who was quite bald, wore the only cap among them. Mrs. Oleson, who had twelve big grandchildren, could still show two braids of yellow hair as thick as her own wrists. Among all these grandmothers there were more brown heads than white. They all had a pleased, prosperous air, as if they were more than satisfied with themselves and with life. Nils, leaning against Hilda's lemonade stand, watched them as they sat chattering in four languages, their fingers never lagging behind their tongues.

"Look at them over there," he whispered, detaining Clara as she passed him. "Aren't they the Old Guard? I've just counted thirty hands. I guess they've wrung many a chicken's neck and warmed many a boy's jacket for him in their time."

In reality he fell into amazement when he thought of the Herculean labors those fifteen pairs of hands had performed: of the cows they had milked, the butter they had made, the gardens they had planted, the children and grandchildren they had tended, the brooms they had worn out, the mountains of food they had cooked. It made him dizzy. Clara Vavrika smiled a hard, enigmatical smile at him and walked rapidly away. Nils's eyes followed her white figure as she went toward the house. He watched her walking alone in the sunlight, looked at her slender, defiant shoulders and her little hard-set head with its coils of blue-black hair. "No," he reflected, "she'd never be like them, not if she lived here a hundred years. She'd only grow more bitter. You can't tame a wild thing; you can only chain it. People aren't all alike. I mustn't lose my nerve." He gave Hilda's pigtail a parting tweak and set out after Clara. "Where to?" he asked, as he came upon her in the kitchen.

"I'm going to the cellar for preserves."

"Let me go with you. I never get a moment alone with you. Why do you keep out of my way?"

Clara laughed. "I don't usually get in anybody's way."

Nils followed her down the stairs and to the far corner of the cellar, where a basement window let in a stream of light. From a swinging shelf Clara selected several glass jars, each labeled in Johanna's careful hand. Nils took up a brown flask. "What's this? It looks good."

"It is. It's some French brandy Father gave me when I was married. Would you like some? Have you a corkscrew? I'll get glasses."

When she brought them, Nils took them from her and put them down on the windowsill. "Clara Vavrika, do you remember how crazy I used to be about you?"

Clara shrugged her shoulders. "Boys are always crazy about somebody or other. I dare say some silly has been crazy about Evelina Oleson. You got over it in a hurry."

"Because I didn't come back, you mean? I had to get on, you know, and it was hard sledding at first. Then I heard you'd married Olaf."

"And then you stayed away from a broken heart," Clara laughed.

"And then I began to think about you more than I had since I first went away. I began to wonder if you were really as you had seemed to me when I was a boy. I thought I'd like to see. I've had lots of girls, but no one ever pulled me the same way. The more I thought about you, the more I remembered how it used to be—like hearing a wild tune you can't resist, calling you out at night. It had been a long while since anything had pulled me out of my boots, and I wondered whether anything ever could again." Nils thrust his hands into his coat pockets and squared his shoulders, as his mother sometimes squared hers, as

Olaf, in a clumsier manner, squared his. "So I thought I'd come back and see. Of course the family have tried to do me, and I rather thought I'd bring out father's will and make a fuss. But they can have their old land; they've put enough sweat into it." He took the flask and filled the two glasses carefully to the brim. "I've found out what I want from the Ericsons. Drink *skoal,* Clara." He lifted his glass, and Clara took hers with downcast eyes. "Look at me, Clara Vavrika. *Skoal!"*

She raised her burning eyes and answered fiercely: *"Skoal!"*

The barn supper began at six o'clock and lasted for two hilarious hours. Yense Nelson had made a wager that he could eat two whole fried chickens, and he did. Eli Swanson stowed away two whole custard pies, and Nick Hermanson ate a chocolate layer cake to the last crumb. There was even a cookie contest among the children, and one thin, slablike Bohemian boy consumed sixteen and won the prize, a gingerbread pig which Johanna Vavrika had carefully decorated with red candies and burnt sugar. Fritz Sweiheart, the German carpenter, won in the pickle contest, but he disappeared soon after supper and was not seen for the rest of the evening. Joe Vavrika said that Fritz could have managed the pickles all right, but he had sampled the demijohn in his buggy too often before sitting down to the table.

While the supper was being cleared away the two fiddlers began to tune up for the dance. Clara was to accompany them on her old upright piano, which had been brought down from her father's. By this time Nils had renewed old acquaintances. Since his interview with Clara in the cellar, he had been busy telling all the old women how young they looked, and all the young ones how pretty they were, and assuring the men that they had here the best farmland in the world. He had made himself so agreeable that old Mrs. Ericson's friends began to come up to her and tell how lucky she was to get her smart son back again, and please to get him to play his flute. Joe Vavrika, who could still play very well when he forgot that he had rheumatism, caught up a fiddle from Johnny Oleson and played a crazy Bohemian dance tune that set the wheels going. When he dropped the bow everyone was ready to dance.

Olaf, in a frock coat and a solemn made-up necktie, led the grand march with his mother. Clara had kept well out of *that* by sticking to the piano. She played the march with a pompous solemnity which greatly amused the prodigal son, who went over and stood behind her.

"Oh, aren't you rubbing it into them, Clara Vavrika? And aren't you lucky to have me here, or all your wit would be thrown away."

"I'm used to being witty for myself. It saves my life."

The fiddles struck up a polka, and Nils convulsed Joe Vavrika by leading out Evelina Oleson, the homely schoolteacher. His next partner was a very fat Swedish girl, who, although she was an heiress, had not been asked for the first dance, but had stood against the wall in her tight, high-heeled shoes, nervously fingering a lace handkerchief. She was soon out of breath, so Nils led her, pleased and panting, to her seat, and went over to the piano, from which Clara had been watching his gallantry. "Ask Olena Yenson," she whispered. "She waltzes beautifully."

Olena, too, was rather inconveniently plump, handsome in a smooth, heavy way, with a fine color and good-natured, sleepy eyes. She was redolent of violet sachet powder, and had warm, soft, white hands, but she danced divinely, moving as smoothly as the tide coming in. "There, that's something like," Nils said as he released her. "You'll give me the next waltz, won't you? Now I must go and dance with my little cousin."

Hilda was greatly excited when Nils went up to her stall and held out his arm. Her little eyes sparkled, but she declared that she could not leave her lemonade. Old Mrs. Ericson, who happened along at this moment, said she would attend to that, and Hilda came out, as pink as her pink dress. The dance was a schottische, and in a moment her yellow braids were fairly standing on end. "Bravo!" Nils cried encouragingly. "Where did you learn to dance so nicely?"

"My Cousin Clara taught me," the little girl panted.

Nils found Eric sitting with a group of boys who were too awkward or too shy to dance, and told him that he must dance the next waltz with Hilda.

The boy screwed up his shoulders. "Aw, Nils, I can't dance. My feet are too big; I look silly."

"Don't be thinking about yourself. It doesn't matter how boys look."

Nils had never spoken to him so sharply before, and Eric made haste to scramble out of his corner and brush the straw from his coat.

Clara nodded approvingly. "Good for you, Nils. I've been trying to get hold of him. They dance very nicely together; I sometimes play for them."

"I'm obliged to you for teaching him. There's no reason why he should grow up to be a lout."

"He'll never be that. He's more like you than any of them. Only he hasn't your courage." From her slanting eyes Clara shot forth one of those keen glances, admiring and at the same time challenging, which she seldom bestowed on anyone, and which seemed to say, "Yes, I admire you, but I am your equal."

Clara was proving a much better host than Olaf, who, once the supper was over, seemed to feel no interest in anything but the lanterns. He had brought a locomotive headlight from town to light the revels, and he kept skulking about it as if he feared the mere light from it might set his new barn on fire. His wife, on the contrary, was cordial to everyone, was animated and even gay. The deep salmon color in her cheeks burned vividly, and her eyes were full of life. She gave the piano over to the fat Swedish heiress, pulled her father away from the corner where he sat gossiping with his cronies, and made him dance a Bohemian dance with her. In his youth Joe had been a famous dancer, and his daughter got him so limbered up that everyone sat round and applauded them. The old ladies were particularly delighted, and made them go through the dance again. From their corner where they watched and commented, the old women kept time with their feet and hands, and whenever the fiddles struck up a new air old Mrs. Svendsen's white cap would begin to bob.

Clara was waltzing with little Eric when Nils came up to them, brushed his brother aside, and swung her out among the dancers. "Remember how we used to waltz on rollers at the old skating rink in town? I suppose people don't do that anymore. We used to keep it up for hours. You know, we never did moon around as other boys and girls did. It was dead serious with us from the beginning. When we were most in love with each other, we used to fight. You were always pinching people; your fingers were like little nippers. A regular snapping turtle, you were. Lord, how you'd like Stockholm! Sit out in the streets in front of cafés and talk all night in summer. Just like a reception—officers and ladies and funny English people. Jolliest people in the world, the Swedes, once you get them going. Always drinking things—champagne and stout mixed, half-and-half; serve it out of big pitchers, and serve plenty. Slow pulse, you know; they can stand a lot. Once they light up, they're glowworms, I can tell you."

"All the same, you don't really like gay people."

"*I* don't?"

"No; I could see that when you were looking at the old women there this afternoon. They're the kind you really admire, after all; women like your mother. And that's the kind you'll marry."

"Is it, Miss Wisdom? You'll see who I'll marry, and she won't have a domestic virtue to bless herself with. She'll be a snapping turtle, and she'll be a match for me. All the same, they're a fine bunch of old dames over there. You admire them yourself."

"No, I don't; I detest them."

"You won't, when you look back on them from Stockholm or Budapest. Freedom settles all that. Oh, but you're the real Bohemian Girl,

Clara Vavrika!" Nils laughed down at her sullen frown and began mockingly to sing:

> "Oh, how could a poor gypsy maiden like me
> Expect the proud bride of a baron to be?"

Clara clutched his shoulder. "Hush, Nils; everyone is looking at you."

"I don't care. They can't gossip. It's all in the family, as the Ericsons say when they divide up little Hilda's patrimony amongst them. Besides, we'll give them something to talk about when we hit the trail. Lord, it will be a godsend to them! They haven't had anything so interesting to chatter about since the grasshopper year. It'll give them a new lease of life. And Olaf won't lose the Bohemian vote, either. They'll have the laugh on him so that they'll vote two apiece. They'll send him to Congress. They'll never forget his barn party, or us. They'll always remember us as we're dancing together now. We're making a legend. Where's my waltz, boys?" he called as they whirled past the fiddlers.

The musicians grinned, looked at each other, hesitated, and began a new air; and Nils sang with them, as the couples fell from a quick waltz to a long, slow glide:

> "When other lips and other hearts
> Their tale of love shall tell,
> In language whose excess imparts
> The power they feel so well."

The old women applauded vigorously. "What a gay one he is, that Nils!" And old Mrs. Svendsen's cap lurched dreamily from side to side to the flowing measure of the dance.

> "Of days that have as ha-a-p-py been,
> And you'll remember me."

VII

The moonlight flooded that great, silent land. The reaped fields lay yellow in it. The straw stacks and poplar windbreaks threw sharp black shadows. The roads were white rivers of dust. The sky was a deep, crystalline blue, and the stars were few and faint. Everything seemed to have succumbed, to have sunk to sleep, under the great, golden, tender, midsummer moon. The splendor of it seemed to transcend human life and human fate. The senses were too feeble to take it in, and every time one looked up at the sky one felt unequal to it, as if one were sitting deaf under the waves of a great river of melody. Near the road, Nils Ericson was lying against a straw stack in Olaf's wheatfield. His own life seemed strange and unfamiliar to him, as if it were something he had read about, or dreamed, and forgotten. He lay very still, watching the white road that ran in front of him, lost itself among the fields, and then, at a distance, reappeared over a little hill. At last, against this white band he saw something moving rapidly, and he got up and walked to the edge of the field. "She is passing the row of poplars now," he thought. He heard the padded beat of hoofs along the dusty road, and as she came into sight he stepped out and waved his arms. Then, for fear of frightening the horse, he drew back and waited. Clara had seen him, and she came up at a walk. Nils took the horse by the bit and stroked his neck.

"What are you doing out so late, Clara Vavrika? I went to the house, but Johanna told me you had gone to your father's."

"Who can stay in the house on a night like this? Aren't you out yourself?"

"Ah, but that's another matter."

Nils turned the horse into the field.

"What are you doing? Where are you taking Norman?"

"Not far, but I want to talk to you tonight; I have something to say to you. I can't talk to you at the house, with Olaf sitting there on the porch, weighing a thousand tons."

Clara laughed. "He won't be sitting there now. He's in bed by this time, and asleep—weighing a thousand tons."

Nils plodded on across the stubble. "Are you really going to spend the rest of your life like this, night after night, summer after summer? Haven't you anything better to do on a night like this than to wear yourself and Norman out tearing across the country to your father's and back? Besides, your father won't live forever, you know. His little place will be shut up or sold, and then you'll have nobody but the Ericsons. You'll have to fasten down the hatches for the winter then."

Clara moved her head restlessly. "Don't talk about that. I try never to think of it. If I lost Father I'd lose everything, even my hold over the Ericsons."

"Bah! You'd lose a good deal more than that. You'd lose your race, everything that makes you yourself. You've lost a good deal of it now."

"Of what?"

"Of your love of life, your capacity for delight."

Clara put her hands up to her face. "I haven't, Nils Ericson, I haven't! Say anything to me but that. I won't have it!" she declared vehemently.

Nils led the horse up to a straw stack, and turned to Clara, looking at her intently, as he had looked at her that Sunday afternoon at Vavrika's. "But why do you fight for that so? What good is the power to enjoy, if you never enjoy? Your hands are cold again. What are you afraid of all the time? Ah, you're afraid of losing it; that's what's the matter with you! And you will, Clara Vavrika, you will! When I used to know you—listen; you've caught a wild bird in your hand, haven't you, and felt its heart beat so hard that you were afraid it would shatter its little body to pieces? Well, you used to be just like that, a slender, eager thing with a wild delight inside you. That is how I remembered you. And I come back and find you—a bitter woman. This is a perfect ferret fight here; you live by biting and being bitten. Can't you remember what life used to be? Can't you remember that old delight? I've never forgotten it, or known its like, on land or sea."

He drew the horse under the shadow of the straw stack. Clara felt him take her foot out of the stirrup, and she slid softly down into his arms. He kissed her slowly. He was a deliberate man, but his nerves were steel when he wanted anything. Something flashed out from him like a knife out of a sheath. Clara felt everything slipping away from her; she was flooded by the summer night. He thrust his hand into his pocket, and then held it out at arm's length. "Look," he said. The shadow of the straw stack fell sharp across his wrist, and in the palm of his hand she saw a silver dollar shining. "That's my pile," he muttered. "Will you go with me?"

Clara nodded, and dropped her forehead on his shoulder.

Nils took a deep breath. "Will you go with me tonight?"

"Where?" she whispered softly.

"To town, to catch the midnight flyer."

Clara lifted her head and pulled herself together. "Are you crazy, Nils? We couldn't go away like that."

"That's the only way we ever will go. You can't sit on the bank and think about it. You have to plunge. That's the way I've always done, and it's the right way for people like you and me. There's nothing so dangerous as sitting still. You've only got one life, one youth, and you can let it slip through your fingers if you want to; nothing easier. Most people do that. You'd be better off tramping the roads with me than you are here." Nils held back her head and looked into her eyes. "But I'm not that kind of a tramp, Clara. You won't have to take in sewing. I'm with a Norwegian shipping line; came over on business with the New York offices, but now I'm going straight back to Bergen. I expect I've got as much money as the Ericsons. Father sent me a little to get started. They never knew about that. There, I hadn't meant to tell you; I wanted you to come on your own nerve."

Clara looked off across the fields. "It isn't that, Nils, but something seems to hold me. I'm afraid to pull against it. It comes out of the ground, I think."

"I know all about that. One has to tear loose. You're not needed here. Your father will understand; he's made like us. As for Olaf, Johanna will take better care of him than ever you could. It's now or never, Clara Vavrika. My bag's at the station; I smuggled it there yesterday."

Clara clung to him and hid her face against his shoulder. "Not tonight," she whispered. "Sit here and talk to me tonight. I don't want to go anywhere tonight. I may never love you like this again."

Nils laughed through his teeth. "You can't come that on me. That's not my way, Clara Vavrika. Eric's mare is over there behind the stacks, and I'm off on the midnight. It's goodbye, or off across the world with me. My carriage won't wait. I've written a letter to Olaf; I'll mail it in town. When he reads it he won't bother us—not if I know him. He'd rather have the land. Besides, I could demand an investigation of his administration of Cousin Henrik's estate, and that would be bad for a public man. You've no clothes, I know; but you can sit up tonight, and we can get everything on the way. Where's your old dash, Clara Vavrika? What's become of your Bohemian blood? I used to think you had courage enough for anything. Where's your nerve—what are you waiting for?"

Clara drew back her head, and he saw the slumberous fire in her eyes. "For you to say one thing, Nils Ericson."

"I never say that thing to any woman, Clara Vavrika." He leaned back, lifted her gently from the ground, and whispered through his teeth: "But I'll never, never let you go, not to any man on earth but me! Do you understand me? Now, wait here."

Clara sank down on a sheaf of wheat and covered her face with her hands. She did not know what she was going to do—whether she would go or stay. The great, silent country seemed to lay a spell upon her. The ground seemed to hold her as if by roots. Her knees were soft under her. She felt as if she could not bear separation from her old sorrows, from her old discontent. They were dear to her, they had kept her alive, they were a part of her. There would be nothing left of her if she were wrenched away from them. Never could she pass beyond that skyline against which her restlessness had beat so many times. She felt as if her soul had built itself a nest there on that horizon at which she looked every morning and every evening, and it was dear to her, inexpressibly dear. She pressed her fingers against her eyeballs to shut it out. Beside her she heard the tramping of horses in the soft earth. Nils said nothing to her. He put his hands under her arms and lifted her lightly to her saddle. Then he swung himself into his own.

"We shall have to ride fast to catch the midnight train. A last gallop, Clara Vavrika. Forward!"

There was a start, a thud of hoofs along the moonlit road, two dark shadows going over the hill; and then the great, still land stretched untroubled under the azure night. Two shadows had passed.

VIII

A year after the flight of Olaf Ericson's wife, the night train was steaming across the plains of Iowa. The conductor was hurrying through one of the day coaches, his lantern on his arm, when a lank, fair-haired boy sat up in one of the plush seats and tweaked him by the coat.

"What is the next stop, please, sir?"

"Red Oak, Iowa. But you go through to Chicago, don't you?" He looked down, and noticed that the boy's eyes were red and his face was drawn, as if he were in trouble.

"Yes. But I was wondering whether I could get off at the next place and get a train back to Omaha."

"Well, I suppose you could. Live in Omaha?"

"No. In the western part of the state. How soon do we get to Red Oak?"

"Forty minutes. You'd better make up your mind, so I can tell the baggageman to put your trunk off."

"Oh, never mind about that! I mean, I haven't got any," the boy added, blushing.

"Run away," the conductor thought, as he slammed the coach door behind him.

Eric Ericson crumpled down in his seat and put his brown hand to his forehead. He had been crying, and he had had no supper, and his head was aching violently. "Oh, what shall I do?" he thought, as he looked dully down at his big shoes. "Nils will be ashamed of me; I haven't got any spunk."

Ever since Nils had run away with his brother's wife, life at home had been hard for little Eric. His mother and Olaf both suspected him of complicity. Mrs. Ericson was harsh and faultfinding, constantly wounding the boy's pride; and Olaf was always setting her against him.

Joe Vavrika heard often from his daughter. Clara had always been fond of her father, and happiness made her kinder. She wrote him long accounts of the voyage to Bergen, and of the trip she and Nils took through Bohemia to the little town where her father had grown up and where she herself was born. She visited all her kinsmen there, and sent her father news of his brother, who was a priest; of his sister, who had married a horsebreeder—of their big farm and their many children. These letters Joe always managed to read to little Eric. They contained messages for Eric and Hilda. Clara sent presents, too, which Eric never dared to take home and which poor little Hilda never even saw, though she loved to hear Eric tell about them when they were out getting the eggs together. But Olaf once saw Eric coming out of Vavrika's house—the old man had never asked the boy to come into his saloon—and Olaf went straight to his mother and told her. That night Mrs. Ericson came to Eric's room after he was in bed and made a terrible scene. She could be very terrifying when she was really angry. She forbade him ever to speak to Vavrika again, and after that night she would not allow him to go to town alone. So it was a long while before Eric got any more news of his brother. But old Joe suspected what was going on, and he carried Clara's letters about in his pocket. One Sunday he drove out to see a German friend of his, and chanced to catch sight of Eric, sitting by the cattle pond in the big pasture. They went together into Fritz Oberlies's barn and read the letters and talked things over. Eric admitted that things were getting hard for him at home. That very night old Joe sat down and laboriously penned a statement of the case to his daughter.

Things got no better for Eric. His mother and Olaf felt that, however closely he was watched, he still, as they said, "heard." Mrs. Ericson could not admit neutrality. She had sent Johanna Vavrika packing back to her brother's, though Olaf would much rather have kept her than Anders's eldest daughter, whom Mrs. Ericson installed in her place. He was not so highhanded as his mother, and he once sulkily told her that she might better have taught her granddaughter to cook before she sent Johanna away. Olaf could have borne a good deal for the sake of prunes spiced in honey, the secret of which Johanna had taken away with her.

At last two letters came to Joe Vavrika: one from Nils, inclosing a postal order for money to pay Eric's passage to Bergen, and one from Clara, saying that Nils had a place for Eric in the offices of his company, that he was to live with them, and that they were only waiting for him to come. He was to leave New York on one of the boats of Nils's own line; the captain was one of their friends, and Eric was to make himself known at once.

Nils's directions were so explicit that a baby could have followed them, Eric felt. And here he was, nearing Red Oak, Iowa, and rocking backward and forward in despair. Never had he loved his brother so much, and never had the big world called to him so hard. But there was a lump in his throat which would not go down. Ever since nightfall he had been tormented by the thought of his mother, alone in that big house that had sent forth so many men. Her unkindness now seemed so little, and her loneliness so great. He remembered everything she had ever done for him: how frightened she had been when he tore his hand in the cornsheller, and how she wouldn't let Olaf scold him. When Nils went away he didn't leave his mother all alone, or he would never have gone. Eric felt sure of that.

The train whistled. The conductor came in, smiling not unkindly. "Well, young man, what are you going to do? We stop at Red Oak in three minutes."

"Yes, thank you. I'll let you know." The conductor went out, and the boy doubled up with misery. He couldn't let his one chance go like this. He felt for his breast pocket and crackled Nils's kind letter to give him courage. He didn't want Nils to be ashamed of him. The train stopped. Suddenly he remembered his brother's kind, twinkling eyes, that always looked at you as if from far away. The lump in his throat softened. "Ah, but Nils, Nils would *understand!*" he thought. "That's just it about Nils; he always understands."

A lank, pale boy with a canvas telescope stumbled off the train to the Red Oak siding, just as the conductor called, "All aboard!"

The next night Mrs. Ericson was sitting alone in her wooden rocking chair on the front porch. Little Hilda had been sent to bed and had cried herself to sleep. The old woman's knitting was in her lap, but her hands lay motionless on top of it. For more than an hour she had not moved a muscle. She simply sat, as only the Ericsons and the mountains can sit. The house was dark, and there was no sound but the croaking of the frogs down in the pond of the little pasture.

Eric did not come home by the road, but across the fields, where no one could see him. He set his telescope down softly in the kitchen shed, and slipped noiselessly along the path to the front porch. He sat down on the step without saying anything. Mrs. Ericson made no sign, and the frogs croaked on. At last the boy spoke timidly.

"I've come back, Mother."

"Very well," said Mrs. Ericson.

Eric leaned over and picked up a little stick out of the grass.

"How about the milking?" he faltered.

"That's been done, hours ago."

"Who did you get?"

"Get? I did it myself. I can milk as good as any of you."

Eric slid along the step near to her. "Oh, Mother, why did you?" he asked sorrowfully. "Why didn't you get one of Otto's boys?"

"I didn't want anybody to know I was in need of a boy," said Mrs. Ericson bitterly. She looked straight in front of her and her mouth tightened. "I always meant to give you the home farm," she added.

The boy started and slid closer. "Oh, Mother," he faltered, "I don't care about the farm. I came back because I thought you might be needing me, maybe." He hung his head and got no further.

"Very well," said Mrs. Ericson. Her hand went out from her suddenly and rested on his head. Her fingers twined themselves in his soft, pale hair. His tears splashed down on the boards; happiness filled his heart.